The Possum Principles

THE POSSUM PRINCIPLES

by

Martin Ramsay

Narrow Gate House Publishers

The Possum Principles

Copyright © 2019

Martin L. Ramsay

Version 1.0 — April, 2019

Version 1.1 — June, 2019

Version 1.2 — July, 2019

Cover design by Balance Creative, Lexington, KY

Published by Narrow Gate House Publishers
PO Box 483
Berea, Kentucky 40403-0483
www.narrowgatehouse.com

Narrow Gate House Publishers is the publication division of CEATH Company, www.ceath.com.

ISBN # 978-1-941099-15-5

Library of Congress Control Number: 2019903985

Chapter 1
In which Ellen gets a job.

Ellen Murphy was talking to her car. "Come on, Gunilla," she said. "Maybe if I can just get this job we can get you to the shop for a tune up. Then you and I can keep going just a little bit longer." The aging Saab 900 didn't reply; it never did. But Ellen kept up the conversation anyway.

"You're a good car, Gunilla, and we've been through a lot together. But it is 1988. I'm 33 year old, for heaven's sake. It's time for me to spread my wings, to make a little money. I can't go on living with Trish and Tommy forever. I just have to get this job." Again there was no response from the car that just kept hugging the road, snaking through the dips and hollows in the Kentucky dawn.

For a fleeting moment Ellen was aware of the beauty around her. Low lying fog was nestled into the valleys of the rolling Kentucky countryside. The autumn leaves were at their most brilliant, and the sun, now decidedly peeking over the eastern knobs, was intensifying their color.

She passed an old rock wall, built without mortar in pre-Civil War times. It bordered the road, then curved up a hill through a stand of ancient oaks and pines. Ellen could barely see, toward the top of the hill, the old mansion sitting up there. It had white columns and a beautiful porch on the second floor. There were double chimneys on either end, and a number of small brick outbuildings. "I've always wondered who lives there, Gunilla, or if anybody lives there. It looks so old, and a little shabby." The car only murmured as Ellen downshifted to go around a curve.

As Ellen neared the outskirts of Oak Lick, she turned left onto a road that directed her to the Powell Manufacturing factory. "It isn't much to look at," she mused as she wheeled Gunilla into the gravel parking lot. "Could do with a bit of landscaping." She took her purse and smoothed her skirt as she exited the car, her heels clicked pertly on the sidewalk. She caught sight of herself in the window in front of the factory and nodded. Ellen had no illusions that she was glamorous, suitable for magazine covers or movies. But she wasn't bad looking, and the suit she had chosen looked professional without being ostentatious. "Not bad for just shy of 30. Maybe I look mature enough to have some experience," she consoled herself. "I just hope I get this job." She thought of Gunilla waiting patiently in the parking lot.

Ellen entered the building and found a small reception area, sparsely but tastefully decorated. A woman in her late fifties looked up from her computer. "May I help you?" The woman smiled and Ellen immediately liked her. "Oh, you must be Ellen Murphy here about the job."

"Yes, I'm Ellen Murphy. Am I here at the right time?"

"Yes, honey, of course you are." The woman's Kentucky accent was as natural as a tobacco patch on a Kentucky hillside. "I'll just tell Rob—Mr. Powell—that you're here. Why don't you sit over there," she indicated a small naugahyde couch in the lobby. "I'm Gladys, by the way. I have to go out into the shop to collect job cards. You don't mind if I leave you for a few minutes, do you honey?"

"No, of course not. I'll be fine." She sat down and picked up a copy of "Gear Week" off of the side table. Gladys went down a hallway and Ellen could hear a murmured conversation, and then a door opening, which let in all kinds of machine noises, clanks and roars from the factory. Ellen was nervously flipping through the magazine, not understanding any of the articles. She was struck by one of the ads, however. It featured a ruggedly handsome movie star who was selling bathroom tissue. "Give your employees the best," the ad said. "Give them Lite Touch toilet tissue." Ellen almost laughed out loud; it was such an odd juxtaposition of subject matter.

Her attention was suddenly grabbed by an oath coming out of one of the offices down the hall. She couldn't make out the word, exactly, but it was filled with frustration. It was a man's voice, deep and full of conviction. "Aaarrgh!!" the voice came again, even louder. Suddenly an object came hurtling out of the door, smashing into the wall of the lobby. It burst into a hundred pieces from the impact, and only then did Ellen recognize it as a keyboard. She could see the coiled cord, still quivering from the impact, and the letters from the keys in a jumble, as if someone had thrown a bowl of alphabet soup against the wall. Ellen clutched her purse, ready to run if the man should decide to come after her next.

She was half way to her feet when the man came out of the office. He strode over to the smashed keyboard and kicked it. Hard. As he turned, he became aware of Ellen perched on the edge of her chair looking like a scared rabbit ready for flight. Ellen was so shocked, she was barely aware of the range of emotions that flew across the man's face. First anger, then embarrassment, and finally a touch of sheepishness. "I don't know what to say." He shrugged his shoulders. "You caught me in a very weak moment." He was tall, wearing a tie but no jacket. "I'm Rob Powell." His long legs took him across the lobby in two paces. He stuck out his hand and Ellen slowly rose, unsure if running might not still be a good idea. "And you are?"

"I'm Ellen Murphy." She gingerly took his hand. His handshake was warm and firm, and he took care not to crush her fingers. He began to look less like a dangerous mountain of dynamite, and more like a man who had had a hard day already at 8:30 in the morning.

"Oh yes. Here about the job, I expect."

"Yes. I can come back later if this isn't a good time." She mentally kicked herself. I want this job; why did I offer to come back later?

"There's never a good time around here. Come into my office and let's talk." He led her into the office, stepping across the dead keyboard as he went. "Do you know anything about computers?" There was desperation in his voice.

"Some," she replied. "I have a degree in business and had several computer courses."

"Do you think there's any hope for this beast?" He glared at the computer on his desk, now missing a keyboard.

"I don't know. The first thing we'll have to do is get you a data entry device—another keyboard. And we'll have to hope you didn't damage anything when you ..." When you ... what? When you went berserk?

He smiled. Sheepishly, again. "I'd be very grateful if there is anything you could do. Maybe we can borrow Gladys' keyboard." He led her back past the blasted keyboard into the work area of the woman who had greeted her. "Can you use this?"

Ellen quickly scanned the computer. It was the same make and model as the one in Mr. Powell's office. "She has some work in process on the screen. We can't just take the keyboard out; she would loose what she's working on. Would it be all right to save her work and shut her computer down?"

"I'm sure it would. And I'm desperate."

"OK." Ellen quickly saved the documents Gladys had open and shut down all of her open applications. Then she initiated the shut down routine. She switched off the power and unplugged the keyboard from the back of the computer. Mr. Powell followed her back to his office where she switched off his computer and plugged the keyboard into his machine. "Let's hope this works," she said ruefully.

She breathed a sigh of relief as the familiar DOS startup sequence began and got past the point at which it would have checked for a keyboard. Windows began coming up. She glanced up at Mr. Powell to see if he understood the significance of what was happening. "This is good, right?"

"Yes," she said, amused by the understatement. "It is very good. Now what were you working on when you ..." When you became a raving maniac? What kind of person would rip a keyboard off of a computer?

"It was a spreadsheet. I was trying to figure out our cash flow and I just couldn't get it to do what I wanted."

"What was the name of the document ... or had you not saved it before you ... before you ripped the keyboard out?"

"No, I'm afraid I hadn't saved it." Ellen was already loading his Lotus 1-2-3 and checking to see what the last documents were that he had been working on. "Or at least I don't think I did."

Ellen spotted a document titled CASHFLOW.123 and loaded it. It came up on the screen. Suddenly Mr. Powell's hand came down on her shoulder. "That's it!" he whispered. "You've done it, Ellen Murphy! You are a genius!" He squeezed her shoulder, then almost danced a jig around the office. "Whooeee!" Now he was almost shouting.

"I'm glad I was able to help." Ellen didn't know what else to say. "I guess I've always tried to be as helpful as possible." It sounded trite, but Ellen truly did believe it.

"Well, look. You came here for a job interview, and I've been a very bad host. You've helped me out more than you know. I can already tell you would be a real asset around here. Do you have a resume or something?" Ellen pulled out the resume she had so carefully printed last night on the expensive rag paper she had bought and handed it to him. Mr. Powell looked at both pages. "Hmmm ..." he said.

Ellen knew it was weak. She had the degree in business. But her work experience wasn't strong. A few jobs here and there, not a consistent pattern of advancement. How would Mr. Powell understand about Trish and the kids? About how desperately Trish had needed her, and how Ellen had been willing to help her sister, because family was so important? How Ellen had put her own career, even her life, on hold to get her sister back on her feet? And now that Carrie was in school, and Nathan was getting so tall and strong and sharp? And how Trish had Tommy, who loved her from the bottom of his heart? And how now Ellen could finally, ten years later, start thinking about what she should do with her own life? And how she really, really needed this job so she could fix Gunilla, still waiting in the parking lot, and get an apartment, and ... and figure out who Ellen Murphy was.

"Hmmm ... " said Mr. Powell again. He had taken off his glasses and was chewing on one of the ear pieces. "Ellen Murphy, what do you want to be when you grow up?"

"I beg your pardon?"

"What are your goals, your dreams, your hopes? What do you want to do with your life?"

"I ... I don't know," she stammered. Had he read her mind? "It's kind of a long story, but I'm just now at the point in my life where I could actually ask myself those kinds of questions." She shrugged. "I don't know the answer yet."

"Have you ever worked in manufacturing?"

"No."

His eyes became bright as he put his glasses back on. "It's wonderful! I get a real kick out of it. You get to see real products going out the door that you know are going to be used to make people's lives better. And its a real challenge to see if you can make it all work ... bring in the right inventory at the right time, schedule the work centers so that you get the most efficient throughput possible, figure out what motivates people to do their best, most satisfying work. And it is real easy to keep score. Either you make money or you don't. I just think manufacturing is one of the greatest pursuits a guy could follow." He laughed at himself as he realized how passionate he had become. "Or a girl, for that matter. Of course it doesn't hurt that my dad was in manufacturing, too. I learned to love it early."

"It sounds fascinating." Mr. Powell looked at her to see if she was being sarcastic, but decided there was genuine interest in her voice.

"I tell you what. I thought I was looking for a secretary. But, frankly, what we really need is someone who has a brain, who isn't afraid to use it, and who really wants to help. It seems to me you fit all three requirements. On top of that, you seem to know your way around a computer. Our computer systems are an absolute wreck." He rolled his eyes to emphasize just how much of a wreck they were. Add to the wreckage one dead keyboard still lying in the hall. "What would you say if I were to offer you the newly created position of Information Manager?"

"Information Manager?"

"Yes. I just made it up. Your responsibilities would be to look at our operation here, figure out how to make it more efficient. That probably means fixing our computer systems, but it may mean other things, too."

"You may think I know about computers, but I don't think I know as much as you think I do."

"Well then we'll learn together. It is high time I learned about them, too. I want someone with a fresh point of view, who isn't stuck in the 'that's the way we've always done it' mindset. And I want someone who can think. Are you the woman for the job?"

"Can ... can I ask how much it pays?" There she was, stammering again.

Mr. Powell named a figure that exceeded her expectations. "You're really sure you want me? Really?"

"Absolutely." He laughed a warm, infectious laugh. "This is going to be great. When can you start?"

"How about tomorrow?"

"Fantastic. We start at 7:30. Be here with bells on!"

Ellen had no intention of wearing bells, or bellbottoms, for that matter. But she smiled in spite of herself. She turned as she was about to leave the lobby. "Oh, Mr. Powell?"

"Yes?"

"Thanks. And don't forget. You owe Gladys a new keyboard."

He laughed again. "So I do. That'll be your first responsibility tomorrow, to get Gladys a new keyboard. See you tomorrow!"

"I don't know, Gunilla," Ellen said to her Saab as she got in. "I don't know, but I think something rather remarkable happened today!"

Chapter 2
We meet the family at dinner.

"Could you pass the potatoes, Ellen?" Tommy was sitting at his place at the head of the table. She passed them, reflecting briefly that things were about to be very different for all of them. This might be the last dinner she prepared for the family. Until now she had been the one who most often did the cooking. But with this new job, that would probably have to change. She sighed. Not that she and Trish weren't used to big changes.

"So, Ellen. We've waited long enough. Tell us about the interview." Tommy's eyes twinkled and Ellen suspected that Trish had already told him that she had gotten the job.

"Aunt Ellen, are you going to wook?" Carrie's little face was framed with bright red hair; the sprinkling of freckles across her upturned nose added to the charm of her five-year-old's lisp.

"Yes," she replied. "Yes, I suppose I am." She smiled around the table at them all. At little Carrie who really didn't need her aunt to be her second mommy any more. At Nathan who was turning into a man right before her eyes. At Trish, her precious sister, who had needed her just as much as she had needed Trish after the tragedy that had killed their parents. And Tommy, dear Tommy, who had walked that tough tightrope of being the husband to a woman whose sister lived with her, who had made Ellen feel welcome and protected, while maintaining enough distance to make clear who was married to whom. "I've been offered the job ..." There was general cheering around the table; they all knew how much she wanted it. "... but I suppose I had better start at the beginning."

She told them about Mr. Powell and the keyboard, about the letters scattered all over the hall and how she had fixed his problem. "He sounds like a nut, El. Are you sure you want to work for him?" said Trish.

"You don't have to take the first job that comes along, you know," said Tommy. "Which job you take can have a major impact on your career."

"Are you going to work with computers, Aunt Ellen?" That was Nathan, already figuring an angle. She could just see the wheels turning in that bright brain of his, thinking about how he could leverage his aunt's new job and his own talent with computers to do something, as he would say, way cool.

Carrie just repeated, "When are you going to go to wook?"

"I start tomorrow. I guess there are going to be some changes around here. I'll have to be at work by 7:30, which means, little bit, that you're going to have to be a big girl and help your mommy get you ready for school." She reached over and gently pulled her niece's hair. "And I don't know what time I get off, but supper may be later than it has been, unless ... "

"I've been meaning to talk to you about that, El," said Trish. "I think it's high time I started carrying my weight in the kitchen. Tommy and I have talked about it and I've talked to my boss. Ambrose, Matheson and Moore is willing to let me cut back to 30 hours a week, so I can be home by the time Carrie gets home from school. With Tommy's promotion, we can afford it. And besides, it's high time you started thinking about your own career. And about, maybe, dating?" Her sister's eyes were twinkling.

"Gross!" said Nathan. "She'd rather spend her spare time working on the computer with me, wouldn't you, Aunt Ellen?"

"Well it sounds like that's settled then," said Ellen. "Trish will be here at 3:00 to welcome little bit home, and maybe I can start looking for an apartment so Nathan can have his own room." There was a silent but intense burst of positive energy coming from Nathan's side of the table. "And Tommy will only have to put up with one woman instead of two."

"Now, Ellen. You know how grateful I am to you for all the help you gave Trish when she needed you. You're welcome to stay as long as you want. We're all family here. But I am concerned about this Powell character. A man with a temper like that may be a rough boss to work for; it sounds like he is expecting a lot from you. I know you know a lot about computers, but you don't have a lot of real world experience." Tommy was big on learning by doing and didn't have much patience for academics who didn't live in what he called the real world. "I just wouldn't want you jumping into something that would make you miserable, just because the money is good."

"It isn't just the money," she replied. "Although I must say it doesn't hurt. I hear what you're saying, Tommy, about my lack of experience. You're right, and I was honest with Mr. Powell, too, but he seems to want me anyway. I guess I impressed him that I can think on my feet. I think he's looking for some fresh blood, too. He said something about not doing things a certain way just because that's how they've always been done. Besides I'm ready for a new challenge. It's time for Ellen to spread her wings a little. And if I get in serious trouble, I can always ask the boy genius here." She reached across the table and poked her nephew in the arm.

Nathan grinned at the compliment as conversation moved on to Trish's day at the law firm and the challenges at the plant where Tommy worked and how Nathan's and Carrie's day at school had been. After the stuffed pork chops and potatoes were done, Ellen brought out the chocolate suicide cake she had made that afternoon. "Hooray," yelled Nathan. "My favorite!"

"Who wants ice cream with it?" said Trish. "Its still warm."

Ellen sighed again, a sigh of contentment this time. She looked around the table at her family, the family she would soon be leaving for a new challenge. She felt the same lump in her throat she had felt that day ten years ago when she had kissed her mother and father goodbye and headed off to college.

Chapter 3
Ellen goes out into the Powell factory, and meets the workers.

Gladys and Ellen arrived in the parking lot at Powell Manufacturing at the same time and walked in together. Already Ellen could hear the deep thumping of the machines working back in the factory. Gladys reached the door first and held it open for her.

"Welcome, honey. Welcome to Powell. It will be great having another woman around the place."

Ellen looked at her." You don't mean you're the only woman ...'"

"No honey, 'course not. But there aren't many of us. And now there's one more." She squeezed Ellen's arm as she went past. "You'll fit in here just like molasses on cat-head biscuits." Ellen grinned. She didn't know what a cat-head biscuit was, but the way Gladys said it made her feel like this might actually work. Suddenly the butterflies she had felt in her stomach as she drove Gunilla to the factory seemed a little tamer.

"So, how many people work here, Gladys?" asked Ellen.

"Two hundred and fourteen, no fifteen, counting you. Not that we have as many as we did back in the glory days. We were as high as 450 at one point."

"Really?" Ellen started to ask her what had happened, when she spotted Gladys' computer, sans keyboard. "Oh Gladys, I'm really sorry. Mr. Powell seemed desperate yesterday when he ... well, I just kind of borrowed your keyboard to get his computer working. I hope I didn't inconvenience you too much." She was talking in a rush. "He said it would be OK and told me to get you a new keyboard today."

Gladys laughed. "Oh, honey. I heard all about it! Who do you think picked up the pieces all over the hall? And that wasn't the first time Rob has sent something to meet its maker. He told me you would get me a new keyboard." She smiled at Ellen, and Ellen felt that it really was OK. "Besides," said Gladys, "I don't really use my computer that much. Give me my Rolodex any day. It never stops working!"

Gladys showed Ellen where to hang her coat and stash her purse. She was even thoughtful enough to point out the women's restroom. "I tell you what," she said. "I usually go make the rounds and pick up the job cards first thing. Why don't you come with me so you can meet some people and get your bearings a little?"

"Sounds good."

Gladys looked Ellen over. "Hmmm ... You'll need some safety glasses." She rummaged around in a drawer and pulled out a pair that weren't too beat up. "And some ear plugs." Ellen struggled to fit the bright yellow bits of foam that were in the package Gladys handed her into her ears. They kept wanting to pop out, but she managed to get them to appear to be in place at least.

They walked past a room with the door closed. "Rob and the other managers are having their weekly staff meeting," said Gladys. "This is a good time to go out on the shop floor. And tomorrow," she added, looking pointedly at the trim pair of heels Ellen had selected with care to match her dress, "Just wear something comfortable. The boys will think you're pretty enough without you having to go to any trouble. Walking in heels can be murder out on the shop floor. Besides, they're not safe." She paused at a door through which the thumping of machinery could be heard even more loudly. "Have you ever been in a factory before, honey?" Ellen shook her head. "Well, welcome to Powell Manufacturing." She pulled open the door and they stepped through.

Ellen's first impression was of the lighting—it was a strange orangey-yellow, plenty bright enough to see, but different somehow, and a little disconcerting. Her second impression was of the room's size. It was at least two stories high, with the odd orangey-yellow lights way up near the roof. And it seemed to stretch back away from her in all directions so far that she couldn't see the end of it. Ellen thought briefly of a tobacco barn with its high rafters ... but this was so much bigger.

Her third impression was of the noise. If the machines had sounded noisy while she was in the office, they were positively furious now. And there were all kinds of activities going on in front of her. Men were driving fork lift trucks with big metal baskets full of things back and forth. Some men were grinding something, shooting a shower of bright orange sparks ten feet across the floor. There were large machines, some almost reaching to the ceiling of that huge place, going up and down. Every time one came down it made fierce noise, and Ellen could feel the thump through her shoes. Away in the distance, Ellen could occasionally see the lightning-blue flash of what she assumed must be a welder. She held her breath in awe and excitement. Suddenly Mr. Powell's remark from yesterday came back to her. 'I just think manufacturing is one of the greatest pursuits a guy could follow. Or a girl, for that matter.' She could see what he meant. This was going to be a challenge. Could she really make a contribution toward helping it all work, toward 'keeping score,' as Mr. Powell had called it? Would she be able to help Powell Manufacturing make money and keep people employed?

"This way!" Gladys shouted, but Ellen could barely hear her through the noise and the ear plugs. She followed along in Gladys' wake.

Gladys seemed to know everyone. She waved at some of the men as they passed, and they waved back. Several waved at Ellen, too. Their first stop was a small office built in the middle of the factory. Gladys and Ellen stepped in to meet a short rotund man staring at a computer terminal, an unlit cigar clamped in his teeth. "Harvey, this is Ellen ..."

"Ellen Murphy." Ellen extended her hand. Harvey stood up and shook it.

"Hey there, young lady. Welcome." He was in his late 50s, balding, a small head and worry lines on his forehead.

"Ellen is going to be working on straightening up our computer systems." Suddenly, Ellen's butterflies were back and a wave of self-doubt rolled over her.

"Well, man, do we need it! This computer is a mess. I can't make heads or tails out of this production schedule. Come here, let me show you what I mean." He indicated that Ellen should come around the desk in the cramped office.

"Now Harvey, she hasn't even got her W-4 form filled out yet. Give her a chance to get settled first. I just came in to pick up job cards." Gratefully, Ellen followed Gladys out of the office after promising Harvey that she would come back after a while and look at what he wanted to show her.

"Gladys, what does Harvey do?" shouted Ellen once they were safely down the aisle.

"Oh. Sorry! I should have said. Harvey is the production manager over the Fabrication area. There's Harvey, in charge of Fabrication, and Leonard over Welding, and Kirby in charge of Assembly. I'll introduce you to all of them." They moved on, Ellen struggling with her heels as she followed Gladys through a bewildering array of machines, racks of parts, lift trucks, and noise.

"Don't look directly at the welding flame, honey," said Gladys as Ellen stared with fascination at the bright blue arc of electricity and the man bent over it with a protective coat and face mask. "It'll fry your eyes, just like looking at the sun." Ellen hastily looked away. "This is Leonard's office," she said as she stopped at the door of another office. Leonard was tall and dark with close-cropped hair and a nice mustache. He appeared to be in his late 20s, perhaps even early 30s and was very friendly. He was apparently delighted that a new computer person would be joining Powell. "We sure need the help," he said. "Poor Whit just can't keep up."

"Who is Whit?" asked Ellen, after they had left Leonard's office.

"Didn't Rob tell you? He's in charge of computers." Ellen tried to digest this bit of news. So, if Whit was in charge of computers, what had she been hired to do? Wouldn't Whit resent her being hired without being consulted? And what about when the obvious happened when everyone, including Mr. Powell, discovered that she knew very little about computers and that Whit was the expert? The flock of butterflies in her stomach became a flock of crows, wheeling and tumbling. Steady, girl, she told herself. Get the facts first. You were looking for a job when you found this one.

They moved on to the last office. Kirby wasn't in, so Gladys just picked up the job cards on his desk and they headed back to the front office.

It was a relief to take off the uncomfortable safety glasses and to pull the ear plugs out of her ears. But, in spite of the discovery of the existence of Whit, Ellen found herself a little exhilarated. Her first factory! It was an exciting place. Ellen found herself wanting to know more about how it worked, what the job cards were that Gladys had been collecting, and what the computer was supposed to be doing to help Harvey and Leonard that it wasn't doing.

"Now," said Gladys, "Let me take you down to Personnel so you can fill in your forms." The Personnel office was down the hall and Gladys introduced her to Rick, a rangy man with a thick, south Georgia accent.

"Rob told me he'd hired you," he said. "Welcome to Powell." The creased brow told Ellen what she was beginning to suspect, that she had been hired by Mr. Powell without much forethought. Rick got out the necessary forms. This Ellen was familiar with; she had held several part time jobs and knew the routine of becoming a new employee. She filled out the paperwork and then Rick showed her to a small office with a desk and two chairs.

At least the desk had a phone and a computer, although it wasn't a very fast one. A few plants, she thought, and pictures of Nathan and Carrie, would spruce it up a bit. She borrowed a phone book from Gladys and began making calls to find a new keyboard to replace the one that had been demolished yesterday. She found one at a computer store not too far away that matched Gladys' model. "Is it OK to go pick it up?" she asked Gladys.

"Sure, honey. They take our purchase orders. Just go get it, sign for it, and bring a copy of the invoice back to me."

In a way, Ellen was glad to be back into Gunilla's familiar seat and to have a little time to think and digest all the new information she had been given this morning. She inserted the key between the seats and drove into Oak Lick where she picked up the keyboard with no problem.

She had just finished installing the new keyboard on Gladys' computer and was booting it up when Mr. Powell poked his head around the corner. Ellen hadn't been aware that he was even in the building, but there he was. "Ah, Ellen. I see you got Gladys' computer going. Good. Now, would you be able to come into my office so we can talk about what you're expected to do here at Powell?"

Yes, and I have a few questions I want to ask you, too, Mr. what-kind-of-a-mess-have-I-gotten-myself-into Powell. But all she said was, "Sure!"

Mr. Powell offered her a seat, and went around and sat in his own chair. He leaned back and studied her for a moment; it gave her time to study him. He was younger than she had originally thought, she realized. Probably not much older than she was. He was medium height and build and looked like he probably worked out or played some form of sport. He was dressed in a pale blue oxford shirt with a tie covered with an illustration of Daffy Duck.

"So what do you think, so far?" he asked. She felt the familiar butterflies again. Why did he always ask questions for which there was no right answer?

"What do you mean, what do I think?"

"What do you think of Powell Manufacturing?"

"Well ... it's hard to say. I've only been here half a day. I haven't really formed much of an opinion, yet." Why was she being timid? She did have an opinion: that Mr. Powell hired people without getting input from others. That she had been hired, possibly, in competition with a man, Whit, whom she hadn't met but who would probably resent the heck out of her. It was really a strange place. And yet ... And yet, she already had a sense of the fascination Mr. Powell had with manufacturing, how it all worked together. How those big metal plates got stamped and ground and formed and welded and assembled to make a product. But what kind of product was it? How customers were receiving things made right here at Powell, things they wanted and needed and were willing to pay for. But what kinds of customers? And how all of that must bring in enough money to pay all the people who worked here and pay the electric bill and the water bill and, hopefully, have some left over.

Something Tommy had said last night at dinner came back to her. 'I just wouldn't want you jumping into something that would make you miserable, just because the money is good.' Mr. Powell was still waiting for an answer. Now or never, she thought to herself. I might as well get this relationship started on a basis of honesty. Better to get fired on the first day, before it really counted, than to wait a week or a month being miserable with the end result still the same.

"Mr. Powell, I know you think I know a lot about technology, about computers. And, in some ways, I do. But I don't want you to have a mistaken impression of my experience. I like a challenge and I'm ready to tackle this one, but you must understand that I don't have a lot of experience. This morning I met Harvey and Leonard and they're both unhappy with their computer system. But I can't fix it right away. I have to learn what they expect it to do. A computer is just a tool, and I need to learn what the task is before I can expect to give any help in making the tool work better. So I'm going to have a steep learning curve."

Mr. Powell looked at her. He just sat there, perhaps waiting for her to say more.

"It seems to me that you haven't been completely honest with me. You didn't tell me about Whit. I don't know what his responsibilities are, but I would say he isn't going to appreciate the fact that I was hired without consulting him. It seemed to me Rick was a little surprised I was hired, too. And Harvey and Leonard are apparently expecting miracles. I don't know how bad the current computer systems are, but I'm not sure you were quite level with me. Mr. Powell, I'm not a miracle worker. But I do like a challenge and I do know something about information systems. I guess, most of all, I seem to have a knack for seeing how things work, not only from a technical standpoint, but from a people standpoint, too. And, like you said yesterday, I'm beginning to find that manufacturing is fascinating. Touring the factory with Gladys this morning got me really intrigued about how it all works together."

Mr. Powell took off his glasses and chewed on one of the ear pieces. Then he smiled. "That's the spirit! That's what I thought I saw yesterday when I hired you." He paused, looking at her. "You're right, I haven't been completely honest, I guess. Not that I was intentionally keeping things from you. But it's time for me to level with you. We need help here at Powell. I've become the leader of a company that, under my dad, was great. But now it is barely breaking even. I know our computer systems aren't great. We use a mainframe system called SOLUTION/400. It does our inventory control, our production management, our purchasing and our shipping, our financials and payroll. And I'm sure it does more than that. But I'm not willing to accept that the average way of dealing with our mainframe system or any of our other problems is going to provide anything but average results. We need some innovative thinking around here, the kind of thinking my father did when he started the company. I happen to think that you are the breath of fresh air that Powell needs. I want you to think out of the box. I think you are going to be part of the solution to our problems."

"I appreciate your confidence and the compliment," Ellen replied. "What you are describing sounds like a wonderful challenge. I just don't want you to have expectations that I can't meet ... to expect a miracle. And what about Whit?"

"Look, Whit is a fine guy. He knows a lot about how to wire a computer network. And he seems to know how to keep our mainframe running. What Whit isn't so good at is looking at the computer as a way to help Powell be successful. He seems more interested in the computer for the computer's sake. You, on the other hand, just said you see the computer as a tool, as a way to help the business. That's exactly what I want to hear, and what I believe, too. Whit is a little bit like a hammer in search of a nail. You, on the other hand, seem more like you believe that you should first look at the problem—is it a nail to be pounded in, or a screw to be driven in, or a pile of dirt to be moved—then decide what tool is best. A hammer makes a lousy screwdriver, and an even worse shovel. Yet I sometimes get the feeling Whit is pounding screws in with his hammer. I want you to look at our problems, and find the best tools to fix what's wrong. It's a big challenge, and I know your experience is limited. But I want a fresh pair of eyes, and that's what you have."

Ellen was beginning to get excited about the prospect of her challenge again. As her mother had once said, 'It's OK to have butterflies in your stomach. You just need to get them to fly in formation. You'll get the energy without the fear.' There was something about Mr. Powell. He seemed to have a vision of what was possible, and Ellen was beginning to share that vision.

"But won't Whit resent me?"

"Ah, yes, there is that to consider. I don't think Whit will be too upset; he'll be glad to have another pair of hands to help out. But don't get sucked into thinking the way Whit thinks. Use your fresh perspective. Don't be a hammer looking for a nail. And I'll talk to Whit," he continued. "Whit will take it better coming from me. I'll try to smooth the way and then I'll take you to introduce him. Meanwhile, would you like to learn a little bit about our business here?"

"Oh, yes! I have to confess, I don't even know what the products are that are made at Powell." She realized how naive she must seem to him. But he put on his glasses again and took out a pad of paper.

"It all started before you or I were born, when my dad had a vision of making life better for farmers, and he invented what became known as the WaterDriver." He leaned back in his chair as if to say this was one of his favorite stories, one he never tired of telling. "From there it really took off. Today most of our products actually go into other machines, particularly cars. We make a lot of automotive components."

Ellen watched him. Clearly he loved this; it was a major passion with him. She did her best to learn the different products he was telling her about.

Chapter 4

Ellen and Nathan discover the hierarchy of data.

Later that day Mr. Powell had taken Ellen out to meet Whit Collette. His office was in another part of the front office. Whit's desk was a jumble of wires and computer equipment and blinking lights and computer magazines. He was tall and lanky with a boyish shock of dark hair across his forehead, even though Ellen would have guessed him to be in his 40s. He smiled easily and the conversation had gone reasonably well. Whit seemed to accept the inevitable that Ellen was hired at Mr. Powell's insistence and that he really could, if he was honest with himself, use someone who would take some of the burden off of him, leaving him free to do what he did best: keep the computer running and string wires from place to place. He seemed relieved when Ellen assured him that she had no expertise with hardware and that she had no intention of horning in on his turf. She understood her role was more to look at the software and how it could be improved to support Powell's business.

When Ellen went home, she was tired, a little worried, but mostly exhilarated. There seemed to be an understanding between her and Mr. Powell. There seemed to be work to be done that she could help with. "And," she crowed to Gunilla, "I have a real job paying real money!"

Trish and Tommy and the kids were happy for her, and things seemed to be going well at the Thompson household. Carrie, while missing her Aunt Ellen, was very glad to have mommy home more. Nathan was just Nathan, happy that Aunt Ellen was happy, and, as always, engrossed in some computer project or other. In fact his only real disappointment with the new arrangement was the times he missed discussing with Aunt Ellen his latest adventure with his computer.

"I want to show you what I'm working on after supper, Aunt Ellen."

"You got it, Ace!" She had been thinking that perhaps she should study some of the manuals she had brought home from Powell, but she needed to spend time with the kids. And, who knows, she thought. Maybe she would learn something from Nathan. He always seemed to be two steps ahead of her.

After she and Trish washed up together, she sat down to play a game of Go Fish with Carrie and Tommy. Then, while Trish read a bedtime story to Carrie, Ellen went over to see what Nathan was working on.

"I got this data base program, Aunt Ellen," he said enthusiastically, the glow of the computer lighting up his boyish face. Ellen noticed how his features were beginning to change. Perhaps he wasn't quite so boyish, after all. He was growing up, and was that a hint of peach fuzz on his upper lip? Ah, time was passing, that was for sure. She turned her attention back to what Nathan was working on.

"Tubby, one of the guys at school, has a paper route, see? So I started setting up a data base of all his customers." He was clicking buttons on the screen so fast that Ellen couldn't follow what he was doing. "See, here's where I put in their names and addresses." He clicked another button. "And here's bills they owe Tubby."

"Hold on there. You put all this in the computer? I'm a little slower than you. Once more with feeling. Give old Aunt Ellen a break. What's a data base?"

He grinned and started again. He liked this side of Aunt Ellen. Sometimes she asked him questions that he already knew she knew the answer to. But it made him think, and he liked that. It made things clearer in his own mind to explain it to someone else. "Tubby used to try to keep track of where his customers live and how much they owe him in a notebook. But I've been reading a lot more about computers. Let's see ... a data base is a collection of bits of data—pieces of information—about a related subject."

Ellen smiled. Quite an academic definition for a fourteen year old. She made a mental note to find that book and read it herself. "So, what is the subject of your data base?"

"Paper routes. Tubby Burnell's paper route to be exact." He went back to the first screen. "A data base is composed of files. This file is a file of customers." He took out a pad of paper and wrote "DATA BASE" at the top of the page. Under this, he wrote, "FILES." He drew and arrow pointing up from one word to the next.

"And a file is ... ?"

"Like, this file is about the people on Tubby's paper route." Ellen saw the screen, displaying information about one Verna Powell. It showed Mrs. Powell's address, her phone number, and other information about her. "Each bit of data is called a field."

"Whoa, Ace. What is a bit of data?"

Nathan pointed at the screen. "Like this bit of data—it's called a field—is the customer's name. And what you type in the field is called the data. That's why it is called a data base." He pointed to another location on the screen. "See, Aunt Ellen? This is the phone number field." He wrote the word "FIELD" on the pad, farther down the page.

Ellen considered how easy this seemed to come to him. Nathan had grown up in a generation with computers around. Ellen hadn't. It made a difference, and Ellen was having to work to keep up.

"So this is the address field for Verna Powell?" Ellen pointed at the screen where it said, "And where it says Three Pines, 1788 Oak Lick Road is the data in that field?" She briefly wondered if Verna Powell and her new boss were related, but Powell was a common name. She didn't recognize the address. She traveled Oak Lick Road to work at Powell Manufacturing, but she didn't know where Three Pines was.

"Right. That's the address field for Verna Powell." He clicked a button on the screen and the information changed. Now it was information about a man named Mason Calico. "Now it is the address field for Mr. Calico."

"So what do you call it when the information is different for each person?"

"Good question, Aunt Ellen. It's called a record. All of the data —all of the fields—you enter about a person is called a record. " He wrote the word "RECORD" on the paper, between the FILE and FIELD he had already written down. Now he drew arrows pointing up from FIELD to RECORD, and from RECORD to FILE. There was already an arrow from FILE to DATA BASE. "This is the hierarchy of data organization." She smiled at the big word; he smiled back because he knew she was proud of him.

Figure 4.1

"So let me get this straight. A field is a bit of information, like a name you enter as data, or the address. Together, all of those tell us about a record. And a record contains information about a specific entry in the file, in this case, a specific person."

"Right. This record is for Mr. Calico. And one of the fields tells us that his address is 421 Dogwood Blossom Trail."

"And a file is this pot full of information about a particular subject, such as subscribers like Mr. Caliso and Mrs. Powell on Tubby's paper route."

"Exactly."

"OK. So I think I understand that. Where, in this example, does the data base come in?"

"Well, a data base is all the fields in all the records in all the files that are related to the same general topic. The topic here is Tubby's

paper route." He tried to slow down to let Aunt Ellen catch up. "Obviously we have to have a file of people on his route. Now I'm working on another file, a file of the bills people owe Tubby. It's like I
have to make another file, because this first file is about Tubby's subscribers, but this second file has a different subject. It's about the subject of bills."

Nathan pulled out his pad of paper again. He sketched a table
with his four rows, adding Database, File, Record and Field as the
row labels. He titled the first column "Tubby's Paper Route" and
filled in "subscribers" in the File rows. Then, in another column, he
wrote "bills" for the File. For the Record row he wrote "name, example: Verna Powell" as a subscriber and under that, in the Field row, he
wrote "address, example: Three Pines."

"Do you see, Aunt Ellen? It kind of, like, builds up, from bits of
data about a particular subject."

"Let me see if I can fill in the other side." She took the pencil
from him and wrote "amount due, example: $5.00" next to Field and
under "bills."

"Exactly! A bit of data about a bill would be how much the person owes."

Database	Tubby's Paper Route	—> (continued)
File	subscribers	bills
Record	name example: Verna Powell	?
Field	address example: Three Pines	amount example: $5.00

Figure 4.2

"But now, Nathan, the next one stumps me. I'm not sure what to write for the record in the bill file."

He grinned again, that fabulous, boyish grin. "That is a tough one. And how you answer that question makes a big difference down the road. Answer it right, and programming is easy. Answer it wrong, and ..." His voice trailed off, as if to say, 'Been there, done that ... and it wasn't fun.'

"So what do I need to know about in order to answer the question well?"

"Well, first of all, whatever you use to describe the file—the subject of the file—should be unique."

Ellen looked critically at the left side of the page. Was a person's name unique? Usually, although ... "What happens if two people are both named Verna Powell?"

"Wow, Aunt Ellen, you ARE good! I hadn't really thought about that. So far, Tubby doesn't have any customers who have the same name. But if he ever did, well, this wouldn't work so well." He leaned back in his chair with his head tilted, staring at the ceiling. It was, Ellen knew, his 'I'm thinking' posture. She'd seen him sit that way for half an hour at a time. And it was time well spent; when Nathan was done thinking, something good was bound to pop out.

"Look, Nathan, I've got some stuff I want to read. This has been great; you've taught me a lot. But you've got some thinking to do, and I have to get up early tomorrow. So why don't we leave it for now, and we'll look at it again tomorrow night?"

"Sure." He wasn't really paying attention, just staring at the ceiling, thinking.

Ellen tiptoed away and found Trish and Tommy sitting on the couch watching a sitcom. "That kid is bright," she announced as she settled into a chair.

Tommy smiled proudly. Even though Nathan wasn't his, biologically, he acted like the boy's father in every way, including appreciating any praise Nathan received. "He'll do in a pinch, I guess," said Trish, her eyes bright.

"Aunt Ellen?" The voice came softly from the now-dark bed-room.

"Yes, honey?"

"You didn't kiss me goodnight."

Ellen got up and went to Carrie to give her the ritual kiss at the close of the day.

Chapter 5
Ellen learns more about the computer system.

The next days at Powell went surprisingly well. Ellen got to know more people, including Kirby, the production manager over the Assembly department that she had missed on the first day. Kirby was about Ellen's age, confident and articulate. Ellen found that he was quite willing to help her learn more about things at Powell. He used the computer to track all kinds of things in the factory, printing out various reports, both for himself, and for the workers in his department, to help them run the business. It didn't hurt that he was extremely good looking with a chiseled jaw line and a dimple on the left side of his chin which showed up when he smiled. Which he did a lot. Ellen began to look forward to her daily rounds with Gladys to pick up job cards because she would get to see his emerald green eyes.

She spent some time with Harvey in Fabrication, trying to understand the computer system. It appeared that there was a mainframe computer somewhere (perhaps in that room full of wires behind Whit's office) that Harvey's terminal was hooked to. As Mr. Powell had explained, the mainframe ran some software called SOLUTION/400. Various kinds of data went into the system from various places, information like customers addresses and customer orders, purchase orders and deliveries, invoices and accounts payable, and much much more. The system was supposed to print out reports to help Harvey run his department. But, according to Harvey, it didn't work very well. In fact, he often referred to it disparagingly as 'POLLUTION/400.'

Harvey wasn't very good at explaining things, so Ellen had to struggle to understand what he was talking about. He used words and acronyms she wasn't familiar with, and, when he tried to explain things, he didn't start at the beginning, he just sort of skipped all over the place, with Ellen trying to keep up and absorb what he was saying.

She decided she had better keep a legal pad with her at all times to
write down things she was learning about and things that she needed
to find out more about.

The bottom line was that the computer system just wasn't providing Harvey the information he needed. "Here, Miss Ellen, you look at
this here." He would point to a report. "I need to know if I've got the
steel I need to run this job for Pentacore. But, see, it says I'm out of
three-quarter inch cold rolled, but I know I've got some. I was just
back in the warehouse and there were sixteen sheets. Now how am I
supposed to know what job to schedule on the presses next? On the
other hand, it says we have that 12-294-03 bracket that we get from
Lark Logistics in stock, but I'll be darned if I can find any. And
maybe that cold rolled is supposed to go to another job. How am I
supposed to know that? You tell me!" And he would push his substantial girth back from the desk, take another pull from his cigar, and
look challengingly at Ellen.

Ellen didn't ever quite know what to say. The cigar smoke in
Harvey's office choked her and made her clothes smell so that even
Carrie noticed it after she went home. All she could do was promise
to see what she could find out about where the data was coming from
and why it wasn't right, and try to be as helpful as possible. Not that
she had much to offer yet, but every day brought new insight and
knowledge.

By the end of the week she was collecting job cards alone, without Gladys. Gladys was grateful; walking on the concrete in the factory hurt her feet and she had plenty of other work to do. Besides,
Ellen felt it helped connect her with what was going on in the factory
and would, ultimately, allow her to be more useful to Powell by understanding how things worked. She suspected that some of Harvey's
problems came from the job cards.

She looked at the cards more carefully. They were a simple form,
printed on card stock. Each card had a job number, a date, a part
number, and a quantity. These were filled in by hand, although she
could tell that the handwriting for the job number and the part number
was different from the handwriting of the date and quantity. She felt a

little like Colombo, playing detective and snooping out what came from where and who did what to whom. She didn't have an old raincoat, and Harvey could keep Colombo's cigar, but she did drive an old, rather unique car, and she did have an intense curiosity about how things got done at Powell that often led her to ask, "Just one more question."

She looked at the job card again and, with a flash of insight, realized that what Nathan had told her the other night related to the job cards she held in her hand. Each card was a record, and each piece of data on the card was a field. For example, there was a field for the part number: 12-308-01 for this particular record. It made it more tangible to hold them in her hand. Each card was a record. Each hand-written piece of information on the card was a field. "I guess I'm holding a file, then," she mused to no one in particular. "I've got a bunch of records here, so it must be a file. But what," she paused to ponder again, "What is the subject of this file?"

She wrote on her legal pad, "Find out the subject of the job card file."

One morning, as she entered the plant and said good morning to Gladys, she could tell something was up. There was a tension in the air. It was even more palatable on the factory floor as she went around collecting job cards. People were tense, jumpy, not as friendly as usual. They seemed to be keeping their heads down, ducking some ominous force that was floating through the air.

Mr. Powell was in Harvey's office when she arrived. And the discussion they were having was heated. She almost decided to change her routine, to go to Leonard's area first. Maybe the discussion would be finished by then. But perhaps she could just slip in, pick up the cards and leave, without attracting too much attention.

"This is absolutely unacceptable!" Mr. Powell was shouting as she opened the door to Harvey's office.

"Look, Rob," Harvey was shouting back. "We're doing the best we can with the information we get! The computer says we had enough to make the deadline, and I double checked the parts. We had plenty of steel in stock! So where is it now? That's what I want to know!"

Ellen quietly eased the job cards off of the corner of Harvey's desk. The argument continued. "I don't know where in blue blazes the steel is, Harvey! All I know is, if we don't make that shipment to Wilco by tomorrow, we'll loose them as a customer! Do you understand what I'm saying, Harvey? We'll loose them as a customer. We can't afford that! Do you understand what I'm saying?"

"Yeah, I hear you. Still doesn't mean that steel is out there. I'm trying to get it through your thick head — it was there yesterday!"

"Are you trying to tell me somebody STOLE our steel?"

"You can think what you like. It was there yesterday. The computer says we had plenty. You think I'm lying to you? Here!" Harvey grabbed the computer keyboard. "Ellen! Show Rob here that I'm not lying!"

Mr. Powell punched the wall, hard. "Dadgonit, Harvey! I'm not saying you're lying. I'm just saying we have GOT to get that order out to Wilco or we'll loose them as a customer!" He hit the wall again. "We will LOSE them as a customer!" A small chunk of the dry wall gave way as his fist hit the wall a third time. Both Ellen and Harvey hesitated, staring at the clear indentation of Mr. Powell's fist in the wall. Mr. Powell was rubbing his fist, wiping off the white dust that coated his knuckles but seemingly oblivious to the pain. Ellen could hear her heart throbbing in her ears and images of a keyboard thrown against another wall hovered around the edges of her vision.

Mr. Powell's jaw tightened. "Look," he said. "You were gonna have Ellen show me something. What is it?" His voice was tight, almost a whisper.

Great, thought Ellen. Put me in the middle of this.

Harvey punched a few keys on the keyboard. "Look." He pointed at the screen with the chewed end of his cigar. "Here's the steel part, that 12-293-50 three quarter inch plate. The computer says we have six in stock. We need 12 for the Wilco order. What do you think, Ellen? Would you bet we've got it or not?"

Ellen stared at the screen.

"I can tell you I wouldn't take that bet," said Harvey. "The computer's never right. If it says we got ten, we got two. If it says we got two, we got twenty."

"What does the computer say about the usage history?" asked Ellen. She reached out and pressed a key to take the computer to a different screen. Whit had been kind enough to show her around some of the screens. Here the system showed a list of work orders, with quantities and dates. "It looks like someone used twelve sheets of this part yesterday for work order 50583." She scribbled the part number and the work order number on her pad, just in case she needed to look them up again later.

"50583!" Harvey consulted a hand written list on a clip board. "That's the Wilco order! Somebody's been using the steel for the Wilco order. Wait'll I see what bozo's been doing ..."

"Isn't that what we want?" asked Ellen. "Somebody should be working on the Wilco order, shouldn't they?"

"You bet your a ..." interjected Mr. Powell. He stopped, eyeing the hole his fist had made in the wall.

"Yeah, but why did they start on it yesterday? I mean, this is NUTS!" Harvey seemed at a loss for words.

"Could we go out onto the floor and see if anybody's working on the Wilco order?" asked Ellen.

"Great idea!" said Mr. Powell. "Harvey! Let's go!" He was out of the door of the office before anyone could respond, striding across the factory floor like Daniel Boone through the wilderness. Harvey and Ellen followed as best they could. She almost stumbled as she tried to keep up in her heels.

Harvey grabbed her elbow. "Here, Miss Ellen, don't fall." His voice was warm and fatherly. "I've been meaning to talk to you about those shoes. I mean they aren't safe. You really should wear something more sensible. Might trip, or something drop on your toe. You're a good looking woman. Don't need heels to fancy you up. Better to be safe, know what I mean?"

"Thanks, Harvey. They're uncomfortable anyway."

Mr. Powell was still ahead of them, heading for the laser cutter. They caught up with him already talking to Herb, the operator.

"Yeah, Mr. Powell, that's the Wilco order right there. I started on it yesterday evening just before end of shift. It's about half done." Herb's hair was tied back in a ponytail, and he was wearing a t-shirt that said, "Go Cats!" on it.

"How many plates did you pull for the job?" asked Harvey, a bit breathless from his trip through the shop.

"Sixteen."

"You did no such thing! You pulled twelve; the computer says so!"

"Nope. Pulled sixteen. Left two in stock." Herb pointed over his shoulder to a pallet. "I've cut seven, number eight is on the laser, and there's eight left to go."

"So you're half done with the job," interjected Mr. Powell.

"Computer says you pulled twelve. Must've told it wrong," said Harvey.

"Nope. Don't tell the computer anything. Just told it I was starting job ... " Herb consulted a dirty, crumpled card taped to the pallet. "... starting job 50583."

Ellen thought she saw what was happening. "Does the computer know how many pieces can be gotten out of one plate?" She addressed her question to no one in particular.

"Sure," said Harvey. "It's in the bill of material. You can get four of the Wilco parts out of one sheet of three quarter inch."

"Nope. You can only get three." Herb emphasized his point by spitting into an empty Ale-8-1 can he had by his machine.

"Well, how many pieces is the Wilco order for?" She addressed this question to Mr. Powell, since he seemed to be the one who wanted it so badly.

"Forty-eight," he replied. "Forty-eight pieces to ship by tomorrow, or we loose them as a customer."

"No problem." Herb turned his attention to the laser as it neared the end of its cycle.

Ellen needed to think. If Herb pulled sixteen plates of steel, but the computer thought he used twelve, and if you could get three finished parts out of a plate of steel, but Harvey thought you could get four ... Something didn't add up. "I've got to get the rest of the job cards up to Gladys." She turned to leave.

"Well at least it looks like we'll keep Wilco as a customer, huh Harvey?" Mr. Powell clapped Harvey on the back.

I'm not so sure, thought Ellen to herself as she headed off toward Leonard's office.

Chapter 6
Ellen feels the need for her own place.

Ellen was grateful for the drive home that evening. "What a day, Gunilla," she murmured to her car as she edged out onto the highway. "I need some time to calm down."

It had been a hectic day. Mr. Powell kept pacing back and forth between Harvey's office, the laser, and his own desk. Ellen was sure that Herb and Harvey both felt that they were being micro-managed. She just tried to stay out of the way, especially after Mr. Powell's little display. Every time she was in Harvey's office the dent in the wall reminded her that she probably wanted to be somewhere else the next time Mr. Powell lost his temper.

The Wilco job had finally been finished. Mr. Powell had seen to it personally that it got onto the transfer truck. Then he went to his office and called someone at Wilco. Though she couldn't understand what was being said, it was clear that Mr. Powell was trying to assure the person on the other end of the phone that a near miss like this wouldn't happen again. Then he had stormed out of his office and back into the shop. Ellen had stayed at her desk, looking at the computer screen and trying to understand what had happened and why.

Despite its age, the Saab purred around the curves. The highway snaked around the rolling Kentucky hills. The sharp cliffs around the tops of the knobs were more visible as some of the early trees were already losing their leaves. The yellows of some of the maples and the shagbark hickories were still holding on, beautiful and brilliant in the late afternoon sunshine. The sky was an irresistible blue and Ellen's heart almost ached with the beauty of it. Fall always did something to her; it reminded her of her childhood when her dad would take her and her sister hiking. She loved the smell of the woods in the fall and the crisp tang in the air. She caught of whiff of wood smoke and looked for the telltale plume of gray smoke above a chimney. She thought she caught a glimpse of a smoky haze drifting near one of the twin chimneys on the old mansion that sat back up off the road. Someone must have decided the cooler weather merited a fire in the wood stove. "Such a beautiful old home," she said to no one in particular. "I wonder who lives there?" The maple trees that lined the long curving drive were losing their leaves quickly, making splashes of red and yellow under each tree.

She found she was leaving the troubles at the factory behind. She reached for the radio dial and found an oldies station out of Lexington. "Put it in drive," the announcer extolled his drive-time listeners. He then spun a tune by the Mommas and the Pappas. Gunilla kept all four tires on the road as Ellen rolled down the window and enjoyed the fresh chilled air on her face and hair.

By the time she reached the house, the sun was getting quite low on the horizon. Trish was already home, but Tommy's truck wasn't in the driveway yet. As she made the turn into the driveway, Nathan came whizzing into the yard on his bike. "Hey, Aunt Ellen," he yelled as he skidded to a stop. "How was work today?"

"Fine, Nathan. A little crazy. How goes the paper route?"

"Good! I got two more customers for Tubby, today."

"Good for you. Does Tubby give you some sort of cut for bringing in a new customer?"

"Yeah, he does. And he's going to pay me for the database I've been working on, too! Maybe I can afford to buy a new graphics card for my computer, huh?"

"You bet. Now let's go see what's for supper."

Aunt and nephew entered through the kitchen door. Nathan dumped his backpack of school books by the door and Ellen laid her purse on the counter under the sign that Trish had put up that proclaimed, "Back door guests ... are best!" Trish was busy at the sink, chopping up an onion.

"Hi, El. How was your day?" The tears in her eyes had no other cause than the onions. Trish pushed back a loose strand of hair with the back of her hand. "Did Mister Temper lose it again today?"

"As a matter of fact, he did. Let me go change and I'll tell you all about it. And leave those onions for me. I always could handle onions better than you could."

She slipped back to her bedroom and kicked off her heels. She got out of her skirt and blouse and pulled on some baggy sweats. No need to impress anybody now that the work day was done. She dug around in a drawer and found some thick socks that were just right for a cool evening at home. She slipped into the bathroom she shared with Nathan and Carrie and washed her face. What an odd mixture of paraphernalia! Her own mascara and makeup were interspersed with the new razor Tommy had bought for Nathan and Carrie's bubble bath that came in a container shaped like a dinosaur. I really do need to be looking for my own apartment, she noted to herself.

Back in the kitchen, Trish was browning some sausage. "Smells good, Sis. What're we having?"

"I thought we'd make homemade pizzas this evening. If you'll finish chopping the onions, I'd be very grateful." Trish sniffed and wiped her still-running eyes on her apron.

"Peetha! Peetha!" Carrie came running into the kitchen tackled Trish around the knees. "Oh mommy, I just love peetha! I love it, love it, love it!"

"Well, I am glad about that, sweetie. 'Cause pizza is what we're having."

"Hello, Carrie," said Ellen. "Did you miss me?"

"Oh, yeth, Aunt Ellen." Ellen was then the recipient of a similar knee-high hug. Ellen patted the little red head.

"I missed you too, Carrie. A day without Carrie ..."

"Is like a day without thunshine!" finished the child. Then, zoom, she was off again, back to whatever it was she was up to before the announcement of pizza brought her into the kitchen.

"How is she doing, Trish?" asked Ellen. "Is it working out OK you being home in the afternoons with her?"

"I really think she's doing quite well," replied Trish. "I know I'm enjoying being home with her. She's a spunky little kid, a real plea-sure to be around." She looked up through her bangs at her sister who was now chopping onions without quite so many tears. "I really am grateful to you, El. For forcing the issue, I mean. If you hadn't gone to work I'm sure I'd still be full time at the law firm and missing all this." She paused. "She does miss you, though," she said quietly.

Was Trish trying to tell her something, Ellen wondered. She used the excuse of the onions to blink away any expression that might give away something that shouldn't be. Tommy came in the back door, just then, and, before he did anything else, grabbed Trish and kissed her, "Why, Mr. Thompson!" murmured Trish. "You'll turn my head." It wasn't a little peck on the cheek, but a long, slow, lingering kiss. Ellen was used to this behavior; it was a ritual with the two of them. Every evening, after work, Tommy would kiss Trish and she would say something like "Oh, Mr. Thompson!" or "My stars, sir, how you treat a lady." Then Tommy would say ...

"Have I told you what a lucky man I am?"

He said it every evening when he came in the door. Only tonight, it was a little harder for Ellen. She turned studiously to her cutting board, chopping fiercely and letting the onion fumes bathe her already tearing eyes. "Hi Tommy," she sniffed. "How was work today?" She kept her back to them.

"Just fine, Ellen. But it does a man's heart good to come home to not one, but two good looking women. How about you?" He patted Ellen on the back. "How was your day at Powell?"

"We had a bit of a crisis, we almost missed a shipment to a key customer."

"Don't I know about that!" Tommy rolled his eyes as if the experience of missed shipments were a common concern at his factory, too. "I'm going to get changed, hon."

"El?" said Trish, after he had gone. "Is something wrong?"

Ellen wiped the tears from her eyes. "No ... not really. Nothing, I guess."

"Come on, El. I know you. What's going on?"

"I don't know, Trish. I don't know! I've got this new job, and I really like it, but sometimes Mr. Powell can be so ... so scary ... he hit the wall today and almost punched a hole through it, and ... and

I'm happy for you and Tommy, but, oh … oh Trish." Suddenly the tears welled up for real.

"Dear Ellen." Trish put her arms around her. "You've been such a trooper. Always doing the right thing. I know Mom and Dad are looking down on you and are so proud of you. But I'm sure they would agree with me: it is time to get on with your life. Right now I feel like I'm the most blessed woman in the world. It was rough when Gary walked out on me and Nathan, but you took care of us, even though Mom and Dad were gone and, by rights, I should have been taking care of you. For Pete's sake, you were just 21! But now Tommy has come along and rescued me – he rescued all of us – and I am so grateful to him, and to you. And I want to give you the chances you gave up when you were taking care of us. I wish I could find another Tommy for you; I wish I could give you every blessing I have and that you deserve. But it doesn't work that way. I know in my heart, El, that there's a Tommy out there for you, but finding him isn't something I can do for you." She paused as Ellen wiped her eyes once more. "What I can do for you, El, is give you my blessing – and Tommy's blessing. You're welcome to stay with us as long as you like, but I truly think it is time for you to take your life back. You've got a good job. Is it time to start, well, maybe dating or something?"

Ellen smiled weakly. As usual, Trish had told her things about herself that she hadn't quite known. Still, there was an emptiness, a longing inside her that she couldn't quite put her finger on.

Dinner was surprisingly subdued. The pizzas were a hit, of course; they always were. The family had the tradition of allowing each person to "decorate" their part of the pizza. Ellen always shared hers with Nathan and Carrie – although she noticed that Nathan was soon going to be needing another slice from her share – while Tommy and Trish split a second one. There was always some good natured ribbing about toppings. Ellen liked mushrooms, but Nathan despised them. They squeak when you chew them, he said. Sometimes he would let Ellen put mushrooms on her part, but sometimes he just couldn't stomach it. The juice might spill over on my part, and that would be gross! He let her tonight, but made a bargain out of it.

"Aunt Ellen, if I let you put mushrooms on your part of the pizza, will you look at my paper route database after supper with me?"

Of course she would. But the mood from earlier hung over the meal. It wasn't sorrow and it certainly wasn't anger. Perhaps it was a wistfulness, thought Ellen to herself. A wistfulness for a life that was ending just as a new one began. The team was breaking up, and she, Ellen, was the cause of it. She was entering her new life, entering with some trepidation, but with a resolve. A new life for her, and a new life for Tommy and Trish and ... a new life.

Chapter 7
Ellen and Nathan learn about the grammar of data.

After supper, Nathan immediately plopped down at the computer and impatiently fidgeted while Ellen finished helping Tommy and Trish dry and put away the dishes.

"Hey, Aunt Ellen. I've got this problem."

"OK, Ace. I'm listening. I don't pretend to be a genius, but I'll do what I can. I've been learning quite a bit at Powell. Maybe I can help."

"Here's the problem. Remember that day we were talking about databases, and files, and records, and fields?" He pulled out the sheet of paper they had sketched on.

"Sure, I remember. In fact I've been meaning to tell you – at Powell I just realized they have the same thing. Just a minute ..." She went to her purse and pulled out a Powell job card. "I've been meaning to show this to you. It's a job card. They fill one of these out for every job they do in the factory."

"Hey, neat!" Nathan held the card up and examined it closely. "So this is one record, right? And here," he pointed to the hand-written notes on the card. "These are fields! Here's a field for 'part number', and here's one for 'customer' and here's one for the 'quantity'!"

Ellen laughed out loud. "You are too smart for me, Nathan. It took me a week to figure out what you just figured out in a second. You are one smart guy!" She tousled his hair.

Nathan beamed, but he did smooth his hair back down. "We make a good team! But here, Aunt Ellen, look at this. I think my problem is similar to the thing I don't understand about this card." He pointed to the question mark they had left in their previous drawing, when they had been trying to figure out what to call the name of the bill record in the paper route data base.

"Well, let's see if we can fill out a column for the job card, shall we? And maybe it would help if we made it into a table." She sketched for a minute. "Hmm, now. What should we put for FILE?"

"I think that's obvious – jobs."

"I agree." Ellen wrote "jobs" in a new column in the FILE row.

"And I know what to put for FIELD," said Nathan. "It could be lots of things, for example, part number, or customer or quantity."

"Yes, I think you're right, Nathan. It's as if the fields are all bits of information about the job card. Let's put down Wilco as an example; Wilco is the name of an important customer for Powell."

Database	Tubby's Paper Route	-> (continued)	Powell Manufacturing System
File	subscribers	bills	job cards
Record	name example: Verna Powell	?	?
Field	address example: Three Pines	amount example: $5.00	customer example: Wilco

Figure 7.1

"OK. But we still have the same problem we do for the bills for the paper route. We don't know what to put for the RECORD. We don't know what it is that makes each record special, what makes it unique." His eyes were beginning to sparkle the way they always did when he was hot on the trail of something.

Ellen laughed. It was great to have Nathan for a nephew. "All right. Last time we were looking at this, you had that look on your face like you were figuring something out. Did you do it? Do you know what we should put in for the RECORD?"

"I think I do, Aunt Ellen, but first, let me ask you something. Do you remember when you studied grammar way back when you were in school?"

"You mean like English grammar? And, listen, you, it wasn't *that* long ago!"

"Yes, English grammar. Do you remember the subject of the sentence?"

"Yeah, the subject of a sentence is what the sentence is about. I seem to remember the subject is a noun."

"Right! It is! The subject of a sentence is what the sentence is about. Isn't that the same as what we're trying to figure out here? What is the subject of the bills file or the jobs file?"

"Yes, I think so. I'm not sure where you're going with this, though."

"Well, the subject of the customers file is the customer's name, right? It tells you what each individual record is about. This record is about Verna Powell. That record is about Ellen Murphy."

"Yes, I see. It's like the subject of a sentence. OK, I'll give you that. Each record has a unique subject that tells you what that particular record defines. So what is the subject of the bills file?"

"That's the question! That's what I've been trying to figure out. It can't be a customer's name, because there could be more than one bill for a customer. It wouldn't be unique. In fact, Tubby sends out bills every month, so every customer will have a bill every month. On the other hand, it isn't the month, either. Tubby has lots of customers – if you just said the subject of the record in the bills file was October, you'd have tons of records with the same subject."

"Right, I'm with you. That makes sense, but it doesn't answer the question."

"Well, I think the answer is the bill number."

"The bill number?"

"Yeah, you know. Like when Mom pays the water bill – the bill has a bill number on it. I looked! She writes the bill number on the check."

"Oh, you mean the invoice number … yes, I can see that you might be right."

"OK, invoice number. Is an invoice the same as a bill?"

"Yes, I think they're essentially the same thing. I guess invoice is a fancy word for bill. But wait a minute. How can the invoice number be the subject of the file? It doesn't tell you anything you need to know, like who the invoice is for, or what month it is for." Ellen was struggling to grasp where this was going. Her instincts told her that Nathan was on to something, that this was important.

"No, it doesn't, but I think I have an answer for that, too. Remember in English grammar you had nouns and adjectives?"

"Yes …" Why did he keep coming back to grammar? "A noun is a person, place or thing. And an adjective describes a noun – it tells you more about the noun."

"Right! And the subject of a sentence is a …" He paused to let her figure it out herself. Suddenly, with a flash, she had it!

"Oh! Oh! I get it! The subject of a sentence is a noun – just like the subject of a file in our database is what the record is about. And the adjective describes the noun, the subject – it tells you more about the noun."

"Right! And, if the subject of the bills file is the invoice number …" He paused again.

"… then there can be other fields that describe the invoice! Like who the customer is and what month the bill is for."

"And how much the bill is for, the amount."

Ellen sat back, almost out of breath. She had it! Nathan had figured out a way to get hold of the data in a database. The noun was the subject of the file – what the file is about – and uniquely defined each record. And the other fields in the file were like adjectives; they provided more information about the subject. "Who would have thought?" She was almost talking to herself. "Who would have thought that English grammar would help me understand databases. You are one smart kid, Nathan. I mean it! This is wonderful!"

Nathan grinned. "Now, are we ready to tackle the job card file?"

"Yes, and I think I know the answer. The answer is the job card number! Just like the invoice number."

"Sure! Give me that job card will you, Aunt Ellen?" She handed it over. "Here it is – this one says 50569."

"Yes. I mean, no. No, that isn't the job card number. That's the order number. Let me see that card." She looked the card over, but didn't see a job card number. As many times as she had carried job cards from the factory back to Gladys' office, she had never noticed that there wasn't a specific job card number. She had just always assumed there was one.

"What's an order number?"

"Well, when a customer orders something that Powell makes, we put in a customer order. Each order gets a number assigned to it. I think they're just assigned sequentially by the computer. The order just before this one would have been 50568 and the next one would be 50570. But, see, the order number can't be the subject of the job file, because it wouldn't uniquely identify the job."

"Seems to me like it would. One customer order makes one job to do in the factory."

"But that isn't the way it works. There may be several jobs required to complete a customer order. See there is a different job card for each machine on the factory floor." She could tell Nathan was now the one who was puzzled. "Let's say Wilco orders some wheels. First, a plate of steel has to be cut by a laser torch. Then the pieces that are cut have to be machined on a Milicron machine. Then some other pieces have to be welded to that. And then some bolts and other parts have to be assembled to it on the assembly line. That's four operations for one customer order – laser, Milicron, weld and assemble. And each of those operations has to have its own job card so the operator – the man who operates the machine – will know what to do and how many to make and when it needs to be done by and all kinds of stuff."

Nathan was examining the job card again. "That stuff is all on here. This one says 'operation 20 – machine.' The quantity says how many to make. The due date says when it has to be done by. All of those are adjectives that describe ... that describe what? The job card? But there isn't a job card number, just an order number."

"Yeah, I don't get it. I have to admit I'm stumped, Nathan. There would be an operation 10 for the laser operation on this part, and this operation 20 for the machining operation, and there are several more, an operation 30 for weld and an operation 40 for assembly."

"Each of those operations has to be done to finish the order?"

"Correct. And done in order. That is why each operation has a number: 10, 20, 30 and 40."

"So each order has a job card for each operation?" Suddenly he got that famous look on his face. He leaned back in his chair, staring at the ceiling.

"Nathan? I think you're on to something, aren't you?"

"Yes," he said quietly. "I think I am. Aunt Ellen, remember back in grammar you could have a compound subject?"

"A compound subject?"

"You know. Like 'Aunt Ellen and Carrie bake a cake.'"

"Oh, yeah, where you have two or more subjects. The subject is both 'Aunt Ellen' and 'Carrie'."

"Right. Don't we have that kind of situation here? If you put two things together – if you compound the subject – you would have a unique way of identifying the job card."

"Like what?" She didn't get it.

"What if you could say that what uniquely defines a job card record is the combination of two things – a compound subject, made up of the order number plus ..." He paused to see if she would get it.

"The order number plus ... " What was he driving at? "The order number plus ... oh! Plus the operation number!"

"Yes! That's it! The order number combined with the operation number – doesn't that uniquely define each job card?

"Let me see. There is only one order number per order, so you wouldn't have more than one of those. And we don't duplicate operation numbers; each one has to be different and in sequence. So, yes! Putting those two things together would make a unique combination. You would never have two job cards that have the same order number and the same operation number! Wow! Nathan, I think you've done it!"

"Thanks, Aunt Ellen. I love doing this stuff." He wrote down on their scratch paper 'order number + operation number.'

"Oh, hey, look at this, Aunt Ellen. We could do the same thing for the bill file. Instead of an invoice number, we could have a compound subject."

Database	Tubby's Paper Route	—> (continued)	Powell Manufacturing System
File	subscribers	bills	job cards
Record	name example: Verna Powell	invoice number	order number + operation number
Field	address example: Three Pines	amount example: $5.00	customer example: Wilco

Figure 7.2

"What would it be made up of?"

"The customer's name and the month of the invoice!"

"Sure, I can see that. Each customer has a unique name – at least until Tubby gets two guys named John Smith both taking the paper. And you only give out one invoice a month so …"

"Wait a minute. That wouldn't be good enough because, when you roll back around to October again, you'd have a duplication so …"

"You'd have to add the year in as well," she finished for him.

"Right! Customer name and month and year would make the invoice unique."

"As long as you didn't have to give out more than one invoice to a customer in the same month and year."

"Oh. I hadn't thought of that. Whew! That could be a problem. I'd better ask Tubby if that ever happens." He glanced up at the clock on the mantle. "Wow! I didn't realize how late it was getting! I'd better get to bed. I've got a test tomorrow at school!"

"An English test?" she teased.

"Maybe." The fabulous Nathan twinkle was dancing through his eyes.

"Well go along to bed, then."

Suddenly he flung his arms around her. "Thanks, Aunt Ellen. Thanks a bunch." And off he went down the hall to brush his teeth.

"No, honey, thank you," she whispered under her breath. "Thank you!"

Chapter 8
We learn about inaccuracies in the bill of material.

The following morning, the tension that had been there the day before was still there. If anything, it was even more pervasive. As she pulled Gunilla into a parking space, Ellen noticed that there was a strange car in the lot, a Porsche. Funny, she thought to herself, I've been here long enough that I know when there is a new car in the parking lot. Not that anyone could help but notice a bright red Porsche.

She went out onto factory floor to collect job cards. Herb was wearing his perennial University of Kentucky Wildcats t-shirt. He paused to watch the machine go through its cycle. Ellen took the opportunity to ask him a question.

"Herb, do you remember that Wilco job yesterday?"

"Sure. Got it done on time."

"Yes, I heard. Good for you! According to what Mr. Powell said, that probably saved us from losing Wilco as a customer."

"Yup." He punctuated his monosyllabic response with another spit into the Ale-8-1 can.

"The order was for how many pieces?"

"Forty-eight, I reckon."

"That's what I remembered, too. So how many plates of steel did you use?"

"Used sixteen. Three per."

"That's what I thought you said. You don't happen to have that print, do you?"

Herb thumbed through a stack of very worn and dirty blueprints, looking for the one Ellen had asked for. "Here it is. Part 29-300-01. Made from three quarter inch plate."

"I don't know much about blueprints, Herb. Where does it say what the part number is of the plate steel it is made from?"

"Here." He pointed with a smudged finger. "Part 12-293-50."

Ellen saw the part number. She also saw what she was looking for. "It says here that you can get three parts out a sheet. Is that what that means?" She was quietly amused by the juxtaposition of Herb's grimy finger and her own manicured one with the new, more subtle shade of red polish she was experimenting with.

"Yup. Three pieces of 29-300-01 from a sheet of 12-293-50."

The laser finished its cycle and Herb almost instinctively unloaded the pieces it had produced, then used the overhead hoist to load up another sheet of steel. "I'm sorry, Herb, you're busy. I'll catch you later."

"Sure." Herb spit in his can again and turned his attention back to the machine.

Ellen continued on her rounds, collecting job cards. Harvey wasn't in his office, but she spotted him across the factory, talking to Kirby, the handsome Assembly foreman. "Hey, Ellen," he said as she came up. "How are you today? You look awful pretty." He didn't have to shout the way everyone did over in Harvey's area where the big presses made so much noise.

"Thanks Kirby. I'm doing well. And how's Harvey, today? " She instinctively touched the round man's arm, but then withdrew her hand, chiding herself. She knew she was a toucher, but not everyone was.

"Not so good, Miss Ellen." He waved his unlit cigar around as he brushed some tobacco off of his front. "Not so good."

"Why, what's wrong Harvey?"

"Harvey is worried about Mr. Van Winkle being here today," said Kirby. "I told him it was nothing to worry about – it'll all work out for the best."

"Who's Mr. Van Winkle? Is he the owner of the red Porsche I saw in the parking lot this morning?"

"That's him! Probably in talking to Rob right now. Probably about that Wilco order yesterday. You remember, Ellen, the one we thought we were going to miss the shipment on?"

"Yes, I remember."

"Harvey thinks Mr. Van Winkle is going to make trouble for us."

"What I can't figure out," said Harvey, "Is how Mr. Van Winkle always seems to know what's going on in the plant. It's like he's got this place bugged or something."

Kirby laughed. "Boy, that's some imagination you have there, Harvey!"

"Well, I don't know, but it just seems weird that every time we have a near miss, Mr. Van Winkle seems to know about it. I've gotta get back and see how Herb is doing on that job." He headed out across the factory floor toward the noisy Fabrication area.

"Now, Ellen." Kirby gently guided her toward his office. "How are you doing? Is working here at Powell suiting you?" There was genuine warmth and concern in his voice.

"I'm doing real well, Kirby. Thanks for asking." She allowed herself to be steered toward his office. "I'm learning a lot. I really find it exciting."

"That's the spirit! You've got a lot of brains and a lot of spunk. I like that in a woman!" Suddenly he was self-conscious. "Oh, I'm sorry. I shouldn't have said that."

"That's OK, Kirby. I appreciate the compliment. Now, can I get your job cards?"

Kirby retrieved them off of the corner of his desk. "Here you go. Listen, any time I can help you if you have any questions about Powell or manufacturing in general, you just let me know, OK?"

"Well, there is something you could answer for me. How does a machine operator know how many parts can be made out of a plate of steel?"

"Oh, you want to know about the bill of material."

"I guess so. What is a bill of material?"

"A bill of material tells you what parts are needed to make another part. For example, give me one of those job cards there." She pulled one out of the stack he had just given her and handed it to him. "OK, now this job card is for a AA-100-10 assembly. See over there?" He pointed through the window of his office to a big wire basket of parts on the shop floor. It had a tag taped to the basket with AA-100-10 hand-written in marker. "That's a basket of this part here."

Ellen saw that the job card specified a quantity of 25 pieces, and it appeared that there were 25 of the parts in the basket. "Yes, I see it." Somehow it pleased her to be looking at a job card that represented a real basket of real parts.

"Now, to make that part, it takes two 13-142-11s, one weldment which is part 15-111-02, and ten bolts."

"How do you know that?"

"Well," his eyes twinkled. "I just know it, but you can also look here." He pulled the keyboard to his computer terminal around and typed a few entries. "This is the bill of material."

Ellen examined the screen. She had seen it before, but now she really studied it. She saw that it was for part AA-100-10 and that there were four lines under that. The first one was for part 13-142-11. The quantity was listed as two. Below that, with a quantity of one, was part number 15-111-02, a weldment. Below that was a line with part 00-012-13, a bolt, with quantity of ten. And finally, there was a line with part 00-012-14, which was listed as a nut. "I think I see. The bill of material lists all the parts that are needed to make another part, and how many of each of those is needed to do it."

"Right! See, I told you you were smart. That's what a bill of material is. Of course, there's more to it than that , but you've got the basic idea."

"OK, then, Kirby. Would you look up another part number for me?"

"Sure! What is it?"

Ellen consulted her clipboard. "Part 29-300-01."

"That's a steel part, I think. One of Harvey's, if I'm not mistaken." He punched a few keys on the keyboard and brought up the part number. "Here it is. Yes, one of Harvey's parts, made out of raw steel plate.

Ellen looked at the screen. It was a simple bill of material. Part 29-300-01, a steel 'blank,' was made from only one other part, three quarter inch steel plate with part number 12-293-50. The quantity was listed as 0.25.

"Now, let me see if I understand this quantity. A quantity of 0.25 means ... means what?"

"The quantity, or 'quantity per' as we call it, tells how many of the component parts it takes to make one of the part itself. So, in that example we looked at a minute ago, it takes ten bolts, oh, and ten nuts – I forgot to say that, didn't I? – to make the assembly. Here, the quantity per is less than one, so that means you can get more than one part out of the component part. In other words, you can get more than one steel blank out of a sheet of three-quarter inch."

"Four, to be exact."

"Right! Since the quantity per is 0.25, which is one fourth, you can get four blanks out of a sheet."

"OK. That's very helpful." She was processing all of this in her mind. "So who draws the blueprints for a part?"

"That's done in the Engineering department."

"And who enters this information into the computer?" She pointed at the bill of material on the computer screen.

Kirby thought for a moment. "I don't honestly know. That's a good question. Maybe one of Whit's people in the computer department? How come you're asking all these questions, Ellen?"

"I'm just trying to understand how things are done in manufacturing, Kirby. Thanks very much. I'd better be getting the rest of the job cards up front or Gladys'll have my head!"

He laughed a warm, open laugh. "Don't worry about Gladys. She's kin. If she gives you any trouble, you tell her she'll have to answer to me! And come back and see me any time. You sure brighten up this place."

Ellen headed back toward the front office, dodging lift truck traffic and grinding wheel flash as she went. She was going to have to think about Gladys' advice to give up on the heels for a more sensible flat. She definitely wasn't ready to give up on the skirts and nice pant suits in favor of jeans. She was enjoying dressing for work. She looked at the red polish on her fingernails in the orange glow of the factory lights. She decided the shade looked good, even in this odd lighting. It was called Persuasion. I think I'll keep that one, she thought to herself.

When Ellen entered the office and removed her safety glasses and pulled the ear plugs out of her ears, Gladys gave her an intense look. "What's going on, Gladys?" Ellen inquired.

"Mr. Van Winkle is here. That's his sports car parked outside." She sat down at her desk and crossed her legs.

"So I've heard. So just who is Mr. Van Winkle?"

"Why honey, he's Rob's uncle. He used to run this factory for a while after Mr. Powell – Rob's father – passed away. Mr. Van Winkle was the one who hired me." She shifted in her chair.

"So why is everyone so nervous? People out on the shop floor seem as jumpy as a cat."

"I heard …" Gladys' voice dropped to a conspiratorial whisper, "I heard that Mr. Van Winkle got wind of the near miss yesterday on the Wilco order. He's here to check up on Rob." She glanced toward the closed office door. Ellen could hear the indistinct rumble of male voices over the thumping of the presses out in the plant.

"As an uncle helping his nephew out, or something more?"

"Oh, much more than that. Mr. Van Winkle owns stock in Powell. He's here to check up on his investment."

"So the two of them don't get along?"

"Let's just say that Mr. Van Winkle is a lot more experienced than Rob. Mr. Van Winkle is a vice president for International Dynamics – a real important man. And he expects his investment in Powell Manu-facturing to give him a good return. When he hears about things like what happened yesterday, he gets unhappy."

Ellen could hear the voices rising inside Mr. Powell's office. Please, she prayed, don't lose your temper.

Suddenly to door to Mr. Powell's office flung open so hard that it banged against the opposite wall. "NO!!" Mr. Powell was shouting. "No, you can't take the Wilco business!"

"But Rob." It was another male voice, one Ellen hadn't heard be-fore. "Be reasonable. Powell just isn't equipped to handle orders like this. You almost dropped the ball yesterday. I'm just offering for

International Dynamics to step in so you don't lose the business out-right. This way, you can save face and, when you get your act togeth-er, go after the business again."

Mr. Powell strode out into the hall. His face was red, just like it has been the day he threw the keyboard out of his office, or like he had been yesterday when he had been talking to Harvey. "And how the heck do you find out about things that happen in this factory, anyway? That was an internal thing – we didn't miss the shipment, not even close! Nobody outside of Powell should have known any-thing about it." He strode down the hallway with his loping stride and slammed out the door to the factory.

The other man stepped out of Mr. Powell's office, gazing at the door that had just crashed shut. He turned to look at Ellen and Gladys, standing with open mouths staring at the drama that had just unfolded. Both women remembered urgent work that was waiting for them elsewhere and scattered. Mr. Van Winkle shrugged, turned on his heel, and went back into Mr. Powell's office.

Chapter 9
At home over Chinese food, Ellen contacts the Klamecks.

When Ellen got home that evening, she realized she was bone tired. Her muscles ached, her feet hurt, and a headache that had threatened to materialize all afternoon now insisted on monopolizing her attention. Neither Tommy's truck nor Trish's car was in the driveway; there was a note on the kitchen counter: "El — Gone to get groceries with Carrie. Nathan on paper route. Put your feet up. Picking up Chinese at Pao Tang's. XOXO — T."

It couldn't have come at a better time. She went back to her room, kicked off her shoes, unbuttoned her dress and let it fall to the floor. She almost didn't pick it up — very unlike me, she thought — so she hung in on the bed post. She shucked her slip and pulled on her beloved sweats.

She found some aspirin in the medicine cabinet in the bathroom and let herself out the patio door off the eat-in kitchen. She eased herself into a chaise lounge. The sun was drifting lower in the sky, its light filtered through the bright red leaves of the maple she and Trish had planted in memory of their mom and dad. It was surprisingly warm for late October. The chrysanthemums were in full glory reaching for the final days of sun before a hard freeze nipped them.

She lay back and let the peace wash over her.

But peace was hard to find. She kept going over the events of the day. She thought about the disturbing sight of Mr. Powell slamming out the door to the factory. She tried to guess about Mr. Van Winkle. If asked, she would have said that he was in his late 40s or early 50s. He certainly knew how to dress — the cut of his suit was impeccable and hugged his sculpted shoulders perfectly. He must work out; people didn't look that good who didn't work at it. His hair had a perfect wave and looked like, even in a tornado, it wouldn't get badly mussed.

Why did Mr. Powell seem to dislike Mr. Van Winkle so?

As she began to relax she recalled the conversation with Kirby. Such a nice guy, and helpful, too. And that information she had learned about the bill of material. That was important, but she couldn't put her finger on it quite yet.

She heard Tommy's truck pull into the driveway. In a few minutes the patio door opened. "Oh, there you are. I thought you must be home."

"Yes. Did you see Trish's note?"

"I did. Slimy Chinese for supper tonight, I guess." Tommy was a reluctant convert to Asian food.

They sat for a moment in silence. "Something bothering you, Ellen?"

She sighed. "Oh, it was a tough day at work. A Mr. Van Winkle, who I gather is Mr. Powell's uncle and a stockholder in Powell, came to the factory today. Everyone was very jumpy. I guess he's a big wheel."

"Mr. Van Winkle? Mr. Robert Van Winkle? Of International Dynamics?"

"Yes, I think that's who they said. Why, do you know him?"

"Know him? No. But I do know of him."

Ellen waited for more information.

"He owns pieces of lots of businesses in Lexington and Louisville. Maybe even some in Cincinnati. But International Dynamics is his main company. Oh yeah. He's a big wheel, all right."

"Well that explains it a bit. I gather he has a ... reputation?"

"Reputation? I guess so. He's very wealthy, very powerful. Politicians and movers and shakers all pay attention when Bob Van Winkle comes to call."

"Is he ... unscrupulous? He seemed like a nice man to me."

"Unscrupulous? As in, a liar and a thief? No, I don't think so. But he didn't get to where he is, you can bet, by being a softy and not taking advantage of opportunities when they came along, even if it meant stepping on someone to do it."

"How do you know this, Tommy?"

Tommy sat down in one of the deck chairs and rested his chin in his hands for a moment. A chickadee landed on the bird feeder out in the yard, gave his characteristic "chickadee-dee-dee" call and then flitted away again. "I don't really know how I know, Ellen. I guess it really is hearsay more than fact. But you know how people talk, especially in the factory. Seems that Bob Van Winkle's name crops up all over the place. He's often on the evening news and things. You know ..."

The sun was sinking lower and the heat of the day was quickly giving way to a bit of chill as the shadows lengthened in the yard.

"Ellen, I've got a ..." Tommy stopped at the sound of tires in the driveway and car doors slamming drifted to the back yard. "Back here, Trish!"

Carrie came careening around the side of the house. "Oh Daddy, Daddy! We got Chineeth food and I got a egg roll!"

"Super, sweetheart." He swung her up into his lap and she wrapped her arms around him and buried her face in his neck.

"Oh, Daddy." Ellen could barely hear her. "I love you."

Ellen always marveled to see how quickly a man of Tommy's strength and masculinity could be touched by a little girl with bright red hair and a lisp.

"I love you, too, peanut."

Trish came around the side of the house carrying a sack from Pao Tang's. "Who's hungry?" She came up on the deck and planted a big one on Tommy, right on the lips.

"I am, but not for that nasty old slimy Chinese food."

"Mr. Thomson!" chided Trish. "You will turn a lady's head if you're not careful."

"Oh, Daddy, you thilly. You know you like Chineeth food!"

"It'll do in a pinch, I guess. But not as good to eat as Carrie's neck." He pretended to nibble on Carrie, which reduced the little girl to helpless giggles.

"Anyone seen Nathan?" asked Trish.

"I haven't seen him yet," said Ellen. "Here, let me help set out plates and glasses and I'll bet he's here before we're ready to eat."

At that Nathan streaked around the side of the house on his bike and ditched it against the side of the deck. He looked up. "What's everyone doing back here?"

"I just came out to enjoy the sunshine and, well ... here we all are."

"I've brought Pao Tang's, Nathan, including an order of sesame chicken."

"Hooray! Let's eat. I'm starved."

"OK, Nate. Why don't you come with me and we'll carry in the groceries from your mother's car and we'll let the women folk set the table."

"Yessir!"

Later as they were dispensing with the last of the sesame chicken and the pork fried rice, Ellen remembered. "Tommy, you started to say something to me when we were on the deck. Do you remember what it was?"

"Hmmm ... " Tommy paused with a forkful of rice halfway to his mouth. "Oh, I remember! And, Ellen I don't want you to take this the wrong way because you know you're welcome to stay here as long as you like."

"I know that, Tommy. But it is time. Do you have a lead for me?"

"I think I might. A guy at work told me that his daughter had been renting an apartment in town, from an older couple. But she's getting married and so is leaving the apartment. The guy at work said he thought it was a very nice apartment, reasonably priced. It is over the top of a garage at an older couple's home. Over on Prospect Street, if I remember right. Seemed to me that might suit you — people around, but not too close, right in town where it is convenient. And, the price sounded right, utilities included."

The butterflies again. Was she really ready for this step? She had a good job, now. And Trish and Tommy sure could use the room she would leave. She swallowed. "Sounds promising. How do I find out more about it?"

"The guy gave me the name and phone number. Kind of a weird name — Klameck." He fished around in the pocket of his work shirt under the embroidered label that said "Tommy" and pulled out a piece of paper. "Here's the number."

After Ellen had read a story to Carrie, looked at Nathan's math with him, and chatted with Trish, she left Tommy and Trish snuggled on the sofa watching a sitcom on TV and went into the kitchen.

The phone rang several times before a man's voice said, "Hello?"

"Mr. Klameck? My name is Ellen Murphy. I understand you may have an apartment coming available?"

"Indeed we do. Are you looking for an apartment?"

"Yes. Yes, I am. Could you tell me a little about it?"

"Well, it isn't large. It is over our garage. We think it is cozy — two rooms, a living room kitchen combination and a bedroom. And a bathroom, of course. Nestled among the trees. It has a little deck, if you like being out in the sunshine like I do. Basically it has everything you need — it just isn't very large."

"I don't have a lot of stuff, but I am looking for an apartment. May I ask how much you rent it for?"

Mr. Klameck told her. "And that includes utilities," he said.

"I think I could manage that. Would it be possible to come and see it?"

"Yes, of course. When would be a good time for you?"

"Well, I'd like to make it a time that is convenient for you as well."

He laughed, a deep, hearty laugh and suddenly Ellen liked him. "My dear," he said. "We're retired. Our time is ... how shall we say ... flexible? At your disposal?"

Ellen smiled into the phone. "Well then, would after work tomorrow be convenient? Say 5:15 or so?"

"That would be just fine. We'll look for you then." Ellen was about to hang up the phone when she heard him speak again. "Miss Murphy? Would it be impertinent of me to ask your father's name? It wouldn't be Moss Murphy, would it?"

Suddenly Ellen had a lump in her throat. "Yes." She almost whispered. "Moss and Dora Murphy are my parents."

"Ah." There was a moment of silence on the other end of the phone. "Fine people. I knew your father. We did some business together. A tragedy. I'm sorry for your loss."

She started to say, "It's OK." But it wasn't, so she didn't say anything.

"Miss Murphy, I apologize for any pain I've caused you. I thought very highly of your father. Your mother too. My wife and I will look very much forward to meeting you tomorrow evening around 5:15."

"Thank you, Mr. Klameck. Good bye."

"Until tomorrow then. Good bye."

Ellen gently replaced the receiver in its cradle.

Chapter 10
Ellen takes an order she shouldn't take.

The next day things seemed less tense at the Powell. Ellen said good morning to Gladys and started to make her rounds collecting job cards.

"Ellen, before you go," said Gladys. "I have a doctor's appointment this morning. I may not be here when you get back. I'm not sure how long it'll take — you know how doctor's offices can be. So just make sure you keep things on the level, OK honey?"

"Sure, Gladys. I'll do my best. Nothing serious I hope?"

"Oh, no honey. Just a check-up. Everything's fine."

"That's good. You look extra nice today. Dressing up for the doctor?" She grinned at Gladys.

"You think so?" Gladys turned a bit to give the full effect. Her skirt came to just the right place on her legs to maximize their toned shape. She had taken even more care than usual of her hair and makeup. And her blouse, well, the darts were in just the right place to emphasize her assets and leaving two buttons undone at the top revealed a hint of cleavage. "I do try to take care of myself."

"Well, you look great. Go have a good time at the doctor, if that's possible!"

"Thanks, honey." She picked up her purse from the bottom drawer in her desk as Ellen headed out to collect job cards. She noticed that the weekly staff meeting was going on; the conference room door was shut and all of the managers seemed to be gathered around the table.

Harvey was already on his second cigar of the day. She could tell because the butt of the first one was already in the ash tray that would be overflowing by the end of the shift. He was staring at the computer screen and simply waved his cigar at the stack of job cards on the corner of his desk.

Leonard was polite and pleasant as usual. Kirby wasn't in his office. Ellen scanned the factory floor for him, but couldn't spot him between the lift truck traffic and the grinder sparks and welding flash. She thought about hanging around until he came back. But that wouldn't be right, she thought, so she picked up his cards and headed back to the front office.

She keyed in the job cards into the mainframe system quickly, then headed for Whit's office. He was up to his elbows in the guts of a computer terminal. "Can I bug you for a minute, Whit?"

Whit set the screwdriver he was holding on the workbench. "Sure. What's up?"

"Yesterday I was out on the floor looking at the bill of material. But I'm confused about how the data gets into the system. I know engineering draws the blueprints and specifies the parts needed to make each new part, and how many parts it takes."

"Yes, that's right. Engineering specifies the child parts that go into the parent part. And they specify the quantity per — the number of each child part needed to make a parent part."

"Oh — like if you were to take apart a part into its component pieces, you'd see its children."

"Right. And how many of each." He swiveled around in his chair to a computer terminal and brought up the SOLUTION/400 system. "Here's the bill of material screen." He pointed. "This is the parent part — the main part on the screen — and these are the child parts." He squinted at the screen. "This is the screen for 13-208-57. It has four children: 14-448-22, 14-449-23, 15-908-33 and 16-001-01. It takes one of the 14-448-22 and 14-449-23 weldments, but it takes four 15-908-33s. And it takes two feet of the 16-001-01."

"Oh, I see ... in this column here." Ellen pointed over Whit's shoulder at the screen.

"That's right. The quantity per column tells you how many of each piece you need."

"I'm beginning to understand. So how does this information get into the computer in the first place, Whit? I mean, who keys in each of those child parts and the quantity per?"

```
SOLUTION/400
Bill of Material Inquiry — Parent/Child
Parent Part:   13-208-57    WELDMENT
    Child Part    Description    Unit   Qty. Per
    14-448-22     WELDMENT       EA     1.00
    14-449-23     WELDMENT       EA     1.00
    15-908-33     PIN            EA     4.00
    16-001-01     CHAIN, 3/4"    FT     2.00
```

Figure 10.1

"I believe that the Engineering department enters the bill of material. But I'm not positive about that. You'd have to check with them."

"I'll do that, Whit. And thanks for the lesson."

Back at her desk, Ellen realized that her fears about Whit resenting her being hired at Powell seemed to be unfounded. Whit was a genuinely nice guy who seemed happy to help a greenhorn like herself.

She logged on to the mainframe and began paging through the bill of material screens she had seen on Whit's terminal. She examined a job card she had picked up that morning and entered the part number in the search box. It showed her a list of child parts similar to the list Whit had shown her. She found that she could select a part on the screen and see its own child parts. She could also see the parent parts if she pressed a different function key. By selecting different part numbers she could browse through the bill of material and get a sense of the variety of part numbers at Powell. By browsing up through the bill of material, from parent part, to its parent, to the parent above that, she could arrive at one of Powell's finished products. By browsing down through the bill of material, from child part, to its child, to its child, she could arrive at a raw material part such as a sheet of steel.

The phone rang on Gladys' desk. Ellen dashed out to pick it up.

"Powell Manufacturing, this is Ellen. How may I help you?"

"Gladys?"

"No, this is Ellen. Gladys is out this morning. Is there something I can do for you?"

"I hope so. This is Karl Smithson at Wilco Manufacturing. I need to talk to someone about our recent order."

"Uh, OK, Mr. Smithson. I'll do what I can to answer your questions."

"Good. Its a simple one, really. We ordered 48 pieces on order 50583 that we received yesterday. But our production volume is taking an upswing. We need eight more of part 29-300-01, and we need it as soon as possible. What can Powell do for us?"

Ellen wrote the part number and the order number down on her legal pad.

"I'll have to check with the production scheduler before I can give you a definitive answer. But let me check in the computer for a second." She hunted for some of the screens she had seen Harvey and Kirby use. She looked up the bill of material for part 29-300-01. She found the child part, 12-293-50, the plate steel she knew Herb used to make the part. "It looks like we have two pieces of plate steel in stock. I'll have to check and make sure those pieces aren't scheduled for another job, but, if they're not, we should be able to make eight parts for you."

"That is good news. We're rather up against the wall, here. We've got a customer breathing down our necks and we really need those eight extra pieces ASAP."

"Well, like I say, I can't promise how soon. But according to what I'm seeing here, the possibilities are good. May I take down your contact information and I'll get back to you as soon as I have the necessary information?"

Mr. Smithson gave her his phone number and extension. He also gave her the purchase order number from Wilco for the eight additional parts.

"I'll call you back in less than an hour with an update," said Ellen and she hung up.

She immediately went in search of Harvey, and found him in his office on the factory floor. Kirby was there, too. "Oh," she said. "I'm really glad I caught both of you." She smiled and Kirby jumped up an offered her his seat, the only chair other than Harvey's in the cramped office.

"Thanks, Kirby." She sat, tucked her legs under the chair, and pulled her skirt down over her knees.

"So what's up, Ellen?" Harvey took one last puff on his current cigar — it looked to Ellen like this was number six for the day based on the number of butts in the overfilled ash try — and stubbed it out.

"I just took a call from Wilco." She paused as both men tensed. "No, no, nothing like that. They wanted to add another order for 29-300-01. Gladys is out this morning, so I took the call from a guy named Karl Smithson."

"Oh, yeah. We know Karl. Good guy," said Kirby.

"They want eight pieces as soon as possible. I looked in the system and see that there are two pieces of the plate steel in stock."

"That would be part 12-293-50," said Harvey.

She checked her legal pad. "Right. So, are there any other jobs scheduled that use that plate steel or could it be used for the additional order from Wilco?"

"Let me see ..." Harvey began pecking on the keys on his keyboard. "Nope. Don't see any other orders that would use that part. Hmmm ... " He pecked a few more keys. "Two in stock. Quantity per of 0.25" He scratched his balding head, then turned to Ellen. "How many do they want?"

"Eight pieces ASAP."

"Right. Yes, we could do that. I've got Herb on the laser on a different job, but he should be finishing up about now. We could schedule this job next without a problem and get the order out to Wilco probably even before the end of the shift."

"Tell 'em we can ship it tomorrow, just to give ourselves a little cushion. And then we can wow them by shipping this afternoon."

"Good idea, Kirby!" said Harvey. "Yeah, Ellen, you can call Karl back and tell him we can accommodate his order and that we'll ship tomorrow. Oh, and remind him that the usual rush charges will apply."

"OK. Thanks, guys. I'm sure that'll make Mr. Smithson very happy."

"Wait a second," said Kirby. "Before you go, hadn't we better enter that order into SOLUTION/400 so we have it on record?"

"Grrrr," growled Harvey. "I hate the computer, but I suppose you're right. Ellen, do you know how to enter an order in POLLU-TION/400?"

"No, I'm afraid I don't."

Kirby said, "Gladys usually enters the orders. But I guess she isn't here to do that, right Ellen?"

"Right. She had a doctor's appointment this morning."

Ellen glanced up just in time to see a knowing look that passed between the two men.

"OK, Ellen. Here's the screen you enter orders on." Harvey pulled up a new screen and swiveled his terminal so Ellen could see. "You put the part here on this line ..." He typed 29-300-01. "And the quantity ..." He entered eight. "And the due date ... we'll say tomorrow." He typed that in. "Now, the customer is Wilco ..." He selected Wilco Manufacturing from the drop-down list. "And do you have a purchase order number?"

"Yes, actually I do."

"Good girl!" interjected Kirby.

"It is 33905."

"OK," said Harvey as he entered the last data. "Does that all look right?:

Ellen and Kirby both examined the screen.

"Something doesn't look right about the address," said Kirby. "When you select the customer from the drop-down list, the system automatically shows the address, right?"

"I think that's right." That was about all the confidence Harvey seemed to be able to muster in the computer system.

"But the shipping address is in Indianapolis. I thought we shipped all Wilco orders to Dayton."

"I thought so too," said Harvey. "But the computer can't be wrong. I mean, no one would have made up an address in Indianapolis if we were supposed to be shipping to Dayton, right?"

"Good point, Harvey," said Kirby. "I guess you're right."

"OK." Harvey hit the Enter button to create the job and print out the job card for the newly entered order. The printer on the edge of Harvey's desk sprang to life and printed a new card. "How about I go out and take this job card to Herb personally to make sure he's finished up with that job he's working on. Then I'll get him working on this new job. And, Ellen, you can go call Karl at Wilco that we'll ship his order tomorrow."

"I'll be glad to do that," said Ellen.

"And I'll go see if I can find Rob and tell him that we've gotten another order from Wilco," said Kirby. "Don't forget to remind Karl about the rush surcharge."

"Sounds like a plan," said Ellen. "We each have our assignments. But before I go, I've got to know what that strange smell is, Harvey. Smells kind of like wet dirt."

Harvey laughed and pointed to the section of dry wall where yesterday there had been a fist-sized hole put there by none other than Mr. Powell himself. "I had maintenance come in and mud over the hole first thing this morning. What you smell is wet dry wall and curing dry wall mud."

"Ohhh ..." Both Ellen and Kirby rolled their eyes as they exited Harvey's office.

Once outside, Kirby stopped Ellen. "There's something I'd like to ask you," he said.

"Ask me? What is it?"

"Well, I was wondering if you ... have you ever been to, that is, have you ever seen a tractor pull? Well, what I mean to say is, would you go out with me?"

"Excuse me?" Ellen wasn't sure she'd heard right.

"Probably a dumb idea. It's just that I have two tickets to the Adams County Harvest Festival and there's going to be a tractor pull on Friday night next week. I had just thought that you might like to go, well, on a date with me ..."

"Go on a date? Why, Kirby, I think that sounds very nice."

"Really?" He was beaming. "Oh, just wait'll you see it, Ellen. You'll really like it. We could eat at the fair grounds and we could look at the exhibits before the pull begins. You'll really go out with me?"

"Sure, Kirby. It sounds fun. When and where?"

"Well, we could leave right after work on Friday. Would that be OK?"

"OK, Kirby. I'm game. I assume I shouldn't dress up too much?"

"Heck no. Though I will say you look mighty pretty. But I guess jeans and a sweatshirt would be better. It can get kind of cool in the evening this time of year."

"Got it. I'll be ready to head out as soon as we're done for the day." His eyes were the most intriguing green Ellen had ever seen, and his face, his whole appearance, was devastatingly handsome.

"Excellent. We'll have a great time. Believe me," he said, "Kirby Anderson does not disappoint!"

Kirby went in search of Mr. Powell and Ellen headed back to the front office to call Karl Smithson with the good news.

Mr. Smithson at Wilco was delighted. "Better than I could have hoped," he said. He even said he was expecting the extra charge for the rush order. "Beggars can't be choosers," he said. "We just appreciate Powell helping us out of a jam we're in."

Ellen then returned to her sleuthing about where the bill of material information was first entered into the computer system. She went to the Engineering department where the three designers worked with large drafting tables creating blueprints for Powell parts. She caught up with Sandy, the head of Engineering. Ellen almost laughed out loud as she spotted the pocket protector in his breast pocket sporting a variety of mechanical pencils and erasers. Could he look any more like an engineer? Yet, against type, Ellen had found in the past that she could ask Sandy a question and that he would answer her as patiently and as accurately as he could.

"What's up, Ellen?"

"Hi Sandy. I'm on the trail of some data. I'm trying to figure out how the bill of material gets into the system."

"You mean who actually enters the bill of material into the mainframe?"

"Exactly. I understand the data comes from Engineering."

"Well, that's partially right. We come up with the data when we do the design work. It all starts with the blueprint."

"Could you show me? You know I'm kind of new to all of this."

"Sure. Here, take this one." He pulled out a large sheet of paper with a drawing of a part and spread it out on his drafting table. "See, this part is for ..." He consulted the box in the lower right corner of the drawing. "... for part 30-902-57. This part is a bracket assembly."

"I see." She pointed to the drawing. "This looks like the part here."

"Right. That's called an orthogonal view. It gives you an idea of what the part looks like in three dimensions, but on a two dimensional piece of paper. These drawings here are from the front, the side and the top of the part. The purpose of a drawing, after all, is to tell the person who is making the part how to put it together. These drawings give all that information."

"Well," Ellen laughed. "I wouldn't be able to build the part. But I know the guys out in the shop sure can."

Sandy's eyes crinkled. "Fair enough. Now, you were asking about the bill of material. See this box here?" He pointed to another box toward the bottom of the sheet.

"Oh, I see. It is a list of parts. Those must be the parts that go into making up this one."

"Exactly! You catch on fast. When an engineer finishes designing a part, he goes over his drawing carefully and makes a table of the component parts — the parts required to make the new part he's designed. That table is called the bill of material. And we put it on the drawing so it is there as a ready reference for the person who is building the part."

"Yes, I see. So this particular, uh, bracket assembly, takes four part numbers to build. Right?"

"That's correct. You see four part numbers in the bill of material table. Two steel parts — one is what we call a steel blank and another is what we call a weldment because it is made of several other pieces of steel welded together. And then there are some nuts and bolts. Four in all, a steel blank, a weldment, some bolts and some nuts."

Ellen could see how the steel blank fit into the weldment based on the drawing, and she could see how three bolts slid through the holes in the two parts and that the nuts were used to fasten the parts together.

"I'm particularly interested in what Kirby and Leonard call the quantity per."

"Oh, sure. See, here's a column in the bill of material table that tells you how many of each part are needed. One steel blank. One weldment. Three bolts and three nuts."

"Yes, I see that now. And that data gets put into the mainframe so that the computer knows that, if you're going to make one of these bracket assemblies, you need one steel blank, one weldment, three bolts and three nuts."

"Precisely."

"So who exactly enters that into the computer. The engineer who designed the part and drew the drawing?"

"No, that's actually done in Production Control. When we're finished designing a part, we send a copy of the blueprint upstairs to Production Control. My guess is that they enter it into the system. We're Engineering. We design the parts and products we manufacture here at Powell, but we don't actually control the data in the computer. That's someone else."

"Oh." She consulted her legal pad. "I kind of thought you did that here in Engineering."

"Nope. Sorry."

"Well, OK then. But, Sandy, would you mind to look at a drawing for me?"

"Sure. What are you looking for?"

She checked her legal pad. "It's part 29-300-01."

"I think that's a steel part. Let's go have a look."

Sandy led Ellen into a back room that was wall-to-wall cabinets made of thin metal drawers. Each drawer was labeled with part number range. Sandy went down the line until he found the drawer he was looking for. He pulled a sheaf of drawings out of the drawer and took them over to the drafting table back in the main room. "Let's see ..." He began thumbing through the drawings, looking at the block in the lower right hand corner. "Here we are." He folded the other pages back so that they could examine the drawing.

"I'm particularly interested in the bill of material. Let me see if I can figure it out and you tell me if I'm wrong."

"Go right ahead." Sandy smiled.

"OK, I only see one entry in the bill of material table. That means there is only one part that goes into making 29-300-01. That part is part number 12-293-50, which, according to this is plate steel. How am I doing so far?"

"Right on target," said Sandy.

"Now, according to this, the quantity is 0.333. If I remember my fractions from school, that means basically one third. In other words, it only takes one third of a piece of plate steel to make one of these blanks. Or, to put it another way, you could get three steel blanks out of one piece of 12-293-50 raw steel plate."

"Exactly right. So what is the issue?"

"Well, according to the computer, the quantity per is 0.25. Here, let me show you." She turned to a computer terminal next to the drafting table and logged on. She brought up the bill of material for 29-300-01, the steel blank.

"Oh," said Sandy. "Oh, I see." He took off his glasses and rubbed the bridge of his nose. "That isn't right. Clearly the quantity should be 0.333, not 0.25. It says so on the print right here." He looked more closely at the print. "Why, this is a part I designed two years ago. I know that quantity is right on the drawing."

"Well, if it is any consolation, Herb out on the laser agrees with you. He says he can get three steel blanks out of one plate of steel."

"Of course he can. The computer program that runs the CNC laser would follow the contours of the part in this drawing. It wouldn't work to try to get four parts out of a sheet of steel."

"Yes, I can see that," said Ellen. "Well, thanks, Sandy. You've been a big help. I think I'd better go talk to the people in Production Control about this. But first, can I help you put the drawings back where they belong?"

"No, I'll take care of that, but thanks for asking." Sandy re-assembled the stack of drawings. "And good luck with fixing that error. It isn't good when the computer's wrong. Garbage in, garbage out, you know."

Ellen went upstairs to the offices on the second floor. Production Control was deserted, but for Annie Angel, the department secretary. "They're all in their weekly production meeting," she told Ellen.

"Would you have one of them call me when they get out? I'm trying to figure out an issue with the bill of material."

"Sure, Ellen. No problem." She wrote a note on a pink While You Were Out pad. "How do you like working here at Powell?"

"I have to say I'm really enjoying it. Thanks for asking, Annie. How about you? Do you like it here?" Annie was about her own age, perhaps a little younger. It suddenly struck Ellen that Annie could be a friend.

"Oh, it'll do, I guess. I plan on working here until Larry Dale and I get married in June."

"Oh, I didn't know you were engaged." She spotted the ring on Annie's left hand. "Nice ring. Larry Dale has good taste, both in rings … and in fiancées."

Annie smiled at the compliment. "Thanks, Ellen. That's real sweet. How about you? You got a feller?"

"No. Not really. I've spent the last few years ... well, since my parents died, I really haven't been able to think about dating because my sister and I ... well, I guess we just had more important things to think about." Then she suddenly brightened. "Oh, but I have been asked out on a date."

"Well, now! Who with? Anyone I know?"

"Yes, actually. Kirby in Assembly asked me out. We're apparently going to the county fair to a tractor pull."

"Ain't that something! You'll have a blast. I just love it when those monster tractors take off. You've been to a tractor pull before, haven't you?"

"Actually no. This will be my first one."

"Oh, you'll have a great time. And they say Kirby knows how to show a girl a good time. Good lookin' and everything. 'Course not as good looking as Larry Dale, you understand."

"Of course. I am looking forward to it. This'll be my first date since I had to drop out of college."

"Well, there you go, girl. You have yourself a wonderful time. And make sure Kirby buys you a deep fried pickle."

"A what?"

"You don't get out much, do you? A deep fried pickle. To go along with your funnel cake." Annie laughed as Ellen retreated back down stairs to her office.

Chapter 11
Ellen takes the apartment at the Klamecks.

"Well, Gunilla, that was an interesting day," said Ellen as she was driving down Prospect Street, looking for the address Mr. Klameck had given her. "I took an order from Wilco — not a big one, you understand, but I have to believe that every order helps. And I got asked out on a date. Just what do you think about that, Gunilla?"

The car maintained its tacit companionship with its owner as Ellen crossed Maple Grove and continued on Prospect.

"Now, let's see." She consulted her pad where she'd jotted down the address. "It should be coming up here pretty soon."

She spotted the house in time to turn into the driveway. It was a charming house, sitting back from the curb, with a carefully manicured lawn and, instead of concrete sidewalks, slate flagstones that gave it a subtle class. There was a stately magnolia tree in the front yard and, best of all, a breezeway between the main house and the garage. There was an architectural rightness about the place, a subtle sense of design that said comfortable, thoughtful and welcoming. The house and the garage both had gable windows on the second floor. Could this be my new home, she wondered? She put the car in park and stepped out.

There was a lamp post between the drive and the flagstone walk surrounded by sedum that had bloomed and were now drying in the late fall sun. A pot of yellow pansies graced the porch as Ellen pressed the doorbell.

"You must be Miss Murphy." The woman's voice was a deep contralto, with an unfamiliar accent.

"Yes, I'm Ellen." They shook hands.

"Won't you come in?" The interior matched the outside. Elegant, yet understated. Classic furniture of deeply polished wood, light hardwood floors, fine carpets. Some of the art on the wall looked slightly familiar; Ellen wished she had paid more attention in the art history class she had before she had to leave the university. "Please come this way," said Mrs. Klameck. "My husband is on the patio."

They stepped out into the afternoon sunshine into a lovely back yard, lined by maples and conifers. A man was sitting at a small metal table reading a book. As Mrs. Klameck ushered Ellen out of the house he looked up and placed a bookmark to mark his page. "Hello, Miss Murphy. Won't you come and sit down?"

He was an older man, perhaps in his early 70s with a very square jaw and a full head of silver hair. He was wearing a sweater over a dress shirt and a tie. Ellen stepped across the patio and joined him at the table.

Mrs. Klameck had stepped back into the house and now returned with a tray. "I thought some tea would be good," she said. "Is Earl Gray acceptable?"

"Um, sure." There was an unfamiliar pungency to the tea. Ellen's experience included the store brand at Robinsons and, on special occasions, some Lipton. Mrs. Klameck poured a mug for her husband and passed it across to him. Then she poured a cup for Ellen.

"Milk? Sugar? Mr. Klameck likes it straight, but I like a little of both." Ellen decided she'd take it straight.

"Very good." Mr. Klameck winked at Ellen and took a sip from his steaming mug. "Now, to business. My name is Jonas Klameck, and I would be pleased if you would call me Jonas. You've already met Mrs. Klameck."

"And please call me Rika."

"I'm very pleased to meet you both."

"So you're looking for an apartment."

"I am." She sighed involuntarily. "I live ... how much do you want to hear?"

"How much do you want to tell?" Mr. Klameck placed both of his hands on the table.

"I don't know." She paused and took a sip of tea. "I'm currently living with my sister and her husband. After ... After ..."

"We know about your parent's death," said Mrs. Klameck. "We're very sorry."

Ellen looked away for a moment and swallowed hard. "After my parents died my sister and I really only had each other. Her husband had left her while she was expecting and I ... well, I had nowhere to go. So we helped each other out. But six years ago Trish — that's my sister — married Tommy. And now I've finally finished my degree and, well, I guess its time for me to start working on my own life. I've landed a job at Powell Manufacturing ..."

Mr. Klameck nodded.

"... and so I really am in a position to be a little more independent. An apartment would give me a chance to be on my own, and moving out would give Trish and Tommy more room, so ..." She looked at both of them, listening intently, as if they really cared. "I don't know why I'm telling you all this." She shrugged.

"Because we care, my dear," said Mr. Klameck. "I knew your father and mother. I suppose you may have even been at a party here at our house."

Suddenly Ellen had a flash of memory. A party, lots of grownups. Singing around a piano. "Was there singing?" she asked. "Around a piano?"

Mrs. Klameck laughed. "Yo ho, that was a long time ago. You remember, Jonas, singing Swedish folk songs around the piano?"

"Of course. Those were good days. So you were here, in this house, Miss Murphy, at one of our midsummer night parties?"

"I ... I'm not sure. The house does seem a little familiar. But I must have been very young."

"Oh, I'm sure you were. But just think, Jonas. Here in our home. *Hur fantastikt!*"

"May I ask? Are you Swedish, Mrs. Klameck?"

"*Du har rätt.* You are correct. And please call me Rika."

"How neat! I've always wondered what Sweden would be like. I have a car made in Sweden." She took another sip of tea. It was cooling now and she could enjoy its strange pungency.

"I thought I heard the distinctive engine of a Saab when you pulled in. I do know my Swedish vehicles." He smiled at his wife.

"Now, ladies, may I suggest, before it gets any darker, that Miss Murphy ..."

"Ellen, please."

"... that Ellen is here on business and that we need to show her the apartment. Do you mind, Rika? I appear to be unable to climb the stairs."

Ellen suddenly became aware that he was in a wheelchair as he rolled back from the table. "I'll just take my book inside while the two of you inspect the premises. Then we can have a chat in the living room to see if everything is satisfactory."

"Of course, *älskling*. You must be getting chilled. Miss Murphy ... Ellen, will you follow me?"

The two women ascended the stairs on the back of the garage to a small deck. From there Ellen could see the trees in the back yard and, through them, the setting sun. The orange and yellow hue of the remaining leaves on the maples was intensified by the glow of the sunset. They stepped through the door into a small apartment with sloped ceilings tucked under the roofline of the garage. It was furnished simply with a small couch, an arm chair, and a coffee table. Two gables on either side expanded the elbow room a bit. One contained a window seat, the other a built-in table with two stools. A tiny kitchen — a two-burner stove, small sink, and a half-height refrigerator — was tucked into one corner. The other corner was occupied by built-in bookshelves. Two doors led off of the main room, one to a tiny bedroom with a single bed built into the space between a closet and the wall. There were drawers under the bed, as well as a built-in dresser. There was a small window tucked under the eve. The other door led to a tiny bathroom with a shower. Too bad, thought Ellen. No bathtub. No chance for long soaks with a good book. But the window seat was charming; she could imagine herself curled up there with Jane Austen or Anthony Trollope on a rainy Saturday afternoon.

"Can you imagine yourself living here?" asked Rika.

"It is tiny, but charming. I really don't need much room. After all, its just me. Its so ... compact. The bedroom makes me think of a sailing ship with every corner utilized."

"I was a child near the sea in Göteborg. We Swedes are used to making use of every inch of space. My husband built most of this himself. We planned it very well, don't you think?"

"It is very homey, for sure. Since it is over the garage, does it get extra hot or cold?"

"We put in extra insulation, even insulation under the floor. And it has a separate furnace — you can set it to your comfort. Although," she paused, "We would hope that you would be cautious since the utilities are included in the rent."

"I understand." She crossed to look out to what must be a southern view. "I love this window seat. Do you suppose plants would grow here?"

"Do you like plants? How nice! I love plants, too. Yes, it is a south window that gets a fair amount of sunlight. I would think you could have some success in this window. The other side — she indicated the nook with the built-in table — would have to have a plant that didn't need a lot of light. Perhaps a Spathiphyllum."

"Yes, I can see that. I have a couple of Peace Lillies that I'm nursing along. I can see them here, in a pretty yellow pot."

"Then you like the place?"

"Yes, I really do. What do you and Mr. Klameck need from me? Is there a lease to sign? I'd really like to rent it, if you'll have me."

Rika laughed. "Ellen, you are charming. Of course Jonas and I will need to talk it over, but I feel quite sure he'll be in favor of renting to you. There are some rules we need to go over, too. I tell you what. Why don't you stay here a few minutes, absorbing the feel of the place. I think that's important, don't you? Imagine yourself here. And I'll go down and have a word with Jonas. Then you can come down in a bit — just let yourself in the back door — and we'll have a nice chat. Just be sure and pull the door shut behind you and make sure it locks."

"Thank you Mrs. Klameck, I mean Rika. That's very kind."

Rika descended the stairs and Ellen sat in the armchair. The sun was sinking fast outside and the shadows in the room were growing long. Ellen sat and absorbed the silence. Would this work? Was she brave enough to leave the protective environment with Trish and Tommy and strike out on her own? Would she be scared at night? Would she be lonely?

"There's only one way to find out," she said out loud. "Give it a try." She suddenly remembered her mother saying, if you're going to do something, then do it. Don't put it off worrying about it. "Yes, Mom. You're right," she whispered. She straightened up, gave the room one last look, trying to commit as many details to memory as she could, and headed for the door.

On the landing she surveyed the back yard. Like the front of the house, it was carefully manicured. She didn't recognize every plant, but enough to imagine that, come springtime, the yard would be a riot of color and green. Now it was painted with the falling reds and yellows of sugar maples and the bright earthy yellow of a shagbark hickory in the corner.

She descended the stairs and opened the back door off the patio, where Rika had turned on a light so she could see her way in the gathering darkness. "Knock, knock," she called.

"In here!" came Rika's voice. Ellen crossed through the kitchen and found them both in the living room. "Am I too early?" The room was cosy, the darkness outside being kept at bay by several cheerful candles.

"Not at all. Come sit down." Mr. Klameck indicated a seat on the sofa. "Rika tells me she believes you like the place."

"Oh, I do. Its charming. You did a beautiful job building in all that furniture so it will just fit."

"We enjoyed doing it, didn't we, my dear?"

Rika smiled. "We certainly did, *älskling*. You sawed and nailed and I sanded and varnished."

"So, you would like to rent it?"

"I would very much, if you'll have me."

"Rika and I have talked it over, and we believe you are the kind of renter we're looking for. But first we must tell you the rules."

"Of course."

"The rent is to be paid by the 10th of each month. We take a very dim view of people who don't pay their rent on time. The utilities are included, even a telephone. We would expect you to reimburse us for any long distance calls you make."

"No pets," said Rika. "We had a renter once with a cat. It took us a lot of cleaning to get rid of the smell. And I'm afraid you must park your car on the street. The driveway isn't wide enough for two vehicles."

"No smoking. No parties or loud music. We're old people. We need our rest!"

"Speak for yourself, Jonas. You may be old, but I am in my prime!"

"Very well, Miss Jean Brodie. Have it your way. But we do value a bit of peace and quiet. We'd prefer you didn't come in very late. This isn't a hard and fast rule, but we generally turn in between 10:30 and 11:00. We'd rather you didn't come in, clumping up the stairs at two in the morning."

"Of course you may have friends over to visit. But no sleep overs. And that goes for boyfriends as well as girl friends."

"I don't have a boyfriend," Ellen volunteered, then concentrated on her hands folded in her lap.

"An attractive, charming girl like you? There will be boyfriends. More than one, unless I miss my guess." Rika smiled at her, then turned to her husband. "Is that all the rules, Jonas?"

"I believe so, my dear. The most important thing is that we get along well. You may be a renter, Ellen, but we hope we'll become friends. We don't rent to just anyone, and we hope that the people we rent to will stay a long time. What do you think? Are the rules acceptable?"

"Certainly they are. In fact, with the kind of rules you've indicated, I think I'll like it here even better. You see, with the exception of the two years I was away at college before my parents died, I've really never been on my own. And even college wasn't really like being on my own — there were all the other girls in the dorm. So, to be quite honest, I'm a little intimidated by living in an apartment all by myself. Your rules actually will help me feel more structured, more safe. And I do hope we can become friends."

"That's settled, then," said Rika. "We're agreed. Now, when would you like to move in?"

"There's really no reason to delay, as far as I'm concerned."

"Why don't we say you'll take up residence on the first of November. That makes the rent easy. And it will give us a few days to get things tidied up. Jonas, I noticed that the paint needs a bit of help. Do you suppose we could get Albert to come and paint the apartment before Ellen moves in?"

"I don't see why not. I'll call him this evening."

"Oh, please don't go to any trouble ..."

"No trouble. We usually paint between renters. We'll have it all freshened up for you before you move in. How's that?"

"Oh, thank you. Thank you both. I'm really looking forward to this. What about a lease?"

"Do you want one?" asked Mr. Klameck.

"No, I mean ... Isn't it customary? I don't need a lease if you don't, but I assumed ..."

"We like to do business with people we think we can trust. And we seal it with a handshake." He rolled his wheelchair forward. Ellen stood and shook his hand. Then Rika came over and shook her hand as well. "Welcome, Ellen," she said.

Ellen left by the front door, Rika standing on the covered porch waving until Ellen had backed the car out of the driveway and was half way down the street.

"Gunilla," she said. "I believe we have a new home."

Chapter 12
Ellen and Nathan work out the bill of material file.

The family was excited for Ellen. But they also recognized that this was a big change, both for her, and for themselves. Carrie was still struggling with Ellen going off to "wook" every day. Nathan knew he would miss his evening chats with his aunt, and he asked if he could show her something on the computer after supper.

"When do you think you might move in, El?" asked Trish.

"They said they'd be ready for me on the first of November." The reality of this was really beginning to sink in.

"I'll take the day off and help move your things," said Tommy.

"Oh, Tommy. I don't want you to have to do that."

"Of course I will, Ellen. Family helps family."

Ellen and Trish washed up while Tommy read to Carrie and checked Nathan's homework.

"I'm really going to miss having you around, El," said Trish.

"Me too." She turned to her sister, as she dried a plate and placed it in the cupboard. "Oh, Trish, do you think I'm doing the right thing?"

"I think so. We knew this day would come. I guess … now that its here ..." Her voice trailed off. "You do need your own life, your own place. And of course we'll get together a lot."

"I know." She stacked away the last plate and began on the silverware. "I guess I'm a little chicken."

"Oh, El. You're one of the bravest people I know. You know you can always come back here if things don't work out. OK?"

"OK." Maybe it really would work out.

Nathan was eagerly waiting for Ellen to come and look at what he was doing. He showed her how his paper route database was coming along. Ellen spied the piece of paper in which Nathan had outlined his "grammar" idea about databases.

"Hey, Nathan. I could really use your help. Remember when we did this?" She pointed to the sheet of paper. "I've got another one to try."

Database	Tubby's Paper Route	—> (continued)	Powell Manufacturing System	—> (continued)
File	subscribers	bills	job cards	bill of material
Record	name example: Verna Powell	invoice number	order number + operation number	
Field	address example: Three Pines	amount example: $5.00	customer example: Wilco	component part number

Figure 12.1

"Cool, Aunt Ellen. I love figuring those things out. What's the new one?"

"Well, it has to do with what they call the bill of material."

"What's that?"

"Well, it's kind of like a recipe, I guess. You know how when your mom makes chocolate chip cookies?"

"Yeah. Sometimes she lets me help."

"Right. You know how it takes a stick of butter and a cup and a half of flour."

"And baking powder and salt. Oh, and sugar!"

"And don't forget chocolate chips! Yes, all that goes into making a batch of chocolate chip cookies. Well, at Powell we have something sort of like that, except it isn't stuff that gets mixed together to make cookies, it is the stuff that goes together to make a part."

"Oh, like a nut and a bolt and a ... I don't know what else."

"But you've got it exactly. A certain assembly may take two nuts and two bolts and a certain piece of steel. Or another one may be cut out of a sheet of steel, and you can get four parts out of one sheet."

"OK, Aunt Ellen. I think I get that. So what's the question?"

"The question has to do with this File, Record and Field thing you've got here. I'm pretty sure the File is the bill of material. And I know that one field is going to be the component part number — sort of like the flour or sugar in a recipe for chocolate chip cookies." She wrote on the chart. "What I can't figure out is what the record is supposed to be. I'm totally stumped."

"Would it help if we think of it like a recipe?" said Nathan. "Sometimes it helps me to think of something different, but kind of the same, you know?"

"Like an analogy. Sure. So if we say a component part is like sugar, then I guess the bill of material is like a recipe. So the File is the recipe for chocolate chip cookies, then one of the Fields is sugar. Or eggs."

"Right.

"So what is the record? Is it another one of your compound subjects?"

"I'm thinking that it is, but I can't quite put my finger on it." He suddenly shoved back his chair. "Just a minute ..." He dashed off to the kitchen.

Ellen heard Trish say, "What are you looking for, Nathan?"

"Mom, can Aunt Ellen and I borrow a cookbook for a minute?"

"Sure, honey. But you'll have better luck cooking in the kitchen than at the computer!"

"Ha, ha." He grinned. "We're trying to figure something out." He brought a Betty Crocker cookbook with its familiar faded red plaid cover and opened it to the tab labeled Cookies. "Here is the recipe for chocolate chip cookies."

They both stared at the page and Ellen became very aware of how much she and her young nephew were of like minds, trying to puzzle out the answer. The ingredients were very familiar to Ellen. How many times had she entertained Nathan and Carrie by making cookies, with Carrie sitting on the counter next to the mixer and Nathan on a chair turned with its back to the counter? On the same page were sugar cookies and peanut butter cookies with variations like putting a Hersey kiss in the middle of a peanut butter cookie.

Wait ... was that it? "Nathan, is it possible that we're not looking at this quite right? Is it possible that the File is all the recipes, not just chocolate chip cookies, and that ... " She had it, but then she lost it again.

"Yes! Yes! That's it! You're a genius, Aunt Ellen. See, the File is all the recipes and the Record is a compound subject, made of the recipe you're making and each of the ingredients it needs."

Ellen didn't see. "Go over that one more time, Ace."

Nathan reached for the pad of paper and wrote.

Chocolate Chip Cookies	Sugar
Chocolate Chip Cookies	Eggs
Chocolate Chip Cookies	Flour
Chocolate Chip Cookies	Chocolate Chips

"See? That's the compound subject: the recipe name plus the ingredient."

"Ah, I'm getting it now. So we could add another recipe to the file." She wrote some additional lines under Nathan's chocolate chip cookie ingredients.

Peanut Butter Cookies	Brown Sugar
Peanut Butter Cookies	Butter
Peanut Butter Cookies	Flour
Peanut Butter Cookies	Peanut Butter

"Right. Two fields, the recipe name and the ingredient name, put
together as a compound subject, make each record unique. And we
could add another field, too." He pointed to the numbers to the left of
each ingredient in the recipe and gave her an intense stare.

"Uh, oh, uh ... like the quantity!"

"Right!" He quickly sketched in that information.

Chocolate Chip Cookies	1	cup	Sugar
Chocolate Chip Cookies	2		Eggs
Chocolate Chip Cookies	2.5	cups	Flour
Chocolate Chip Cookies	1	bag	Chocolate Chips
Peanut Butter Cookies	1	cup	Brown Sugar
Peanut Butter Cookies	1/4	pound	Butter
Peanut Butter Cookies	2	cups	Flour
Peanut Butter Cookies	1	cup	Peanut Butter

"Oh," said Ellen. "And you've written two things here, a quantity
and of what at Powell they call the unit of measure. See? Cup, bag,
pound. Each of those make one of our fields, don't they?"

"Yeah, this is so cool!"

"So now let's go back to my problem at Powell. It is like a recipe,
too, right? If a component part is the ingredient, then what is the
Record? It is a compound subject, I'm thinking."

"Me too. For the cookies, it was the combination of the recipe
name and the ingredient. For manufacturing, it is the combination
of ... the ... I don't know what it is called ... the thing that is being
made, and the component part."

"That's called the finished good or finished part. And you're
right. I see it now. It is the combination of the product being made
— the finished good — and the component part." She paused to look
at the sheet.

"Oh, and we have quantities and units of measure in manufacturing, too. We call the quantity the quantity per. And the unit may be a
sheet of steel or a single nut or bolt. So, like the part I've been chas-

ing takes three nuts and three bolts and ... " Suddenly what had been nagging her all day came into focus. She was almost talking to herself now, but Nathan was tracking right along with her. "The quantity per doesn't have to be a whole number." She looked at Nathan. He knew what a whole number was. "We have these big plates of steel. There's this big laser that cuts parts out of it. Kind of like when we roll out Christmas cookies and cut several cookies out of one rolled-out sheet of dough. So the quantity per would be ..." She paused.

"Like one third or one fourth?"

"Exactly! In fact, you've just nailed a problem we have. We have a blueprint that says the unit of measure should be one third, but the computer says it is one fourth. So every time we load a sheet of steel in the laser cutter, the computer thinks we can make four pieces, but we can really only make three. Which means that we're always falling behind." Suddenly she smacked her head with her hand. "Which also means that I may have a big problem tomorrow at work."

"That doesn't sound good."

"It isn't. I accepted an order today, but I'll bet we don't really have enough steel. The computer says we do, but I know that isn't right. We aren't going to have enough steel to make the Wilco order."

Chapter 13
Mr. Powell and Ellen track down the Wilco order.

The next day at Powell Ellen tried to be proactive. She managed to beat Mr. Powell to work so that she could catch him as he came in. She confessed what she had done. She'd taken an order for eight extra pieces from Wilco. She'd conferred with both Harvey and Kirby and they'd agreed the order could be placed. But she was convinced that the computer had the wrong quantity per and that the two sheets of steel wouldn't be enough to ship all eight parts.

She saw his face begin to flush, saw the veins stand out in his neck. She knew his temper was about to blow. She tried to calm him down. "Could we go out onto the shop floor and see what's going on? Maybe ..." She didn't really have anything else to offer.

She watched him calm down a bit. "Right," he said through clenched teeth. "Better we get the facts." He headed out toward the factory door.

Rather than going to Harvey's office or Kirby's area, Mr. Powell went straight to the laser. "Herb!" he shouted above the pounding of the presses. "Did you get an order for eight extra pieces to go to Wilco?"

"Yup."

"Well? What happened? Did you make the order?"

"Wasn't easy."

"But you made it?"

"Yeah, I made it. But I had to borrow a sheet of steel from the CoreGen order to do it."

"What do you mean?"

"I think I know," interjected Ellen. "You were a sheet of steel short. You needed to make eight parts. You had two sheets in stock. But that only made you six, because you can only get three parts out of a sheet of steel, not four like the computer says. You needed another sheet to make the last two pieces."

"Yup," said Herb. "She's right. That's 'zactly what happened."

"So the order shipped?" asked Mr. Powell.

"Dunno. I finished my part." And that, apparently, was all he had to say about it.

"How about we go check with shipping?" asked Ellen.

"Yes, we'll do that," said Mr. Powell. "But first, Herb, I gotta know. This means we'll be short on the CoreGen order, right?"

"Yup."

"Humph!" He scratched his head and Ellen suddenly realized how young and vulnerable he could look. "Let's go check with shipping, then I've got something else to check on." Suddenly he was off, striding across the factory floor, with Ellen scurrying along as fast as she could in her heels.

"Hasn't anyone told you not to wear heels in the factory?" he asked over his shoulder. "Could be dangerous." Over the din in the factory she didn't hear him say, "But you sure look good in them."

The two men who worked the shipping dock were clearly taking it a bit too easy. When Mr. Powell rounded the corner they suddenly snapped to, trying to look busy and covering up for loafing. Mr. Powell had more important things on his mind. "Guys, did eight pieces to Wilco ship yesterday?"

One of the men consulted a computer screen. But the other one answered immediately. "It was here ready to ship when I got here this morning. I loaded it myself on a LTL BestWay truck. I'd say it went out of here about 30 minutes ago."

"OK," said Mr. Powell. "That's good. Well done. But guys, if you don't have anything to do, there are bins that need to be organized." He pointed to a pile of parts in metal tubs against the wall. "There are always things to do, right?"

"Right," one of them said sheepishly. The other one nodded, and stepped over to begin sorting through the parts.

"OK, Ellen. Crisis averted." He headed toward the office door. "But we're not done yet. We've got to check on the CoreGen order."

They climbed the stairs to the second floor where the Production Control offices were. "Hey, Annie," Mr. Powell said as they entered the area. "Is Luther in yet?"

"He just got in," said the secretary. "You can go on in. Hey, Ellen. How was the big date?"

"Oh ... " She blushed. "It isn't until the weekend."

"Well, I want to hear all about it," said Annie.

"Big date?" asked Mr. Powell.

"She's going with Kirby to a tractor pull at the Fairgrounds. Ain't it exciting?"

"Um, yes. Exciting." Mr. Powell looked at Ellen in a way that made her feel just a little bit uncomfortable. "Let's go check with Luther."

They stepped into Luther's office, who was clearly a golfing aficionado. From the posters on the walls to the nicknacks on his desk, everything shouted golf.

"Hey, Rob. What's up?"

"I need to ask you about a CoreGen order."

"I know the one. That's a nice big order."

"When is it due?"

"Next week sometime, I think. Hang on, let me check." He pecked on the keyboard to log into the system. After a few more pecks, he announced, "Thursday next. The 10th."

"Any problems you're aware of with that order?"

"None that I know of. Why? What's going on?"

Mr. Powell ignored the question. "And what is the usual lead time on sheet steel? Ellen, do you know that sheet steel part number?"

She consulted the legal pad that seemed to go everywhere with her these days. "Yes, it's 29-300-01."

"Oh," said Mr. Powell. "Sorry. You two probably haven't met. Luther, this is Ellen. She's our new Information Manager. And this is Luther. He heads up Production Control."

"Pleased to meet you." Ellen held out her hand.

Luther shook it and said, "I've seen you around. Welcome to Powell. I hope this guy isn't giving you too much of a hard time." He winked at Mr. Powell.

"No, I'm enjoying working here. But I really would like to know about that part."

"Oh sure," said Luther. "The lead time on sheet steel is usually about two weeks. Do we have a problem?"

"Possibly," said Ellen. "We were short one sheet of steel for a Wilco order that just went out this morning. We had to borrow it from the CoreGen job. It'll put the CoreGen job short if we can't replace it soon."

"I see what you mean. The CoreGen order is due Thursday next, but if I order steel today, it won't be here for two weeks. At least not with the standard lead time. That'll be cutting it too close."

"Right," said Mr. Powell. "Way too close for my comfort, anyway. Any possibility we can expedite some steel?"

"Sure, that's always possible. But the steel supplier likes to charge us a premium for rush orders."

"I know they do," said Mr. Powell. "But Luther, you're the master wheeler-dealer. See what you can do, OK?"

"I'll do what I can. That shipment of steel for the CoreGen order should arrive day after tomorrow. I'll see if I can talk them into adding one more sheet to the order. Is one piece all you need?"

"I think so," said Mr. Powell. "Right, Ellen?"

"Yes, that's right. But we need to consider one more thing."

"What's that?"

"That the bill of material in SOLUTION/400 is wrong. That Wilco part should have a quantity per of 0.333. Instead it has 0.25. I know it is wrong because I checked with Sandy in Engineering. I saw the blueprint, and I've seen Herb cut out the pieces on the laser."

Luther did some more pecking on the keyboard. "I see what you mean. The quantity per definitely says 0.25. It should be 0.333 you say?"

"Yes."

"I'll just fix that right now. My password lets me fix the bill of material." He pecked on the keys a few more times. "There. Fixed," he announced.

"Good deal," said Mr. Powell. "Thanks, Luther. So, is the weather getting too cold for golf?"

"Never too cold for golf! Why I remember when I was golfing out at Boone's Trace and the wind was so ..."

"If you gentlemen don't mind, I've got some more checking to do," said Ellen and she began to back out of the door.

"I'll come with you," said Mr. Powell. "And thanks for your help, Luther. I really mean it."

"No problem!" said Luther. "That's what I'm here for."

As Mr. Powell and Ellen walked back down the stairs, he said, "I wanted to tell you how impressed I am with the detective work you did there. You may have saved us a big mistake that would have cost us a lot of money and perhaps even lost us a customer. I'm grateful."

Ellen looked at him. Did he really mean it? Everything in his face seemed sincere. There was no trace of irony or anger. "Thanks. I think I'm getting the hang of this."

"I think you are, too. Come to my office some time and let's talk about what you're learning. Not right now, but sometime soon."

"Sure," she said. "I'd like that. Right now, though, I want to track down how that error got into the bill of material in the first place. Errors like that could be catastrophic."

"Catastrophic. A calamity, even." He smiled. "You go get 'em, tiger. We'll talk later." He turned down the hallway toward his office, leaving Ellen clutching her legal pad and wondering what he meant.

Chapter 14

Mr. Klameck challenges Ellen to find the five principles.

The move into the apartment went surprisingly well. Tommy did take the day off, and Ellen was well organized. She had pre-packed everything she could and labeled each box where it should go. She had very little furniture to move since the apartment was already modestly furnished and Trish and Tommy could use things she left behind. Nathan would move into her old bedroom and use her bed and dresser. She brought her mother's rocker and night stand.

It had been a bit challenging to decide what to take for the kitchen. Trish generously suggested she take their parents' china. In the end, however, they decided the apartment was too small to merit a twelve piece full service set. There wouldn't be any place to store them.

Her clothes were also a challenge. The small closet wasn't really big enough for everything and she had to get creative with using some of the built-in drawers under the bed for sweaters.

In the end, however, it began to feel like home. She brought in her plants and found good places for each one. She hung the water-color her mother had given her when she left for college in a nice spot near the door. It was an image of a lighthouse, done in mauves and grays in a remarkable way. Ellen loved the way the artist had created a mood of light and air. And even more importantly, she hung the photo of her parents near her bed. Every morning she would wake to see them, clearly in love with each other and beaming down at her.

"Why don't we give you time to work on getting things just the way you want them. Tommy and I will go out and get some pizza from Gabrielli's and ..."

"Peetha!" interjected Carrie. "I love peetha! 'Spethially from Gabriellieth!"

"We'll bring it back here, OK?"

"That would be great, Trish. Thank so much for your help, Tommy."

"That's what family is for." He hugged her and then herded his family out the door and down the stairs.

Ellen sat down for a moment in her mother's rocker. She was tired, but strangely happy. She looked around the room. The evening sun was slanting through the western window, bathing the room in mixture of cadmium yellow and raw sienna. The quiet wrapped itself around her like a warm, cozy quilt.

There was a gentle tap at the door. "May I come in?" It was Rika. She opened the door. "No, no. Don't get up. You look so relaxed."

Ellen smiled. "I am. Tired, but happy."

"It looks like it suits you very well. You seem to have settled in nicely."

Ellen sighed. "I do so appreciate you letting me rent the place. I plan to be very happy here."

"I hope you will be. If there is anything you need, Jonas and I would be most pleased to assist."

"Thank you."

"We'd like you to join us for dinner tonight if that's possible. A little welcome celebration."

"Oh ... "

"You had plans."

"Well, its just that Trish and Tommy — that's my sister and her husband — just went out for pizza."

"I see." Her disappointment was genuine. "Perhaps another night, then. Soon?"

"Of course. I'd like that very much." Suddenly she brightened. "This may be crazy, but would you like to join us? You could meet my niece and nephew, too."

"Mr. Klameck and I would enjoy that. But he would have a bit of a problem with the stairs, I'm afraid. It is a nice evening. Could we move the party to the back deck? I would be glad to provide some

lemonade. And maybe I could put together something ... a salad, perhaps. Maybe a dessert."

"Oh, that would be great! And Trish and Tommy would like to
meet you both."

"That's settled, then. I'll dash off and pull together something to
go with pizza. And I'll let Mr. Klameck know that our plans have
changed ever so slightly."

As soon as she was gone, Ellen went to the phone and looked up
the number for Gabrielli's. "Hello? Gabrielli's? Are Trish and
Tommy Thompson there? They'll have a young teenage boy and a
five year old red-headed girl with them. Trish is wearing a ... They
are? Oh, great! Could I talk to Trish a second? Thanks."

She waited, listening to the murmur and buzz of the restaurant.
Then she heard Trish's voice. "Hello? Is anything wrong? Who is
this?"

"Its only me, Trish. Listen, change of plans. Mrs. Klameck came
up and invited me to dinner."

"Oh, then, you should go with them."

"No, no! I want to be with you, too. But we decided together to
move the party out onto their back deck. Mrs. Klameck—Rika—is
going to make a salad. But I was thinking, it might be good to add
another pizza to the order, or at least bring some breadsticks."

"Oh, OK. I get it. Sure. That'll be fun. Let me run and turn that
order in so we don't have to wait too long."

"OK, Trish. Thanks. I think you'll like the Klamecks. I know
they'll like you."

The dinner started off a bit timidly. The Klamecks were very
pleasant, but Rika's salad included olives and bleu cheese dressing,
something Nathan detested. But Gabrielli's pizza lived up to its reputation and gradually people relaxed. Tommy and Mr. Klameck talked
about manufacturing, and Ellen realized that Mr. Klameck must have
worked in manufacturing at some point in his career. Trish and Rika
warmed to each other; Trish was easy to like and never met a stranger,
while Rika was as gracious a hostess as could be desired.

It was very pleasant on the Klamecks' back deck. Despite being early November, the weather was unseasonably warm. There had already been two killing frosts, so the flying insects that would have been exasperating in September were completely absent. Daylight was fading fast, but Rika had placed several candles around, washing the group with the warm glow of flickering blue tapers.

The party really began to warm up when Carrie suddenly took a shine to Rika and charmed her with her precocious questions and precious lisp. Mr. Klameck happened to ask Nathan what he enjoyed doing in his spare time and Nathan had gone into a long explanation of his database project which captivated Mr. Klameck. At one point he looked across at Trish and said, "Your young man here is very intelligent. His grasp of the foundational principles of information technology are remarkable for his young age." Then he turned back to Nathan and continue the conversation as if they were peers. Ellen found herself listening in, realizing some of what they were talking about applied to her work at Powell.

When the meal was over, Trish endeared herself to Rika by beginning to tidy up without even asking. Rika tried to dissuade her, but ended up slipping back into the house and emerging, a few minutes later, with a magnificent chocolate cake. Nathan, with uncharacteristic frankness, said that it more than made up for the bleu cheese. Ellen was afraid Rika might have taken offense, but she threw her head back and laughed so genuinely that Ellen knew it would be OK. "I hope you'll visit your Aunt Ellen frequently, Nathan, and that you'll be our guest again for dinner many times. And I promise never again to subject you to the indignities of bleu cheese dressing." Nathan smiled but continued to attack his cake with a gusto that would not be denied.

Trish began making noises about it being a school night, and Tommy admitted that he did have to get up pretty early to get to his work. The departure was warm and real, Tommy and Trish thanking the Klamecks for a lovely time and the Klamecks thanking the Thompsons for the pizza. Nathan solemnly shook hands with Mr. Klameck and Carrie once again charmed everyone by turning and waving as she walked down the drive holding Trish's hand. "Thank you vewy, vewy much," she said. "Good bye, Aunt Ellen. Come and vithit me vewy, vewy soon, OK?" Ellen promised that she would.

"Well," said Rika as she began gathering up the dessert plates and forks and Ellen started gathering up the glassware. "You have a charming family. I can see why you're reluctant to leave them."

"They're the best," said Ellen.

"Ellen," said Mr. Klameck. "I wonder, do you have a moment? I'd like to discuss something with you. Rika, would that be acceptable?"

"Of course, *älskling*. I'll just clear away these dishes. There isn't much here. You sit down, Ellen. I know that look. He has something on his mind."

"Let me just help you carry these ..."

"No, indeed. I have a feeling Mr. Klameck may have something important to ask you." She winked and headed inside.

Ellen was suddenly nervous. Had she broken one of the rules without even knowing it?

"Sit down, my dear. You look like you're in trouble. I assure you, it isn't anything like that." Ellen sat. "No, I just wanted to ask you about the project young Nathan was telling me about. He says you've been helping him with a database project he's working on."

Ellen laughed. "More like he's helping me. Seems like every time he figures out something in his database, it is just what I need to know in my job."

"Can you give me an example?"

"Well, it was a bit odd, but I thought it was brilliant." She explained Nathan's ideas about using grammar to explain about fields, records, files and databases. The more she explained, the more Mr. Klameck asked questions and the more Ellen found herself checking her own understanding. Then Mr. Klameck began asking questions about her work. He clearly knew about her job, about bills of material, about the challenges of making production schedules. By his questions, the relationship between Nathan's grammar idea and what she was seeing on the factory floor at Powell came sharply into focus.

"My goodness!" she exclaimed. "You're really helping me here, Mr. Klameck. I'm seeing connections clearly now that were kind of vague in my head before."

"I'm glad."

"Would you mind if I ran up to my apartment and got my notepad? I'd like to make a few notes."

"Of course, of course."

She dashed off and was showing him the diagram she and Nathan had worked out when Rika joined them, carrying a coffee pot and three mugs on a tray. "Coffee, anyone?"

"Thank you, my dear. A perfect end to a perfect day. As you would say, 'the dot over the i.'" Rika poured and handed around the cups. "Do you realize, Rika, what a treasure we have here with us tonight?"

"The Thompsons are wonderful people. I enjoyed this evening very much."

"They are, indeed. But I'm talking about Ellen here. She's quite something. That nephew of hers is a clever boy. But Ellen is applying these ideas to her work in rather special ways. It reminds me of the old days."

"Ah, the old days. Mr. Klameck was rather well known in his day."

"Now, Rika. Let's not go into all that."

Rika looked at Ellen. "Ask me later. I'll tell you more about Mr. Klameck. But, Jonas, you have that sparkle in your eye. I haven't seen it for years."

"Ha! The sparkle, indeed!" He smiled broadly and swatted the table with the flat of his hand. "The sparkle! Ha! Rika, could I ask a favor of you? In my desk, in the lower right hand drawer, there is a notebook. Would you get it for me?"

"Of course, my darling. For you, anything." She stood and lightly kissed the top of his head.

"I have something I want to give you." When he saw the chagrin on Ellen's face, he said, "Oh it isn't anything wonderful. But something that may be useful to you. And I have a challenge for you."

"A challenge?"

Rika returned with the notebook and laid it in front of her husband. "Is this the one?"

"The very same." He flipped through the pages and Ellen could see that they were blank. It was nicely bound with what appeared to be real, tooled leather. "Ellen," said Mr. Klameck, pushing the notebook across the table toward her. "I'd like you to have this."

Gingerly Ellen took it, feeling the quality of the leather and smelling its bookish scent. "It smells ... wise."

"Ah, what a good word. I hope it does provoke wisdom. Ellen, I would like you to have this notebook, and I hope you will use it. I've been keeping it for just such a person as you. And here you are, sitting at our table as if you've always been here. I hope you will use this notebook much as you have been using your legal pad, there." He indicated the pad she and Nathan had used. "A bound notebook is a better way of recording thoughts, making observations, developing conclusions. Things don't get lost. Don't be afraid to write in it. It may look a bit intimidating, but I hope you will come to treat it as your friend, as the recorder of knowledge, of the wisdom, to use your word, that you acquire. I hope that this notebook can become the journal in which you record the journey I hope you will take."

"Journey? I'm not ..."

"Not a physical journey, but a quest for knowledge. You have already come so far. Farther than you probably understand. If you will allow me, I would be pleased to serve in some modest capacity as your guide. I, too, have been down the road you are undertaking. I may be able to point out a road sign or two."

"I'm not sure I understand."

"Ellen, your work at Powell is very important. In fact, as we wind down 1988, as we near the close of the 20th century, I believe the kind of work you are engaged in will prove to be some of the most important for business success. You've already begun the quest. Understanding the structure of data, teasing out the idea of 'compound subjects' as you and Nathan call them, is a stunning accomplishment."

His gaze was intense. Ellen could tell this was important, that it meant a great deal to him. "I would like to challenge you, Ellen Murphy, to find the five key principles of business information technology systems. I believe I know what they are, and you have already discovered the first one, even though you may not have put it into words yet. I would like to challenge you to observe closely, think deeply, and explore passionately. Capture what you find in this notebook. And, when you're ready to discuss what you're discovering, I'll be available. What do you say?" —

"I'm ..." She traced her finger along the edge of the cover. She opened the notebook and inhaled the clean scent of paper and fine leather. She looked at the blank pages. What, exactly, was he asking her to do? Was she capable of doing it, even if she understood it? She looked up and, for a moment, their eyes met, mentor to student, apprentice to sherpa, older friend to younger friend. "I'm not sure I have what it takes. Or even that I really understand what you're asking."

"As I have it worked out, there are five key principles of business information technology. I call them BITS — Business Information Technology Systems. I'm asking you to go on a quest to discover all five of them. You'll discover most of them, I'll wager, at work. But I think working with young Nathan will help you sharpen your thinking. And I'll be here, any time you want to bounce ideas around."

Ellen caressed the cover of the notebook. "It sounds challenging ... exciting. Fun, even. This idea is bringing out a sense of excitement, of discovery. There has definitely been something going on at work, and with Nathan. I can't quite put my finger on it. BITS, you say. Five of them."

"Yes. Five basic principles of Business Information Technology Systems. And, as I observe, you are well on your way to uncovering the first one. As you go through your day, observe, think, record, write down your thoughts in the journal. You'll find all of them. I have every confidence."

"I love the fine workmanship of the notebook, and appreciate it. And, I guess all I can promise is to do my very best." She paused. "I know I'll need a lot of help."

"Of course. Any time. I will look forward to chatting with you whenever you need me." He wheeled his chair back from the table. "And now, my dear, if you don't mind, I find that this sparkle in my eye has made me rather tired. I think ..."

Rika was up immediately, ready to wheel him into the house. Ellen stood and started gathering coffee cups. "Please, Ellen. Just leave those. I'll get Mr. Klameck into the house and come back to collect those later. You go get settled in to your new home. I hope you sleep well. *Godnatt, sov gott.*"

Ellen saw that she was serious. "I'll say goodnight then. And thank you for a lovely evening. And for my notebook." She held it to her chest. "I'll do my best to be worthy of it."

Chapter 15
The Wilco order was shipped to the wrong address.

The alarm went off. Ellen stretched. For just a minute she wasn't sure where she was. The patterns that the streetlight threw on the ceiling were unfamiliar.

Then she remembered. She was in her new apartment. And, after taking a day off to move, after the physical tiredness of hauling all those boxes up the stairs, she needed to get up and go back to work. She lay just one more minute, counting her blessings and thinking of her mom and dad. And, unbidden, the notebook Mr. Klameck had given her came to mind. She wondered what this day would bring.

Getting ready for her first day of work in her new apartment would take some getting used to. She didn't have her morning routine figured out yet. She started the coffee percolating while she showered. She sat down in her robe and let her hair dry a little while she ate some toast with strawberry jam. The coffee tasted extra good and she found she was humming a little tune as she brushed out her hair and finished dressing.

As she left for her first day of work as an independent woman with her own apartment, she gathered the notebook from the counter where she had left it by the door. The Klamecks' windows were dark; only the streetlight was burning.

Gunilla started like a champ. There was something restful about the early morning as winter approached. The days were getting shorter and shorter; it wouldn't be light for an hour yet. The air was crisp and clean. The only people on the road were people like herself, people going to work.

The lights of the Powell parking lot welcomed her in and the lights through the windows looked warm and inviting. She headed for her desk and hung up her coat. She turned on her computer and checked the bill of material. Sure enough, the quantity per for part 29-300-01 was still correct. She flipped over to the order screen to check on the order to CoreGen. Everything looked right. The order had processed through steel and was on schedule to be shipped on time. Luther's efforts to expedite the extra steel must have worked. She also checked the Wilco order. It, too, had shipped as expected. She breathed a sigh of satisfaction. Maybe things were finally starting to go right.

Now she could focus on figuring out how the bill of material error had gotten in there in the first place. It occurred to her that, to figure the source of the error, she should follow the process all the way through from the drawing of the blueprint to the entry into the computer. She pulled out the notebook Mr. Klameck had given her. She opened it to the first page. She hesitated for a moment before placing any marks on its pristine surface. "Mom used to say that every journey begins with the first step." She wrote her name and the date on the front page.

Then it occurred to her that the journey Mr. Klameck had talked about had actually begun when she and Nathan sat down at the computer that day and began to figure out Nathan's "grammar" ideas. She pulled out her legal pad, the one that was now beginning to look a bit ratty and worn. She decided that it would be right to capture those early ideas into her notebook as well. She spent some time copying the drawings and ideas and, as best she could recollect, dated each entry. She found that the sheer fact of copying the work and tidying it up helped her understand it even better. When she had finished, she began a new page devoted to the process of moving from a blueprint at Powell to its entry into the mainframe computer system. She hoped this was the kind of thing that fit into the challenge Mr. Klameck had laid down yesterday evening.

She was just finishing up when she heard a roar from Mr. Powell's office down the hall. His voice, and his rage, were unmistakable.

Almost immediately her phone rang.

"Ellen Murphy."

"Ellen, this is Rob. I need you in my office. Right NOW!"

"Uh ... OK. Be right there." As she hung up, she realized her hand was trembling. What could be wrong now?

The scowl on Mr. Powell's face as she entered his office spoke louder than words. It was bad. Kirby was there, sitting in the corner chair as far from Mr. Powell's desk as he could get.

"Ellen," said Mr. Powell. "We need your detective skills here. We've had a major screw up. Again. You know that shipment that was supposed to go to Wilco? Well, after all that work, it didn't arrive."

Ellen hesitated. Hadn't she just checked that order? Didn't it show shipping on time? That was the order they'd had to borrow some steel from the CoreGen order to complete, but they'd made up for that by bringing in more steel to complete the CoreGen order. And that order was already through steel and on into Assembly, looking like it would ship on time. "I, uh, I checked the order this morning ... " She hesitated. Was this some kind of trap? "It looked like it went out OK."

"Well, they didn't get it. I just got a call from Karl Smithson in Dayton, wanting to know where the heck his parts are. I could have sworn we shipped them. But I guess we screwed up." He looked at Ellen. "You're new here, so you may not know. Wilco is a key customer. This screw-up probably means we'll lose them." He pounded his fist on his desk. "We can't afford that!"

Kirby looked at Ellen, Ellen looked at Kirby, then back at Mr. Powell. And then the light bulb went off. "Did you say Dayton?" She saw that Kirby suddenly saw it too.

"Yeah, Dayton. Karl Smithson works for Wilco. In Dayton. Why?"

"Because we shipped the order to Indianapolis, if I remember correctly."

"That's right," said Kirby. "We thought it was odd at the time, but the computer said Wilco orders were to go to Indianapolis, so that's where we had it sent."

"You have GOT to be kidding me." If possible, Mr. Powell was getting even more angry. "We went to all that trouble to get the extra parts out the door, and then we send it to the wrong place? I can't believe this is happening!" He threw his hands up in the air.

"Let's take a look at the computer, could we?" Ellen was beginning to see how valuable it was to go to the source of the data. "Let's see what the system has for Wilco's address."

Mr. Powell pecked on his keyboard and brought up the Wilco contact and shipping information. "Well I'll be ..." he said. The billing address showed Dayton, but the ship to address showed Indianapolis. "This is coming back to me, now." He scratched his chin. "Wilco started out in Indy, but they opened a second plant in Dayton several years ago. Most of our production goes to Dayton, but the original address was Indianapolis." He stroked his chin some more. Almost to himself he asked, "But how could our orders have been shipping to the right place until now?"

Ellen didn't have an answer for that one, but she wanted to find out. Kriby seemed clueless.

"Tell you what," said Mr. Powell. "I'll call Karl and tell him what happened. I'll try to salvage our reputation. Maybe the fact that the parts did ship to a Wilco plant, even thought it was the wrong one, will help him cut us some slack." He looked over at Kirby. "You're sure, you're absolutely sure, Kirby, that the order shipped."

"Yes, sir. I am positive the order went out on time." He hesitated. "Of course, what happened after it left here is something I don't know."

"OK. Does that sound like a plan, then? Maybe we can recover from this."

"Sounds good," said Ellen. "If it is OK with you, Mr. Powell, I'll dig into how the shipments go to Dayton most of the time, except for this one shipment."

"Sure, sure. That's good, Ellen. You do that." He looked at both of them. "Everyone know what to do, then?"

"Yup," said Kirby. He scooted past Ellen and left.

"OK," said Ellen. "I'll try to keep this from happening again."

"OK. Thanks, Ellen." He was visibly calmer now. "Why don't you stick around while I call Karl."

"Uh, OK." It wasn't what she would have preferred to do, but she had taken the original call.

Mr. Powell dialed the phone. "Hello, Karl? Yeah, Rob Powell here. I've been digging into what happened to your order." He paused while Mr. Smithson said something. "Yeah, I know, Karl. You were counting on us coming through for you. I have Ellen Murphy in the office with me; she's the one who took your original phone call."

"Hello, Mr. Smithson," said Ellen in the background.

"What happened, Karl, is that we shipped the order on time, but we shipped it to your Indianapolis location rather than to Dayton. We screwed up, Karl, and I really apologize. We tried to meet your additional requirements and come through with the extra parts for you, but we dropped the ball when we shipped the order to the wrong location."

Ellen could hear more words from the other end of the phone, but she couldn't make out what Mr. Smithson was saying.

"Oh. That's good, Karl." Mr. Smithson said more. "All right, then. I really apologize for this, Karl. And you have my word that we'll do everything we can to make sure we don't make an error like that again. Fair enough?" He paused. "We appreciate Wilco's business, Karl. You're very important to us. I promise you we'll do everything we can to strengthen the relationship." There were more words on the other end. "OK, then, Karl. Thank you. Thank you very much. Goodbye." He hung up.

Mr. Powell gave Ellen a lopsided grin. "Apparently Karl had found out that the shipment was in Indy. And, good news, they have a intra-company truck coming from Indy to Dayton this morning, so the parts will be in Dayton by noon today. So Karl's happy. Although we did make him more than a little nervous."

"Whew! That was close." Ellen meant it. "I really want to find out what happened, though. I'm becoming more and more convinced that it is critical that the information in the computer be correct." She pulled out her notebook. "Remember the bill of material issue?"

"Yes, I do. You did a really good job of digging that one out. You're just like Columbo!"

She smiled. "Yeah, and just one more thing ... " He chuckled and she smiled.

"What's that?" He pointed to the notebook.

"Oh, this was a gift someone gave me yesterday. He was suggesting I use it to track my research into computer systems. I was just looking over the information about the bill of material issue." She consulted the notebook.

"Good idea," said Mr. Powell.

"Yes, I'm coming around to thinking it is a good idea, too. So I'm treating this shipment error as another research project." She wrote down the date and some basic facts about the Wilco order. Then she wrote, 'How do ship-to addresses get entered? How do Wilco orders get shipped to Dayton instead of Indianapolis?'

"Agreed. You go get 'em, tiger! Do your best Peter Falk."

Ellen gathered up her notebook and headed out to the shipping dock.

The guys on the shipping dock were no help. The ship to address was simply printed on the shipping documents they received from the front office. They simply followed orders.

"Where do these documents come from, then? How do they come to you?"

"We get a printout that is in our mailbox every morning," volunteered one.

"I think they are printed on the mainframe printer overnight and someone puts them in our box in the morning," said the other.

"Yeah, that sounds right," said the first one.

"OK, thanks," said Ellen. She wasn't getting any useful information here. She headed back to the front office, thinking that Whit might have some ideas.

She poked her head in Whit's office door. "You got a minute, Whit?" she asked.

The Management Information Systems Manager looked up from his work. He had a screwdriver in his hand and was deep into the innards of a computer. "Sure, Ellen. What can I do for you?"

Ellen was pleased. There didn't seem to be any bad blood between them, despite the potential overlap of their work. "I'm trying to track down the shipping documents. We had some bad data today on an order, and I'm trying to figure out where the data comes from. I thought I'd start with how the shipping documents get generated."

"Oh, yeah. Good idea. Users sure know how to screw up data, don't they?" He riffled through a stack of green bar paper that looked like it was headed for the shredder. "We had a bad run the other day, so I think I have some scrap samples around here somewhere. Ah, here it is." He pulled a report out of the stack. "Are we talking about this?"

Ellen looked the report over. "Yes," she said. "That's it." It was titled 'Shipping Manifest' and had big letters spelling out 'MRP072' on the cover page. "Can you tell me about how it gets generated?"

"Sure. It is part of the nightly process that runs automatically every weeknight. This one gets generated by a job called MRP072." He pointed to the first page of the report. "See here? It says this goes to shipping, so we just fold it up and put it in their box." Ellen knew he was talking about the cubby holes in the mail room.

"Great. That's what I needed to know. Now, do you know where this data ... " She pointed at the ship to address on one of the shipping documents. "Where this data comes from?"

"Hmmm." Whit examined what Ellen knew were fields from the record representing this order. "I'm not for sure. I'd have to do some research in the system, but I would think that possibly order entry puts that data in."

"I don't believe I know where the order entry department is," said Ellen.

Whit chuckled. "Well, there really isn't one. That's basically Gladys. She's the one who usually enters the order." He paused. "At least that's what I think. What do I know?" He shrugged. "I'm just the computer guy."

"Ha! Don't underestimate yourself. Thanks, Whit." He went back to taking apart the computer and Ellen went in search of Gladys in the front office.

"Well hello, honey. How you doing?" Gladys' warm smile always put Ellen at ease.

"Doing fine, Gladys. Thanks for asking"

"Are they treating you OK? Is Rob treating you OK?"

"Sure. I'm really enjoying working at Powell."

"So what can I do for you?"

"Well, I'm trying to track down how some data gets into the system. The manifest that goes out to shipping, do you know how the ship-to address gets entered?"

"Well, sure I do," said Gladys. "I enter that data."

"Oh, good," said Ellen. "I was having a hard time figuring that out. So let me ask you about an order for Wilco from a few days ago. It was supposed to go to Dayton, but it went to Indianapolis by mistake. I know you didn't enter that one because I was with Harvey and Kirby when they entered it. They thought it was a bit strange that the order was to ship to Indianapolis because they knew Wilco orders usually go to Dayton."

"Oh, honey, that's easy. I just ignore what the system says. I always use this." She pulled a Rolodex file across her desk and showed it to Ellen. She flipped to the W cards and found the card labeled Wilco. "See?" she said. "Here's the card for Wilco. It shows the address in Dayton. I always override what the system says and enter the correct address from my Rolodex."

"Oh. So let me get this straight. The system tells you an address to ship to, but you always override that and manually enter an address from your Rolodex?"

"Exactly. I mean everyone knows the data in the computer is wrong. This Rolodex." She caressed it almost fondly. "This Rolodex has the real addresses in it."

"Which would explain why Harvey and Kirby saw the incorrect Indianapolis address, but didn't know to override it."

"That's right." She winked at Ellen. "They need me, you see. This place wouldn't run without me."

"I'm sure you're right. But tell me, wouldn't it be easier to get the address corrected in the computer system?"

Gladys laughed. "Honey, that would take an act of congress! I know someone has to keep the right addresses on file, so I just take it upon myself to keep this Rolodex up to date."

"I see. And if we could find out how to update those ship to addresses so that they are correct, it would be a good thing, right?"

Gladys laughed again. "I suppose it would, honey. But good luck with that. I personally, don't think it can be done."

"Thanks, Gladys. I'll let you know if I find anything out." She headed back to her office and opened her notebook. What had she learned just now? Clearly the data in the computer system had to be right. Sandy's statement about 'garbage in, garbage out' rang true. But there was more to it than that. Gladys' Rolodex bothered Ellen. It was great that she had a file with the correct addresses, but it seemed to Ellen that there was something fundamentally wrong with this approach. Perhaps she was going to need to talk to Mr. Klameck about things even sooner than she thought.

Chapter 16
Ellen tackles the first two of the five principles.

There was a definite bite in the air as Ellen left work. Ellen had hung around for a while, hoping Mr. Powell would return to his office so she could share what she'd learned from Gladys.   But it was getting late.

She pulled her coat around her as she wished goodnight to some of the other workers who were leaving Powell at the same time. The western sky was painted a glorious palette of reds, pinks, roses, corals, and oranges. "Red sky at morning, sailors take warning. Red sky at night, sailors delight," she mumbled as she unlocked Gunilla. "I hope this means we'll continue to have good weather."

Darkness fell rather rapidly as she drove the winding road from Oak Lick back to the Klamecks' home and her apartment in Laodicea. The wind was picking up and leaves were skittering across the road as she drove. They looked like little creatures, scurrying home to their dinner.

"Oooh!" she said out loud. "I forgot to stock the refrigerator!" Luckily Robinson's Supermarket was still open and she was able to do some quick shopping before she pulled into her space in the front of the Klamecks' house. She locked her car, lifted the paper sack of groceries and clamped her notebook under her elbow.

As she was climbing the stairs to her apartment, she glanced down at the Klamecks' back deck. She saw Mr. Klameck was sitting in his wheelchair, a cup of coffee at his side. He spotted her and hailed her.

"Good evening, Mr. Klameck!" she called.

"Hello, Ellen," he called back. "Good day at work?"

"Yes, actually." She paused on the stairs. "I think I'm beginning to figure things out."

"Do you have a minute to talk about it? I'd like to hear what you've learned."

She looked at her bag of groceries. "Um, sure. Just let me put these groceries in the fridge."

"Why don't you join us for dinner? I'm sure Mrs. Klameck has made enough. She cooks as if there are six people around the table."

"I don't ... that is ... well, I don't want to be a mooch. I've bought some groceries and I've got to get used to fixing my own dinner. But I wouldn't mind joining you, if you're really sure. There are some things I'd like to talk over with you."

"Wonderful!" Mr. Klameck seemed genuinely pleased. "Oh Rika!" he called. "Set another place at the table. We have a guest for dinner!"

Ellen put her groceries away as quickly as she could and cast a longing glance at her slippers. Her heels clunk, clunk, clunked back down the stairs. "How are you this evening, Mr. Klameck?"

"I'd be better if you'd call me Jonas." He laughed. "Come on. Rika has already called us in to dinner. How about you drive."

Ellen took the handles of the chair and wheeled Mr. Klameck into the dining room. Rika was setting a steaming bowl of potatoes on the table. "Oh, Ellen! How nice you're joining us. You can see, we have plenty. This will be such fun! I'll just get a few more things ... " She ducked back through the door to the kitchen.

"Here, Ellen. You sit here." He indicated the place to his left. "I always sit here where there aren't any chairs in the way."

Rika brought in the last of the food and sat down. "We always say a Swedish grace before we eat," announced Mr. Klameck. "I hope you won't mind."

"Not at all!"

The Klamecks joined hands and prayed in unison.

"I Jesu namn till bords vi gå
"Välsigna Gud den mat vi få
"Gud till ära, oss till gagn
"Så få vi mat i Jesu namn."

"I know it is a bit trite," laughed Rika as she passed the dishes around. "We're having Swedish meatballs tonight."

The meal was tasty and the Klamecks made Ellen feel right at home. "And will there be dessert tonight, my dear?" Ellen had to smile at the earnest pleading on Mr. Klameck' face.

"Of course, *älskling*. We wouldn't want that sweet tooth of yours to starve to death, now, would we?" She excused herself to fetch the dessert.

"Now, Ellen. Tell me about your day. What have you discovered?"

Ellen briefly explained about the mix up with the order being shipped to Indianapolis instead of Dayton. She told him how Harvey and Kirby had been concerned about the Indianapolis address, but hadn't known what to do about it and had entered the order anyway. And she discussed how she had followed the process through and had discovered that Gladys kept a separate Rolodex file of customer addresses. She was about to tell Mr. Klameck her conclusions when he stopped her.

"Just a moment. I think I know what you're going to tell me, and you're right. You've found the first principle. But before we discuss that, may I complement you? I want to point out that you did something that very few people would think to do. You actually tracked down what happens. You started at a point you knew, the shipping dock, and followed the process through the MIS department — do they still call it Management Information Systems or something else these days? — and ended up discovering where the real action happens, with the administrative assistant. That's good work, Ellen, and you must remember that technique."

"Thank you. I felt a little like Colombo on the Sunday Mystery Movie; I kept asking 'just one more thing' until I found the answer."

"Exactly! Always be like Colombo and I'm certain you'll find all five of the principles I mentioned."

Rika returned with apple pie and coffee, to rave reviews from her husband, echoed by Ellen. "That is the dot over the i," said Mr. Klameck.

"Hmmph!" Rika smiled at Ellen. "He just wants a second helping, and wants to make fun of my Swedish."

"My dear, Ellen was just telling me about her day at work. You might find this interesting," said Mr. Klameck.

"I'm sure I will," replied Rika, refilling their cups and giving Mr. Klameck a small second slice.

"So, Ellen, you discovered a Rolodex file that didn't contain the same information as the mainframe. What is your conclusion?"

Suddenly Ellen felt self-conscious. Was she on the right track? "It seems to me that, well, it seems so simple, but the information has to be right. It has to be correct, otherwise mistakes happen, like happened with the shipment to Indianapolis instead of Dayton. Is that the first principle?"

"Yes, yes it is." Mr. Klameck beamed. "But I would like to explore that a bit more, if I may." He smiled over at Rika.

"Ellen, you must understand Jonas. He's an old, scruffy consultant at heart. He always wants to dig a little deeper. You're a bit of a Colombo yourself, aren't you, Jonas?"

"I should hope so!" he exclaimed. He turned to Ellen. "You say the information has to be correct, and that is exactly right. But why does it have to be correct?"

"Well, mistakes happen if it isn't right. Is that what you mean?"

"Exactly. Mistakes happen. But let me ask you about the two men you say entered the order. They were concerned that the shipment to Indianapolis wasn't correct, but they weren't sure. They went ahead and entered the order, despite their misgivings."

"That's right. They thought it was strange, but they accepted what the computer said."

"You see, this is what happens where there is more than one information system in play." He was warming to the subject. "You know one information system is the mainframe, what do you call it?"

"SOLUTION/400."

"Ah yes, SOLUTION/400. But I wonder, can you tell me what the second information system is?"

Ellen thought a moment. Then, just like Nathan had explained about the paper route, she saw it. "Gladys' Rolodex, of course!"

"Exactly!" He winked at Rika. "So there are two databases having to do with where orders should be shipped. One is electronic, in SOLUTION/400, and the other is non-electronic, a Rolodex on Gladys' desk. So what happens when they don't agree?"

"Well, they ... don't agree. The computer says ship to Indianapolis, but the Rolodex says ship to Dayton. I guess Kirby and Harvey didn't know what to believe. They thought Dayton was right, but the computer said Indianapolis."

"Again, you are exactly right. When there is one database that overlap one another — we say when there is data redundancy — then problems of accuracy are bound to arise, because ..." He paused to see if she could finish the sentence.

"Because ... Oh! Because the databases will get out of sync. They won't agree with each other."

"Again, exactly right. When there are redundant databases, over time, the databases will diverge. They will get, as you say, out of sync with each other. And the problem is that workers don't know which database is correct."

"So saying the data has to be right implies, if I'm understanding you, that there is no overlap of data. No data redundancy."

"Yes, a thousand times yes!" Again he looked at Rika. "Did I not tell you, my dear, that she was very sharp?"

"You did, Jonas. That you did."

"And, Ellen, you have now discovered the second principle of business information technology system."

"I have?"

"Indeed you have. The second principle is that the data system must be non-redundant. Any time you have overlap, like you do with the mainframe and Gladys' Rolodex, you have violated the second principle."

"I guess that makes sense." She excused herself and retrieved the notebook where she had laid it by the back door. "I want to write this down."

"I would hope you would. But before you do, let's go back to the first principle. We haven't quite got it nailed down yet."

"What do you mean?"

"Well, you said that the system's data must be correct. And that is exactly true. And then we explored the idea that redundancy of data pushes a system, over time, to be incorrect. We don't know which system to believe. And we'll talk about why that happens some other time. But for now, let's concentrate on the purpose of the system. What purpose does it serve to have accurate data in the system?"

"Well, it lets us know what to do. It lets us know where to ship orders." She thought about Herb on the laser machine. "It lets us know what to produce in the factory, and how much material will be needed for each production job, and it lets us know when we need to order more material, more steel, to complete those jobs. It just ... it lets us know everything about what we're doing."

"How right you are! I don't want to put words in your mouth, Ellen, but would *you* accept the idea that the business information technology system is a *model* of what is actually happening in the business?" He stressed the word model as if it were very important.

"I guess so. Let me think about that." She thought about the job cards she carried around each morning. Those were something real she held in her hand, but she knew there was an equivalent record in the mainframe system for each job card. And she knew that the system had records for shipping manifests that got printed and used on the shipping dock. And she knew that the bill of material in the system was a representation of what was already on the blueprints in Sandy's engineering department. Just about everything that was done at Powell was represented in SOLUTION/400 in one way or another. "Yes, I guess that's so. The computer system represents the real world in one way or another."

"The computer system is a model of what really goes on. And that's why accuracy is so important. If the computer has inaccurate data, then it no longer represents or models the real world, which can bring disastrous results. Didn't you tell me about a bill of material error in which the quantity per for a steel part was incorrectly entered into the system?"

"Yes, and it was almost a disaster. That was when I started thinking about the importance of data accuracy."

"Right you are. So here is how I would state the first principle. See if you agree. The business information technology system must model the business it serves. You see, stating it that way encompasses not only the need for accuracy, but the need to have reality reflected as closely as possible in the computer's data."

"I like that." She took pen in hand and began to document the first principle.

Principle One: The business information technology system must model the business it serves.

"I particularly like the idea of it serving the business," she said.

"I'm glad you do. To me, that is an important concept. The system exists to serve the organization, not the other way around. So often, in my career, I've met technologists who seem to have it backwards. They forget that their job is to serve the business. Instead you often end up with the tail wagging the dog."

Rika laughed. "That is such a strange expression in English. How can a tail wag a dog?"

"It can't," said Mr. Klameck. "But that's the point. Sometimes technology people appear to be attempting the impossible, forcing the organization to meet their needs rather than the other way around."

Ellen said, "Now I've already forgotten the second principle. It had something to do with redundancy."

"Correct. Simply stated, the second principle is that the business information technology system must be non-redundant."

"Oh, right." She entered that into her book as well.

Principle Two: The business information technology system must be non-redundant.

"Wow," she said as she finished. "Two already! Surely the other three aren't as easy as that."

"I would say that they are perhaps a bit more difficult, particularly the fifth principle. But I have confidence that you'll figure them out. You've done a marvelous job of teasing out the first two. Most people never understand these fundamentals. They're doomed to experience technology always causing a problem rather than, as we've been saying, serving the business."

"So to put these to use, I need to look for data redundancy and for ways in which the information system doesn't model the business, particularly in the area of data accuracy."

"Right you are!"

Rika got up to start clearing away the dishes. Ellen stood up, too. "Dinner was delicious, Mrs. Klameck. Rika. Thank you so much. Let me help with the dishes."

"That really isn't necessary."

"I tell you what, my dear," said Mr. Klameck. "Let's let her be a part of the team. You see," he turned to Ellen. "Rika usually washes and I dry. And we both put things away. But why don't you dry and I'll put things away, and we'll be done just that much faster. What do you say?"

"I would love to help," said Ellen.

"I would appreciate the female company," said Rika. "Sometimes Mr. Consultant there gets too deep for me." She tossed her head at her husband. "Besides, I want to hear more about your family."

And so they washed, dried, and put things away together, Ellen chatting comfortably with Rika at the sink while Mr. Klameck wheeled in and out of the kitchen, putting things in their place as Ellen finished drying them.

Suddenly Ellen was aware: she had a new family to be a part of. This one didn't replace Trish and Tommy and the kids by any means. The Klamecks were in addition to Trish and Tommy. A new sense of peace and confidence was beginning to blossom.

When she returned to her apartment above the garage she sat at her little kitchen table, thought about her parents, about working at Powell, and about what Mr. Klameck had said.

Chapter 17
Ellen discovers bar codes.

The next day at work Ellen couldn't find Mr. Powell. She made the rounds, stopping to chat with Harvey and several of the other guys. Kirby wasn't in his office but could be seen on the far end of the plant talking to one of his assembly operators, a younger woman with red hair.

She learned from Gladys, as she returned to the front office area, that Mr. Powell had been called to meet with some customers in Georgetown and wasn't expected back until late in the afternoon. She made good use of her time by getting clearer in her mind how the process for taking orders, entering them into the computer, scheduling work, and shipping an order to the customer all worked. One of her classes in school had used a technique for documenting processes in a flowchart using special meaningful shapes. Drawing the process out on a sheet of paper helped her to see the big picture and the interconnections between various parts of the process.

Whit Collette, the MIS manager, stopped by her office and spotted what she was working on. "I thought I was the only one at Powell who knew anything about flowcharting," he said. "Wait right there. I have something I'd like to give you."

When he returned, Whit held out a piece of stiff plastic with holes cut in it. The holes were the same shapes Ellen was using to draw her flowchart. She had been hand-sketching the shapes: a rectangle for individual component processes, a diamond for a decision, a shape that looked like it was a piece of paper torn off on the bottom for a printed report, a circle for a data tape. Ellen could see that using the plastic template would simplify drawing up the flowchart and make it neater to boot.

"I'd love to borrow this and redraw my flowchart," she said.

"Its yours to keep," said Whit. "The IBM rep gave me several when we bought the new computer. It's an extra and yours now."

"Gosh, Whit. Thanks! This is nifty." Whit went away with a smile on his face and Ellen spent the rest of the day, diagramming the process with her new template, or going out into the shop, or following up on details in the office to make sure she had the specifics right. By the time the clock was moving toward 5:00 PM, she felt like she really understood the process and was even beginning to see some places where it might be improved.

As she left the Powell parking lot, heading home from Oak Lick, a beautiful sunset was again painting the western sky. Ahead she could see a cloud in the sky that seemed to be moving back and forth, up and down. As she got closer she realized it was a huge flock of blackbirds, wheeling and turning, seemingly with one mind. They gathered, flocked, changed direction, divided into two flocks, then merged again with chaotic precision that fascinated and amazed her. How could individual creatures behave in such a way?

"Keep your eyes on the road, girl," she said to herself and to Gunilla, even as she continued to watch the dramatic ballet being played out above her.

She stopped in at Robinson's to do some more serious shopping and buy some of the staples she knew she wanted to have in her tiny kitchen.

As she was checking out, Barney, the owner's son, was fiddling with a gadget attached to the cash register. "What's that you've got there, Barney?" she called out as she was getting ready to get in line.

"Oh, hey Ellen. Come over here. Let me check you out. You can be my guinea pig."

"You calling me a pig, Barney?"

"Ha! You're not still sore over that little incident during our senior year, are you?"

Ellen grinned. It had been a harmless prank and she and Barney were still friends. "Just kidding, Barney. Seriously, what is that?"

"It's this new thing called a bar code reader. You know those little black stripes you see on some packaged food?" He picked up a can of kidney beans out of her buggy. "See, here's one."

"Oh, yeah. I've been seeing those. What are they? What are they for?"

"Well, I'm not sure how it works, but this gadget here ..." He indicated a thing that looked like a gun, with a red beam of light coming out of its barrel. "This here's the reader. You wave it over those black lines, they're called bar codes, and bingo! It reads the code." Barney held the reader in front of the bar code on the can of kidney beans and, sure enough, it beeped and the display on the cash register said "beans, kid 15 oz $0.79.".

"Wow!" said Ellen. "That's amazing!"

"It sure is!" said Barney. "This is 1988. You've got to stay up with the latest technology. I've been trying to get the old man to let me try it for about a year now. He's finally let me get one and install it. I'm just ready to test it. Want to be my first?"

"Sure!" said Ellen.

Barney took each item out of Ellen's buggy and passed the scanner over the bar code. In most cases the price came up on the screen and that was all he had to do. No keying in of the price, not hunting for missing price tags. A few times he couldn't get the code to read, and some items simply didn't have a code — such as on the fresh vegetables she was purchasing. But it certainly went more quickly than even Myrtle, Robinson's long-time checkout clerk who was a whiz at the cash register, could do it.

Barney pushed the total button on the register, and Ellen's total was immediately displayed. "Tell you what," said Barney. "For being the first customer to try out the new bar code system, I'll give you a ten percent discount." He winked at her as he entered the discount into the cash register.

Ellen pulled the money out of her purse and paid him. "That's very nice, Barney. Thanks." He counted out her change. "But tell me, how does it work? I don't mean how does that scanner work — that's way more than I'm sure I can understand — but I mean the process. Do you have a computer with all of these codes in it somewhere?"

"Sure we do. There's this group called the Uniform Code Council. As independent grocers, we're members through our association. That council keeps track of all the bar codes on all the packaged food items. We buy a database of those codes. That database will tell our computer that the code I read off that can of kidney beans is actually the code for a 15.5 oz. can of red kidney beans for that specific manufacturer. In the database in our computer, which is up there ..." He pointed to the mezzanine office in the back of the store. "I program in the cost of every item we sell. Then, when I scan the bar code, the cash register knows what I've scanned and how much to charge for it."

"That is fantastic, Barney. And so much faster, too."

"You bet! Faster and more accurate. No more mis-keyed prices. And, on top of that, I can now tell how many items we sell each day, without having to take a physical inventory." He handed her the sales receipt, with each item she had purchased along with the price listed neatly, line by line. "You remember when I had to break a date with you our junior year because I had to do an inventory for my dad?"

"Uh, yeah. You broke my heart." She smiled to let him know she'd gotten over it.

"Sorry. Really, I am. But, see, my dad was losing control of boxed cereals and we had to do an emergency inventory to make sure how many boxes of corn flakes and shredded wheat we had in stock. We had to count every single box by hand. Now, with the bar code system, each time a cashier scans something, the computer knows to deduct one from inventory. Now I can know when I need to reorder corn flakes or kidney beans because the inventory is up to date."

"I see what you mean. That is really neat! If everything works as planned, you'd be able to say that there are 14 boxes of corn flakes left on the shelves and you'd better order more when that number goes down to ten."

"Exactly! That's called a stocking minimum. We set a stocking minimum on each item, depending on how quickly it sells and how long it takes to get a replacement — we call that the lead time."

"We call it a lead time at Powell, too. Only we're ordering steel, not corn flakes."

"I didn't know you were working at Powell. I hear that's a good place to work."

"It is. I like it a lot. And I think this bar code thing could be helpful in our work, too. Tell me, do all the bar codes get printed on the box by the manufacturer?"

"More and more they do, but everything isn't covered. At least not yet. So we have a bar code printer up in the office. We can print our own stickers to put on things that don't have a bar code. For example, you know those bags of yeast?" He indicated a small bag with a twist tie in her shopping bag. "We buy that in bulk, and then put our own bar code label on the bag so it will work with the bar code scanner."

"So you can make your own bar codes. Hmmm ... I haven't heard of anyone in our business putting bar codes on things, but you're giving me an idea. Hey, Barney, thanks a lot. It has been great to talk to you!"

"You too, Ellen. Next time you come in I plan to have these scanners in both checkout lanes. See ya!"

"Well, Gunilla," she said to her car as she placed the groceries in the passenger seat. "That was very interesting!"

When she arrived at her apartment, there was no sign of the Kalmecks on the back deck. So Ellen went up her stairs and into her cozy little home. She changed into jeans and a sweater and went about cooking herself some dinner. At first the quiet bothered her so she turned on the radio. But the DJ started getting annoying so she turned the radio off again, and began to appreciate the stillness of her own place.

After she'd washed and put away her supper dishes, she sat in her mother's rocker and read Caddie Woodlawn all the way through. She stretched, rubbed her eyes, looked at her watch and suddenly realized she was tired. She dressed for bed, brushed her teeth, and snuggled down in her little bed. Thoughts of Nathan and Carrie winged through her mind. Before she knew it, the alarm clock was ringing.

Breakfast was still a simple affair: coffee, toast, and her favorite strawberry jam. She added a bit of blueberry yoghurt that she'd bought at Robinson's the night before. Which started her thinking about the bar code reading system Barney had shown her. The idea from yesterday was beginning to become clearer.

The drive in to work was peaceful. Initially she had the radio on, but she turned it off so she could think. Would stickers with bar codes printed on them stay put on pieces of steel?

The sun was beginning to peek over the eastern knobs as she neared the outskirts of Oak Lick. School busses were already queuing up at the middle school and traffic on the bypass was building toward what served for Oak Lick's morning rush hour.

She hung up her coat and stashed her purse in her desk drawer and immediately went to Mr. Powell's office. He wasn't there. She went to the front office. Gladys was there, checking her eye liner in her compact mirror. "Good morning, Gladys," said Ellen.

"Why, hello, sweetie. How are you today?"

"Fine thanks. Just looking for Mr. Powell. Have you seen him yet this morning?"

"No, honey, I sure haven't. But let me check ..." She consulted a desk calendar. "Sure enough, he has a morning meeting today with Mr. Van Winkle in Lexington. I wouldn't expect him back until after lunch."

"Oh, OK. Thanks." She headed back to her office.

She sketched out her ideas for using bar codes on a piece of paper, then she went down to see if Whit Collette was in his office.

"Hey, Ellen." He looked up from the computer terminal he was working on. The cowl was off of the monitor and several circuit boards were laid out on his desk. "What's up?"

"I saw something yesterday I'd like to get your take on. I was in Robinson's last night and they have this new thing called a barcode scanner. It reads those little black lines you see on cans of food, I think with a laser or something. Do you know anything about that?"

"Ya gotta love a girl who likes bar codes!" He winked. "I didn't figure anyone else around here even knew what they are. Yeah, I know a bit about them. I've been keeping up on the developments with UPC and code 3 of 9. I'd love to play with them, but there's just no need for that here. They're for grocery stores and such like."

"Maybe ... I was kind of thinking there might be a way we could use them, but first we'd have to be able to print a bar code. Any way we could do that?"

"Let me see ..." He reached on the shelf up above his desk and pulled down a catalog. "I think I saw something the other day ..." He began flipping pages in the catalog. "There it is! I knew I'd seen one." He turned the catalog around so that Ellen could see, too. "It's a dedicated bar code printer, see? And it has the specification that would allow our mainframe to talk to it. Kinda expensive, just to print little labels, but there it is."

Ellen looked at the price. It was expensive. Too expensive. "Wow, that is a chunk of money. Too much for us. But, just since I'm looking, how much do those readers cost?"

"Oh, they're more reasonable." He flipped pages in the catalog again. "Here's one that connects between the monitor and the keyboard. You could think of it as an automated typist. It sends a signal to the monitor containing whatever it reads in the bar code. It is as if you'd typed that same number on the keyboard."

"Is that how that works? I thought the bar code contains the data, but it just contains a number? Last night a Robinson's, Barney scanned the label on a can of kidney beans and it came up with the size of the can and the price."

"I think the bar code just contains a number. Then the database on the computer can match that number with an inventory code, or something like that, and the inventory record contains the size and the price and probably much more."

"Oh, I think I get it. And could that number be just any old number — it doesn't have to be inventory, does it?"

Whit leaned back in his chair and laced his fingers behind his head. "No," he mused. "No, I guess it doesn't. It could be any number, and, if the program were prepared to accept it, that number could

be matched with any number in the database. Like ... Like ..." His
imagination failed him.

"Like a customer order number?"

"Yeah, like a customer order number. Sure. Or just about anything else, for that matter."

"Better and better," said Ellen. "In terms of the system, then,
we'd have to know what numbers we wanted to print using a bar
code. And we'd have to make sure the system was ready to accept
those codes when they were scanned in."

"I think that's right," said Whit. "That would be like a heat
seekin' missile. 'Course we're a long way from anything like that
here at Powell, right?"

"Right. But it is fun to think about."

"It sure is." He picked up his screwdriver again and shook his
head. Almost as if addressing the computer, he said, "You have the
most interesting ideas."

Chapter 18
Ellen learns about Powell's trouble ... and goes on a date.

Later in the afternoon Mr. Powell stuck his head in Ellen's office. "Got a minute?" he asked.

"You're back!" She said. "How was the meeting?" She grabbed her notebook and a pencil and followed him to his office. "What's up?"

"I had a meeting with Bob Van Winkle today. You've met Mr. Van Winkle?"

"No, not really. I saw him ... once. He was here in the plant one day."

"Right. He's my uncle. He ran Powell for a while after my Dad ..." He paused and swallowed. "After my Dad died. Before I was out of college."

She waited for him to continue.

"We had a meeting this morning in Lexington. At his office." He paused. He turned and looked at her intently. "Look, Ellen. I need to tell you some things. But." He paused again and adjusted his tie. Abruptly he stood up and closed the door. "I feel like I can trust you. I hope I'm not wrong."

"I certainly hope you can, Mr. Powell. But, what's going on? Or, I guess what I really should say is that I don't want to know. I don't think you should tell me something you're uncomfortable talking about."

He pointed his finger at her. "That is exactly why I trust you. You have integrity." He lowered his finger. "Look, I need someone who doesn't have a dog in the fight. Someone I can trust."

"Fight?"

"Perhaps that's too strong a term. Disagreement, perhaps. Bob Van Winkle and I see things differently. I want to grow Powell Manufacturing and provide work for people. Good work. Uncle Bob thinks we're a sinking ship and that his company, International Dy-

namics, should take over Powell. Uncle Bob doesn't think we can cut
it and that we might as well give up now. I'm just not ready to quit."

"Does he want to take over the company? Would that mean you
would be out of a job?"

"Yes, me and lots of other people. I'm not worried about me. He
would pay to purchase the company and our assets. I'll be able to
figure something out. It's the rest of the people I'm worried about.
People like you ..."

"You know I'm grateful to be working here at Powell, but I could
probably find another job ... at least I hope I could."

"I want you to work here. You're smart. The way you think
makes us better..." He stopped and looked out the window.

Ellen's voice was hushed. "Are things really bad?"

"Mmmm. Good question." He stroked his chin. "They aren't
good. We barely stay in the black. Some months we actually lose
money. By my calculations, unless things change, by early March
we'll be out of cash. I'll be forced to sell out to Uncle Bob and lay
everybody off. Uncle Bob wants our customers, our assets, our intel-
lectual property. He doesn't want our people." He sat down in his
chair again. "I've always believed that, as long as we pay our people
and pay our suppliers, we don't necessarily have to make a big
profit." He paused again. "Of course I owe my mother a living. The
shares in Powell that my dad left her are her living."

"I see."

"And Bob Van Winkle owns shares in Powell, too. He definitely
wants us to be profitable because he wants a good return on his investment."

"That complicates things," she said.

"It does. And so I go back to what I said earlier. Bob Van Winkle
and I see things differently."

"And, if I'm remembering my business classes in college correctly, shareholders get a say in how the company is run."

"You're right, of course."

"May I ask who holds the majority share?" She stopped. "I'm
sorry. That's none of my business."

"See, that's what I'm talking about. I want to enlist your help. And to do that I need to share some confidential things with you. Are you ready for me to trust you with some information?"

"Uh, mmm. I mean I passionately want to help. I want Powell to succeed. But do you have to? I mean, I'll hold what you tell me in confidence. But isn't there someone else you could talk to?" Her brows were knitted in concern.

"See that's it. There are lots of good people here. But you have perspective. People like you, they like that you listen to them. You see things and you figure out what they mean. You're the one."

She was suddenly self-conscious. "I don't know what to say."

"First of all, say that you'll do me the favor of calling me Rob? Mr. Powell was my father. And then tell me you're as trustworthy as I believe you to be."

She looked at her hands folded in her lap. "Being honest is important to me. And so is keeping my commitments. If you tell me things that I can't share, then I'll keep that confidence. I can understand that you need someone to talk things over with. But ..." She paused again and looked him full in the face. "But, really, isn't there someone else?"

He held her gaze as the clock on the wall measured the seconds. Tick. Tick. Tick. Tick. Finally he said, "Ellen, you are the one."

She looked down again in acquiescence. "All right, Mr. Powell." she all but whispered. "Rob."

Suddenly there was a knock on the door.

"Who's that?" growled Mr. Powell. "Come in!"

Kirby poked his head in the door. "Sorry to interrupt. You ready?" He was looking at Ellen, not at Rob. He had a motorcycle helmet under his arm.

Ellen started to ask what for and then, in a flash, it hit her. The date. Kirby had asked her to go out with him on Friday, and today was Friday. How could she have forgotten? She hoped that she was able to hide any confusion from her face. "Sure!" she said brightly. "Give me just a few minutes to finish up here and I'll be right with you." She looked at the clock on the wall. Five minutes after five!

Where had the time gone? "How about I meet you in the lobby in ..."
She looked at Rob. "Five minutes?" she said.

"Sure!" Kirby sauntered off, whistling an off-key tune.

Rob looked at Ellen intently; she could feel his gaze on her. She
looked up and locked eyes with him. "What?"

"Nothing," he mumbled and turned his attention to a stack of papers on his desk.

Clearly the mood had been broken. And Kirby was waiting.

"You go on and have a good time," said Rob, brushing an imagi-
nary eraser crumb off of the page. "I'll think about this more over the
weekend and then maybe get with you on Monday. OK?"

"Yes, thanks. That would be good." Ellen gathered up her notebook and headed back to her desk. She got her purse out of the drawer and pulled on her jacket. Luckily she had chosen an outfit this
morning that could, conceivably, be considered a date outfit. The
dark purple wool skirt was sliming and short. The heels matched her
purse nicely and she knew that heels gave her walk an interesting little wiggle. The white blouse was fitted and flattering. She stopped in
the ladies room to brush her hair. The blouse also had a scoop neck
that emphasized her décolletage without being immodest. She wished
she'd worn a little necklace, but there wasn't anything she could do
about that now. She fixed her lipstick and applied a little more eyeliner. She stepped out of the ladies' room, ready for a night on the
town.

She met Kirby in the lobby. "You kids be careful, now," grinned
Gladys. "Don't do anything I wouldn't do!"

Ellen blushed, but Kirby said, "You behave! I'm just taking this
nice girl to the tractor pull at the fairgrounds."

Ellen heard, "You big spender, you!" as Kirby held the front door
open for her.

In the parking lot Ellen suddenly wanted to die. She looked at the
motorcycle parked in the skinny little parking spot near the door and
saw the second helmet, one that matched the one Kirby had under his
arm, and she suddenly realized the mode of transportation Kirby had
planned. Had he said something about that and she'd just forgotten?

Her mind raced. She glanced at her short skirt. She'd never ridden a motorcycle, but she'd seen girls do it. It required some rather indecent wrapping of legs and arms around the guy who was driving. Should she suggest they take her car? No, this was a date. That just wouldn't do.

She squared her shoulders as Kirby handed her the second helmet. She pulled it down over her ears and snapped the chin strap. "OK, Kirby, here's the deal. My skirt is a mite short for this kind of travel. But if you'll get on and close your eyes, I'll do my best to climb on and maintain my dignity."

"Gosh, Ellen. You're a sport. I didn't even think that you might not be dressed for this. I'm afraid it's all I've got."

"I understand. Now you get on and close your eyes. Then I will get mounted." She wished she'd used a different word immediately after it left her lips.

"I'll be facing forward. I won't see a thing." He easily swung his leg over the seat and waited.

It was an ordeal. Before she was able to get enough swing in her leg to straddle the bike, she almost had to pull the skirt up to the top of her thighs. But she managed it. Only after she was settled, with her bare legs snug on either side of Kirby's hips, did she catch just a glimpse of his snapping green eyes in the rearview mirror on the handle bar. And then she realized, to her horror, that Whit Collette, Rick Baker and Harvey Green were all standing in the lobby, no doubt getting ready to leave for the day, but openly watching the floor show she'd just put on. She groaned and wrapped her arms around Kirby's burly chest. "Let's get out of here, Kirby."

He started the bike and revved the engine. "Hang on!" he yelled and popped out the clutch. The bike surged forward, the front wheel lifting off the ground. Ellen shrieked and held on even tighter. A wild, maniacal laugh was ripped from Kirby's mouth by the wind as the bike rapidly gained speed heading out of the parking lot.

"Oh Lord," prayed Ellen. "What have I gotten myself into?"

The ride was fast and crazy. Kirby seemed like a different person, speeding and passing cars with abandon. The wind was blowing up

Ellen's skirt and down her blouse. Her bare legs were freezing. She gripped him even more closely, trying to hunker down out of the wind behind his body. But that seemed to only inspire him to drive faster.

One car they passed had four teenage boys riding in it. The driver honked his horn and give her a big thumbs up.

She was so relieved when they pulled into the fairgrounds that she didn't even think about the dismount. She just scrambled off the bike, smoothing her skirt and hugging her arms to her chest to get warm.

Kirby grinned at her. "I just love riding my bike!" he exclaimed. "Don't you just love it?" His enthusiasm was obvious.

"It was ... exciting," she stammered. How was she going to get home, when the temperature dropped? At least it would be dark and no one would catch her flashing them with her bare thighs.

"Let's go get something to eat!" Kirby grabbed her hand and led her toward the food wagons that had been set up. "Aren't you starved? I sure am! What would you like? A hot dog? Hamburger? Bratwurst? How about some cotton candy or a funnel cake later?"

There was quite a crowd of people with kids running in and out, farmers who looked like they'd just come from the barn, and women dressed in everything from nice dresses to flannel shirts and jeans. The number of blue Future Farmers of America jackets and 4-H t-shirts per capita was a lot higher than at the mall in Lexington. There were lots of young couples, too, just like Kirby and Ellen, strolling along, holding hands and licking ice cream cones.

"Hey there, Kirby!" The girl that drawled his name was attractive with a tight t-shirt. She was wrapped around the strong silent type with a trucker hat and a pair of Liberty overalls.

"Oh, hey, Marisa. I haven't seen you in a while."

Marisa giggled. "Silly, that's 'cause you're working all the time. You don't have fun like we used to."

There was an uncomfortable silence as Ellen tried to disentangle herself from Kirby's arm and he tried to pull her in even closer.

"Hey, Tyler. I ain't seen you in a while." That was Kirby's attempt at conversation.

Tyler of the overalls barely managed to say "hey." Apparently that was all he was planning to contribute to the conversation.

Ellen stuck out her hand. "I'm Ellen. I work with Kirby."

"Well hey there, honey." Marisa shook Ellen's hand. "Aren't you the purty one? Where you been hidin' her, Kirby? You need to bring her down to the Manhattan Club on Thursday nights. I'll betcha she'd fit right in!"

"Uh, I don't know, Marisa. I'm kind of not into the Thursday night scene any more."

"Oh, you old stick in the mud! A little beer, a little pool. Why, shoot, sugar, that's about as good as it gets. Unless it's what me an' Tyler have planned for later, don't we honey?" She hugged her arms around her man, who lapsed into an even more profound silence even as his cheeks glowed red in the fading sunlight.

"See ya!" she said brightly, and tugged Tyler toward the parking lot.

"We used to date in high school," said Kirby by way of explanation. "She was my first ... uh, prom date."

"I see." They weren't holding hands any more, which relieved Ellen. "Did you say something about getting something to eat? I'm suddenly hungry."

Kirby brightened. "You bet! Let's have hamburgers, OK? Lucy Mae's wagon makes the best, with fresh meat and everything."

They ordered hamburgers with everything and an order of fries to share. Kirby paid. They took their food and made their way to the tractor pull arena. They found a seat in the bleachers, fairly high up, after Kirby had greeted several people he knew. They had barely gotten settled when one of the tractors came into the arena. Ellen couldn't make out what the announcer said over the noise of the engine. Some men hooked what looked like a big heavy sled to the rear of the tractor and then the real noise began. The driver of the tractor revved his engine and the noise became unbearable. Flames started shooting out of the exhaust pipes on the side of the engine and the tractor suddenly started moving down the track in the middle of the arena. It seemed impossible, but the noise got even more deafening as the tractor attempted to pull the heavy sled as far as it could.

When it finally could go no farther, the crowd went wild, the announcer burst into unintelligible yammering to add to the din, and the sled was unhitched.

"What just happened?" screamed Ellen in Kirby's ear.

"Why honey, have you never seen a tractor pull?" He put his arm around her and pulled her close so he could speak directly in her ear. "A lot of boys like to tinker with tractors and then show off how strong they are at a tractor pull. That sledge ..." He pointed to the heavy weights now being pulled back down the field in preparation for the next contestant. "That sledge has weights on it that move forward the farther it pulls, making it harder and harder for the tractor to go. He goes as far as he can. Whoever goes the farthest wins."

Ellen paid closer attention as a blue tractor came into the arena and was hooked up to the sled. Again, the noise became unbearable as the engine was wound up to full speed and then the tractor ground down the runway as far as it could go.

"Looks like the blue one went farther than the green one," said Ellen.

"You're right. Ford beats John Deere every time in my book. But we're bound to see Massey-Fergusons and White New Ideas, and all kinds. Just watch to see if anybody gets a full pull." He pointed to a marker at the far end of the field. "If anyone gets a full pull, then there'll be a pull off. That's when it really gets exciting!"

The next tractor was red and had "Makin' Bacon" painted on its cowl. It did even better than the Ford had done. They watched several more pulls. It seemed to Ellen that they were getting progressively farther, except for one fellow who didn't make it half way down the field before this tractor stalled. The driver could be seen later kicking the tire of his tractor as if he held a personal grudge against it.

Then two tractors in a row pulled past the Full Pull marker and Kirby got excited. He stood up an yelled along with most of the crowd. Ellen kept her seat and tried to keep her knees together as she gathered up the trash.

"Oh boy, did you see that!" said Kirby as he sat back down. "Now we've got us a real tractor pull. That was my buddy Mick on that last one. Mick is a mighty fine mechanic!"

"What happens then?" asked Ellen.

"Anyone who gets past the Full Pull marker goes to the second round and they have a pull off. Whoever pulls the sledge the farthest, even if it is way past the Full Pull, is the winner. There's one more tractor in this round."

"Round?"

"Yeah. That was the single engine class. Next we have the super-charged class. And, if we're lucky, we might even see some four wheel drive class, but I don't know if any of those will be here."

"So this is just the first round?" Ellen said faintly. But Kirby didn't hear her. He was already on his feet, cheering on the last tractor in this first round.

Ellen suddenly realized that she was bored. The noise and the fumes of the tractor exhaust were beginning to give her a headache. She didn't want to spoil Kirby's evening, but she'd seen just about enough of very large, noisy engines trundling down a short strip of dirt in a show of testosterone-laden strength.

When the first round finished and Kirby's friend Mick got second place, Ellen said she was going to go in search of a Ladies Room. "Sure, babe," said Kirby. "I'll keep your place for you."

The night air was cool and refreshing. She realized she was feeling a bit queasy, too, and walked away from the arena and its incredible noise. Kids were still running, shouting, chasing each other and having a wonderful time. She wandered over toward another building and found that restrooms were available.

She didn't want to go back into the arena just yet, so she found a picnic table bench to sit on. She listened to the sounds of the night insects with their steady, monotonous drone. One bug was making a "buzz-zupp, buzz-zupp" rasping sound. Another chorus was softly trilling. Somewhere across the field she could hear a Chuck Will's Widow. The sounds suddenly made her think of her father, holding her on his lap even when she was eight or ten, and teaching her about the night sounds. "That's a katydid," he would say. And she would listen and learn to identify it. But the Chuck Will's Widow was both of their favorites. "Lot's of people think that's a Whip-poor-will," said her father. "But it isn't. Do you hear that faint 'chuck' at the beginning of his call? He's saying 'chuck will's widow' and that 'chuck' at the beginning tells you he's not a Whip-poor-will."

Ellen had been fascinated and had snuggled into her daddy's chest. "Tell me more, Daddy. I want to learn more."

"I know you do, darling. I'm so proud of you." And suddenly, in the middle of the fairgrounds where she hardly knew a soul, sitting at an old beat up picnic table, tears filled Ellen's eyes. She hadn't cried for her parents in several years, and suddenly the ache, the pain, was back in force. She pulled an old tissue out of the pocket in her skirt and blew her nose. "I miss you Mom. I miss you Dad. I love you both," she whispered into the darkness.

Her mind shied away from remembering that awful day. She'd been called out of her chemistry class by the dean. She'd gone numb. She couldn't remember much about that day, or the weeks afterwards. She and Trish had gone through the motions, planning the funeral, making arrangements. It wasn't the kind of things two young daughters should have to do, but they did it. Friends had helped and they had relied on each other. Trish's first husband hadn't been much help and, within a year, he had abandoned a pregnant Trish, leaving his wife to give birth to Nathan all by herself. That's when Ellen had moved in to help out. It had been years before she could return to college. She changed her major from Biology to Management Information Systems because she thought it would be more practical.

And that had led her to the job at Powell. Her mother's words, quoting Julie Andrews in the Sound of Music, came echoing back to her. "Wherever God closes a door, somewhere He opens a window." Perhaps Powell was her open window.

She dried her eyes and headed back to the arena. Kirby was still in the same spot, standing with most of the crowd, yelling and cheering. He grinned at her and motioned her to come stand by him.

The tractors that were pulling now didn't even look like tractors. They were huge beasts with oversize tires and suggestive slogans painted on their sides. One was called "Planting it Deep" and the one with four engines was called "Four Play."

Thankfully the pull was wrapping up with a final contest between two behemoths that made the very bleachers tremble.

Kirby was enthusiastic about the evening. "Did you have a good time?" he asked naively.

"Sure I did," said Ellen. "Thanks, Kirby. I've never done anything like this before."

The ride home was uneventful, with Kirby carrying the conversation, when Ellen could even hear him over the wind and the bike engine and the ringing in her ears from the tractor pull. The night was cooling down rapidly.

When they pulled into the abandoned Powell parking lot, Gunilla was sitting patiently in its lonely space. Kirby offered to take her out for coffee, but Ellen declined. "I'm afraid I didn't dress warmly enough and I'd really like to get home and get into some warm clothes."

"Well all right, then." He held the door for her as she got into her car. "Thanks for going with me, Ellen. You're a real sport. Next time we'll do something a little more like a date."

Next time? Did she want there to be a next time? Ellen wasn't sure. "Thanks, Kirby. Thanks again. That would be nice." Maybe she did.

For a moment she thought he was going to lean over and kiss her as she sat in the driver's seat, but he didn't. Instead he closed the door and gave her a cheerful salute. She started the engine and headed home.

Chapter 19
Ellen and Rika have a *fika*.

The phone rang. What time was it? Ellen struggled to get from her bed to the little kitchen and the phone. "Hullo?" She was aware she barely sounded coherent.

"Hey, El. Aren't you awake yet?"

"Mmmm." Ellen stretched and yawned. "What time is it?"

"It's already eight-thirty! Don't tell me you were still in bed." Trish's voice was teasing.

"Well, it is Saturday. And I usually get up so early now to go to work at Powell." She paused. "That sounded kind of lame, didn't it."

"Yup." Trish was no help at all.

"Well, I guess the fact is, I was sleeping in. So there. You caught me."

"Well, you deserve it. I'm only kidding. Say, didn't you have a big date last night? How'd it go?"

"Oh, yeah. That was ... interesting. Ever been to a tractor pull?"

"A what?"

"A tractor pull. Guys with tricked-out humongous overgrown tractors try to make the most noise possible while pulling a heavy weight down a track. Can you hear the desperate enthusiasm in my voice?" Ellen yawned again.

"You have got to be kidding! He took you to a tractor pull?" Her laughter was infectious and Ellen found herself smiling.

She told her sister about the incident with the motorcycle and the short skirt, and Trish was appropriately empathetic. Ellen had learned a lot of what she needed to know about boys from Trish, so they had a shared bond about dating and other matters that concerned the opposite sex.

"What are your plans today, El?"

"I hadn't really gotten that far, Trish. I've been working so hard that, well, I thought I'd just take it easy today." Suddenly she remembered the strange conversation with Rob just before leaving on the date with Kirby.

"Well, you deserve it, kid. Say, why don't you come over for supper tonight? Nathan has some things he says he wants to talk over with you, and Carrie just misses you. Tommy and I would love to see you, too."

"That sounds nice, Trish. I'd like to be with you guys. Usual time?"

"Usual time. Love you, sis."

"Love you, too." Ellen hung up and headed for the shower.

She was just pulling on her favorite worn sweatshirt when there was a knock at the door. It was Rika.

"*God morgon.* Good morning, Ellen. May I come in?"

"Of course. Please!" She ushered her landlord into her tiny apartment. She wondered how Rika seemed to look so elegant and pulled together. She was suddenly aware that she hadn't put on her makeup and that her clothes looked extremely casual. "I was about to put some coffee on. Would you like some?"

"A *fika*! That would be wonderful. Jonas isn't much of a coffee drinker in the morning so I don't make it very often. We Swedes do love our coffee."

"I would be glad to have someone to drink a cup with." She busied herself measuring out the grounds and pouring the water.

"How have you been, Ellen? Your job seems to keep you very busy."

Ellen laughed. "That's a true statement." She bustled around, getting out mugs and pouring milk into the little creamer pitcher her mother had given her. And because she had company, she got out the little matching sugar bowl, poured some sugar into it and set both on the table along with two dainty spoons.

"These are beautiful!" exclaimed Rika. "Where did you get them?"

"From my mother," said Ellen. "They were hers when she ... died. I had always loved them, and Trish said I should have them."

"They are lovely," said Rika. "And I'm glad you have something nice to remember your mother by. Do you know where she got them? They look familiar."

"I believe my father brought them to her as a present when he returned from one of his business trips. It never occurred to me to try to figure out where they came from."

"They look like Rörstrand. Do you mind?" She lifted up the sugar bowl to examine its underside. "Yes. This set was made in Lidköping. Here is the Rörstrand mark." She looked over the top of her glasses at Ellen. "It is beautiful Swedish porcelain made by Rörstrand in the town of Lidköping. Lidköping is on the south shore of the big lake Varnen. I grew up in Göteborg, not so very far from Lidköping."

"How nice to know that. I wonder when my dad would have traveled to Sweden. I don't remember that, but then I didn't always know where he was going, just that he was gone on a business trip."

"How well I understand. Jonas used to travel a great deal. He would bring me little gifts, too. Leaded crystal from Prague, an umbrella from Thailand."

The coffee was finished and Ellen poured each of them a mug. "Mmm," said Rika appreciatively. "This is perfect, just perfect, Ellen. Thank you!"

"You know," said Ellen. "We need a little something sweet to go with this ..."

"You were reading my mind!" said Rika.

Ellen rummaged around in her cupboard and brought out some little pastries she had bought at Robinsons. She put two on a little plate and set them on the table.

"Oh, how nice," said Rika. "I'm so glad you are living here with us, and I hope that I am not intruding. It is just that, well, I miss a bit of female companionship every once in a while."

"I ... I don't know what to say. My mother and I used to sit over coffee like this. Trish never enjoyed it as much as I did, but I could sit with my mother for an hour, solving the world's problems. She said that if only people would listen to the solutions she and I came up with, we could fix a lot of what was wrong with the world. Of course she was kidding, but with her I really did feel like we could figure out just about any problem we were having."

"What a wonderful memory, Ellen. And I appreciate your sharing this time with me. You and your mother were close?"

"Very close. I adored her. Perhaps she got tired of me hanging out with her, but she never let on. She always had time to sit over coffee and listen to me. We were a very close family. Trish was maybe the more independent one, but I loved both of my parents. My daddy was always teaching me things and encouraging me to try new things, but my mother seemed to completely understand me."

"You must miss her very much."

Ellen looked away at this simple statement and stared at the morning sunlight angled through the eastern window. It made the pattern on the carpet stand out in sharp relief, even as it illuminated the motes of dust moving gently on unseen air currents. "Yes. I miss her." Unbidden tears rimmed her eyes again.

"I'm sorry. I did not mean to bring up painful memories."

"Not painful, exactly," said Ellen. "It's just that I still miss them, even after all of these years." Tears now twice in twenty-four hours. What was going on with her?

"I didn't know your mother so well, but if you are anything like her, she must have been a very wonderful lady. I did know your father more."

"You knew my father?" Rika had her full attention. "Oh, of course. From the summer parties."

"Yes, from the midsummer night parties, that's right. Both he and Jonas worked for the same company."

"Mr. Klameck worked for Allied Fabrication?"

"He wasn't on the payroll, but he was a frequent consultant to Allied Fabrication. That's why we ended up moving to Laodiciea. And I would say we became friends. At least we were more than casual acquaintances. We attended several dinners together. Your parents seemed like special people. And Jonas had a great deal of respect for your father. In some ways, even though he was a bit too young, I believe that Jonas almost regarded your father as the son he never had."

"My goodness! I had no idea."

"I tell you what. Why don't you come to dinner tonight and you can ask Jonas to tell you more."

"That would be ... oh, wait. I can't. Trish already invited me to supper at her house."

"And of course you must go." Rika patted Ellen's hand. "But I would love to have you to dinner again soon."

"You and Mr. Klameck are so nice to me. I really appreciate it. But isn't it me who should be inviting you to dinner? After all, it is my turn, isn't it?"

"Nonsense. Between our four eyes I love cooking for others. You're just an excuse!" She winked at Ellen. "Besides, Jonas would have a bit of difficulty getting up the stairs!"

"Oh, yes." She was flustered. She hadn't meant to bring up her landlord's disability.

"I've just had a brilliant idea! Why don't you plan on having Thanksgiving dinner with us? I love what Americans do with that holiday." Her enthusiasm was infectious. "Oh, please say yes! I would love to have an excuse to cook a big turkey dinner. And, if you like, you could come and help me. I'd love to have the company, and ..." She stopped as she saw the look in Ellen's eyes. "What is it, Ellen?"

"It's just ... It's just that Trish and I always have Thanksgiving together, especially after Mom and Dad were killed. It sounds wonderful, and I would love to be with you in the kitchen. But Trish ..." Her voice trailed off. How could she explain how important Thanksgiving had become, especially after the accident?

"Of course you must be with your sister and her family on Thanksgiving. Of course. It goes without saying. I wonder ... do you think they would all be willing to come here for Thanksgiving? I completely understand if that isn't your wish. Thanksgiving is a time for family. But Jonas and I, we would consider it to be a great honor if you would all join us."

"Oh, I ..." What could she say? What would Trish say? It could be very nice. She had already experienced Rika outstanding culinary talents. But it was such a change, perhaps too much of one in a year with so many changes already. "Thank you, Rika. From the bottom of my heart. But ..."

"But, no." The disappointment was evident in her voice.

"Not no, just maybe. I really would have to talk to Trish and Tommy first."

"Of course, of course."

"Would Nathan and Carrie be invited too?"

Rika grinned and reached her hand across the table, covering Ellen's younger one with her own more worn one. "Of course, Ellen. Of course. It goes without saying. We mustn't break up the family." Rika squeezed Ellen's hand. "Jonas loves your nephew. And little Carrie is too sweet for words. You talk to Trish this evening when you have dinner with her. I hope you'll all say yes, but I understand. It must be a family decision."

Chapter 20
Nathan's paper route system confirms the first two principles.

"She's here! She's here!" Ellen could hear Carrie's voice through the door. Clearly the little girl had been watching for her.

Should she knock? This wasn't her home any more; it didn't seem quite polite to barge right in. On the other hand, this had been her home with Trish for so many years it seemed awkward not to just open the door.

Carrie solved the problem for her by struggling to open the door herself. Ellen stooped to Carrie's level and Carrie rewarded her by throwing her arms around Ellen with the complete abandonment of childhood. "Hello, sweetheart. I've missed you."

"Oh Aunt Ellen. I love you." Her warmth and genuineness would have been apparent to anyone, but Ellen buried her nose in the child's neck and hair, breathing in the innocence and the scent of her unabashed sweetness.

"And I love you," she whispered.

"Hey, El." Trish was drying her hands on her apron, the same one she had worn over a decade ago when they both would cook with their mother. Ellen stood and Trish gave her a big hug.

"What can I help with?"

"You'll be amazed at how domesticated I've become. Tommy says my cooking has improved, although, when he wants to razz me, he says I still don't measure up to the meals you used to make when you ... when you lived here." She paused and looked at Ellen with all of the deep connection that only close sisters can share. "How are you doing, El? I mean, really, how are you doing?"

Ellen shrugged. "Really, I think I'm doing quite well. I like working at Powell a lot. It is interesting and challenging, and I've met some interesting people."

"Like the motorcycle jockey you went out with last night?"

Ellen laughed. "Well … maybe." How did she feel about Kirby? "More like some of the people at the plant, Mr. Powell and the others. And the Klamecks are really super nice. Oh! That reminds me …"

Tommy entered the kitchen then. "Oh, hey, handsome. I didn't hear you come in." Trish puckered up and Tommy gave her a big kiss right on the mouth.

"Mr. Thompson, I shall positively die for love!" Trish said it in her best Scarlett O'Hara voice.

"Hey, Ellen. You here to help your sister learn to cook?"

Trish swatted him playfully on the bottom. "You bugger. Get out of here. You said my cooking was improving."

"Only kidding, honey." He kissed her again, then hugged Ellen. "Seriously, Ellen. She really is getting to be as good as you. You'll have to watch out or she may take your 'chef of the family' title away from you."

"I'm glad, although I will say I've missed cooking with you all. Say, that reminds me. What would you say to having Thanksgiving with the Klamecks? Rika invited us this morning when she came up for coffee. I think they're a little lonely. Mr. Klameck would apparently like to talk to Nathan some more." Carrie waltzed back into the kitchen with one of her dolls for no apparent reason. "And who wouldn't want to be around Carrie?"

"I don't know …" Trish looked at Tommy.

"It could be fun. I kind of liked Mr. Klameck. He wasn't the stuffed shirt I thought he might be. But what do you girls say? I'm just the man of the house. You were doing Thanksgiving together long before I came on the scene."

"Would you like to do Thanksgiving there, El?" Trish was letting her make the final decision.

"I think I would. Rika says she'd be happy if we would like to help out in the kitchen and I think she'd put on quite a spread. She seemed really eager to have us come. I think it would be fun to cook with her … we might even learn some Swedish chef secrets. That is, Tommy, if you wouldn't be too bored with Mr. Klameck while we are cooking."

"Does he like football?"

"I … I honestly don't know."

"Well, let's hope he does. The Dolphins and the Jets are playing. It should be a good game."

"Well, that's settled then," said Ellen. "I'll let the Klamecks know we accept the invitation."

"Hern de fern de bar-be-queue!" said Tommy in his best Muppets imitation of a Swedish chef.

Dinner was fun and Trish's cooking skills had clearly improved in Ellen's absence. But there was an undercurrent of melancholy, too. The old gang — Trish and Ellen, enhanced by Tommy — was no more. The conversation sounded more like a reunion than a return to the old ways. But even as each of them was sad in their own way to move on, there was a sense that the next chapter was important and inevitable. The old gang couldn't last unaltered, could it? "I kind of wish it was back the way things were," said Trish, in response to Ellen's concerns over the changes they were all going through.

After dinner and dessert of apple cobbler, which Tommy declared to be superb, Carrie wanted Aunt Ellen to read her a story, which she was only too happy to do. They curled up on the couch, just as they used to do, and read "The Tawny, Scrawny Lion" followed by a book about sounds. Ellen always did her best to imitate the indicated noise — from the sound of a vacuum cleaner to a police siren to feet walking across gravel. Carrie was appropriately appreciative and giggled as Ellen contorted her mouth to try to reproduce each sound. They finished up with a very old favorite, Richard Scary's "I Am a Bunny." Then Carrie was off to bed and whispered "Aunt Ellen, I love you" as Ellen leaned over to kiss her.

Ellen thought she'd have a chance to sit and chat with Trish and Tommy, but clearly Nathan wanted some time with his Aunt. Tommy winked at her and Trish crossed the room to the TV to turn on *Simon & Simon* while Ellen visited with Nathan in her old room.

"So what's been going on, Nate?" said Ellen as she sat down on the bed — her old bed — so she could see the computer. She pulled her focus away from noticing how much had changed, even though it was the same room she had slept in for years, back to Nathan.

"Oh, Aunt Ellen! I've been doing the neatest stuff with Tubby's paper route system. You remember that stuff we were doing with the cookbook and your bill of material?"

"Sure I do. That was really helpful, Nathan. I even used it at work."

"Really? That's cool! Do you still have your pad of paper?"

"Ha! I've got something even better — but it is out in the car. Let me run get it, OK?"

As she entered the living room she caught Trish and and Tommy in a prolonged kiss on the couch. "Ahem!" she coughed. Tommy caught her out of the corner of his eye, winked, and motioned her to keep moving. Ellen laughed. "Ah, young love!" she muttered as she went out to collect her notebook.

Database	Tubby's Paper Route	—> (continued)	Powell Manufacturing System	—> (continued)
File	subscribers	bills	job cards	bill of material
Record	name example: Verna Powell	invoice number	order number + operation number	
Field	address example: Three Pines	amount example: $5.00	customer example: Wilco	component part number

Figure 20.1

"See, Nathan? Mr. Klameck gave me this notebook because he said I needed to keep a record of what I was learning. I copied all of our diagrams into the notebook as well as making some notes of my own."

"Wow, Aunt Ellen. This is great!" Nathan's hungry eyes skimmed the pages, absorbing as he went. He came to the page where Ellen had copied the Database, File, Record, Field diagram. "There! That's the one. I've come up with a problem ... well, not really a problem, but something I think I need to do differently."

"How's that?"

"Well, originally, I had planned to put the subscriber's name and address in the file along with the amount due. But you remember we decided we'd have a file of subscribers and a file of bills?"

"Yes, I remember. The subscriber file would have the name of the subscriber — first name and last name — their address, and some other fields, although I'm not quite sure what they are."

"Right. And the bills file would have that invoice number we talked about and the amount due. And I added the month and the year. The invoice number would uniquely identify the bill, but the month and the year ... oh, and the subscriber names, combined, would ..."

"Using your compound subject idea, would also uniquely identify the record. Is it OK that a file has an invoice number, which is unique, and a compound subject of the subscriber plus the year plus the month, also which is unique?" She asked the question more to herself than to Nathan, but Nathan had an answer.

"I think it is OK. The invoice number is convenient, kind of like a code name for the record. But the subscriber/year/month combination is what really identifies the record." He drew a box around the fields that made each record unique.

"I think you're right. Just like at Powell. Remember when we looked at that job card? The job card has a number — kind of like the invoice number for the paper route — but we also decided that the 'noun' of the file was a compound subject composed of the order number from the customer plus the operation number."

"Oh, yeah. I remember. So at Powell the unique identifier is the job number, just for convenience, but it really is a code name, a model, like, for the order number plus the operation number."

"Bingo! So your paper route idea is, I think, spot on. Two files, one for subscribers and one for bills." She stopped as her mind caught up to what he had just said. "Wait a minute, Nathan, what did you say? A code name, a … what?"

"I think I said 'model.'"

"You did!" She started turning the pages in her notebook. "There it is!" She pointed to the First Principle as Jonas had dictated it to her.

Principle One: The business information technology system must model the business it serves.

Nathan read the words to himself, then read them again. He looked at her with a question on his face.

"See, you're designing an information technology system for Tubby's paper route. That's the business, and clearly you are 'serving' Tubby — that's important. You're helping him out. But this way of looking at subscribers and bills in two different files, it 'models the business' better than the way you had originally planned to build the system. You figured out a better way, and that's really good."

Nathan was clearly pleased, but he wasn't completely tracking with her. "Mr. Klameck gave me this notebook because he wants me to find the principles of business information technology systems. He calls them BITS for short. He says there are five. He knows them, but he isn't telling me because he says I — we — have to figure it out for ourselves. This is the first one, the business information technology system must model the business it serves. You're demonstrating that right now in the way you're thinking about Tubby's system."

"I think I'm following you, but I'm going to have to think about that some more."

"Sure. I'm not sure I totally grasp it, either. But I do know that it is important."

Nathan pointed to the adjacent page. "You've already found the second one, too?"

"Yup. Mr. Klameck says the first two aren't too hard, once you get the hang of it. Does this make sense to you?" She pointed to the second principle.

Principle Two: The business information technology system must be non-redundant.

"I'm not sure, but I think so. When I decided I needed two files, it was because I realized I would have to repeat the customer's name and address again and again, each time there was a new month and a new bill."

Ellen smacked herself on the head. "Of course! I get it, now. There are all kinds of ways a system can be redundant, and that isn't good. It would be wasteful to repeat the name and address each time. And one of the records could have the wrong information." She told him about the Rolodex file that Gladys kept and how it was redundant with the data in SOLUTION/400 and what problems it had caused. "I'm really beginning to see why Mr. Klameck says this is an important principle."

They both sat and looked at the page again. "I tell you what, Nate. How about we sketch out the noun and the adjectives for your two files?"

"That would be great! I've already been working on that." He pulled out a piece of paper covered with the awkward scrawl of a young teenage boy. "See, for the subscriber file, I have the name, address, city, state and zip. For the bill file I have the bill number, the year, the month and the amount due. But I'm thinking I'll need to add the amount paid, when Tubby gets the money."

"Yeah, that's important. Remember — serve the business. I'm betting Tubby doesn't deliver papers just for fun. He'd like to make some money, right?"

"You bet! And me, too! When Tubby first writes the bill, the Amount Due is written in and the Amount Paid is empty. Later, when the subscriber pays their bill, the amount paid gets written, too."

Subscriber File	Bills File
Name	Bill Number
Address	Year
City	Date
State	Amount Due
Zip	Amount Paid
	Subscriber Name

Figure 20.2

"Makes total sense. But now I have a question, and I don't know the answer to it. How do you connect the bill file to the subscriber file?"

"You just ... oh, wait. We said the bill file needed the subscriber in it, too." He wrote down 'subscriber name' on the list under the bill file.

"Um, Nathan. Is that a good idea? I mean, what if Tubby had two subscribers with the same name. You said he didn't, but what if?"

"It's more than a what if, Aunt Ellen. Just yesterday Tubby told me he had two Jeff Greens as subscribers. One is a farmer who lives out on Three Forks Road, the other lives in town and is a college professor."

"How about that? So using names won't work because it would violate the second principle. We'd have redundancy."

They both sat and thought about that problem and then Ellen observed the classic Nathan behavior. He tilted back in his chair and stared at the ceiling, deep in thought. She didn't disturb him; she knew that something good was about to happen. When he came back to earth, he asked a simple question: "Could there be a subscriber number, just like there is a bill number?"

The brilliance and simplicity of it took Ellen's breath away. "Of course. That's it! How perfect!" Without thinking she grabbed the pencil and scribbled 'subscriber number' in the subscriber file, and marked through 'subscriber name' and replaced it with 'subscriber number' in the bills file. Then she realized the gaffe she had committed. "Oh, Nathan. I'm sorry. That was your diagram and here I went and marked all over it."

Nathan grinned. "That's OK, Aunt Ellen. Isn't this a team effort?"

If it wouldn't have offended him she would have hugged him right then and there. "Thank you Nathan. It sure is nice to have a boy genius on the team."

They both looked at their work, appreciating what they had accomplished. Then another problem occurred to Ellen. "Uh oh. I've got another problem. How do you link the two tables together? I mean, it seems to me that the bills file would have to know about the address of the subscriber if Tubby were going to print out bills to mail."

"I see what you mean. I had actually been thinking about that, but you've just made it clearer. You remember that grammar idea I had?"

"Oh no, Ace! Does this mean I have to go back to high school English again?"

"'Fraid so." He grinned. "What do they call the part of speech that joins two sentences together?"

Ellen wracked her brain. It just wasn't coming. She was stumped by a middle schooler. "I give up."

"A conjunction," he said triumphantly. "The two files are joined by a conjunction." He drew a line between the subscriber number in both files and put arrows on either end. "I have to read up on how you do that, but I think I know. Can I tell you about it the next time we get together?"

"Wow. You bet!" She couldn't resist tousling his hair. "You really are a genius, you know."

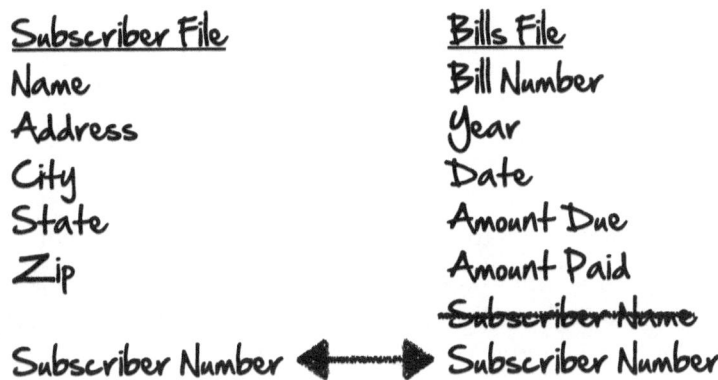

Figure 20.3

He only grinned as she gathered up her things. "Good night, Nathan."

"Good night, Aunt Ellen. Thanks."

"Thank you," she whispered so as not to wake Carrie as she closed his door.

Trish and Tommy were still sitting on the couch holding hands. It didn't seem like they were very interested in what was on TV. "The coast is clear," she said. "Go to bed."

"Goodnight, Ellen! Love you!"

"Love you, too. 'Night, Tommy." She let herself out the front door.

Chapter 21
Thanksgiving is celebrated with the Klamecks.

Thanksgiving was a great success. Ellen had gone over early to help, and had found Rika to be an organized and effective chef. Clearly she knew all of the US traditions, raising cranberry salad and pumpkin pie to a high art form. Rika had insisted that Ellen wear an apron she had made and Ellen realized it was a match for the one that Rika was wearing. Ellen knew her way around a kitchen, of course, but she found herself a little intimidated by Rika's artistry. She tried to be helpful, and clearly Rika enjoyed her company, chatting as they diced celery, laughing as the onions made them cry.

Jonas rolled in at that moment and said, "What's this? Are you girls weeping?" Of course they explained about the onions and Rika handed him a knife and a cutting board.

"Just for your impertinence, Jonas, you may dice the final onion." She tossed her head. "I have more important things to do!"

Jonas gamely pulled his wheelchair up to the table and began dicing away. Obviously he'd done that a time or two, and Ellen smiled to herself.

"And what are you smiling at, my dear?" Jonas pointed his knife at her.

"You two." Ellen grinned. "You remind me of my parents. They were quite a pair, always teasing each other. But Trish and I knew they really loved each other. You two seem like you might actually like each other, too."

"I don't know about all that," he replied. "She seems to tolerate me well enough. But she keeps threatening to trade me in for a younger model."

"You old goat," said Rika, coming over and kissing him on the top of the head. "I've just about got you trained. I would not want to have to start all over again." She returned to the sink where she was washing out the mixing bowl she had used to make the pumpkin pie filling. "Now get those onions chopped! We haven't got all morning."

A few moments later, she cried, "Oh, Ellen! I think our company is arriving. I think I see your sister and little Carrie getting out of the car. Why don't you go and greet them and bring them in through the front door."

Ellen did as she was told and soon the house was filled with Carrie's giggles and Trish and Ellen's chatter. "As you can see, my dear," said Jonas, indicating a pile of diced onions, "I have completed my assignment. May I be excused to go with young Tommy and Master Nathan into the living room to check on the pre-game festivities?"

"I suppose," said Rika. "Now that I have some more capable help." She tossed an apron to Trish that matched the one she had given Ellen earlier. And Carrie was thrilled to find that there was a matching apron for her, too, in just her size.

The house began to smell amazing as the turkey began turning a golden brown and the pumpkin pies were removed from the oven to cool. The dressing went together and then Rika looked at the girls. "Now for a very important question ... does the dressing go inside the bird, or is it baked separately?"

Ellen and Trish looked at each other. "Funny you should ask," said Trish. "Our mom always baked it in a shallow baking pan. I know that's kind of unusual, but that's what she did."

"Perfect!" said Rika. "I want you to show me. I had already put some stuffing in the turkey, but this baking in a pan, I don't know about that. I've baked it in a casserole, but not in a pan."

Ellen and Trish showed Rika how their mother had greased a jelly roll pan with Crisco and then patted out the dressing. "It seems a little dry for this," said Trish. "Could we dip a little of the broth out of the turkey pan?"

"That's what Mom always did," explained Ellen.

Rika had already set the table and the sisters remarked on the beauty of the place settings. The plates were bright white in the center with an intricate dark blue pattern around the edge. There were cups and saucers, bread plates, and little salad bowls to match. The cutlery was a simple and streamlined design. Rika beamed with pride. "They're Swedish," she said. "A wedding present from my sister."

Soon they were bringing things to the table: sweet potatoes, green beans, corn, dinner rolls that Rika had made from scratch, cranberry salad as well as a green salad. "This truly is a feast," Tommy said appreciatively.

Jonas sat at the head of the table with Rika to his right. He lifted the carving knife and fork in the air and Ellen realized everyone was holding their breath for this dramatic moment when the feast would begin.

"May we give thanks?" Jonas asked. They all nodded. Of course!

Jonas laid down the utensils reached for his wife's hand. "Oh great Lord, we know that every good thing comes from Thee. We thank Thee for this bounty, for the fruit of the earth. We thank Thee that we have work to do and we thank Thee for the hands that have prepared this feast. We thank Thee for the friends gathered around this table and ask your continued blessing on each household represented here. Most of all we thank You for loving us. We praise You. We give thanks to You. Amen."

Ellen found herself whispering "amen" as well. It had been a long time since she had felt this way. It had been a very long time since she had said amen.

The meal was a great success and even Tommy protested that he couldn't eat another bite.   "All right, then," said Rika. "If that's the best you can do, I suggest you men retire to the living room and the ladies will tidy up a bit. Okay with you?" She looked around the table. "I'll be in later to watch the game. I want to make sure that Dan Marino leads the Dolphins to victory."

Tommy raised his eyebrows. "What?" asked Rika. "You don't think a Swedish lady knows about American Football?"

Tommy grinned and raised his hands in protest. "I'm not saying anything, ma'am," he said. "I just think New York has a stronger offense and will take Miami."

"Ha!" exclaimed Rika. "We'll see about that! Mr. Marino is a very good looking man and my money's on him."

The ladies cleared the table and put the leftovers away. "You girls are such a help!" Rika said. She gathered them both into her arms and hugged them. "I've had such a wonderful time today. Thank you for coming, Trish. I know this isn't what you ordinarily do for Thanksgiving."

"Oh, my!" said Trish. "The meal was absolutely wonderful and these aprons …" She hugged Carrie to her. "You've been such a wonderful hostess, making us all feel so welcome."

"I've loved having you! And I so much appreciate having your sister right next door. I finally have some female companionship." Her eyes suddenly got a little misty. "I am so thankful that you've come into our lives."

"Now," she said, briskly. "We have a football game to watch. Mr. Tommy and I have a difference of opinion about the outcome."

Carrie was settled into an easy chair where Trish hoped she might drift off to sleep and take a nap. The rest of them watched the game. By the end of the first half, New York was leading 24 to 14 and Rika was visibly disappointed. Tommy did his best not to rub it in.

As the half time show got under way, Jonas said to Ellen, "Young Nathan here has been telling me about his idea for conjunctions in databases. I wonder, would the two of you like to move into the dining room with me and tell me more about it?"

"Didn't you want to see the game?" asked Ellen.

"If you want to watch the game, that's fine. I just sensed that perhaps football wasn't quite your thing."

"Please, Aunt Ellen?" said Nathan. "Football's fine and all, but this database stuff is way cooler! Besides, I know Mom likes football way more than you do."

"You're right about that. It's fine with me."

The three of them returned to the dining room table and Jonas got out a tablet of paper and a pencil and handed them to Nathan. "Now, Master Nathan, show me what you're thinking about."

Nathan explained about the paper route and the two files he was wrestling with, the bill file and the subscriber file. He explained how he and Ellen had come up with the idea of using a subscriber number instead of the subscriber name because of the two Jeff Green subscribers.

"The first principle," said Jonas. He looked at Ellen.

She nodded. "Nathan knows about the quest for the Five Principles. I tried to explain that using subscriber numbers instead of names allows us to model the business more accurately."

"Correct." Jonas looked at Nathan. "You wouldn't want to turn down a new subscriber just because they happened to have the same name as an existing subscriber."

Nathan nodded.

"Now, young Nathan," said Jonas. "Tell me about this conjunction idea. It sounds intriguing."

"Well," said Nathan hesitantly. "You know I had this idea about using grammar and parts of speech to describe a database."

Jonas nodded. "Absolutely brilliant."

"It seems to me that we need a way to link the two files together, the bill file to the subscriber file. If we don't, we end up having to keep the address of the subscriber in the bill file. Which Aunt Ellen tells me violates Principle Two."

"It does exactly. Having a subscriber's address in two places is redundant. That violates the second principle. Instead it should be housed only in the subscriber file. The invoice file — you call it the bill file — should be linked to the subscriber file and get the address from there when it needs it. So you just have to link the two files … is that what you meant by a conjunction?"

"Yeah. It seems kinda simple now that you explain it that way."

"Nathan, look at me." He held Nathan's gaze. "Figuring out how to make something that is complicated simple is one of the hardest things to do. This idea of a conjunction is brilliant. Why don't you tell me more about what you have in mind?"

"Well, I just kinda thought that, just like in English grammar where a conjunction joins two sentences, that a conjunction could join two files."

"Exactly!" Jonas looked over at Ellen. "Have I not said that this young man is brilliant?"

"You have, Jonas. And I agree."

Jonas stroked his jaw line. "Absolutely brilliant," he murmured to himself. "A conjunction for a join." He looked up at Nathan again. "You're spot on, Nathan. Computer scientists describe it in much more complicated ways, but calling it a conjunction is brilliant in its simplicity." He indicated the pad of paper. "Why don't you draw out your two files and let's take a look."

Nathan scratched his head, chewed on his tongue in the endearing way Ellen had become so fond of, and sketched out the two files just as he and Ellen had drawn them earlier. Finally he drew a line between the subscriber number in the two files. "That's the conjunction," he said. "Right there!"

"Indeed it is. If I were still running my consulting practice I would offer you a job right now." He looked at Ellen. "Perhaps I should wait until you're in high school." He looked at Ellen again. "Ellen, I think you should take Nathan with you to Powell sometime. It would do him good to be inside of a manufacturing plant and understand the data that describes the processes that are happening there."

"Oh yeah!" breathed Nathan.

"Who knows?" said Jonas. "Perhaps he will help you nail down the elusive Principle Number Three!" He winked at Ellen.

Just then Rika came waltzing triumphantly into the dining room. "Aha!" she chortled. "I knew Mr. Marino would come through! Miami made 20 points in the third quarter and now leads New York 34 to 24."

"Congratulations, my dear. I'm sure you and Mr. Marino are both very happy. I'm not so sure about Tommy, however."

"I shall endeavor to be graceful, Mr. Klameck. You need have no fears that I will embarrass you by gloating unduly."

"Now, Nathan," said Jonas. "Let me show you how a conjunction might be used in a factory." He took the pad and sketched out a parts master file, listing the part number, the description of the part, the unit of measure.

"That looks like a parts file," said Nathan.

"Indeed it is. Well done! Of course there is more information than I've sketched out here, but I wanted to use this file before I sketch out the next file." He filled in some part numbers: 101, 102, 103, 104.

He than began listing the fields in a file that included parent part number, child part number, and quantity per. Ellen saw what he was doing and suddenly realized she really needed to be paying attention.

Part Number	Description	Unit of Measure
101	Assembly 1	Each
102	Steel plate	Sheet
103	Bolt	Each
104	Nut	Each
105	Assembly 2	Each
106	Valve	Each
107	Hose	Each

Parent Part Number	Child Part Number	Quantity Per
101	102	0.25
101	103	4.00
101	104	4.00
105	102	0.50
105	106	2
105	107	2

Figure 21.1

"Hey!" said Nathan. "That's like the recipe file me and Aunt Ellen worked out!"

"Aunt Ellen and I ..." Ellen choked back her correction as Jonas talked over her.

"Recipe file? What a clever idea! Of course it is a recipe file, but a recipe for making parts in a factory, not a Thanksgiving dinner."

"Yeah, that's what we figured. You put the two parts together — like chocolate chip cookies takes sugar or chocolate chips ..."

"Yes, exactly! And a recipe specifies the amount ..."

"The quantity per!"

"... and this bill of material file does the same."

"And we figured out we could make a compound subject, and ..."

"A compound subject? I'm not familiar ..."

"Yeah, you know. Two nouns together make a compound subject in a sentence."

"Is this more of your grammar idea?" Jonas looked at Nathan, and then at Ellen.

"Yeah. We figured out that a recipe book is like the database and there is a record for each ingredient, with a compound subject."

"And what is the compound subject?" asked Jonas.

Suddenly Nathan hesitated. "We, uh, thought it was the recipe, like chocolate chip cookies, and the ingredients, like sugar."

"It is exactly. And calling it a compound subject makes so much sense." He pointed to his diagram. "See, it's the same here. This recipe is for a part, let's call it 101, and it contains three parts, let's call them 102, 103, and 104. And here's another recipe for part 105. It contains the same part, 102, and 106 and 107 as well."

Nathan nodded. "Yup, I see that."

"Now," he pointed his pen at Nathan, "Watch this!" He drew a line from the parts master to the parent part in the bill of material file. "There's your conjunction!"

"Oh, yeah I see! Can you do that? Link two files together like that?"

"You sure can! And your idea of calling it a conjunction makes it so easy to understand. But I want you to see that you can have more than one conjunction. See, you can also have a conjunction between the parts master and the child part."

"Oh, I didn't know that! That would sure be handy!"

"More than handy, it is essential for constructing good databases, databases that meet the requirements of the first two principles of BITS — Business Information Technology Systems."

They chatted some more, then all three drifted back to the living room where Trish was snuggled up in Tommy's arm and Carrie was snoring softly.

The fourth quarter didn't go so well for the Dolphins. With Ken O'Brien's leadership, the Jets scored two more touchdowns, making the final score 38 to 34, New York. Rika stood, walked over to where Tommy was sitting, and solemnly shook his hand. "You are a better predictor of football than I am. I am humbled in your presence. How about something to eat?"

Tommy was pleased by the banter, but Trish stretched and said, "Mmmmm. Shouldn't we be going and get out of your way?"

"Absolutely not! I will not hear of it. It is tradition, is it not, that the evening meal on Thanksgiving is comprised of leftovers? Jonas and I always scrounge for supper after a big turkey dinner. He always makes a turkey sandwich and ..."

"I love turkey sandwiches!" interjected Nathan.

"So, that's settled, then. Ellen, Trish looks so comfortable there. How about you and I pull some things out of the refrigerator? We'll call you when it is ready. Jonas, why don't you introduce Nathan to the game of Jotto while the others rest?"

Ellen found herself enjoying Rika's company even more. They developed a comfortable repartee and almost seemed to know what the other was thinking as they worked to pull out turkey, leftover dressing, and vegetables. Ellen heated up the gravy so it would be hot and Rika pulled out a plate of brownies.

"More dessert?" asked Ellen.

Rika laughed. "Perhaps I got a bit carried away, I was so excited about your coming. I couldn't resist making a second dessert for the evening meal."

By the time Carrie had woken up and had eaten some more "tuwkey" with "gwavy" everyone was completely stuffed again. Trish insisted on helping clean up the kitchen and by the time she,

Tommy, Nathan and Carrie were saying their goodbyes, the kitchen and dining room were as spotless as ever.

"Now then," said Rika, after they'd gone. "Some tea."

"Oh, no. I need to leave you both in peace," said Ellen. "You've had a big day!"

"A wonderful day, wouldn't you say, Jonas? I can't recall when I've enjoyed Thanksgiving so much."

"Indeed, my dear. A wonderful day. And may I say what a terrific cook you are?"

"You may, *älskling*," she said. "You are a lovely man." She patted him on the head. "Let me go get the tea things."

Rika lit candles "like we do in Sweden" and the chilly darkness outside just served to emphasize the warm coziness inside as the three of them drank their tea and reviewed the day.

Chapter 22
Can Powell take on a new order from Wilco?

Somebody's radio was tuned to a station that was playing Christmas music as Ellen slid out of her coat and placed her purse in the bottom drawer. The managers were in their staff meeting, so she headed out to the shop to pick up job cards. She realized that she was becoming quite adept at wearing safety glasses and ear plugs. She'd even finally swapped her heels for some Chelsea boots she had splurged on. She was sure Harvey would approve.

"Hello, Ellen," he said around his cigar. "Things going OK?"

"I think so, Harvey. Thanks for asking. How are things in Fabrication?"

"Same old, same old. You know. The computer has the wrong information but we keep making parts."

"If anyone can do it, you can!" Ellen picked up the job cards and headed toward the blue arcs and sparks of the Welding department.

"Morning, Leonard!" she called out. Leonard was outside of his office talking to one of the welders as Ellen trekked by.

"Oh, hey girl! Lookin' good this morning," he answered back.

"You, too, Leonard. I'm just picking up your job cards."

He gave her a thumbs-up and Ellen found the neat stack of cards on the corner of his desk, exactly where they always were.

Then she headed for the Assembly department.

She halfway hoped Kirby would be down at the far end of the assembly line, and halfway hoped he would be in his office. They hadn't had much chance to interact at work; Kirby always seemed to be somewhere else when Ellen was on the shop floor. He hadn't called and Ellen was confused: Had he not had a good time? Was Ellen not his type?

She was also confused about how she felt about Kirby. He certainly was good looking. He had given her a nice evening, even if a tractor pull was somewhat unconventional for a first date. She wasn't sure if she wanted him to ask her out again, or even if she wanted to see him again.

Kirby was in his office.

"Oh, hey, Kirby," she said. "I just came to pick up your job cards."

"Thanks, Ellen." He indicated the job cards in the basket on his desk. She was about to just pick up the cards and leave when he spoke again. "Did you ..." He hesitated and swallowed. "Did you have a good time the other night?"

Despite the oddity of the date, Ellen told the truth. "I did, Kirby. I really did enjoy myself. I've never been to a tractor pull and I found it ... interesting. I enjoyed being with you."

Kirby smiled. "So, if I asked you out again, you might say yes?"

"Depends. Are we talking mud wrestling? Or maybe the roller derby?"

"Actually I was thinking of skeet shooting." He grinned. "Just kidding. I think I owe you a steak dinner in Lexington."

"That would be nice," she said.

"Great!" he responded. "Let me see what the work schedule looks like next week or two, and I'll call you."

"That would be real nice, Kirby." She picked up the job cards as she realized she was beginning to enjoy the idea of dating a good looking man who knew how to have a bit of fun. "Thanks. See you around."

She headed back to the front office. Unbidden, her mind conjured up an image of Kirby sitting across the table from her in a nice restaurant. The lighting was dim, and there was a candle on the table. The candlelight, if possible, made him even more handsome. He had on a crisp white shirt and tie with a nice sport coat. They held their menus and, almost as if by accident, his hand brushed hers as they ordered.

Ellen shook her head. Let's not get ahead of ourselves, she told herself. So far it was only one date, and at a tractor pull, no less. But a girl can dream, can't she?

As she closed the noise of the shop behind her, Rob came out of his office. "Oh, there you are, Ellen."

"Is there something I can do for you?"

"I hope so," he said. "We have an important new order — a big one. Karl Smithson from Wilco called. One of their big suppliers is booked up and can't fulfill a big order they need. It may be small stuff to the other supplier, but it is a big deal for us. Good profit, and the manufacturing process is right in our lane."

"That's great!" said Ellen. And she meant it. "So, is there a problem?"

"That's just it. I don't know. We have the drawings from Wilco's engineering department. They're even willing to ship us the tooling if we can do this order for them. Karl even hinted that, if we do this well, they'd be happy to let us be their supplier of record for that part from now on. So we have to make sure we don't screw it up."

"That sounds good, too. There must be something you're not telling me."

"Well, we have the raw material. That's easy. It is all plate steel and our suppliers can easily get us what we'll need. What I'm worried about is the manufacturing time. Do we have the tooling capacity to do this job and get it done on time?"

"Do you mean, like, if we do this job, we'll have our machines occupied doing this job, which means they aren't available to do something else?"

"Right. You catch on quick. There's this thing we call m-time, short for manufacturing time." He explained that the company has an m-time is for every part calculated by Sandy McDonald and his engineering team. But there would be two problems with the new part. First, the m-time would have to be calculated. "Sandy's group will be working on that as soon as I get these drawings to them," he said, indicating a roll of blueprints in his hand. "Second, we don't know what other jobs we have scheduled that would have to be set aside in order to push this one through. I don't want to promise Wilco we can do something when we can't or, worse, make a bunch of our other customers mad because we delayed their job to do the Wilco job."

"I kind of think I'm following what you're saying. It would mean looking at the data for the scheduled jobs we have and seeing if any of the tooling that is needed would be impacted by the Wilco job."

"Exactly. Do you think you could look into that for me? I need an idea of what impact this would have, preferably by close of business today. Worst case, I'd need to know first thing tomorrow morning so I can tell Karl if we can do the work or not."

"Won't we have to have Sandy's numbers first? I mean before we could figure out if we have the capacity?"

"Yes, of course. Let's go and see Sandy now. Maybe he can give us a quick read before his team does the detailed manufacturing analysis." He headed down the hall to Sandy's office and Ellen realized he was assuming she was following him. She almost had to trot to keep up.

Rob explained the situation again to Sandy and told him what they'd need. Sandy went out into the open area where the engineers worked. There was a big table in the middle of the room and he spread the blueprints from Wilco out there. Ellen and Rob watched as he scratched his head, pointed here and there on the drawing, and mumbled under his breath. "Well?" said Rob.

"Hey Butch! Come over here." Sandy motioned to one of the engineers at a desk in the corner.

"Yeah, Boss?"

Sandy explained the situation. "Do you think the three and a half ton press can handle this?"

"We'll have to build the tooling ..."

"No," said Rob. "Wilco will send us the tooling."

"What gauge steel are we talking here?" He and Sandy examined the specifications in the box in the corner of the blueprint. They started talking engineering jargon. Rob seemed to be tracking along with them, but Ellen was at a loss.

"So we can build it?" asked Rob.

"Yes, we think we can," said Sandy. "Butch and I need to check a few more specs, but our initial guess is that we can build this part, assuming they really will send us the tooling. Do you agree, Butch?"

"Yeah, I agree."

"That's good," said Rob. "Now the next question is do we have the capacity to do the work. I've asked Ellen to do some checking with what we have in the master schedule. We don't want to get this part to Wilco late, and we sure don't want to miss a shipment to any of our other customers. Would it be possible to work up the m-times for the part by this afternoon?"

Butch rolled his eyes, but Sandy said, "Yeah, Rob. We can do that. We understand that this is an important job for Powell, don't we, Butch?"

Butch saluted. "Yessir, Boss!"

"That's the spirit. Thanks, Butch. I really appreciate it." Rob looked at Ellen. "What questions do you have, Ellen?"

"Uh, well …" She was thinking furiously, thinking about the first principle and how the m-time would fit into the way Powell did business. She was also thinking about the second principle and how the mainframe system files that would apply here were set up. "I guess I'd need to know which work centers this part would go across. Would it only be the three and a half ton press, or are there some other processes? And I'd need to know the manufacturing time — the m-time — for each work center. Oh, and …"

Sandy cut her off. "We don't break down m-times that way. We calculate the total m-time for manufacturing the entire part, regardless of which work centers it goes across."

"Oh," said Ellen. "But won't it make a difference depending on how much time is needed on each work station?"

"In an ideal world, yes," said Sandy. "But we don't have that kind of detail here at Powell. SOLUTION/400 doesn't support it. We just look at the entire m-time for a part."

"I see what she's saying, Sandy," Rob added. "If the part took most of its m-time on one work center, and very little time on a second work center, it would have a big impact on the capacity of the first work center, but not on the second."

Ellen touched Rob on the arm. "You said it much better than I could. That's exactly what I mean. If we're going to know what kind a capacity issue this is going to generate, we'd need to know which work centers will be impacted by how much."

Sandy nodded his head. "Yeah, I see what you mean. I tell you what — and, Butch, I want to make sure you're in agreement here — how about we calculate the m-time like we always do, but we also give Ellen a list of the work centers that will be impacted and an unofficial idea of how much time might be required on each. Butch?"

"Yeah, that seems fair. Unofficial, of course, but I understand where Ellen is going with this."

"Great, gentlemen," said Rob with a smile. "And lady." He nodded at Ellen. "So do we think we can have this by the end of business today?"

"I really can't start analyzing until I know which work centers would be involved, can I?" Ellen still wasn't sure she knew what she was doing, but her instinct was that she could do it.

Sandy said, "Officially, you're right. But Butch and I can tell you, can't we Butch, just from looking at the drawing, that the press will have the bulk of the work. You could start looking into the schedule on that work center. And we'll have you a list of the other work centers by, say 3:00 PM. That OK?"

"Well ..."

"Make it 2:00, OK?" said Rob. "Ellen has some heavy calculating to do, and we need to let Wilco know for sure by close of business."

"Yeah." Butch saluted again.

"Sandy?"

"Yes, Rob. I understand. Butch and I will get right on this."

"Thank you." Ellen was truly grateful. She wanted to help, but still was unsure. Again, the confidence these men placed in her moved her, and she didn't want to let them down.

"Great, we'll leave the blueprints with you," said Rob.

"And I'll start working up some preliminary capacity estimates on the press work center." She smiled specifically at Butch. "And, Butch, I'll come to you if I have dumb questions?"

"You betcha, Boss!" His smile mirrored hers.

Chapter 23
Ellen researches capacity on the press.

Ellen put down her pencil and rubbed her temples. She closed her eyes, willing the green numbers that were dancing across the computer terminal to go away. She opened her eyes again. They were still there, and she could feel her blood pressure, along with her temper, beginning to rise.

She looked at her pad of paper again. She had made a list of every order that was scheduled to go across the press over the next 30-plus days. She'd had to go out to the shop floor to ask Harvey Green for help.

"Harvey, is there a way in SOLUTION/400 for me to find out all the work orders that are scheduled for the three and a half ton press for the next month or so?"

He had been kind, in his gruff way, letting his perpetual cigar languish in its ash tray while he showed her a screen called the Machine Load report. "The three and a half ton press, that's work center 117." He pointed to the place on the screen where you could search for a particular work center. The list of parts had been long. While it was early December, with the Christmas shut-down coming up, Ellen thought she had better look at any work order due between now and January 31st. Harvey agreed. "Even though we schedule the shop right through the holidays, taking into account the Christmas shut-down, things always seem to slow down. I guess the guys aren't quite running at full capacity after a little too much Christmas dinner and celebrating. It takes 'em a while to get up to full speed."

Ellen had dutifully written down each part and order on her legal pad, and then had headed back to her desk to do more research. As she was heading toward the front office door, she saw Kirby heading her way.

"Hey, good lookin'," he called.

"Hey yourself."

"I've been thinking about that steak dinner. I don't want to wait a couple of weeks. Would you be available Friday?"

"This coming Friday?"

"Well … yeah. That's what I had in mind. I thought I'd take you to the Cork and Cleaver."

"I've heard that's really nice."

"Oh it is. Real nice. And it'll be even nicer if you'll be my date."

She smiled. A real date to a nice restaurant. When was the last time she had really gone on a date, discounting the tractor pull which she and Trish had both agreed really couldn't be counted as a genuine date? There had been Bob Forsyth during her sophomore year in college after the tragedy. Her mind suddenly put on the brakes and wouldn't go there. Bob had been nice, but more than a little handsy, and Ellen had broken it off, realizing she was probably clinging to Bob to fill the void left by her parents. Truthfully, she needed to be with Trish. She hadn't been able to handle college or Bob.

She forced herself to think about it: a real date. The first one she'd had in almost ten years. Her heart beat a little faster and she blurted out, before she could change her mind, "Yes! Yes I'll go out with you on Friday."

"Great!" He was grinning so big Ellen was afraid for his cheek muscles. "Just great! I'll pick you up at 5:30? Can you be ready by then?"

"I'll try to leave work right on time. I'll try not to keep you waiting."

"I don't want to rush you. Would 6:00 be better?"

Ellen was impressed by his courtesy. "That would make it a little easier, if that's OK. Do you know where I live?"

"Uh, actually, no, I don't."

"I could come meet you somewhere."

"Not on your life. This is a date. There will be no motorcycles or diesel fumes. I will pick you up at 6:00 PM if you'll just tell me where to come."

"Its an apartment on Prospect Street." She gave him the number. "It is an apartment above the garage there."

"I think I know it. White house on the left just before you go down the hill? Big magnolia tree in the font yard?"

"Yes that's the one."

"Excellent, just excellent. I'll see you then, OK?" He winked at her and sauntered off toward the welding bays whistling "Don't Worry, Be Happy."

There was a little bounce in Ellen's step, too, as she headed back to her office. The bounce lasted until she crashed into the data she was supposed to be looking into for the Wilco order.

It had proved so tedious. Pulling data out of SOLUTION/400 was like pulling teeth out of a hen. She had to go from screen to screen to screen to try to get the data she needed. First she had to look up every part number for every order that was scheduled to be worked on by the press. Then she had to find out the m-time for each of those parts on another screen. Then she had to look up what operations went into the part through the bill of material. For each operation, she had to look up the work center. A lot of them were work center 117 — the press — which was no surprise. But there were other work centers, too. She saw a lot of references to work center 103 as well as a handful of others. Then she had to multiply the number of parts that were ordered by the m-time for the part to get the total m-time that would be needed.

She rubbed her temples again. 'Think, Ellen, think. What would Jonas do?' He'd keep the main goal in focus, she thought to herself. And what is the main goal? Oh, yes, to decide if we have enough capacity on the press to take the Wilco order. She started adding up the m-times for all the parts and came up with 212 hours, just through January 3, four weeks from today. When she added the additional orders through January 31st, she realized something had to be wrong.

"The guys work eight hours per day, five days a week," she said to herself. "That's a potential of 40 hours per week, if they keep the press running all shift long. I don't know if they do that, but Harvey would know. But 212 hours in about four weeks, that's way more than 40 hours per week times four weeks or 160 hours. We already have a problem even if we don't take the Wilco order."

She decided to go back out to the factory and check with Harvey again.

Harvey took a long drag on his cigar. "You're asking a good question," he said. "Yes, work center 117 is a busy one. We do tend to keep it running all shift. And don't forget, sometimes we have to ask the guys to work overtime, or work on a Saturday. Mr. Powell doesn't like it when we do that, because we have to pay time and a half, double time on Saturday. But ya gotta do what ya gotta do, know what I mean?" He looked at her to make sure she was tracking with him. "But I think the real reason the numbers look so large is because you're dealing with m-times for the complete part, not just the m-time for work center 117, the press."

She had to think about that. "So this part here." She pointed to the first part on the list on her legal pad. "It has operations on the drill press, then the press, then a milling machine, and then weld."

"That's right. So the total m-time …" He looked at her sheet. "The total m-time of 0.88 hours for that part is the total m-time for all four of those operations: drill, press, machine and weld."

"But don't we need to know how much time each of those four operations take, not just the total of 0.88 hours?"

"You're a smart gal, Ellen. That's exactly what's needed. Us old guys that have been doing this since before you were born kind of have it in our brains. You'll learn it, kid. It just takes time."

"But shouldn't the mainframe be able to tell …"

He cut her off. "That piece of crap? It couldn't tell you what day of the week it was if you told it today was Wednesday."

She looked at him.

"Sorry, honey. I shouldn't have said crap in front of you. But you gotta call 'em like you seem 'em, know what I mean?"

"Yes, well. I …"

He cut her off again. "You're actually right, you know. If SO-LUTION/400 were worth half of the millions we pay for it, it would be able to tell you how much m-time to account for for each operation, not just the total. But like I said, it is a piece of …" He reached for his cigar and put it in his mouth before he could finish his own sentence.

"Thanks, Harvey. You always come through for me and help me understand how things work." She left the blue cloud of cigar smoke that defined Harvey's office and headed back up front again.

She went looking for Butch in engineering. "How is your work coming along, Butch?" she asked.

Butch looked up from the blueprint he was studying. Ellen could see it was the Wilco part they'd been discussing earlier.

"I think I'm about done with my calculations. I think we're going to be able to build this for Wilco. At least technically we're going to be able to build it with the machines we have. I see four operations: drill, press, weld, and assembly. That's assuming, of course, that Wilco really does send the tooling for the press. We've assigned it part number 37-558-01." Ellen wrote that number in her notebook. "How about you?" asked Butch. "How are the capacity calculations coming?"

"Actually I had a question about that," said Ellen. "In looking up the orders that are scheduled to go across the press, it looks like we're over capacity already, even without taking the Wilco order. But then, in talking to Harvey, we realized the m-time values I'm using are for the entire part, not just the operation on the press. You had said that before."

Butch nodded his head. "Go on," he said.

"Well, it seems to me, to me and Harvey, that we really have to know how much time each of these parts ..." — she indicated her legal pad with the orders for the next month and a half — "really need to spend on the press. Right now, if I just use the total m-time, we're already over capacity. Harvey tells me we run the press fairly constantly, but we're not getting further and further behind like my calculations would indicate."

"Right. I understand what you're telling me and we just don't have that data. All we have is the total m-time for the part, regardless of which workstations the part goes across."

Ellen felt her jaw muscles tighten. "But, Butch, can't you give me some idea? Like this first part here, 37-301-01. It goes across four workstations, the 103 drill, the 117 press, the 595 milling machine, and then assembly. According to the computer, it has an m-time of 0.88 hours. Of those 0.88 hours, what would be your guess as to how many of them are actually on the 117 press?"

"You mean like a percentage?" asked Butch.

"Well, yes, if you want to think about it that way. What percent of the 0.88 hours are on each of the four work centers?"

Butch scratched his head. "I don't rightly know ..."

"Just a ballpark, Butch. Anything. I'm desperate here. If I don't have any more information that this, I'll have to tell Rob I don't think we can take the Wilco order. In fact, I'd have to say that I think we're going to miss some shipments of other customer's orders as well because we're already over capacity on the 117 press." Ellen was surprised at her own firmness over this. She realized she was playing the 'I'll tell the boss' card and, had she thought about it beforehand, she probably would have tried to figure out a better way to encourage Butch's cooperation.

"I don't know ..." But scratched his head again. "See, the thing is, it really doesn't take that long to press a part. Thirty seconds would be a long time."

"Only thirty seconds?" Ellen was incredulous.

"You hear that sound out there?" Butch indicated the wall of his office. On the other side was the factory, and Ellen could hear the deep thump-thump-thump of one of the machines, the one that vibrated the floor every time it thumped.

"You mean the thump, thump, thump?" She kept time with the throb of the sound.

"Yeah, that's it. That's the three and a half ton press operating. Each one of those thumps is another part."

"That fast? Each one of those thumps is another part? That's even faster than 30 seconds!" She looked at her watch. "More like five seconds per part!"

"Right," said Butch. "Some parts take longer than five seconds to press out. But, like I said, 30 seconds would be a long time."

"I'm beginning to get the picture. So if we estimated 30 seconds per part for the parts on my list, here ..." She indicated her legal pad with all the orders on it. "That wouldn't take much time at all, would it, Butch?"

"I guess not."

"Do you have a calculator?" Butch pulled one out of his desk drawer. "Let's see. Thirty seconds is half a minute. And there are 60 minutes in an hour." She divided 0.5 by 60. "That's a really small number: 0.0083. And 0.0083 divided by the total m-time of 0.88 hours is ..." She did some more calculations. " ... is 0.0095. Or, put another way, less that one percent, 0.95% to be exact, of the total m-time is on the 117 press. Have I got that right?"

Butch was an engineer. Math like this was second nature to him. He took the calculator back from Ellen and ran the numbers himself. "You betcha! You've got it right. And that's using the conservative estimate of 30 seconds per part. Most of these will be even less than that."

"So using that logic, only 1% of the m-time on each of the orders on my list here would actually be on the press." She looked at Butch directly. "Am I making a mistake here?"

"No, I don't think so," replied Butch. "That feels right in my gut. Press parts go pretty quickly."

Ellen had another thought. "So why does Harvey say the 117 work center stays so busy? I calculated 212 hours of m-time for the next four weeks. But if only 1% of the time is needed for the press, that's only 21 hours. There are 160 hours available in a four week period, right? That's 40 hours per week times four weeks."

"Yessir, you're right. But don't forget the tooling swaps."

"Tooling swaps?"

"Yeah. For a press to work, you have these big dies. There's a top die and a bottom die. You slide the sheet of steel in between the two, down comes the press, and presto! You've got a part. But swapping those dies out for a new part is a bear."

"How big of a bear? Smokey Mountain black bear or Rocky Mountain grizzly?"

"Grizzly."

"So how much time does it take to swap out the dies, on average?"

"Oh, I'd say it takes half a day by the time the boys unbolt and remove the old dies, get the new dies installed — they have to place them in with a lift truck, you know — and get them lined up. Then they have to run registration blanks to make sure everything is lined up perfectly. Yeah, it can easily take a half day. Sometimes even more."

"So four hours, on average. Let me see ..." She did a quick count of the orders she had on her sheet. "I think I have 27 orders here, give or take. That's 27 tooling swaps, right? One for each new part number?"

"Yup."

"So 27 tooling swaps times four hours per swap is ..." She took the calculator again. "That's 108 hours! Add that to the 21 hours to actually make the parts and ..." She looked at the calculator screen to make sure. "Aha! That's 129 hours. Getting closer to the 160 hours we have available. Now I see why Harvey says the press is always busy. Not so much for making parts, but for swapping out the tooling."

"And remember, I said half a day, maybe more. I think you've found your answer."

"I think we have, Butch. Thank you. So I think I can tell Rob — make sure you're in agreement with me — that we can probably handle the Wilco order. It may stretch us a little bit, but it isn't something we can't handle. We'll have to do the tooling swap with the tooling from Wilco."

"Right. And the thing I worry about is whether or not Wilco will really send us the tooling."

"I'll make sure to emphasize that with Rob."

"And the tooling swap will probably be longer. It always is the first time you run a new part. Lots of little nuances that have to be

worked out to make the part just right. But once you've got the tooling in place, Katie bar the door, you can crank out the parts like flip-
pin' flapjacks."

"This is great, Butch. I really appreciate it." She turned to leave.
"Oh, sorry. Just like Columbo, that TV detective."

"Yeah, he's good. Peter Falk plays him, with the frumpy overcoat
and the cigar."

"Yeah, that's the one. He's always saying, 'Just one more thing.'
Butch, what about the other work centers? Like the 103 drill, does it
take that long to swap out the tooling?"

"Oh, no. There's really not much tooling on a drill. The bit just
has to line up in the right place and drill the holes. No tooling, per se.
Of course, it takes a lot longer to actually drill a hole than it does to
press out a part. But tooling swaps on a drill are a cinch. Nothing to
worry about there."

"Really great, Butch. I'll go write up my report and give it to Rob
so he can tell Wilco we'll do the order. I'm sure he'll be pleased.
And I'll make sure he knows how much this was a joint effort."

"I appreciate that. I guess I can get back to my regular work
now."

Ellen returned to her office to check her assumptions and her math
one last time and to type up a neat little report for Rob. She was able
to keep the report to a page and a half. At the bottom she typed,
'Recommendation: Accept the order from Wilco. Powell Manufacturing has the necessary excess capacity on the three and a half ton
press.'

A management staff meeting was just breaking up when she went
in search of Rob. She found him outside of the conference room as
the other managers were headed to their offices. He invited her down
to his office and was delighted with her findings as she explained her
logic to him. She pointed out that the actual pressing of the parts
would not be the issue, but warned that the tooling swap would be
what would eat the capacity. She also reminded him that, without the
dies from Wilco, nothing could start rolling.

"You're right, of course. I'll remind Karl Smithson of that when I call him. And I'm impressed that you know what a tooling swap is."

"An hour ago, before Butch helped me, I had never heard the term."

"Well you learn fast. Some time when you're out in the shop, get Harvey to let you watch a tooling swap. It's kind of a big deal and, for obvious reasons, we try to minimize the swaps all we can."

"I'd like that. Anything else?"

"I don't think so. Thanks, Ellen. This is going to be one call to Karl Smithson I'm going to enjoy. Usually I'm calling him with bad news. This will be a nice change." He looked at his watch. "And fifteen minutes to spare before five o'clock."

On the drive home Ellen was feeling rather proud over herself until she had this nagging feeling that Butch had said something that was important, something that she had missed. What was it? She couldn't think but she just knew she had overlooked something vital.

Chapter 24

Jonas helps Ellen understand an operational bill of material.

Her usual parking place on the street in front of the Klameck garage was available. Ellen eased up to the curb with a maneuver that had become familiar. She grabbed her purse and notebook and headed up to her apartment. She could see Rika through the kitchen window washing dishes. "That means they've finished dinner," she thought to herself.

She glanced in the fridge to make sure there'd be something to eat later, and changed quickly into jeans and a sweater with a nice turtleneck underneath. She picked up her notebook off of the counter and headed across the driveway.

Ellen had barely tapped on the back door when Rika opened it, almost as if Ellen had been expected. She greeted Ellen with her usual broad smile. "How delightful!" she said. "I thought I had seen you come in. Have you had your dinner?"

"Yes. That is, well, no, but I didn't come to bum a meal. I just had something interesting happen at work today that I'd like to get Jonas's opinion on, if he isn't too tired."

"Tired? That old elephant?" She laughed and almost bodily drew Ellen into the room. "Jonas, we have a visitor!" she called. "Here, let me take your coat."

And, before she could protest, she found herself in the cozy den. There was a nice log fire burning on the grate and Jonas came wheeling around from the kitchen.

"Ah, Ellen. I was just thinking about you, wondering how you're doing on the quest."

Ellen held up the notebook as evidence. "Making progress, a page at a time," she said. "But that isn't really why I came. I was wondering if I could talk something through with you. We had an interesting opportunity at the plant today, and I wonder if I could bounce a few things off of you."

"Nothing could make me happier. Here why don't we go into the dining room where we can spread out on the table. Rika, dearest, could you fetch me a pad of paper and a pencil, just in case Ellen gets over my head and I need to write something down?"

"Of course, *älskling*." She bent down and kissed him on the top of his head.

Jonas pulled up to his customary place at the head of the table and Ellen chose the chair opposite the one she had seen Rika use most often. "So now, Ellen, what is this opportunity we're going to explore?"

Ellen explained about the possible new order and what it would mean. "I don't know this, but it seems to me we could use the business."

"Of course," agreed Jonas.

"And it could lead to more business in the future. The thing is, we weren't sure we had enough capacity to take the order. We don't want to disappoint the customer, and we certainly don't want to delay any order commitments we've already taken."

"Exactly the right attitude," said Jonas. "So who is analyzing the factory's capacity to take the order?"

"I am. Or I was. I told Mr. Powell just before I left work that my analysis said we had the capacity to tell the customer we could accept the order. He was going to telephone them and accept."

"Ah," said Jonas, noncommittally.

"The thing is, something just doesn't feel right. I'm afraid I've made a mistake, and that's why I wanted to go over my thinking with you, if that's OK."

"Nothing could make me happier," he replied. "I thrive on a challenge — and opportunity, as you called it — like this." Rika returned with the pad and pencil and laid it in front of Jonas. "Thank you, my dear. Have I ever told you that you are a treasure and that I would be completely lost without you?"

"You tell me that every day, sir. Occasionally I believe you. Most of the time I think you're just laying on the Klameck charm."

The radiant smile that lit up her entire face told Ellen that she enjoyed her husband's appreciation of her, despite their comfortable banter.

Rika headed back into the kitchen and Ellen turned her attention back to the Wilco order.

"The problem is that engineering has been calculating the m-time for the new part and ..." Ellen stopped as Jonas placed his hand over hers on the table.

"May I stop you and give you some feedback?"

"Ah, well, of ... of course." Ellen wasn't quite sure how to take the question, or what might be coming next.

"You see, Ellen, I respect your mind and your instincts. I see in you the makings of a remarkable person who will use technology, business acumen, and your sense of people to do some very good things. That's why I want to see you do well. And so I am eager to help you become even sharper, if you'll take what I have to say and consider it."

"I, uh ..."

"I've alarmed you. My apologies. I assure you, my intentions are good. I want to help you grow. When you were explaining the situation to me just now, I wonder if you remember what you said."

Ellen's brow wrinkled. She respected Jonas. Even liked him. If he saw potential ... Oh, she'd been talking about the work engineering was doing. "I think I was talking about engineering developing the m-time for this new part ..."

"Yes, that's exactly what you were saying. Ellen, do you think I know what an m-time is?"

"I guess I assumed ..." Suddenly she was embarrassed. "Don't you?" she asked quietly.

"I think I do, but it is always best to eliminate jargon as much as possible when explaining something to someone who may not know what you're talking about. You don't want to make them feel foolish or stupid." He stopped. "Not that you have done that to me," he laughed. "I just wanted to point out that helping people understand is a major objective if you're trying to solve a problem. They may not completely understand what you're talking about, but, to avoid embarrassment, they may not ask you. And then where would you be? You'd possibly be talking past each other and not even know it.

"I, on the other hand …" He shrugged his shoulders and gave her a cross-eyed grin. "I embarrass myself daily, so why don't you tell me what an m-time is, just so I'll know."

Ellen smiled. It was going to be OK. He really was helping her. "M-time is short for manufacturing time. It is the amount of time, usually expressed in minutes, that it takes to manufacture a particular part."

"Excellent," said Jonas. "That's rather what I thought. And it is interesting how many different labels there are for that concept. Some companies call it production time. Others call it unit machine load. I've heard it called PBOM — short for Production Bill of Material. There are lots of different ways to say it, and m-time is as good as any."

He looked at her again. "By the way, another thing to learn, is that you have to pick up people's vocabulary quickly. You call it m-time, and I suppose everyone at Powell does, too." Ellen nodded. "But if you go to another factory, they may call it something else. You need to learn the local vocabulary and start using it as rapidly as possible. Someone with your intelligence can do that. Most people don't even know they're using a specific vocabulary." He paused. "Am I telling you too much?"

"Oh no, not at all! I'm just so, well, overwhelmed that you apparently think so highly of me. I'm really nothing. I don't have the training or the experience or …" She finished lamely.

"That may be true, Ellen, but you have a mind. A very good mind. And a great instinct. The fact that you sense something is wrong at the factory is remarkable. You don't know what it is, but you know it is there, and you're going to keep digging until you find it. You being here tonight is evidence of that. You have rare raw qualities that I would enjoy helping to refine, if you'll allow me."

At that moment Rika appeared with a roast beef sandwich on a plate, along with a little green salad and some boiled potatoes. "Dinner," she announced. When Ellen started to protest, Rika held up her hand. "Tut, tut, tut, young lady. You told me you had not had dinner. This isn't much, but you can't think these massively important thoughts that my husband is forcing you to think on an empty stomach. Water, iced tea, or milk?" she asked.

"Thank you, Rika. Water would be fine."

"There, you see?" said Jonas. "Didn't I say that my wife is a treasure? An absolute treasure?" He reached out and gently touched Rika's hand. "Thank you, my dear."

They turned back to the discussion. "Let me ask you a question. How many tools, work centers, machine codes, manufacturing centers — there are lots of words to describe that as well — is this part going to need to go across to be manufactured?"

"Oh, that's a good question. I asked engineering and they said it was four: drill, press, weld, and assembly." Jonas wrote those four words down the left side of his paper. "It is the press we're worried about," she continues. "That press runs pretty much full time, and this new part is going to require the press."

"Understood. Now tell me about your software. Do you keep the m-time for each of the four work centers?"

"I asked that question, too, and the answer is that we do not. Our system only allows for an m-time for the finished part, not at each stage in the manufacturing process."

"Pity," said Jonas. "And that just won't do. Remember the First Principle? The business information technology system must model the business it serves." Ellen said it along with him. "This m-time only on the finished part would seem to violate the first principle. Would you agree?"

Ellen paused. This was important, she could tell. Then she had it. "Yes! Yes, I do see. If we don't have an m-time on each of the four operations, how can we know for sure that we won't have a capacity problem on the press?" Jonas smiled. "We can't. And that's the problem. That's what I was trying to get at with the engineering guys, but this is a better way of saying it. The best that the engineer I talked to could do was tell me that it doesn't take long to press out a part."

"That's often true," said Jonas. "As you know, I've been in a factory or two. Big presses are impressive, both in the noise they make and the speed with which they can stamp out lots of parts. The problem is usually in the set up, particularly when exchanging tooling to produce a different part."

"Wow, you have been around." Ellen hadn't meant to sound naive, but it came out that way. "I mean, that's exactly the issue we settled on. The real challenge is how many times do we have to change setups — we call them tooling swaps — while we are supposed to be producing this new part? And, even more importantly, do we have the capacity to squeeze another setup in?"

"And what did you conclude?"

"That we do have the capacity. Barely." She showed him the calculations she had made with Butch. "So, you see, if we really pay attention to the setups, we think we can do it."

"I am inclined to agree. But never forget that Murphy is sure to strike."

"Murphy?"

"You've heard of Murphy's Law? If anything can go wrong, it will."

Ellen laughed. "That's funny." Then she stopped. "But kind of true," she said more seriously.

"Indeed. We must always be on the lookout for Murphy. But let me ask another question about your system — does it record the amount of time for setups? I suppose this could be the equivalent of the m-time, but for setups. Call it the s-time."

Ellen thought. "No ... at least I don't think so. I'll have to check tomorrow." She wrote that down in her notebook.

"You can see why I'm asking. For the press, at least, m-time is much less significant to capacity than s-time."

"It sure is. I do see what you're saying."

"If the system does not support recording s-time and provide capacity calculations based on them, I'm afraid we have another violation of the First Principle."

"I'm beginning to see how important this First Principle is," said Ellen, making more notes in her notebook.

"Indeed. Now, let me point out one other concern." Jonas pointed to his pad where he had written down the four operations: drill, press, weld and assembly. "We've talked about the press, and that you think you have capacity to take this new order. But what about the other three operations? Can you be equally confident about them?"

"They guys in engineering don't seem concerned about anything but the press." She stopped and sat straight up in her chair. It was there again: that nagging feeling that something was wrong.

"What is it, Ellen? You have good instincts. What are you thinking about?"

"It was something Butch said …" It almost slipped away, and then she had it. "He said that there wasn't much to worry about when it came to tooling and setup on the drill. But he said … he said that it takes a lot longer to drill a part than it does to stamp it on the press."

Jonas didn't say anything. He waited.

"Oh, gosh, Jonas! It could be that we have enough capacity on the press, but we don't have enough capacity on the drill! Isn't that what it means?"

"It could very well."

Suddenly Ellen was deflated. Her chin sagged into her hands, her elbows propped on the table, the sandwich left only half eaten. "Oh, gosh. I'm such a klutz! And I told Mr. Powell we had the capacity. But we may not. Oh rats! Rats, rats, rats!"

"There, there, child." Mr. Klamick touched her hand. "I don't think it is bad as all that. You did an excellent job on analyzing the press. Now tomorrow you'll go and look into the drill capacity. It may be that the drill is an underutilized work center and there will be no problem. Or, if it is used consistently, the good news is that drills are fairly common. You might even be able to outsource the drill operation to one of the tool and dye shops in the area."

"But that would cut into our profits."

"Yes, it might. But some profit is better than none, I presume. Besides, no sense in borrowing trouble. You know what you need to look into tomorrow. And I would hope that your boss would be impressed that you figured out where else you needed to look. The engineering department may know instinctively there isn't a problem, or they may just be too nearsighted to see what you've seen. Either way, it doesn't bear worrying about any more tonight." He pushed his pad across the table as if to put it out of sight and out of mind. "Now I suggest you finish your sandwich and I shall see if Rika has some little morsel saved back. Oh, Rika, my dear?"

"Yes, *älskling*?" She came from the kitchen, untying her apron.

"There wouldn't happen to be any small morsel we could cap off this invigorating discussion with, is there? And perhaps some tea?"

"As if you didn't know, you silly man." She turned back to the kitchen and immediately returned, bearing a tray with tea things and some wedges of cake that looked like it had almonds and caramel in it.

"You both are too much! I give up!" said Ellen.

"That is as it should be," said Rika, seating herself at the table next to her husband. "There is absolutely no point in resisting a Swede with tea and cake."

Chapter 25
Ellen and Annie go to lunch.

The next day Ellen went straight to Rob's office but couldn't find him. She checked with Gladys.

"Honey, he's gone to a meeting in Lexington," Gladys told her. "Probably be gone all day. Can it wait?"

"Well, I suppose. I wanted to talk to him about the new Wilco order."

"I hadn't heard about that one. A good order for us?"

Ellen explained about the potential order without going into all the details of the m-time calculations.

"That sounds really good, honey. Wouldn't it be great if Rob can land that order?"

So Ellen went back to her office and began the same tedious research she had done yesterday, except this time she was focusing on work center 103, the vertical drill, rather than on work center 117, the three and a half ton press. The good news was that there weren't as many orders that made use of the drill, so it didn't take as long. On the other hand, many of the products that used the drill also used many more work centers, not just the drill and the press, welding and assembly. There were usually seven or eight operations for parts that also used work center 103. In one case Ellen counted 12 operations.

She wasn't sure if that meant anything so she went back to Butch again.

"Butch, do you have a minute?"

"Sure. What's up?"

Ellen showed him her list of orders and explained what she was doing. "A lot of these parts have a lot of operations. I've looked up the m-times, but, because we don't know what portion of the total m-time is used by each operation, I'm not sure whether we're likely to have a capacity problem on the drill."

"Yeah, kind of like yesterday, huh?" He scanned the list of parts. He marked three of them lightly with the mechanical pencil from his pocket protector. "I'm not sure about these three. The rest look fine. The drill is a small part of their total m-time."

He went over to a computer terminal and looked up the three parts. "The first two are OK," he said. "None of these parts need a lot of time on the drill. I'd say most of them you'd be safe in saying less than ten percent of their m-time is on the drill. None of them would be more than twenty percent." Then he stopped. "Now this part here ..." He pointed to the third part he had marked. "This one is different. It is actually part of a disc brake assembly. It uses one inch cold rolled steel, blanked, and then drilled. There are sixteen different holes in this one." He looked up at her. "You know what that means?"

"Uh, that the part will spend a lot of time on the vertical drill?"

"Bingo! You nailed it. I would say better than fifty percent of this part's m-time is spent on the drill. Maybe even sixty percent. If you're going to have a problem, it will be because of that 47-405-03 part." He went over to the wall of cabinets where Sandy had pulled out the drawing to look at the quantity per. Butch scanned down until he found the drawer he was looking for. He thumbed through the blueprints in the drawer and pulled out one, taking it over to his drafting table where he could spread it out.

"See this here? That's your 47-405-03 part. See these holes here? Those are all made by the drill. Oh, and my bad. I missed four. There are sixteen 3/4 inch holes, but there are also four mounting holes, 3/16 inches in diameter. Which means ..." He looked up at Ellen. "Which means ..."

"Yet another setup?"

"Right again. Two different diameter holes, two different bits on the drill press, two setups. Like I said, if you're going to have a problem, its with this 47-405-03 part."

Ellen looked at her list of orders. "Looks like there is only one order for that part, and it is for a quantity of fifty."

Butch looked relieved. "Well, then. Maybe it won't be a prob-lem."

"I hope not. Thanks for your help, Butch. I'll go finish up my calculations, just to make sure. How long is a setup on the 103 verti-cal drill?"

"Oh, not more than thirty minutes, usually half that."

"OK, I'll base my calculations on that, then." She thanked him again and headed back to her office.

Later Annie Angel, the Production Control department secretary, put her head in Ellen's door. "How's it going, Ellen?"

"It's going fine, Annie. How about you?"

"I was just going out to get some lunch. I'm tired of packing a sack so I just decided I'm going to treat myself today. I wondered if you'd like to come along and keep me company."

"I ... well." She eyed her own sack lunch. She knew very well what it contained: a peanut butter sandwich and an apple. Nothing inspiring. But still, she needed to watch her pennies. "I brought a lunch, and ... I've got to finish up this report for Rob." She indicated the computer screen.

"Looks like its mostly done to me," said Annie. "Besides, I need a girlfriend to go out with, someone to talk to." She paused an looked at Ellen straight on. "Couldn't you use someone to talk to, too?"

Unbidden thoughts ran through Ellen's mind. Since her mother had died, she'd really only had Trish to talk to. No real girlfriends. Nobody, really. And she knew Annie from working together on vari-ous projects. She was a straight arrow; you never had to guess where you stood with Annie. She was the most honest person Ellen had met in a long time. That drew her, and she found herself smiling.

"Why not?" said Ellen. "That sounds fun. The peanut butter sandwich can wait for supper."

"Oh, great!" enthused Annie. "I was kinda hoping I could talk you into going to Ma Kelly's."

"Ma Kelly's?"

"Ain't you never been to Ma Kelly's? Girl, you are in for a treat!
Come on! Let's go!"

They took Annie's car and Ellen wasn't sure about the restaurant.
It looked like an old, beat up storefront on the wrong side of the
tracks. Inside was worse. Graffiti covered the walls, but people were
sitting down, cheek by jowl, and seemed to be enjoying their food.
"It's just good ol' home cooking," explained Annie. "You just go
through the line and tell 'em what you want. The lady at the end tells
you how much it costs — and, believe me, it won't be much."

The ladies who were dishing up were all grandmother types,
wearing aprons and literally dishing up off of the stove. Ellen chose
meatloaf, green beans and corn. Annie selected fried chicken —
"Could I have a drumstick?" she asked — collard greens and fried
okra. And the meal was so cheap, Ellen wondered why they didn't
come here every week.

"Why, girl, we could do that if'n you wanted to," said Annie.

As they carried their plates and silverware, looking for a place to
sit, Ellen was fascinated by the graffiti. It seemed that everyone in the
world had wanted to put their name on the wall. Every single surface,
from floor to ceiling, was covered with people's names, dates, and
wisecracks. Why would anyone want to put their name out there for
everyone to see, she wondered. Still, it was different and Ellen was
intrigued in spite of herself.

They found a spot in a corner. "This is good," said Annie. "We
can talk here." Everyone else was ignoring them and digging into
their food, which suited Ellen just fine. One of the grandmother types
came around and asked what they wanted to drink. "Why, sweet tea,
of course!" said Annie before Ellen could respond. Why not, thought
Ellen. When in Rome …

The sweet tea was delicious, and so was the meal. As Annie
said, it was just good home cooking. The graffiti over Annie's head
spelled out "MOM" in big, bold scrawly letters. Suddenly Ellen had
to look away so Annie wouldn't notice.

But she noticed anyway. "Girl, what's wrong? You look like
you lost your best friend."

Ellen didn't — couldn't — say anything. She swallowed again. "It's nothing," she said.

"Oh, I know what nothin' looks like. And this ain't nothin'. Nothin' is when a boy tells you he loves if you'll just let him. But he just wants inside your drawers. He's nothin'. This ain't nothing. It ain't nothin' when you come home and find your momma black and blue in the face and cryin' 'cause your daddy hit her. That ain't nothin', even if'n she says it is. It ain't nothin'. And the way you look, that ain't nothin'." Annie reached out and covered Ellen's hand with her own. "It's OK if you don't want to talk about it. But I'd be proud to listen if it would help." Her eyes were gentle and her smile was warm.

"It's my mom," Ellen whispered.

"What about your mom, honey?"

"She's gone."

"You mean like, she's done passed?"

Ellen nodded. "My daddy, too."

"Both of 'em?" Her shock was palatable. "How long ago?"

"That's the thing. It was nine years ago this month. A long time. I should be over it by now."

"Aw, honey. Nobody every really gets over a thing like that. Losin' both your momma and daddy. It just has to become part of who you are. You don't get over it." She took a drink of tea. "Can I ask, how did they die? Did they die together?"

Ellen nodded again. "They were on their way to a Christmas party. There was ice and an accident. I was away at college. I remember Dean Kellog coming to find me in Chemistry class. It was awful ..." A lone tear overflowed her left eye, slid down her cheek and dripped into the meatloaf.

"You poor child," said Annie. "I didn't know. And I'm so, so sorry. I wish we could bring them back, I can tell how much you miss them."

"I guess it is the time of year and this food. It is a lot like my mom used to make."

"And like my granny used to fix. I guess that's why I like coming here." Without taking here eyes away from Ellen she said, simply, "My mother was a drug addict. She gave me away when I was a baby."

"Oh, heck!" Ellen was truly surprised. "I had no idea. At least I had time with my mother. At least I knew she loved me." Ellen's hand flew to her mouth. "Oh, I've said the wrong thing. I didn't mean that your mother didn't love you. I was being very insensitive. Oh, I am so, so sorry ..."

Annie laughed. "Now, listen, Ellen. I'm no worse for wear." She hugged herself across her chest. "My granny raised me, and she did a good job, God rest her soul. I've got me a fine feller' who is going to marry me. What kind of mess my momma made of her life was her business. Doesn't mean it has to stick to me."

"I don't know how you can be so ... so ..." Ellen took one of the sugar packets from the bowl and twisted it between her fingertips.

Annie laughed. "Why, I've had lots of practice with tragedy," she said. "You're just gettin' started." She laughed again. "Now who is saying the wrong thing? I didn't mean I was implying that your life is going to be one big tragedy. I mean, well, it just takes time to get over things. You don't get over it in a year, or even nine years."

"I guess that's right."

"Looks to me like you've got some things going for you. I mean you're pretty, an' smart, an' ..."

"Oh, Annie!"

"I'm serious, Ellen. You are pretty. You just don't know it. But the men at the plant do."

Ellen's look of confusion made Annie laugh again. "Oh, Ellen. You really are the whiskers on the cat. You have no idea, do you?"

"No idea about what?"

"About boys, an' how to use your feminine ways, and ..." She arched her eyebrows. "About the birds an' the bees."

"Oh, Annie!"

"I tell you what, Ellen. Me an' Ronnie Dale, we've been saving ourselves for marriage. But give me a couple of months after we're

hitched and, why, I'll bet you I can answer all kinds of questions."
She took a long draw from her tea glass. "I don't mean to embarrass
you. I like you a lot and I hope we can be good friends. I figure God
made man and woman in His own image for a reason. I think it
pleases Him when two folks get married and enjoy each other. You
ever read the Song of Solomon?"

"The what?"

"The Song of Solomon. It's in the Bible. You oughta read it
some time. It's real interesting. And how about that Kirby? He's a
good looking drink of water, ain't he? Are you and him going out
again?"

"Well, he did ask me to go to dinner with him to a nice restaurant
in Lexington ..."

"Now that's what I'm talking about. A right proper date. You
gonna dress up real pretty, wear some makeup?"

"I guess. I hadn't really thought that far ahead."

"Well, it is high time you did. Do you have a pretty dress?
We're about the same size, if you don't. I'd be proud to lend you one
of mine. And makeup? You got some pretty red lipstick?"

"I do, yes. I think I'm OK. I just hadn't thought about it."

"Well it's time you did you some thinking on it. Girl, I think you
deserve a nice date with Kirby. And many more, too."

Late in the afternoon Ellen was still worrying with the drill press.
She had already printed out the report for Rob and had put it on his
desk. He still wasn't back from Lexington. She kept looking at the
data from one side and then another. "I don't think we have a problem," she said to herself. "But it wouldn't take much. There's not a
lot of margin."

"You talking to yourself?" It was Annie, with her coat and
gloves on.

Ellen looked up and grinned. "I guess I was ..."

"Long as you don't start answering yourself. Then everyone 'ud
know you was crazy." Annies infectious smile found itself reflected
on Ellen's face. "I really enjoyed going to lunch with you, Ellen. I

hope I didn't embarrass you. You know me ... open mouth, insert foot. I'd like to do it again."

"Oh, I would too!" That came out with more enthusiasm than she had expected. It had been good to talk to Annie. And, Ellen thought, she could be a good friend.

"I'll hold you to that," replied Annie. "Ain't you about ready to head home? It's after five o'clock."

"Is it?" Ellen looked at her watch. "I had no idea. I've got a few more things to check on."

"I know you like your job. Hey, I like mine, too. But this place doesn't own us. Come five o'clock, it's time to head to the barn. And time to think about what shade of lipstick you're going to wear when Kirby takes you out to that fancy restaurant." She winked. "I'm just sayin' ..." Ellen could hear her shoes tapping on the linoleum floor as she headed for the lobby and the front door.

Later, through the window, Ellen watched Annie get into her car and drive away. The parking lot was thinning out fast. And then she saw Rob's car pull in. She heard the front door and heard his steps going into his office. She almost got up to see if he'd seen her report about the vertical drill, but then she stopped.

It sounded like a human lion, a roar filled with such rage that she wasn't sure she was hearing right. And then a chair, Rob's chair, came sailing out of his office door and crashed against the hallway wall. And that was followed by what could only be called screaming.

Ellen grabbed her coat and purse and, as quietly as she could, tiptoed quickly to the front door, let herself out, and almost ran to Gunilla in the parking lot. She had driven several miles before she realized she was gripping the steering wheel like it was a life preserver and that her heart was still beating wildly and her breathing was rapid and shallow.

Chapter 26
Ellen is accused of leaking confidential information.

The next morning Ellen was putting away her coat and purse when her phone rang. "Ellen Murphy," she said into the receiver.

"Ellen, I need you to come to my office right away." Somehow she knew he'd call. And she was beginning to dread having to go to his office. He could be so nice. But then, last night. His temper. She could feel her heart rate building as she walked down the hall to Rob's office.

Sandy and Butch were there, standing. Rob was seated and it looked like one of the wheels on his chair had been broken off in last night's violence. Ellen thought he was holding one leg rather stiffly so the chair wouldn't tilt on the bad leg.

"What's this about?" Sandy was asking.

"I want each one of you to tell me who you talked to about the new Wilco order. We talked about it day before yesterday, and each one of you did some research on whether or not we could handle the order. I want to know who else you told." He tone was terse, and Ellen could see a vein on his neck throbbing.

"Nobody." Sandy shrugged his shoulders.

"Me either, Boss." Butch looked at Ellen. "Ellen and I discussed the order in the engineering room. But we didn't talk to anyone else. Why, what's this about?"

"Ellen, who did you talk to besides Butch?"

"Just Butch. No, wait. I did talk it over with my landlord night before last."

"Your landlord?" Mr. Powell's voice was incredulous. "Your landlord? Why in the name of all that's holy would you talk about Powell Manufacturing business with your landlord?"

"He's a retired consultant. He's helping me learn more about how manufacturing works."

"Did it not occur to you that the information was proprietary, that you shouldn't go blabbing it all over town?"

"I didn't go ... I'm sorry." What had she done? She suddenly couldn't remember. What had she said that was out of line to Jonas? "I didn't say anything that was specific about the order. At least I don't think I did ..." She looked down at her shoes. "I shouldn't have done that. I don't think he would have told anyone else."

"Well, clearly he did." He looked at each one of them in turn. "We've lost the new Wilco order."

"What?" Sandy was incredulous. "How could that happen? I thought the order was ours if we had the capacity. And we've calculated that we do have the capacity, right?"

"We were underbid. I met with Karl Smithson yesterday afternoon in Lexington. He told me the bad news."

"But who? How?" Sandy was taking the lead on getting to the bottom of this.

"Karl is too much of a straight arrow to say, but I'm pretty sure it is International Dynamics that got the order. Karl said it was a company in Lexington and the only one I know that has presses like we do is International Dynamics." Mr. Powell looked at Sandy for confirmation.

"That sounds right. ID is the only company I know of that could do that work. Butch, do you know of anyone else who could handle that part?"

"Not me, Boss. I think International Dynamics make sense. But how did they find out about it? Did Smithson put the order out for bid? I thought he wanted us to do the work. How could they have underbid us? Don't we have a lower overhead than they do?"

"Exactly!" said Mr. Powell. "Karl told me it was a late, unsolicited bid that came in yesterday morning just before lunch."

"Unsolicited?" The tone of Sandy's voice was bordering on disbelief.

"That's what Karl said. He got an unsolicited bid that was cheaper than ours. So he had to take it." He paused again and Ellen swallowed. "So, Ellen, who does your landlord know at International Dynamics?"

"I ... I have no idea!"

"Well we sure could have used that bid, and the follow up work that would probably have come afterwards," said Mr. Powell. "I don't have to tell you what a loss this is. Let's watch ourselves, people, and not let this happen again." He looked each one of them in the eye, ending with Ellen. "That's all."

And, just like that, they were dismissed.

Ellen was nearest the door and she took the opportunity to bolt. Gladys looked up from her desk as Ellen rounded the corner in the lobby, but Ellen was in no mood for conversation. She found herself, sitting at her desk, staring at a blank computer screen. She wracked her brain. What had she said to Jonas? And why would he share it with anyone, let alone someone at International Dynamics? It just seemed so out of character. And yet there it was ... someone passed on the secret information, and it had to have come through her conversation with Jonas. Both Sandy and Butch denied talking to anyone. They could keep their mouths shut. Why do I have to be such a blabbermouth? Talking is overrated. Keep your nose to the grindstone and your eyes straight ahead.

Ellen stifled a cough or a hiccup. On top of everything, Mr. Powell was really, really angry with her. And rightly so. She knew that the company needed new business, and she had lost it for them. For him. She knew how passionate he was about the company, about succeeding. She'd seen his temper when things didn't go his way. She's seen how that temper of his could quickly explode out of control. And now he hated her. If she was honest with herself, she was scared. Scared that he would fire her. Scared that he would take his anger out on her. Scared that their budding friendship had been destroyed by one careless, stupid conversation.

Before she was really aware of what she was doing, she was pulling on her coat. "I've got to go out for a bit." She tossed the words at Gladys as she flew past and out the front door.

Again she was driving, clenching the steering wheel, and this time she didn't even know where she was going. She just had to get away, away from Mr. Powell's anger, away from his disappointment in her.

She found herself back at her apartment. She climbed the stairs two at a time and didn't look to see if she could see Rika through the kitchen window or if she had noticed and wondered why Ellen was home at this time of day.

She sat in her mother's chair, clenching and unclenching her hands. It seemed the most natural thing to do to simply ask Jonas who he had talked to. But if he told her, she would be so disappointed in him. And if he denied it, her disappointment would have even been more profound.

She called Trish.

"Are you busy?"

"A woman's work is never done," came the breezy reply. "I'm trying to bake bread."

"Would ... would it be OK if I came over?"

"Of course, El. What's wrong?"

"Nothing. Everything. Oh, I'll explain it when I get there."

Trish was up to her elbows kneading bread dough when Ellen let herself in the kitchen door. She looked up and wiped a bead of sweat off of her brow, leaving a white flour streak in its place. She had her hair done up in a kerchief.

"Well, don't you look domestic," Ellen commented as she hung her coat on its customary peg by the door.

Trish laughed. "I'm really getting to like this homemaker stuff," she said. "Baking bread, cooking, cleaning. If you can believe this, I have actually cleaned the grout in the hall bathroom with a toothbrush."

"Will wonders never cease." Ellen tried to find the right balance of light teasing in her voice, but it came out strained.

Trish divided the dough into three equal portions and placed each one in a bread tin. "There," she said. "That needs to rise a bit more and then it'll be ready to bake." She poured a cup of coffee for Ellen and topped off her own. "Sit down and tell me what's up."

Ellen sat. The familiarity of this kitchen suddenly tumbled over her. It was like the first time they had gone to Myrtle Beach as a family. She had ventured out too far and had been knocked flat by a big wave. Her dad had grabbed her and held her up above the churning sandy froth as she coughed and sputtered and tried to regain her sense of normal. This kitchen — Trish's kitchen, not hers any more — was so familiar, so comfortable, so safe. She wanted it back. She wanted the ocean waves to quit pounding her into the sand. "I'm afraid I might get fired."

"What?" Trish stared at Ellen, her mouth wide open. "What?? Why? I thought things were going so well ..."

"They were. At least I thought so. But I made a bad mistake ..." She told Trish about the Wilco order and the conversation with Jonas and how Powell had lost the bid. "And you can't tell a soul, Trish. Not even Tommy. Promise me, please. Because I'm already in trouble for telling Jonas. But I'm so confused and scared. I just had to come talk to you."

"And rightly so." Trish leaned over and hugged her sister. "Don't worry. I won't tell anyone. But I'm glad you came to me. You and me, we're sisters. We always did understand each other. But is it really that bad?"

"I think it is." She told Trish about what she had witnessed the previous evening, when the chair had come careening out of Mr. Powell's office. "I swear, Trish, he was screaming."

"He sounds unstable. Maybe it would be just as well if you left Powell."

"But I like the job ... most of the time. And I need the money, if I'm going to be able to live on my own."

"Now you listen to me, El. You're always welcome back here. I know we said it was time for you to move on. But I've been missing you. A lot. You're a way better cook than I am, and, believe me, Tommy tries to be nice about it, but I think he'd be happy to hear you were coming back."

"I don't think …"

"Seriously, don't even think twice about it. If you need to come back here, that'll be fine with everyone. The kids would love to have you back."

It sounded so good, so tempting, so right. She could just chuck it right now, quit her job, never have to face Mr. Powell again, and stop the churning waves that kept battering her life. Coming home. Maybe …

She found her resolve in her coffee cup. It had just the right amount of cream because Trish knew exactly how she liked it. And everything would be simple, back to normal. Easy. Trish would take care of her, and she would take care of Trish.

And yet, would it be easy? Or would that just be the simple way, the cowardly way? But not the right way. She felt the undertow of her own sister, her own flesh and blood, pulling her back, pulling her down. Trish meant well, but no. Trish needed to continue building her home with Tommy and Nathan and Carrie. And she, Ellen, needed to stand on her own two feet. There was no father any more to hold her up out of the fray and catch her breath. Sitting there in Trish's kitchen, gripping a mug of perfectly blended coffee, she found that she was at an important crossroads.

Trish was talking. " … and if Mr. Crazy-Pants ever gets violent with you, why, you've just got to come back here. I know we've talked about you being ready to move on with your life, but you can always, always …" Trish grabbed Ellen's hand with a desperate fierceness. "You can always, always come back home."

"Maybe," said Ellen. "You're very good to me, Trish. It is tempting, but I've got to figure this out." Jonas said she had good instincts. Could she trust him about this? Could she trust him, period? Would things work out at Powell? Or was this the end already, just months after she'd started?

"Your support means everything, Sis." She stood and hugged Trish fiercely. "And good luck with the bread," she hollered as she headed out to face her dragons.

Back in front of her apartment, she pulled into her customary space. The magnolia tree suddenly didn't look like a tree that added a simple elegance to the home, but a sentinel guarding the house from intruders. Guarding the house from her.

Magnolia leaves littered the yard and Ellen stooped to pick one up. They were large and tough, not the papery leaves of maples or oaks, leaves that would turn into compost, but like slabs of plastic that would outlast the pyramids of Egypt. She bent the leaf between her hands; it didn't want to yield. The magnolia leaf could not be formed as she desired; she could not impose her will upon it. Instead, it fought back, hard and inflexible. In disgust she threw it down on the ground, only to realize that dozens, perhaps a hundred of equally un-yielding leaves littered her path forward. She shrank back from the enormity of the obstacles before her and, as she looked up, she saw hundreds more. She held out her hand in a useless gesture, intimidat-ed by so many waxy, green, intransigent barriers to her desires. She kicked some leaves out of her way and stomped up the stairs to her apartment.

She deliberately sat in a different chair so that she didn't have to see any magnolia leaves through the window. Again she found her-self clenching and unclenching her hands. Think, Ellen, think. What is the right thing to do? What would her mother advise her? Unbid-den, she found herself asking what Jonas would suggest. She shoved that thought away: she had no business wondering what someone who might have betrayed her would say. And yet there was no history with Jonas to suggest anything other than a man of integrity.

She glanced at her watch. Twelve o'clock! She had been away from her job for half of the day. There was no excuse for that. Re-gardless of what Mr. Powell thought of her, she had no reason for shirking her responsibilities on her job. "The job cards!" she said out loud.

Again she grabbed her purse and was heading back down the stairs when Jonas' voice sliced through the chaos in her head. "Ellen, are you OK?" He was in his wheelchair on the back deck, a blanket over his legs, reading a book.

She looked up. She didn't want to say anything. She wanted to slip past the sentinel magnolia with its landmine leaves, skirt Jonas' calm questioning, drive away somewhere, anywhere. But she was too polite, too well behaved to ignore him.

"I fear something is amiss," he said. "You're not usually home at this time of the day."

Reluctantly she crossed the breezeway to him. "Yes, I've got a bit of a problem."

"Is there any way that I can help?'

"No. Well, maybe. Mr. Klameck, if I ask you a question, will you give me a straight answer?" There was a hitch in her voice that she hoped he hadn't noticed. But he was sharp. Very sharp. Undoubtedly he had noticed. She knew she was naive, but not so naive as to think he might have overlooked a small giveaway clue in her voice.

"The only answers I believe in are straight ones." He looked at her, cocking his head every so slightly. "This looks difficult for you. I would hope you would just ask your question. I will commit to doing my very best to give you a straight answer."

Perhaps he did know that the stakes — at least for her — were enormously high.

"Two evenings ago we had a conversation about the capacity at Powell to accept a new order."

"Yes, we did."

"Did you discuss that conversation with anyone, particularly with someone who might work for a Powell competitor?"

He took a moment to answer. "No, Ellen, I did not discuss that conversation with anyone. Anyone other than Rika, that is. And the conversation with her was very brief and contained no details." He motioned to her to come sit down at the table. "It seems to me that something has gone wrong. It is none of my business what exactly has happened. But let me offer some observations. First, there was a time when I knew many, many people who worked for fabrication plants like Powell. But those days are gone. My contacts have moved on to other organizations or retired. Some are deceased. So my contacts in the business now, that I might talk to, are limited. Second — and this is simply my word which you may chose to believe or not — I am not in the habit of repeating information I may learn from conversations with people. I've been a consultant for much of my career. Not keeping proprietary information to myself would have been an excellent way to undermine any future work I might have with a client. I learned long ago to keep things confidential as a matter of course. Third, if there has been a breach of confidentiality — which I believe there has been, based on the seriousness of your question — it may be useful to think about other avenues by which the information may have been leaked. I would offer to help you think that through, but I recognize that my credibility may be somewhat strained with you right now."

Rats, Ellen said to herself. Again with the tears. Jonas's soliloquy rang so true that she was again moved for reasons she would have found difficult to explain. His explanations made sense. Either he was really, really smooth or he was exactly what he seemed to be: an experienced, intelligent man who had no more betrayed her than he was able to walk across the back patio. "I don't know what to say," she said aloud.

"You need not say anything. You must make up your own mind what you think about what I've said. I cannot cajole or bribe or force you to think anything. I can merely note my own observations. What I say is within my own circle of control. What you think about it is certainly within my circle of concern — I care very much about you — but it is not within my circle of control."

"You have been nothing but trustworthy with me ..."

"Trust is something earned," he said. "It is not granted quickly. Easy trust is a cheap thing. Real trust must be cultivated. And," he looked up at her to be sure he had her attention, "It can be destroyed like that." He snapped his fingers. "My intentions are to continue to earn your trust. I hope I have not destroyed it."

"Without saying more than I should, let's just say that we lost the bid for a new part, the one that utilized the work centers you and I were discussing night before last. And, as near as we can tell, our competitor found out about it in some underhanded way. I was afraid I had told you too much and that perhaps you ..."

"A natural assumption. You are right to consider every possibility. I am clearly on the list of suspects. But, unlike you, I can know for sure what I did and did not do. I know for sure that I did not discuss it with anyone else. You can't be sure I am telling the truth, but I know that I am. And thus my mind is already wondering about who else might have known about the confidential information and have conveyed it to a third party."

"That's what I've been wondering, too. Each of us who knew about the project was grilled by Mr. Powell this morning. He's really upset, as you can imagine. Everyone else denies talking to anyone. I was the one who volunteered that I had talked to you. And now I am suspect number one, and you are identified as a co-conspirator."

Jonas smiled. "I've always wanted to be infamous." he said. "But I have to say that I think it is unlikely that the other people who knew about the project did not share the information in some way. In my experience, people are not that careful. It may have been a casual conversation but, in the hands of a sharp spy, a few bits of information can be pieced together in surprising ways."

"Thank you, Jonas." She stood up to leave. "Now I really must get back to work. I've been gone way too long already."

At the plant she ditched her coat and purse quickly and headed out to the shop floor. It was in the middle of lunch break, so people weren't in their usual workstations and most of the machines were not running.

She waved at Herb Coffey, sitting on a steel beam with several of his buddies, eating a sandwich and drinking an Ale-8-1. Ellen wasn't sure, but it seemed that he was still wearing the same "Go Cats!" t-shirt he was wearing every time she saw him. She tried to make her wave nonchalant, hoping not to betray the emotions roiling inside her.

She picked up the job cards on the corner of Harvey Green's desk in Welding and found Leonard Pfieffer sitting at his desk, also eating a sandwich. "Hey, Ellen," he said. "You're late."

"Yeah. Sorry. I had kind of an emergency."

"Everything OK?"

"I hope so."

"Have you had lunch? Sharonda made some mighty good chicken salad and you'd be welcome to the other half."

"Oh, no thanks, Leonard. I don't want to take food away from you."

Leonard patted his stomach. "I'm living off the fat of the land. Sharonda feeds me too well. This is mighty good, but I really could do with only half. Come on, sit down and have a bite. Unless you'uns is scared that she put possum in it or something like that."

"Oh, you!" She punched his arm and sat in the only other chair in the tiny room, a hideous blue plastic molded thing with a crack that seemed designed to snag pantyhose or pinch a leg.

They sat in silence, munching on the chicken salad. Was one expected to carry on a conversation, or was it OK just to chew and think? Leonard rescued her. "How's that chicken salad?"

"Mmmmph," Ellen mouthed around a big bite. "It's amazing, Leonard. Really! You tell Sharonda that I really, really like it."

"Well, I'm glad to know it. I wasn't sure if a little 'ole white girl could handle such a masterful blend of seasonings an' ingredients." He grinned at her. "We folks have been eatin' fine cuisine like this for generations, even though we don't use possum any more. Hard to come by possum these days," he commented, almost to himself.

"You are a nut, Leonard. But, seriously, I know chicken salad and this is some of the best I've ever had. You're really nice to share it with me. But I've got to get the rest of the job cards picked up. Thanks again, Leonard!"

"Any time, Possum. You come on back and we'll see what Sharonda packed."

Ellen was a little disappointed that Kirby was nowhere to be found, but she did find his job cards, making her run complete. She headed back to the office, but stopped by the pop machine. She had enjoyed the chicken salad Leonard had shared, but she needed something wet now. "Why not?" she asked herself as she punched the button for Ale-8-1. "Herb has put me in the mood for twice the sugar and three times the caffeine."

She breathed a sigh of relief as she passed Mr. Powell's office. His door was closed and the lights were off. It was high time to get back to work and wait to see if this business with the lost Wilco order would blow over.

Chapter 27

Ellen looks at bar code readers and discusses dates with Rika.

After Ellen finished the job cards she had an idea. She would make a form that would track set up time and actual m-time for key operations in the shop. She fiddled around using her spreadsheet software to make some nice columns and rows for the data she was hoping to collect. Then she printed off three copies and took them out into the shop.

First she went to see Herb at the laser. She wondered if he owned any shirt other than ones from the University of Kentucky. As usual, he was spitting into an Ale-8-1 can. Ellen tried not to think of what disgusting concoction was brewing in the can. "Herb," she said. "I need your help."

"Sure, Possum. What do you need?"

"Possum?"

"I dunno. I reckon you've got a new nickname. Kinda fits, don't 'cha think? Leastways, Leonard seems to think it does."

"Possum? Really? I mean … possum?"

"Yup." Herb spit into his can. "Was there something I can do you for?"

"Oh, yes. I'm hoping you can keep track of your work for a few weeks." She showed him her form. "See? What I'd like you to do is write down every job you do — the order number and the part you're producing. But, most importantly, I'd like you to write down the time when you start a new setup, the time you finish the setup, the time you start the job, and the time when you finish it. Do you think you could do that?"

"Looks like a lot of paper work to me."

"Well, I know I'm asking something above and beyond. But I'm really trying to get a handle on how long it takes to set up for each order and how long it takes to run each order."

"I dunno …"

"You've heard of m-times, Herb?"

"Of course. They ain't worth the paper they're printed on."

"That may be ... but they're all we've got. I'm trying to make them more accurate by getting real data from you guys who actually run the machines."

"Yeah, I could see that." Herb shrugged. "I think us operators are the only ones who really know what's going on around here."

"There's a lot of truth to that," responded Ellen. "Will you give it a try. For me?"

"Well, since you didn't blow a gasket when I called you Possum, I reckon I can try it."

"You're the best, Herb!" She went off in search of David Palmer, the operator of the 117 press, and Joe Bob Walker at 103 vertical drill. She explained what she was after to both of them and asked if they would be willing to help her. They both said they would try.

When she got back to the office, Mr. Powell's door was still closed and the lights were still off. Ellen found herself releasing a pent-up breath as she walked past his door. "At some point I'm going to have to face him," she thought. "But I would just as soon it wasn't today."

She went down to see Whit Collette. "Hey Whit," she said as he looked up from his computer screen.

"Hey yourself. How's it going?"

"Oh, pretty good. I'm getting more and more familiar with the SOLUTION/400 screens. Kind of getting more acclimated."

"That's very good. There's a lot to learn."

"Don't I know it. I'm just working the main screens right now — parts master, bill of material, customer orders, shop orders. But I'm learning a lot." She switched gears to the reason she wanted to talk to Whit. "Whit, you remember those bar code readers we were looking at a while back?"

"Sure do." He reached up to the shelf above his desk and pulled down the catalogue. "What are you looking for."

"Well," she said. "This really isn't Powell related. But I've got a nephew who is a bit of a computer whiz kid. I was wondering if there was a scanner that would work with his computer that I could get him for Christmas."

"Well, now, that is a different kind of Christmas present!" Whit nodded approvingly. "Most kids would want the new U2 album or a talking Alf or a Nintendo."

"Yes, he's a special kid. I'd kind of like to encourage him by getting him something he'd get a kick out of. Do you think that company would sell a scanner to me rather than to a company?"

"I don't see why not," said Whit. "I tell you what. Why don't you take the catalog and see what you can find. Then give them a call. It can't hurt. Just bring me the catalog back when you're done."

"Perfect. Thanks very much."

That evening she fixed dinner for herself. She made a nice stir fry with broccoli and snow peas and bit of leftover chicken, just like Jasmine Chin had taught her. It was quick, easy, and she liked the way it tasted.

She was just washing up the last of the dishes when there was a knock at the door. It was Rika. "Are you busy?" she asked.

"No, not at all. I'm just tidying up from supper."

"It smells like something good."

"I had a friend from China in college. She taught me some Chinese cooking just using an iron skillet. It's quick, easy, and tastes really good."

"Better, I fear, than what I fed Jonas tonight."

Ellen laughed. "Now, you know I don't believe that. You're an outstanding cook!"

Rika smiled. "You're very sweet to say so. But you are a very good cook, too, Ellen. Look, I brought some pastry." She held out a dish covered with a dainty blue and yellow napkin. "I hoped we might have another fika."

"That would be lovely," said Ellen. "I'll make some coffee."

"I rather hoped you would," said Rika as she uncovered the Swedish pastries and placed them on the table.

Ellen busied herself getting out cups and saucers, spoons, milk in a cunning little pitcher she'd found at one of the craft shops in Laodicea, and the sugar bowl.

When the coffee was perked and the pastries placed on individual plates, Ellen looked at Rika. "I suppose that my conversation this morning with Jonas is why you're here. Is he terribly hurt?"

It was Rika's turn to look at Ellen. "I'm afraid I don't know anything about that. Jonas did not tell me that you and he had spoken this morning."

"Surely he did. We had a problem at work and I had just about concluded that he had shared some things we had discussed in confidence. I all but accused him of being a spy." She stared into her coffee cup, took a sip, and looked over the rim at Rika. "I'm very sorry," she whispered. "He deserved better from me."

"I am very sincere, Ellen, when I say that I know nothing of this. Jonas made no mention of it to me."

"Does he seem to be OK?"

"Of course. Trust me, he is fine."

Ellen rested her forehead on her hand, her elbow on the table. "I've done it again." She almost said it to herself. "First I don't trust Jonas, now I don't trust you to be telling me the truth." She looked up at Rika again and shoved her hair out of her face, tucking it behind her ear. "I'm sorry, Rika. The problem seems to be with me. I don't seem to be very trusting right now."

Rika reached across the table in a gesture that had become both familiar and comforting. "There, there, dear girl. Life is throwing a lot at you right now. A new job, a new apartment, a new landlord." She stopped and smiled. "Although I will say that the new landlord is very, very happy that you have come into our lives. You have brought a joy, a ray of light, that we have not had for many a year. I bless the day you asked about the apartment, Ellen."

"Thank you." She looked down again, fearing to ask, but compelled to do so. "So what did you want to see me about?"

Rika threw back her head and laughed, as if it was the most comical question in the world. It was not derisive laughter, nor was it mocking. Nor was it even at Ellen's expense. Instead, it seemed that Rika was genuinely amused — delighted even — by Ellen's question.

"If you must know, I am here because I did not want to share my other pastry with Jonas. He has a terrible sweet tooth, as you probably have noticed. We had one of these at supper. If he knew I had more, he would want another one. Besides, I was hoping you might offer to brew some coffee — delicious, by the way, and perfectly brewed — and that we might just have a chat. Woman to woman, so to speak." Now it was her turn to be a bit serious. "I love my husband with immense devotion. But sometimes I simply crave the company of another woman. Is that so bad?"

"You and Jonas are amazing to me. How long have you been married?"

"Forty-eight years."

"Oh wow. That is wonderful! And you clearly are still in love with each other."

"Indeed we are."

Ellen sighed. "I hope, when I get married, it can be that kind of a love. A love that will last."

"It can be, if you choose it to be. So many people think that marriage is about falling in love, about the roses and moonbeams, about the fleeting feeling of romance. But marriage is actually work. Sometimes it is hard work. But I can tell you, it is worth the effort." Her eyes gazed off into the distance, as if she was seeing down through the years, seeing the rough patches, the different seasons, in her marriage to Jonas. "Yes, it is worth the effort …"

After a time, Ellen asked, "More coffee?"

"Oh, I am so sorry. I was daydreaming a bit, remembering our early years together." Suddenly she was back, her eyes focused on Ellen as she held out her cup for a refill. "And what about you, Ellen? It sounds like you do hope to marry. Are there any young men on the horizon?"

So Ellen told her about the date with Kirby that would happen tomorrow night. "Oh, the Cork and Cleaver," said Rika. "A very nice place. They have a wonderful salad bar as well as divine steaks." They discussed what Ellen might wear, how she might fix her hair, what jewelry would add to her ensemble. Ellen realized that, while no one could replace her own mother, Rika was, in a way, filling that void in her life. They giggled as women will do when thinking about going out with a man, compared notes, contemplated how things might go.

"He wants to come pick me up here," said Ellen.

"It is only right that he should do so. A young man should call for a young lady that he is courting. Would you like — how do you American's say it — would you like for me to have Jonas just casually polishing his shotgun on the front porch when the young man comes to call?"

"Oh, goodness, no! I mean, he ..."

Rika laughed again in her rich contralto. "Of course I am only jesting," she said. "Jonas does not even own a gun. I just thought we should perhaps put the fear of God into him when he arrives. No funny business, agreed?"

"Oh, agreed! I don't want ... that is, I hope he doesn't think ..." She stopped, lamely. "Rika, do you know anything about the Bible?"

"Why, yes, I suppose I do. Why do you ask?"

"My friend Annie asked me if I had read the Song of Solomon. She said it was in the Bible, but I had no idea what she was talking about."

Rika smiled. "I believe your friend Annie is very wise. Yes, I know about the Song of Solomon. Is Annie married?"

"No, but she's engaged to be married. In the spring, I think. Is the Song of Solomon about ... sex?"

"You are a delightful child. So mature, and yet so breathtakingly innocent. I take it you have not been with a man in that way?"

Ellen felt the heat rising in her cheeks. The room seemed very hot, and she found that her pulse was pounding in her temples. "No," she whispered. "I've never even ..."

Again Rika reached across the table and covered Ellen's smooth hand with her wrinkled one. "And that is as it should be. Believe me, Ellen, please believe me, that there are things a man and a woman should discover together, with each other and only with each other, and only after they are married."

"I know, but ... how do you know ..."

"I know this: that a date with a young man who is going to take you to dinner is not a prelude to something more. If he wants that, he is not the man for you. But, if he treats you with respect, cherishes you, that is the way it should be.

"The Song of Solomon isn't about sex, exactly. It is about marriage. It is beautiful poetry about King Solomon and his wife. They speak beautiful words to each other about their courtship, about their wedding day, and, yes, about their wedding night. But they also speak of trouble in their marriage and how they overcome the problems they have. Do you have a Bible, Ellen?"

"Yes, I guess I do. It is probably at my sister's house."

"I would be pleased to lend you one if you don't," said Rika. "But let us discuss one thing before you go on this lovely date with your young man. How far are you willing to let him go?"

"Excuse me?"

"How far are you willing to let him go? I mean, are you willing to let him kiss you? Are you willing for him to place his hands in certain places?" She rested her hands on her own bosom. "Are you willing for him to go farther than that?"

"Oh, Rika!"

"I'm sorry to ask such a forthright question, but I have learned, in my vast experience ..." She smiled and Ellen noticed the wrinkles around her eyes that made them dance but also gave her an air of well-earned experience. "I have learned that it is far better to decide ahead of time how far you are willing to let him go, than to try to decide in the heat of the moment. Believe me, in the heat of the moment, you may go much farther than you ever intended. And, if he is like most young men, he will be even less able to hold back than you will. So I suggest you decide now: how far are you willing to let him go?"

"I ... I don't know."

"Exactly. So why don't you decide now? Would you like him to kiss you?"

"I ... I suppose I would."

"And that's fine. How about more than that?"

"No, I don't think so. I know so little about ... that stuff."

"I rather suspected as much. So, if he kisses you, you will enjoy that. But if his hands stray to places they should not, well, you can decide right now that you will firmly put an end to that. Yes?"

"Yes!" The knot that had been building in Ellen's stomach, building for days ever since Kirby had asked her to go to dinner with him, suddenly unwound, like a spring let out of its casing. The tension was released; she felt relief. "I really didn't know what to expect. You've helped a great deal, Rika. I know nothing about ... about the things of marriage. But I realize now, it was worrying me. Knowing how far I'm willing for him to go — how far I'd like him to go — and knowing where the line is. That helps a lot!" It was her turn to touch Rika's hand, a gesture that was becoming familiar between them.

"I am so glad I could help. You are someone I have grown to care very much about and, if my poor words of wisdom help, I am very touched." She placed her hand over her heart in unconscious empathy. "Now, please don't misunderstand what I have said to mean that you should not have a good time. I expect you to be charmed by the young man's attention and to have wonderful conversation as befits a young man and a young woman who are beginning to explore a relationship they might have. And I expect you to eat a big, juicy medium rare steak, too!"

"Ick, not medium rare. Well done!"

"Ah, you poor child. You believe that a steak must be burnt beyond recognition. Some day you will come to know the delights of a perfectly prepared medium rare steak. But perhaps not tomorrow night!"

"Nope, I draw the line both at a guy who gets too hands-y and at steak that bleeds on the plate!"

They both laughed and enjoyed the last of their coffee.

Chapter 28
Ellen goes to the Cork and Cleaver with Kirby.

The following evening, Ellen rushed home from work so that she could get ready. She showered, brushed her hair until it shone, and put on eyeliner and lipstick. In uncharacteristic abandon, she applied some light rouge to her cheeks. Observing the effect in the mirror, she thought it didn't look half bad. "Now, decision time," she said out loud. "Final choice of clothes." She was in the process of pulling out several possible outfits when there was a tap at the door. Was Kirby here already? "Just a minute!" she squealed, grabbing her robe and shoving her arms through the sleeves. She squinted through the door peephole and was relieved to see Rika standing on the landing.

"Come in!" she said. "I'm trying to decide which outfit to wear."

"I know you are in a hurry, and I won't stay. But I wanted to bring you these." She held out some sparking diamond earrings and a simple chain with a diamond caught lightly in a setting of six prongs that allowed the facet's brilliance to be displayed unencumbered. Ellen caught her breath as Rika placed the jewelry in her hand. "I would be pleased if you would wear these tonight ... assuming they will go with what you had planned to wear."

Ellen could feel the heft and quality of the chain. The diamonds seemed almost to be living things in her hands, illuminated in a thousand different directions. "They're beautiful," she breathed.

"Actually, I am a scalawag," said Rika. "By lending these to you, I am assured of you returning them tomorrow. Which means," she winked, "I will get a full report, yes?"

"Yes! Yes, of course. They really are gorgeous. Are you sure ... ?"

"Have you not learned, yet? When a Swede sets out to do something, they are not to be thwarted. Will they work with your outfit?"

Ellen showed her the different possibilities: a pants suit with a scoop neck blouse and jacket, a quality white blouse with ruffles around the neckline and sleeves and a nice A-line skirt, or what could only be described as a little black dress. "I'm leaning toward the dress, but it is cold outside, and the hem comes just to my knees."

"Ah, what we women suffer to look good. I agree, the dress is the simplest of the three, but the best choice. Ellen, do you know how a jeweler who wants to really show off a beautiful piece displays it on a simple black velvet cloth? I think you are the same. You are a beautiful jewel, and the simple black dress shows you off to the best effect. Might I see it on?"

Before she had even thought about it, she had discarded the robe onto her mother's chair and slipped into the dress. "May I help?" Rika asked, and zipped her up. Ellen put in the earrings and Rika fastened the necklace for her. "It hangs at the perfect length," she said. "Not so high as to feel like it might be choking you, not so low as to get lost in your décolletage. It looks lovely." She looked over Ellen's shoulder into the mirror. "You ... you look lovely." She gently kissed the top of Ellen's head. "Now I must go. I wouldn't do for your young man to find me here fussing over you."

"Thank you!" Ellen called after her as Rika clattered down the steps and across the breezeway.

Rika hadn't been gone more than a few minutes when Ellen heard a car stop in front of the house. Looking out the window, she saw a handsome black Mercedes pull up. The lights went out and, in the twilight, she could see Kirby exiting the driver's side. He was wearing a black suit and looked very sharp indeed. Ellen grabbed the coat she had decided on — nice looking, and warm enough to make up for thermal deficiencies in the dress — and stepped out onto the landing. "Up here, Kirby," she called.

He looked up at her and stopped. As she carefully descended in her black heels, she realized he was watching every move. He seemed to be rooted in place, just past the curb, in suspended animation while his eyes tracked each step she took.

"Wow!" he said, when she had gotten to the bottom of the steps. "Wow, wow, wow. You look amazing!" He held out three red roses. "These are for you."

"Thank you, Kirby." She breathed deep of their eternal scent, the same scent that drove poets to rhyme and artists to paint.

"Here, let me get the door for you."

As his back was turned, Ellen caught Rika watching her, framed by the lighted kitchen window. She grinned and then found herself in the plush, warm, opulent seat of the automobile. She almost told Kirby she'd never been in a car this nice. Not even close. But she decided perhaps she didn't need to tell him everything. She smelled the roses again as she buckled her seat belt.

"To the palace, princess," he said as he started the engine and pulled away from the curb.

The Cork and Cleaver exceeded Ellen's expectations. The lights were low, each table had a candle, and there was a fireplace with a real fire burning, giving the restaurant a sophisticated, woodsy ambience. Ellen had been smart enough to pause when Kirby parked the vehicle. Sure enough, he came around and opened the door for her. The sun had long since gone down, and the lights of Lexington felt sophisticated and inviting. Kirby gave the hostess at the Cork and Cleaver the reservation for two he had made. She took their coats. Kirby's eyes traveled up and down, obviously appreciative of the way Ellen looked. He didn't look so bad himself, now that she had a chance to see him more fully. He was really quite good looking. He had a nice strong jaw and his nose turned up ever so slightly, giving him an impish quality. His eyes only added to that impression. They were an exotic green and seemed always to be smiling or teasing. His hair was dark and full, with a bit of curl, especially up top, that made him appear rakishly insouciant. Perhaps he really was: he chatted up the hostess as they were seated, but promptly switched his attention to Ellen as he held her chair for her.

The table was Ellen's daydream reified. It had a white tablecloth, dark cloth napkins, fresh flowers around the candle, and hefty cutlery that hinted at the solid meal to come. Ellen was pleased that her seat allowed her to watch the soothing flicker of the flames in the fireplace. But Kirby was good to look at, too.

"Hungry?" he asked as they looked at their menus.

"Oh, yes," said Ellen. In her daydream, their hands had brushed as they studied their menu, but, as she crossed her legs, her foot brushed against Kirby's pants leg. Had he noticed? Would he think her too forward? She concentrated on the menu. "I love steak," she said. "But I don't know much about the different cuts. What are you having?"

"Hmm," he said. "Lots of nice choices. I'm not sure yet."

Their waitress turned out to be a man, neatly dressed in a jacket and tie. He called Ellen "miss" and asked if they would like a cock-tail. Ellen tensed, realizing that alcohol could change things signifi-cantly. She hadn't had much experience with drinking. Her parents were both teetotalers and her only brushes with booze had been at a few frat parties where she'd seen the seamier side of alcohol-induced silliness. She'd tried beer and thought it smelled foul. Hard liquor, as she had told her friend Jasmine, seemed more like a chemistry lab gone bad than something good to drink.

Kirby must have sensed her discomfort, suggesting a bottle of wine instead. He and the waiter-cum-sommelier conferred over the best choice and ended up selecting a red that the waiter highly rec-ommended with beef. Ellen caught a glimpse of the price and sud-denly wondered if Kirby could afford this meal. She didn't know what his salary at Powell was, but this was not going to be an inex-pensive dinner.

"How about an appetizer?" asked Kirby. "I've been looking forward to some calamari. Would that be OK?"

Ellen had no idea what calamari was, so she said, "Sure!" enthu-siastically.

The wine arrived and was decanted for Kirby to taste. He pro-nounced it excellent and complimented the waiter on the recommen-dation. Glasses were duly poured for both of them and Kirby held up his glass. Ellen lifted hers in response. "To us!" said Kirby, gently tapping her glass and producing a pure musical tone that sounded like what might come from a fairy godmother's magic wand when she grants the scullery maid, who is really a princess, her fondest wish.

Ellen smiled and sipped. It really wasn't too bad. Kind of like grape juice that had been left out of the refrigerator too long, but not seriously objectionable. Kirby grinned. If anything, the curl in the center of his forehead was even cuter and his eyes were even greener.

The waiter returned to take their entree orders. Kirby ordered a filet mignon. When Ellen looked at him, he suggested she do the same. Again Ellen saw the prices on the menu and worried. "But," she told the waiter, "The petite cut, please."

"And how would miss like that prepared?" asked the waiter.

"Oh well done, please." Ellen knew she had done something wrong the moment she uttered the words. The waiter's face only flickered briefly, but Kirby actually frowned.

"The chef is very good at making sure a well done cut is still tender," the waiter explained. Clearly aficionados of all things beef would never place an order for a well done steak. Kirby restored their good graces to the waiter by ordering his filet rare. "Help yourselves to the salad bar," said the waiter, indicating a room off to the side.

Kirby stood and held Ellen's chair again. He guided her to the salad bar, placing his hand in the small of her back, and Ellen experienced a tingly sensation that was not at all unpleasant under his touch.

When they returned to their table, the appetizer had arrived. Kirby speared one of the battered rings with his fork and held it to Ellen's mouth. She gamely took it, finding the taste a bit chewy, but intriguing. "OK," she said, as Kirby helped himself to several. "I give up. What are we eating?"

Kirby grinned and his eyes sparkled. "Calamari. Here, have another one." He fed Ellen another one off of his fork. "They're good with a little cocktail sauce, too." He indicated a small bowl of red sauce. "Good?"

"Not bad," she replied. "It has an interesting taste, but it is kind of … uh, chewy."

Kirby laughed again. "Gosh, Ellen, you're something! You're just straight up, you know? Honest. I like that. Not to mention that you're drop-dead gorgeous!"

"Thank you, I think. But, really, Kirby, what is calamari?"

"You really don't know? Why, squid, of course."

Ellen's stomach did a flip-flop. Get hold of yourself, girl, she told herself. You said you wanted to go on a fancy date. Well, you're on one now, and eating squid. Keep it together.

She reached for her wine glass and washed away the taste of the calamari. With an effort, she smiled at Kirby. "Well, what do you know? I have to say, this is the first time I've ever eaten squid." She skewered another breaded ring and placed it on her appetizer plate. But she didn't put it in her mouth.

Ellen really did enjoy her salad. The lettuces were fresh and varied (what Tommy would have called "designer greens") and the different vegetables and toppings available seemed infinite. She had chosen bleu cheese dressing and found that it was outstanding. What Nathan Thompson, ace programmer, didn't know wouldn't hurt him. "Do you think they make it here?" she asked Kirby.

"I'm sure they do. They take pride in making everything from scratch," he said. "But I can't figure out why you like that moldy stuff when you're not sure about calamari." He indicated the uneaten piece on her plate. He made a dramatic show of eating two calamari at once.

"How about you try some of my bleu cheese?" she teased, waving a fork full of spinach leaves coated with dressing in front of him.

"I give," he offered. "You eat the moldy dressing, I'll eat the rest of the calamari."

Their steaks arrived and Ellen tried not to watch the red liquid oozing out of Kirby's as he sawed away on it. Hers was done completely, just like she had wanted it, and was pleased that it was, indeed, tender and tasty. They both ate in silence for a few minutes. Then Kirby offered up a new topic.

"How are you liking working at Powell?" he asked.

"I really like it! I find it fascinating how all the pieces work together. I guess I get to see the big picture because I collect and process all the job cards. I love how it all runs, like a giant machine, to produce products that our customers pay us for. Of course, it doesn't always work perfectly, and that's part of the fun, too — how to make it better. It's like a great game, with how much profit we make as the way to keep score, and I get to be a player in the middle of it."

"Sounds like you really enjoy it," he said drily.

"Oh, I do! I love the welding flash and the sparks coming off of the grinders, I love the massive thump of the press, and I love the lift trucks whizzing around, delivering material to the different machines. I love the tractor trailers lined up at the loading dock, ready to take our shipments of finished goods to wherever the customer needs them. Don't you just love it, Kirby?"

"Maybe not as much as you do." He focused on slicing off another hunk of meat, transferring it to his mouth, and chewing methodically. Once he had swallowed, he noted, "I work for a paycheck. I'm not in love with it. Don't pay me, I won't work. And I'm always looking for an angle to make a little more."

"Oh? Like what? What kind of angle?"

"Nothing in particular." He focused on another piece of his steak. "Let's just say I enjoy brokering deals when there's something in it for numero uno." He made a show of gripping a piece of his fillet mignon off of the fork with his teeth and holding it there just a moment before taking it completely into his mouth. "But let's talk about something other than work. What do you think of my tie?"

Ellen examined the tie critically. "I like it," she pronounced. Her father had worn a tie every day to work and he had shown her the finer points of men's neckwear. "The width is just right. You're a well-built guy, and your tie isn't skinny, out of proportion with your body type. And it certainly isn't so wide as to be ridiculous. It also nicely matches the width of your jacket lapel. That's important."

"You sure know a lot about ties," said Kirby. Suddenly Ellen felt his foot tracing past her ankle and up her calf. Kirby didn't blink, didn't give any sign that it was anything but an accident. "What do you think of the color and the pattern?" he asked. Perhaps he didn't even realize he had touched her so intimately.

"Uh, I'm partial to blue, but red is classic, and contrasts nicely with your dark suit. I hear that red is considered a power color. The diagonal stripes are very traditional — I like that — but the mix of stripe widths and the two different shades of red makes it distinctive. Certainly not boring." Perhaps she had only imagined Kirby's foot against her leg.

"You have excellent taste! Now, shall we have some dessert?"

Ellen had protested, but Kirby had insisted on an "apple skillet" — a warm apple pie in a small iron skillet with high quality vanilla bean ice cream. She had agreed to share it with him, but felt awkward dipping into the same dish as him. Kirby ended up eating most of it.

She excused herself to go to the ladies room and, when she returned, Kirby had already paid the bill and seemed ready to go.

The drive down I-75 was uneventful. Satiated from the excellent meal and caressed by the luxurious seating of the Mercedes, Ellen found herself growing drowsy. But when Kirby suggested they go to his place, she came wide awake. "Uh, no. No thanks. I don't think so. That's very kind, but ..." Even to her ears it sounded lame. But she wasn't quite ready for what she thought he had in mind. When he placed his hand on her bare knee — her dress had ridden up a bit — she felt quite certain she knew what he hoped for. "No, Kirby," she said with more firmness. "It has been a wonderful evening and I've enjoyed your company and the meal immensely. But I'd like to go home now, please."

"OK," he said gamely, placing both of his hands on the wheel.

At the Klamecks' house, Kirby again opened the door for her and escorted her to the stairs up to her apartment. "Aren't you going to invite me up?" he asked. It was dark, so Ellen felt more than saw the charm of his eyes, his easy smile, his rakish curl of hair.

"No, I can't. I'm not allowed to have guests."

He snorted. "You're a grown woman! A beautiful grown woman." Suddenly she was in his arms and his lips came down on hers. She felt the nearness of his body, the firmness of his embrace, the salty sweetness of his mouth. It was new, heady, overwhelming, and she found herself responding. But then she felt his hands sliding down her back, going farther than they should have.

She gasped and pushed away. "Thank you for a very nice evening, Kirby. Good night!" She fled up the stairs, fumbling with her key to get in, coming just short of slamming the door and throwing the lock. She leaned against the door for a moment, panting, heart racing, alarmed, confused. Then she peeked out the corner of the window. In the light of the streetlight, she could see Kirby was still standing at the foot of the stairs. Finally he shrugged, sauntered to his car, and drove off.

Ellen took off her heels and sat down in her mother's rocker, wondering what had just happened.

Chapter 29
Mr. Van Winkle visits the factory.

Saturday morning Ellen dropped by to return the jewelry to Rika and give her a full report. "Hmmm," Rika had tutted. "Did you think he went too far?"

"Yes! His hands … "

"Went too far." Rika nodded. "Too far, indeed. We must watch this young man. Will he ask you out again?"

"I don't know. I hadn't even thought about that. Maybe I turned him off by pushing him away."

"If you did, he isn't the caliber of young man I would hope for you. Do you want him to ask you out on another date?"

"Maybe. I'm not sure. Not if I have to fight him off with a stick. But, until he got all fresh, we had a lovely time. I enjoyed it. It was nice to go out, to be appreciated."

"Indeed," said Rika.

Later, she visited Trish. She wanted a full report, too. "Yes, he kissed me good night. But he went … well, his hands went where they shouldn't have."

"Uh huh. Let's call it what it is. He was horny."

"If you say so."

"I know a little more about this than you do, El. I've got the kids to prove it. And listen, El! Just because a man wants something doesn't mean you have to give it to him. Do you hear me?"

"Yeah, I hear you. I know you're right. It was scary, but kind of exciting, too."

"Oh, I'll bet it was. But … right time, right place, right person. Right, El?"

"Right."

Monday at work she headed out to collect job cards and to see how Herb and the others were doing with the form she had given them. The sheet she had given Herb was considerably more dirty than when she had brought it to him. It had clearly been folded several times. "Thanks for doing this, Herb," she said as she looked at his sheet.

"Uh huh," said Herb.

"Uh, could you help me understand what you've written here?" His handwriting was a barely legible scrawl. But the bigger problem was that clearly Herb hadn't documented every job he had done. "I see here you did 20 pieces of part 29-011-03. And you finished that job at 10:15. But the next job doesn't start until 12:30. What happened in between?"

"Well, I was shore workin'!" said Herb.

"I'm sure you were. Did you maybe forget to write down some other job you did before lunch?"

"Probably. Maybe. Can't be sure."

"OK. It sure would help me, though, if you could list every single job and setup you do all day long." She smiled up at Herb.

"Well, I'll try, Possum. No promises."

It was the same story with David at the press and with Joe Bob at the vertical drill. They had tried, but hadn't captured a full day of work, just a few entries here and there. Ellen collected what they had, hiding her frustration, and gave them new sheets to use for the week.

She went by Leonard's office to pick up his job cards and found him hunched over the computer monitor and scribbling notes on a pad of paper. She walked right up behind him and punched him on the arm.

"Ow!" he exclaimed, rubbing his arm. "What was that for?"

"For telling Herb to call me Possum."

"I may have mentioned to him how you liked Sharonda's possum sandwiches."

She punched him again. "Ow, girl. You do that a hundred more times and you may actually hurt me. You ain't riled, are you?"

"No, I guess not. You're a good enough guy. But ... Possum? Couldn't you think of something a bit more ... more feminine?"

"Nope. You're Possum. It fits you. You hang back, might even play dead. But when you're riled, buddy, look out! Besides," he said, suddenly very interested in his fingernails. "To a boy possum, a girl possum looks awful purty." He looked up and grinned at her.

"Oh, you!" She punched him again, just for good measure.

On the way back to the office she saw Mr. Powell heading toward Assembly. She took the long way around through Welding and successfully avoided him.

In her office, she got out a calculator and started calculating the times for each job that had been recorded as well as the setup times, when the guys had managed to remember to write them down. Then she started looking in the mainframe system, comparing the data there with the actual data coming off of the shop floor. In the end she had to give up. There just wasn't enough data to draw any meaningful conclusions.

She went down to see Whit Collette.

Whit was going through reports that had printed off the big line printer. These were stacks of what Whit called "green bar" paper. The paper was a long continuous sheet, folded back and forth on itself like the folds of a fan, with small holes on either edge that allowed the paper to be pulled through the printer. Each report began with a front page with the name of the recipient in block letters. "I go through the reports that print overnight," Whit explained. "I tear them apart and then deliver them to the proper department." He indicated a report with a big "ENGINEERING" on the front page. "This is the report of new part numbers that were created last week and the m-times."

"Oh, I know about that report!" Ellen reached for the green bar paper, flipping pages. She was searching for part 37-558-01, the Wilco part that had been stolen away from Powell by International Dynamics. "Found it!" she exclaimed. "And what m-time did engineering assign?" she asked herself. She traced her finger across the line of data. "OK, 1.38 hours. Seems reasonable ..."

"You always talk to yourself like that?" asked Whit.

"Oh, sorry!" Ellen laughed. "We just had a big mess about how long it would take to manufacture this new part and I was just curious what time Sandy and Butch ended up assigning to it." She handed the report back to Whit. "Thanks for letting me look at that. Actually, Whit, the reason I came down here was to ask you about that bar code printer we talked about weeks ago."

"I remember." He pulled the same catalog off of the shelf they had looked at in early November. "I think we were looking at this one here." He pointed to a standalone model.

"Right, I think that's the one. What I was wondering, Whit, is if there is a way for our regular printers to print bar code."

"Oh, I don't think so. The 1403 printer here uses a print band that has raised letters and numbers embossed into it. I don't think it could print a bar code. Maybe the new laser printer could, though." He pointed to a Hewlett-Packard LaserJet.

"What kinds of things do you print on the LaserJet?"

"Well, the release of SOLUTION/400 that we upgraded to last summer included the ability to print job cards on eight and a half by eleven paper. We haven't made the switch yet from the old job cards, but that's one of the things I'm working on."

"You mean the job cards I go collect every morning, those could be sheets of paper instead?"

"Yup, that's my understanding."

"And do you think that a bar code with the job number could be printed on the page?"

Whit scratched his head. "In theory, I think it could. But there are a lot of unanswered questions. Can we modify the print routine to include the bar code? Can we get bar code software that will work? Will it work with the laser printer? Lots of questions, Ellen. Or should I say Possum?"

Ellen flushed. "Wonderful. Just wonderful. If even you have heard it, it appears I've acquired a lovely nick name."

"Oh, yeah. It's all over the plant. I think you're going to be Possum for life."

"Aargh!" she screamed. "Not what I had in mind."

"Could I give you some advice?" Whit asked. "Don't let it get to you, or at least don't let them see it gets to you. If they see it gets under your skin, they'll tease you unmercifully. But if you take it, they'll probably forget about it. And, besides, the fact that they've given you a nick name means they like you. Nick names are more a sign of being accepted than anything around here."

"I guess. But ... Possum? Oh, my word!"

"I can think of a lot worse," said Whit. "Really, it isn't a bad nick name, as nick names go. A guy who worked here a few years ago was stuck with Mutt. Even his wife started calling him Mutt. And of course there's Fish Bait. He works in Assembly."

"I guess I'll have to buy a stuffed toy possum and put it in my office to show them I can take a joke."

"That's the spirit, Ellen! Now about this bar code printing ..."

"Yes, about that. I was kind of hoping you could look into what it would take to print the order number as a bar code on the job cards, or job sheets, or whatever we would call them if they were printed on the LaserJet."

"I could do that," said Whit.

"You see where I'm going with this? If we can print the operation number on the job sheet, then the guys could use those inexpensive bar code readers to record each setup and each operation. Right now I'm trying to get them to fill out a form I made, and ..."

"Let me guess. They don't do a very good job."

"That's putting it mildly."

"Every time I've tried to get them to fill out some form, I fail miserably. I guess it is because the guys in the shop are really good with machines, but not very good with paperwork."

"Yes, that makes sense. So if they could start and finish each operation by zapping a bar code, I think we could get a lot more data."

"I think you're right. And I think it is a good idea. Let me look into it and I'll get back to you." Whit put the catalogue back on the shelf and took down the operator's manual for the LaserJet. "By the way, did you end up ordering that bar code reader for your nephew?"

"Yes, I did. I'm hoping it arrives before Christmas. Otherwise I'll have to put an empty box under the tree with a note that says the bar code reader is on its way."

Whit brought her back from her Christmas daydreaming. "Tell you what. I'll look into printer bar codes with the LaserJet and you work on figuring out how the scanners can fit into the flow of work through the shop."

"That's a great deal, Whit. Done! And I appreciate it.'

"No problem … Possum." He grinned and she smiled back at him.

As she entered her office, she spotted a red Porsche pulling into the parking lot. The driver pulled into one of the visitor slots and Ellen saw Bob Van Winkle extract himself from the sports car.

"Uh oh," she thought to herself. "He usually means trouble. Keep your head down."

She was so engrossed in her work that she forgot all about him being in the plant until Annie said, "Did you bring your lunch?"

Ellen looked at her watch. "My goodness. I had no idea it was after 12:00. Yeah, I brought mine."

"I did too." Annie held up a brown lunch sack. "Want to go down to the cafeteria and eat together?"

"Sure!" Ellen extracted her lunch sack from the bottom drawer of her desk and followed Annie out the door and toward the lobby.

As they entered the lobby, they saw Mr. Van Winkle was bent closely over Gladys' chair. He seemed to be whispering to her. When they saw Annie and Ellen, Mr. Van Winkle stood up and Gladys looked away and smoothed her hair.

Annie and Ellen continued to the cafeteria and only then did Annie say, "Did that seem odd to you?"

"You mean Gladys and Mr. Van Winkle?"

"Yes." Annie opened her lunch sack and pulled out a sandwich wrapped in wax paper.

"Uh huh. It did."

"I wonder what they were talking about," said Annie.

When she returned to her office after lunch, Ellen could hear shouting coming from Mr. Powell's office. Even though the door was closed, she could hear two voices, both raised in anger. "Please," she whispered. "Keep your cool. Don't lose your temper."

Chapter 30
Ellen and Jonas discuss the third principle.

As Ellen parked Gunilla at the curb and was walking up the driveway, Rika tapped on the kitchen window and motioned her to come inside. Rika opened the front door wearing her perennial apron. "Come in, Ellen. I have something for you."

Ellen set her purse and notebook on the hall chair, hung her coat on the coat tree and followed Rika into the kitchen. There on the table was a large brown package. "The UPS man delivered this today," Rika explained. "It was addressed to you, so I accepted it and kept it inside. I hope that was OK."

"Of course, and I appreciate it." She looked at the return label. "Oh, it's the bar code scanner! It came in time for Christmas." Seeing the blank look on Rika's face, she explained. "It is a piece of computer equipment for Nathan. It's to be my Christmas present for him and I was afraid it wouldn't arrive in time. Do you have a knife or a scissors I could use to open it?"

Rika found a pen knife in one of her meticulously organized drawers and handed it to Ellen. Ellen sliced through the tape and opened the lid to find excelsior protecting another box. She carefully brushed away the packaging and lifted out the inner box. She held it up to inspect the image of the bar code scanner on the front.

"May one ask what that is?" Jonas's deep voice startled them both.

"*Älskling*, you startled us!" scolded Rika. "He likes to sneak up on me with those rubber wheels of his. I don't hear him coming," she explained to Ellen.

"Pish tosh, my dear. I'm merely wondering what that clever looking device is that Ellen has there. I assume this is the contents of the UPS package?"

"Yes," said Ellen. "Rika was kind enough to accept it. It is a bar code scanner that I'm planning to give to Nathan as a Christmas present."

The expression on Jonas's face went from mildly interested to genuinely engaged. "This sounds fascinating! I would like to learn more. Rika, my dear, I wonder ..."

"I'm already ahead of you, Jonas. I could see it coming from the look in your eye." While Ellen and Jonas had been talking she had already pulled out a third china plate, water glass, and silverware. "Ellen, it appears that you will be staying for dinner. My husband insists on it." She winked at Ellen.

"Oh but I couldn't! You're always having me over and ..."

"Ellen," said Rika sternly. "We are friends, yes?"

"Yes. Yes, of course."

"And do you believe that two old people occasionally like to have their drab, dreary, elderly ..."

"Speak for yourself," interjected Jonas.

"... elderly days enlivened by you, a friend, a charming young person?"

"Well, I suppose so. But ..."

Rika held up a finger and stopped Ellen with one simple gesture. "And do you believe that two such older people can eat all of ..." She paused dramatically to open the oven door. Wonderful smells wafted out and Ellen found her stomach reminding her that lunch had only been a simple sandwich and an apple. Inside the oven Ellen could see a large casserole of some sort. "There is plenty of this chicken and broccoli casserole. And I've made a nice green salad. It isn't sophisticated fare but, as you can see, there is plenty."

"And we do so enjoy your company," said her husband. "Besides, I really do want to learn more about this gift for Nathan."

"Oh, you two!" The laugh lines in the corners of Ellen's eyes belied her severe tone. "It would be my pleasure to stay. The feeling is mutual; I enjoy your company as well. Let me run across the breezeway and change shoes, if I may. And I'll bring back some brownies. I made them yesterday evening."

She dashed across the breezeway with her purse, leaving the notebook for the conversation that would inevitably follow. She slipped off her heels and, while she was at it, shucked off her skirt and blouse, pulling on a comfy pair of jeans and a long-sleeved t-shirt instead. Her feet now cradled in well-worn loafers, she dashed back just as Rika was taking the casserole out of the oven. "Here are the brownies," she said. "Now what can I do? Set the table?"

"Yes, please," said Rika, indicating the stack of plates and silverware.

Ellen knew her way around Rika's kitchen well enough that she had filled the water pitcher (no ice, for, as Rika had said once, "Only Americans want their water frigid.") and poured each glass by the time Rika came in bearing the casserole and salad.

The Klamecks sang the Swedish grace they always sang as Ellen reflected how comfortable she felt in their home.

After brownies — which Rika had warmed and to which she had added a scoop of ice cream — Jonas said, "Now, Ellen. I want to learn more about this device you've purchased for young Nathan."

Rika began clearing dishes, her eyes clearly communicating to Ellen that she should remain with Jonas and talk.

"I'm going to try not using jargon as you have taught me, Mr. Klameck."

"That's fine, Ellen, but can you not call me Jonas?"

"I'll try." She swallowed. "Jonas." She tried to look at him and smile, but failed. Taking in a breath, she continued. "Have you seen the little black lines we're seeing more and more of on grocery items? Canned goods, cereal boxes, things like that?"

"Indeed I have."

"Those are called bar codes. I don't understand how it works exactly, but a laser can interpret those lines and read the code they contain. So those black bars of various thicknesses are interpreted as a twelve digit number."

"So each bar code actually contains digits that can be read electronically?'

"Exactly. And the device I bought Nathan for Christmas is one of those laser readers. Hook it to a computer, point it at a bar code, pull the trigger, and the computer knows the twelve digit number in that particular bar code." She passed the box containing Nathan's gift down the table to him.

"This is truly wonderful," said Jonas. "I have been looking for something like this for a long time. Can the bar codes contain any data whatsoever?"

"I believe so, but I'm not positive. I know that one big issue is the standard by which the bar code is configured. The bar codes we see on grocery items follow the UPC — that's Universal Product Code — standard. Another standard, called 3 of 9, is more flexible and can include letters and symbols as well as numbers. And 3 of 9 can be different lengths, too."

"And could these bar codes be printed on an ordinary computer printer?"

"I don't think just any printer could do it. But we believe the laser printer we have at work could. We're looking into that. My hope is that we can print bar codes on the shop orders — the paper documents that tell machine operators how much of something to build. My idea is to give the machine operators a bar code scanner so that they can read each job card as it comes through. We would be able to get a lot more useful data that way."

"Such as?"

"Well, as we discussed before, we really do need to know how long it takes to produce each part. What we call m-time. And we also need to know how long it takes to do a setup for each part. My idea is to have the machine operators scan the bar code on the work order, so that the computer will know which job the operator is working on, and then an activity code from a standard page. Right now I'm thinking we need four codes: start setup, end setup, start production and end production. I'm hoping, although I haven't confirmed this yet, that the bar code reader will know what time and date it is, so that the operator can just read those two items …"

"The shop order number and the activity code …"

"Right. And the bar code reader will record the precise time the code was scanned."

"Ellen, I think this is brilliant. In fact, in my younger days, I used to dream that such technology would become available. There really wasn't any way to accomplish what you're contemplating here. We had to ask people to record their data by hand. And that wasn't ever particularly successful."

"Let me show you something …" She rifled through her notebook until she found the form she had picked up from Herb and the other operators. She laid it in front of Jonas, smoothing out the numerous creases and hoping that the smudges and stains of questionable origin wouldn't offend him.

Jonas laughed. "Ah, Ellen! This indeed brings back memories. Do you know I tried something almost like this fifteen years ago, and had to give it up. The data was just so poor."

"Look!" She pointed at some of Herb's chicken scratching. "I can't read that entry. And it looks like he was doing nothing for over two hours here. But I know Herb, er, the operator. He works constantly. He wouldn't ever loaf around for two whole hours."

"This is music to my ears and artistry to my eyes. I had the same miserable luck trying to capture similar data. We're birds of a feather, you and I. I'm just a wee bit older than you. I remember when IBM came out with the punch card reader that could be placed in the factory. We thought we had found the holy grail because the machine operators could run a punch card through the reader each time they started a new job." Jonas paused for a minute and Ellen could see in his eyes that he was revisiting progress in the past. "But this bar code thing, this is much, much better. Instead of having to attach a punch card to each shop order, you can print the bar code right on each piece of paper. Fabulous!" He held the bar code reader box in his hands with a tenderness that surprised Ellen. "I don't suppose …" he said. Then, "No, it is a gift for young Nathan." He looked up at Ellen. "Soon after Christmas day, I would be very grateful if young Nathan would bring over his new toy and show me what he's learned."

"I'm sure he'd love that," said Ellen.

"Now," Jonas said, setting the box down and rubbing his hands together. "I would like to let you know that you have found the third BITS principle."

"I have?"

"Indeed you have. It has to do with what you've been exploring: getting data into the business information technology system."

"You mean like reading a bar code?"

"Like reading a bar code. But I've just been reading a book that makes me think I need to adjust the wording of the third principle. I wonder, would you hand me that book that is on the bookshelf, just to the right of the pipe and tabor?"

"Pipe and tabor?" Ellen looked in the bookshelf and saw a small drum and what looked like a whistle. "You mean this?"

"Yes, that's it. The pipe and tabor were used in Shakespeare's day ... but we can talk about that later. Right now I want that new book by Shoshana Zuboff."

"This one? In the Age of the Smart Machine?"

"That's the one. I recommend you read it, Ellen. But right now I want to explain a word that the author coined. She's a very smart professor at the Harvard School of Business. The word is 'informate' — a combination of information and automation. A process is said to be informated when it is both automated and captures useful data — information — at the same time."

He paused for Ellen to digest this. "Does that mean that what I'm trying to do in the shop with the bar codes is, is 'informated?'"

"Indeed it does. While it isn't perfect — I expect the day will come when the machine itself will report on its progress rather than requiring the operator to scan the bar code — it is a major step in the right direction."

He opened the book and Ellen saw that many passages were underlined and highlighted. There were extensive notes in the margins. When Jonas read a book, it was almost as if he was having a dialogue with it. "Here we go," he said. "Zuboff says that information technology is unique in that it can translate activities, objects, and events into information. She calls that process informating." He looked up at Ellen as she wrote the word in her notebook. "I rather like that word."

"Yes, but what does it have to do with the third BITS principle?"

"I used to say that the third principle of BITS was that the system must be constructed so that it gathers data that is both accurate and timely. But I want to incorporate this idea of Zuboff's. Let me see …" He looked off into a random corner of the ceiling across the room, and Ellen was struck by how similar he looked to Nathan when her nephew was thinking hard.

"How about this?" asked Jonas. "The business information technology system must be informated so that it gathers, no, so that it *creates* data that is accurate and timely." Ellen started to write but Jonas stopped her. "I'm missing something having to do with the automation of the process, having to do with the effort …"

Again, he looked off into the distance and Ellen waited. She realized the clock on the mantle was softly ticking. The only other sound was the soothing crackle of the fire on the hearth. Then Jonas snapped his fingers. "The business information technology system must be informated so that it requires less effort than equivalent nontechnical systems and creates data that is accurate and timely."

"Wow," said Ellen. "Let me see if I can capture that."

Principle Three: The business information technology system must be informated so that it requires less effort than equivalent non-technical systems and creates data that is accurate and timely.

"We might be able to improve that — it seems a bit wordy — but it captures the essence, don't you think?" he said.

"I'm still trying to digest what it means," admitted Ellen.

"We've already talked about the word informated. But I want to get in there the idea that, if a process doesn't require less effort to do, people won't do it and it won't succeed."

"Oh, I just thought of an example! Have you seen the new bar code scanner they have at Robinson's Supermarket?"

"No. Tell me about it." Jonas didn't seem troubled in the least that she would assume he had been grocery shopping in his wheelchair.

"They have a bar code scanner built right into the table where you buy your groceries. It scans those UPC codes I was talking about and automatically puts the price into the cash register. According to Barney Robinson, it also deducts the item from the store's inventory so that they always have an up-to-the-minute picture of what is in stock."

"Marvelous! And you say that is at Robinson's today? Rika must allow me to go with her the next time she goes marketing. I have to see this marvel for myself."

"Isn't that a good example of an informated process? Myrtle — she's one of the checkout ladies — can scan each item with much less effort than she would have to use to key in the price of each item. And, in doing so, the system is creating data that is both accurate and up-to-the-minute."

"Precisely, my dear. Precisely!" He beamed at her. "Do you know what a marvel you are?" He sighed and, almost to himself, said, "Don't you just love this?"

"Oh, and by putting bar code readers on the shop floor, the machine operators will use less effort than if they have to write it all down on my forms." She was almost talking to herself as well.

"Yes," he replied. "And you'll get data that is both more accurate than this ..." He indicated the smudged, much abused form. "And it will be more timely, too."

Their sense of accomplishment was almost tangible.

"I do see a problem," said Jonas. "Right now the shop operators can ignore your form and invest the least effort of all. Using the bar code scanner has a bit of cost — I don't mean financial cost, I mean the cost of the effort. So you may find that the men are reluctant to use the scanners."

"What can I do?"

"I suspect the newness of the technology will make it exciting for a while. But that will wear off. Hopefully before then it will have become a habit. But you may need to put some teeth in it. There is a corollary to the third principle which states that it may be necessary to tie a process to something else — for example, the operator's pay is tied to how many hours they report with the scanner. Let's hope you don't have to go that far."

"I'm not sure how Mr. Powell would feel about that. Not to mention Human Resources."

"You are correct, of course. But perhaps a bit of one-upmanship might do the trick. You could post charts of the number of hours reported by each operator in the break room. A bit of rivalry might develop that would help incentivize using the bar code scanners."

"I see what you mean. It isn't a decision I have to make right away, is it?"

"No, but it is always best to think of contingencies in case the primary strategy starts developing a weakness."

With impeccable timing Rika appeared with the tea tray and Ellen closed her notebook, very pleased that the third principle of business information technology systems had been hunted down and captured.

As they sipped their tea and chatted like old friends, Rika looked at Ellen and asked, "May I ask you a question, Ellen?"

"Yes, of course."

"This is an important question, and one that I am asking because I know that Jonas will never ask it."

"Now Rika ..." said Jonas. There was a weariness in his voice Ellen had not heard before.

"No, Jonas. You need to know. I need to know." Ellen tensed. This was not going to be an easy question. "And I want to know," continued Rika, "Because Ellen means so much to me." She looked at Ellen. "I believe in being direct."

"Oh dear ..." whispered Ellen under her breath.

"Ellen, we — Jonas and I — would like to know what you think of us after your suspicion that Jonas or I had betrayed information you told Jonas in confidence. Are you still suspicious? You see, we have come to care for you a great deal. And so your opinion of us matters."

"We would understand it if you still thought we were not to be trusted. But we would like to know where we stand." Jonas laid both hands on the table, palms down. He looked at his hands and his shoulders slumped. With great effort, it seemed, he raised his head and looked across the table at Ellen. "We would very much appreciate it if you could be truthful with us."

The mantle clock's ticking was the only sound in the room. Ellen looked from Jonas to Rika, and back to Jonas again. She almost laughed at how vulnerable they both looked. Did she have some kind of power over them? Did they truly care what she thought? Except for Trish, there was no one left on the planet who really cared. Yet here were her landlords, looking at her with trusting naiveté. Were they vulnerable? Yes. But was it funny? Not at all. The gravity of their friendship and the trust that must be there settled around her shoulders like a weight. "My yoke is easy and my burden is light," she whispered to herself.

"You both deserve an answer." Ellen reached out a hand to each of them, and she found herself holding Rika's hand and Jonas's hand. And she saw they were holding each other's hands, too, making a little circle of three. "It is true. I did not trust you at first. But that was only because, logically, I couldn't think of any other way for the information to leak out. But I know you." She smiled at the two of them. "I know you wouldn't do this thing. You didn't deserve to be treated that way, and I'm sorry. Will you forgive me?"

Jonas's eyes were bright. "There is nothing to forgive. You were correct to be suspicious, and I hope that some day you will find the real culprit. But let's say no more of this, eh? Can we say it is water under the bridge and just leave it at that?"

Ellen's response was simple, but affirming and clear: "Yes. I'd like that." Within herself she recognized the commitment she had made. Jonas Klameck had proven himself to be more than trustworthy in every encounter. She had no reason to doubt him and every reason to believe in his integrity. As of this moment she was choosing to trust him.

Making that decision and moving on felt good, freeing. As of now there was one less variable to worry about, one less unknown to consider. And that was that.

Chapter 31

Powell gets another opportunity to produce a part for Wilco.

The next day Ellen had barely gotten settled in when her phone rang. "Ellen Murphy," she answered.

"Ellen, this is Rob. Could you come to my office?" Ellen froze. This was it. The other shoe was going to drop.

"Now?" she squeaked.

"Yes, please. If you could."

"OK." It came out as a croak. She cleared her throat. "OK. I'm coming." The corridor seemed to lengthen with each step. The criminal takes her last walk to the judge's chambers where sentence will be passed. There will be officers to take her away. "Blindfold? Cigarette?" Be strong, she said to herself as she chewed the inside of her cheek. At least they cannot take your dignity.

She knocked and entered Mr. Powell's office. Sandy and Butch were already there. She'd done this scene before, and would just as soon avoid a repeat.

"Oh, hi Ellen," Mr. Powell said. Dare Ellen take a faint ray of hope from the lightness of his tone? "Come in. Shut the door and have a seat." He indicated the remaining chair. He turned and faced the three of them. "OK, gang. We have another opportunity. I just got another call from Karl Smithson at Wilco. He'd like us to bid on another part for them. This one, as near as I can tell, has a better profit margin and a bigger volume. In other words, this one is even better than the one we lost a couple of weeks ago." He grinned a lopsided grin and said, "Obviously I'd rather not repeat what happened to that one."

Three heads nodded in agreement.

"So here's the deal," continued Mr. Powell. He unrolled a blueprint so that Sandy and Butch could look at it. "Same questions as before. Can we build this? Do we have the capacity to manufacture it without adversely affecting any of our existing delivery commitments?"

Butch pointed to the drawing. "I don't see anything that looks like we need the press."

Sandy agreed. "Rob, did Smithson say anything about tooling?"

"Nope, nothing about tooling. As I understand it, it should be laser cut out of plate steel and drilled in several places. There is a weldment that gets welded on, but the most complex thing is that the part requires several assembly elements."

"Right," said Sandy. "I see that. Looks like four nuts, lock washers and bolts. Then … what's this here? Oh, a clamp with a hose …"

"Two clamps and two hoses, which get routed through a hole in the weldment and then attached to this valve block." He looked at Sandy. "Lots of assembly work …"

"Yeah, I'm seeing that. What's this part for, Rob? Any idea?"

"Karl said it was something for hydraulics in one of their lifts."

"That makes sense. Anything you see, Butch, that scares you?"

Butch scratched his chin for a minute. "I don't think so, Boss. Nothing we haven't done before, just not on this scale with this many components. The assembly will be tricky to spec out."

"Ellen, that's where you come in." Mr. Powell looked at her. "You did a good job on figuring out our capacity with the m-times Butch worked out. You'll need to do that again, except for …" He looked to Sandy for help.

"Well, we'll need to check the laser cutter, the drill press, welding, and, most of all, assembly."

"I can do that," said Ellen. Her confidence was gradually leeching back. The tone and questions didn't imply that her pink slip would be in today's paycheck. "But how do we go about figuring how Assembly will be affected? Does Assembly have an m-time, too?"

"It does," said Sandy. "But you're right — it is a little different. We can figure the m-time, but the big challenge is scheduling the line. A part may be able to move down the line fairly quickly if there is nothing in front of it. But the assembly line gets clogged up with parts that are hard to assemble or that have missing component pieces. Kirby is the guy who keeps it running as smooth as possible." Sandy paused for a minute, then asked, "Rob, I think this project is going to need to involve a few more people. These hoses, if I'm not mistaken, are a specialty hydraulic hose. I think we need to get purchasing involved in sourcing those right away and figuring out what lead time we can get."

"Agreed," said Mr. Powell. "I think involving purchasing up front makes sense."

"And I think we need to get production control involved. They manage the master schedule and, once we get the m-times calculated, we'll need to get Luther and his people to see what kind of production load SOLUTION/400 produces after the weekly MRP run."

"Again, I agree," said Mr. Powell. "But I think we should limit the number of people who are involved to a small team until we have a signed purchase order from Wilco. We don't want to lose this one. As my Dad used to say, 'Loose lips sink ships.'"

"We'll have to involve Kirby."

"Of course. That's a given," said Mr. Powell. "Let's just not discuss this with anyone outside of the company, OK?" Ellen expected a pointed look from him, but it did not materialize. He made his remarks to the room in general, not specifically to her. Yet every accusation Mr. Powell did not say out loud, she heard in her own head multiplied tenfold.

"OK, Sandy. You're in charge of Operation Silk Stockings …" He looked around the room. "What? Hydraulic hoses. Stockings. Hose stockings." He laughed at them. "Come on guys, I'm not that weird."

"Speak for yourself," said Sandy under his breath.

"I heard that," said Mr. Powell. "Now, as I was saying, Sandy, you're in charge of Operation Silk Stockings. Go get purchasing and production control up to speed, and, when you're ready, you can get with Kirby to focus in on the Assembly impact. Any questions?"

There were none.

"All right, then. It's Friday and of course I'd love to be able to call Karl Smithson before the weekend." He looked at the three of them for confirmation. "But if we can't, we can't. I hate to ask this, with Christmas coming and all, but, if we have to put in some time this weekend to get this figured out, let's do that. At the very latest I want to be able to give Wilco an answer first thing Monday morning. Let's go make Operation Silk Stockings a success!"

Sandy, Butch and Ellen held a brief strategy session in the hall. Sandy would go talk to purchasing and production control. Butch would begin working on the m-times for the laser and drill. He would also work on a jig design for the welding operation. Ellen would start researching loads on the laser and drill, waiting for Butch's m-times as soon as he had them figured, so she could do the final calculations. Then she would talk to Kirby about the assembly line.

As Ellen walked back to her desk she realized three things. First, the debacle with the lost Wilco order now seemed to be in the past, possibly even forgiven. Second, she still had a job! And third, she thought to herself as she sat down and turned on her computer, she knew how to do this. She'd done it before, and each time she got better at it.

Despite the tedium of her task, she worked her way through it, looking up orders that used the laser cutter and then the drill press. For each order, she looked up the part and wrote down the m-time. "I'll have to get a sense from Butch about what portion of each of these m-times are for the laser cutter," she thought to herself. She was less sure about the welding operations. "I'll have to ask Butch about that, too."

By late morning she had all her data together. Unless the m-time portions were surprisingly large, there didn't seem to be any problem on the laser cutter or on the drill press. She went down the hall to see Butch.

"Hey. How's it going?"

"Good so far. I've done the calculations for the laser cutter and for the drill press. But, like before, I need your best guess about what portion of the m-time is required on those two machines." She handed him her list.

Butch scanned the list and made a few marks on the sheet. "I'd say less than ten percent on the drill, and probably more like five percent on the laser cutter," he said. "But I need to check on these few — I'm not as familiar with them."

He went to his computer and looked up a few parts. Then he went over to the blueprint cabinets and found one. "Uh huh," he said to himself. "Yes, looks good." He looked up at Ellen. "I think every one of these is under ten percent on those work centers. The laser cutter is probably less. More like five percent, like I said. Setups are easy, too. The press is where the setups can get you."

"OK, that's good, Butch. We don't have a problem on those, then. But what about Welding? I mean it isn't quite like other work centers, right? You have a welder — more than one, if I understand Leonard correctly. So what amount of time does a weld take? And what is the setup like?"

"You're right. Leonard has ten or so guys on his crew, all welding. Not every one is trained for all welds, but the weld on this new Wilco part is a simple one. I've already got the jig designed to hold the two pieces of metal in place while the welder puts down a bead. You following me, Boss? Or should I say, Possum?"

Ellen groaned. "Leonard has a lot to answer for. Is there anyone who hasn't latched on to the Possum nickname?"

"Not that I know of, unless it would be Rob."

Ellen sighed, remembering Whit Collette's advice. "Possum it is then. But what about these welds — do they take a long time? How about the setup?"

"This weld is fairly quick and easy. Some can get pretty complicated when there are multiple pieces of metal and multiple welds. But this Wilco part just has two pieces of metal and one weld."

"And setups?"

"A setup for a welder pretty much means just putting the jig on the welding table. Nothing too complicated."

"So, it sounds like welding probably isn't an issue, either."

"Right. The real challenge, in my mind, is going to be Assembly."

"We were planning on going out to talk to Kirby later on. Should we go talk to him now?"

"I don't see why not, Possum. I'd like to see you in your native habitat." He rolled up the Wilco blueprint and held the door open for her.

The shop was the familiar buzz of activity. Ellen felt comfortable on the factory floor now, even liked the smells and sounds of welders arcing and grinders sending off their shower of orange sparks. There was a metal smell, mixed with a faint whiff of smoke and machine oil, all bathed in the yellow-orange light of the sodium vapor lights up in the rafters. She had developed a sixth sense about lift truck traffic and knew when to step out of the way. She'd also permanently given up her heels, wearing more comfortable — and safer — shoes to work now.

As she and Butch headed toward the back of the shop, they passed Herb on the laser cutter. He hoisted his Ale-8-1 can in salute. "Hey, Possum," he called.

David Palmer was waiting for a lift truck driver to install a new tooling setup in his press. "Lookin' good, Possum!" he said as they passed.

"Wow, Boss. I think they kind of like you," commented Butch.

"Like is kind of strong. At least we're friends. I've decided the Possum thing is something I'm just going to have to live with."

"Not every girl gets nicknamed after a marsupial," said Butch.

Kirby was in his office. He looked up. "Hey Butch. What's up, Possum?" He winked at Ellen.

"We need your help to figure out something," said Ellen. Butch rolled out the Wilco blueprint on Kirby's desk.

"We've got a chance to produce a new part for Wilco. Rob is really keen to win this bid, so we're doing the research of what it would take to produce it."

"And whether taking on this order would interrupt work we already have scheduled," added Ellen. "We're looking at our capacity as well as what it would take to manufacture it."

Kirby looked at the blueprint and whistled. "Lots of assembly here."

"Right. That's why we're here. To get your take on it."

"What's the profit margin on this part?" asked Kirby.

Butch scratched his chin. "Well, I don't really know. But it must be good, otherwise Rob wouldn't be so keen on it. What's your take on the time it will take to manufacture this one?"

Kirby traced his finger across the drawing, noting the hydraulic hoses and other details. He and Butch discussed several of the finer points and Kirby took out a pad of paper, sketching out the steps on the assembly line. "Let's see," he said. "I think it would take five stations on the line." He listed the sequence that the parts would be installed. "I assume the weldment would come from welding?"

"Right," said Butch. "Harvey's group will do the initial machining of the steel. Then Leonard and his team will weld the two pieces up. You'll get the weldments from Leonard, and we'll have the other parts — the hoses and the like — delivered to the assembly line. Does that sound right?"

"Yeah, that sounds right. Let's see … I think we should call it 30 minutes per piece on the assembly line."

"Thirty minutes!" Butch was indignant. "I could do it myself in twenty."

"Oh, yeah? Well look here …" Kirby went over the steps again, suggesting times for each step.

In the end Butch reluctantly agreed. "It still feels long to me, but you're the boss."

Just then Gladys opened the door and came in. "Oh, hey everybody. I didn't know we was having a party out here. I just came out to get the timesheets. But let me go back and get some Dixie cups. Kirby, you got any of that 'shine in your bottom drawer?"

"Now Aunt Gladys, you know I don't have any liquor here at work."

"I'm just funnin' with you, honey. Lighten up!" She smoothed her skirt. "But, really, what are y'all doing out here?"

"We're looking at a possible new part we might take on for Wilco," said Butch.

"But Mr. Powell wants us to keep it quiet, OK?" said Ellen. "This isn't something we're to talk about outside of the plant."

"Oh, gotcha!" said Gladys. "Real hush-hush. I get it." She winked broadly and tapped the side of her nose. "Did you get that, Kirby? Mum's the word."

"Oh, I got it, Aunt Gladys. I'll keep my mouth shut."

"I think we're done here, right Ellen?" asked Butch.

Gladys picked up the timesheets off of Kirby's desk. "I'll walk back with y'all." Butch held the door for her.

"Ellen, hang on a second, if you don't mind," said Kirby as the others exited. "I wanted to ask you ... " He paused until the door closed. "I wanted to ask you if you have lunch plans today. It won't be a steak dinner, but would you like to go up to Fast Ernie's and have lunch with me? My treat."

"I brought my lunch, but I suppose it won't spoil if I put it in the refrigerator. Kirby, is Gladys your aunt? Did I hear that right?"

"You didn't know that? Sure, she's my dad's sister. I'll pick you up at your office a few minutes before noon."

"Kirby, what are you driving?"

He laughed. "Not my motorcycle, if that's what you mean." He eyed her skirt that barely came to her knees. "We'll take my car."

"OK, but just one thing. I've got to get these calculations done for Mr. Powell. If I feel like I've run into a problem, I'd probably better eat lunch at my desk and keep working. So I might have to take a rain check."

"You're a smart girl. You'll get it figured out. I'll be there just before twelve. Now, scoot, Possum. Get back to work!" He smiled that charming smile and his dimple showed.

Ellen couldn't help but feel warm and tingly inside as she walked back to her office up front. This Possum thing, especially coming from Kirby, was kind of growing on her.

Fast Ernie's was the lunch counter in a sprawling country store that pretentiously called itself the Centerville Mall. Lots of factory workers went there for lunch because Fast Ernie's was fast, the sandwiches were good, and they didn't cost too much. Fast Ernie was behind the counter, wearing a jaunty soda jerk hat. You told him what kind of bread you wanted — white or wheat — and he pulled out two slices. Next you told him your spread — mustard or mayo were the common choices — and then what meat you wanted. Ernie stocked all kinds of meat — ham, roast beef, hard and soft salami, turkey, and more. You also got to pick from a variety of cheeses and finally — Ellen's favorite part — you got to pick your vegetables. There were sliced onions, tomatoes, lettuce, pickles, banana peppers, and, for the granola crowd, choices like alfalfa sprouts and sunflower seeds. Ellen usually ended up saying, "Throw in the whole garden." There was no extra charge, regardless of how many veggies you added. Ernie would put it together right in front of you, slip your sandwich into a plastic baggie, and write the price on the outside with a Sharpie marker. Ellen never could find any consistency in Ernie's pricing. The same sandwich could vary as much as a dollar in price, but Ellen didn't complain. A great sandwich was $2.75, tops. She figured, what's a dollar between friends?

She placed her order — ham and Colby cheese with all the veggies — and Kirby followed her, placing his order for roast beef on white bread. They took their baggies over to Bonnie, the cashier. "Want a Coke?" asked Kirby.

"I'd love a Pepsi if they have one." Kirby fished two bottles out of the tub of ice by the cash register. Ernie knew how to create an impulse buy.

"Will that be all, kids?" asked Bonnie.

"Chips?" asked Kirby.

"Not for me, thanks." Kirby got a pack of barbecue potato chips and threw in a pack of Nabs. "For later," he said.

Bonnie rang up the bill and Kirby paid. "There's a table over in the corner," Ellen pointed. They made their way through the lunch crowd, said hello to Herb and some of his buddies who were chowing down. Ale-8-1 was the drink of choice at that table.

"So tell me about this new Wilco order," said Kirby when they had gotten settled.

"There's not much to tell. First we have to make sure we get the order," said Ellen around a mouthful of ham and cheese.

"Yeah, but is it a big order? I mean, am I going to have to hire some temporary workers on the assembly line?"

"I really don't know," replied Ellen. "I'm just supposed to figure out what kind of impact it will have on our capacity."

Kirby chewed on his sandwich and then washed it down with a swig of Pepsi. "Probably be too disruptive. Might be one of those things we think we want but we really don't."

Ellen considered this but couldn't come up with an appropriate response. So she changed the subject. "How come we call any soft drink a Coke, even when it's a Pepsi?" She saluted Kirby with her icy bottle and took a sip.

Kirby laughed. "We do, don't we? We say, 'Do you want a Coke?' and it could be a Pepsi or a Sprite or an Ale-8-1 like Herb over there. I don't know why we do that. You're smart Ellen. You tell me."

"I really don't know. I suppose it has to do with Coke being based in Atlanta, in the South, while Pepsi's headquarters are some-where up north. New York, I believe."

"I didn't know that. Makes sense. But of course there is a Pepsi bottling plant in Corbin. You order a Coke in Corbin, you're likely to get shot."

It was Ellen's turn to laugh. Kirby was easy to talk to, fun to be with.

"Say, Ellen, I've been meaning to ask you. Would you be my date for the company Christmas party?"

"Christmas party?"

"Yeah, you know. Sometime during the week before Christmas there is always a company Christmas party. I think this year it is go-ing to be at Halls on the River next Tuesday. People don't have to have a date, but I'd sure like to take you. I'd like to think of you as my girl. People dress up, there's a nice meal, Rob makes a dumb speech and then there's dancing. There's a cash bar, but the company pays for everything else."

"I guess I didn't know about it …"

"Please say you'll go with me."

Suddenly Trish's words rose up and niggled in her ear. You can always, always come back home. But wasn't it Trish who had also suggested she should start dating? Before she allowed herself to over-think it, she said, "Sure, why not! Sounds fun."

"You bet! It'll be great, you'll see."

Chapter 32
The Powell Christmas Party.

Kirby picked Ellen up in the Mercedes at 5:30. Mr. Powell had let everyone go home early to prepare. Ellen had sensed a building anticipation on Monday for the Powell Christmas party and by Tuesday everyone was excited to the point of distraction.

"Does everyone come?" Ellen had asked Annie.

"Just about. Folks from the plant, the supervisors, us folks up here in the office, even management. They all come and most of them have a good time. A lot of 'em bring their wives. I'm bringing Ronnie Dale. Say, you've never met him have you? You're in for a real treat!"

"I'll look forward to that. What's the dress code? Kirby is taking me and I want to wear the right kind of outfit."

"That Kirby is a lucky fellow. Persistent, too! Most folks wear nice Christmasy stuff. Some of the men will have sport coats and ties. There's always a lot of fun with some of the crazy ties some of them will wear. Lots of green and red. Herb had a tie last year with that Green Eggs and Ham guy on it."

"Like Dr. Seuss? But what do the girls wear?"

"Well, some dress nice with Christmas sweaters or a nice pant suit. Some of 'em dress what my Mammaw would have called 'slutty' — you know, backless or see through and the like."

"Well, I won't be wearing anything like that."

"Ain't that the truth!"

Ellen had settled on a simple red sheath dress with a white cardigan over her shoulders. She had some earrings that looked like candy canes that picked up the red in the dress, and she wore a silver choker with a poinsettia worked in silver that fit the dress's scoop neckline just perfectly. Red heels completed the outfit.

Kirby approved with a low whistle as he helped her out of her coat. "Wow, Ellen. You get better looking every time I see you."

"Thanks, Kirby." His compliment had been genuine, if a bit sophomoric in its delivery.

"I'll go get us some drinks."

"Just ginger ale for me, please." While Kirby was gone, she mingled, saying hi to Harvey Green who introduced her to his wife, Susan. She spotted Leonard and went over to say hello to him as well.

"Oh, hey, Possum. Lookin' good. I want you to meet my first wife, Sharonda."

"First wife?" Ellen said vaguely.

"Oh, honey, don't pay him no mind. He's always sayin' that." Sharonda grinned a wide, welcoming smile. "He should have said his first and only wife." She punched Leonard on the shoulder.

"Ow!" he said in mock pain. "What'd I do?"

Sharonda took Ellen's hand in hers and shook it. "Did I hear him right? Are you the one they call Possum?"

"Thanks to Leonard, apparently I'm stuck with it."

"Well I'm pleased to meet you. Leonard and all the boys say you're doin' a real good job. And don't worry about bein' Possum. Why my grandmother could make the best possum pie ..." She winked at Ellen. "When I can get away from this hunk of real man, I'll tell you what his brothers used to call him."

"Uh, I think we'd better dance," said Leonard, dragging his bride onto the floor.

The band was from Dayton and were doing a good job cranking out George Harrison's 'Got My Mind Set On You' and Michael Jackson's 'The Way You Make Me Feel.' They threw in some do-wop from the 50s, which Ellen's Dad would have loved. Ellen was intrigued that the lead singer was a girl and that one of the guys was playing flute like Ian Anderson.

Kirby found her and handed her a drink. Ellen knew immediately it wasn't ginger ale. It was something much stronger and, when she had the chance, she set it down. "Let's dance, Baby!" He took her hand just as the band launched into 'Crockodile Rock.'

Ellen had to admit, Kirby was a good dancer. Not only did he move well, he pulled her in as well, twirling her under his arm and grabbing her by the waist for a couple of turns. She grew self-conscious as she realized people were watching them. The band was good at getting the audience involved, inviting everyone to sing along on the "laaah, la la la la la" chorus. By the time the song ended, Ellen was quite breathless.

As they headed off the dance floor, Ellen bumped into Rob Powell. "Oh, sorry," she said.

"Good evening, Ellen. Having a good time?" He looked classy in his suit, white shirt, and tie covered with Christmas trees.

"I am. Thanks for organizing this." She indicated the folks milling around, waiting for the meal to begin. "Folks seem to really enjoy it. And me too."

"It's been a tradition since when my Dad ran Powell. It's an important part of our culture." He touched her arm. "You enjoy yourself, OK? Hey Kirby." He acknowledged her date and moved on.

The buffet lines were just about ready and Mr. Powell stepped up to one of the band's microphones.

"Could I have everyone's attention for just a second?" he called. "We're about to eat. I just wanted to say a few words." Whit Collette said something Ellen couldn't hear. "Yeah, thanks for that, Whit. I cut my speech down from an hour to 45 minutes this year." There was good natured groaning in the audience.

Ellen realized that Gladys was standing beside her. "Hey, Gladys," she whispered. "Merry Christmas!"

"Same to you, honey, same to you." Gladys gave her a little hug. "I'm so glad you're here with us, with Kirby."

"We've had a good year at Powell," Mr. Powell was saying. "Not the best year we've ever had, but a solid good year. And if it weren't for all of you, we would't be able to do anything, much less do it so well. So thank you. Thank you and merry Christmas!"

"Merry Christmas!" responded the crowd.

"Before I ask David to come up and bless the meal, I want to share some good news with you. Some of you may know we've been working on bidding on a new product to make for Wilco. Well, I'm very happy to say that we landed the order." He grinned as impromptu applause broke out around the room. "That's right! This is some good news just in time for Christmas. Right after the new year, you'll be seeing a new part move through Fabrication and Welding, and especially in Assembly. Right, Kirby?" He looked over at Kirby. Ellen was standing with her hand tucked in Kirby's arm. Gladys was standing on the other side of Kirby. Ellen was watching Mr. Powell, but, when he looked at Kirby she was inexplicably embarrassed. It seemed to happen in slow motion: she dropped her hand away from Kirby's arm. As she did so, she saw a strange look on Gladys' face. Gladys wasn't looking at Mr. Powell but at Kirby. The look on her face was odd. Was she happy that Kirby's Assembly department had more work to do? Or was it something else, something that caused her to be less than pleased? Kirby didn't seem to notice Ellen had released his arm; he was in an eye duel with the man on the stage.

"Like I said, this is a big deal for us here at Powell," continued Mr. Powell, his voice booming through the band's speakers. "I just got the call from Karl Smithson at Wilco this morning that they were awarding us the business. So congratulations to all of you. If we can continue to build our reputation for quality and for on-time delivery, we'll see more of this kind of order. I don't have to tell you that's good for business.

"Now," he continued, "I've asked David Palmer of Fabrication to come and bless the food. Then we can eat. Brother David," he said as he welcomed David onto the stage.

David prayed and everyone headed for the buffet line. The band took a break so that people could talk while they ate. When Ellen had her plate, she saw Annie waving at her from across the room. She made her way over to Annie. "We saved you and Kirby a seat," said Annie.

Ellen wasn't sure that Kirby would have chosen to sit with Annie and her fiancé, but Ellen relished the idea of sitting next to her friend and led Kirby that way.

"Ellen, this is Ronnie Dale," said Annie with obvious pride. "Ain't he just finer than frog hair split four ways? And Ronnie Dale, this here's Kirby."

"Nice to meet you, Ronnie Dale," said Ellen, shaking hands with him. "Annie seems to think you're something special."

"Aww ... I kinda like her, too." His arm slid easily around Annie's waist and drew her to him, giving her a little squeeze.

Ronnie Dale turned out to be quite a talker. He was very interested in farming and animals. By the time they had covered Angus vs. Holsteins and ways to prevent a hen from going broody, it was time for dessert.

Kirby brought Ellen a second mixed drink. Ellen pretended to take a sip, then quietly set it down.

Mr. Powell was at the microphone again. "We're like a big family here at Powell," he said. "This annual Powell Christmas Party has been a tradition for years. My father instituted it. It is an opportunity to relax a bit, enjoy some nice food and a great band ..." He saluted the band and the lead guitarist saluted back. "I want you to enjoy yourselves. Enjoy the music. We have a cash bar open, but I don't want you to enjoy that too much." Laughter drifted around the room. "Seriously, if you've overindulged, or if you have a friend that's had too much, please have the restaurant folks call you a cab. Marcie over there ..." He pointed to a tall redhead in a black catering vest. "... Marcie and her team will be glad to make sure you have appropriate transportation. Right Marcie?"

Marcie gave him a thumbs up.

"OK, then. Let's have the band come on back up." The band was eager to get back to it. The drummer was already settling in and the lead guitarist was strapping on his axe. The lead singer, in a simple green peasant blouse and skirt, her hair held back with a green bandana, was ready at the microphone. "Merry Christmas everyone! Have a great time. Here's Susan and the boys with 'Chelsea Morning.'"

Ellen suddenly realized that Mr. Powell had hopped off of the stage and was heading for Kirby. Oh no, she thought. Now what? There's something going on here that I don't understand.

"Ellen?" He was talking to her. "May I have this dance? You don't mind, do you, Kirby?"

"Uh …" Kirby wasn't quite on his A game. "I guess not. That is, if Ellen …" He looked at her lamely.

"What about it, Ellen? Care to cut the rug?"

"Sure, why not." He led her out onto the dance floor.

He wasn't as flashy a dancer as Kirby. 'Chelsea Morning' had an odd beat that didn't quite lend itself to regular dancing, but it wasn't a slow dance either. "Do you know how to foxtrot?"

"Not really …"

"Let me show you. It works well with this kind of four-four rhythm." He took her around the waist, holding her right hand in ballroom position. "I step forward and you step back. The rhythm is slow, quick quick, slow, quick quick." In no time Ellen had gotten the basic idea and they were dancing in sync, Rob leading and Ellen being very content to follow. As the song was coming to an end, Rob threw in a few extra moves, making some half-turns but never letting go, never letting her flounder.

When the song ended, Rob gave a little bow, still holding her hand. "Thank you, Ellen. We may have to do that again some time."

"That … that would be nice," she said as he led her back to her seat.

Kirby had been dancing with one of the girls from Assembly who was dressed just as Annie had described — a short, backless dress that clearly didn't have any place for a bra. When the band kicked off '25 or 6 to Four' Kirby kept dancing with her. Ellen was happy to sit one out and share conversation with Annie and Ronnie Dale, observing who was dancing with whom, what they were wearing, and who seemed to have had a bit too much to drink.

As the evening unfolded, Kirby danced with Ellen occasionally, but he also danced with the prettiest girls in the room. Whit Collette asked her to dance once, but she quickly realized it was a mercy dance — Whit wasn't a particularly good dancer and seemed secretly relieved when it was over. Annie and Ronnie Dale seemed content to watch. "Don't you kids want to dance?" asked Ellen.

"I'm not much of a dancer," explained Ronnie Dale.

Kirby came over with another drink for Ellen. She protested, but he admonished, "A little toddy for the body! Now drink up!"

Again, Ellen pretended to take a sip. "Haven't you about had enough, Kirby?"

"I am shocked at you, woman," he said in a fake dramatic tone. "Shocked, I say! The night is still young, and Kirby has just begun!" He dragged her onto the floor for another dance, but clearly the alcohol was having an effect; his moves weren't a sharp as they had been earlier and he was beginning to be unsteady.

The next dance was a slow dance, and Kirby held her close. But his inebriation made her feel more like she needed to prop him up.

After a few more dances and another drink — Kirby didn't bring her one this time — Ellen said, "Kirby don't you think it's time to head home?" The crowd was thinner now. The band seemed willing to play as long as there were dancers on the floor, and they were taking requests.

"Home? The evening is young!"

"But Kirby, we have to be at work tomorrow morning, and I'm afraid you've had a bit too much."

"Non-schenshe! The night is young, and Kirby has just begun!"

"I think you're past beginning and well into it. Where are your keys, Kirby?"

"Are you going home with me? Now that's what I'm talking about."

"I'm going to help you get home." She held out her hand. "I'll drive."

"No need for that, woman. I'm fine."

"No, you're not." She looked over at Annie for support, who gave her the slightest nod. She knew she was right. "Give me your keys."

Ellen was surprised that he did. "Come on, big guy. Let's get you home."

"Home, home on the range," sang Kirby. As they retrieved their coats he pointed at Ellen and said to the hostess, "She's goin' home with me."

"I'll be driving and leaving him there," Ellen said firmly.

As she was driving the Mercedes toward Kirby's house, he suddenly said, "Pull over, Ellen. Oh, I'm about to puke. I don't want to get it on my carpet." Ellen pulled over in time for Kirby to deposit the contents of his stomach on the side of the road.

She found his house in spite of his rather incoherent directions. "I'll drive your car to work tomorrow," she said. "Can you get yourself to Powell some other way?" She made sure that he got safely into his apartment and ignored his mumbled attempts to get her to come inside.

Then she drove back home and parked the Mercedes on the street behind Gunilla.

Chapter 33
Ellen faces the Klamecks about the car left overnight.

Wednesday morning Ellen drove Kirby's Mercedes to work rather than taking her Saab. She'd have to figure out a way to get home — maybe Annie would give her a ride. She dropped his keys off at his desk when she collected job cards. He wasn't anywhere to be seen.

While she was at it, she stopped by the laser cutter to see if Herb was doing any better at logging his production and setup times. If there was an improvement, it wasn't much of one. She swapped his smudged form for a new one, planning to calculate what she could from his data. In her heart she knew it would be mostly futile.

She didn't have much better luck with Joe Bob Walker on the drill press, or with David Palmer on the press. His prayer for the meal last night did give her the opportunity to learn that he was, indeed, an ordained minister and pastored a small Baptist church in the southeast end of the county.

The party the previous night did seem to have taken a lot of people's energy. While people were getting their work done, there wasn't as much buzz and good-natured camaraderie as usual. Herb only called her Possum once.

Ellen took what little data she had from the three machines and tried to make some sense of it. She realized that what she really wanted was to compare what the men had recorded about their work with data out of the mainframe. She logged on to the system, looking for a screen or a function that would give her what she wanted. "This is silly," she said out loud. "I know the system has data about orders that have gone through those three machines, but I sure can't find it."

In frustration she went down to Whit Collette' office. "What's up, Possum?" he said.

"Whit, I'm stumped." She explained what she had been doing with the log sheets for the three machines.

"Good idea," replied Whit. "How's that going?"

"Not well. I know the guys just aren't recording all their time. I know they're busy and lots of times they forget. I thought I could fill in some of the blanks by comparing what they did document with what's in the mainframe. But I can't find any screen that will let me see historical data about shop orders that have gone across specific machines."

"Hmmm," said Whit. He logged into the system himself. He searched through some of the screens Ellen had used, and a few she hadn't. In the end, though, he came up as empty as she did.

"Would there be a way to get at the data directly?" Ellen asked.

"You mean like bypassing SOLUTION/400 and going directly to the data tables?"

"Yeah, I guess. I'm not even sure what I'm asking. I know the data I want is in there. It seems crazy that we can't get at it."

"I know what you mean. But the vendor of SOLUTION/400 takes a pretty dim view of its customers messing directly with the data tables. I guess the thinking — and I see the logic in it — is that we might inadvertently mess something up. And then we'd have a real mess on our hands. I guess you could say they're protecting us from ourselves."

"Maybe ..." Ellen wasn't so sure. "I'm not asking to update the data or anything, just get access to look at it. Seems like our data is kind of being held hostage by the vendor."

Whit chuckled. "Secretly I might agree with you. But I would never dare to say that at the annual SOLUTION/400 user conference. I would get ushered out of the room by some over-muscled types with SOLUTION/400 name badges on."

"Well thanks, Whit. You're always willing to listen to my crazy ideas."

"They're not crazy," said Whit. "Maybe just ahead of their time. And not possible, at least today."

Ellen went back to her office and tried several other angles at teasing something useful out of the logs from the shop. In the end, though, she had to admit defeat. She made an entry in her notebook about not being able to get data she needed off of the factory floor, and not being able to extract it from the mainframe, either.

Annie was happy to give Ellen a ride home. "It's on my way," she said. "I'm meeting Ronnie Dale for dinner at Gabrielli's in Laodicea, so it would be easy to drop you off." On the drive home they commiserated over Kirbys less than stellar behavior the night before.

After Annie dropped her off, Ellen walked up the driveway toward the stairs to her apartment. As she passed the Klamecks' kitchen window, she saw Rika motioning her to come in. Ellen started to knock on the door but Rika beat her to it, opening the door and saying, "Come in, Ellen. I'm afraid we need to talk to you."

Ellen went into the living room as directed and found Jonas, apparently waiting for her. He motioned her to a seat and Rika sat down, too, opposite Ellen.

There was an awkward silence. Jonas cleared his throat, then said, "Ellen, do you recall sitting in this room when you first came to us, wanting to rent the apartment over the garage?"

"Yes, of course."

"And do you recall that we laid down some ground rules?"

"Yes. What's this about?" She sat with her hands clenched in her lap.

"Ellen," Rika inserted. "We're very sorry to have to do this. But rules are rules and we cannot have them broken. We must ask you to leave. Please be packed and out of the apartment by the end of the month.

Ellen's mouth dropped open. She tried to speak, but her mouth was dry. Words wouldn't come. She had come to love these people. Why were they doing this to her? A tear slid down her cheek. "May ..." she squeezed. "May I ask what I've done?"

"You'll recall that we said there were to be no overnight guests," said Jonas.

"Yes, but ..."

Rika held up her hand, stopping the words that were hard enough for Ellen to form. "We both saw the car last night. I know, because I saw him pick you up, that this is the vehicle of your boyfriend ..."

"A Mercedes, I believe," added Jonas.

"The car was there the entire night, Ellen." Rika paused. Her eyes were threatening to spill over as well. She looked down and sniffed, reaching for a tissue. "I'm very disappointed, Ellen."

"We both are," said Jonas.

A glimmer of hope shone like a small flashlight in a dark forest. Perhaps they could be made to understand. She smiled crookedly. "It wasn't like that at all."

The both sat, silent, waiting for an explanation.

"The Mercedes is Kirby's car. That's his name: Kirby. He invited me to be his date at the Powell Christmas party last night. While he was at the party, he had way too much to drink. I asked for his car keys and managed to get them. I drove him to his apartment, dropped him off, then drove his car here because I had no other way to get home." She lifted her chin. "You see, it wasn't like that. He didn't spend the night. In fact, his behavior last night did not impress me. I doubt I'll be seeing him socially again."

"What did you do with the car this morning, then?" asked Jonas.

"I drove it to work and left my car here. I dropped the keys off on Kirby's desk, and a friend gave me a ride home after work." She looked from Jonas to Rika and back to Jonas again. "That's what happened. I know trust is earned, and perhaps you do not trust that I am telling you the truth right now. I know for sure that Kirby did not spend the night. You can't be sure I am telling the truth, but I know that I am." She heard herself using the argument Jonas had used about himself and the issue of the Wilco order. "Is there anything I can do to earn back your trust?"

The ticking of the clock on the mantle was the loudest sound in the room. Even the crackle of the fire was muted. The three of them sat in silence for some time.

Finally Jonas spoke. "It seems to me I had this conversation not too long ago with a young lady who gave me the benefit of the doubt.

Your version of the facts seem plausible." He looked at Rika who nodded almost imperceptibly. "I am willing to accept your explanation. Rika?"

"Yes," whispered Rika. "Yes," she said louder. "Ellen, you can see how seriously we take our ground rules."

"I do, and I agree. I will never intentionally violate them. I wish you could believe me."

"You have shown yourself to be a young woman of integrity," said Jonas. "That counts for something."

"That counts for a lot," said Rika.

Ellen dared to hope. "So, may I stay in the apartment? You won't kick me out just before Christmas."

Rika smiled and looked at Jonas. "No, my dear," he said. "We won't do that. And thank you for the grace you've shown two old curmudgeons. You could have gotten angry."

"No," said Ellen. "Not angry. But hurt."

"Yes, I can see that," said Rika. "Come, let's put it behind us, shall we? How about you stay for dinner. I've made some fresh spanakopita."

"No, no thank you," said Ellen. "I really have some things I need to do for work." She saw Jonas sitting up a little straighter in his chair, so she hastily added, "And I have some tidying up in the apartment I've been putting off."

Later, after a sad meal of tuna fish and Ritz crackers, she sat in her mother's rocker, staring into the rapidly falling darkness outside on Prospect Street. She berated herself for treating the Klamecks so badly. Their concern was real, their forgiveness genuine. It was shabby to turn down their dinner invitation simply because they had hurt her by not trusting her.

While there was no mirror on the wall, she felt that there was. And the face staring back at her was condemning her for her own selfishness and self pity.

Chapter 34
Christmas day.

Since her parents had died, Christmas Day had not been a day of joy and celebration for Ellen. The simple pleasures of childhood — the anticipation, the smell of the tree, her Mom's baking, her Dad letting her sit on his lap while she enthused over some present — had all been eroded by her parents' absence. She loved being with Trish and Tommy; she was thrilled when Nathan and Carrie were excited about their presents; she enjoyed cooking with Trish and sitting down to a meal of turkey and corn and dressing and all the things their mother used to cook. But, since the accident, everything had taken on a bittersweet hue.

Ellen was convinced that Trish had similar feelings, although they perhaps did not debilitate her as much as they did Ellen. After all, Trish had Tommy and the kids. Ellen had them too, in a way, but it just wasn't the same.

On Christmas morning, she set her alarm clock early and was over at Trish and Tommy's house just about the same time they were being drug into the living room by two excited kids. "Oh, Ellen! Your timing is perfect," said Trish, pulling her into the house and taking her coat. Ellen's clothes were comfortable, but everyone else was still wearing their pajamas. If I lived here, she thought to herself, I'd be in my gown and robe right now.

But the morning was fun. Nathan was over the moon with his bar code reader and Trish had to scold him to get his nose out of the instruction manual and be a part of the family.

Trish and Ellen cooked and Tommy played with Carrie on the floor, helping her give names to all the Fisher Price little people in her new village set. Nathan went off to his room and worked on getting the bar code reader installed until Trish called them all for dinner.

After grace, it seemed like someone had pressed pause on the VCR. Everyone looked around the table at each other, savoring that they were back together again. Ellen wished she could save up that feeling and take it out again whenever she was blue. But then the mood broke and the feeding frenzy began. "I believe," said Tommy between mouthfuls of mashed potatoes and gravy, "That the Murphy girls have outdone themselves. This is the best Christmas dinner yet!" Trish and Ellen both said thank you, but Ellen remembered Christmases long ago and her mother's cooking that couldn't be matched.

"I got the bar code reader working," Nathan confided in Ellen.

"Really? So fast? I always knew you were a genius."

"It wasn't that hard, really. It just kind of sits between the keyboard and the computer. What you read on the bar code is like you had typed it on the keyboard. But I'm already thinking of ways this could really be helpful for Tubby's paper route."

"Like how, Nate?"

"Well, like I could print the invoice number on the bottom of each invoice we mail out. Then, when they send in their payment with the bottom half of the invoice, I could just scan the bar code. The system would then know which invoice it is and whose account should show the payment. All I'd have to do is scan the bar code and type in the amount that was paid."

"That sounds terrific, Ace. Remind me to tell you about BITS Principle number three."

"You found another one?"

"Yup. And it has to do with what you and Tubby are doing. I'll have to look up the exact wording in my notebook, but the idea of grabbing data as you're doing something else is at the heart of it. Just like you're planning — processing payments, and using the bar code reader to simplify the whole operation."

"Cool!" said Nathan, who was promptly distracted by his mother's offer of another serving of dressing.

After the dishes were washed, dried and put away, Ellen said to Trish, "Do you mind if I run over to the Klamecks to wish them a merry Christmas? I was kind of rude to them the other day."

"You rude? El, I can't believe that. You don't have it in you to be rude."

"Well, let's just say they invited me to dinner and I turned them down because they had hurt my feelings." She ended up having to tell Trish about the whole business with Kirby's car being left overnight and the conclusion the Klamecks had jumped to.

Trish laughed. "Oh, that's too much. I was the one who got in trouble. You're the straight arrow. What a hoot that they would think that of you."

"It didn't feel so funny at the time," said Ellen ruefully.

"No, I don't suppose it did. Hey, I tell you what. Why don't we all pile in the car and go visit them. Mr. Klameck sure seems to enjoy Nathan and I think Carrie has Mrs. Klameck wrapped around her little finger. Hey, Tommy," she called. "What say we all go over and visit the Klamecks for a few minutes?"

"Sounds good. I wonder if Mrs. Klameck will be watching the Aloha Bowl."

"I'd like that," said Nathan coming out of his room. "I bet Mr. Klameck would like to hear about my bar code reader."

"I know he would. In fact, he specifically asked for a report after you received it. You see," she whispered, "He and I looked at it before I wrapped it up and put in under the tree for you."

"That's settled, then," said Trish. "Coats, everyone. It's cold outside."

The Klamecks were more than delighted to see them all. They were welcomed in, pressed to partake of tea and cake (with milk for Carrie) and given little gifts. Trish, unbeknownst to Ellen, had brought a gift from the family for the Klamecks, so Ellen rushed across the breezeway and brought her gift to her landlords, a small original watercolor done by a local artist.

The hug between Rika and Ellen spoke volumes; all was forgiven on both sides.

Jonas was extremely impressed with Nathan's bar code reader and quizzed him at some length. At one point, he asked Ellen to recite the third principle. She had to get her notebook to make sure she quoted it correctly.

Principle Three: The business information technology system must be informated so that it requires less effort than equivalent non-technical systems and creates data that is accurate and timely.

Nathan looked at the ceiling for a while as he ingested this. "What's informated mean?" he asked.

"You take that one, Ellen," said Jonas.

"Well, let me see if I get this right. To informate something means to capture data at the same time that you're doing some tasks. So, as you're processing invoice payments for Tubby, the process will be informated because you'll be capturing data about the payment. Or, like I'm hoping to do at work, use a bar code reader to capture data about when the men start working on a certain job."

"Or," added Jonas. "Ellen tells me there is a new gadget at Robinson's Supermarket that captures data at the checkout counter."

"Oh, yeah," said Nathan. "I've seen that when Mom is grocery shopping. That looks neat."

"It is neat," agreed Jonas. "And think, young Nathan, what is happening when that jar of bleu cheese dressing ..."

Nathan made a face.

"My apologies, young man. I seem to recall you having an aversion to bleu cheese dressing. What is happening when that jar of pickles is being scanned by the bar code reader?"

Nathan thought for a moment. "I guess the computer looks up the price, 'cause it's at the checkout counter ..."

"Exactly! That is a process being informated. During the checkout process, the price data is looked up. What else?"

Now Nathan had to think harder. "I don't know. Is it ... does it have something to do with ordering more pickles because they sold one?"

Jonas smiled at Ellen. "I tell you, Ellen. This nephew of yours is quite the thinker. It is a pleasure to talk to him. You're right, young Nathan. We call that inventory. The computer is deducting one jar of pickles from inventory. And when the pickle jars in inventory get too low, Barney Robinson knows he needs to order more pickles."

"I'll have to think about that," said Nathan. "But I kinda get the idea."

"And another thing. Robinsons could start keeping track of what kinds of things are bought together."

"Like chocolate bars, marshmallows and graham crackers?" asked Nathan.

It was Jonas's turn to think. Then he snapped his fingers. "Of course! For s'mores. My goodness. I haven't had one of those in decades. But yes, exactly. Data like that could be very useful information, for example, for laying out the shelf displays. Perhaps putting marshmallows by the graham crackers, even though they aren't crackers, might encourage people to think about s'mores and buy some marshmallows, too."

Jonas stroked his chin and then addressed Ellen. "You know, Ellen. It seems to me that, if Robinsons could assign an account number to each of their customers ..."

"They do have a rack they keep the ledgers for people who buy on account. I bet those have an account number," interjected Nathan.

"I'm sure you're right. But consider this: if almost every customer had an account, and if Robinson's could scan a bar code for that account — maybe off of their account ledger, Nathan — then they would not only know what items are often purchased together, but they would also know who purchases what."

Ellen considered this. "Like Trish buys chocolate milk, but I buy white milk?"

"Exactly. So they could mail a coupon to Trish for chocolate milk and have a reasonably good chance that she'd want to use it. But if they mailed that same coupon to you, Ellen, it would probably be a waste of effort."

"I see what you mean. Marketing could get pretty sophisticated. Still ..." She paused.

"Still what?"

"Well, I'm not sure I'd like Robinson's knowing everything I buy. Seems kind of ... creepy."

Jonas laughed. "I wouldn't worry about it. I'm sure we're a long ways away from Robinsons or any other business tracking what we buy. It is interesting to think about, hypothetically, and, as you say, kind of creepy at the same time."

Rika managed to convince Trish and her brood that they must stay for supper. "It's just leftovers," she demurred. But Ellen knew that Rika's leftovers were better than most people's main course.

After supper, Trish, Tommy, Rika and Carrie played Sorry!, with Carrie sitting on Rika's lap and moving the "piethes" where Rika indicated. Jonas, Nathan and Ellen attempted Scrabble, but Jonas' superior vocabulary blew his competitors out of the water.

When Ellen finally got to her own apartment, had a good hot shower, and was in her nightgown, she sat down in her mother's rocker and realized it had been a better day than she expected. Perhaps she had been dreading Christmas Day. Having Trish and her family helped, but so did the warm welcome of the Klamecks. "I'm not forgetting you, Mom and Dad. I still miss you so bad it hurts," she whispered. "But perhaps I'm finally growing up just a little bit."

Chapter 35

Bar code readers are installed at the Powell factory.

Because Christmas fell on a Sunday, Powell employees got their Christmas Eve and Christmas Day holidays the following Monday and Tuesday. Almost everyone opted to take their New Year's Day holiday on Friday, leaving just Wednesday and Thursday as work days. But most people chose to take those days as vacation days so that they could be off all week.

Because Ellen hadn't earned enough vacation days yet, she went in to work on Wednesday. The plant was mostly deserted, although she did find Whit Collette in his office.

"What are you doing, Whit?" she asked.

"Trying to escape the madness at home," he said with a smile. "The after-Christmas chaos with five daughters is a bit much. I came to work to get some rest!"

"I had no idea you had five kids. How old are your girls?"

"Two, four, seven, ten and thirteen. What they say about the terrible the terrible twos and the fearsome fours … all true."

"Any plans for number six?"

"We'd kind of like a boy, but I believe Mrs. Collette would shoot me first." He smiled. "So what brings you in today? Surely not escaping the after-Christmas madness."

"No, quite the contrary. It was kind of quiet at my apartment and, frankly, I don't have enough vacation time yet to take off the two days. So I thought I'd come on in and do a little more work on bar codes."

"Oh, yeah. How did that bar code reader work out for your nephew?"

"He was thrilled. It worked even better than I had hoped. In fact, it gave me some ideas I want to look into."

"Like what?"

"Remember those log sheets I was trying to get the guys in Fabrication to fill out?"

"The ones where you wanted to get data out of the mainframe so you could compare them?"

"Yes, those are the ones. I was thinking ... what if we could put bar codes on the shop orders like you and I have talked about, and then put one of those bar code readers at each of the machines? Then logging a job would be a simple as scanning the bar code on the shop order."

Whit stretched his legs out in front of him and laced his hands behind his head. "Have a seat," he indicated. Ellen sat in his guest chair. "Let me see if I have this right. If we switched from our current shop order cards to the new feature in SOLUTION/400 that lets us print shop orders on plain paper, and if I could figure out a way to print a bar code on the shop order — and it would only have to be the shop order number, right? — then if we put a bar code reader at each machine, have the guys scan that number when they start each new job, and ... and then we'd have some really good data about the flow of work through the Fabrication shop."

"Yes, exactly."

"That's a lot of ifs," he stated. Ellen nodded, waiting.

"So, let's see ..." Whit was thinking out loud. "We'd need a computer terminal for each of the bar code readers, right?"

"Yes, I thought about that. Even though the bar code readers aren't particularly expensive, getting three more terminals may be prohibitive."

"I think I can help you out there. Come with me." Whit launched himself out of his chair and unlocked a door Ellen hadn't really noticed before in the corner of his office. Inside was a small room lined with shelves containing various kinds of computer equipment.

"What is this place, Whit?"

"Well, it isn't quite the computer graveyard, but I use parts from these to fix other computers and equipment if they break. And I believe ..." He stopped and counted, touching different computer terminals as he went down the row. "Yes, we've got three old terminals that will do. The screens are getting dim, but that isn't the main point. It's the bar code connection that is important, right?"

"I guess so. You mean you have some used terminals we could use out in the shop?"

"Sure do. Interested?"

"And how! Now I just need to get some bar code readers ordered. But, oh ..." She paused as the realization hit her. "I don't actually know how to order something like that, or even if I'm allowed to. I'd buy them myself but ..." Her smile was thin. "Well, let's just say I'm getting on my feet, financially speaking."

"Come with me," said Whit, and Ellen followed him out of the room back into his office. He crouched down under his desk and came up with a familiar looking box.

"Is that ...?" Whit was delighted at the astonishment on her face.

"Yep. When you ordered that one for your nephew and I saw where you were heading with this idea, I thought it would be a good idea to get some bar code readers. After all, I'm the head of MIS. I've got the budget to spend."

"Oh, Whit! You're wonderful! We can try out this one and, if it goes well, maybe expand it to the other two machines?"

Whit held up his hand to stop her and pulled out four more identical boxes.

"You bought five? FIVE? Oh, wow! This is great! I figure we only need three."

"Yeah, I didn't know how many you might be thinking of, and there was a price break if I ordered five." Whit shrugged. "So I did."

"Whit Collette, I could kiss you!"

"But what would Mrs. Collette say?"

"Only kidding, but this is fantastic, Whit. You are so insightful. I can't tell you how grateful I am."

"Aw, shucks, kid. Come on. How about we start doing some testing on how this works. If we're really good, we might even have something to deploy out to the shop before everyone comes back after the first of the year."

They spent the rest of the day, testing the bar code hardware connection, looking at various screens in SOLUTION/400 where the bar code data would be most appropriate, and Whit working on his bar code printing routine. By 5:00 PM, they were well satisfied with what they'd accomplished and agreed to continue their work the following day.

The next day their enthusiasm continued even stronger. By lunch they were close to figuring out a process that would work. As Whit continued to fiddle with his bar code printing routine on several sample shop orders, he would occasionally give Ellen a sample printout to test with the bar code readers. In between, Ellen began typing up a list of the steps that Herb and the others would need to follow.

"Uh oh," said Ellen.

"What uh oh? That doesn't sound good," said Whit.

"As I'm typing up this procedure, I'm realizing several scenarios I hadn't thought of. For example, what if it gets to be 5:00 and the job isn't done yet? We can't just leave the ticket open. It would be as if the press was running all night long, but not producing any parts. We need some kind of transaction to show that a job is partially completed so that they can close down for the night, and then start up again the next morning."

"I think I can help there," said Whit. He showed her a screen in the system that did just what Ellen had envisioned. She tested the bar code reader; it read the shop order number. But the operator had to indicate how many parts had been produced so far. Then the ticket could be reopened later.

"This will work," she said, as she added those optional steps to her document. "And it will help not just at the end of the day. For example, if they have to stop for a shop floor meeting or for some other reason."

"Right you are," said Whit. "Here, try this one," he added, handing her a sheet of paper that came off of the laser printer.

Instead of just scanning the page, Ellen followed her procedure to test it out. She pretended she was operating the laser cutter, the first operation in the sample process Whit had set up. First, she brought up the screen for starting a job in SOLUTION/400. Then she clicked the search button and scanned the bar code off of the shop order Whit had printed. That, she found, brought up the proper shop order and she was able to click the button to start the job. "It works perfectly," she reported to Whit. Then, pretending the job was finished, she simply clicked the finish button. But even as she did so, something was nagging in her mind, something she was forgetting.

"I see it," said Whit, looking at his own computer terminal. "When you said the job was complete, it shows up in the queue for the drill press. Until you did that, it was still in the queue for the laser cutter. This is pretty slick." He punched a few buttons and the laser printer hummed to life, spitting out another shop order. "Now," he said, "Pretend you're the drill press. See if you can start the job and finish it for that work center."

Ellen logged in for work center 103, the vertical drill press. She brought up the same search screen she had a minute ago, but this time as a different machine operator. Again, the scan of the bar code on the shop order brought up the proper work order. She clicked the button to start the job.

"Yes," said Whit. "The status has changed for that shop order from pending to in process." Ellen noted the job as complete. "And now it's gone from the queue," reported Whit. "Just a minute ..." He clicked a few buttons. "And there it is in the next work center's queue, the 117 press." He grinned. "This is going to work! What say we get some lunch to celebrate?"

They grabbed a quick lunch at Fast Ernie's. As they were eating their sandwiches, Ellen had an idea. "Whit, this is a little off the wall, but do you think it would be OK if my nephew Nathan could come to the plant and help us install the computers and bar code readers out on the shop floor? He's a really smart kid, and he's never been inside the plant. Besides, it was really him who got this whole thing rolling."

"Well, kids probably shouldn't be in the factory when it's running. But it isn't running right now, and I know it would mean a lot to him."

"And to me."

"Oh, why not? I like helping kids learn about real work."

"As soon as we get back to the plant I'll call him and go pick him up."

"Why don't we just swing by and pick him up now? Ernie would let you use his phone right quick."

"Good idea!"

After Ellen had called Trish and explained what she wanted to do, everyone was on board. Whit drove to Trish and Tommy's house and Nathan bounced out of the front door, clearly eager for this adventure.

When they got back to the plant, there were three cars in the parking lot: Ellen's Saab, a red Porsche, and a car she didn't recognize.

"Uh oh," said Whit.

"What is it?" asked Ellen.

"That's Mr. Van Winkle's car next to Rob's. That usually isn't a good thing. Let's just quietly go down to my office and leave them alone."

Ellen was relieved, but not surprised, that Nathan took it all in stride. He was just excited to be in the factory and to see all the computer equipment in Whit's office. Whit explained how Ellen's purchase of the bar code reader for him had been the beginnings of an idea to install bar code readers in the factory. Pretty soon they were talking shop, comparing computer models and peripherals. Ellen was only halfway paying attention when she saw Mr. Van Winkle get into the red Porsche. He revved the engine and scattered gravel as he blazed out of the parking lot. A few minutes later, Mr. Powell came out of the plant. If he noticed Whit's car now in the parking lot, he didn't give any indication. He plodded to his car, got in, and drove away at a slower pace than the Porsche had.

"Whew," said Whit. "They're gone. Now maybe we can do what we came for."

Whit had a wheeled trolly onto which they loaded the first computer terminal and bar code reader.

The factory was dark with a few safety lights providing limited illumination. And it was eerily quiet, a big change from the way Ellen was used to seeing it. "There is usually a lot going on here," Ellen told Nathan. "The lights are on, there are lift trucks driving everywhere, welding sparks ..."

"It's really cool," said Nathan. "Thanks, Aunt Ellen, and thanks, Mr. Collette, for letting me at least see inside. I've always wondered what it would be like. And maybe, when I'm older, I can come back and see it in action?"

"I'm sure you can," said Whit. "Right now, let's get this first terminal installed."

Ellen let Nathan be Whit's assistant since Nathan actually knew more about the bar code reader than she did. Whit had brought along a sample shop order and he let Nathan test the reader. It worked as expected. "One down, two to go," said Whit.

By the time they had finished installing and testing the third terminal it was getting on toward 5:00. Ellen looked at her watch. "Oh, Nathan. I need to get you home. Your mom will be looking for you."

As they headed back to the front office, Ellen realized there was a light on in Mr. Powell's office. He must have come back, and had heard the door to the factory close. He came out into the hallway. "What's going on?" he asked, taking in Whit, Ellen and Nathan.

"Oh, hi Mr. Powell. I didn't know you had come back. This is my nephew Nathan. I was just showing him the factory since nobody was here. I hope you don't mind."

"As long as nothing is going on, I guess it's OK." His tone wasn't completely approving, but Nathan stuck his hand out and Mr. Powell shook it. "What are you doing here, Whit?"

"We've been working on a project that Ellen cooked up. I think you'll like it."

"Oh?"

"Ellen has this idea that we need to keep closer tabs on parts as they go through the factory."

"Like the kind of detail we needed to know if we could take the Wilco order," Ellen added.

Mr. Powell looked at her sharply. That Wilco order still was bothering him.

"We've actually just installed some bar code readers in the factory for the press, the laser cutter, and the drill press. Nathan here was a big help. He's a bit of a bar code expert, so we thought it would be good to have him along."

"You did what? Maybe you'd all better come into my office and explain yourselves."

Whit and Ellen sat in the guest chairs. Mr. Powell sat in his big executive chair behind his desk. Nathan hopped up and sat on the credenza.

"Now, start from the beginning." Whit and Ellen took turns explaining the idea of capturing data at the source, of the need for an easy way to get data into the system, of Whit's programming to allow the laser printer to print a bar code on the shop orders, of Ellen's process for the three machine operators. Ellen emphasized that she had a procedure written that she would use for training on Monday when the crew came back to work. She also noted how helpful Nathan had been.

Mr. Powell had the decency to say, "We thank you for your help, young man." Nathan just ducked his head.

Ellen went on to say how valuable the data would be for identifying what new parts Powell Manufacturing could take on.

Mr. Powell listened intently. "That actually sounds good," he said. "I see why this could be helpful. But I have a couple of questions. First, how did you pay for the equipment?"

"I paid for it out of my discretionary budget," said Whit. "The cost was modest, and it seemed to me the benefits could really help us."

"OK, as long as you had it in your budget. That's your call, Whit. Second question: have you run this by Harvey?"

"Uh oh. That's what it was," said Ellen.

"That's what what was?" asked Mr. Powell.

"All day I've felt like I was forgetting something. I thought it had to do with the process, but it was that, in my enthusiasm for getting this done, I forgot to keep Harvey in the loop. That's my error."

"Yes, it is. I don't like people doing something that is going to affect someone else's department without discussing it with them first." Ellen felt his stern eyes focusing on her and her alone. "I'm not sure that Harvey is going to like this. So I'd suggest you be here bright and early Monday morning, Ellen, and see if you can't help him to understand why you're so keen on this."

"Yes, sir," replied Ellen. "I certainly will do that."

Later, over dinner, Ellen enjoyed hearing Nathan recount to his parents the adventures he'd had at the Powell factory that afternoon. But as far as her boss was concerned? "Two steps forward and three steps back," she muttered into her chicken pot pie.

Chapter 36
Bar codes take off in the machine shop.

She'd practiced her speech to Harvey as she slept, as she show-
ered, as she fried an egg and made toast, as she brushed her teeth.
She even picked out clothes that she perceived Harvey would approve
of — sensible shoes, conservative skirt, high collar and a sweater.
She picked her mother's simple pearl earrings. "Wish me luck,
Mom," she whispered. "I'm in kind of a jam."

But Harvey had been remarkably agreeable. Perhaps it was because she started by apologizing and by taking responsibility for what
was done. But what really seemed to win him over was the argument
that collecting data this way would help to make the mainframe computer system have more accurate information they could use to run the
shop more efficiently. "Now that's what we need. This piece of trash
…" — he indicated the computer monitor — "Sure needs something.
And you say it won't take the guys but a few seconds to do?"

"No, sir," she replied. "Would it help if I offered to show you?
With your approval, I need to train Herb, David and Joe Bob in how
to use the bar code reader. You could come with me and we could
show them now, and you could see that we're really not talking about
a significant burden."

"I tell you what, young lady," he said, flourishing his cigar like a
conductor's baton. "You've been straight with me. I'm willing to
give this a go. Let's go talk to the guys." He came around the desk
and held the door open for her.

"Thank you, Harvey. I really appreciate it."

As soon as they were outside of Harvey's office, the sounds and
smells of the factory roared around Ellen. "There's just something
about this," Ellen thought to herself. "Why do I like this so much?"
The sound of a grinding wheel accompanied the scattering of sparks
that sprayed across the aisle in front of her. The liminal thud she
could feel through her shoes told her the press was operating. "Must

be a fairly short m-time job," she calculated to herself, mentally timing the press cycles.

They came to David at the press first, but, as Ellen had intuited, he was busy feeding parts into the press as fast as they would go. "Let's go check with Herb at the laser cutter. David looks busy," she shouted into Harvey's ear. He nodded, not bothering to take out the earplugs he wore to protect his hearing.

Herb was relaxed, watching the laser cutter do its work. By now Ellen knew her parts well enough to know that the laser cutter had quite a bit of work yet to do. Unless there was a problem, the laser cutter was on autopilot right now. It was a good time to talk to Herb.

Herb grinned at her as she and Harvey walked up and said, "What's up, Possum?"

Ellen glanced at Harvey, but he didn't bat an eye. Either he was familiar with the moniker the shop floor guys had pinned on her, or he hadn't heard. Ellen launched into her pitch.

"Herb, I've got something I'd like for you to try ..."

"Like them sheets you had me filling out?"

"Well, sort of. But I think this is way better, and a lot quicker too."

"That's good, Possum. 'Cause I ain't no good at filling out paperwork. Right Harvey? I know how to run the laser cutter, but paperwork ain't my thing."

"I'm going to have to agree with you there, Herb," said Harvey.

"Herb, what I'd like you to do is to use this new computer terminal we installed over the Christmas break ..."

"I been wonderin' about that. David and Joe Bob noticed, too."

"Exactly. We're asking the three of you to do something for us." She showed him how the job cards now had a bar code in the corner. Then she showed him how to scan the code.

"Now that's slick," he said. For Herb, that was high praise. "An' I don't hafta fill out the dad blame form no more?"

"Nope. The bar code reader makes that obsolete. Every time you start a new shop order, I want you to just scan the bar code like I showed you. Think you can do that?"

"I dunno, Possum. Looks pretty tough. I'm not sure a hillbilly like me can figure out how to squeeze the trigger on that there laser gun."

"Oh, Herb, I really think …" And then she caught the twinkle in his eye. It was going to be OK. "Harvey, what do you think? Will this take too much of the men's time?"

"Looks as easy as pie, young lady. Possum." He hid his smile behind his cigar hand, but the crinkles around his eyes gave him away. So he did know about the nick name.

"Now there's one other thing," added Ellen. "When you finish a job, you need to go to this screen here …" She showed him the second screen she and Whit had worked out. "And you need to log the number of pieces you made." She sensed the question in Herb's mind. "The reason we need to do that is that you might come to the end of the shift and not have finished a job, so we need you to record the number of pieces you did finish. Or maybe you get called to a meeting … Does Herb ever call production meetings?" she asked innocently.

"Huh!" was Herb's reply.

"OK, so if you get called away for any reason, just log the number of pieces you finished up to that point." She reviewed. "Scan the bar code when you start each job. Log the number of pieces you finished, either when you finish the job, or if you have to stop work for some reason. Can you do that for me, Herb?"

"I reckon I can, Possum."

"OK, Herb. Thanks. Harvey? Any issues you see?"

"I think you've covered it all. And I'll keep after the men to make sure they do it, right Herb?" He pointed his cigar at Herb's face.

"Yessir," replied Herb. "Anything to make Possum happy."

They had similar results when they caught David waiting for a change of tooling on the press, and with Joe Bob when he was between jobs on the 103 vertical drill.

They headed back to Harvey's office. Once inside, Harvey said, "You handled that well, Ellen. Good job. And I can see why this is important — we need good production data. I'll keep after the men to make sure they do it right."

"Thanks, Harvey. It is an honor to work with you."

"Just one question ..."

"Yes?" Ellen tensed for the other shoe to drop.

"Where did Possum come from?"

Ellen laughed out loud. "I think you had better ask Leonard that one," she said, as she slipped out the door.

As she headed back to her office she passed Mr. Powell's office and saw that he was in. She tapped lightly on the door frame. He looked up.

"Got a second?" she asked.

"Sure," he said. His voice was not laced with the prickliness Ellen had experienced when he had caught her, Whit and Nathan in the shop over the Christmas break. "Have a seat."

"I just wanted to report that I've worked things out with Harvey and that he's being very supportive. He says he sees the need for better data that the bar code readers will bring us. He and I went together and trained Herb, David and Joe Bob and they seem to be on board, too." She took a breath, realizing she was talking too fast in an effort to get it all said. "We'll see how it goes, but I wanted to apologize to you, like I did to Harvey, for not running this by him first."

"Yes, you should have done that. Try to remember that in the future, OK? But, really, Ellen, I've been thinking about what you're doing here and I can see it could have a very beneficial effect for us. The more information we have on how material moves through the factory, the better we'll be able to control it. We'll be able to reduce wasted time and materials, and improve our efficiency. That's always a good thing. So, while I don't approve of the way you went about doing it, I fully support the creative idea behind it and what it can do for Powell Manufacturing."

"I, uh, well, I guess it is a bit early. This may be a great big flop. But we've got to do something to get a handle on what's happening in the shop."

"True enough. To me, in some respects, the shop is like a great big black box. We know what customer orders and raw materials go in the front end, and we know what finished products ship out the back, but we know very little about what happens inside the inscrutable black box that is the factory itself."

"Wow, that's a good image. I hadn't thought about it exactly like that. You've put into words what I've been struggling with. We need to know what goes on there on the shop floor."

Later, in her office, she drew a picture in her notebook of a box with raw materials flowing in, finished products flowing out, and a big question mark on the box. "Trying to open up the black box," she wrote under the illustration.

After lunch there was a knock on her door. It was Mr. Powell. "May I come in?"

"Of course." She had a guest chair in her office. It wasn't nearly as nice as the one in his office, but he sat in it without being prompted.

"I've been thinking about your bar code scheme. Tell me again what we're going to be able to tell from this."

Ellen went over the plan with him, this time in great detail. He stopped her frequently, asking questions to make sure he understood properly. He wanted to know if the system would accept the data from each machine center. He wanted to know if the plan to use bar code readers could be expanded to other parts of the factory. He wanted to know if Ellen would be able to get information out that would tell how much time each individual part took to go through each operation. He wanted know if she would be able to compare the data recorded by the machine operators with the m-time that Sandy McDonald and his engineering department had come up with.

When she had finished the explanation, he said, "OK, I think I've got the picture. And I have to say, this could be very promising. Karl Smithson at Wilco and several of our other customers have been asking about actual run data, not just theoretical data from our engineering team. You see where I'm going with this ..."

"I'm not actually sure that I do."

"If I can go to Karl Smithson and our other customers with actual process data, with data that shows we know exactly how long it takes each part to go through each process, I think we can impress them with our detailed knowledge and, frankly, I think it will win us more contracts."

"That would be good," she said.

"It would be very good," he smiled. "We really need to get some more orders or it will …" He stopped mid-sentence. Ellen saw his hand involuntarily move to his mouth; his fingers to his lips as if he was physically trying to prevent himself from saying more. "Let's just say," he continued, "That it would be very good."

"I'm all for that. I want Powell Manufacturing to succeed."

"I know you do, and I appreciate that more than you know. So let's really get this bar code thing going and going well." He crossed his legs. "What can I do to help?"

"I don't really know that there's anything, Mr. Powell …" It was her turn to pause as she considered the opportunity he was giving her. "Well, you could …"

"Yes?"

"You could tell Harvey Green that you support what we're doing. He seemed to buy in, but it wouldn't hurt for the boss to say so, too. I mean, Mr. Powell, I really did mess up by not talking to Harvey first. And I'm sorry about that. And he does seem to be supportive. But a little extra encouragement from you would help."

"Consider it done. That's a good idea. Now what about the guys that are actually using the bar code readers? Who did you say they were?"

"Herb on the laser cutter, David on the three and a half ton press, and Joe Bob on the vertical drill."

"Right, those three. I'll stop and have a chat with them, too. It won't hurt them to know that someone other than Possum is also watching for their results."

Ellen about fell off of her chair and she realized her face had turned red from her neck to her forehead.

"What?" he said. "You didn't think I knew about that? You're famous around here, Possum."

"Oh my word," Ellen whispered to herself.

"I like it. Kind of cute, kind of feisty, quiet when it needs to be, ready to defend itself if it comes to that." He looked at her in a way she couldn't quite interpret. "Kind of like you." Ellen clenched her hands together in her lap under her desk where he couldn't see them.

"Now, I've got an important question and I don't know how complicated this is. This is really the question I came in here to ask you, but I wanted to make sure I understood all the ins and outs of the bar code deal before I asked it."

Ellen's mouth went dry as she tried her best to look impassive. Trish had always said she was a lousy poker player. She hoped her face wasn't giving her away right now. She couldn't even begin to guess what this crucial question was.

"Have you thought about doing the bar code thing on the assembly line?"

The air whooshed out of Ellen's lungs. OK. That was the question. The assembly line. Her mind started gearing up … that would mean another bar code reader. Whit had two left he hadn't used yet. But wait …

"We'd need to put a bar code reader at the first station on the assembly line."

"I figured that."

"But wouldn't we …" Her mind was racing to connect the dots. "Wouldn't we need to have another one at the end of the assembly line?"

"I hadn't gotten that far in my thinking about it …"

"Because there are two different people who work at station one and whatever is the last station …"

"Usually station nine, although it depends a bit on which product is being assembled."

"So the person who works station nine is not the same person who works station one. The person who starts the production wouldn't be the same person who finished it. So I think we'd need a bar code reader at the end of the assembly line, too."

"I see what you're saying. In the machine shop, the same operator — Herb or David or Joe Bob — starts the job and finishes it."

"Exactly," she affirmed.

"But on the assembly line it is two different people. One in station one and one in station nine."

"That's the way I see it."

"So we need two more bar code devices ..."

"Actually Whit ordered five. He got a price break at five, so we have three in the machine shop right now, and two still in their boxes."

"How perfect is that!" He sat back in his chair, beaming.

"Like it was meant to be," she echoed softly.

"How quickly can you get it set up?" he asked.

"Let me work with Whit. There may be some problem I'm not seeing. But it seems to me that most of the hard work has already been done. Whit already has the bar codes printing on each shop order. And we have the equipment ... oh, I forgot."

"What?"

"We need a computer terminal to connect the bar code readers to. I'm not sure how many spares Whit has."

"Check with him, OK? If he needs one or two, I can use my discretionary budget line to purchase them. I think this is important, don't you?"

"Yes, I think so." Her tone was a little vague, and Mr. Powell picked up on it.

"It *is* important," he said, "Because the new Wilco part is so heavily dependent on the assembly line. If we can control the machine shop, that's one thing. But we really need to get our arms around what's going on with the assembly line. That's where the bulk of the m-time goes for this particular part, so it makes sense to focus especially on that." He paused to make sure she was with him. "Now, just like with Harvey, we need to run this by Kirby before we pull the trigger."

"I can talk to him."

"Are you sure about that?" Suddenly memories of the Christmas party surfaced. She could see Kirby weaving around the dance floor. Mr. Powell knew Kirby had brought her to the party. Who knew how much else he knew. A cassette tape of 'Chelsea Morning' began playing in her head.

She nodded her head once, firmly. "Yes, I'm sure. It is my responsibility to tell him about this, just as it was my responsibility to talk to Harvey."

"Good girl. But if you need my support, just like with the other folks, I'll talk to him and to the people and the assembly line to back you up. Fair enough?"

"Yes, fair enough."

"Alright then. You'll talk to Whit and make sure there aren't any wrinkles with deploying bar codes to the assembly line. If you need help with computer terminals, you come to me. And you'll also prepare Kirby and I guess the people on the assembly line, right?" She nodded. "Meanwhile, I'll go add some support to the guys who are already using bar codes: Harvey and the guys in the machine shop. Does that about cover it?"

"I think so," she said, and her smile was genuine. She realized her hands were no longer on her lap but resting relaxed on her desk as she pulled a pad of paper toward her to make some notes.

"Thanks, Ellen." He stood up to go. "I'm really glad you're here." He started for the door, then turned. "Really glad," he said. "Oh, and there's one more thing."

"Yes?"

"Can you please call me Rob?"

Chapter 37
Kirby agrees to Assembly Line Bar Codes.

Ellen's phone rang. "Ellen Murphy," she said into the receiver.
"Hey, El." It was Trish.
"Trish? Is something wrong?"
Trish laughed. "Why would anything be wrong?"
"It's just that … well, you don't usually call me at work."
"Is that a problem?"
"No, not at all. You just caught me off guard. I was suddenly worried when I heard your voice."
"Nothing's wrong at all. Tommy just said we should celebrate the new year by going out for pizza tonight. We were wondering if you'd like to come along."
"Oh, that would be nice. Sure, I'd love to. What time?"
"You get off work at five, don't you?"
Ellen looked at her watch. It was a quarter to five now. Where had the afternoon gone? After Rob had left her office, she'd gone down to talk to Whit Collette. He was both pleased to have a reason to unbox the other two bar code readers, and that Rob had offered to provide funding for a computer terminal or two if needed. "But, honestly," he said, "We don't really need it. I have several older models that will do just fine. But I'm really pleased to know he is getting behind this project." They'd discussed ins and outs of measuring production in Assembly, and Whit had agreed that two bar code readers, one at the beginning of the line and the other at the end, would be required. They'd explored functions within SOLUTION/400 and had convinced themselves that the same approach would work.

She had then gone out into the factory to look for Kirby. She found him talking to Harvey, which made her approach easier. Harvey had backed her up. "It really doesn't take any time at all to scan the work order, Kirby. You won't lose any productivity, and my guys seem to get a kick out of zapping the job cards." Ellen had explained what they were trying to do and how it would work, with Harvey chiming in occasionally.

Kirby had proved surprisingly difficult to convince. Despite Harvey's assurances, he thought it would disrupt his workers on the assembly line to have to stop and use the bar code reader. When he said he didn't think his team would be able to learn how to do it, Harvey jumped in. "Now Kirby, Herb Coffey on the laser cutter has it figured out. And if Herb can do it, well ..." He let the conclusion hang in the air as Kirby rose to the bait. Assembly line people were smarter than machine shop operators; everybody knew that. If Harvey's machine shop operators could learn this, then surely Kirby's superior assembly line team could. "Besides, Ellen will train them, won't you Possum?" He waved his cigar expansively across the shop seeming to indicate her skill in training hourly employees knew no bounds.

"I just don't think it will be very accurate," protested Kirby. "I mean there's not really an m-time per se on the Assembly line. I kind of think it will be a waste of time."

"It could be," admitted Ellen, trying to see his perspective. "But we won't know if we don't try. Besides, we really need to get our arms around the new Wilco part. It spends a lot of time on the Assembly Line."

"You got that right," groused Kirby. "We should have never taken that part. Too complicated on the Assembly line. We're not set up to deal with those kinds of parts."

"I know Rob was really glad for the business ..."

"Oh, I'm sure he was," said Kirby. "But we still may regret taking the order."

"Please, Kirby," said Ellen. "I'm asking you to allow Whit and me to install two bar code readers, one at station one and one at the end of the assembly line. And I'll train your people how to use the new equipment. We really need the data ..." She wasn't sure what more she could say to strengthen her case.

"I tell you what," said Kirby, looking at Harvey with his eyebrows knit. He turned to Ellen and faced her directly. "If you'll go on another date with me," he said, "I'll let you install that equipment."

"Oh, Kirby, I don't know ..." The last personal interaction she'd had with him was after the Christmas Party. The sound of him retching, of his dinner splattering on the side of the road, was a strong and unpleasant memory. She'd all but decided that she wanted no more to do with him in any kind of romantic sense.

"Simple deal," he said, matter of factly. "A date — and I'll take you somewhere nice — or no dice."

She turned to Harvey for support, but his eyes telegraphed his position clearly: take one for the team. What's one date when this much is at stake, he seemed to be saying.

"Promise it will be somewhere nice?" Kirby's half smile placed his dimple on full display. What could it hurt? They'd had a nice time at the Cork and Cleaver. "I'd be willing to go back to the Cork and Cleaver."

"Deal," said Kirby, sticking out his hand. "We may go to the Cork, but I've got another nice place in mind I think you'd like, too. It is upscale, maybe even nicer than the Cork and Cleaver."

"Deal," repeated Ellen, shaking Kirby's hand. "Whit and I will install the equipment tomorrow and I'll do the training after we get things up and running. Fair enough?"

"Fair enough," he agreed. He held onto her hand longer than necessary. "You're my witness, Harvey," he said.

"I'm your witness," agreed Harvey. To herself, Ellen was wondering what she'd gotten herself in to.

"Ellen, are you there? Hello? El!"

"Oh, sorry, Sis. I was thinking about a conversation I had earlier this afternoon. I've been asked out on another date."

"No kidding! Same guy?"

"Yes, same guy. And he's promised somewhere nice for dinner."

"Tell you what, you tell me all about it over supper. You can come, right?"

"Sure I can come. That'll be fun. What time?"

"Can you be at Gabrielli's by 5:30?"

"I should be able to do that.

"Great, El. The kids will love seeing you. Heck, I'll be glad to see you myself."

The family was already seated in their usual booth by the time Ellen arrived. It was a long booth, big enough to accommodate all five of them, and Trish liked it especially because it was on the front side of the restaurant where she could see who came and went. The booth was divided from the back of the restaurant by a tall half wall on which Mr. Gabrielli had placed various potted plants: schefflera, peace lilies, and vining pothos. Carrie was standing up in the booth as Ellen entered, waving to her excitedly.

"Aunt Ellen, Aunt Ellen," she yelled. "We is over here!"

"I see you are, sweetheart," she replied as she swept the little redhead into her arms for a big hug. "And how are you, Ace? Still bar coding?"

"You bet, Aunt Ellen! That bar code reader was the neatest present ever!"

"That's great, Nathan. And I've got a little bit of news to tell you, too." She turned to Trish and Tommy, snuggled up together on their side of the booth. "And how are you two?"

"We're good, El. I'm glad you could come."

"Me too," said Tommy. "How's the job?"

"Well, going rather well, I think." She took off her coat and hung it on the peg at the edge of the booth. "What I wanted to tell Nathan is that Mr. Powell likes the bar code idea we installed when you were at the factory so much that he wants Mr. Collette and me to install two more on the Assembly line."

"That sounds positive," said Tommy. "Nathan has been telling me more about what you all did last week."

"That's cool!" said Nathan. "I don't suppose there's any chance I could …"

Ellen mussed his hair. "Probably not. You've got school and the plant is back in operation. So I don't think they'd let you in."

"Yeah, you're probably right." His voice betrayed his disappointment. "Still though," he said, brightening. "They liked the idea enough to add some more bar code readers."

"Right you are," said Ellen.

"Who's hungry?" asked Trish. Carrie raised a chubby hand in the air and Nathan proclaimed that he was starved. Ellen hopped up and fetched some menus, just in case. They really didn't need them; the family almost always ordered an extra large pizza to share. But just in case everyone studied their menu. Maybe inspiration might strike.

"The usual?" asked Tommy.

"Extra large pizza, half pepperoni and half grizzly style but hold the anchovies, right?" asked Trish.

"I love peetha!" lisped Carrie. "I love it, love it, love it!"

"I know you do," said the little girl's mother.

"I'll go place the order," announced Tommy. He held up his hand as Ellen opened her purse. "Nope, Ellen. Our treat. It is good to see you again."

"Well thanks, Tommy. I appreciate it."

"Mommy, I gotta potty," announced Carrie.

Trish sighed. "OK, sweetie. Thanks for telling me." She scooted out of the booth and held out her hand to her daughter. "Ellen, we'll be right back."

"Well, I guess it is just you and me, Ace," said Ellen. "What shall we talk about?"

"Have you found any more of those BITS things you were looking for?" asked Nathan.

"Yes, I …" Suddenly a phrase came wafting over the divider between their table and the booth on the other side of the wall. Ellen couldn't see who was speaking, but the words grabbed her attention.

"… Karl Smithson at Wilco." It was a male voice, a fairly ordinary one. But it was the words that made Ellen press her finger to her lips at Nathan. She glanced over the wall with her eyes and Nathan seemed to understand.

Why would someone be talking about Karl Smithson at Wilco here in Gabrielli's Pizzaria? Very few people in Laodicia would have heard of Wilco, let alone Karl Smithson. Ellen knew she shouldn't, but she strained to hear more.

The conversation was hushed, more of a murmur, between two men. Occasionally a phrase would become intelligible: "...I can get that information..." she heard one man say, then "...we won't be surprised again..." Then the other voice spoke: "...can't keep going much longer..." The first voice again: "...someone on the inside who will let us know..." Then: "... we've got an excellent fly on the wall ..." It sounded to Ellen like the plot of a spy novel rather than a conversation in a small-town pizza parlor.

She had just about made up her mind to go around to the other side of the half wall to see who was talking when Tommy returned. "Number 43," he announced, placing the plastic number on the table so the wait staff would know where to bring the pizza. "Shall we go get the drinks, Nathan?"

"Sure, Dad." Ellen smiled to herself. Nathan called Tommy his dad, even though Tommy wasn't his biological father. But in every other way Tommy was Nathan's dad. Raising a boy without a man, without a father figure, wasn't good, and Ellen was so glad for Trish and Nathan that Tommy had come along when he did.

And precocious Carrie had been the result. The child in question was returning to the table with her mother. "I pooped!" announced Carrie for everyone's edification.

"Good for you," said Ellen. "And I'm sure you washed your hands."

"Oh yeth, Aunt Ellen. I did. Mommy thays that is vewy impowtant."

"Mommy is a very wise lady," said Ellen, winking at Trish and Tommy.

"Aren't you the cutest thing?" said a lady who was passing by the booth. She paused to pat Carrie's red tresses.

"Thank you vewy much," said Carrie solemnly.

The lady complimented Trish on raising such a polite daughter and then moved on as their pizza arrived. Ellen watched as Nathan devoured more than his share. "I'm thinking an extra large may not do us much longer, Mr. Thompson," observed Trish. Tommy allowed as how she might be right.

Trish pumped Ellen for information about her upcoming date with Kirby. "There isn't really more to tell," shrugged Ellen as if it wasn't such a big deal.

"But he made a date with you on the condition of you doing that whatever-it-is in his area? I think he really likes you," teased Trish.

"Sounds like a manipulator to me," said Tommy.

"Oh, he's not so bad. Quite good looking, and willing to take me somewhere nice." She didn't tell them about the incident on the side of the road after the Christmas party.

After the last slice of pizza was eaten and the family prepared to leave, Ellen eased around the half wall to see if the two men were still there. But the opposite booth was empty. She spotted a credit card receipt lying on a tray in the booth and was moving in to see if she could pick up a name when the waitress came and scooped it up.

Ellen came back around just as Trish was finishing bundling Carrie up in her coat. "It is very cold outside, sweetheart," she told her daughter. "You need to put on your mittens, too."

It was cold, colder than when they'd first come in. The temperature appeared to be dropping. Ellen said goodbye to her family and headed for her car.

On the short drive over to Prospect Street Ellen wondered what she should do with the information she'd overheard. It had just landed in her lap; she hadn't gone looking for it. Perhaps she should have ignored it. But it seemed so strange to mention Karl Smithson's name. Perhaps she'd misunderstood. But, no, they had also said Wilco. It seemed like something a bit underhanded was going on, but she could't figure it out.

Nor could she figure out what to do with the information. She could do nothing: just sit on the information and tell no-one. But that didn't give her a sense of peace. Somebody was planning something and somebody else needed to know. The question was who?

As she was steering Gunilla into her customary parking place on the street, she saw Rika in the kitchen window. "I need to drop in to say hi anyway," she rationalized.

Her knock on the back door brought Rika scurrying, drying her hands on her apron. She'd been drying dishes. "Oh, Ellen! How wonderful! I'm so glad you stopped by. Have you had supper?"

Ellen explained about the family pizza night at Gabrielli's. "Oh, how nice," said Rika. "I was just about to put the kettle on and I made some *kladdkaka* because it just seemed to be that kind of day. Is it still so cold outside?"

"Yes," said Ellen, taking off her coat and scarf and hanging them on the coat tree. "And getting colder." She reflected how comfortable she felt in this house. The faint whiff of wood smoke from the fireplace, the cheerful candles set here and there, Rika's Swedish red wooden horses in the bookshelf all combined to invite her in.

Jonas came wheeling in from the other room. "Is that Ellen I hear? How very nice. I've been hoping for an update."

"Oh, *älskling*, why don't you and Ellen go into the dining room and I'll bring the tea things and a nice slice of the *kladdkaka* I made this afternoon."

"Have you ever had Rika's *kladdkaka*, Ellen?" He winked at her. "It is not to be missed."

"I'm sure that's true," said Ellen, as she followed him into the dining room.

"You brought your notebook, I see," he remarked.

"I hardly go anywhere without it."

"So how are things at the plant? How is the bar code project coming along?"

"Coming along well, I think. We're just getting started so I don't really have any data yet." She explained about the three machine centers and then told him about Rob's idea about the assembly line.

"Let me make sure I understand about that," said Jonas. "This new part you're producing for Wilco requires a lot of assembly?

What was your term? M-time, was it? The majority of the m-time for this part is on the assembly line?"

"Exactly. So we really need to get a handle on that part of the process, too."

"I couldn't agree more. Do you intend to place bar code readers at each station on the assembly line?"

"I don't follow …"

"As the part moves down the assembly line, do you need to keep track of how long each station on the line takes?"

"Oh, I see. That would be nice …" She looked off into the distance. "That would be really nice, but I'm afraid we only had two spare bar code readers."

"Ah, so you intend to place one at the beginning of the first station and one at the end of the assembly line when the part is complete."

"That's exactly what we're doing! How did you know?"

"It stands to reason, doesn't it? If you're not able to gather data on the finite level of each station, at the very least you can track how much time the part takes as it travels from the beginning to the end of the assembly process."

"That's exactly how Rob — Mr. Powell — thought about it."

"Your Mr. Powell sounds like a very intelligent fellow."

"Oh yes, I think he's quite smart. And he really cares about the company."

"How old would you say he is?" asked Rika, bringing in a tray with a tea pot, mugs, and three plates of an intriguing chocolate something with a dollop of whipped cream and a strawberry on top. "I'm sorry about the strawberries," apologized Rika. "It is hard to get good ones this time of year. Of course in Sweden, we were sensible enough to wait until summer to make desserts with *jordgubbar*." She sat down and poured tea in each of the mugs. "Did you know that, in Swedish, it literally means 'old men of the earth?' Isn't that comical?" She laughed and passed the mugs and the pastry.

"Now," said Jonas, "I expect to see an expression of transfixed delight on your face, my dear, as befits one's first taste of *kladdkaka*."

He picked up a morsel with his fork and Ellen giggled as he closed his eyes, grinned broadly, and rumbled "mmmm" deep in his chest.

"I suppose that was a face of transfixed delight?" she teased, tasting for herself. Her eyes flew open wide and she looked at Rika. "Oh, it is good, Rika. Really, really good!"

"There, you see?" said Jonas. "Did I not tell you?"

Rika beamed and then said, "But you haven't said how old your Mr. Powell is?"

"He's uh … well, I guess he's about my age, a little older."

"Ah ha!" crowed Rika.

"Ah ha, what?"

"Oh, nothing. Only I don't know why I hadn't put it together before now. This Mr. Powell is about the right age to be the son of Harold Powell, wouldn't you say, Jonas?"

"Of course you're right. Harold Powell and I used to be good friends before he passed. And his son — I believe his name was Robbie — was always hanging around. He doted on his father. His mother must still be living, I suppose. Wasn't her name something interesting, Rika? A double name."

"Shelby something."

"That's it. Shelby Lynn. I wonder what became of her after Harold died. And I don't think I've seen young Robbie but just a few times since, oh, since he went off to college."

"His first name is Rob. And he did mention that his father had died some time ago."

"Must be the same fellow," said Jonas, finishing up the last of his dessert. "So he's running things now, eh? And you work there. Well, well."

Their desserts finished, they turned their attention to the warming astringent tea. "Mr. Klameck — Jonas — I'd like to get your advice about something."

"Of course, my dear. What's on your mind?"

"Shall I clear away?" asked Rika.

"Oh no, not at all. In fact you may have some ideas, too. You see, I overheard a snatch of conversation this evening at Gabrielli's that I don't understand. But I think it is important."

"Oh?"

"I heard two men talking. They were in the booth opposite where we all were sitting, but there's a partial wall between the booths, so you can't see across. I heard the words Karl Smithson and Wilco."

"Wilco is in Dayton, isn't it? Why would someone here in Kentucky be talking about Wilco?"

"That's just it. I can't figure it out. And Karl Smithson is in Wilco's purchasing department. He's the one who places the orders with Powell Manufacturing. So it seems to me they had to be talking about something that Wilco would buy."

"More precisely, something that Powell would sell and that Wilco would buy," contributed Rika.

"Possibly, but I suppose there are other manufacturing companies around the area that Wilco purchases from," said Ellen.

"True," said Jonas. "Let's see. I'm sure Allied Products used to sell to Wilco. And I would imagine International Dynamics is a supplier to Wilco. There may be others."

"So we can't assume they were talking about Powell Manufacturing," Rika said.

"Did you hear anything else?" asked Jonas.

"I did. Just little bits of the conversation. It was noisy in Gabrielli's, and the men were talking rather softly. But every once in a while, I'd hear a word or two."

"Like what?"

"That's the trouble. My memory is already fading. I seems like they were talking about getting information. And one man said something about having somebody on the inside — that's what he said: 'on the inside.' 'Like a fly on the wall,' he said. The other man said, 'It can't keep going like this.' And the first man acted like he had been surprised or like something hadn't gone the way he planned. His voice sounded angry. It was like a dialogue out of a spy story or something. I just don't know what it means, or even if it is important."

"I'm not sure what it means, either. It could have been an ordinary business dinner. But it does seem a bit, oh, I don't know, sinister. You're sure you heard correctly?"

"I can't be sure. But that's what I thought I heard. What do you think I should do?"

"I'm not sure there is much you can do. You really don't know anything. You didn't get a look at them, I suppose?"

"No. I tried. As we were leaving, I went around the wall to see who was at the booth, but they had already left. There was a credit card receipt lying on the table." Jonas raised his eyebrows. "But the waitress came and took it off of the table before I could see whose name was on it."

Rika chuckled. "Perhaps if things don't work out at Powell you can become a private detective."

"It is probably nothing," said Ellen. "But it just feels ... off. Like something is up."

"That is your remarkable instinct coming into play," said Jonas. "If your instinct is that something is wrong, it probably is. But you just don't have enough to go on, do you? You can't very well make unfounded accusations."

"No, certainly not. But do you think I ought to alert Rob — Mr. Powell?"

"My advice is not yet." Jonas looked at Rika. "What do your instincts tell you Rika? You're much better at this than I am."

"I think I agree. But I would be watchful. If one thing is off, something else will be, too. You'll know it when you see it. But as for alerting your Mr. Powell, I think it might be premature."

"I agree," said Jonas. "But do keep us posted if you discover anything else. And let me know how the bar code project is coming along. I'm very curious about that." He set down his empty tea mug. "And now, my dear ..."

"Of course, *älskling*. You're tired."

"I'm so sorry," said Ellen. "I've stayed too long."

"Not a bit," said Jonas. "Stay as long as you like. But my dratted limbs seem to wear me out faster than they used to. So if you
don't mind, I'll say goodnight."

Rika started to gather the tea things but Ellen stopped her. "It's
my turn to wash up," she said. "I'll do the tea things while you see to
Jonas. I'll let myself out."

"I will allow this," said Rika. "But only because I consider you
to be family rather than a guest."

Ellen was familiar enough with where things went in Rika's
kitchen that she was able to wash the mugs and plates and silverware
and then put them where they belonged. She could hear the murmur
of voices down the hall as she let herself out, locking the door behind
her. She climbed the stairs to her little garage apartment, pulling her
coat tighter about her. It was cold and getting colder, but the night
was clear and she could see the stars over the tops of the trees. She
shivered as she inserted the key in the lock and let herself in.
"Whew!" she said to no one in particular. "It's cold!"

She checked on her plants. The long winter nights left them a bit
in need of sunshine, but they seemed to be doing well enough.
"Spring will be here sooner than you know," she said to her schefflera. "We just have to be patient."

She went ahead and dressed for bed putting on her puffy house
slippers and robe for extra warmth. She curled up in her mother's
rocker, thinking she might read for a bit to get sleepy. But she ended
up just sitting and thinking.

There was a lot to think about. The conversation she had overheard at Gabrielli's had ominous overtones. But perhaps it meant
nothing. She had had some success at the plant today, getting Harvey
to support her with the bar code readers in the machine shop and helping convince Kirby to let her install the same equipment on the assembly line. And then there was that date that Kirby had extracted in
exchange for it. "Maybe I should have made him work a little harder
for it," she mused out loud. "But he is awfully handsome. A girl
could do much worse. Mom, I wish you were here to talk about it."
She felt the familiar stab of pain, but it wasn't as acute this time. She

did wish her mother was still alive to talk with, but it no longer seemed to immobilize her. "I really am not forgetting you, Mom. And Dad. I'm just trying to come to terms with the fact that I'm on my own now. I think that's what you raised me to be — my own woman. But I sure do miss you." Unbidden she could almost hear her father's voice saying that he was proud of her. The fact that Rob had liked her idea about the bar code system and had expanded it into other areas would have thrilled him. "And Rob doesn't seem to be so mad at me now. I don't like it when he's angry with me."

"And I'm on a quest to find Jonas's five principles," she reminded herself. "Three down, two to go."

She stretched, yawned, and went to turn down the covers of her little built-in bed. "It really is a nice apartment," she said as she crawled under the covers. The sheets were frighteningly cold, almost taking her breath away. But her mother's quilts piled up would warm her soon enough. Before she knew it she was asleep.

Chapter 38
Kirby welches on his date with Ellen.

That week at work, Ellen tried to be patient. "I've promised myself I won't peek at the data we're collecting until we have at least a week's worth," she told Whit Collette.

"Makes sense to me," he replied. "That would be kind of like a gardener who plants potatoes, and then keeps pulling the plants out of the ground to see if any potatoes have grown yet."

Ellen kept herself busy collecting the old style job cards and trying to better understand how processes worked at Powell. She was finding herself consciously looking for Principle Four.

She also found she was growing more adept at spotting the first three principles in action. Gladys' Rolodex, for example. She knew that the Rolodex was a clear violation of Principle Two because it was redundant with the information contained in the mainframe. And, as Jonas had pointed out, the data in the computer system and the data on Gladys' desk did not match, with the result that an order had been shipped to Indianapolis instead of Dayton. A Wilco order at that.

"But Gladys hangs on to that Rolodex like a monkey with a banana," she thought to herself. "I don't see an easy way to convince her that we need to update the mainframe with her data and then use the mainframe as the definitive information about shipping addresses." She had not broached the subject with Rob yet, and she wasn't sure she should.

She got out her notebook and reviewed Principle One: the system must model the business it serves. Whit Collette had sure served the business when he had the right equipment to support the bar code readers. And his work on printing bar codes on the shop orders themselves was wonderful. But in what ways was the mainframe not modeling the way Powell ran its business as well as it could?

She decided she really needed to learn more about how SOLU-TION/400 tracked work on the assembly line.

And perhaps there would even be other ways that bar code technology could be used that she hadn't thought of yet. She looked up Principle Three again. She didn't really have her mind wrapped around what it all meant: The business information technology system must be informated so that it requires less effort than equivalent non-technical systems and creates data that is accurate and timely. The idea of informating a process was still new to her. "Although," she admitted to herself, "What's happening in the machine shop area is an informated process, I suppose."

She worked with Whit Collette to get the bar code readers and the computer terminals ready to install on the assembly line. Kirby still seemed less than pleased, but he stuck by his bargain. He did, however, frequently remind Ellen that she would have to "pay up" soon. He said it loud enough so that people around could hear, and it embarrassed Ellen until she looked into his twinkling green eyes and swooned, ever so slightly, over his dimple. Then it seemed like it was OK. She liked the attention he gave her, that he appreciated the way she looked. His innuendos were harmless enough.

She made a new friend on the Assembly line, a girl named Rachel Hemingway. She was in her late 20s and, based on the absence of a ring, not married. She was tall, pretty, redheaded, and spoke her mind. Ellen found herself growing closer to Rachel who worked in Station One in Assembly and quickly grasped what Ellen was explaining.

"You're trying to make sure that every order that goes down the assembly line gets clocked in," she said.

"That's a really good way of putting it, Rachel," said Ellen. "Yes, we want to make sure every order gets the bar code treatment."

"I can do that. I know I like to get paid. If I don't clock in, I don't get paid, so I reckon this is kind of like that for these parts."

"Spot on, Rachel!"

James who worked as a combination quality inspector and last assembly line station worker wasn't quite so sharp. Ellen had to show him how to read the bar codes several times, and she wasn't sure he really had understood what she meant about reporting the completed quantity, even if it was just because it was quitting time or the team had to attend a meeting. She made a mental note to check back with James frequently just in case he was having trouble.

By the time Friday rolled around, Ellen felt like the bar code readers were really getting in the groove. She promised herself that she would take her first peek at the data on Monday.

Meanwhile, Kirby announced that, because it was Friday, he intended to collect his date with her. "Just like that," she teased. "Without even asking me?"

"Oh, I've already asked you," said Kirby. "And you said yes. Harvey was my witness, remember? Now I've decided that today's the day I'll be collecting. I'll pick you up at 6:00 tonight. Don't keep me waiting!" He winked one gorgeous green eye and flashed his dimple before striding off down the assembly line, leaving Ellen sputtering for a retort.

Ellen ate her lunch in the cafeteria with Annie Angel. She spotted Rachel Hemingway coming in and asked her to join them. Rachel and Annie already knew each other and by the time they were biting into their apples, there was a growing bond between the three women.

"Oh that Kirby," laughed Rachel. "Yeah, he's easy on the eyes. But not too many of the girls take him seriously. He's all the time talking about getting into their panties ..."

"Rachel!" admonished Annie.

"Now, I don't know if he actually does or if that's all big talk. None of the girls I hang out with have, you know ..."

"Well, I promised him I'd go out with him tonight," said Ellen flatly.

"You never!" said Rachel. "Well don't that just take the cake."

"You be careful, girl," said Annie with genuine concern in her voice.

"Oh, I will. I think Kirby's actually more of a talker. I've been out with him a couple of times; he didn't really try anything major."

"It just don't seem fair ..." sighed Rachel.

"What doesn't?" asked Ellen.

"That all the good lookin' ones are also the womanizers. I reck-on their looks give them the big head and they think they're God's gift to women."

"Not Ronnie Dale," said Annie. And that led to a conversation in which Annie extolled the many virtues of her fiancé and the impending nuptials. By the time break was over they had discussed every possible angle from the bridal gown to the flowers to the honeymoon.

That evening Ellen was faced with the same dilemma: what to wear? She almost called Rika to ask for advice. "No," she admonished herself. "You're a big girl now. You can stand on your own two feet and decide what to wear." She ended up selecting the A-line skirt with the nice white blouse with the ruffles. She went bolder with the jewelry this time since the clothes weren't as sophisticated. She rather thought the skirt had a Navajo theme so she chose a chunky necklace and matching dangly earrings with turquoise her father had brought her from a business trip. She pulled her hair back into a pony tail and held it in place with a leather thong that also had a southwestern motif.

She glanced at the clock. Five minutes to 6:00. She looked out the window for Kirby's Mercedes, just in case he was early. At least she was ready on time. He had said, after all, not to keep him waiting.

Her phone rang. She assumed it was Trish, the only person who really ever called her. Had she told Trish about the date with Kirby, she wondered. She'd give her a quick heads up, and then call her when she got home. "Hello?"

"Hey, Baby." It was Kirby. "I'm real sorry to have to do this to you, but something's come up. I'm not going to be able to take you out tonight."

"You're ... not? Is everything OK?"

"Sure Baby. Everything's fine. I just can't make it tonight. I'll let you know when. You still owe me one, right?"

"Uh ... right," she said faintly.

"OK, Ellen. Thanks for understanding." The phone clicked in her ear.

She looked at the clock. 6:02. She sat down in her mother's rocker, smoothing her Navajo skirt and playing with her necklace. Suddenly, the apartment seemed very small. The light was all but gone out the window. There were shadows in the corner by her little built-in bed and under the tiny breakfast nook table. She sighed. She wasn't going to cry, it wasn't worth that. She sighed again and folded her hands in her lap. Maybe she would call Trish, but maybe not. She was embarrassed; she'd been stood up. She felt lifeless, useless, aimless.

She put her hands on the arms of her mother's rocker, almost willing her mother to speak to her through the piece of furniture.

And then it was almost as if she had. Ellen remembered what her mother said when she had complained that there was nothing to do. "There's always something you can do," her mother had told her. "When you don't know what to do, do something for somebody else."

"Thanks, Mom," she whispered. She got up and took off her jewelry and clothes, hanging them up in her little closet and pulling on a sweatshirt and jeans. "Cookies," she said. "Oatmeal cookies for the Klamecks." She started digging around to make sure she had the ingredients. It would use her last egg, but that was OK — she needed to go grocery shopping tomorrow anyway. She'd just have cereal for breakfast.

The cookies went together quickly and she had a couple of trays done in no time. She put them in a pretty basket with a nice cloth, pulled on her coat, and descended the stairs to knock on the Klamecks' door.

"How nice to see you, Ellen," said Rika, answering the door.

"I just made some fresh oatmeal cookies and thought I'd bring you some. I'm not here to intrude."

"Nonsense," said Rika, pulling her into the room. "I was just about to make tea, yes? Jonas!" she called. "We have a visitor!"

"I hope it's Ellen," came a voice from the other room.

"You shouldn't say that, *älskling*. What if it was someone else and they would be hurt because they are not Ellen?" She took Ellen's coat as he came wheeling into the room. "But, of course, it is Ellen. Aren't we fortunate?"

Jonas wheeled across to Ellen and held out his hands to her, taking her cold slender hands in his larger gnarled ones. "I'm always glad to see you, Ellen."

"I've brought fresh cookies," she said.

"What could be better? Rika do you think …"

"We might have some tea?" she finished. "I was just about to put the kettle on. You two settle in and I'll be right back."

Jonas was interested in how the bar code experiment was going. "I don't know yet," confessed Ellen. "We did get the bar code readers installed on the Assembly Line and the key personnel trained. But I'm making myself wait until Monday before I start looking at the data. I have to admit, I'm a little apprehensive. Will the data be useful, or will it be like what I collected off of the hand-written sheets?"

"It will be better than the hand-written sheets," said Jonas. "Because you have informed the process. I like to think in terms of what I call process-effort."

Ellen pulled out her notebook that went everywhere with her, even when she was delivering hot homemade cookies to her landlords.

"Any business process takes effort to complete. A process is where certain inputs are transformed into certain outputs: a plate of steel is transformed into stamped out steel blanks, for example. Or a group of raw parts is assembled on the assembly line into a finished product. But none of these processes happen on their own; they take effort. Effort on the part of the operator of the press that stamps out the steel. Effort on the part of the workers on the assembly line to produce the finished product. If you can capture data in such a way that a process takes even less effort, then you really have something."

"Like at the supermarket," said Ellen. "It is easer to check a customer out by scanning the bar codes on their purchases than it is to hand-enter each item on the cash register."

"Precisely!" said Jonas. "That is a perfect example. Now, Ellen, do you suppose that your hand-written sheets took more effort or less?"

Rika returned with the tea and with Ellen's cookies arranged artfully on a beautiful china plate. She poured tea and handed around cups and saucers, then passed the cookies.

"Oh my," said Jonas, after biting into one. "These are heavenly. She does not make it easy on an old man with a sweet tooth, does she?"

"No, I fear not," said Rika. "But they are very good. And it was so kind of you to bring them," she added. "Now, what were the two of you discussing?"

"I was asking Ellen if she thought filling out a hand-written report sheet took more or less effort than not doing so."

"I've had a chance to think about that," said Ellen. "I suppose it took more. The guys had to stop and fill in the sheet. It wasn't much more, mind you, but I suppose it was a little bit more."

"I imagine you are correct about that. For machine shop workers to stop and fill out a report by hand probably cost them — and I don't mean cost in terms of finances, but in terms of the effort required. It certainly didn't save them any effort like in your grocery store example. So what do you suppose the result would be?"

"I know what the result was. More than half the time they didn't bother to fill out the form at all."

"Even though, as you say, it didn't take much more effort?" Ellen nodded. "Then may I suggest to you that there is an important consideration for Principle Three here: Informating a process is very difficult if you increase the effort required, even if it is just by a little bit."

"I suppose you're right. And now you've got me worried about the bar code process. There's effort there, too."

"Of course there is. But is it more or less than using the hand-written report sheet?"

"Oh, less, for sure. With the hand-written sheets, they had to stop what they are doing, pick up the pencil, write down several columns of data, and then get on with the real work."

"Compare that with the bar code process."

"It is much easer. They simply scan the bar code — pull the trigger on the bar code reader — and they're done."

"So less effort by far than the hand-written sheets, but not without a tiny bit of effort."

"That's right. Do you think they'll do it? Am I going to have anything like complete data on Monday?"

"I don't think we can say one way or another. Human behavior is interesting — and hard to predict. In your favor you have what I call the 'gee whiz' factor. People like using new 'toys' — and the bar code guns will be seen that way. On the down side you have the fact that effort is required. Which side is more important is something I hesitate to predict."

"Could it help that the boss — Mr. Powell — told them how important he thinks it is?"

"Did he do that? That is helpful. It may not be enough, but every little bit helps to tilt the scales in your favor." He reached for another cookie and earned a stern look from his wife. "Ideally, Ellen, you look for ways to informate a process by decreasing the effort of the process. Like at the supermarket. But that isn't always possible. When it isn't, you look for ways to influence human behavior in favor of using the informated process. Giving them new toys — which convey a bit of prestige, bragging rights, if you will — can help. Having the boss support it is another. An even better way is to tie the process to something they care very much about."

"Like what?" Ellen nodded as Rika offered to pour another cup of tea for her.

"Like their paycheck. You're familiar with Hollerith cards?"

"Oh, the punched computer cards that you can feed through a reader so that the computer can interpret them? We used those in college some, but they are beginning to be obsolete now that we have 8 inch diskettes that can hold many cards on one floppy disk medium.

"Exactly. Those cards had their origins in the weaving and textile industry in England as a way to control looms, but it was Herman Hollerith who proposed, in the late 1800s, using the card to store data. Hollerith went on to start a company which merged with several other companies to become, in the 1920s, what we know as IBM today. It was an amazing innovation for its time." He paused to let Rika refill his teacup. "Some years ago, we put in a system at a manufacturing plant where the machine operators were supposed to run a Hollerith card through card readers we installed in the factory when they started each new job."

"Oh, that's a lot like what we're trying to do with the bar code readers."

"Indeed it is. Whether the operator is inserting a Hollerith card in a card reader, or scanning a bar code, the objective is the same — to informate the process. Our experience is similar to what I fear you may find, that people couldn't quite make themselves go to the trouble to remember to read the card as they started each new job."

"What did you do?"

Jonas winked at her. "We tied the readers to their paycheck." He smiled. "They cared about their paychecks, of course, so we turned those bar code readers into time clocks as well. To get paid people had to clock in to work using those same readers."

Ellen had to think about that. "That seems a little ..."

"Manipulative?" asked Jonas.

"Well, yeah. It does, to be honest."

"And I don't disagree with you, my dear. But we were desperate to get the data, and the plant manager is the one who actually suggested it. We didn't really do anything they weren't already doing. They were already clocking in and out; we just changed where and how they were doing it. It made a difference. Oh, that and the performance charts we published."

"Performance charts?"

"Yes. We did it anonymously by machine group, but we published how many hours of work, on the average, each machine group generated per day. We posted the data as a graph on the bulletin board where everyone could see it. It became a bit of a race to see who could generate the most hours."

"I could see how it might have that effect."

"At least in this case it did. There is a caution I'll give you, but that's a story for another day." He rolled back from the table. "You ladies enjoy each other's company. As for me, I think it is about time for me to think about turning in."

"Oh, I've stayed too long again ..."

"Nonsense. Our conversations always invigorate me."

"They do," agreed Rika.

"Let me do the washing up, again," offered Ellen.

"Jonas, would you mind if I talk to Ellen a minute? Then I'll be along."

"Of course, my dear. I'll say goodnight, then." He rolled toward the hallway.

"Goodnight, Jonas," said Ellen. She began gathering the tea things.

"Leave it," said Rika. "It's just a few cups and saucers. I'll do them in the morning. Everything else is already done." Ellen stopped and looked at Rika, puzzled. "Sit down, Ellen. I want to ask you something."

Ellen put down the tea things and sat in her chair.

"If it is not being two impertinent, I would like to know what is going on with you. Just between four eyes."

"What do you mean?" asked Ellen.

"Between four eyes is a Swedish expression. You might say 'just between the two of us.' I can't help but notice that something seems wrong. I am delighted you brought these lovely cookies ..." She indicated just two that had not been eaten. "...but it is unusual, would you not agree? You've never done that before and thus I deduce that something is amiss."

"Oh, Rika ..."

"You do not have to tell me if you do not want to. But it seems to me that you could use a friend and a sympathetic ear."

Suddenly Ellen was telling her about Kirby, how good looking, even sexy, he was, but what kind of reputation he had. And then she told Rika about the concession Kirby had extracted from her for the date and that tonight was the night he had intended to collect on his demand, but that he had canceled at the last minute.

"And how did that make you feel?" asked Rika.

"Well, hurt, I guess. I mean I can't figure out if I really like him or if I just want him to like me because he's, well, because all the girls seem to think he's something, and here he is interested in me. I was kind of looking forward to our date this evening and, well, it made me mad that he canceled so easily."

"Did he say why?"

"Not really. Just that something had come up. Oh, I don't know, Rika. I'm all mixed up."

"Is this the same young man who picked you up the night you wore that lovely black dress?" Ellen nodded. "And the same one who you had to drive home from the company Christmas party because he'd had too much to drink."

"Yes." Her voice was resigned. She realized it didn't sound very good.

"Hmmm," said Rika.

"Hmmm, what?" asked Ellen.

"Nothing. Just hmmm."

"But what should I do?"

It was Rika's turn to ask, "What do you mean?"

"I mean, should I keep on dating him? I had just about decided I wasn't interested in dating him any more. What should I do about this date he says he's going to 'collect' from me?"

"Yes, I don't care for that terminology. Young men should not collect dates from young ladies. They should treat young ladies with respect and care. But I think the heart of the matter, Ellen, is how much you like and care for this young man."

Later, as she was drifting off to sleep in her little built-in bed, Ellen continued to ask herself Rika's question. Did she like Kirby? And how much did she like him? She didn't know the answer.

Chapter 39
Ellen can't get access to the bar code data.

By Thursday morning Ellen was ready to tear her hair out. "Aaargh!" she groused at no one in particular. She went down the hall to Whit's office.

"Whit, I'm stumped!"

"Oh?" He looked up from the computer screen he was looking at.

"I can not for the life of me figure out how to get the bar code data out of SOLUTION/400!" She flopped into Whit's guest chair. "I've been trying since Monday and I give up. Help!"

"Well, let's see what we can find in the manuals." One whole bookshelf in Whit's office was filled with identical three-ring binders, each with a neatly typed label stuck on the spine. Whit ran his fingers across the manuals. "Let's see, now. The bar code readers are entering data into the Operation Process manual and ... oh, here we are. It should be in this one." He pulled the binder off of the shelf and placed it on his desk. He flipped open the manual and found the table of contents, scanning several pages. "Hmmmm ..." he said, tapping his fingers on the desk. He turned to the back of the manual, looking in the index. "Do you remember the actual screen name, Ellen?"

"I thought it was OP130. Or was it OP103? I guess I'm not totally sure."

"Doesn't seem to be here," said Whit. He rolled his wheeled desk chair over to the bookshelf again. "I wonder if it is in the Machine Load module." Again he retrieved a big binder, scanned the table of contents and was forced to go to the index. "Ah," he said. "This might be promising." He turned to a particular page in the manual.

Ellen pulled her chair around so that she could see what Whit was looking at. Whit was scanning the page until he found what he was looking for. "Machine production data is entered through the OP130 screen," he read. "The data is stored in file ML3072, see page 379." Whit dutifully turned to that page. "Ah, this looks right."

Ellen scanned the page. It reminded her of the work she and Nathan had done with the paper route and the cookie recipes. It clearly was a file, containing fields for the work center, the shop order, the quantity produced, the start date and time, the end date and time, and the time elapsed. She almost asked, "What's the subject noun of this file?" but converted her language to more standard terminology. "What is the key field in this file?"

"There really isn't a key," said Whit. "SOLUTION/400 uses mainly VSAM files. Those are flat files with no key. Basically, they can contain any data they want to. But here," he pointed. "These asterisks indicate that the table entries should be unique if they are combined."

"A compound subject," Ellen said under her breath.

"Excuse me?"

"Just some terminology my nephew Nathan came up with. He calls this a compound subject because more than one field combined makes up the key." Whit started to object. "I know, I know. It is a VSAM flat file, so it really doesn't have a key. But for the company to note these four fields with the asterisk, well, that kind of tells us something, doesn't it."

"Yes, I suppose it does," said Whit. "Let's see. I get that the work center — we would call it the machine number — plus the shop order number would be needed to identify a record. But I don't see …"

"Oh, I do. A minor light bulb just went off in my head because of what I've been teaching the guys in the machine shop and on the assembly line. If they're halfway done with a job, they have to report it. Then, when they start up again to finish the job, they have to make another entry. So an order could have more than one work center and shop order number entry, but each with its unique date and time. So, when you put all four together — work center, shop order, start date and start time — then you have the record uniquely identified."

"I'm with you. That makes perfect sense. Now, let's see if there are any report programs that get access to this data." He pulled a third three ring binder from the bottom right shelf and went straight to the index. "I'm looking for ML3072," he said. A moment later he commented, "I don't see any entry for that file. You know what this means?" He looked at Ellen. "It means we have to build a program to extract the data ourselves."

"How hard is that?" Whit shrugged. "Whit, you've already got so much to do. I don't think you should waste any more time on it."

"That bar code data isn't much good if we can't get at it, is it?"

"Well ..." The word hung in the air. The conclusion was obvious. "It gets to me," Ellen added. "It seems like our data is being held hostage inside the computer." Suddenly she had a sense of deja vu. "Whit, didn't we look for something along these lines before Christmas? Before we put in the bar code readers? I'm having this sense that we've done this before."

Whit sighed. "Yeah, Possum, we did. Only then we were looking for work order logs. Pretty close to what we're looking for now, but not exactly the same."

They sat in silence, Whit staring at a page in one of the manuals, Ellen hoping for some kind of divine inspiration.

Then Whit said, "I wonder ..."

"Wonder what?"

"I thought there was a utility ..." He went back to the bookshelf and pulled yet another thick three-ring binder off of the shelf. He skimmed the table of contents, then turned to a page about a third of the way into the document. He scanned a few more pages. "This looks promising, too," he said.

"What does?"

"It looks like there is a way to define a VSAM table so that you can pull data out of it." He looked up at her. "Ever heard of RPG?"

"Uh, no. Oh, wait! Isn't that a programming language? I think they talked about it briefly in one of my classes."

"Yes, that's right. It stands for Report Program Generator. It is a really strange language, but I think it might help us out here. We might be able to use this utility and write an RPG program to extract the data."

"Whit, if you could do that, I would write you a certificate saying you are genius."

"Aw, shucks, Possum."

"No, really, Whit. That would be fantastic."

"Tell you what. Give me some time to read up on this. I used to write some RPG code before I became the guy-who-fixes-everything around here. I'll let you know by the end of the day if I think I can pull something off."

Ellen stood up, restraining herself from hugging him and settling for a nice pat on the arm. "You're saving me once again, Whit. Thank you for anything you can figure out."

"Aw, shucks, Possum. What would the missus say?"

Back in her office, Ellen tried to strategize what she would do if Whit was successful in getting the data out of the system. She was still unhappy about how the data seemed to be locked away inside the computer. The more she thought about it, the more upset she got. "This just isn't right," she said out loud. "A decent system ought to have a way to get information out ..."

She grabbed her notebook and began to write, documenting the shortcomings of the SOLUTION/400 system and identifying the key characteristics of a good information technology system. Her pen paused mid-sentence. She snapped her fingers. "That's it!" she exclaimed. Again, she had said it out loud.

"What is?" asked Rob Powell. She had been concentrating on her work that she hadn't heard him at her office door. "Sounds like you're on to something. Maybe something related to the bar codes?"

"Oh, hi Rob. Yeah, I was just ... well, it is kind of related to the bar codes, in a way."

"How's that coming? Are you getting good information from the bar code readers?"

"Honestly, not yet. How much do you want to know?" asked Ellen.

"Tell me as much as you want to tell me, Ellen." He came in and sat in her guest chair. "I think this is an important project."

So Ellen explained why she had waited a week before she started looking at the data. Then she explained how inaccessible the data appeared to be. "I've looked on every screen in the mainframe I can think of, and I can't find it. So I went and talked to Whit. He did a lot of research in the SOLUTION/400 manuals, and he came to the same conclusion I did — we just can't get at our own data."

"That doesn't seem right."

"It certainly doesn't! So Whit is working on using a special language called RPG that might help us get access to the data. But it really depends on what Whit is able to accomplish. It's making me think maybe I had better learn RPG, too."

"If that's what it takes to get access to the information, you may need to do that. I'm glad we have you — I certainly couldn't learn that RGP stuff." His grin was lopsided, as if to say he was admitting to his own shortcomings, but hoped she wouldn't hold that against him.

"RPG," she corrected.

"OK, RPG. So is that what you were excited about when you said, 'that's it!'?"

It was Ellen's turn to smile sheepishly. "No, it had to do with my notebook." She pulled it toward her. "Have I told you about this notebook?"

"You told me a friend gave it to you. I've noticed you carry it with you most everywhere."

"Yes and he's encouraging me to find what he calls the five principles of business information technology systems. He wants me to document my quest, as he calls it, in the pages of this notebook."

"That sounds important."

"I actually think it is. So far I've found three, and I think today I figured out the fourth one."

"Oh really?" Rob sat forward in his chair.

"Yes. It has to do with getting data out of a system. The third principle has to do with capturing data and getting it into the system

— like we're doing with the bar code readers. I'm thinking that the fourth principle has to do with getting data back out. I was just jotting down some thoughts in my notebook here. Our mainframe system is not very good at allowing us to access our own data. Which is why Whit's doing the research he's doing right now."

"I've never thought SOLUTION/400 was perfect. It has plenty of flaws. But I know we have to have something. We can't run the factory without some kind of system for tracking inventory and orders. But maybe there's something better out there." He paused and pressed his fingertips together, frowning. "But whether or not we could afford to switch is another question."

"Well, it seems to me like switching to a different software system would be a real challenge. It's not just the software, its the …"

"… people, the training." Rob finished her sentence.

"Exactly! New procedures to figure out, new screens to learn."

"Can you imagine the agony Harvey Green would have to go through?"

"I don't know that he would survive …"

"He'd probably quit first," said Rob. "So we're agreed, at least for now. We don't need to replace SOLUTION/400 any time soon."

"It seems like that would be a major undertaking, just because we have a problem getting data out of the system."

"Right. So you and Whit are working on that. And I have every confidence you'll figure it out. You know you're a tiger, Ellen, when you are on the trail of figuring something out. You'll figure this one out, too."

"I don't know …" She knew it sounded lame as soon as she said it.

"Well I do. I know you can do it." He stood up to leave. "And I'll be really interested in the results you find when you do figure out how to get the bar code data back out of the system."

"I'll check with Whit again this afternoon to see how he's coming."

"Thank you, Ellen. Thank you very much."

After he left, Ellen sat staring at her notebook but not really seeing it.

Ellen ate lunch at her desk and then began sketching out what
she would do with the bar code data if she could get her hands on it.
"This may be a complete exercise in futility," she said under her
breath. But thinking through how she would subtract the start time
from the end time to get the number of minutes, and how she would
divide that by the number of pieces produced to get the time per
piece, helped her go another layer deeper in her thinking. She realized that time per piece was the same thing as m-time. She also started thinking about ways to compare the actual data from the bar code
readers with the m-time carried in the mainframe bill of material.
"Since we don't have m-time on a per machine basis, I'll have to take
any times for work centers that don't have bar code readers from the
bill of material. That won't be very accurate. We'll just have to see
… that is, if Whit can access the data."

She was so focused on her work that she didn't realize how late
it had gotten when Whit appeared in her doorway. "Always
working." He shook his head. "You know what they say … all work
and no play turns a possum into road kill. Do you know what time it
is?"

Ellen looked at her watch. After 5:00 already. "Oh, Whit, I'm
sorry. I should have come down to see how you were getting along."

"No problem, Possum. The good news is that I think I'm going
to be able to do it. I had to add some special access methods to
VSAM, but preliminary indications are that I can access the files using RPG. I'll know more tomorrow. Then I'll have to build the program. I assume you'd prefer the data in Lotus 1-2-3 format?"

"I should have thought about that. Yes, it would be nice if I
could get the data in spreadsheet form."

"I'm not sure I can do that. I may have to give it to you in a
simple text file format. Could you handle that?"

"In college I worked with text files a bit. I'd have to know
which columns contained which data."

"Of course. I'll let you know where the data is. Have you ever used dBase?"

"In college, just a little bit."

"That may be the best software for what you're wanting to do. But one step at a time. I'll know more tomorrow."

"Thanks, Whit. You're a genius."

She wrapped up her work and headed home.

Chapter 40
Ellen and Jonas nail down Principle 4.

The weather had turned staggeringly cold. Ellen took off one glove to try to find a weather report on the car radio, but she hastily put it back on. An announcer on WLAP suggested that the temperatures would plunge into the single digits that night. "An arctic blast of cold air will infiltrate the region," he said. "And, folks, we're in for a long one. Temperatures are not predicted to get above freezing all this week."

"Brrr," said Ellen as her mind turned toward thinking about what to fix for supper. On a cold night like this some hot soup would be her preference, but that would take too long to make. "But I'm not sure I can face another peanut butter sandwich. I already had one for lunch."

As she pulled onto Prospect Street in Laodicea, she committed herself to making a grocery list. She would stop by Robinson's Supermarket tomorrow on her way home from work.

Rika waved to her from the kitchen window as Ellen walked up the drive. She motioned for Ellen to come to the door.

"Come in, Ellen. My, it is getting as cold as above the Arctic Circle in Sweden," said Rika. "Would you be willing to have supper with us tonight? Jonas is dying to know about your *rotvälska* — those what do you call those things?"

"Bar code readers?"

"Yes, that's it! How about it? I've made some *ärtsoppa*, traditional Swedish yellow pea soup. We're supposed to have it on Thursdays, but it was so cold, I thought it would taste good tonight."

"That sounds ... interesting. But I'm afraid I don't have much to tell about the bar code readers. I wouldn't want to eat under false pretenses."

"Nonsense! Besides, I've made *pannkakor* for dessert. Come, let me have your coat and you go sit by the fire while I finish in the kitchen."

"Oh, let me help you," said Ellen, hanging her coat on the usual hook by the back door.

"No need. It is almost all ready. You just go warm yourself. Oh, Jonas!" she called. "Ellen is here!"

Ellen sat in the stuffed chair by the fire. It was exactly what she needed: a warm, comfortable chair, the quiet hiss and crack of the fire. She felt the tension draining from her shoulders.

Jonas wheeled in. "Ellen, this is so nice. Rika has made a big pot of *ärtsoppa* for supper."

"So I heard."

Jonas laughed. "Oh, my dear. It may not sound very appealing. In fact," he whispered, "it looks a bit repulsive. But, oh, does it taste good. Warms the body on a cold night like this. The Swedes know what to do with cold weather, that is a fact."

"I'm willing to try it," she replied.

"Good for you. Now tell me all about what you've been discovering with your bar code data."

Before she could respond, Rika came into the kitchen, drying her hands on her apron. "Dinner is ready!"

Rika had lit candles. "To drive away the dark," she said. Each place had been set with a large, flat bowl of a rather unappealing yellowish porridge. There was a covered tureen on the table with a large ladle and a big loaf of bread on a cutting board along with a bread knife. They sat, Rika and Jonas sang the blessing, and Jonas passed a dish that looked like it had grainy, brown mustard in it. "This is senap," he said seriously. "It is an important part of the meal."

"Uh, what is it?" asked Ellen.

"Essentially it is hot mustard," explained Jonas. "Swedes eat it with pea soup. Here, let me show you." He scooped a large spoonful and placed it on the edge of his bowl. "Each person can add as little or as much as he likes. I like a lot." He grinned.

"Yes, Jonas, you do like a lot. Remember when you were consulting with Saab in Trollhättan how you looked forward to Thursdays when they would serve *ärtsoppa* along with big helpings of senap?"

"As I recall, there was a dispenser that looked rather like an udder on a cow. You would step up, grab it like you were going to milk it, and squirt a lovely pile of mustard into your soup."

Ellen delicately tried a small spoonful while they were talking. "Why, this is really good!" she exclaimed.

"Was there ever any doubt?" asked Rika, a twinkle in her eyes. "Now you must try it with a little *senap*."

"Oh, I'm not so sure ..." But she did try some and she found that the bite of the mustard was a wonderful combination with the more bland tasting soup.

"Rika, why do Swedes eat *ärtsoppa* on Thursdays?" asked Jonas.

"I'm not sure anyone really knows. But we do: all across Sweden, on Thursdays, everyone has *ärtsoppa*. It is just what we do." She cut the loaf of bread and offered it around. "Some say that it is from before the Reformation," she continued. "It was a way to fill up before the fast on Friday. I'm not sure I believe that, however."

"I think it is a fine tradition. It is a very democratic thing to eat, too, is it not? Everyone in Sweden, from the king to the lowest janitor, eats *ärtsoppa* on Thursdays, yes?"

"That is correct. No matter who you are or what your occupation, pea soup is the order of the day. Even the Army and the Navy serve pea soup on Thursdays."

"Another reason I like it," said Jonas, polishing off his bowl.

"Would you like some more, *älskling*?"

"I wouldn't say no," said Jonas, winking at Ellen.

"Ellen, how about you?"

"No thank you. I think I'll keep working on this one. It really is good, but I think one bowl will do me."

"You are a very good sport, Ellen," said Rika as she dished up another serving for Jonas. "The truth is that Jonas did not start out liking *ärtsoppa*, but it grew on him. Didn't it my love?"

"Indeed," said Jonas, dishing out more mustard. "Why," he said, indicating the candles, "Do you suppose that Swedes do so much with lighting candles?"

"That is easy," said Rika. "Sweden is so far north that, in the winter time, it gets dark very early. The cheery little lights of the candles help make everything more cozy. Swedes love to entertain in the winter time, inviting their friends over for dinner. And they always light candles. Just like we've invited you over, Ellen."

"It certainly does feel cozy being with you all. I'd like to say that you shouldn't invite me over so much, but I enjoy it so that I can't say that."

"The good news," said Jonas, "Is that the best is yet to come. Because with pea soup always comes ..."

"*Pannkakor*," finished Rika.

"And just what is *pannkakor*?" asked Ellen.

"Pancakes. Swedish pancakes. They are like crêpes, served with jam and loads and loads of whipped cream."

"That sounds yummy."

"Oh, it is," said Jonas. "Just you wait."

"Everyone finished?" asked Rika. "I'll go get *pannkakorna*."

Ignoring Rika's disapproving look, Ellen got up and started clearing the table. She had just finished stacking things by the sink in time for Rika to bring a tray of the thinnest, most delicate pancakes to the table. She indicated to Ellen that she should bring the bowls of a bright red jam and whipped cream.

Ellen watched in fascination as Jonas demonstrated how to place some of the jam — "It is lingonberry jam," said Rika — onto a pancake, smother it with whipped cream, and then fold it up. She suspected that the look of delight that spread over his face as he took his first bite was completely involuntary.

"I don't think I've ever heard of lingonberry jam before," said Ellen, helping herself.

"It is a small berry that grows wild in Sweden. The plant is low to the ground and we Swedes love the taste."

"Count me in," said Ellen, enjoying the tangy sweet taste of the jam on the light pancakes. The candles winked and radiated their cheery light while the thermometer outside continued its downward slide. The house creaked and settled in for a protracted chill. The fire in the other room clunked as another ember dropped through the grate, then whispered of honest heat that kept winter at bay. The mantle clock hypnotically ticked, then struck eight o'clock.

Ellen jumped up to clear away, saying she had stayed too long, but Rika announced that she would make tea. "On a frigid night like this, tea is a requirement. Earl Grey, I think." That was to no one in particular, a simple statement of fact.

"Before you go, Ellen, I really would like to hear how the bar code project is going," said Jonas.

Ellen sat down after taking the dishes to the kitchen. "There isn't much to tell. I've been totally stumped trying to get data out of the system. In fact ..." Suddenly she felt a sense of urgency to discuss what she'd found out with Jonas. "I think I might be on to the fourth principle."

"Oh?"

"Does it have something to do with getting data out of the system?"

"Well done, Ellen. It does, indeed. I knew you could find it." Rika returned with a steeping pot of tea and three delicate cups. "Did I not tell you, Rika, that this one has a sharp mind?"

"You did indeed, Jonas. I never doubted you." She sat down and poured the tea.

"So tell me how you are thinking about the fourth principle," said Jonas.

"Well, I think a good system should make it easy to get data out of the system. The third principle has to do with capturing data and getting it into the system. The fourth principle, I think, should enable you to get data back out."

"Exactly. And why would you want to get data out of the system?"

"Well, because. Because we need to know things, things that will help the business run better, smoother, more profitably."

"What kind of things do you need to know?"

"Well, right now we're trying to figure out if the m-times, the time it takes to manufacture a part, are realistic."

"Because …"

"Because, if they're wrong, we may take on a new product that we don't really have the capacity to produce. On the other hand, we may find that we could actually produce more than we think we can. We just don't know. So many questions!"

"And that is the key word, Ellen. Questions. The reason you need to get data out is so that you can answer critical business questions."

"That makes sense. We have a lot of questions about the m-times in the factory, and the bar code data we're collecting can help us answer those questions."

"Precisely. Ellen, have you ever thought about the difference between data and information?"

"Hmmm." Her brow furrowed as she tried to think about that. "I guess data is … well, just data. But information is something … something you can use. Like, if we could get these questions we have answered, that would be information."

"You nailed it, that is precisely right. In the presence of a question, access to data can be used to answer those questions. When that happens, we call the data information. For example, it is cold outside. Suppose I could provide you with a file containing the high and low temperature for each day for the past five years. That might be interesting data, but it is just data. Now suppose you are a farmer and you are planning to plant corn. What you need to know is the average date in the spring beyond which the temperature is at least 45 degrees. That would be your earliest safe planting date. And that is a question: when can you plant your corn? The data I have could be used to answer that question and provide you with very important information for your farming operation."

"You Americans," Rika laughed. "You say corn when you mean maize — corn is what you call wheat. And 45 degrees? That is blazing hot because you insist on using that odd Fahrenheit scale."

Jonas laughed with her. "Have it your way, my dear. We're planting maize, not corn. And we want the temperature to be above, oh seven degrees celsius. Is that better?"

"Much better. More tea?"

"Yes, please. But Ellen, would you do me the favor of getting a folder for me? It is in the file cabinet, probably in the top drawer, marked Goldratt."

Ellen went and looked. "Goldratt, Eliyahu?" she asked.

"That's the one. I seem to remember some very interesting work …"

"Is that the funny little man who smoked cigars?" asked Rika.

"Indeed. You remember him? We met him in New York. And I've crossed trails with him several times since."

"Was he from Israel? I seem to remember him wearing a yarmulke."

"Yes, a brilliant physicist from Israel who turned his mind to manufacturing problems. His book, 'The Goal,' was a huge success. And now he tells me he is working on a new book." Jonas began paging through the folder. "Ah, here it is. He told me he was working on a book that he is tentatively titling 'The Haystack Syndrome.' It is an allusion to finding a needle in a haystack." He looked up at Ellen. "You'll like his subtitle, Ellen. 'Sifting Information Out of the Data Ocean.' Does that sound like what we're talking about?"

"Yes, it sure does," she said, reaching for her notebook. "But what is the wording of the fourth principle?"

Jonas was lost in thought, scanning handwritten notes in the folder. "What? Oh, sorry. I can see I'm going to have to refamiliarize myself with Goldratt's brilliant theories. The fourth principle. Hmmm, let's see. How would you word it?"

"Uh, maybe 'BITS must allow access to data?'"

"Close, but I think we need to include this idea of information in the wording. How about, 'The Business Information Technology System must encourage access to data in a way that creates information.'"

"Yes, that's much better. Let me get that written down." She wrote in her notebook:

Principle Four: The Business Information System must encourage access to data in a way that creates information.

"I like that," she announced. "Unfortunately SOLUTION/400 does not encourage access. In fact, it discourages it."

"And in an economy based on knowledge, workers need access to information for decision-making more and more."

"That makes sense to me. I'm hoping we have some more opportunities to make some decisions about whether to take on new products or not. But first, I've got to get that data." Jonas looked at her. "So that I can answer our questions and turn that data into information we can use."

Jonas smiled.

Chapter 41
The Wilco order is in jeopardy.

It wasn't until well into the following week that Whit finally came to Ellen and announced, "I think I have some data you can use." Ellen looked up from the RPG manual she had been studying. "I know I suggested giving you data in Lotus 1-2-3 format, but it occurred to me that you're really going to want to match the data from the bar code readers with m-time data. Am I right?"

"Yes, that's what I intend to do anyway. We'll see how good the data is."

"That will mean extracting the data from the bill of material tables as well, won't it?"

The half-smile on Ellen's face was simultaneously apologetic and rueful. "Uh, kinda. Yeah."

"That's kind of what I thought, when I got around to thinking about it. So if I extract the data and give it to you in Lotus 1-2-3 format, you'd have to do ... what?"

"I've actually been thinking about that. I guess I'd have to get the m-time data the same way. But then what would I do? Manually go through each line, looking for a match? I guess I could do that ..."

"But that would be really tedious and prone to human error. I have a different idea."

"I'm all ears."

"You said you had a little bit of RPG experience."

"Yes, in college. Experience is a rather strong word. More like it is something we talked about in one of my classes." She held up the manual that was on her desk for him to see. "But I've been reading up on it."

"Well done. So here's my idea. What if, instead of extracting the data in Lotus 1-2-3 format, you build a program that would match the bar code data with the m-time data."

"Me build a program? Surely you jest."

"I think you can do it, and I'll be glad to help. But the key thing is I have finally figured out how to set up an RPG program so that it can access the bar code data. The SOLUTION/400 people sure didn't make it easy, but, in the end, I was successful."

"So I'll make you out a certificate that says you are a genius, because you are. I will sign it and date it — even frame it."

"No need to frame it, and only on the condition that you sign it 'Possum.'"

"Oh you!" But Ellen was happy. She might actually be able to get at the data. "So how do I get started?"

"Mind if I pull up a chair?" He pulled Ellen's guest chair around to her side of the desk so that they could both see the computer monitor.

Before they knew it, it was almost noon. "We've made some real progress, Ellen. And I think you're really getting the hang of RPG."

"I couldn't have done it without your help. But I'm beginning to see how we could compare the m-time with the actual production data captured with the bar code readers. I don't know what it will tell us, but my instinct says it is going to be important for Powell Manufacturing."

"I agree. Now, what say we take a break and go get some lunch?"

"Sure, that would be good."

"Ever been to Ma Kelly's?"

"Oh, I love that place. Annie and I like to go there."

"Well grab your coat, because it is cold as blue blazes out there."

Whit had just stood up when Kirby stuck his head in the door. "Hello Whit. Hey good lookin'" The greeting to Whit lacked the enthusiasm of Kirby's address to Ellen.

"Oh, hi Kirby."

"I was wondering if I could take you to lunch."

"Oh, I'm sorry. Whit and I had just made plans to go to Ma Kelly's."

"Don't let me spoil the fun for you kids. I'll just get some crackers out of the machine."

"Don't be silly, Whit. We said we were going to lunch, and we will. But would it be OK if Kirby came along, too?"

"Hey, I don't need a pity date," said Kirby.

"Oh, Kirby. It's not a pity date. It's not even a date, for Heaven's sake."

"Wow, you've got a crowd here." It was Annie, joining the other three. Ellen's office was getting a bit tight.

"Hi, Annie. We were just making lunch plans. Thinking about going to Ma Kelly's."

"Ha, girl! I was just coming to ask you if you'd like to go to Ma Kelly's myself."

"Well, then. You should join us," said Ellen. "Right guys? The four of us can go to Ma Kelly's and talk shop. It'll be fun."

Kirby didn't look excited about the prospect, but he tagged along. Whit drove all four of them in his car. Kirby smoothly opened the door for Annie on the front passenger side, forcing Ellen to sit in the back with him. "He planned that," noted Ellen to herself.

Once during the ride, Kirby's hand brushed hers as it lay on her lap. Ellen glanced up at him, but he was staring straight ahead as if nothing had happened.

Everyone at Ma Kelly's was wearing a heavy overcoat because of the cold, which made things even more crowded. But it was fun, as always, and the food was good. The kitchen ladies had made a big pot of chicken and dumplings. Ellen chose that as well as some cooked carrots and fried cornbread. Everyone had sweet tea; it would have been a sacrilege to have anything else, but Kirby got a cup of coffee, too.

Ellen glanced at the graffiti covered walls as they threaded their way through the crowd to find a table. She spotted the "MOM" scrawled above the table where she and Annie had sat the first time they came to Ma Kelly's. She swallowed hard and followed her group to the table where Kirby had staked a claim.

Kirby held the chair for Ellen, then quickly took the one next to her so that Whit and Annie had to sit on the other side. Ellen was against the wall so that she was blocked in by Kirby. His leg brushed against hers, but there was nothing in his eyes that gave away what was happening under the table. Desperate to deflect attention away from herself, away from any hint that she and Kirby were a couple, she blurted out, "Did you all know that Annie is getting married in June?"

"Is that a fact?" said Whit, setting down his glass of tea. "Congratulations, Annie! That's wonderful. Anyone I know?"

"I don't think so," said Annie. "His name is Ronnie Dale Tease. He thinks it's funny, me giving up being an Angel to become a Tease." She grinned and laughed.

"Ha! That's a good one," said Whit.

"I never heard you say Ronnie Dale's last name before, Annie," said Ellen. "Are you kind of worried about giving up your Angel name?"

"Not a bit," said Annie. "I love him, and he loves me. That's good enough. I'll be his Tease for the rest of my life."

"Is he one of the Teases from over Poor Holler way in the southeast corner of Adams County?" asked Whit.

"Why yes, yes he is. His daddy is Elmer Tease. Do you know them?"

"I sure do," said Whit. "Isn't Elmer the one that stirs off sorghum in the fall? I go get a couple of gallons from him every year. He's a good man."

"He is that. And he's right smart to stir off molasses, for sure. Folks all around come to get Elmer Tease's sorghum when he's stirring it off. Ronnie Dale helps him and some day I reckon he'll be squeezin' the cane and boiling it down himself."

"I hope he pays attention to how Elmer does it. Elmer sure has the touch. Is Elmer still using the mule?"

"Old Beck? He sure is! Ronnie Dale has tried to get his daddy to use a tractor to squeeze the cane, but Elmer won't have it. He likes sitting there, feeding the mill, and watching Old Beck go round and round."

"Good for him," said Whit. "Some traditions are worth holding on to."

Ellen put down her fork. "All right, you two. I give up. I have no idea what you are talking about. What's sorghum? And what does a mule have to do with it?"

Annie laughed her merry, unfiltered laugh. "Girl, you need to get out more." She laughed again. "You tell her, Whit. My food's gettin' cold."

"Sorghum is kind of like sugar cane. Sugar cane requires a warmer climate than we have here in Kentucky, but sorghum grows well here. Farmers grow it in a field, then, when the weather turns cool, just before the first frost, they cut the sorghum cane with long knives, strip off the leaves, and bring it to a mill, like the one Elmer has. A mill is basically two rollers mounted close together. By feeding the stalks of cane through the mill, the sorghum juice is squeezed out. It looks green and nasty and you wouldn't think it would ever amount to anything. You ever seen sorghum cane squeezed, Kirby?"

"Nope."

"Well, the rollers can be powered by a tractor motor, but the old fashioned way, the way Elmer does it, is to have a mule that is hooked to a long pole. The mule walks around in a circle and powers the mill. It is quite a sight to see the mule going around and around and the mill operator sitting on a little stool feeding in the stalks of cane, and the green juice oozing out into a barrel."

Annie took up the tale. "You pour that juice into a big pan — a pan as big as this table or even bigger — and you build a fire under it. And if you've got the touch, like Elmer has, you can boil down the juice 'till it gets golden brown and sweet as can be. Do you like molasses, Kirby?"

"Not really."

"Too bad. I just love it!"

"You can't beat it on fresh cat-head biscuits on a cold morning," said Whit.

"OK, I've got to ask that one, too. What is a cat-head biscuit?" asked Ellen.

"You tell, her, Kirby. Your aunt is rumored to make the best ones."

"She does make good biscuits," agreed Kirby. He turned to Ellen. "A cat-head biscuit is formed by hand. You don't roll them out and cut them, like Yankees do. You pinch off a gob of biscuit dough, about as big as the head of a cat, and put in on the pan. Cat-head biscuits are bigger than regular drop biscuits. Aunt Gladys makes them in late May when the strawberries are coming in. We put fresh mashed up strawberries on our cat-head biscuits and it is about the best eating there is."

"My granny used to make a dodger an' ... you know what a dodger is Kirby?" asked Annie.

"Yep," he said.

"Well, I don't," said Whit. "What's a dodger?"

"It's like a biscuit, only much bigger," said Annie. "My granny would make a panful of biscuits. Then she'd take the leftover dough and make it into a dodger on a second pan, about this big around." She indicated the size with her hands. "You can slice a dodger long-ways and put strawberries on it. That's what we used to have instead of shortcake. Biscuits or a dodger with fresh strawberries in the springtime is something special."

"And if you like sorghum — which Kirby doesn't ..." Whit grinned at Kirby to let him know he was just teasing. "A cat-head biscuit with sorghum and butter is just the thing in the fall or the winter."

"Is there a recipe I can get?" asked Ellen. "I'd like to try to make biscuits like that."

"Girl, you don't need no recipe. You just gotta practice. Tell you what, I'll come over to your place some Saturday and we'll make us a batch. Deal?"

"Deal only if I get to come along," said Kirby.

"I'll be bringing sorghum," said Annie. "And we know you don't like sorghum."

"How about some hot maple syrup?" he asked.

"Nope," said Annie. "That ain't traditional. I don't know why you're so all fired keen to try my biscuits." She glanced at Ellen. "Well, now that I think about it, I believe I do know why you're so interested."

"I make no apologies," said Kirby. "Ellen's my girl and I don't care who knows it." Ellen could feel the flush going up her cheeks. She didn't know what to say. Whit raised his eyebrows in an unspoken question. Ellen wanted to protest, but seemed unable to speak. She lowered her eyes to her plate. What had looked delicious before now appeared unappetizing.

"Did you all know," Kirby continued, "that Ellen owes me a date?"

"Oh?" said Whit.

"Yes. We made a deal. In order for her to put those ray gun things on the assembly line, she had to agree to go on a date with me." He grinned, letting them all know he had the upper hand. "Harvey was our witness, wasn't he, Babe?"

"You promised it would be somewhere nice." That was all Ellen could find to say.

"Sure, sure. Real nice," said Kirby.

"And you've already stood me up once," said Ellen. Both Whit and Annie's eyebrows went up. What was their problem? It was just a date, right?

"Oh, Babe. You understand. Something just came up. It couldn't be helped." Kirby wasn't conceding any ground. He was still in charge. "I tell you what. I'll collect that date from you a week from Friday. I'll take you somewhere real nice, too. I promise."

"Well ..."

"Oh, come on, Ellen. A deal is a deal. You know you owe me."

"I guess. OK. Six o'clock?"

"Six o'clock. Don't make me wait." He grinned, going into full dimple mode. Annie looked at Ellen. It was a look that Ellen couldn't quite read.

Ellen spent the rest of the afternoon compiling RPG programs, looking up error codes in the manuals Whit had let her borrow, feeling an adrenaline rush as she figured out some detail and despair when she was stumped.

Just before 5:00 PM her phone rang.

"Ellen Murphy."

"Ellen, its Rob. Can you come down to my office?"

"Now? I mean, sure, I'll be right there."

Butch and Sandy were in Rob's office when she arrived. She started to make a smart comment about "deja vu all over again" but decided against it. Rob's face was serious.

"I've called the team back together," he said, "Because I've had a call from Karl Smithson at Wilco."

"I take it that it isn't good news," said Sandy.

"No. No, it darn well isn't." Rob's face was flushed and, from where she sat, Ellen could see his hands in his lap. His fists were clenched as if he were desperately trying to hold onto something. Maybe his temper. "Karl says one of our competitors — he wouldn't say who — has offered to produce that new part cheaper than us." The tips of his ears were getting red. Ellen silently sent him calming thoughts. Without warning, Rob's fists whipped out of his lap and banged on the desk. Ellen jumped and Sandy's eyebrows went up.

"Did he say how much cheaper?" asked Sandy.

"No, he didn't. It must be enough to make Karl be willing to go through initial runs and quality testing with a new vendor."

"We can figure this out, Rob," said Ellen quietly. She was hoping to calm him down a bit. "Has Wilco already made a decision to switch, or do we have a chance to keep the business?"

"I guess we still have a chance. But it just frosts me, it absolutely frosts me to think about how somebody could …" He sighed. "Karl says it's just business, and I guess it is. Still …" The words hung in the air like the exhaled fog of tobacco smoke from Harvey's cigar.

"Did you get the feeling that our competitor — whoever the sons of guns are — know more than they should? Like, do they know our pricing and are undercutting us unfairly?"

"I just don't know. Could be. It seems so strange. It is like somebody knows too much." He looked up at Ellen.

Uh oh, she thought to herself. Here it comes.

"We need to be really, really sure and not involve anyone else in this," said Rob. He was still looking at her. "Is that clear?"

"Sure," said Sandy. And Ellen and Butch voiced their agreement, too.

"What I'd like the three of you to do is to go over the numbers again and see if there is any way we can reduce our price. I hate to, for two reasons. One, we need the margin we're getting on this order. And two, I just don't like … well, it's the principle of the thing. We ought to be quoting fair and accurate pricing to our customers from the start, and not have to be forced into price concessions like a used car salesman." He raised his clenched hands and rested his chin on them, his elbows on his desk.

He looks thoroughly dejected, thought Ellen. "We can certainly go over the numbers again, can't we guys?" Sandy and Butch both nodded. "And I've got that bar code data that may tell me something I missed."

"And I heard you, Boss, about keeping this to ourselves," said Butch. "But we'll have to involve Kirby if we're going to go over this again. I thought his assembly line timings were a bit padded. I think that's a place we can look for some savings."

"You're right, of course," sighed Rob. "But please, let's keep it to the absolute minimum." He looked at Ellen again. "It just feels like our competition knows too much."

"How much time do we have?" asked Sandy, eyeing the clock on Rob's credenza that read 5:08.

"Karl said he'd like to have a response from us by close of business on Friday. What's today? Wednesday. So that gives us less than two days."

"You want we should stay this evening?"

"No." Rob took off his glasses, pinched the bridge of his nose and sighed. "No. Why don't you all go home and get some rest." He rubbed his temples. "We'll be fresher in the morning when we can think."

"That sounds like a good plan," said Sandy.

"We'll work on it first thing, Boss," said Butch. "I'll go out and work with Kirby as soon as the shift starts tomorrow morning."

"Thanks, Butch. I know you will."

"And I'll be reviewing the data from the bar code readers."

"Good, Ellen. You do that. And Sandy, do you think there's any chance that purchasing can negotiate better pricing on the raw materials?"

"I'm not optimistic," said Sandy. "It is worth a try, but I don't think we want to actually change sources to something cheaper. That might impact quality."

Rob stood up. "You're right, of course. OK, folks. Operation Silk Stockings, phase two, begins now."

Ellen went back to her office, determined to get a first report out of the RPG program she was working on before she went home.

She was still working when Rob entered her office. "Haven't you gone home yet? I thought I made it clear that you didn't have to stay tonight."

She looked up just as yet another compile completed — but only two errors this time. She was making progress!

"Yes, I know what you said. But I really want to make sure I have some data to look at tomorrow first thing. I'm so close." She pointed to the screen. "Only two errors in the compile. I'm getting close!"

"You are a real tiger, aren't you? Well, suit yourself. But don't stay too late. It's already 6:30." He turned to go, then turned back again. "Say, you wouldn't like to grab a quick bite to eat somewhere and then come back to finish up, would you. It might help if you took a break."

"Why, thanks. That's very nice. But I really think I'm close to being done."

"No problem. Goodnight, Ellen."

He turned and was gone. Suddenly the office seemed very quiet and Ellen almost wished she'd taken Rob up on his offer.

But, 45 minutes later, Ellen had a clean compile and the RPG program was running. She went down to Whit's office in time to hear the familiar "splat, splat, splat" of the 1403 printer pulling green bar paper through and the characters being pressed onto the page, one whole line at a time.

She tore off the report and glanced at it. She knew what she was going to be looking at this evening. But she would do it in sweat pants and an old sweater, not here at work. And she'd do it after dinner.

She closed the front door, listening for the click that meant it was locked. The wind was picking up, making it even colder as she trudged across the parking lot to Gunilla. She laid the green bar report on the passenger seat along with her purse and started the car.

"Good car," she said, as she patted the dash board. "The heated seats in a Saab sure are nice on a night like this."

Chapter 42
Ellen works on her bar code data.

Ellen was usually a creature of habit. After work she would change into more comfortable clothes and fix herself some dinner. Admittedly cooking for one was rather dull, so the meals were, by her own admission, uninspiring. She always washed the dishes immediately after eating so that they wouldn't be left for later. She also fixed her lunch for the following day, placing it in the Tupperware lunchbox Trish had given her and storing it in the refrigerator. After supper she had a weekly routine. Monday she went out to the Tie-D-Wash laundromat and washed clothes. Tuesday was business night. If there was a checkbook statement to balance, she would take care of that. If there were any bills to pay, she would do that, too. She also watered her plants. Wednesday she cleaned the apartment, except for the bathroom. Thursday was reserved for cleaning the bathroom. Her thinking was that a clean bathroom on Thursday was preparation for Friday, when there might be a reason to go out with Kirby or get together with Trish and Tommy and the kids.

After the task of the evening, she would often read until she got sleepy and then head for bed, usually by 9:30 or 10:00. The alarm clock rang early for her workdays at Powell.

Today was Wednesday, the day for cleaning the apartment. After supper — leftover lasagne from Monday — she looked around and decided the apartment could wait. She had a vague sense of unrest, in need of a change.

She sat down in her mother's chair and looked around. The apartment looked clean enough. "I know, Mom." She looked at her mother's picture. "Have a schedule and stick with it. But it doesn't really need cleaning."

She had come to love this little nook above the garage, above the trees. The blonde wood of the built-in furniture was so different from what she was used to. But it seemed light and uplifting, not heavy and dark. She loved the way her little bed was built into the wall with the drawer space underneath. She loved the window nook with its cushions, and the schefflera in the big pot on the floor as well as the peace lilies that were actually blooming on the built-in table. She sighed. She did love it here, yet there was a sense of ennui that lurked in the dark corners and threatened to grow.

She couldn't quite bring herself to take it out and look at it, whatever it was. She decided instead to take a shower, an unusual choice. Showers were for mornings when she was getting ready for work. Yet tonight the thought of humidity and warmth called to her. The hot jets of water on her back eased the tense muscles and warmed her against the frigid temperature outside. She washed her hair and toweled it dry, winding her mane up in a towel and wrapping her thick terrycloth robe around her.

It was dark and cold outside and she remembered Jonas's remarks about candles. "Candles would be nice," she said to herself. She lit the three tapers in the candle holder on her table as well as a pillar on the kitchen counter and one on the night stand by her bed.

She sat down at the little table and pulled out the green bar report she had retrieved from the printer just before leaving Powell that afternoon. She had sorted the report by work center, then by part number, so all of the similar parts were together. She had added a calculation to subtract the start time from the end time to get an elapsed number of minutes. She had also divided the elapsed minutes by the number of parts produced to show what the real m-time was.

As she poured over the report, some patterns began to appear. Time on the 103 vertical drill were extremely consistent. Some parts took twice, or even three times as long as others, but the factor of doubling or tripling was very consistent. "I suppose these parts have two holes or three holes to drill," she said out loud. "Make a note of that, Ellen."

The 117 press was not quite as consistent, and there weren't any multiples of two or three that she could find. Ellen tried using a calculator to compute the average m-time. The variance for each bar code transaction was relatively small.

The Assembly Line data was a different story. Where both the vertical drill and the press were relatively consistent, the Assembly Line data was all over the place. Ellen started noting the high and the low for each part number. Some part numbers varied by as much as 45 minutes. One part might take 18 minutes to produce, where that same part, on a different day or a different run could take an hour and a half. She'd need to get the Engineering m-times for these parts from Butch tomorrow. She also wanted to check with Kirby to see if he had an explanation for the wide variance of times on the Assembly Line.

"This calls for the notebook," she said to the empty room. She got it from under her purse and wrote notes to herself:

1. Check on vertical drill multiples. Are they related to the number of holes drilled?

2. Get Engineering's m-times for all parts listed (from mainframe? ask Butch?)

3. Compare average m-times from bar code data with m-times from Engineering. Make a spreadsheet?

4. Ask Kirby if he understands why Assembly part times vary so widely.

She put her pencil down and gave in to daydreams about Kirby.

He certainly was handsome. That dimple of his. And his easy smile, his careless charm. And don't forget, she reminded herself, he's a really good dancer. He'd made her look good at the Christmas party, even if he had kept bringing her all those drinks. Rob was a good dancer, too, she reminded herself. He was just … different. Rob was serious, even sophisticated. Kirby was fun, lots of laughs, always ready for good time. You could count on Kirby. With Kirby you knew what to expect. Well, sort of. She had begun to think that, despite his charm and good looks, she didn't much care for him. But she found herself changing her mind. In a way she knew that Rachel

Hemingway was right — Kirby did kind of have a one-track mind, especially when it came to women. But at least he was consistent. He didn't lose his temper. He just …

She thought about their upcoming date. What was he planning? Where was he planning on taking her? He was always a bit enigmatic, like he was going to get her into some situation that might be a little outside of her comfort zone. But that was part of the allure, the magic which was Kirby. Who would have ever thought she, Ellen Murphy, would be riding on the back of a motorcycle in a short skirt in freezing weather to go to a … a tractor pull? Or driving home his plush Mercedes because Kirby had gotten sick on the side of the road and getting in trouble with her landlords? With Kirby you never knew, yet you always knew. He'd be charming, he'd be a flirt, he'd probably make a pass, or two or three.

She swallowed and dared to ask herself: is that what you want? Do you want a man like Kirby? Do you want the excitement, the thrill, the buzz that came from flying in Kirby's circle, being drawn to his burning light and feeling its heat and attraction?

She heard footsteps on the stairs outside the door, followed by a tap on the door. Ellen got up. It was Rika. "Rika, how nice to see you. Is everything all right? Please excuse my appearance." She pulled the towel from her hair and felt it. Not too damp.

"Oh yes. Everything is fine. Jonas had a bit of an upset stomach, so he went to bed early. I wasn't quite ready for bed yet, so I thought I would bring you these and see if you might be up for a cup of coffee or some tea." She handed Ellen a tray of rectangular cookies.

"I certainly would. I'll put the kettle on. What are these delicious looking things?"

"A simple Swedish butter cookie. I was feeling a bit bored and you know me. Cooking is like therapy to me."

"I love your therapy. Although my waistline sometimes doesn't!" Ellen got out the tea things and put some milk in a little pitcher. "Please, sit down. The water will be ready soon."

Rika sat. "Ellen, do you have a hair brush?"

"Yes, of course. Do you need one?"

Rika laughed. "Not for me. For you! Would it embarrass you if I offered to brush out your hair?"

"I ... er. I can brush my own hair out. But is that something you ... you want to do?"

"I would love to. I used to brush my daughter's hair ..."

"You have a daughter?" The tea kettle began its piercing whistle. Ellen rushed over to take it off of the stove and to put the water into the teapot with the teabags. She made sure she had everything: cups, saucers, spoons, sugar, milk, and Rika's Swedish cookies. She brought them to the table. There was pain on Rika's face and Ellen waited.

"Yes," she finally said. "I had a daughter. We had a daughter. She had beautiful hair, long and blonde. I used to brush her hair each night before I read her a story."

Ellen poured the tea, waiting.

"She was our world, Jonas's and mine. And then she died."

Ellen almost dropped her cup into the saucer. "She ... died?"

"Yes." Rika suddenly looked very tired. In the candlelight there appeared to be dark circles under her eyes. The angle of the flickering lights emphasized her wrinkles.

"Oh, Rika. I'm so sorry. You seem ... tired." Suddenly she stood up and went around behind Rika's chair. She began to massage her neck and shoulders.

"Ahh, Ellen. That feels so good." In the mirror by the door Ellen could see her close her eyes. Ellen kept kneading her tense trapezius muscles.

"Yes. She died. When she was seven. Of spinal meningitis. And we were never able to have any more children." Rika sniffed. "I don't know why I'm telling you this."

"You don't have to," said Ellen quietly. "But I'll listen if you want to tell me about it."

"There isn't much to tell. She was a happy, active child and then, within a week, she was gone. Jonas and I went through a very dark time. But it was in that valley of death that we found the Lord.

Or maybe He found us. In the end we finally came out the other side, stronger, more devoted to each other than ever." She sighed and Ellen felt the tension in her knotted muscles beginning to relax. "We tried to have more children. I love children. And Jonas adores them. But it never happened. The useless doctors could never explain what was wrong. We finally had to accept this and move on. Jonas became a consultant well known in the US and throughout the world. I became his cheering section, his biggest fan and supporter."

"I'm so sorry, Rika. What was your daughter's name?"

"Ellinor. Very similar to your name."

Ellen was still, taking in this knowledge, feeling Rika's pain through her hands resting on her shoulders. "I didn't know."

"No, of course you didn't. And I've depressed you. I am sorry. Please, come sit down and drink your tea before it gets cold." She shrugged her shoulders experimentally. "*Åh*, you have *magiska fingrar*, magic fingers." She cocked her head from side to side. "Oh, that feels so much better. Thank you, Ellen." She nudged a cookie towards Ellen. "And when we finish our tea, I would very much like to brush out your hair, if you will let me."

The rafters of the garage groaned as the temperature outside continued to drop. The stiff magnolia leaves rattled in the wind. Yet inside the companionship between the two women, one younger, one older, was palpable. They drank their tea and Rika told Ellen about Ellinor, simple stories of a mother and daughter. Ellen listened intently, noting the glow of the candle coming from the night stand through the bedroom door and how it seemed to illuminate a circle around Rika's head.

Suddenly Rika clapped her hands lightly together. "Enough story telling. Your hair needs to be brushed or it will go, how do you say it, frizzy. Where is your brush?" Ellen retrieved it from her dresser and sat on the floor in front of her mother's rocker while Rika sat in the rocker and brushed out Ellen's hair with slow, rhythmic strokes.

They sat in silence for some time, until Ellen said, "Rika?"

"Yes, Ellen?"

"How did Jonas lose the use of his legs?"

The cadence of Rika's brush paused, then resumed. "I am not sure that I should tell you."

"Oh, I am sorry. I shouldn't have asked that. It is too personal."

"No, my child. It is not personal to me. I am not sure that I should tell you because it involves you."

"Me??"

"Yes, you. Do you really want to know?" Suddenly Ellen's heart was filled with dread. The shadows in the corners loomed large, threatening to overpower her. The ennui she had felt earlier became full of foreboding. Her unrest ripened into the first flickers of fear.

"Maybe I don't want to know."

"I think perhaps, since you asked, that you are ready to know. You are stronger than you think, you know. Much stronger."

"I don't feel strong. But now I don't think I can not know."

"*Precis så*. Exactly so. I think the time has come for you to know. It was many years ago, near Christmas time. A group of us were going to a party in Lexington."

"Oh no, Rika. Not that ..."

"Yes, I'm afraid so, dear Ellen. The same accident, the same drunk driver that killed your parents destroyed my Jonas's ability to walk."

Ellen suddenly flung her head into Rika lap, wracked with sobs. Images of her mother, her father slid through her mind. Conjured up pictures, images she had never seen but that had been built up in her subconscious in the days, the weeks, the months, even the years that followed the accident, inserted themselves behind her closed eyes. She saw visions of flashing red lights, of mangled metal, of her parents' bodies being pried loose from the wreckage and being placed on stretchers to go, not to the hospital but to the morgue. Her mind was like a tape recorder playing the same scenes over and over and over. She couldn't stop the tape from playing. She would try to reach out and press the pause button, but the images kept playing out. She clutched Rika's skirt with a desperate ache that was always there, but rarely seen.

"There, there, child." Rika stroked her hair. "There, there." There was a raspy quality to Rika's voice, and Ellen knew, without seeing, that she was crying, too.

"Oh, Rika. I am so, so sorry. Sorry for Jonas, sorry for my parents. Sorry for me. Sorry about Ellinor. I'm just ... sorry."

"As am I." She paused, and then said quietly, "No, not sorry. Sad. It wasn't my fault, it wasn't your fault. We have nothing to be sorry for, even though we're sorry these things happened. I am sad more than sorry."

Ellen raised her head from Rika's lap and looked up at her. Her eyes were red and there were tear traces down her cheeks. "Why did it have to happen?"

"That I do not know. I take great comfort from knowing that the Lord is in control, even though there are times when I have a hard time understanding it. I know He loves me, and He loves me through the pain. He doesn't take the pain away, He shows me He is with me IN the pain. Am I sad? Yes. Is it good to cry sometimes? Yes. Is it good to have a dear friend to cry with? A thousand times yes." She cupped Ellens chin in her hand and raised her face so that they were looking directly into each other's eyes. "I am grateful for you Ellen. You are a treasured friend to me. I know for a certainty that one of the best gifts God gave us this side of Heaven is true and abiding love for each other. Thank you." She bent and kissed Ellen on the forehead.

"And now," said Rika. "I must go. I need to check on Jonas. And you must go to bed for you have a work day tomorrow, do you not?" Ellen stood and offered her hand to Rika. She took it and Ellen helped her up.

"I don't want you to go," said Ellen.

"Nor do I. But we all have our duties to perform. You will work. I will see to my husband. But ..." She suddenly pulled Ellen into a full embrace. Ellen realized how much she craved physical touch like this, a touch that was based on — what had Rika called it — a true and abiding love. "I thank you for this evening. You have helped me more than you can know."

Later, lying in bed and looking up at the shadowed photographs of her parents on the wall, her attention was drawn to the window. The moon must almost be full, she thought, for there was a light outside that seemed brighter than a street light. She found herself praying in a way that was different and strange and strangely comforting. "Lord, if you're there, help me to understand. And help me to be a better friend. And please take care of Jonas and Rika."

During the middle of the night Ellen woke up, dreaming that the flashing red lights of her vision were in the room with her. She fought off the fear that was like a tangible force swirling around her bed, turned her face to the wall, and tried to go back to sleep.

Chapter 43
Something is wrong with the Assembly times.

Before she had taken off her coat the next morning, Butch was in her office wanting to talk about the Wilco order. "I don't get it," he said. "I've been over the assembly times again and again. I think Kirby is sandbagging us. It shouldn't be taking that long to build this new Wilco part."

"I'm glad you stopped by, Butch. Let me show you what I've been doing." She pulled off her coat and pointed to the report she had generated with her RPG program. "These are all the actual times from the bar code readers ..."

Butch took the report from her hands. Ellen started to protest, but let him absorb what he was looking at. "Could we look this over together and you tell me where I've made incorrect assumptions?"

"Huh? Oh, sorry." Butch looked a bit sheepish. "This is great stuff. We've never had anything like this before. Didn't mean to grab it from you. It's just, well, its really good."

"Thanks. Here, let's start with the vertical drill press." She showed him her calculations. "I notice that the times are quite consistent except these here that are almost exactly twice the average time, and this one ..." She pointed. "This one is three times the typical time."

"Let's see ..." Butch scanned down the page. "Mind if I use your computer terminal?"

"Help yourself!"

Butch logged in and began checking some part numbers. "Ah," he said after a bit. "The ones with double the time have two drilled holes. And that triple time one has three holes." He looked up at her. "That kind of consistency really makes this data credible."

"I'm glad you think so. And I was wondering if the times had to do with the number of holes. So how do those actual times recorded by the bar code reader match up to the official m-time?"

Butch consulted the computer some more. "Mind if I write on this?"

"Not at all," said Ellen.

Butch looked up each part number in turn and wrote a number in the margin. "These are the actual m-times on the bill of material," he explained. When he was finished he looked over the list, comparing his times with the time indicated by the bar code read at the start and end of each production run. "Whadayaknow," he said. "Hmmmm …" He looked up at Ellen. "Almost all of these m-times and the bar code times match up really well. They aren't identical. I wouldn't expect them to be. But they're close. Really close. This is cool!"

Ellen smiled.

"But look at this one part here. The m-time is two minutes and 20 seconds. But the bar code time has it at one minutes and 2 seconds, give or take. That's not even close."

"What does it mean?"

"I'll tell you what it means. It means, I think, that we've calculated the m-time wrong. We've been saying it will take longer to produce than it actually does."

"What's this I hear?" It was Rob. He was passing Ellen's door and overheard the conversation.

"Hey, Boss, come in here and look at what Ellen has done." Butch showed Rob the report with the actual bar code times and the comparison to the m-times in the computer. "We were talking about this one here," said Butch, indicating the particular part number. "I believe we in Engineering have overestimated the time it takes to produce this part on the horizontal drill."

Rob studied the report carefully. Then he looked up at Ellen. "This is amazing work, Ellen. You did this? This is like gold. We can use this kind of information in so many ways. We can tighten up our production estimates. We can balance the shop load better. We can tell our customers with certainty what it will take to make a product. Speaking of that, have you gotten anywhere on the Wilco part yet?"

"We're coming to that," said Ellen. "If you don't mind, I'd like to look at the press, first." Butch turned to the next page of the report and began studying the data there. Without saying a word, he started looking up part numbers again in the system, writing down the official m-times for each one. Rob and Ellen watched over his shoulders.

"They're not as consistent as the horizontal drill," commented Ellen.

"No, not quite as consistent. But I wouldn't expect that. The vertical drill is a CNC machine. It runs off of a computer program. The press is operated more manually. I would expect there to be more variability. Still, Ellen, these numbers are darn good. The variation isn't too much. And, I'm happy to say, right in line with Engineering's calculated m-time." He looked up at Rob. "That's good, right?"

Rob smiled and patted him on the shoulder. "You do good work, Butch. Am I right that the next page is assembly? That's the third place we put the bar code readers, right? Where the bulk of the work on the Wilco order is done?"

"Right." Ellen turned the page. Suddenly she was nervous. The numbers in Assembly were not nearly as consistent as she would have liked. And she couldn't explain it. Perhaps Butch could.

Butch was already looking up m-times for each part. There weren't as many part numbers, even though the number of individual bar code transactions went onto a second page. When he finished, he looked up at both of them. "This kind of has me puzzled." He pulled a pad of paper from Ellen's desk and began to make notes. "Look here," he said. "I've written down each Assembly line part number with its official m-time. Then I've listed each bar code transaction." He began circling some times drawing a square around others. Ellen caught on that he was circling the highest and putting a square around the lowest actual time recorded by the bar code readers for each part number.

"In every case, the longest bar code time is longer than the m-time," observed Ellen.

"But the shortest bar code time is quite a bit shorter than the m-time. In some cases ..." He pointed to the report. "... here, here and here, the bar code time is a lot shorter. Like half as much or even less."

Rob looked from Butch to Ellen. "So do you know what this means?"

The wheels in Ellen's head were turning, but she couldn't quite grasp it. She wished she'd gotten a better night's sleep so she could be sharp this morning. That bad dream about the flashing lights had kept her awake.

"It means, Boss, that either the people on the Assembly line aren't nearly as good as the machine shop people at recording data with the bar code reader, or ..."

"Or it takes less time to make some of these parts on the Assembly line than we thought," finished Rob. "Is that the Wilco part there?" He pointed to one of the part numbers on the report.

"Yes, Boss. That's it."

"So, Ellen," said Rob. "What does this mean about the Wilco order?"

She made a stab at an answer. "It may mean that we actually can reduce the m-times for that Wilco part. Which means we might be able to reduce the price to Wilco, and still ..."

"And still what?" he asked. He was grinning, like they were in on a secret that nobody else understood.

"And still ... and still keep our profit margin," she finished.

"I love it, absolutely love it when you talk like that," said Rob. "You guys understand what so few people do. For the first time in over 24 hours, I'm feeling cautiously optimistic."

"It's probably good to be cautious, Boss. I think we need to figure out why the assembly line has so much variation in it. And we need to figure out if those low numbers are right — or if we're missing something."

"Good point, Butch. But humor me just a little bit, OK? I could use some good news."

Ellen pulled out her notebook and consulted her list of questions from last night. She showed them to Rob and Butch. "We've already answered the first one. The vertical drill multiples are because of the number of holes being drilled. And Butch has done the second one by looking up the m-times for each part." She looked at him and smiled. "Thanks, Butch. And your chart here on the notepad is the bulk of question three. Why don't I plan on making that spreadsheet and doing more of the calculations?"

"Good idea, Ellen," said Rob. "And that's a good list, by the way."

"Ellen, shall you and I plan on talking to Kirby about number four?" asked Butch. "We could pick his brain."

"We could," said Ellen. "But I have a different idea. Do either of you know Rachel Hemingway?"

Butch shook his head, but Rob said, "Tall, usually works station one in Assembly?"

"That's her. I kind of know her now. She seems really smart and pays attention to what is going on around her. What if I asked her first, in a casual way, before we go talk with Kirby? I think we might have more information if I could talk to Rachel first."

"It can't hurt," said Rob. "Why don't you do that."

"OK," said Ellen.

"Hey, Boss?"

"Yes, Butch?"

"Ellen did good, didn't she? I mean with this report and all."

"She sure did." Rob put his hand on Butch's shoulder and took Ellen's hand. "I want you both to know that I really appreciate what you all have done here, and what you're going to do." He squeezed Ellen's hand before he let it go. "Maybe we can keep that Wilco part from going to the competition. And maybe we can even get some more!"

Ellen had just started working on the spreadsheet when her phone rang.

"El, is that you?"

"Trish. What's going on? You sound worried."

"I got a call from Tommy at work. He said there's a rumor going around that Jonas Klameck has had a heart attack."

"What??" Ellen couldn't believe what she was hearing. She fell back in her chair. "Surely I would have known."

"They said it happened in the middle of the night. They took him by ambulance to the hospital."

"Is he all right? He isn't ... he didn't ... I mean, he's OK, isn't he?" Suddenly it hit her. The flashing red lights. They weren't part of a dream. That was the ambulance come to take Jonas away.

"I don't know any more than that, El. I just thought you'd want to know."

"Oh, I do. Thanks for telling me." She was already reaching for the phone book when her sister hung up.

"Hello, is this the hospital? Yes, could you tell me if you have a patient, Jonas Klameck?" She spelled the last name. "You do? Is he ... how is he? In ICU?" She breathed a sigh of relief. At least he hadn't died. "Yes, thanks. Thanks very much."

She gathered her purse and coat and went down to Rob's office. He was there, staring at the computer terminal. "Knock, knock," she said. He turned around and smiled. "Rob, I'm really sorry. I've just learned that my landlord had a heart attack last night and I really need to go and see if his wife is OK. She doesn't have anyone else here in town."

Rob's smile became serious. "How is he?"

"I don't know. I just called the hospital and they said he was in ICU. I've just got to go and be there for them both."

"Of course, I understand. I would do the same thing if it were me. Go, with my blessing. And I hope he pulls through."

"Oh, me too. Me too, Rob. And thank you."

The drive to the hospital was a blur. She didn't remember pulling Gunilla into a parking place, nor did she really remember asking the receptionist for directions to the ICU. Her awareness only really came back when she stepped off of the elevator and saw Rika, sitting all alone at the end of the hall, looking like her world had completely fallen apart.

Ellen half ran to her. Rika stood as she saw Ellen coming toward her and they fell into each other's arms. "You came," sobbed Rika. "I knew you would." She buried her face in Ellens neck. "Now it is your turn to be a comfort to me." Ellen held her and let her cry.

Later they sat together and Rika told Ellen about the night before. "You recall he went to bed early, not feeling well. In the middle of the night, it got much worse, and became localized in the left side of his chest. He was having trouble breathing and I realized it could be a heart attack. I called the hospital and they sent an ambulance. I rode with him." She smiled ruefully at Ellen. "Of course I will not be going anywhere as long as Jonas is here, but I do not have the car." She chewed on her lower lip. "I guess I could walk."

"Whenever you need to go — to get some clean clothes or whatever — I'll drive you." She realized Rika's housecoat was showing below the tail of her overcoat. Ellen surmised she was probably still in her pajamas underneath.

"You're very kind."

"But right now, how is he? What do the doctors say?"

"A bunch of *rotvälska* is all. I can't understand what they are saying. Elevated enzymes. ST changes. I don't know what it all means. But I know it is serious. Very serious."

"Have you seen him?"

"They only let me go in for five minutes every hour. He's lying very still, with wires hooked up to him everywhere and monitors beeping and alarms going off." She teared up again. "Ellen, what will I do if I lose him?"

"We're not going to think about that right now," said Ellen firmly.

They sat, side by side, talking occasionally, Ellen holding Rika's hand in hers. The fluorescent light overhead was buzzing annoyingly, giving Ellen a headache. She looked down at the yellowed linoleum on the floor, at the dog-eared magazines that were two years out of date on the table. Ellen looked at her watch. Almost lunch time. Should she try to convince Rika to go down to the cafeteria and get something to eat? She probably wouldn't go, but she needed to keep up her strength.

For the second time in less than 24 hours she found herself praying. "Lord, if you're listening, please take care of Jonas. His wife needs him. I need him. Let him be OK, please."

The elevator dinged and it was Rika who saw the man walking toward them first. "Why Robbie Powell, is that you?"

"Yes, Mrs. K, it's me. How are you? More to the point, how is Jonas?" Then he stopped as he spotted Ellen. "Ellen? Is this ... are the Klamecks your landlords?"

"Hello Rob. Yes, I live in the apartment above the Klamecks' garage. You didn't know? How do you know the Klamecks?"

Rob hugged Rika. "I'm so sorry," he said. "When Ellen told me that her landlord had had a heart attack I had no idea it was Jonas. When I did hear it was him, I came as fast as I could get away. What do you need? What can I do for you?"

"Nothing, Robbie. There's nothing any of us can do. This is in the Lord's hands."

"Of course it is. But there surely is something we can do. Have you been here all night?"

"Since about 3:00 AM."

"Would you like me to take you home so you can get a shower and some clothes?"

Rika drew her coat around her. "I look a mess, don't I? But I can't, I won't leave Jonas."

"Mrs. Klameck?" A nurse had come around the corner.

"Yes?" The dread in Rika's voice broke Ellen's heart.

"Would you like to come in and see your husband for a few minutes? Doctor says it would be OK."

"Oh, yes. Yes, please!" The relief in her voice was almost tangible.

"Rika, how about you go in and visit with Jonas. Then, when you come out, I'll stay here with him while Rob — Mr. Powell — runs you home so you can get what you need. Would that help?"

"I really don't want to leave, but yes. Yes, I think that would be good. That is, if you're willing, Robbie?"

"Of course, Mrs. K. Anything you need."

"Right this way, Mrs. Klamek." The nurse gestured to the imposing double doors of the ICU.

After she was gone, Ellen sat back down and Rob sat opposite her. "Well," he said. "How about that? You and the Klamecks! Well, well."

"So how do you know the Klamecks?"

"Oh, Mr. K and my dad were great pals. Mr. K was this big shot international consultant and my dad had a little manufacturing business and somehow they hit it off. I remember going to their house for midsummer night parties when I was a kid. Do they still live in the house on Prospect Street, the one with the big magnolia in front?"

"That's the one. And I have this vague memory of going to a midsummer night party there, too. I think I must have been quite young."

Ellen smiled, remembering the soft summer twilight and playing hide and seek with the other kids in the yard. She remembered a picnic table in the yard with things to eat and punch. She remembered the adults sitting in Adirondack chairs, chatting and enjoying themselves. She remembered one boy, standing by his mother's chair, not wanting to play with the other kids. "Were you ... were you very shy, as a kid?" she asked.

"Painfully so," Rob replied. "I didn't really grow out of it until college."

"I remember a boy, standing by his mother and not wanting to play hide and seek with the other kids ..."

"And a girl came and said, 'Come on! Let's play.' and my mom gave me a little push. It was the bravest thing I think I'd ever done up to that point, to go with her. I ended up having a good time. That little invitation from that girl, well, it may have changed my life." He looked off into the distance. "I wish I could thank her."

"You can," she said simply. "I think I was that girl."

"You? Really?"

"I remember a boy with a striped shirt and jeans. His mother had on a green organdy strapless dress with a very full skirt. She was sitting in the chair in the yard with a drink in her hand and I remember thinking how elegant she looked. And then she hugged her boy and said, 'Go on. You can play with the nice little girl. You'll have fun.' And he did!"

"That was my mother. She still has that dress. And she tells me, although I have no proof of this, that she could still wear it if she wanted to." He winked.

"So we met as children. What about that?"

"And we both know the Klamecks," he added. "Say! When you said you had told your landlord about the Wilco part we lost, it was Mr. K you told. Right?"

"Of course!"

"And here I had this idea that you were telling some random stranger about our business at Powell. I apologize, Ellen. That was out of line. Mr. K is as trustworthy as they come."

"You didn't know. If I had known you knew the Klamecks I would have explained. He's been so good to me, helping me learn about the manufacturing business and how to think about information systems. He's the one who gave me the notebook." She pointed to it, tucked under her purse on the end table next to the June 1986 issue of Newsweek. "He's the one who sent me on the quest to discover the five principles of business information technology."

"My goodness! And how is the quest coming?"

"Four down, one to go. He just can't die, Rob. He has to point me to that last one!"

Rob crossed over and sat in the chair next to her. "I can't promise that he won't because that isn't up to me. But he is a strong man, strong in spirit. If anyone can pull through, he can."

They sat for a few minutes in silence when Rika came back around the corner. Ellen stood up. "How is he doing?"

"Perhaps just a little better. The doctor is pleased with what he's seeing on the EKG now. I told Jonas you both were out here. He wants to see both of you."

"Oh, I don't know …" Ellen was suddenly apprehensive. She'd never been in an ICU before, let alone spending much time in a hospital. Even though her parent's bodies had never been sent to the hospital, somehow she associated hospitals and emergency rooms and all the medical paraphernalia with her parent's deaths. And she wasn't sure she wanted to see Jonas all hooked up to wires.

"Come on, Ellen. It will do him good to see you." Rob took her elbow and guided her toward the nurse that was holding the door open for them. "I'll be just a minute, Mrs. K, and then I'll take you home, OK?"

Jonas was pale and his shirt was off. There were wires taped to his chest and an IV running into his arm. Another nurse was checking his blood pressure. "Just a minute," she said. "No longer. But he insisted on seeing you. He's a hard man to say no to." She smiled down at her patient.

Jonas reached for Ellen. "I'm so glad to see you, Ellen." His voice was husky and weak. Not the commanding voice she was used to. "And Robbie Powell. How nice to see you again. Sorry it had to be under these circumstances." He waved his hand around at the medical paraphernalia surrounding him.

"Hello, Mr. K. It is good to see you, too. Although I'd like to plan to get together again when you get out of this place."

"You can count on it, my boy. And I see you know our Ellen?"

"Absolutely. She's with us at Powell Manufacturing and doing a fabulous job. And Ellen was just telling me that you've been the one advising her on some of the brilliant ideas she's brought to work."

"Modesty forbids, my boy. She's brilliant in her own right."

"Uh, hello? I'm standing right here," said Ellen.

"Of course you are, my dear." Jonas smiled and Ellen felt like it transformed his whole demeanor. She took hold of his hand.

"I want you to get better," she said. "I have one more principle to find."

"Oh, well if you say so," he replied. "I had rather thought I would shuffle off this mortal coil, but since you insist, I'll make it my business to recover from this rather insulting episode and come home so we can continue the quest."

"Oh, you!" She squeezed his hand and Rob grinned.

"OK, folks." That was the nurse. "That's enough. Let's let our patient rest now."

"Of course," said Ellen. "Goodbye, Jonas. I'll make sure Rika doesn't get too tired out. And I'll be back just as soon as they'll let me in." She surprised herself and bent over to kiss his forehead. "You just get better, you hear?"

"You are the master," he replied, giving her hand another squeeze before she stepped back from the bed. "And you, my boy," he said to Rob. "You take care of this young lady. She's special."

"Don't I know it," said Rob. "Goodbye, Mr. K. I'll be seeing you later, too."

Rob took Rika home and Ellen sat in the waiting area, idly flipping through a Time article about Garrison Keillor. She had pulled out her notebook and was looking through it when Rob returned. "Aren't you going back to the plant?"

"I will, after Rika gets back and after I take you both to lunch. She's going to shower and change clothes, maybe pack a few things and bring her car over here so she'll have it at the hospital."

"I suppose I should get back to work, too. My boss is this horrible taskmaster ..."

"Isn't he just?" His eyes twinkled. "If I were you I'd tell him a thing or two ... No, seriously, can we talk about business for a few minutes while we wait for Rika?"

"Sure. What's on your mind?"

"That new Wilco part we're producing. With the work you did and Butch's research, we felt comfortable reducing the price by about eight percent. Sandy and Butch were in my office when I called Karl Smithson at Wilco. We gave him the good news, and he appreciated it very much. Sandy and Butch did a good job of explaining to him how we had been able to offer the reduction. We wanted to make sure that he knew we weren't just giving in to pressure, but trying to do the right thing by accurately reflecting our costs in our pricing. Butch told him about your bar code data and the actual production data you'd been able to gather. Karl was impressed. He says he'd like to meet you sometime."

"So that's done? Do we get to keep the business?"

"Yes, Karl said the business was still ours. He said he would be able to report to his boss that the unsolicited offer from our competitor had been met by the current supplier. I reminded him again, we weren't doing this so much because of pressure from the competition, but because we want to offer Wilco a fair price. Your bar code data allowed us to have new data that adjusted the price."

"Any idea who the competitor is?"

"No, Karl wouldn't say. But he did slip and say something about Lexington. I feel sure it is my Uncle Bob's company, International Dynamics."

"Would he do that to you? Underbid his own nephew?"

"In a New York minute."

Rika got off the elevator, looking much more like herself with a nice belted tunic and pants with heels. She was carrying her overcoat and a large bag. "How is he?" she asked. "Any change?"

"There's been no word," said Ellen. "No change."

"I think we can honestly say that no news is good news," said Rob. "Now, Mrs. K, what about something to eat? My guess is that you missed breakfast and now you've missed lunch, too."

"That's where you're wrong, young Robbie. I actually fixed myself a sandwich at the house after I took a shower. And I packed myself some snacks." She indicated her oversize carryall. "How about you kids? Would you like something to eat?" She sat down and imitated Mary Poppins, pulling out plastic containers of things to eat, several books, a blanket and a small pillow. "See?" she said. "I have everything I need."

"You're certainly prepared." Ellen noted her fresh lipstick and earrings. No one could ever accuse Rika of not looking good.

"How about it? Robbie? Something to eat?"

"If you don't mind, Mrs. K, I have some things I need to discuss with Ellen. Business things. Would you mind if I take her out for a quick bite? Then she can come back. I'll have to get back to the plant."

"Of course, of course. That sounds lovely. But, Ellen, don't you need to get back to work, too?"

"Well ..." She looked at Rob.

"It's entirely up to you, Ellen. Feel free to stay here with Mrs. K. Or you can come back to work, then we'll both come down and check on her and Mr. K at the end of the day."

"You've already responded to Wilco. That was going to be my work today, getting that data ready for you."

"You were going to check with that girl on the assembly line. Rachel, was it?"

"That's true. I want her to look at the data and do a reality check on it."

"Oh you kids," laughed Rika. "Jonas would love to be out here talking with you about these kind of things. This is, what do you say, right up his alley."

Ellen laughed, too. "He'd better hurry up and get better or he's going to miss all the fun. Rob's really on to something but I'm sure Jonas would have plenty of perspective to add."

"I tell you what," said Rika. "When you come back, we'll see if we can't get the nurse to let you both in to visit at the same time and you can give him an update. Having something like that to think about would be better than any medicine they could give him."

"That sounds like a plan, then," said Rob. "Ellen and I will go and get a bite to eat and we'll be back around 5:00 this evening. Sound good?"

"But you have to promise to call me if there's any change. Promise me, Rika. Here's my number at work." She scribbled her number on a piece of paper she found in her purse.

"OK, I promise. I'm feeling so much better since you both have come. I was pretty defeated when you first came. But I'm doing so much better now. You've restored my confidence. You've restored my faith." She reached out to both of them and pulled them into a hug. "Thank you. Thank you both." Ellen hugged Rika back and realized that Rob had his arms around both of them, hugging Rika, but hugging Ellen, too.

Chapter 44
Ellen gets information from Rachel.

They went to Fast Ernie's for lunch. Apparently Ernie knew Rob; he called him Robbie and the two of them chatted for a few minutes before Ellen and Rob placed their order.

Ellen found being with Rob was beginning to be more comfortable. He didn't treat her like an underling, more like a colleague. He enjoyed talking about the business, but then Ellen enjoyed that, too. When they had finished, Rob said, "I'll take you back to work in my car. Then we can drive down to the hospital this evening and you can pick up your car then. Does that suit you?"

"Sure, that's fine."

Back at work, Ellen hung up her coat and decided she'd use a slightly devious tactic. She went to see Annie.

"Got a minute?" she asked.

Annie looked up from her work. "For you, girl, always. What's up?"

Ellen sat down in Annie's guest chair. Because her desk was out in the open, outside of Luther's office, Ellen had to be a little careful.

"You get together with Rachel for break, don't you?" she whispered.

"Yeah, sure. Every once in a while. We're friends. Why are we whispering?"

"I'm doing a little research and I think Rachel might be able to help me with it. But I don't want people to know what I'm digging into. It's a little project I'm doing for Rob."

"Oh, real cloak and dagger stuff. I get it. So what do you need from me?"

"I was wondering if I could just happen" — she made air quotes with her fingers — "to be with you when you go to break with Rachel. If you can make it look kind of, well, coincidental, I'll ask

Rachel my questions real casual like and maybe I can get the information I need without anyone really noticing."

"Ellen, I swear, you are such a hoot. I git mixed up in the daggonest things when I'm with you."

"But can you do it? Get me hooked up with Rachel in a casual way, I mean?"

"Course I can. I was named after Annie Oakley, doncha know."

"Were you really?" Ellen's eyes must have betrayed her gullibility.

"No, silly. But it makes for a good story, don't it?"

"Oh, you!"

"Be back up here about twenty-five minutes after two. We'll go to the break room. Assembly takes its break at 2:30 and we'll just wave Rachel over and have her sit with us. Will that work?"

"Perfect, Annie. You're a peach."

"Actually," said Annie with a dignified air. "I'm an angel."

"But not for long!" said Ellen as she left.

Annie's plan worked beautifully. They had chosen a table with three chairs against the wall. Rachel came in with the rest of the Assembly Line crew and she almost didn't have to be invited; she came over with a bag of barbecue potato chips and an Ale-8-1 she got out of the vending machines. Ellen had printed out a fresh copy of her bar code report and had torn off the two pages dealing with the Assembly line. She had it in front of her as Rachel sat down, studying it.

"What cha got there, Ellen?" asked Rachel.

"Oh, this? Its the report from those bar code readers we've put on the Assembly line. I really appreciate what you and James are doing, scanning each order as it comes through. This is what it looks like." She turned the report around so Rachel could see. "Here's the time you scanned each order onto the line. And this column here is the time that James said it completed. And here's the quantity of parts that were produced."

"Well, ain't that a trip! Look at that, Annie! Little ole' me, makin' data!"

"We're gonna have to get you a badge that says 'Data Queen' on it, I'm thinking," said Annie.

"I was looking at this report, Rachel, because I can't quite figure something out. See here on this part? Sometimes it takes over an hour to complete, and other times it takes less than twenty minutes. See? Here's another one. The times vary from 45 minutes to two hours. Do you suppose James doesn't always report the parts right when they're finished? I mean, that would explain it, I suppose."

"Let me look at that again," said Rachel. "Are these the actual times that I scan the order on? And this column here is when James scans it complete?" Ellen nodded. "I don't think it's that," said Rachel. "I watch James pretty close. If he gets distracted and forgets to scan, I remind him." She looked up at Ellen. "I know this stuff is important."

"It is important. Maybe even more than you realize."

"Look a'here," said Rachel. "See how them orders that are done earlier in the day take longer than the ones towards quitting time?"

Ellen looked. Rachel was right, and she hadn't noticed it before. The m-times got shorter, in general, as the day wore on. "Why is that, Rachel?"

"Cause Kirby don't want us wearing ourselves out early in the day, in case we need more git-up-and-go later in the day."

"Interesting. So let me ask you this ..." She pointed to the new Wilco part. "Is it possible to make this part faster — like this report is showing later in the day — or does it take longer?"

"Oh, no. We could make it faster. We just don't. That's that new part, isn't it? The one with all the hoses?"

"Yes, that's it. I was just wondering about putting the hoses on and whether it can be done faster without losing the quality."

"Oh, we don't lose quality. We're proud of our work. James tests every one before he passes it off of the assembly line. We don't want no leaking parts. Those come back from the customer and we have to fix 'em again."

"That's exactly right."

"Kirby tells us to be extra slow with that one. He says it's real important to get that one right. He says he don't want nobody breaking no speed limits."

"Huh. I just want to make sure what this data is telling me — that we could make the parts faster, and with good quality, if we really needed to."

"Yeah, for sure. Why are you asking? Are we fixing to get more orders?"

"Keep it to yourself, Rachel. But, yes, that's what we're working on. We're hoping to get more orders, but we don't want to go after them if the assembly line can't handle the load."

"Oh, sister, we can handle it. We like it better when there's plenty to do. We'd rather work faster than drag our feet, wouldn't we Snake?" Rachel's crew was beginning to head back out to the factory.

"Hey, Rachel!" Ellen called after her. "Keep it to yourself for now, OK?"

"Sure thing, Possum!" She laughed as she headed out.

"Snake?" asked Ellen.

"Lots of people have nicknames here," said Annie. "I happen to know Snake's real name is Willard Duval. But everyone just calls him Snake."

After returning to her office, Ellen had to think about what she'd learned. She made a spreadsheet of the data, plotting production time vs. time of day. While it wasn't always a sure thing, there was a definite trend that things sped up the closer it got to 5:00 PM. She could at least confirm to Rob that the offer they'd made to Wilco to reduce the price based on faster than expected assembly line times was backed up by her research.

But what to do about this information about Kirby's directions to the Assembly line crew? That didn't seem right to her. But maybe that's how things were supposed to be. If Jonas were available, that would be the kind of thing she would talk over with him.

That reminded her of Rob's plan to drive both of them back to the hospital. She looked at her watch: 4:18 PM. As if on cue, Rob knocked on her open door and walked in. "You about ready to go?" he asked.

"Just about. When were you planning on leaving?"

"I have a few things to finish up. Say in about 15 minutes?"

"That would be great. And I'll have something to talk about while we drive."

"I'll look forward to that."

On the drive to the hospital Ellen explained about the correlation between time of day and speed of production. She had decided not to mention Rachel's name, even though Rob could probably guess Ellen had talked to her. And she certainly wasn't going to repeat Kirby's instructions to the team. Right now, that was hearsay. But the data was real, and she decided to stick with the facts.

"So you're telling me the closer we get to quitting time, the faster the assembly line runs?"

"That's what the data suggests."

"Huh. That's interesting. Strange, even."

"What it means, though, Rob, is that your offer to Karl Smithson is fully supported by the data. The assembly line could run faster. It could produce the product in less time. So the cost savings is fully justified."

"That's good work, Ellen. Really, really, really good work. This order might postpone having to close the plant down. It isn't a silver bullet, but it helps." He looked over at her. "I am so glad you came to Powell," he said as he pulled into the hospital parking lot.

Jonas was steadily improving, according to the doctors. He was on blood thinners to help prevent another clot from forming. And he was alternately charming and demanding to the nurses. "He's driving them mad," said Rika. "Isn't it wonderful? That's my old Jonas back."

Ellen tried to convince Rika to go home and sleep in her own bed but she seemed determined to make a bed out of a couple of chairs in the waiting room. "I've brought a pillow and a blanket," she protest-

ed. Even Jonas tried to get her to go home, but she dug her heels in
and refused. "My place is with you," she had told him. "If you are
here, here I will be as well."

In the end, they had to let her do what she wanted to do. It was
getting late and Ellen realized she was getting hungry. Without any
prompting, Rob said, "Come on, then, kid. If Mrs. K has made up her
mind, we can't change it. She outranks us. But at least we can split a
pizza at Gabrielli's. Can we bring you something back, Mrs. K?"

"No, my boy. Thank you, but I have everything I need. I am like
one of your boy scouts — always prepared."

The nurse came out to say that Rika could go in and see Jonas
again, so Ellen and Rob headed to the elevator. "Want to drive over to
Gabrielli's or would you like to walk?" asked Rob. "It's just a couple
of blocks."

"Oh, let's walk. It would do me good to stretch my legs."

"Good choice. But bundle up. In the words of Dean Martin,
'Baby, It's Cold Outside."

She smiled at the reference and they walked briskly down the
hospital driveway to the warm, garlic-infused humidity that was
Gabrielli's. They shared a pizza, discovering they had similar tastes:
grizzly all the way, hold the anchovies.

After dinner Rob walked her back to her car, held the door for
her as she got in, and made sure it started and was rolling before he
headed for his own vehicle. At home everything seemed quiet. Even
though she wouldn't necessarily have seen the Klamecks when she
came in, she felt their absence. She knew they weren't across the driveway and it just felt wrong.

Ellen stopped by to see Rika as she went to work the next morning. "No, they are not very comfortable," she said about the chairs.
"But Jonas continues to improve, praise God," she said. "He may
even get out of ICU this evening."

"This evening. Oh, I forgot. I'm supposed to go on a date with
Kirby this evening. I'll cancel it."

"You will do no such thing!" said Rika. "I'll be fine. Jonas will be fine. You go and have a nice time. Is Kirby that young man with the Mercedes?"

"Yes, that's him."

"You go and enjoy yourself. But be careful!" Rika warned. "Remember our talk about how far you are willing for him to go!"

"I'll remember, Rika. Thank you. Now I had better get to work."

At work, Ellen made a spreadsheet that was similar to the data that Butch had scratched on her legal pad. Having the data in spreadsheet form made it easier to do calculations, like what was the percentage difference between the bar code times and the Engineering Department m-times. But it only served to confirm what they already knew — that the vertical drill press times matched up extremely well and the press was close, but with more variation.

The Assembly Line was another story. She marked the high and low times for each part, just as Butch had done, and she noticed that the m-time was always closer to the lower time than to the high time. She tried to picture the Assembly line in her mind's eye. Sometimes it would go faster. Sometimes it would go slower. But why?

She also set about refining her RPG program. At least in this part of the SOLUTION/400 system, the design of the data followed Principle Two. The data containing the m-times for each part was in a single, non-redundant location. By matching the part number on the order for each bar code entry with the data from the system Bill of Material, she was able to add the m-times for each part so that Butch wouldn't have to look it up next time.

As she stepped out into the shop to collect job cards, she realized how comfortable the factory had become. The deep thump, thump, thump vibrating through the soles of her shoes told her that the three and a half ton press was running. She was so used to looking away from the intense blue of the welding flash that it had become second nature. Some of the guys hauling baskets of parts here and there waved to her. "Hey, Possum! How's it going?" She noted a pile up of parts over in the Fabrication area and Harvey Green waving his cigar around at several of the workers. Uh oh, she thought to herself. We've got a quality problem in Fabrication. I hope they can get that resolved soon.

She picked up the cards in Harvey's office and then headed over to Leonard's area. "Hey Possum. What's shakin'?"

"Not much, Leonard. Just picking up job cards."

In the Assembly area she stopped by to say hi to Rachel and found her in the middle of scanning a new order with the bar code reader.

"Is that still working for you, Rachel?" she asked.

"Oh, hey, Ellen. Yep, it sure is. Slick as a ribbon."

"That's good. You let me know if anything ever acts up, OK? Is Kirby in his office?"

"I think so. He was out here on the line just a few minutes ago."

Kirby was in his office as Ellen knocked then went in to collect his job cards. "Oh, hey, Ellen. I was hoping to see you today. Ready for our big date?"

"I'll be ready by 5:30. But I'd like to know where we're going so I can leave a phone number with my landlady. Her husband is in the hospital and she may need to reach me."

"Oh, that's a surprise." He adopted a German accent. "Ve cannot divulch zat information."

"Come on, Kirby. This is serious. I really want her to be able to reach me if there is a change."

"Well, OK, kid, since you asked so nice. I've got reservations for us at Brownings for 6:30. Satisfied?"

"Brownings is really upscale, isn't it? I've never been there. It's over by the Campbell House, isn't it?"

"Best steak in Lexington, in my humble opinion. I think you'll like it. Nothing's too good for you, Baby."

"OK, Kirby. I'll be ready."

"Wear something sexy for your man, OK? Say, I hear we managed to hang on to the Wilco order for that new part."

"Excuse me?" Ellen wasn't sure she'd heard him right.

"That new Wilco part, the one with the hoses. We didn't lose it to … we're still producing it for them, right?"

"Uh, yeah. That's my understanding." She grabbed the job cards and headed out. "I'll see you tonight."

Ellen had to call the long distance operator to get the number for Browning's Restaurant on Harrodsburg Road, but she finally got it. On the way home from work she stopped by the hospital again. Jonas wasn't in ICU and she found him in a bed on the second floor. Rika was sitting in a chair by his bed, reading to him. The other bed in the room was empty.

"Ellen!" exclaimed the patient. "You are a sight for sore eyes. Look, Rika. Here's Ellen come to see us."

"She's been here a lot, Jonas. You just didn't know it in ICU."

Ellen crossed to the side of his bed and took his hand. "How are you doing?"

"Apparently I'm improving. Or they got tired of me in ICU. But let's talk about something interesting. What are you finding in your bar code data?"

"Jonas, I insist," said his wife. "No business for at least one more day. I know you love it dearly, but the doctors say you really need to take it easy."

"Maybe tomorrow," said Ellen. "Right now, though, I've got a hot date I have to go get dressed for. Do you need anything?"

"Not a thing," said Rika. "They are taking very good care of us here."

"I'm glad to hear it. Rika, here is the number of the restaurant where I'll be tonight just in case you need anything. Don't hesitate to call. And I'll be back here in the morning. Maybe, if you're really good, Jonas, I'll tell you what I'm learning from the bar code data."

"I am breathless with anticipation," he said.

"Shush!" said Rika. "I do not like teasing about being breathless. I have already seen enough of that when the ambulance came."

Ellen decided on her nice pant suit, the one with the scoop neck blouse. Kirby had said wear something sexy, but it was so cold out that wearing a dress was more than she could contemplate. The pant suit was made of fine wool, a gray that went well with her skin tone. She added a simple string of pearls and some chunky bright green earrings. She was just finishing applying her eye shadow when she heard Kirby's Mercedes pull up on the street. She grabbed her coat and headed down the stairs to meet him.

"Hey, Baby. Looking good!" he said as he held the door for her. The plush warm interior of the Mercedes was luxurious. Ellen settled back into the soft leather and relaxed. This will be fun, she thought to herself.

"A little music?" asked Kirby.

"Sure, why not?"

Kirby pushed the cassette tape that was resting in the player all the way in. The unmistakable voice of Barry White purred through the speakers. Was he trying to send a message with the song, "Can't Get Enough of Your Love, Baby?"

Interstate 75 wasn't too busy and Kirby knew a shortcut through some residential areas that brought them out near the Campbell House hotel and Brownings. Instead of pulling into the parking lot of the restaurant, Kirby chose the larger parking lot of the Campbell House. "Easier parking," he explained.

The hostess was a cute girl in a little black dress and black stockings with a seam up the back. "Nice to see you again, Mr. Smith," she said when Kirby held the door for Ellen. "I've got your usual table ready for you."

"Wow," said Ellen after they were seated. "They know you here. You must be a big shot." Kirby smiled. "But what's with the 'Mr. Smith?'"

Kirby flashed his famous dimple. "I figure they don't need to know all of my business, so I just tell them my name's Smith. Keeps things nice and anonymous, you know?"

The menu was a huge affair, more like a book than a dining selection. The selections were wide ranging from many different cuts of steak to several types of seafood to pasta dishes. "Gosh, Kirby. There are so many choices, I don't know where to begin."

"You just let me take care of things, Baby. I know what you like." He motioned the maitre'd over. "Could we start with a couple of cocktails? Martinis, I think. With Tanqueray, please, and very dry. Can you manage that?"

"Certainly, sir." The maitre'd glided away silently.

"But Kirby, I really don't like to drink. I'd rather not."

"What you need is to relax a bit. A Tanqueray Martini is as classy as they come."

When the waiter returned with the drinks, Kirby ordered prime rib for himself, rare, and then looked at Ellen. "You enjoyed that fillet mignon at the Cork and Cleaver. Want to do that again, or try something different?"

"I was wondering about some fish?"

"We have an excellent Dover sole, this evening, madam," said the waiter. "In my opinion, it is one of our best offerings."

"That sounds very nice."

"Would madam prefer it broiled, pan seared, or prepared blackened in the Cajun style?"

"What do you recommend?"

"Does madam enjoy seasoning with some heat, some spice?"

Ellen wrinkled her nose. "Not so much," she said. "It burns my mouth."

"Indeed, madam. Then might I recommend the broiled preparation. We serve it with a nice lemon butter sauce and some capers on the side."

"That sounds good," said Ellen.

Kirby added sautéd spinach and grilled mushrooms as sides to share as well as a baked potato for each of them. He also ordered a house salad for both of them. "I suppose you'll want bleu cheese?" he asked.

"Yes, please. But that's a lot of food, Kirby!" said Ellen.

"I don't want you to go hungry. Drink up!" He raised his glass in a toast. "To us!" he said, and took a healthy swallow. Ellen raised her glass and put it to her lips, but didn't take any of the liquor. The smell brought back old memories working on experiments in the chemistry lab with her college chum Jasmine.

The salads were artistically arranged on chilled china plates. Ellen enjoyed hers very much. Kirby was less enthusiastic about his. "I'm not so much into the rabbit food," he explained. "I'm waiting for that prime rib." The enthusiasm in his green eyes was irresistible. He really is a dream boat, Ellen thought to herself. I'm a lucky girl to have him lavishing this much attention and spending this much money on me. She leaned back in her chair and sighed contentedly. "This is nice, Kirby. Thank you for bringing me."

"A good looking, desirable woman like you? You deserve it!" Kirby raised his glass again and drained it.

Like magic the maitre'd appeared. "Another one, sir?"

"Sure, why not? And another one for the lady … hey, Ellen! You're going to have to pick up the pace if you're going to keep up." The maitre'd turned to go but Kirby stopped him. "We haven't ordered any wine with dinner." The maitre'd turned back.

"No, sir. It would be my pleasure to assist you, sir." There was a brief conference about the best selection. Apparently Ellen's choice of fish had thrown a monkey wrench into the works. Kirby's steak required a red, but her fish demanded a white. Kirby almost ordered two bottles, but Ellen protested that she really didn't want any wine. Ultimately, with an able assist from the maitre'd, Kirby ordered a bottle of pinot noir for himself and a carafe of chardonnay for Ellen.

The maitre'd quickly returned, poured a bit of the red for Kirby to taste. He approved and the maitre'd filled his glass half full. He then poured some of the chardonnay for Ellen. She didn't know what was expected but she tasted it and pronounced it "very good." It was chilled and she actually did think it tasted pleasant. Her glass was also filled — it was a different shape than Kirby's — and she took another sip.

"I wonder why wine glasses are different shapes?" she asked, attempting to get the conversation started.

"I don't know," said Kirby. "I just like what they do to me." He took a sip of his wine and followed it with a Martini chaser. "So how do you like working at Powell?"

"I really enjoy it. There are lots of nice people, the work is interesting … what's not to like?"

"That's great, but do you ever want more? I know I do."

"It suits me fine right now," she replied. "When we went to the Cork and Cleaver, you said something about brokering deals. What did you mean by that?"

"Oh, nothing you'd be interested in …" He paused as their food arrived.

Ellen had a hard time looking at the mass of quivering pink flesh on Kirby's plate, but her sole looked wonderful. She picked at a bit of fish with some of the sauce on it. "Oh, wow! That is really good!" she exclaimed. The waiter hardly broke a smile and she knew she'd over reacted.

"I said that there wasn't anything you'd be interested in, but maybe I was wrong," said Kirby as he spooned some of the mushrooms onto his plate. "Here, help yourself to the spinach. Most people don't like spinach, but I liked it fixed the way they do here at Brownings."

"You were wrong about what?" asked Ellen. Her fish really was outstanding.

"You might be interested in helping me broker a little deal. There'd be something in it for you, of course. Nice dinners like this …" He waved his Martini glass around the table and took another sip. "Maybe even some real cash money."

"I don't know … I'm not much of a risk taker. I don't have any spare funds to invest."

"You have something even more valuable: information. Take, for example, that new part we're producing for Wilco, the one with all the hoses. What kind of price did we end up quoting to Wilco? You'd know the answer to that, and that's useful information."

"Kirby, that sounds like spying. Is that ethical?"

"I'm just kidding. Just testing you to see if you're loyal to the company. Besides, anyone with access to a computer terminal can look up the list price in the mainframe Bill of Material, right?"

"I guess so. But I wouldn't want to be the one who shared that information."

"Of course you wouldn't. But I tell you what you could do. You could let me know when there are any more parts that come in for bid from Wilco or any of our other customers, especially those parts that are going to affect my area. I mean, it's only fair to give me a heads up when there is a potential new part that might impact the Assembly line, don't you think?"

"Maybe. I guess so ..."

"Of course it is. Fair, I mean. I'm responsible for getting the work out on the Assembly line, right? So giving me a chance to know what's coming so I can make the necessary adjustments, that would just be the right thing to do. I can count on you, right?"

"I ... I guess so." She looked down at her plate. The fish didn't seem as appetizing now. She took a sip of the white wine. "Could we talk about something else?"

"Sure. I'm sorry. I've bored you. Let's talk about you and me. What is your favorite weekend getaway destination?"

"I ... I've never been on a weekend getaway. Actually, I've not been on a vacation since ... well, since I went off to college."

"Oh, that's a shame. A real shame! A pretty girl like you needs to get away every once in a while. Tell you what: let me look at my schedule and see if I can't get off on a Friday when you can get off, too. You've earned some vacation days by now, haven't you? Then we'll go away together, just the two of us. Gatlinburg, maybe? No ... tell you what, we'll go to Nashville. We'll do Opryland and go to the Grand Ole' Opry. I've got a friend who works back stage, so we can meet some of the stars. We'll stay at the Opryland Hotel. Have you ever been there? It is a-may-zing!" He paused to finish off his martini. "You'd like that, wouldn't you?"

"I ... I guess so. Would ... would we have separate rooms?"

Kirby tilted his head back and laughed like that was the funniest thing he had ever heard. Then he looked at her with his green eyes, his curl of hair hanging like an upside down question mark. Ellen could hardly breathe. "Oh, Baby, that would miss the whole point of a weekend getaway, wouldn't it? You're such a tease!" He reached across the table and squeezed her hand. "Gosh you sure look sexy tonight."

Kirby continued to talk, unaware that Ellen had gone silent. He ordered one more martini after Ellen had declined dessert. He also finished off the rest of Ellen's wine. "Can't let it go to waste, now, can we?"

Ellen excused herself to go to the ladies room. When she returned, Kirby had paid the bill and was waiting for her with her coat. The maitre'd wished them a pleasant evening and they stepped out into the frigid January night.

As they walked across the parking lot toward Kirby's car parked next door, he said, "Let's go look at the Campbell House lobby. Have you ever been inside? 'Course its nothing like the Opryland Hotel, but it's pretty nice."

Ellen started to protest, but then thought the better of it. Perhaps she could figure out a way to get Kirby's keys. The prospect of him driving her home sent shivers down her spine. "Oops!" said Kirby, tripping over the curb and grabbing on to Ellen for support.

The Campbell House looked like an antebellum mansion with white columns on the front porch. Inside it was warm at least. The lobby had a certain faded charm. It had been elegant, genteel even, in its day. But now it looked a little tired, a little shabby.

The desk clerk looked up as they entered. "Good evening, Mr. Smith! So glad to see you again. And I see you've brought a lovely young lady with you. We have your usual room all prepared for you."

"His name isn't ..." But Kirby cut her off.

"Thanks, Alex. You know how to treat your regulars. We just came in to take a look around." Ellen saw, out of the corner of her eye, Kirby actually wink at the clerk.

He escorted Ellen over to the fireplace. "Why don't you have a seat here and warm up by the fire — not that you're not hot already — and I'll take care of a few arrangements." Kirby went back to talk to Alex. She couldn't hear the conversation, but she saw Alex hand Kirby a key. In a moment Kirby was back. "I won't be a moment. I'm just going to make a quick pit stop. Then we can really start enjoying our evening." Before Ellen could find her wits to ask what he meant, Kirby had slipped around the corner under a sign that pointed to the restrooms.

Ellen launched out of her chair and went over to Alex. "Alex, I'm afraid there has been a mistake. Or at least a misunderstanding. I don't know what Kirby Anderson — his name isn't Smith — expects is going to happen here this evening, but it isn't going to happen with me. He's too drunk to drive back to Laodicea, and I was just trying to figure out how to get his car keys from him. Is there a way for me to get back home and leave him here to sleep it off?"

"I understand completely, miss. Mr. 'Smith' often brings young ladies here. But we here at the Campbell House want no part of an unwilling liaison." He picked up the phone. "Hey Roger, you're about to get off work, aren't you? Yes … you live in Laodicea, right? Good. Look, would you mind to give a young lady a ride? She's in a bit of a jam. You would? Oh, thanks, Roger. I'll have her meet you by the west service door."

He turned back to Ellen. "I assume you'd like to be gone when Mr. Smith comes back from the restroom? If so, please step this way. A nice gentleman, Roger Chenault, lives in Laodicea. He's about to get off work and would be glad to give you a ride. It that acceptable?" Ellen heard the distant sound of a toilet flushing.

"Alex, you are a gentleman. Thank you." She slipped through the door marked 'Employees Only' as Alex pointed toward the service entrance. The door had barely closed behind her when she heard Kirby's voice say, "Alex, I've misplaced my date. Did she go to the restroom, too?"

Ellen didn't stop to find out how Alex handled that — or to give him a chance to change his mind and betray her. She walked quickly

down the bare corridor to a set of utilitarian double doors. A man in
an employee uniform with 'Roger' embroidered on the shirt pocket
was standing to the right of the doors. He was in his late 50s with
gray hair and a gray mustache. His face was lined from hard work but
it was an honest face. "Are you Roger?"

"Yes ma'am. Are you the young lady what wants to get to Laodicia?"

"Yes, Roger. I am. My name's Ellen." She held out her hand to
him. He wiped his palm on his pant leg before tentatively shanking
hers. "I'm so grateful to you."

"Hit's my pleasure, ma'am. Are you ready to go now? You got
any luggage nor other kit you need to nuss home?"

"Nope, just me. Are you ready to go? I'd kind of like to get out
of here."

"Yes'm, I'm right smart ready to get home myself." He held the
door for her and she stepped out onto a loading dock. If anything it
had gotten even colder. Roger led her down a short flight of stairs to
his pickup truck. It wasn't a Mercedes, but it looked a lot safer to
Ellen right now. Roger even held the door of the pickup for her.

As they rounded the side of the building, Ellen saw Kirby's Mercedes still sitting in its place. She even thought she caught a glimpse
of Kirby himself, looking out of the front doors. Instinctively she
slouched down in the seat, even though she knew Kirby couldn't see
into the cab of Roger's pickup.

Soon they were down Harrodsburg road and turning onto New
Circle. "Can I ask what yer needed to get out of town so quick for?
Ain't none a my business, o'course."

"Oh, I don't mind," said Ellen. "My date for the evening apparently had a room reserved at the Campbell House and expected me to
join him there after dinner. He's not the kind of man who takes no for
an answer."

"Amen. Don't know what's gotten into men these days. Ex-
pectin' to get the milk for free without buyin' the cow."

Roger turned out to be easy to talk to. He was genuinely concerned about Ellen and glad to give her a lift. He seemed to take it on

as his personal mission. Ellen asked him about himself and he was happy to share. He's worked at the Campbell House most of his adult life and had worked his way up to head of maintenance. He had a wife he'd been married to for 38 years and two grown sons. One was married and expecting Roger's first grandchild. Ellen kept asking more questions so he wouldn't ask her any, and Roger was only too happy to oblige.

As they exited the Interstate at Laodicea, Ellen told him she'd like to go to the hospital. He raised his eyebrows, but she explained that she had a friend she'd like to visit before visiting hours were over.

In the hospital parking lot, Ellen tried to pay Roger for his trouble. "No, ma'am. It wouldn't be right to take your money. Jesus said when you do it for the least of these. You remember that, ma'am. And someday you can pay me by doing a good turn for somebody else. Is that fair?"

"More than fair. You're a good, good man, Roger. I'm deeply grateful."

As she waited for the elevator, the near miss of this evening began to crash in on her. By the time she had reached Jonas' room, she was almost physically shaking.

"Why, Ellen, dear, what's wrong? You look like you've seen a ghost. See? Here is Jonas sitting up and trading lies with young Robbie. He's just fine. You don't need to worry."

"What a relief!" feigned Ellen. It was a relief to hear Rika's Swedish accent and to feel her genuine concern. "How are you, Jonas?"

"Having a wonderful time with young Robbie, here. He's been catching me up on your bar code project."

"Rob, you're not supposed to tell him anything. I was using that as leverage to make him behave in the hospital. Now you've undermined my one big asset."

Rob smiled. "I see you have the same kind of relationship with Mr. K that I do."

"How was dinner, Ellen?" asked Rika.

"Uh, it was … OK. I'll have to tell you about it later." There was no way she was going to explain what happened in front of Rob. Or even Jonas.

An announcement over the loudspeaker said that visiting hours were now ending. "I guess that's our cue. Rika, are you going home tonight to sleep in your own bed?"

"No. My place is here. Besides," she whispered to Ellen. "I stretch out on this other bed. It is quite comfortable. The nurses look the other way. Let us hope that they do not need to admit someone else to this room!"

Ellen and Rob walked to the elevator together. "Rob, can I ask a favor? Would you give me a lift home?"

Something in the set of Ellen's jaw or the paleness of her complexion stopped him from asking the obvious questions. Instead, he simply said, "Of course. I'd be happy to."

Parked in the driveway in front of her apartment there seemed to be something hanging in the air that needed to be said. But neither of them found the words, so Ellen got out, thanked Rob and trudged up the stairs to her little nest.

She sat in her mother's rocker for a long time before she finally got up to put on her pajamas and brush her teeth. In bed, she thanked the Lord for protecting her and for sending Roger.

Chapter 45
Ellen hangs out at Trish's house.

The next morning Ellen drove over to the hospital to see Jonas. Rika was beginning to look a little worn — lack of restful sleep, Ellen surmised — but Jonas seemed to be bouncing back well. "However," Rika said to him firmly, "There will be some changes when they let you go home. Fewer desserts, for one thing."

"But my dear, your culinary prowess is beyond resistance!" he replied. Ellen left them doing their pretend arguing and drove to Trish's house.

"Can I hang out here for the day?" she asked.

"Of course," said Trish. "I'd love it! But what's going on? That's not quite like you, El."

"Pour me a cup of coffee and I'll tell you about it." She sat down at the kitchen table and Trish joined her. "So you see," she said when she had finished, "I don't really want to be at my apartment today just in case Kirby comes looking for me. I don't think I could face him."

"Oh, you poor thing. Men can be such jerks, can't they?"

"Who are you calling a jerk?" That was Tommy, looking adorably tousled. "Good morning, sweetheart." He gave Trish a kiss right on the lips. "What's for breakfast?"

"Oh, rats! Ellen came by." That was obvious. "And I hadn't got around to breakfast yet. Here, let me pour you some coffee and I'll work on something." She was up and getting a cup out of the cupboard when Tommy stopped her.

"Tell you what," he said. "You girls look like you could use a good sister talk. I was going to take the kids to the skating rink anyway this morning, so how about I take them to the Dixie Diner for breakfast first?"

Ellen was amazed at how perceptive Tommy could be. Maybe all men weren't jerks. Kirby certainly was. But why couldn't a nice one show up in her life? "Tommy, that would be wonderful. How about Ellen and I have a nice meal for you all when you get back from the rink?"

"Sounds like a plan to me." He winked at Ellen and bellowed down the hallway. "Kids! Nathan! Carrie! Rise and shine! Waffles at Dixie Diner if you can be ready in ten minutes."

The effect was instantaneous, although Nathan was torn when he realized Aunt Ellen was there. He wanted to stay home, eat cereal, and show her his latest database innovations. In the end, though, he went with Tommy and Carrie after Ellen had promised him that, after lunch, she'd take a look with him.

"He's so good to take the kids off like that," said Ellen.

"Amen," said her sister. "I've got me a real keeper, there."

They spent the morning reviewing the events of last night, at times being indignant, disgusted, or just flabbergasted at the cheek Kirby had. "Some of the girls at work say that's what he's all about. I didn't really believe it until last night. And I guess he's had some success — that's an ugly thing to call it, success — or he wouldn't have tried it with me."

"What do you think he'll do now?" asked Trish.

"I don't know and I don't care."

"I actually think you should care. Might he try to retaliate for you humiliating him like that? Shouldn't you be thinking about how to protect yourself?"

"I'm not going to tell anyone. You're the only one I've told, and please keep it to yourself. I'm not going to retaliate and I won't be humiliating him. I just don't want to see him again."

"Don't you think he's pretty humiliated already? Think about it. He takes a pretty girl out ..."

"Oh Trish! Really!"

"No, I mean it. You're pretty, El. He takes a pretty girl out and expects her to sleep with him in a hotel room he's already reserved and, I assume, paid for. He's also sprung for an expensive dinner. Don't you think he's feeling pretty sore about it, even if nobody else knows?"

"When you put it that way ..."

"And how can you avoid seeing him? Don't you have to work with him?"

"Yeah, that's true, too. But at least I can minimize our interaction at work. I certainly won't go out with him again."

"I should think not."

They didn't come up with any obvious answers. Since it had been a while since the sisters had really had a chance to chat, the conversation drifted to other topics. "What about other guys, El? Any other prospects on the horizon?"

"Not really. I was kind of thinking Kirby was maybe the one. I mean he is exciting. He's really good looking. Have I ever told you about his green eyes? And that cute little curl ..." She drew and upside-down question mark on her own forehead. "Oh, and his dimple. When he smiles, I just melt ... except not any more. Oooh, he makes me so mad!"

"No other guys at all?"

"They're all either too old or married. I guess there's Herb Coffee. I don't think he's married. He runs the laser cutter at work. Nice enough guy, but ... but, no." She said it firmly. "Oh, and I guess there's Rob Powell."

"Rob Powell as in the owner?"

"Yeah," she sighed. "He's single. And smart. And reasonably good looking. But, oh, does he have a temper."

"Oh, is he the one that threw the keyboard and broke it? The one who punched a hole through the wall?"

"Yeah, that's the one. He's really fun to be around and he is really good to challenge me and let me run with some of my ideas. He's scary, too."

"More scary than a guy who assumes you're going to spend the night with him at a hotel?"

"Well, when you put it that way, maybe not so much."

By the time Tommy got back with the kids, Trish and Ellen had made hamburgers with Ellen's secret ingredients (finely diced onions and some Worcestershire sauce), homemade mac and cheese, and a big green salad. "The kids must have skated ten miles today," said Tommy. "I'll bet they're starved."

"If you'll fire up the grill — I know it's cold, but I'm counting on you, sir — we'll be ready to eat soon."

Tommy kissed Trish on the mouth again. "Why, Mr. Thompson! You'll turn my head if you're not careful."

"That's the plan!" he said as he carried the platter of burgers and the spatula out to the back deck.

Trish lightly broiled the hamburger buns while Ellen set the table.

"Mommy, Mommy, gueth what?"

"What, sweetheart?" Trish got down on her knees to look Carrie in the eye.

"I won the limbo contetht!"

"You did?"

"In her age group," Nathan added sagely.

"How low can you go!" Carrie quoted in her deepest voice and then dissolved into giggles.

"Oh, you. You're my precious little girl." She hugged the little redhead.

Before long they were all gathered around the table like old times. Ellen had set the table like she had always done, but she realized from Nathan's slight awkwardness that there must be a new table arrangement now in her absence. Times were moving on.

After they'd washed up, Ellen went back to her old room to find Nathan working on his computer. He gave her the grand tour of the system he was writing for Tubby's paper route and Ellen noted that there appeared to be several weeks worth of live data in the system.

"Nathan, this is really impressive. I'm serious. You've done really, really well here. Tell you what, Ace. Let's see how the system stacks up against the five principles of business information technology."

"That would be great! I've been wanting to know how you're doing on that," he said.

"So first," said Ellen, "Does the system model the business it serves? In this case, what is the business?"

"Tubby's paper route."

"Of course," said Ellen. "And do you know what we mean by 'model the business?' Does it work the way the business does?"

"We talked about that before, but I think it does. Remember I set up two files, one for subscribers and one for bills? That was better than the way I first did it."

"Right, I remember."

"I had to add another file, too. Sometimes people don't pay their whole bill. Like they owe $8.00, but they only give Tubby $5.00. So the bill isn't paid, but I have to keep track of the $5.00 that was already paid and the $3.00 they still owe."

"How do you do that?"

"I made another file called Payments."

"What's the noun of that file?" He smiled that she remembered his way of thinking about files using grammar.

"It is a compound subject," he said. "At first I used the subscriber number — remember that, Aunt Ellen? How we came up with a number instead of using the name because there could be more than one person with the same name? — but now I just use the bill number."

"Don't you have to have the subscriber number?"

"Sure, I have to have it. But it doesn't uniquely specify the bill. The bill number alone does that.

"But does it? When that person finally pays their other $3.00, won't that have the same bill number?"

"Uh oh. I hadn't thought about that ..." He leaned back in his chair in classic Nathan thinking posture. Ellen waited. "Oh, I've got it! It has to be the bill number plus the date — that makes the subject unique in the payment file."

"I believe you are right, Nate. Well done! Now what about the second principle, that the system must be non-redundant?"

"Well, we kind of worked on that ..."

"Yes, you did. And from what I'm seeing, from what you've told me about the payment file, you're doing a good job of that. You're adjusting and changing the system as you learn new things. Now, are you ready for the third rule?"

"You bet!"

"The third rule is that the system has to be built in a way that it is easy to capture data. The bar code readers you helped with at Powell over Christmas break are an example. We can scan those bar codes and get data into the system really fast."

"I think you're gonna like this, Aunt Ellen." He pulled out his own bar code reader, the one Ellen had gotten him as a gift. "Look at this screen." He showed Ellen a simple screen that had the bill number, the amount, the date, and a place to record a check number or the word 'cash.' "See?" he said. "I just scan the bill number off of the piece of paper they send back to Tubby." He demonstrated with a sample bill. The system looked up the subscriber ID off of the bill number, then placed the subscriber's name on the screen.

Ellen couldn't help herself. "Oh, that is so COOL!" Nathan beamed.

"Then I just enter the amount and the check number — or cash, if they paid by cash, and the system puts in today's date. I can replace the date if the check like came in the mail yesterday, but I didn't get it entered until today."

"Nathan, this is fabulous! I would say your system meets Principle Three very, very well."

"So what's the fourth principle?

"Well, just like Principle Three is about getting data into the system, Principle Four is about getting data out. The system has to be built so that you can easily get data out?"

"Like what kind of data?"

"Well, let's see. I imagine Tubby might like to have a report of which people owe him money so that he could try collecting when he's out on his paper route."

"Yeah, I thought of that, too." He rummaged around the papers on his desk and pulled one out. "Like this?"

Ellen scanned the printout. It was done in monospace Courier type on a dot matrix printer: not particularly elegant, but functional. All the information was there — the subscriber's name and address and the amount they owed as well as the amount they had paid so far, if any. "So this uses your new history file, too?" she asked, pointing to one of the entries.

"Yes, Mason Calico was who I was thinking about when I told you that example. He owes $8.00, but only paid $5.00. He told Tubby he didn't have any ones. And see, this one here, Verna Powell, owes the full $8.00, but that is because the bill just went out — Tubby hasn't collected that one yet."

"You are a boy genius! I'm so proud of you. And so, if Tubby wanted to know how much money he collected during the last week, both in checks and cash, could you do a report of that?"

"Hmmm." He tilted back in his chair again. "Yes, yes I think I could. And that's a good idea, Aunt Ellen. Tubby would really like that."

"And the fact that you are thinking about how to do that shows you're using the fourth principle very well. I'm actually working on those kinds of reports myself at work."

"So what's the fifth principle?"

"I haven't figured it out yet. Mr. Klameck tells me that I will, but so far I haven't found it."

"I know you will, Aunt Ellen."

"Thanks, buddy. Your confidence in me means a lot. Now I have an idea."

She and Nathan went back into the living room. "How about I take the kids to a movie?" she asked.

Carrie was immediately bouncing up and down. "Oh yeth, yeth. I love movieth!"

"What's playing?" asked Trish.

"There's a new Pippi Longstocking movie out that I'd like to see. It would be appropriate for Carrie. Nathan might not love it ..." She looked at Nathan. "But, you see, Pippi Longstocking is Swedish, and

I'm kind of interested in Swedish things right now because of my
landlady being from Sweden. What do you say?"

Everyone agreed. "Between the drive to the theater in Oak Lick,
the movie, and maybe a snack afterwards, you've got at least three
hours," Ellen whispered to Trish and Tommy. "What you do with the
time is your own business."

Chapter 46

Ellen discovers the gossip that is being spread about her.

Monday morning Ellen managed to collect the job cards without running into Kirby. He was at work, but was at the far end of the Assembly Line when she made her rounds. She spotted him at a distance, grabbed the job cards from his office, and headed back to the front office before he could speak to her. Herb Coffee gave her a huge grin, a big thumbs up, and said, "Way to go, Possum!" as she went by.

She managed that little maneuver for several days in a row. "I know I can't dodge him forever," she said to herself. "But maybe the more time that goes by, the less he'll feel the humiliation."

On Thursday she met Annie and Rachel in the cafeteria to share lunch. "I'm a little surprised at you, Ellen," said Rachel. "You ain't the kind of girl I thought you was after all."

"Excuse me?" said Ellen. "What are you talking about?"

"Yeah," sighed Annie. "I was wondering too what was going on."

"What do you mean, what's going on?"

"About you and Kirby," said Rachel. "At the Campbell House in Lexington."

"Oh, that. So Kirby's talking, huh? Well it is a good thing I had your warning, Rachel, or I would have been in real trouble."

"I guess everyone's got a different idea of trouble," said Rachel. "Spending the night with Kirby would be trouble, if you ask me. But if you ain't worried …"

"Spending the night?? Spending the night??" Ellen's voice got louder and shriller so that several people at nearby tables looked at her. "I didn't spend the night." She made a real effort to lower her voice. "I got out of there quick when I realized what he was trying to pull off."

"That's not what Kirby's telling around the factory," said Rachel. "He says the two of you spent the night together. He's bragging about it."

Ellen almost choked on her sandwich.

"You mean it ain't true?" asked Annie. "I prayed and prayed it wouldn't be ..."

"Of course it isn't true." Ellen was fierce, glaring at the other two women. "Of COURSE it isn't true. What kind of girl do you think I am?"

"Maybe one of a dozen others who couldn't quite fight off the Kirby Anderson charm," said Rachel. "I didn't want to believe it, but Kirby's telling everyone who will listen what a great night he had with you."

Ellen started to get up, "I'm going to give that rat a piece of my mind ..."

Annie pulled her back down onto the bench. "Don't go off half cocked Ellen. First, why don't you tell us what really happened. Then we'll work us up a plan."

So Ellen was forced to relive that night again, trying as accurately as she could to recount what had happened. "And so a guy named Roger, Roger something, gave me a ride home in his pickup. He was just getting off work and he lives here in Laodicia. He was a real life saver."

Annie put her hand to her heart. "I am so relieved. I didn't want to believe it, but the rumors are as thick as molasses in winter." She reached out and touched her friend on her shoulder. "We believe her, don't we Rachel."

"Of course we do. We just didn't have any other story agin' Kirby's tale."

"The thing is," said Annie. "What are we going to do about it? Ellen's reputation has been drug through the mud. What do you think, Rachel?"

"Well ..." said Rachel thoughtfully. "It kinda seems to me that if Ellen says it ain't so, people might suspect her of not telling the truth.

What did Will Shakespeare say? 'Me thinks she doth protest too much.'"

"Shakespeare, Rachel? Really?" said Ellen.

"What? You don't think us mountain girls know about Shakespeare? English lit was my favorite class in high school. But ole' Will's got a point, don't he? If you protest too much, it'll make people think what Kirby's saying about is really true."

"That's a good point, Rachel. I want to go and pop Kirby on the nose so bad, but it might be better to be a little more strategic."

"That's right," said Annie. "We got to come at him sideways, like. Besides, Scripture says we got to turn the other cheek. Don't it say that, Rachel?"

"It does. 'Vengeance is mine, saith the Lord.'"

"Now hold on girls! I've got to get back at Kirby for what he's done to me. Are you saying I shouldn't get even?"

"That's what we're sayin'," said Annie. "A feller like Kirby will step in his own doo-doo sooner or later. You've just got to hold your head up, keep on the straight and narrow, and be patient. He'll get his sooner or later, and you won't have to lift a finger."

"But how can I face people?" Suddenly the image of Herb saying 'Way to go, Possum.' took on a new context. Her face turned red again with anger and shame.

"We can help you there," said Rachel. "We can pass the word around that Kirby's spreading lies about you. Not everybody'll believe us, but it's a start."

"And I'm serious, girl. You got to keep doing your job and hold your head up high even though you know what some people are whispering about you. You think you can do that?"

"It'll be hard. I want so bad to …"

"Me too," said Rachel. "In fact, several of the girls in Assembly will be right there with you. They've gone out with Kirby. Remember what I told you about him wanting to get in their panties? Some of 'em found out the hard way, just like you did. But getting back at Kirby is liable to backfire on you. You got to put this in the Good Lord's hands."

As she walked back from lunch to her office, she suddenly wondered if Rob had heard the rumors and what he must think of her. Somehow that mattered to her. "Oh, but he's the head guy. He probably doesn't hear the shop floor gossip," she consoled herself.

Ellen threw herself into her work. In the weeks that followed, she became more of a recluse, spending more time in her office developing additional RPG programs to analyze the bar code data. She managed to avoid Kirby as much as possible when collecting job cards, and was grateful when he was off for a vacation day or whatever his reason was for being gone. The volume of data was becoming substantial with the passage of each week, so she had a lot more to analyze. She wasn't sure what she was looking for, but she felt she would know it when she found it.

She also started writing RPG programs to extract data for some of the other managers, too. For the head of purchasing she wrote a program to extract all of the steel orders for the past 12 months, sorting them first by gauge of steel, and then by vendor. "We'll use this to go after some price concessions from some of our vendors," he told her. "When we show them the volume of business we do, and consolidate it by gauge of steel, I think we'll have some good leverage. Thanks, Ellen."

For Luther Holtzmann, the Production Control Manager, she wrote a program to analyze all of the work for the past six months by machine center, clearly establishing tooling swaps on the three and a half ton press as a critical bottleneck in the factory. "You're working magic, there Ellen. You've confirmed what I've always kind of suspected. We really need to put some effort into making sure the press is kept busy all the time every day and that we minimize those tooling swaps every way we can."

Word was getting around and other mangers were coming to her with requests to extract data for them. "I'm starting to see the real power of the Fourth Principle," she said to herself. "These guys are asking good questions that they really need answers to. I'm helping them make good decisions and that's got to be good for the company."

She was beginning to take real pride in being able to answer questions as they came up.

Sandy McDonald had her come to one of the weekly staff meetings and explain to Rob and the other managers some of the finer points of a report she had done for him. When he introduced her, he said she had worked some 'Possum Magic' to create the report. Ellen tried to take that in stride, since her value to the company seemed to be widely respected by the managers.

Jonas was home from the hospital by now and they had settled into a routine. Rika was totally focused on making sure Jonas did his physical therapy and that he ate right. Ellen was a frequent guest for dinner, something she enjoyed immensely. She never told Rika about what had happened that night at the Campbell House; she was trying to put it behind her. She did badger Jonas a bit, however, asking for hints about the Fifth Principle. He just laughed and said, "You'll absolutely know it when you see it. It is perhaps the easiest of the five, and yet the most difficult to see. It is right in front of your face, but you just don't know it yet." To Rika he said, "Oh, this is fun, my dear. Such a bright young woman, and so much fun to talk with. It feels like the old days." Rika just smiled and suggested another serving of kale and almond salad.

The winter days stretched on and Ellen found herself getting tired of the cold, dark weather. She took a cue from Rika and often lit candles in her apartment. She read a lot in the evenings, reading all six Jane Austin novels again. Or she went to visit Trish and Tommy. Valentines Day came and went, and she wondered if she'd ever have someone special in her life.

Chapter 47
The snow storm.

"They're giving snow on Channel 27." Annie poked her head in Ellen's office. She already had her coat and scarf on. "Don't you be staying late, now. You get on home, you hear?"

Ellen looked up from the spreadsheet she was working on. "Oh, right. Thanks for telling me, Annie. I think I did hear something about that on the radio this morning."

"I'm just sayin' …" said Annie, and she was gone.

Ellen must have lost track of time; she realized it was already four o'clock and there were some fat flakes of snow drifting down. She had downloaded another batch of bar code data and was looking for patterns.

"Hey, Ellen. You still here?" It was Whit Collette. Ellen looked up. She glanced out the window and realized darkness was beginning to fall outside.

"Oh, yeah. I guess I lost track of the time."

"I think you and I are the only ones left in the building," said Whit. "Well, except for Rob. I think he's still in his office. You need to go. I live right here in Oak Lick, but don't you live in Laodicea?"

"You're right. I really ought to be going." She started to show Whit what she was working on, but he held up his hand to stop her.

"It can wait. The roads are getting slick already." He pulled a wooly toboggan over his ears. "See you Monday."

Ellen looked at a few more data points and then began to gather her purse and coat. She clicked off the light in her office and noticed how dark and still it seemed. No machines pounding out in the shop, no buzz of conversation, no clicking of keys on keyboards. It was so still she could hear the quiet but ominous pecking of the flakes of snow blowing against the window. The only light in the hallway was coming out of Rob's office. She turned away from the lobby and walked toward his office.

"I'm the last one out except for you. Want me to hit the lights? I think maintenance already locked the doors."

Rob looked up from the pad of paper and rubbed his eyes. "What time is it?" he asked.

Ellen looked at her watch. "Five-thirty," she said. "Hadn't you better head home, too? They say it is going to snow."

He looked out his own window toward the empty parking lot. Only two cars were there and Ellen realized that the snow was already several inches deep. She had better head home, and soon. "I'd say it already is snowing. And coming down fast. You go on. I'll make sure everything is snug for the weekend, OK?"

"Sure," she said. "But don't stay too long. It looks like it could get rough out there." She didn't mean to come across as someone who was overly concerned, just as one colleague to another. I don't even know where he lives, she thought. Does he have a long drive, or is he like Whit and he's just a short distance from home? "Good-night!"

"Goodnight, Ellen. Have a nice weekend."

The snow was over her shoes as she picked her way across the parking lot to Gunilla. It was coming down so thickly that she had to keep blinking her eyes when the big flakes stuck in her eyelashes. By the time she got the engine started and the wipers going, her feet were wet and her cheeks were numb. "Whew, Gunilla!" she said to her car. "Let's go home!" Gunilla made the scrunchy, squeaky noise of tires breaking new snow on pavement.

By the time she got out on the state highway, the snow had intensified and Gunilla's lights were no match for the blowing snow. The patterns of the flakes floating inexorably in unison were mesmerizing. First they went left, then right, but always down and down, adding to the inches piling up on the road. "Concentrate, Ellen. You've got to concentrate." She gripped the wheel. No radio now; her Dad had taught her how to drive in snow. She needed to hear the tires on the road. The only sound was the whisper of the heater fan motor and the thunk-thunk, thunk-thunk of the wipers. "Wow, this is ridiculous," she said out loud. "I can hardly see the road."

She had driven the route so many times that she knew it quite well. She was coming to the stretch with the old rock wall border and the old mansion up on the top of the hill. Suddenly she was looking at the lights of a snowplow coming toward her. She squealed as she tried not to slam on her brakes. She knew that would make her lose traction. The snowplow seemed wider than the road and she had to steer quickly to the right to avoid the huge blade as it thundered past her, barely missing her mirror and making an awful scraping roar. She tried to correct back to the left, but it was too late. She felt the skid and then the right front tire tip over the edge of the road, followed quickly by the rear one. Suddenly she was at a dead stop, tilting badly to the right, and with the rock wall immediately outside the passenger window. Clearly she was in a ditch, and a deep one.

Ellen tried putting the Saab in first gear, but the wheels immediately spun. She tried reverse, with the same result. "Now what?" she said out loud. She sat there for a minute, seeing the snow coming down as hard as ever. There was a brief moment of panic — was she going to freeze to death in her own car? No! She was more resilient than that. But what could she do? She struggled to open the car door and push it uphill. It was a job to get out with Gunilla lying at such an angle. She put her foot down and realized that her pretty shoes were no match for eight inches of snow. She struggled out of the car to assess the damage. The silence of the blizzard was deafening.

Without a flashlight, it was difficult to see anything, but it did seem that the car was well off the road. She couldn't walk far in those shoes and she hadn't brought anything better to change into. Did she have any other warm things? She tugged her scarf closer around her neck and tucked it down in her coat. She pulled her hat down over her ears, even though it wasn't exactly a fashion statement.

Suddenly she was aware of a car coming toward her, from the Oak Lick direction. She'd never hitchhiked before, unless you counted Roger giving her a ride home from the Campbell House. Regardless, this was probably a good time to start.

She waved her hands and then stuck out her gloved thumb. Hopefully the driver would see her and not run over her.

The car slowed down and pulled along side her. The window opened on the passenger side and a familiar voice said, "Have a little problem?"

"Yes, a snowplow came along on my side of the road and I dodged it but I ended up in this ditch and now I'm stuck and I really need ... Sorry. I'm babbling. What I really need is to get to a phone to call someone to come and pull me out."

"Is that you, Ellen?"

She peered into the interior of the dark American Motors Eagle. The dashboard illuminated his face just barely. "Mr. Powell? I mean, Rob?"

He laughed. "That's me. I think you could use a little help. Come on, get in."

"But what about my car?"

"I don't think it is going anywhere tonight. We'll call a wrecker to come pull you out in the morning. Right now, though, I think we need to get you somewhere warm. And I know just the place. Do you have anything you need in your car? Probably better turn off the lights and lock it, just in case."

Ellen did as she was told, grabbing her purse and the notebook, and then slid into the passenger side of the blissfully warm car. "Oooh," she breathed, trying to keep her teeth from chattering.

"I'm really glad I came along when I did," Rob said as he put the car in drive.

"I am too. I'm not sure what I would have done."

"Well, I know what we're going to do right now. We're going to get you some warmer clothes and a hot meal." He suddenly turned off the highway onto a narrow drive that went up a hill.

"Where are we going? And how is your car pulling this hill? It is slick out there," she said ruefully. "I know from personal experience."

"This Eagle has full time four wheel drive," he replied. "It can go places most cars can't. Built on the Jeep platform, you know. As to where we're going, why, we're going to my home. You're about to meet my mother!" He looked at her and grinned.

"You live … here? In this old … I mean, in this mansion? Wow!"

He laughed out loud. "I'm glad you approve. It isn't quite a mansion, but it is a grand old home that dates back from before the Civil War. It has been in my family for three generations, counting me."

The drive was long and curving and, at one point, to Ellen's horror, the back wheels started fish-tailing. Rob expertly steered into the skid and, after a few tense moments, got the car back under control and heading up the hill.

He pulled up behind the house and, before Ellen could get herself organized, he was around at her door, opening it, and offering his hand to steady her on the slippery pavement. "Come on in," he said. "My mother and grandmother would love to meet you."

They stomped their feet on the back porch steps. "I'm sorry not to be bringing you in the front door as befits a first-time guest. But I figure those shoes wouldn't be interested in trekking around to the front of the house just for formality's sake."

"I'm just grateful for a chance to get in out of the snow and maybe get out of my wet shoes."

Rob opened the door with a flourish and yelled, "MO-ther! I'm HO-me!"

"Is that you, Robbie? I was worried. The weather has gotten so bad, I …" An attractive woman wearing a nice sweater and a wool skirt came around the corner. She was drying her hands on an apron she had around her waist. "Oh," she said. "And who have we here?"

"Mother, this is a stray kitten I picked up on the side of the road. Can I keep her, huh? Can I, huh? Can I?"

"Oh Robbie, you foolish boy. Does this beautiful stray have a name?"

Ellen held out her hand. "Hello, Mrs. Powell. I'm Ellen Murphy. I work at Powell and I've had a bit of an accident at the foot of your driveway. A snowplow and I disagreed over which side of the road belonged to him, and … Well, Mr. Powell was nice enough to rescue me from certain death."

"Oh, how delightful! Mr. Powell was my father-in-law. But this young rascal ..." She patted his face affectionately. "This young rascal has provided us with a rare treat. I'm so glad he rescued you." She shook Ellen's hand. "Welcome to Three Pines."

"Who is it, Shelby Lynn?" An older woman, also wearing an apron, came around the corner.

"Mother, Robbie has brought home a guest for dinner. Do we think we can accommodate one more?"

She was a petite woman, hardly five feet tall, with a precious round face that was all wrinkles and smiles. She clasped her hands as if she could not imagine anything more pleasant. "Of course, of course. It isn't often we get guests up here on the hill. I'm so delighted that you've come." She took both of Ellen's hands in her own. "What is your name, child?"

"I'm Ellen Murphy. I am very pleased to meet you. I work for Mr. Powell at Powell Manufacturing."

"How wonderful!" she said. "And you must call me Verna. I'm Robbie's grandmother."

Between the three of them, they bustled about and got Ellen to take off her wet shoes. Her coat was hung where it could drip and dry. Mrs. Powell the younger brought her some cozy house slippers and a shawl and Ellen was finally beginning to feel toasty.

"Dinner is just about ready," said the younger Mrs. Powell. "Mother, what else do we need to do?"

"I'll just set another place and I believe we can sit down."

They sat and, without a word, reached out and took each other's hands. Ellen, at the foot of the table found she was holding the slim hand of Rob's mother on one side and the wrinkled hand of his grandmother on the other. They all bowed their heads in unison and Rob asked a blessing on the food.

The conversation flowed easily. Mrs. Powell the younger was a skilled conversationalist, bringing Ellen into the conversation without giving her the third degree. By the time dinner was over, Ellen was managing to remember to call her Shelby Lynn, instead of Mrs. Powell. The grandmother was so genuinely friendly that using her first name just came naturally. Throughout dinner, Rob joined in the conversation when prompted, but every time Ellen looked across the table, there he was, watching her and smiling.

When dinner was over, Ellen offered to help with the dishes. The ladies were quick to find her an apron and make her feel at home. In no time, Ellen felt like a member of the team. Just as they were wrapping up, Rob came back in and announced, "It is coming down even harder, if you can believe that. I think we've got ten inches on the ground and no sign of it stopping. I've brought in extra wood, just in case we lose power."

Ellen realized now that there was the faint tang of woodsmoke that gave the old house a rustic charm. "Will I be able to get home?" she asked.

"Honestly, Ellen, I don't think that's a good idea. I slid coming up the drive, and that hardly ever happens with my four wheel drive. That means it is really slick out there. Getting you home might be … difficult." He looked at his mother for support.

"I have an idea, Ellen, that I hope is acceptable to you. How about you stay here for the night? Then, in the morning, after they've been able to clear the roads and we see how things are in the daylight, Robbie can run you home and see about getting your car pulled out of the ditch."

"Oh, I don't know …"

"Now, now, honey," said Verna. "It won't be that bad. We can come up with some spare clothes, can't we Shelby Lynn?"

"Of course we can, Mother. I have a wonderful flannel nightgown that I've never worn, big and warm and just right for a night like this. I think I may even have a spare toothbrush, just a little used." She laughed and reached out and patted Ellen's shoulder. "I"m only kidding! It hasn't been used. They gave it to me at the dentist's office last month. What do you say?"

"Well …" It seemed so awkward to Ellen, staying at her boss's house with his mother and grandmother. "I don't know …"

Rob took her hand and pulled her toward him. "Come here. I want to show you something." He led her around the corner, past the back door, and into a huge living room. The ceilings were so high they seemed lost in the shadows, but there was a wonderful fire burning cheerfully in a wood stove and it was giving off blissful amounts of heat. "Take a look out the window." He led her to a window that seemed to go floor to ceiling. She could feel the cold coming off of the glass as she and Rob stepped closer to it. The snow was coming down as fiercely as it had been when she'd been run off the road. More than that, the tracks Rob's car had made coming up the drive were almost completely filled in. "I really don't think you're going anywhere tonight."

"I see what you mean. Oh, Rob, I'm so sorry. I didn't mean to intrude on ..."

He cut her off. "Now listen here, Ellen Murphy. We would take a stranger in who was stranded out on a night like this. But you're no stranger. No stranger at all. It's settled, OK? You'll stay here and I'll take you home in the morning, assuming we can get out." He winked at her. "Oh, MO-ther!" he called. "The stray kitten has decided to stay."

"Oh good," said Shelby Lynn as they returned to the kitchen. "See here, Ellen? We have a gown and a towel and washcloth, and a toothbrush, and this cunning little toothpaste tube I picked up at an airport somewhere."

"You're all so kind, taking me in like this ..." She looked around at all three of them. "I'm very grateful."

"Would you like to make a phone call, honey?" asked Verna. "Is there someone who needs to know where you are? A husband, perhaps?"

Ellen laughed. "Oh, no. No husband. Or boyfriend, either. But it would be good to call my sister and let her know what's happened."

Shelby Lynn showed her where the phone was and then gave her some privacy. "Hello, Trish? ... Yes, it's me. Listen, I had a little accident. I was ... No, no, I'm not hurt. But my car is stuck and there's no way for it to get pulled out tonight. ... Yes, right. ... No, I'm trying to tell you. Rob, er, Mr. Powell came along and found me and brought me to his house ... No, no, it's all right. His mother and grandmother are here, too. They've invited me to stay the night and I really don't have any other options." She listened as Trish talked it through and came to the same conclusion. "OK, Trish. I just thought you ought to know where I am. … Yes, all right. … Right. … Kiss the kids and Tommy for me. Goodbye."

While she was at it, she called Rika and explained the situation. "Yes, so a friend from work happened to come along — I'll be staying with them, tonight. I just didn't want you to worry when you realized I hadn't come back to the apartment." Why hadn't she told her it was Robbie Powell's house she was at? She rang off and went back into the kitchen.

"We have decided," said Shelby Lynn, "that it would be best if you take Robbie's bedroom. It is upstairs, and the only bedroom up there. And it has its own bath. You'll have more privacy that way. Robbie will sleep on the sofa in the living room and keep an eye on the stove during this brutal weather."

"Oh, I couldn't!"

"Yes you could, and you will," said Rob. "It is decided. I'm not your boss here, so I can't order you around." He winked again. "To my way of thinking, though, this makes the most sense."

"It's just …" She looked around the room at all three of them again. "You're all being so nice to me, and …"

"That's what friends are for, child." Verna gave a firm nod, as if to indicate she would brook no opposition. Ellen nodded and couldn't help stifling a yawn.

"You're tired, aren't you?" Shelby Lynn said. "I was thinking I might put on some water for tea, but I'm wondering if you'd just like to turn in now."

"What time is it?" asked Ellen. She looked at her own watch. Almost 9:30! But they were all so nice. "Well, maybe one cup." She smiled, and found her smile reflected in all three faces.

"I'll put the kettle on," said Verna.

"And I'll get the tea things," said Shelby Lynn. "Robbie, why don't you show Ellen where she'll be sleeping. I hope you made your bed this morning!" She patted his face.

The brief cloud that crossed his face reminded Ellen that she sometimes forgot to make her own bed, too. For his sake, she hoped he had remembered. "My room is up the stairs around here." They passed through the living room, past a large door that Ellen presumed was the front entrance. The stairs were wide and grand as befitted an antebellum mansion. A modest chandelier hung over the broad wooden treads. They turned on the landing and Rob opened the door. "This is my room," he said briefly.

The bed was made. Ellen glanced around the room as she laid the gown and towels on the bed. There was a desk with a computer and two pictures in frames. One was clearly Shelby Lynn and a man that Ellen presumed was Rob's father. The other was older in faded black and white. The seated man was dressed in clothes from the early 1900s. There was a petite young woman, a girl, really, standing beside him with her hand on his shoulder. She wore and wide-brimmed hat with a feather, a nice dress for its day, and high buckled shoes. With a flash, Ellen recognized it was Verna as a young woman. "Is this your grandmother?" she asked.

"Yes, that's Mammaw and Pappaw, on their wedding day."

"How wonderful!" she exclaimed. "It's a great picture. I'm sure you're proud of it."

He picked it up and looked at it. "They were a great couple. They worked hard and scrimped and saved and bought Three Pines. I've never seen such a team."

"What is the history of this place? You said it was built before the Civil War. How did they come to own such a grand mansion?"

"Oh, it's a great story. He was a poor farmer and she was the proverbial farmer's daughter. They must have loved each other from a very young age. They married young. He was 18 and she was 16. But they were a real force to be reckoned with. They worked very hard and were able to purchase this place when it came up for sale. The owners had fallen on hard times and they were able to get it at a bargain. Then they worked some more and turned this place into a real working farm with a beautiful mansion."

"It is beautiful!"

"Did you know that this house was used as a hospital in the civil war?"

"I had no idea."

"Some day I'll show you the dent made by the cannon balls on the front wall." He pulled back the carpet that was beside the bed and pointed to a stain on the bare wood floorboards. "They say that is the blood of a confederate soldier who died in this room after the battle." He looked up at her. "I'm sorry. I shouldn't have told you that."

Ellen stared at the faded stain. "No." she said. "No ... that's OK. It is fascinating history ..." She paused again. "Kind of creepy, though."

"Yes, and probably just a legend that isn't true. This house was used as a field hospital after the battle, though. But sometimes it creeps me out just a little bit, too." He flipped the rug back over the stain and grinned up at her. "Why do you think I keep a rug over it?"

He indicated the bathroom. "And, just in case, here's a candle and some matches. The way this storm is going, it wouldn't surprise me if the power went out."

They went back downstairs where the ladies had laid out the tea things. "What kind of tea do you like?" asked Shelby Lynn.

"I ... I'm afraid I'm just learning about tea. I like it, but ... "

"Oooh, honey. You're just like me," chortled Verna. "I love tea, but give me plain 'ole Lipton. Here, come sit by me."

Chapter 48
The night at Three Pines.

The room was very cold by the time Ellen changed into the borrowed gown. The blowing snow was still coming down relentlessly as she took one last look out the window. There was a strange orangish cast to the landscape. It should have been dark, and yet, with all the snow, it seemed that the light from the house downstairs was being reflected again and again, giving an eerie glow to the scene.

She wanted to browse the many bookshelves in Rob's room, but she was cold and tired. The sheets were frigid as she slid between them, giving her bare legs a burning sensation. She pulled the thick quilts up under her chin and shivered. How would she ever get to sleep?

But she must have, for, when she awoke, the wind was rattling the windows and she realized that it was really cold, much colder than it was before. She looked at her watch. 3:30 AM. So she had been asleep. But, my goodness was it cold! She fancied she could see her breath when she exhaled.

The tea drove her to the restroom despite the cold. She flipped on the light, but nothing happened. Perhaps the electricity really was out. She fumbled with the match and got the candle lit. Her hands shook from the cold.

The thought of the wood stove downstairs drew her. She wrapped Shelby Lynn's shawl around her shoulders and tried to be as quiet as possible as she felt her way down the stairs, using the candle for light.

It was definitely warmer in the living room. The dancing flames in the wood stove gave the room a cozy glow. She was trying to quietly slip into a chair in the corner when a voice spoke from the couch. "The power's out."

"I'm sorry. I didn't mean to wake you. I thought the power was out. It is frightfully c-cold upstairs." She shivered.

"I'm sure it is. This may be a mansion, but insulation is not something it offers. I'm glad you came down. I was hoping you might sleep through it, but I wouldn't want you up there freezing to death."

"What about your mother and grandmother?"

"They both have rooms that were added on later. They're well insulated and, until the power went off, were well heated. But in the original structure, no insulation and only fireplaces for heat. And now …" He indicated the stove. " … this lovely beast." He sat up and brought a blanket to her. "Here. Wrap this around you while I throw another log on old Bessie here."

"Thanks." In the light of her single candle and the glow of the stove, she could see that he still had on his dress pants from work, but that his dress shirt and tie had been discarded over the back of a chair, leaving only a t-shirt. "Aren't you cold, too?"

"Oh, I suppose. A little. But its not bad, and old Bessie here will be pumping out more heat in no time." He returned to the couch and pulled a blanket up around him.

They watched the fire through the glass door of the wood stove, gradually catching the logs and gently increasing the heat output. They didn't say anything. The old regulator clock on the wall was like a metronome, counting off the minutes quietly in the corner. In a flash she understood it must be a manually wound clock since it was still ticking. Ellen realized that the wind outside seemed to have died down a bit. A sense of peace, blissful, unexpected and completely comfortable established itself in the room.

When Rob spoke, it was almost as if he was reluctant to break the mood. "Ellen," he said, almost in a whisper. "Are you happy?"

"Oh yes," she sighed, and then caught herself. "Oh, I mean, that is … do you mean at work?"

"I suppose. Partly. Work is a big chunk of our lives. But I really meant you, as a person. Are you happy with your life, with what you're doing with your life, with the directions your life is taking?"

In a corner of her mind, Ellen realized that this was an intensely personal question. And yet, in this place, in this darkened room with only the sound of the clock and the crackle of the fire, at this time, stranded in a snowstorm with this man who had rescued her, with only two of them talking … it seemed like the most natural question in the world.

"I think so …" She began tentatively. But as she spoke into the velvety shadows that played around the corners of the room, she grew in confidence. She tucked her knees up under her gown so that her thighs pressed against her, hugging her knees to her as the room began to warm up. Her initial hesitance gave way to transparency as she explained about Trish and Tommy, about finding her own place, about how important and rewarding her work at Powell was to her.

Rob let her talk. Occasionally nodding or asking a clarifying question. He didn't ask about her relationship with Kirby, but, had he asked, she would have willingly told him.

He told her about his dad and going off to college and his dad suddenly being diagnosed with cancer. Fast, inoperable pancreatic cancer. How he had been thrust into the leadership of the company before he felt he was ready. He spoke passionately about his desperate desire to save the company, for the people who were employed there, to safe-keep his mother's investments, as a way to honor his dad. He was very candid with her; when he had finished talking about it she understood deep in her soul how important it was to him and also how dire things were.

They talked of meaningful things, of plans and dreams, of silly things. The conversation flowed easily and freely. Something about the magic of this time made it all seem so right. She realized, drowsily, almost subconsciously, that she was beginning to see Rob more as a friend and a colleague and less as a boss and an employer.

Chapter 49
After the snow storm.

They must have slept. Ellen became dimly aware that the light had changed. The dark windows were now pale grey and a pre-dawn glow suffused the room. The fire was mostly embers, now, although the heat coming off of "old Bessie" was comforting. She stretched.

"You're awake." Rob made a simple statement.

"I guess I dozed off."

Rob smiled. "I'm glad you did. We both needed some sleep. But I really enjoyed our chat." He looked at her with those intense eyes of his. "Really, I mean it."

"I enjoyed it, too," she said quietly. They both sat for a moment, watching the embers in the stove.

"I need to put more wood on the fire, but I have an idea." He got up and moved across to the stove, opening its door and placing three more logs inside.

"Oh?" she asked.

"I need to check out the animals after this storm. Come with me."

"Animals? You have a farm?"

"Yup. A horse, some goats and chickens. They'll have had a rough night and I need to make sure they're OK, give them some feed and make sure they can get to water. I'd like you to come."

She looked down at her flannel gown. "Is it far? I don't think that I'm dressed exactly ..." She let the thought dangle lamely.

"Yes, you're right. But I think we have what you need. There's a pair of insulated overalls in the back hall and an insulated pair of boots. We'll put one of my work coats around you and I think you'll be fine." He grinned and held out his hand. "Come on. I want to show you some things, things I care about."

She couldn't resist, although getting stuffed into a pair of overalls while dressed in a flannel nightgown was a new experience. By the time she was all bundled up, she realized how ridiculous she must look. Clunky old farm boots, overalls, and a bulky winter coat that was several sizes too big and that smelled of animals and hay made quite a picture, she was sure. But Rob was delighted as he pulled an old hat down over her head and gave her a pair of insulated gloves. "You look absolutely stunning," he said. "You think I'm kidding you, don't you? But I'm not. You look really special." He took a basket off of a hook and opened the back door.

The brightness as they stepped out took their breath away. The storm was obviously over, having spent itself during the night. In its place, the air was bitterly cold, but the sun had now come up, illuminating everything and making the snow so bright it hurt to look. It was breathtaking. Ellen suddenly found her throat was tight and there were tears in her eyes. "Ohh," she breathed. "It's beautiful!"

Rob just stood there, looking out at the barn and the fields behind the house. Finally he turned and looked at her. She couldn't read his face, but clearly something had touched him. "Isn't it beautiful?" she asked.

He swallowed. "Amazing. Stunning. I can't find the words ..." He looked at her again. "Come on. I'll introduce you to the animals."

The snow was a good twelve inches deep and required some high stepping to get through it. Rob finally suggested that he go first and that she follow in his footprints. They reached the barn and Rob lifted the latch so they could slip inside. Ellen heard the low nicker of a horse and the cluck of chickens.

"Hello, Henry," called Rob. The horse nickered again, and Ellen saw him, looking over the half door of his stable. Rob stroked his velvety nose. "How are you doing, boy? Was it a cold night?" Henry responded with what was clearly a ritual, moving his massive head in alignment with Rob's hand.

"Henry, I'd like you to meet Ellen. Ellen is a very special lady. Ellen, this is Henry. Henry is a horse, although sometimes he gets confused about that."

"I'm very pleased to meet you, Henry," she said gravely. "Please forgive my appearance. If I had known I was to meet a person of your stature, I would have dressed more appropriately."

Henry snorted and Rob laughed out loud. "That's horse for 'you silly woman' and 'I'm glad to meet you, too,'" he said. He forked some hay from an open bale into Henry's manger and put a measure of feed in his trough. "Now I'd like to introduce you to the girls." He moved down to the next stall. Ellen heard a "maa-aaa-aaa?" Was it sheep?

She peered over the door and saw two goats. "Ellen, meet Taylor and Bell. They are Nubian goats. You can tell by their long droopy ears." They came over to Rob and he scratched their heads. "Please don't embarrass them by telling them how silly they look. They think they are humans, too, and they wonder why everyone doesn't wear their ears hanging down past their chins like they do."

"Would they let me pet them?"

"Absolutely! Here." He moved aside so the could reach into the stall. At first the goats shied away, but curiosity got the best of them. She scratched their heads like she had seen Rob do, enjoying the rough texture of their fur.

"Hey!" she exclaimed as one of them started nibbling on her coat sleeve.

"Now, girls!" Rob said. "Leave Ellen's coat alone." Then to her he said, "It is not true that goats will eat a tin can. However, it is true that they will at least taste just about anything else. They're intensely curious and actually very clever."

"I think they're wonderful." They were both dark brown, with some white markings. She asked which one was which, and Rob pointed out the white blaze on one's forehead that distinguished Taylor from Bell.

"They're named after Kentucky counties," he said. "My Dad started naming all our goats after Kentucky counties. Since there are 120 counties in all, we haven't gone through all the names yet. By the way, these ladies are expecting. Come spring, they'll both be giving birth, most likely to twins."

"How neat," said Ellen. "Congratulations to both of you!" The goats eyed her with their slightly creepy pupil slits running side to side.

Rob gave them some feed and checked to make sure the water hadn't frozen.

"And now, for our next creature category," he announced with a flourish. "Come meet the chickens."

"And do they think they're human, too?"

"Uh, no. Chickens are not the brightest animals on the planet. I doubt they know they're chickens, let alone thinking they're people."

He gathered eggs into the basket and scattered some feed for the chickens.

"So," he said. "What do you think?" Henry had stuck his head out of his stall again, and was looking at her expectantly, like he, too, expected an answer.

"I think this is really something, Rob. I love the smells and the warmth and ... " Henry nickered. "And I love you, too, Henry." Henry snorted in appreciation. "Rob, I can't quite figure you out."

"What do you mean?"

"Well, you run a successful business that employs lots of people. Yet you have a mother and grandmother that you clearly dote on. And you have a farm and animals you take care of. You're a ... you're an intriguing man. With lots of facets."

"Why, I was just saying to myself the other day, I was saying, Rob, my man, you have facets! Yessir! That's exactly what I said — facets. Most women, most people, wouldn't find you interesting, but you do have one thing going for you — facets."

"Oh, Rob. You're teasing."

"Actually, I'm not. I'm glad you appreciate my ... facets. But right now, I'd appreciate some breakfast. Are you hungry?"

Ellen was suddenly aware that she was famished. "I sure am."

"Good! Have you ever had a really, really, REALLY fresh egg?" He held up one from the basket to emphasize his point. "Behold, the egg. A perfect ovoid containing an unrivaled combination of protein and vitamins. The entire world in one smooth, brown shell. I give you … drum roll, please … the egg! And, besides. One of my other facets is that I'm a mean cook. Come on! I'll show you."

As they entered the house, stamping snow off of their boots and exhilarated from the march back from the barn, Ellen smelled something wonderful: bacon. It seemed the most heavenly scent one could ever hope to inhale.

"Bacon!" said Rob. "Did the power come back on? Oh, MO-ther!" he called. "I'm HO-me!"

"Oh, there you kids are!" Shelby Lynn came around the corner wearing a different apron over a lavender housecoat. "I wondered where you'd gotten off to."

"Did the power come back on?" asked Rob. "And here I told Ellen I was an excellent chef."

"It smells wonderful!" added Ellen.

"No power yet, I'm afraid. But we made good use of the wood stove. Sorry to steal your cooking thunder, Robbie." She looked at Ellen. "Next time we'll let him do the cooking." She led them into the living room where Verna was tending a sizzling iron skillet with popping strips of bacon. "How are we doing, Mother?"

"Just about done. I'd say Ellen has time to, perhaps, tidy up a bit. You'd like that, wouldn't you, child?"

"Oh, goodness!" Ellen realized how frumpy she looked. She was still wearing the coat that was ten sizes too big, along with the overalls and the hat Rob had pulled down over her ears.

"Now, honey. Don't you worry. You look like the perfect farmwife. Many's the day I've come in from the barn looking like that. But I figure you might like to change before breakfast." She pointed the fork she was using to turn the bacon at Ellen. "As long, mind, as you hurry. This bacon is making me hungry!"

Ellen ran upstairs and changed back into the clothes she had worn yesterday, folded up all the borrowed clothing, made the bed, and ran a quick comb through her hair. When she brought the clothes downstairs, the table was being set on the coffee table in the living room. "I thought we'd eat in here," said Shelby Lynn. "It's nice and warm while the kitchen is a bit on the cool side."

For the second time since leaving Trish and Tommy's house, Ellen found herself relaxing. With Jonas and Rika it had taken a little time. But now she felt completely at home with them. With Rob and his mother and grandmother, the feeling came more quickly. They were so easy, so welcoming. It was as if they had just assumed that, of course, she would fit in and be a part of them.

After they did up the breakfast dishes, Verna suggested a card game. "Honey, do you know how to play Canasta?" she asked.

"Oh, my goodness. I do! Although I haven't played in years. My Dad used to love playing Canasta. When we couldn't talk my mother and sister into playing, we'd play two handed Canasta, just the two of us." Then she paused. "Oh, wait. It has been so long I'm afraid I've gotten rusty on the rules. Black threes and red threes are different, right?"

Verna rubbed her hands together. "Ho, ho, Shelby Lynn! I think we are going to have our first foursome in Canasta since I don't know when. Now, Robbie, you sit here across from Ellen. You'll be part-ners. And Shelby Lynn and I will proceed to trounce you young whipper snappers, won't we Shelby Lynn?"

Shelby Lynn apparently enjoyed the game, too, because she got into it, playing fiercely in partnership with her mother-in-law. Ellen didn't embarrass herself too badly, although she and Rob lost the first two hands. On the third hand she surprised Rob by asking if she could go out, leaving Verna and Shelby Lynn with a lot of cards that counted against them. "I'll have to remember that," said Verna as she dealt the next hand.

By the time Verna and Shelby Lynn reached 5,000 points, Rob and Ellen were only a couple of hundred points behind. "Well!" said Verna, leaning back in her chair. "I can't say as when I've had such a good time playing Canasta." She patted Ellen's hand. "You'll come back again, won't you? I want to do this again. And soon!"

Shelby Lynn stretched and looked at the clock. "Is anyone hun-gry? It is half past noon already."

"Oh, my. I should have been out of your hair long ago! Do you think anyone could come and pull my car out now?"

"Nonsense!" said Shelby Lynn. "We've absolutely loved having you. And you're welcome to stay as long as you like. Spend the night again tonight if your car is still stuck."

"I tell you what," said Rob. "Let me go hike down to the road and see how things look. then we can decide what to do."

"And we'll see about putting some lunch on the table without electricity," said Shelby Lynn. She caught a glimpse of herself in the mirror over the mantle. "Look at me!" she wailed. "I look a fright. And I'm still in my housecoat! This will never do."

Ellen and Verna started planning what they could do for lunch while Rob headed out to check the road. In a few minutes, Shelby Lynn was back, dressed in a slimming forest green corduroy jumper with a dark blue cardigan. She was tying on an apron when Ellen saw her. "Wow, you look great even when the electricity's off." She instantly regretted saying it, but Shelby Lynn enfolded her in a big embrace.

"I like this girl, Mother. Don't you?"

"I sure do, Shelby Lynn. I sure do."

They pulled out bread and cheese and some slices of ham. "I think we have a little potato salad that should be used up before it gets too warm," said Verna.

When Rob came stomping back in, blowing and shaking snow off of his booths, the women were just putting the finishing touches on a light luncheon, again on the card table to be near to the wood stove. "Well, Robbie?" asked Shelby Lynn. "How is it out there?"

"Not too good," Rob said ruefully. "It looks like a snowplow has been through once. It is a solid sheet of ice, and there is no traffic on the road at all. Our driveway would be tough going. I might be able to slide down, but I don't know about getting back up again." He looked at Ellen. "I'm afraid you're stuck here for another night, Ellen. I did check on your car, though. It looks to be resting comfortably, but a tow truck is going to have to have more traction than it can get right now to pull it out."

"Oh dear, I'm so sorry …" She looked around at the other three. "I'm sorry to be such a bother."

"Why, honey, you're like the first warm day of spring. We haven't had this much fun in years. Now then, who wants to see if Robbie can grill us a gourmet grilled cheese sandwich on top of the woodstove."

Ellen raised her hand, grinning.

"That's the sprit! Now then, Robbie. Let's see some of that culinary magic you say you possess." Verna handed him the spatula.

The meal was simple but delightful. The company was even better. After lunch, Verna said she'd like to lie down and Shelby Lynn said she'd like to write a few letters before the afternoon light was all gone.

Rob asked Ellen if she'd ever played Jotto. She hadn't, but she vaguely remembered Nathan and Jonas playing it. It was a simple word guessing game involving only words of five letters. Rob easily won the first two games until Ellen got the hang of it. Then they were fairly evenly matched, although Rob stumped her with "snath." "No fair!" cried Ellen. "That's not a word!"

"Au contraire. Look it up." He pointed to a massive volume on the bottom shelf. It was a Webster's Unabridged Dictionary, third edition.

"Oh," she breathed. "I've heard of these, but I've never actually held one."

"You don't actually hold it," laughed Rob. "It's too massive."

Sure enough, snath was a real word — the curved shaft of a scythe. "See, I knew that because I've actually used a scythe," he said.

But Ellen got him in the next round with "ennui" — she figured a double letter and three vowels would be harder to guess. "Well played," Rob complimented her.

By now they were both on the couch, curled up on either end, Ellen with a blanket over her lap and Rob totally relaxed like she had never seen him at work. "Facets," she thought to herself.

"Oh, hey. We'd better go check on the animals again before we lose daylight," said Rob after they were tied four to four.

"You mean …"

"Yep. We get to stuff you back into the overalls and barn coat. And I get to pull an old hat down over your head. Come on! It'll be fun!"

She couldn't resist his enthusiasm, so, for the second time, she climbed into the overalls — although at least this time she had clothes on instead of a flannel nightgown with nothing underneath. Henry was happy to see them and the goats were ecstatic. "I didn't know goats wag their tails like a dog," said Ellen.

"How do you know dogs don't wag their tails like a goat?"

"Oh, you!" She threw a handful of hay at him, which fluttered uselessly to the ground.

"Don't start something you can't finish!" Rob grabbed a handful of hay to throw back, but then dropped it into Henry's stall. "I guess we'd better go back in."

"Ok, if you want to."

He leaned over the stall door, watching the goats. He scratched their heads absentmindedly. "I really don't want to," he said to himself. And Ellen watched him, lost in thought until he turned, saw her standing there, and took her hand to lead her back to the house.

Chapter 50
Kirby's plans are revealed.

The power had come back on sometime during Saturday night. Rob was finally able to show off his skill with eggs. While everyone knew it was time for the party to be over, there was genuine reluctance on the part of Verna to let Ellen go, and Shelby Lynn hugged her again and whispered, "Please, please come back soon."

It had been a job getting home on Sunday morning. The roads were still very slippery, and Rob talked Ellen into letting him drive her back to Laodicea. It wasn't until Monday that she was able to get her car pulled out after she'd asked Annie for a ride to work.

By Thursday the snow was mostly gone, but people were talking about the big snow for weeks afterwards.

It was several weeks later, looking at some data, that she noticed something that sent a shiver down her spine. She had been looking at that odd fact that the assembly line could produce the same part faster toward quitting time. The data continued to show that trend, except for the occasional exception. And those exceptions were what caught Ellen's eye. Could it be? She went down the hall to see Rick Baker, the human resources manager.

"Rick, this may be out of line, but could you tell me which days Kirby Anderson was absent in the last two months?"

"I don't think that is something I can share with you," Rick said. "That's confidential."

"I kind of figured you might say that," said Ellen. "So let me ask you this. If I gave you a list of six days over the past two months, could you confirm that Kirby was out of the plant on those days?"

"Maybe ... What are you up to?"

"I have a weird theory. If my memory serves, something that happens in the factory corresponds to when Kirby is out of the plant."

"Go on. You've got my interest."

Ellen showed him her data. "See, using the bar code readers, I'm able to tell how long it takes the Assembly Line to produce different parts. The thing is, they speed up as the day goes on. Except for this day ..." She pointed to a line in her report. "See, on this day, the Assembly Line was performing at high speed all day long, not just toward the end of the day. And here. And here again." She turned the page. "And here, and these two days back to back. That was when it hit me. I think I remember Kirby being out of the plant on those two days, so I wanted to see if the other days correspond to when he was out as well."

Rick pulled out a three ring notebook and started turning pages. Ellen tried not to look, but she recognized the pages as the weekly attendance log each salaried employee had to turn in.

"OK, I'm neither confirming or denying that those days Kirby was out of the plant. But just for the sake of argument, let's say he was, what are you suggesting?"

"I hesitate to say this, but the data suggests to me that his presence is slowing the line down. It's as if him being here somehow makes the Assembly Line less productive."

"That's what I thought you were suggesting."

"It's not so much me as what the data shows. I mean it is pretty dramatic ..."

Rick held up his hand to cut her off. "I see the data. And I understand what it implies. Now my advice to you to is to go back to your office and work on something else for a while. I'm going to see Rob and I'll get back with you, one way or another."

Chastised, Ellen returned to her office. She tried to work on other things, but her mind kept coming back to what she had seen in the data. She couldn't help herself; she started looking at the patterns over the course of a day when Kirby was on site. She made a graph with parts per hour on the Y axis and hour of the day on the X axis. She removed data from the six questionable days. No matter which part she plotted, the graph always started low and ended up higher. Then she plotted the six days when she suspected Kirby had been absent. That graph was always a fairly straight line across the top of the page. The productivity on days without Kirby were as good as or better than the productivity toward the end of the shift when Kirby was there.

It wasn't exactly a smoking gun, but something sure smelled fishy. She remembered Jonas telling her to use her instinct. Her instinct was ringing a distinctive alarm. Something was wrong at Powell Manufacturing, and Kirby was at the center of it.

Her phone rang.

"Ellen Murphy."

"Ellen, it's Rob. I need you to come down to my office, please. Bring the data you showed Rick earlier."

"Right away."

When she got there, Rick was still in the office. Both he and Rob looked deadly serious. "Ellen, without naming names or making any accusations, show me your data."

Ellen did her best to be clinical. She pointed out the days when productivity was high all day. She pointed out the rest of the days when productivity started low, but increased as the day went along, but never as high as the six high productivity days. She tried to end on a neutral note. "On these six days, something in the factory was different. Productivity was higher." It was a statement of fact. No accusations, no calling anyone out, no recriminations, no payback. She just let the data speak for itself.

"Rick tells me I am not allowed to tell you anything about a particular individual." He looked at Rick who nodded, every so slightly. "Let's just say that we have met with several individuals from a particular department in the shop and they have confirmed, after some questioning, that a particular individual has been directing them ..." He looked at Rick. "Allegedly directing them to deliberately slow down their work. Obviously this cannot be tolerated." He looked at Rick again. "How am I doing?"

"Doing well, Rob. No names, no accusations. 'Allegedly' is the right word to use."

"OK," said Rob, sighing and rubbing his temples. "Ellen, let's just say that we're grateful, I'm grateful, that you brought this data to our attention."

Rick spoke. "And the fact that you're the one who discovered this data does not need to leave this room." Ellen hadn't thought about that. Might she be called a whistleblower? Might some see this as payback for what he tried to do at the Campbell House? She sat in her chair, knees pressed together, hands clenched in her lap, lips in a thin line.

"Are we clear about that?" asked Rob. Ellen nodded. "Good. Then I'd like you to go back to your office and keep a low profile. Rick and I will take it from here."

Ellen did as she was told and tried to focus on something else. It wasn't easy. About 4:30 she looked up to see Rick walking with Kirby to his Mercedes. Kirby was carrying a cardboard box. He put it in the trunk of the car and Rick watched him drive out of the parking lot.

Soon after that Gladys' voice went out on the intercom requesting all managers and supervisors to meet in the conference room for a brief meeting.

At 5:00 the door to the conference room was still shut, so Ellen collected her coat and purse and headed home.

The next day she also tried to be invisible. She wanted to stay as far away as possible from what she imagined must be some serious drama going on out on the factory floor.

Annie came by at lunch and asked her to come with her to the cafeteria. "Oh, I don't think so, Annie. See, there's some stuff going on and …"

"I know," said Annie. "I think you'll be glad you did."

In the cafeteria Ellen sat with Annie and Rachel. Before they had barely tackled their sandwiches, Rachel wanted to know, "Have you heard the news?"

"What news?" Ellen feigned ignorance.

"That Kirby Anderson was fired yesterday! See, I told you. You just have to be patient and wait on the Lord's timing."

"Fired, huh? Not having a job will be pretty hard on him. He likes his nice things, expensive things. I feel kind of sorry for him."

"Sorry for him!" Rachel was indignant. "After what he did to you?"

"Still ..." said Ellen. "Oh I guess I'm glad I won't have to keep out of his way when I'm in the shop. Any idea why he was let go?"

"I know exactly why," said Rachel. "He was fired because they finally found out what he was doing."

"What was that?"

"Slowing down the assembly line. He told all of us to slow it down every morning. Then, if he saw we weren't gonna make minimum production, he'd let us go faster after lunch. We knew it weren't right, but he was our boss. What could we do?"

Just then Gladys' voice came across the intercom. "There will be an all-employee meeting in the cafeteria in 15 minutes," she said. "This is a required meeting for everyone."

"Easy for us," commented Annie. "We're already here!"

People started streaming in from the shop floor as well as from the offices. Gladys came in; Sandy McDonald, Luther Holtzmann and Rick Baker came in together. Harvey and Leonard came in off of the factory floor.

Rob entered the room and held up his hand for quiet. The room was very crowded — standing room only — so he climbed onto a stool so he could address the crowd. Rick Baker from Human Resources stood beside him.

"Kirby Anderson is no longer employed at Powell Manufacturing," he said. "He was escorted off of the property yesterday afternoon. We discovered that Kirby was deliberately slowing down the assembly line so that our productivity would suffer." He paused to gather his thoughts. "Folks, I want you to understand something: that is not acceptable behavior. Slowing down the Assembly line, or doing anything less than our best, anything that harms production, is wrong. We all work here." He pointed to several people. "Harry works here. Mildred works here. Barry does. So does Snake. I work here. Every one of us who work here depend on each other to do our best. If we don't, we lose customers, and that means we can't make payroll, we have to lay people off, we might even have to shut down the plant. Doing less than our best, or deliberately trying to hurt our work here puts all of our jobs at risk. It just can't be tolerated, and that is why Kirby was terminated. We're not trying to overwork anyone here; we have good working conditions and pay that is above average for our market." He looked down at Rick for confirmation. "But we do want to work hard. We want to be productive. Kirby wasn't letting us do that." He looked around the crowd; he had their attention. "Now, I want you all to know that Leonard Pfieffer will be taking over as shop supervisor for both Welding, which he already had, and Assembly. Come up here, Leonard."

Leonard came forward out of the crowd amidst applause.

"Leonard, I have every confidence in you. I know this is a big responsibility, but I've watched you work. You have everyone's respect, you're smart, and people genuinely like you. You're going to be great at this." Leonard ducked his head. "Is there anything you'd like to say to the folks before I make another announcement?"

"Not really. I'll … I'll try to do a good job, if y'all will help me." Heads nodded around the room along with a chorus of "we will" and "got you covered, Leonard."

Rob got down off of the stool and shook Leonard's hand. "Now," he said, "We kind of think that Leonard could use a little help with this big new job. Rachel Hemingway, would you come up here?"

Rachel's eyes went wide as she looked across the table at Annie and Ellen. "Go on," said Annie. "Don't keep the boss waiting."

Rachel walked over to where Rob was standing. Her apprehension showed in her body language, the way she walked slowly, shoulders slightly hunched.

"Rachel," said Rob, "We've noticed what a fine job you've been doing. And we think Leonard is going to need a pair of eyes and ears on the Assembly line. So we're asking you to become Assistant Assembly Line Supervisor, reporting to Leonard, and with responsibility for day-to-day operation of the line. What do you say?"

The room burst into even louder applause than they had given Leonard and Rachel's apprehension was clearly gone. In its place was a 1,000 watt smile. Rob shook her hand and told her he was looking forward to seeing what good things she would do.

Rob held up his hand for quiet one more time. "Now," he said, "Before we head back to work, are there any questions? Anything you'd like to talk about?"

"Will Rachel get a raise?" someone hollered from the back of the room.

Rob grinned. "Here at Powell we believe pay should be commensurate with responsibility. Yes, Rachel will get a raise. Rick will work out the details." He looked around the room again. "Other questions?"

"I heard Powell was having a hard time. Are we gonna close?"

"Not if I can help it. It is no secret that we are struggling to be profitable. Which is why I'm so set on everyone doing their best. When someone does something like Kirby did, it sure doesn't help. I don't want to put all the blame on Kirby, for sure, but we need to step up our game, and that includes me. I'm always looking for new customers and expanding our existing customers' orders."

"What about that new Wilco part? That's good, right?" That was from James Tucker, the final inspection worker on the Assembly line.

"Yes, James. That one is very good. And we almost lost it because we thought it took more labor to produce than it actually did. We were able to reduce the price a bit and keep Wilco as a customer. That just shows, again, why everyone working at their top performance is so important." He paused to see if there were more questions. "I should add," he said, "That we are pursuing some additional Wilco parts. It is too early for me to announce anything, but I hope to be able to give you some good news soon about that."

"When can we get one of them bar code whatcha callits in Welding?"

Rob laughed. "You like those, huh? That's the brainchild of Ellen Murphy ..." He pointed to Ellen sitting at the corner table with

Annie. "Ellen, any reason we shouldn't be expanding the bar code readers to other areas of the factory?'

"Uh, no, not really. You give the go ahead and Whit and I will get them put in place."

"Good deal," Rob said. "I say go ahead. Y'all are going to be so high tech you won't know what to do with yourselves."

He waited a few moments for any other questions. "All right, folks. Let's get back to work. My door is always open if you need to talk about something. And let's make sure we give Leonard and Rachel our support, OK?" The crowd began to move out. Rob shook Leonard's and Rachel's hands again and Rachel returned to the table where Annie and Ellen were sitting.

"Congratulations, girl!" said Annie. "You know you deserved that."

"Well done, Rachel. I had no idea this was coming, but you'll be absolutely great at it."

Rachel sat down. "I don't hardly know what to say. It ain't hit me yet."

Chapter 51
Dinner at the Klamecks with Rob.

Later, as she was walking back to her office, Ellen saw that Rob's door was open and that he was alone in his office. "May I come in?" she asked.

He smiled. "Of course! Come in. Have a seat."

"Thanks," she said. She looked around his office. It looked like a man's office: very little that was personal. She did recognize Shelby Lynn in the photo on his credenza, standing next to a man she assumed was Rob's father. It wasn't the same photo he had in his bedroom, but it was the same couple.

There was a painting of a sailing ship on the wall. While it was an oil in dark blues and teals, quite different from her lighthouse watercolor with its mauves and grays, she was startled to recognize they both had the same theme in their paintings. Rob's was of a tempest-tossed brigantine, running before a gale and desperately on the lookout for a lighthouse which could be seen in the far, far distance, just beyond the rocks splitting the waves and gnashing their teeth to chew up the ship. Ellen's painting was of a lighthouse, serenely standing firm against whatever winds may blow to protect those struggling sailing ships.

Other than the photo of his parents and the ship painting, everything else was all business. Unlike Luther's office upstairs that left no questions about his sole and consuming hobby, golf, Rob's office said very little about the man. Yet from being stranded at Three Pines during the snow storm, Ellen knew there were facets — there was that word again — to this man that few people knew.

"What can I do for you, Ellen?"

"Oh, sorry. I was just admiring your painting. I have a watercolor of a lighthouse that my mother gave me. I was just thinking about the nautical theme …" She forced herself to focus. "I guess we're in some kind of rough waters right now."

"You could say that," he agreed. "It has been a bit rough."

"I wanted to tell you how well I thought you handled that all-employee meeting today," she said. "That was touchy, and I want you to know how impressed I was. Not that you need my approval," she added.

"And yet it means a great deal to me," said Rob. "Was it really OK?"

"More than OK," she replied. "People could have been upset that Kirby was let go … although I have a hard time imagining that, based on the kind of reputation I'm learning he had. But you didn't let people get upset. You just told the truth, and you told why it mattered to them. And you were totally transparent."

"Transparency is one of my … facets."

She giggled out loud. "Oh, you! Always so quick-witted. Being hilarious is another of your facets. But I only know that about you because I saw you in a different environment away from work."

"Speaking of getting away from work, what are you doing this evening? Could I take you to dinner as a way of saying thank you for discovering certain facts — the details of which shall not be disclosed — that led to what I hope will be a significant improvement in productivity on the Assembly line?"

"Oh, I don't know, Rob. Is that appropriate? I mean, I work for you …"

"Well, if you don't want to, that's OK. I would like to just have dinner with someone I hope is a good friend. I'd like to say thank you for what you've done. But I know you and Kirby had been … seeing each other."

Ellen suddenly colored. How much did he know? What had he heard? She would be dismayed if she thought Rob had heard the rumors about her and Kirby at the Campbell House. She would be absolutely mortified if she thought he believed them.

"I think I can safely say that chapter of my life is over," she whispered.

"Well, in that case, won't you please have dinner with me? I would enjoy your company. I really would. But if you don't want to …"

His expression was so pitiful that Ellen had to laugh again. "You are absolutely pathetic!" she chided. "Who can say no to that long face? Sure, we can go to dinner, if you like. I'd like to talk over some things with you and it might be nice to do that away from the plant."

"Excellent," he beamed. "Would you like to leave here from work in my car, or would it be better if I picked you up at your place?"

"Maybe it would be better to pick me up. That way I could change … What kind of clothes should I plan on wearing?"

"Nothing fancy," he responded hastily. "Just be comfortable. This is just two friends having dinner together. I mean, it's not like it is a date or anything."

"Not a date," she echoed. "Right. Not a date."

Later, as she was driving home, she was grateful that the days were getting longer. The sun didn't set so soon after she got back to her apartment. And she was beginning to have some hope that the gloomy days of winter were retreating.

She selected a nice pair of slacks with a pretty blouse and a cardigan as her ensemble for the non-date. She was contemplating what kind of earrings to wear when she heard footsteps on the stairs. She glanced out the window, but didn't see Rob's car parked on the street or under the streetlight.

There was a knock on the door. It must be Rika, she thought. Just in time to help me select the right jewelry.

She opened the door and was amazed to see Rob standing there. "How did you …" she sputtered. "Come in. I'm just about ready."

He came in to her tiny apartment and suddenly she hoped he would like it as much as she did. It was very different from Three Pines, and it mattered to her that he would like its cozy atmosphere and careful design.

"Wow! What a great apartment," he said. "This is really, really neat. Oh, by the way …" He held out a tiny bouquet of dainty yellow flowers. "These are for you." They weren't in a vase or paper, as if they had just been picked.

"How very lovely! Where did you find crocus?"

"You know the vacant lot down the street?"

"Yes." She drove past it every day on her way to work.

"I happen to know that there used to be a house there that burned in the 40s. No one has ever built back. But the owners must have planted crocus along where the walkway used to be. Every spring they have the earliest crocuses of anyone."

"How sweet!" Her response was unguarded and transparent. "I have always loved flowers. Did you pick these just now? For me?"

"Yup. I parked down the street and picked them because I thought you might enjoy them."

"I certainly do," she said, getting a shallow dish out of the cupboard and filling it with water. She arranged the intensely yellow flowers so that their stems were in the water but their heads were on full display.

"Later there will be hyacinths and then daffodils and narcissus. And, by early May, there should be tulips blooming, just in time for the Derby."

"You continue to amaze me. Who knew you would know so much about flowers, and where to find them on a vacant lot?"

"I like to think of this as yet another of my many facets." He grinned and moved across the little living room to her painting of the lighthouse. "Is this the painting you were talking about?"

"That's it. My mother gave it to me when I went off to college."

"I can see why you like it." He stepped back to admire it. "I love the color palette. It is subtle, almost washed out as if it is in very bright sunshine. You can almost feel the hot day, and hear the breakers just over the dunes. Your mother had good taste."

"I think so. But it just means a lot to me since she gave it to me."

"Of course. And the oil in my office was something my Dad acquired and had in his office. I guess you could say I inherited it. It reminds me of him every day." He gave the painting one last silent look. Then he turned. "So …"

Ellen got her purse and coat. "I think I'm ready if you are."

"I am indeed." He opened the door for her.

The air was nippy, but clean and fresh. There was the faint tang of new life in the earth. Bulbs were waking up from their winter nap and thinking about reaching heavenward. Trees were shaking off their hibernal torpor and feeling the sap begin to move. Ellen stopped and took a deep breath. Rob stopped with her.

"Smell that?" she said.

"Yes. What is it?"

"Spring. Spring!" She almost sang it.

"My beloved spoke and said to me: Arise, my darling, my beautiful one, come with me. See! The winter is past; the rains are over and gone. Flowers appear on the earth; the season of singing has come."

She stood there on the landing, looking at him, looking at the Klamecks' back yard and the flowers she knew would soon be blooming there. "That's beautiful, Rob. Did you write that? Another of your facets?"

"I wish. No, that's from the Song of Solomon in the Bible."

"The Song of Solomon. I seem to remember Annie telling me I should read that. If it is that beautiful, I'll have to do that. Quote it again, please."

Rob obliged as they descended the stairs. Then, instead of walking toward the street, he crossed under the breezeway and knocked at the Klamecks' back door.

Rika opened the door, drying her hands on her apron.

"I hope we're not late, Mrs. K."

"Not a bit of it, Robbie. It is so nice to see you again. And from the look on Ellen's face, I am quite sure you managed to pull this off, as you American's say, without her having a clue."

"I believe I did. Tell me, Ellen, did you have any idea that we were having dinner at the Klamecks?"

"I … I don't know what to say," stammered Ellen. "Did the two of you cook this up? I thought we were going out to dinner …"

"Oh, well. If you would rather go eat some third rate food in a fourth rate restaurant, that's fine with me," said Rika. But her tone told Ellen she wasn't offended.

"Oh, Rika. You know how much I love being with you and Jonas. I just didn't …" She turned on Rob. "How did you arrange this, you devious man?"

He shrugged his shoulders. "I just called up Mrs. K. and told her I was taking you to dinner tonight. And I may have hinted that an invitation to dine with her and Mr. K wouldn't be a bad idea. Lucky for me, she is very quick and immediately invited us for dinner. Which I instantly accepted."

"Facets," mumbled Ellen. "Devious facets."

Rika pulled them into the house out of the cold and began demanding their coats. The smell in the house was divine. There was the fundamental scent of some kind of roast, with overtones of rosemary and sharp cheese. The fireplace gave a tangy counterpoint with its smoky notes. Ellen breathed a deep sigh of satisfaction.

"Glad to be here?" asked Rob.

"Oh, Rob. This is the best. What a good idea. You'll love the Klamecks."

"I already do. Remember, I knew them too. And frankly — and I think this is the real reason Rika invited us — I think Mr. K would like to talk a little shop with you."

The man himself rolled into the room. "Hello, my dear." He took Ellen's hand and actually kissed it. "You don't know how I've missed our little chats. This dratted heart attack has set me back. But I'm better than ever now. And Robbie," he turned to address Rob. "I'm so delighted you're back in our lives. Welcome! Welcome! Shall we go in and see if Rika has prepared anything that is at least edible?"

"I heard that," came Rika's voice from the kitchen. "If you're not careful, you will receive only bread and water for your supper."

"Well, we wouldn't want that, now, would we?" He winked at Rob and Ellen and beckoned them to follow him into the dining room.

Rika had used her good Swedish china that she had used at Thanksgiving and Ellen knew this meant, to Rika at least, that this was an important and special dinner. She had placed a blue runner down the middle of the table and was just lighting the blue tapers in the centerpiece. "Have a seat everyone, and I'll bring in the food," she said.

Ellen asked if she could please help and Rika allowed it. The roast with potatoes, carrots, onions and celery went in front of Jonas. There was fresh baked bread, green beans, and a green salad with little shrimp sprinkled through it. "We will sing, and then Jonas will carve the roast," announced Rika when everything was in place.

The Klamecks sang their Swedish grace as Ellen, who had heard it enough to follow along, gamely tried to join in. Rob was simply intrigued. Then Jonas attacked the roast with gusto. In turn, each one passed their plate to him and he loaded it up with meat and vegetables that smelled heavenly. The other dishes were passed around and Rob was asked to cut pieces of bread. "And butter," said Rika firmly. "Fresh bread must have good, real butter."

The meal was delicious, the conversation was amusing and engaging, and the feeling around the table was warm and comfortable. Ellen loved it and found herself wondering if she could ever create a home like this. Or if she'd ever get the chance.

"Now, Ellen," said Jonas as Rika returned to the kitchen 'to make tea and put the finishing touches on the dessert.' "Tell me about work. Robbie and I had some nice chats while I was in the hospital, but I want to know what exciting things you have been working on." He looked at Rob. "Perhaps the boss will indulge a curious old man who loves manufacturing?" Rob simply smiled.

Where to begin? She began by telling him about the data she had been getting from the bar code readers and about the difficulty of getting the data out of the system. "I think we've done a good job with Principle Three," she told him. "But Principle Four needs a lot of work."

"OK," interrupted Rob. "Stop right there. I keep hearing about these principles. So what are Principles Three and Four?"

Ellen looked at Jonas, but he indicated she should do the explaining. "I'll try," she said. "But you have to fill in the gaps, Jonas." He nodded and Ellen quoted, "Principle Three: The business information technology system must be informated so that it requires less effort than equivalent non-technical systems and creates data that is accurate and timely."

That led to a lively discussion about what it meant to "informate" a process. When it had run its course, Rob had a much deeper appreciation of what had happened when Ellen and Whit had installed the bar code readers. He had a deeper appreciation of how hard she had worked to get them accepted by the different operators.

"You did a great job," Rob said. "That request during the all-employee meeting to get bar code readers into the rest of the factory was pretty impressive."

"Do you mean to tell me that you have people actually asking to have these bar code readers installed in their work stations?"

"Yes, I guess we do, Jonas. During the meeting someone asked Rob when they could get a bar code reader." She looked at Rob. "I believe I heard the boss say that we should roll them out as soon as possible."

"I did say something like that," said Rob.

"Congratulations, my boy. This is really remarkable. I predict good things will come from this."

Rika returned with a steaming teapot and a dessert that looked like strawberries and ice cream, but Ellen realized it was more than ice cream. "Homemade this afternoon," whispered Rika to Ellen when she quizzed her. The men were continuing to talk about the Powell factory.

"But we've only talked about Principle Three. I want to know about Principle Four. And I assume there are Principles One and Two as well?"

"And Five," said Ellen. "Which I have not discovered yet, and Jonas won't tell me."

"She'll know it when she sees it," said Jonas. "Go ahead, Ellen. Tell him Principle Four."

"The Business Information System must encourage access to data in a way that creates information," she quoted.

"Now that one I understand better," said Rob. "I know you had a hard time getting the data out of the mainframe, didn't you, Ellen? I think our system doesn't do very well in that regard. But, Mr. K., I'm going to tell you about some information Ellen discovered. I'm not going to name any names, but she figured out how someone was deliberately attempting to sabotage our productivity." He explained about the patterns Ellen had found in the data and what it implied that Kirby had been doing. He concluded with, "We let him go yesterday and promoted from within to cover the position."

"I wonder," said Jonas. "Could that have had something to do with the conversation you overheard at the restaurant, Ellen? Have you told Robbie about that?"

"No, as we discussed, I didn't pass it on. But it does seem that, given what's just happened, it might be important." So Ellen explained to Rob the conversation she had overheard in Gabrielli's with its sinister overtones.

"But you don't know who it was?" said Rob. "It wasn't Kir … er, the individual who was let go yesterday?"

"I'm confident it wasn't him, but I don't know who it was. I'm sorry, Rob. I know it would be good to know that. At the time it just seemed too bizarre, too unsubstantiated to worry you with. Now it seems like I might have got it wrong."

"We got it wrong," interjected Jonas. "I counseled Ellen to not bring forward something that seemed to have no foundation." He looked down at his strawberries and ice cream.

"I've just had a thought," said Rob. "Remember when we had the leak about the Wilco order? And I thought you, Ellen, had been the one who leaked it to your landlord?"

Jonas looked up from his dessert. "To me?"

"I didn't know it was you at the time, Mr. K. Ellen just told me that she had discussed with her landlord a new part from Wilco we were trying to win. Clearly someone got wind of our bid and under-bid us. We lost out to the other company, and I wondered if you were the leak. Now I know of course it couldn't have been you, but, I wonder, could it have been Kirby? Ellen, do you happen to remember discussing the order with ... " He looked at the Klamecks. "Please forget that I said a name. Ellen, do you remember discussing the or-der with the individual who was let go yesterday?"

"No, I ... wait a minute. Butch and I must have talked to him about that part to get his input. I think ... I guess I'm not sure." She shrugged her shoulders.

"I think we've found our leak," said Rob. "The question is, who was he leaking the information to?"

There was silence around the table as this question was given grim consideration.

In the end, it was Rika who hinted that it might be time for Jonas to be thinking about retiring for the evening. "I am a bit tired," he admitted. "I don't have the stamina I once did. But I have thoroughly enjoyed this evening. And perhaps, my dear, we can invite these two young people again because ..." He grinned at Robbie. "Ellen needs to explain about Principle One and Principle Two."

"She sure has some 'splainin' to do," Rob said in his best Ricky Ricardo imitation.

Ellen got up and started clearing away dishes. "Now Ellen ..." said Rika.

"No way, Rika. You know I'm going to help."

Rika sighed with mock exasperation. "If you insist."

"And I'll help, too," said Rob.

"You and I, Robbie, will carry the dishes in while the ladies wash and dry. Then I'll show you where to put things away."

And that's just what they did. Rob put on a show with a dish towel over his arm and a fake French accent, keeping the other three in stitches. The four of them together made quick work of the dishes.

Who would have thought, Ellen said to herself, that washing dishes could be so much fun?

They said goodnight, and Rob started to walk Ellen up the stairs to her apartment. "Rob, your car is way down the street. How about I walk down with you to keep you company, and then you can drive me back up here?"

"I would like that very much, if you won't get too cold." She took his arm and they started down the sidewalk. They walked in companionable silence and Ellen was almost sorry when they got to the car. Rob opened the door for her to get in, and opened it for her again up at her apartment. There was a brief moment when they just stood there together. And then Rob said, "I hope this wasn't a bad idea. I did want to take you to dinner."

"Oh, Rob. I've been taken to dinner several times lately and none of them came close to this evening." Before she could stop herself, she reached up and kissed him on the cheek. "Thank you."

She almost flew up the stairs to her little apartment.

Chapter 52
A day on the farm.

Spring seemed suddenly to have arrived in Kentucky. There was a freshening of the air, the scent of growing things, budding things being carried on the breeze. The clouds were soft and puffy and the sky seemed infinitely high and wide and boundlessly blue.

Ellen stepped out on her little deck, still in her pajamas with a housecoat and slippers on. The fragrant fog coming off of her coffee mug warmed her nose and cheeks as she held it close. She inhaled deeply; complex overtones of the coffee were intertwined with the counterpoint of delicate woodsy scent on the wind. She let out her breath, a deep, contented sigh. It was a Saturday morning and all seemed right with the world.

An AMC Eagle came up Prospect Street and Ellen watched as it swerved into a parking spot behind Gunilla. Her heart skipped a beat.

Rob got out and waved to her. "High time you were up and about!"

"Rob Powell, I'm not even dressed yet! Go away!"

The look of consternation that contorted his face made her laugh. "I'm only kidding. Well, about the go away part. The not dressed yet part is true. What in Heaven's name are you doing here?"

"I've been sent," he said, recovering.

"Sent?"

"Yes. Henry has been asking for you. He wants to know why you haven't been back. I've come to take you to him."

"Henry? My dear friend Henry? The one with the rather longish face and the mohawk haircut?"

"The very same. So will you come? My mother and grand-mother have also been asking for you. You've been invited to luncheon, but I think they may not approve of your current attire."

"I told you, I wasn't dressed yet, silly."

"So you had best get a move on. Do you have any more of that coffee?"

"Yes, of course. Would you like a cup?"

"I thought you'd never ask. It is hard for a man with as many facets as I have to keep up if he hasn't had his coffee." He bounded up the stairs. "Good morning!" he said, standing in front of her.

Ellen tugged her robe closer together at her throat. "Good morning." She turned and looked out over the Klamecks' back yard, out at the trees, at the knobs in the distance. "Isn't it beautiful?" She breathed in another deep breath of the spring air.

"Beautiful," he agreed. But there was just a pause after he said it before he turned and followed her gaze out over the back yard. The daffodils were sending green shoots up in earnest and the yellow blooms of the forsythia were already showing.

"OK, let's get you that coffee," she said, turning and heading indoors. She selected a mug that was a bit more masculine than her delicate cup and poured. "How do you take it?"

"Just black," he said. Suddenly he looked contrite. "Look Ellen, I'm sorry. I've come barging in here unexpectedly. It just seemed like such a good idea to come and fetch you as a surprise when I left the house. Now I realize I'm intruding." He took a sip of coffee. "But, really, Mother and Mammaw really did ask if you'd come to lunch. I thought you might like to see the farm when it isn't under a foot of snow."

"You're not intruding. It sounds glorious. And on such a glorious day, too. But really, I have to get dressed."

"Shall I go back down to the car?"

Ellen considered it. Then she said, "No. Just make yourself comfortable. I'll try not to take too long." She went into her little bedroom and shut the door. Trying to hurry, and also not to make too much noise — who knows what Rob might be thinking? — she selected a trim pair of jeans, a blouse in a blue print and a woodsy green sweater vest.

When she came out, Rob was looking at her bookshelf. "I see you like Jane Austen."

"Among others. Yes, I really like Jane Austen." She crossed to her jewelry case on her small desk in the living room. She selected a pair of dangly gold earrings and a simple gold chain.

"Is it unmanly to admit to liking Jane Austen?" he asked.

"You? I suppose not. I don't think I know any men who read Jane Austen, though."

"One of my facets," he said. "I like the feisty women characters. Emma is my favorite. And I'm a sucker for happy endings."

"You are indeed a man of facets," she said, working to get the necklace to fasten.

"Here, let me help," he said. And before she could protest, he had it in place. "Ready?"

She put the coffee cups in the sink and glanced around the room. "I think so!"

"Great! I'm looking forward to today," he said, holding the door open for her.

As they descended the stairs, Ellen caught Rika looking out through the kitchen window at them. She waved, and Rika waved back.

The drive was just as glorious as Ellen had anticipated. She leaned back in the seat and watched the scenery float by, enjoying the luxury of not being the one behind the wheel. "I think Kentucky is beautiful," she sighed.

"Me too."

"I know we're in for some more rough weather before Spring is really here, but I love days like this."

He smiled over at her and said again, "Me too."

They remarked on the Kentucky road names. "Tates Creek," said Rob. "Named after Daniel Boone's friend who went missing one year. They found a skeleton in a creek the next year when they re-turned to hunt. Thus, Tates Creek."

"I may be forced to live there some day," said Ellen, indicating the sign pointing to Possum Kingdom. Rob snorted.

"Where do you suppose that one came from?" he asked, directing her attention to Shake Rag Road.

"Oh, I know that one. My Dad told me that there used to be an
old railroad near here. There was a woman who used to come out and
wave at the engineer with her dish towel as the train went by."

"No kidding! I never knew that one. Maybe Mammaw will
know about that."

Rob turned into the driveway between the two stone fences
where Ellen had been run off of the road in the snow storm. This time
she was able to enjoy the trees lining the lane and the rolling fields on
either side as well as the stately home that was Three Pines.

Shelby Lynn and Verna were delighted that she had come, although Rob had to admit to applying some pressure. But he wouldn't
let her stay long. "Come on! I want to show you the farm." He insisted she change out her nice shoes for a pair of rubber boots that
came two thirds of the way up her calves. "Almost as sexy as overalls
and an old coat," he remarked. Ellen heard Verna snicker behind her.

The farm was a new experience for Ellen everywhere she turned.
Rob took her by the hand and showed her the old slave quarters. "My
parents spent their wedding night there," he remarked and Ellen
wasn't sure if he was teasing or telling the truth. He showed her the
well, the ice house, and the woodshed. He led her across the fields
down to the creek to the back of the field. The daffodils were blooming, here, well ahead of the flowers in Rika's back yard. He showed
her the draw where the Confederate soldiers had outmaneuvered the
Union troops, flanking the main force and pushing the larger Union
army back toward Oak Lick, abandoning their cannons as they went.
He showed her a rock, supposedly carved by Daniel Boone's brother
Squire. "It's old," he said. "But not that old. We don't think it is
genuine." Everything he showed her intrigued her, enthralled her, delighted her. Each object, each tableau seemed more extraordinary
than the last.

At last they returned to the barn to visit Henry and the goats.
Henry nickered his greeting as they took turns feeding him oats out of

their bare hands. One of the goats was lying in the corner, breathing hard. "Oh, Ellen," he said softly, putting his arm around her shoulder. "Taylor's in labor. If we stay quietly we might get to witness a true miracle."

They watched quietly in wonder as Taylor panted and heaved. And then, without any fanfare, a tiny little goat slipped out and twitched, already struggling to get upright. The doe's tone changed dramatically to soft, reassuring noises as she licked the afterbirth away from her kid's face. There were tears in Ellens eyes as she leaned against Rob's shoulder. "I've never seen anything like it," she whispered.

The little goat had long floppy ears, just like its mother. "It's a girl," Rob announced. "We like girls. They give milk and have more little goats."

And suddenly, without warning, a second kid slipped out, dropping the distance from Taylor's back side to the soft hay below. "Oh!" was all Ellen could say.

"Goats usually have twins," Rob explained. "If she hadn't had a second one, I might have had to help out. But it looks like they're doing fine." The firstborn was already trying to stand on shaky legs.

"Can they get up that fast?"

"By the time we finish lunch, they'll both be dried off, standing, and nursing. Looks like the second one is a girl, too. You've brought us luck, Ellen. But I do think we'd better go in and see if lunch is ready. And Mammaw will want to know that Taylor has had her kids. I'm betting Bell will have hers within a few days."

Rob kept his arm around her shoulder as they walked the path they had walked a month ago in the deep snow.

Both Verna and Shelby Lynn were pleased to hear about the new goats. "Do you suppose Mrs. K. would like me to give her one as a gift so it can mow the grass in her back yard?" asked Rob.

"She'd probably love it until it ate all her flowers. They'll eat just about anything, you know," Shelby Lynn said to Ellen.

Lunch was simple yet elegant. Shelby Lynn had clearly been schooled in proper table settings, presentation of food, and good etiquette. Ellen wasn't exactly uncomfortable, but found herself wishing that she might learn some of Shelby Lynn's gentility and skill at entertaining.

Verna confirmed the story about the origins of Shake Rag Road and proceeded to rattle off more strange and comical Kentucky place names. She named Gravel Switch and Mousie, Thousandsticks and Blackey, Betsy Layne and Big Hill, Bugtussle and Burning Fork, Hazard and Hazel Green, Squib and Sprout. Shelby Lynn pointed out that, within an hour's drive, one could visit London, Paris, Athens, Frankfort and Versailles. "I know in France it is 'vair-SIGH', but here it's just 'ver-SALES'," she laughed.

"And tell, me, honey, how do you pronounce the capitol of Kentucky? Is it 'LEWIS-ville' or is it 'LOU-a-vull?'"

Ellen almost fell for Verna's joke, starting to say that any Kentuckian worth his salt would know that it is pronounced 'LOU-a-vull' but caught herself in time. "Verna, shame on you! The capitol of Kentucky is Frankfort!"

Verna laughed out loud, enjoying the joke immensely. "You're a good 'un, Ellen. A real keeper." She looked across the table at Rob.

"I wonder if the woman who shook her rag at the engineer was married to him," Shelby Lynn asked vaguely. "I wonder if they were happy."

"Now why would you ask that, Mother?" asked Rob.

"Oh, I don't know. If your father had been the engineer, I would have gone out and waved at him every time he went by."

"Yes, you would have," said Verna. "You loved him, and Harold loved you. Not everyone gets to enjoy that kind of love." She said it to the room in general. It was as if she were quoting an ancient proverb that had been proven true down through the ages.

"I consider myself fortunate," said Shelby Lynn. "Even though Harold was taken from me much too soon, I got to know what true abiding love is. If I had followed my family's wishes, I probably would have married some well-to-do horse person and had plenty of money, but have been miserable."

"Look at Uncle Bob," said Rob.

Shelby Lynn sighed. "Yes, Robbie. You're right. My brother is an important man in Lexington, has more money than he knows what to do with, but true love seems to have eluded him. Alyson is a sweet girl, in her way. She probably married him, at least in part, for his money. She's given him children, keeps his house tidy and keeps herself looking good. When Bob needs to go to a function, he can always count on having Alyson draped on his arm. And she looks the part. But true love? No, I don't think so." She looked at Verna. "Am I wrong to say they deserve each other?"

"No, you're not wrong," said the older woman. "Bob has a wandering eye and has … well, we'll say no more about that. Let's just say that he's not committed to his wife and leave it there."

"That's true, Mother. Not everyone is blessed with the kind of men we've had in our lives. And have." She patted Rob on the shoulder. She made an obvious attempt at changing the subject and brightening the mood. "Now who would like more tea?" she said, offering the pitcher around.

It was a good lunch and a good time. Before he took her back home, Rob took Ellen back to the barn. Sure enough, both kids were on their feet, nursing away, with mother hovering over them, making her soft noises and continuing to lick them. Rob gave her some extra feed and made sure that there was plenty of water. "Giving birth is thirsty work," he said.

"Oh, Rob. That was so special. I've never seen anything like it." Ellen floundered for words to express her wonder and appreciation.

Rob collected eggs and offered them to Ellen. "I have yet to make you one of my superior omelettes. Next time," he said, placing a little basket of five, brown still-warm eggs in her hand. Would there be a next time? Ellen found herself hoping intensely that there would be.

She said goodbye to the Mrs. Powells and promised to come again soon. Rob drove her home as the late afternoon sun illuminated the branches of the trees that were swelling with buds.

As he pulled in behind Gunilla and trotted around to open her door, Ellen spotted Rika again in her kitchen window. Suddenly shy, she didn't linger for the kiss she felt sure would be coming and instead hugged him. But it wasn't a quick hug — it was a hug that lasted more than a few moments. "Thank you for the loveliest day I've had for a long time," Ellen whispered into his chest. Then she untangled herself and walked quickly to the stairs, waving at Rika as she passed.

She knew Rika would surely come over later for conversation and coffee. For now, though, she wanted to sit in her mother's rocking chair, savoring the day. She took out each scene, each memory and handled it like a precious jewel before placing it back in the vault of her mind where she knew she could take them out an look at them any time she wanted. Her mind flitted briefly to Kirby, and then recoiled. All the good looks and dimples and incredible green eyes in the world could not hold a candle to the warmth, the easy companionship she had with Rob.

Unbidden, the conversation she had with Rika came back to her. "How far are you willing for him to go?" She realized she had come to a decision. So far and no farther until she was married. Would she like to be married? After a day like today, yes, she would.

She heard Rika's footsteps on the stairs. Ellen got up to put on the coffee and mentally prepared her explanation for Rika. After all, she had broken one of the rules this morning. While there hadn't been a sleepover, Rob had been in her apartment rather early in the morning. She had learned that coming clean right away was the best approach.

Chapter 53
Three potential new parts for Wilco.

At work, Rob was professional. Their developing friendship was something, Ellen could tell, he preferred not to display to everyone in the company. She appreciated that, although Annie was much too astute not to notice that he seemed to spend more time around Ellen. "We're just working on lots of projects together," said Ellen when Annie confronted her about it.

"Mmmm," was all Annie would say. But the twinkle in her eyes betrayed that she understood much more than she was saying, perhaps even more than Ellen understood herself.

Ellen's phone rang and she answered it. It was Rob. "Meet me out in the Fabrication Shop, please." What was that all about, Ellen wondered as she headed out onto the factory floor.

She spotted Rob looking at a basket of parts near the vertical drill. She had to yell over the thumping of the press, the whine of the grinders, the squeal of the lathes. "What's up?"

He pointed at a basket of parts, shouting back. "I'm getting a little paranoid. I'm beginning to wonder if my office and the conference room are bugged. I figure we can talk out here without anyone overhearing us. Just pretend we're talking about the parts in this basket." He lifted the paperwork wired to the side of the basket and looked like he was studying it.

"I doubt anyone can hear us out here, including me," said Ellen, cupping her ear to hear. "What do we need to talk about?"

"I've had another part we might start producing, this time for Pentacore. I didn't bother you with it because it was a simple part that Butch could handle by himself. Somehow International Dynamics underbid us by just one half of one percent. One half of one percent!" The telltale vein on his neck stood out. "That's too close to be a coincidence. We don't have the same relationship with Pentacore that we do with Wilco, so I couldn't salvage the business on my good looks and your data." Ordinarily he would have grinned, but this was too serious. "I'm just about convinced that, even though Kirby is gone, we still have a spy in our midst. Any idea who?"

"I haven't a clue. I mean I really thought it was Kirby. Even the way he talked to me at …" She let it drop, remembering Kirby's encouragement during dinner at Brownings for her to tell him whenever Powell Manufacturing was bidding on a new part. Rob didn't pick up on what she started to say.

"Well, let's keep our eyes and ears open. We've got to stop this leak if this company is going to survive. Meanwhile — and this is really what I wanted to talk about — Karl Smithson has given us three more parts to bid on. They're complicated parts, and I want you to start researching them with Butch. He's the only other one I'm going to loop in on this — so we can limit the exposure. In fact, I want you to do this very quietly. Don't let anyone know what you're working on, OK? These are the kind of products we need to turn this company around, and I don't want to lose them because somebody knows too much and tells the wrong person."

"I understand. I'll be finishing up installing the rest of the bar code readers with Whit, but I'll also work on this with Butch. And I won't leave my work lying around where anyone could happen to see it."

"That's exactly what I mean. Thanks, Ellen."

They parted, she going to collect job cards and he heading back to his office.

Toward noon Butch stuck his head in her office. "Might it be a good idea if we went somewhere off site and talked over lunch?"

"Good idea, Butch. Are you ready to go now?"

"You bet. How about Fast Ernie's?"

"Sounds good."

Fortunately it wasn't a particularly busy day at Fast Ernie's and they were able to find a table with some privacy. Butch sketched out what the parts looked like on his note pad and gave Ellen a list of machines that he thought would be involved. Ellen wrote them down in her notebook.

"I'll start researching our capacity on each of these machines using data from the mainframe and, when I have it, I'll try to give you a rough idea of the process times we might be looking at," she said.

"Sounds good. And I'll work on developing the m-times for all three. Oh, and I'll start researching pricing for the raw materials. The steel will be easy: we already use the right gauge steel. Some of the other components, though, I'll have to source."

"Will there be any issues with tooling?" asked Ellen.

"There might be. I think one of the parts will need to be stamped out on the press. I'll keep an eye out for that, too."

Ellen considered that. "Because we know the press is the bottleneck and, if we have to do a lot of tooling swaps, it will affect productivity."

"For sure."

They said out loud what they already knew: that Rob wanted this project kept very quiet so that no one else found out about it. Each one of them finalized their own game plan and then they headed back to the factory.

Ellen spent the afternoon researching the load on each of the work centers Butch had defined. She was getting quite adept at this kind of data analysis, writing several small RPG programs to help report the data she needed.

She also started looking at bar code data from the affected work centers. By now, Whit had installed bar code readers in most of the major work centers in the factory. While some hadn't been on-line for long, Ellen was able to get a sense of the amount of time required to produce a variety of products on each work center. She started making a spreadsheet with her estimated m-times for each work center.

She dialed Butch's number. "Hello, Butch. Can you talk?"

"Uh, that's a negative, Boss."

"OK, then. Just listen. I've taken each of the work centers you outlined for each of the parts and have looked at the capacity. I'm not seeing anything that concerns me in that area, with the obvious exception of tool swaps on the press. Good so far?"

"Good so far."

"What is more interesting is that I've also looked at the bar code data coming off of each machine. Most of the machines are fairly consistent on how much it takes to produce a part. The drill press still has multiples, depending on how many holes have to be drilled, and the laser cutter has some variance, I suppose, based on the length of the path it has to cut."

"You're making lots of sense."

"Good. So, here's the thing. I've come up with an m-time for each part based on the individual machines. What I've done is add up the estimated m-times on each machine to get a total. Have you come up with your estimated m-times?"

"I just finished."

"That's great. You don't say anything else. Just give me the m-time for the first part." Butch quoted a number. "Oh, good. Very close to what what I calculated. Makes me feel like I'm on the right track. What about the second part?" Again, Butch told her his m-time. "Again, really close. I was higher on the first one. I'm lower on this one. And the final part?" Again Butch stated a number, to which Ellen replied, "Oh, now that is higher than what I got. I must have missed something."

"That part goes down the Assembly Line. Maybe I'm so used to having to pad the numbers for Assembly that I'm the one who is off."

"Well, at any rate, we have a pretty good guess about the time to manufacture each one. What about the raw materials? Were you able to get an idea of cost?"

"I think so, but maybe there are too many to ..."

"To read over the phone. I get it. So could I pick up a copy from you now?"

"I'll bring it down to you." In a few minutes he was in her office with a handwritten report showing each of the three parts, the raw material items that would be needed for each, and the cost.

"Oh, this is really great, Butch. And if we add the m-times, broken down by work center, we can give that to Rob and he can ..."

"What are you kids working on?" It was Gladys making her "rounds" as she called it to say hi to people.

Ellen tried to unobtrusively cover Butch's sheet of paper with another one. "We're comparing notes on the m-times coming from the bar code readers with what Engineering has on file," she said brightly. She hoped it was a convincing response. It was true; it just wasn't the whole story.

"Honey, those bar code thingies are just the cat's meow, aren't they? You can really figure all that out from them? Well I'll be!"

"Yep, its pretty neat stuff what Ellen has done there," said Butch, trying to back her up.

"Well, y'all have a nice day!" Gladys headed down the hall to say hello to other departments before she left for the day.

"I don't know who exactly Rob thought we should be cautious of," said Ellen. "But I guess that means everyone, even Gladys."

"I doubt she's anyone to worry about. Still, Rob did say to keep it quiet. You did a good job of redirecting. Are we about done would you say?"

"Yes, I think so. Would you be comfortable if I make up a sheet like we were talking about, showing m-times, raw material costs, and any capacity issues? I'll give you credit for all the work you did, but I'd like to get that to Rob today."

"Sure. No problem. I know he knows we both worked on it. And I'm happy to have you write it up. Saves me the work!" He smiled.

"All right then. I'll get that done before I go home tonight. If he's still here, I'll give it to him tonight. If not, I'll give it to him first thing in the morning."

"I'll say good night, then." Butch left and Ellen started a new spreadsheet on her computer.

By the time she had it finished, she realized it was getting late. "I'd better see if Rob is still around." She must have said it out loud because Rob's voice answered.

"He is," Rob said.

"How long have you been standing there?"

"Oh a few minutes, just enjoying watching you work. What have you got?"

"Is anyone else around?"

"Nope. We're the last two people in the place. You worried?"

"That someone might overhear? Yeah, maybe. Butch and I took your cautions to heart. We met off site to review what we needed to do, and we worked independently until the very end. I'm just combining our work into one report to give you."

"So, you have something to show me?"

Ellen printed out her spreadsheet and invited Rob to sit down and review it. She explained her process for calculating m-times, and that she had verified them with Butch's calculations. She showed how Butch had researched each raw material that went into the parts and how much those would cost. "So," she said, "I think we have pretty much all of the information we need to make the bid, right?"

"Almost," he replied. "We've got to add overhead and then we'll have it all. Do you have supper plans? I've got an idea."

"No, nothing special. I was just going to fix something at home."

Rob held up a finger, indicating she should wait, and began dialing her phone. "Hello, Mrs. K.? This is Rob. Robbie. ... Yes, I'm fine, and you? ... Say, Ellen and I have something we'd like to talk over with Mr. K. If Ellen and I picked up some lasagne and breadsticks from Gabrielli's, could we invite ourselves over to dinner? ... Of course you have! I should have known. .... Well, I don't want to impose, but I really would like to go over some things with the Master Consultant. ... Yes, all right then. ... OK, we'll see you shortly." He hung up the phone. "I was trying to bring dinner in to them, but of course Mrs. K has already made some fabulous meal. That woman sure can cook! We've been invited to dinner again. Would that be all right with you?"

"Sure, I love being with the Klamecks. And I'm very curious what you want to talk with him about."

"I'll explain as we drive. Be sure and bring all of the material related to the Wilco bid. Oh, wait. You have your car here. I guess we'd better drive separately, although I would enjoy going down to Laodicea together."

They ended up going separately, although Rob followed Ellen all the way down. It wasn't like he was tailgating her, but more like he was keeping an eye out in case she had some kind of problem. Ellen parked in her usual place and she realized Rob must have parked down by the empty lot again. That gave her time to run up to her apartment and swap out her work shoes for something more comfortable. She was just coming back down the stairs when Rob came sauntering up with a handful of daffodils.

"These are for Mrs. K.," he announced. And then, with a flourish, he produced from behind his back one solitary narcissus.

Ellen inhaled deeply. "Why is it that narcissus smell so, so good, and daffodils don't hardly smell at all?" She took the delicate flower from his hand. "Thank you, Rob. You really are quite special, you know."

"Can't help it," he said. "I've got these facets, you see ..."

She grinned and dug her elbow into his side. They knocked on the Klamecks' door. Rika was just finishing setting the table and adored the flowers. She immediately put them in a vase and placed them in the center of the candles on the table. She got a delicate bud vase — "This is leaded crystal Jonas brought me from Prague," she said — and put Ellen's lone narcissus in it.

Dinner was delicious as always. Ellen was constantly amazed at how Rika seemed to be able to double the size of a meal to accommodate guests, and make it look effortless. The conversation during dinner did not center on work. There seemed to be an unwritten rule that business talk happened after the dishes were cleared away.

There was coffee and dessert, of course. As Ellen was helping Rika clear away and bring in the dishes for the apple tart she'd made, she heard Jonas say to Rob, "So what, may I ask, is the topic for conversation tonight?"

"I need some advice on pricing some new parts," said Rob. "Could I convince the venerable consultant to hang out his shingle for the son of a friend? I'd be more than willing to pay your going rate."

"Tut, tut," said Jonas. "I'm retired. No need for that. Besides," he said, "The pleasure of having you young people around my table provides more remuneration than mere consulting fees." He indicated Ellen who was carrying in a tray of dessert plates and the apple creation, while Rika followed with coffee cups and saucers. "Ellen has been a bright spot in our lives ever since she moved here. And you, my boy, are always welcome. I enjoyed working with your father, and I hope to work with you as well. What is on your mind?"

Rob explained about the three new Wilco parts and made it very clear that Powell Manufacturing was in a financial bind and really needed to win these bids. Then Ellen explained how she and Butch had analyzed the possible costs, Butch focusing on raw material costs and she focusing on data coming from her bar code readers. She showed Jonas the report she had made.

"May I make a comment, Robbie? Do you notice how Ellen instinctively knows how to present data? In this one sheet of paper she has provided quite a lot of information, yet it is pleasant to look at, arranged nicely on the page so that the eye instantly grasps what is included. And notice that she has not included superfluous information that doesn't add anything. Ellen is very talented and I think you should do everything you can to keep her."

Ellen blushed, while Rob simply replied, "I intend to."

Then they got down to the questions Rob wanted to ask. "First, he said, I'd like to go over my direct cost calculations with you. Then I'd like to discuss how you think overhead should be allocated."

"Both excellent topics, and vital if you are to develop a fair and competitive bid to give to Wilco."

Amid complements to Rika for yet another stunning dessert triumph, they talked about labor costs, allocating indirect costs based on labor hours or on raw material content, or doing some kind of value added accounting. They even talked about the necessity of accrual accounting versus the benefits of cash accounting. A lot of it was over Ellen's head but, in the end, using the numbers Butch and she had developed and with the addition of some multipliers Rob knew from his long experience with Powell's financials, they came to a price for all three parts that everyone was comfortable with. "Those prices each give us a healthy margin," said Rob, "without being greedy. I don't want to gouge Karl Smithson, but I want to make a fair profit, too."

"Exactly," said Jonas. "I call it the 'point of indifference.' If you're charging too much, then you find yourself really excited and hoping the customer will go for it, because you'll make a windfall. If you're charging too little, you'll come to hate the work because you're not making enough, or even losing money on every one you sell. At the point of indifference, you don't hate it for being too low, nor do you covet it because it is too high. It seems we've arrived at the point of indifference for all three parts."

"I'm going to remember that," said Rob. "The point of indifference ..."

"Now, if I may," said Jonas, "there was the matter of the first two principles we were going to discuss."

"Right!" said Rob. "I'm all ears."

"Ellen, can you explain Principle One to Robbie?"

"Sure," said Ellen. "The business information technology system must model the business it serves." She went on to explain the idea of a model. "Rob, would you say that SOLUTION/400 is a good model of our business at Powell?"

"Uh ..." Ellen realized she might have gone too far by questioning her boss. She glanced at Jonas who was beaming like he'd never had such fun. "Uh, not exactly," said Rob.

"In what ways does it not model our business?" If anything, Jonas' grin widened even more. He was loving this.

"Oh, oh, wait!" Rob snapped his finger. "The m-times! We need them to be based on each work center and all we have is a total m-time for the part. Is that it?"

Ellen looked over at Jonas again. "I believe, Jonas, that Mr. Powell is a fairly intelligent man. He understands."

At this Jonas laughed out loud. "Robbie, my boy, not only is she bright and organized, but I think she's got your number. Of course you're right. When the system fails to model the business, it always causes problems. Has the fact that your system doesn't allow you to have m-times per work center caused you any business issues?"

"And how!" said Rob. "We lost business, and we were over-inflating some of our processing times on the Assembly Line because we couldn't track that. It was Ellen's bar codes that gave us the insight we needed."

"No hard feelings, Rob?" asked Ellen. "I was just treating you the way Jonas treats me. He never gives me the answer. He just keeps asking questions until I figure it out for myself."

"An important consulting technique," noted Jonas. "Also known as the Socratic Method."

"No," said Rob. "No hard feelings at all. In fact, you've got me thinking — we also don't have any way to track or measure setup times, which we know are also very important." He turned to Jonas. "Ellen helped us see that our capacity issue on our big press is actually in the turnaround time on our setups, not on the actual stamping out of parts." He thought a minute more. "Is it time to get serious about replacing SOLUTION/400?"

"I can tell you that implementing new software is very expensive," said Jonas. "The cost of the software itself is just the tip of the iceberg. You would need to do some analysis, but my initial answer is to say 'make do with what you have.' We could have a whole discussion about software modification, but perhaps that can wait for another time. I'd like to get to Principle Two."

"Before we do," said Ellen, "I think it is important for Rob to hear that part about serving the business. Jonas has taught me that the system exists to serve the business, not the other way around."

"That's a really good point. When I meet up with other heads of small manufacturing companies, they often complain about how they're being held hostage by their systems. Their MIS guys tell them they can't do that because the system won't let them. That seems crazy to me."

"It is crazy, Robbie," said Jonas. "The system must serve, not be the master. Now, on to Principle Two. Ellen, if you would, please."

"The business information technology system must be non-redundant," quoted Ellen. "That one is fairly easy to understand, but not so easy to implement."

"I agree," said Jonas. "Can you think of any examples, Robbie, where you have redundant information?"

"No ... oh, wait. Yes I can! Does Gladys' Rolodex count as a redundant system?"

"Of course it does. Well done, Rob! You caught on a lot quicker than I did," said Ellen. "Remember the incident where we shipped parts to the wrong Wilco factory?"

Rob groaned, "Oh, do I! And all because Gladys was keeping a Rolodex, a redundant system, on her desk. That was a close one. And I can see how important that principle is."

"So, now Robbie, you know the first four. I am sure that Ellen will tell you when she finds the fifth one."

"Couldn't you give me a little hint?" asked Ellen.

"Now where would be the fun in that, my dear? The adventure is in the finding."

Rob thanked the Klamecks for a lovely evening and Ellen began to clear away the dessert dishes. "Hold on a moment, Ellen," said Jonas. "Robbie, may I make a suggestion?"

"Of course."

"I've been thinking about the pricing for the three Wilco parts we were discussing earlier. Why don't you take Ellen with you when you present the numbers to Mr. Smithson? I'm not sure if you had intended to give him the numbers in person, but I would advise you to do so. You can read his body language, identify any problems and correct them right then. If you take Ellen along, she can impress him with how carefully she was able to develop those costs. I think it would impress any customer. It shows a level of thoughtful analysis that I think is, unfortunately, quite rare. And it doesn't hurt," he said, turning to Ellen, "that you are so utterly charming and forthright."

"I think that's a great idea," said Rob. "If I can get an appointment with Karl tomorrow, would you be up for a trip to Dayton, Ellen?"

"I … I guess so. I've never done anything like that. I have talked to him on the phone, but that's about it."

"Besides," added Rika. "It never hurts, when dealing with a man, if the young lady is attractive."

Rob's "amen" was lost under Ellen's protests and sputtering.

"I only speak the truth," said Rika. "In this world there are men and there are women. And if the young lady is, as you say, easy on the eyes, that can't hurt. I believe it was Academy Award winner Edith Head who said, 'You can have anything you want in life if you dress for it.' So wear something nice tomorrow, yes?"

"Rika, you are too much." But she was watching Rob who was watching her as she said it.

"All right, then. I'll call Karl first thing tomorrow morning and, if he can see us, we'll make the trip to Dayton. Thank you for the very good advice, Mr. K. And Mrs. K., as always, an incredible feast. You both are too kind. Ellen, can I walk you across the breezeway?"

They ended up walking arm in arm down to Rob's car and then riding together up to her stairway, just as they had the other night. Rika was watching out her kitchen window as she washed the last dishes, so Ellen just wished Rob a good night and waved to Rika.

Chapter 54
The trip to Dayton.

Karl Smithson was only too happy to meet with Rob and Ellen. "What time can you be here?" he asked.

"If we leave now we should be there about 11:00," said Rob. "Would that work? We could discuss the pricing, then take you to lunch."

"If you're buying, I'm in," said Karl.

"I'll buy lunch, but I hope you'll buy the parts from us," joked Rob. But he was more than halfway serious.

After they hung up, Rob said, "Ready to go?"

"Yes. I've got all my paperwork and I printed out some extra copies of the costing report."

"All right, then. After you!"

They rode in Rob's car. At first Ellen was a little nervous — it was her first real business trip. But Rob was so easy to talk to that the miles flew by. "I've always found that windshield time is a really good opportunity to talk about business and to get to know each other," he commented.

Ellen's nerves started again as they pulled into the Wilco parking garage. Rob led the way. They had to get guest name badges at the front security desk and have Karl Smithson paged. He appeared quickly, welcoming them, shaking Rob's hand and clapping him on the back. He shook hands with Ellen, too, and seemed to assume she was an equal colleague. It had occurred to Ellen that she might be treated as an extra. Rob was the boss. She didn't want to think in those terms, but she was afraid she might be treated as 'just a girl.' But that wasn't Karl's style at all. He was respectful and jovial, fairly tall, balding and with rather thick glasses. He had a sandy colored mustache and deep set blue eyes. Ellen quickly took the measure of the man and liked him.

Karl ushered them into his office and offered them a seat. "How about a soft drink or some water?" he asked. "Or coffee?" Both Rob and Ellen declined, but Karl picked up his phone. "Marsha, would you mind to bring our guests some water? And a diet Coke for me." Then they got down to business.

Rob led off, explaining how much Powell Manufacturing valued Wilco's business and that he hoped to be able to continue to earn Wilco's trust as a preferred supplier. He then asked Ellen to explain the work she had been doing to develop the pricing. She realized that the practice she had last night explaining it to Jonas had helped prepare her for today. They started with the blueprints, then moved to the raw materials, building up to the individual work centers.

"You need to explain about the bar code project," prompted Rob.

So she explained about that, too, and she realized Karl was really interested. At one point he stopped her. "Wait, you mean you've got this on every work center?"

"Not every single one, but almost every one."

"And you're gathering this data for every batch of parts?"

"Yes."

Karl looked at Rob. "This is way ahead of anything we have at Wilco. I'm blown away by this." He turned back to Ellen. "This is really impressive, Ellen. When you get tired of working in a two bit town like Oak Lick and are ready to come to the big city, I hope you'll give me the opportunity to offer you a job. I'll bet we can pay you more than Rob is paying you." He winked at Rob.

"That's very kind ..." Ellen started to say, but Rob cut her off.

"Karl, if you think you can poach my employees, my best employee, then the deal is off."

"Oh, hey, I'm only kidding. Except I'm not. This is really, really good work. You've made a believer out of me — your pricing is based on solid, solid evidence, and you have given me confidence that you know what you're doing and can deliver. That's what I want to hear."

"So, do we get the business?"

"Unofficially, yes. But officially I have to look at two more bids. You understand. It's company policy."

Rob sighed. "Yes, I understand. It's just that I don't want to lose your business because someone underbids us by a few pennies. I had hoped that Ellen's work would prove to you that we're not basing our pricing on some wild guess. Nor are we trying to get the business just by underbidding someone else. Those are our prices and we're proud of them. They're fair to both Wilco and Powell."

"And Ellen's work does prove that. I'm serious. This is really impressive work, Ellen. You've convinced me, but I have to follow company rules. You understand. And I can see that you're not up for a job change right now ... Don't get steamed, Rob. I just want you to know what an impressive person you've got on your team."

"Oh, I know. I know in so many ways. But right now we just want a fair shot at earning your business, OK? So how about some lunch?"

They ended up at a nice seafood restaurant. Ellen tried to re-member her table manners as her mother had taught her, but Karl and Rob clearly enjoyed each other's company and they included Ellen in their banter. Karl, it turned out, had a small farm and raised sheep. He and Rob were able to compare the relative merits of sheep versus goats, and Ellen was able to describe watching the baby goats be born. "Just like that?" asked Karl. "Sheep need a lot more help than that."

On the drive home, Rob said, "So how do you think that went? I always like to debrief a meeting after I leave."

They both agreed it went fairly well and that they had a good chance of getting the business. "But I hope you don't think I'm going to take a job with Wilco, despite the nice things Karl said," said Ellen.

"Well, you would be within your rights to explore it. In fact, as your friend, I would say you should always take a look at promising offers that come along. But, as your employer, I can say without a doubt that we would be much worse off as a company if you chose to leave. Then again, as your friend, I would personally hate to see you go. You've come to mean a great deal to me."

They lapsed into easy silence, each mulling over their own thoughts. "You really did nail that presentation to Karl," said Rob, almost to himself. "We need to get you in front of more customers."

Back at the plant it was getting close to quitting time. Gladys was still at her desk in the lobby, but was tidying up her work area. Ellen wanted to check on a few things and she needed to make sure the job cards had been taken care of. "Thanks for going with me," Rob said. "I think we have a very good chance of getting the business," he said. "Thanks to you."

The next morning, as Ellen was putting her purse away, she had the odd feeling that things on her desk weren't quite as she had left them. She couldn't be sure, and she dismissed it as excitement from her business trip to Dayton.

She had lunch in the cafeteria with Annie and Rachel. "How's the new job going, Rachel?" she asked.

"Right well," said Rachel. "It ain't much different than before. Only now I can speak up when something ain't right. If somebody is slacking off, I know it and I can go poke 'em, like, and tell 'em to get with it."

"Do you think people will resent you for that?" asked Ellen.

"Sure. The lazy ones will. But the good ones appreciate getting to work more steady-like, and turn out better work."

"If anyone can get the lazy ones to do better, it's you, Rachel," said Annie.

"Thanks, girl. I hope so. And if they can't — or won't — why, then maybe they'd be better off working somewhere else."

"You're tough, Rachel. And smart. Just what Powell Manufacturing needs."

"Hey, we're like the female three Musketeers," said Annie. "All for one ..."

"… and one for all," repeated Rachel and Ellen in unison.

Late that afternoon, Rob called. "Could you come to my office? I think you'd like to be a part of this."

Butch was in his office when she arrived. And Karl Smithson was on the conference phone. "Shut the door," he told Ellen. "OK, Karl. Ellen's here now. What were you saying?"

"Hey, Ellen. I was just telling Rob that Wilco is officially offering the business to Powell."

"Hooray!" said Ellen, and Butch grinned. "That's great! Thank you, Karl."

"There is one little thing," said Karl. The mood in the room suddenly became more serious.

"What's that?" asked Rob.

"Yours wasn't the lowest bid. Each of the three parts had a bid from another supplier that was just a few cents less than your bids."

"You have got to be kidding me," said Rob. Ellen could see the vein on his neck beginning to throb. "Just a few cents?"

"Yes. A nickel or less difference between the two bids. Now I'll let you draw your own conclusions about that, but I thought you ought to know. By the way, we didn't feel that the other offer was credible. It lacked the careful research that you showed me yesterday, Ellen."

"And don't forget Butch," she added. "He did a lot of the research, too."

"Right. Thanks, Butch. So, Rob, the bottom line is that you've got the business if you want it, and I'll be getting you the purchase orders tomorrow. How soon can you start production?"

"Oh, we want the business. Butch, what do you think about startup?"

"Most of the raw materials have about a two week lead time. I think the bigger holdup will be getting the tooling made."

"We may be able to help with some of that," said Karl. "I think we may have some of the tooling already. Or at the very least you can talk to our engineers and see if we can help out with tooling. Could I put you in touch with them, Butch?"

"You bet, Boss. That would be very helpful."

"OK, then, Rob. Tomorrow I'll get you the purchase orders and Butch, I'll have one of my engineers contact you. Fair enough?"

"More than fair," said Rob. "As we say in Kentucky, that's better than plumb."

"Uh huh. You folks south of the Ohio River have some strange expressions. All right then. Congratulations," said Karl, and he left the call.

The three of them, Butch, Rob and Ellen, sat looking at each other for a moment. "Well done, you two," said Rob. "Very well done. I'm grateful. Everyone who works here should be grateful. Can I take you both to dinner?"

"Sorry, Boss. I'd rather go with you, but I've got Boy Scouts tonight. Getting the new Tenderfoots ready for their first campout."

"And I've been invited to Trish and Tommy's for supper," said Ellen. "Another time?"

"You can count on it," said Rob.

Chapter 55
Ellen recognizes Uncle Bob.

The next morning Ellen noticed the red Porsche in the visitor's parking lot. Rob's Uncle Bob must be in the plant today. She remembered how jumpy people were when he was on site, so she made a quick trip to the ladies room to make sure her hair was brushed right and that her makeup was in good shape.

As she exited the restroom she saw Gladys listening. Ellen could hear it, too. Rob's voice raised in anger, and another man's voice that she assumed was Bob Van Winkle's. "I can assure you, there are no flies on the wall," he said.

Ellen froze.

Where had she heard that before? Oh, yes! That conversation she overheard at Gabrielli's. Was this the same voice? The more she listened, the more she became convinced that it had been Bob Van Winkle and another man she had heard while sitting at the table with Nathan.

"Gladys, is …"

"Is what, sugar?" asked Gladys.

Ellen realized she had better be careful. Very careful. "Never mind …" She headed back to her office.

She tried to work on some of the projects she had going, but she had a hard time focusing. If that had been Bob Van Winkle that she overheard at Gabrielli's, and if she was interpreting what she heard correctly, there could be huge implications. She needed to make sure of her facts. It wouldn't do to accuse someone as powerful as Bob Van Winkle unless she was absolutely sure. He could swat her like the proverbial fly on the wall.

She just didn't know what to do.

It was a tough day. She ate her lunch at her desk and felt miserable. On the one hand, she could be wrong about Mr. Van Winkle. If so, it would be very bad of her to accuse him of — of what? Spying on Powell? But hadn't Rob said that Mr. Van Winkle owned a part of the company? How could someone spy on what was theirs to begin with? On the other hand, it just didn't feel right. If Mr. Van Winkle was obtaining information about Powell Manufacturing that he was using in some way to hurt the company, that would be wrong, too. But why would he try to hurt something that he owned? It just didn't make sense.

And then there was the family angle. Bob Van Winkle was Rob's uncle, Shelby Lynn's brother. What would she have to say about all of this? Ellen could see it possibly tearing the family apart. She wouldn't want that for Shelby Lynn, or for Rob.

There were the employees to think about, too. If Mr. Van Winkle was, for some crazy reason, trying to put Powell Manufacturing out of business, a whole lot of people would be out of a job. These were people she cared about— people like Annie and Rachel, Leonard and Harvey, Butch and Sandy, Herb and David and Joe Bob, even Whit and Gladys. The more she thought about it, the heavier her heart grew. She felt like she was carrying a massive weight, a weight that had been placed on her shoulders without her looking for it.

What could she do? What should she do? Who could help her to know? She thought briefly about Rob — but he was too closely involved. It wouldn't be fair to him unless she knew for sure. She thought about Jonas. His advice was always sound and well measured. But she wasn't sure she should take this to him — it was a different kind of problem. Then she remembered her sister. Trish worked for Ambrose, Matheson and Moore and so might know something about the legal ramifications. Trish might be able to advise Ellen if she was going to need an attorney. And Trish would keep it to herself.

It wasn't 5:00 yet, but Ellen decided to leave early. She gathered her purse and told Gladys she was leaving early. "Everything alright, honey?" she asked.

"Sure. Fine." In the parking lot, the red Porsche was still there. She tried to ignore it.

The sky was clear as she drove toward Laodicea, but there were dark, sinister clouds to the west. That suited her mood — there were definitely clouds on her personal horizon.

Trish was home, baking bread and delighted to see Ellen. "Hey, El. Can you stay for supper? I'm trying a new chicken cacciatore recipe I got out of Southern Living."

"I'd love to stay, if I can help. And if you're sure you'll have enough."

"Oh, I think I've got enough here to feed a small army. Please stay."

"Sure, that would be really nice." Carrie came bounding in and wrapped her arms around Ellen's knees. "Hello sweetie. I needed to come and get some sunshine. Because you know what they say. A day without Carrie is like ..."

"A day without thunthine! I love you, Aunt Ellen!"

"Love you, too ..." But Carrie was off again to whatever she was pretending with her dolls.

Ellen sighed.

"What's wrong, Sis? I know you. You look like yesterday's mashed potatoes."

"Yeah, I've got some heavy stuff going on at work. Do you mind if I bounce it off of you before the others come home? Maybe we could talk while you cook?"

"Sure. Maybe you could chop the vegetables while I get this chicken ready. You know where the aprons are."

So Ellen began chopping onions and carrots and garlic cloves while Trish braised the chicken. And Ellen explained about the conversation she had overheard in Gabrielli's while Trish had Carrie in the bathroom.

"But you couldn't tell who it was?"

"No, but one of them said he had a fly on the wall, like he was spying on the company. And I heard that same phrase again today and I recognized the voice — or at least I think I did."

"Who was it?"

Ellen's face was completely transparent. The agony, the doubt, the hurt, the concern all showed in her expression. "It was Rob Powell's uncle, Bob Van Winkle."

"Oh." Trish let that sink in. Then, again, "Oh. Oh, that's bad."

"Right! Why would he be trying to hurt the company? It's his own flesh and blood that runs the place. Maybe I got it wrong, but I don't think so. Trish, I just don't know what to do! I need your advice."

"Let me think about that a bit ..."

"Do you think I need to see a lawyer? You work in a law firm. What do you think?"

"Maybe. Maybe you need representation, but I think that's premature. I wonder if it wouldn't be good to write down what you know. Document it, you know? Stick to the facts as you know them."

"Yeah, that's a good idea. But should I tell anyone? Just pretend it didn't happen? Do I tell Rob?"

Trish's eyebrows went up. "How close are the two of you? Do you trust him?"

"Yes, I trust him. I trust him a lot. And ... yeah, I'd say we're getting closer."

"I see ..."

"I mean he's a really nice guy. I'd say he really has integrity. And he's interested in lots of different things, fascinating things. He treats me very nicely. I really like being with him. I ... oh, hang it all, Trish, I like him. I like him a lot."

"I kind of thought so. And I couldn't be happier for you. Tommy says he has a good reputation, even though he is known for having a temper."

"Yeah," said Ellen ruefully. "I've seen his temper in action. Tommy's right about that. But still ... he's really wonderful." Again, her face could not hide her enthusiasm. I don't think I'll ever be able to play poker, she thought to herself. When I like somebody, I can't hide it. And when something bothers me, everybody knows.

"Here's what I suggest, then," said Trish. "I would say you should write up what you know. And then I would say you should talk to Mr. Powell."

"What if I'm wrong?"

"Well, how sure are you?"

"I'm pretty sure. Mr. Van Winkle's voice sounds the same as the voice I heard in Gabrielli's. That was a few months ago, though. But they both used the same words. 'A fly on the wall' is what the man said in Gabrielli's and what Mr. Van Winkle said today at the plant."

"Lots of people say 'a fly on the wall.'"

"Yes, that's true. But put that together with what sounded like the same voices and I think it is more than just a guess. I'm pretty sure it was the same man in both cases."

"OK. I just wanted you to make sure. Then I say write up your documentation and then talk to Mr. Powell."

"OK, Sis. Thanks for the advice." Ellen kissed her on the cheek as Trish was assembling the meal into a large dutch oven.

"I think this is under control. Why don't you go check on Carrie while I get the table set?"

Ellen went and played house with her niece. Ellen was, at times, the mommy, the big sister, and the teacher in Carrie's role-playing. Ellen loved the little redhead and dreamed that someday she might have a daughter, too.

Nathan came in from school full of boyish energy. When he discovered Ellen was staying for supper, he demanded some time at the computer with her. Since Tommy wasn't expected for half an hour or more and the chicken had some cooking to do, she joined him in her old room as he was turning on the computer.

"Tubby's going crazy," he announced. "He likes my system a lot, but he's taken on a second paper. In addition to the Lexington Herald-Leader, he's also now delivering the Louisville Courier Journal. That's completely messing up my software."

They discussed what this change in Tubby's business meant for Nathan's system. "Do you remember Principle One?" asked Ellen.

"I think so. Isn't that the one where the system has to model the business it serves?"

"Extra points, Ace. That's it exactly. Tubby's business is changing, so you'll have to modify it to continue to model the business, right? Have you thought about what you'll have to do?"

"I know in the Bills file I'll have to add which paper the subscription is for. But there's more to it than that. Will I need a subscription file so the system knows which subscription each customer has?"

"That might be a good idea ... I'd have to think about that."

"I'm thinking the answer is yes. Which, if I did that, would mean Tubby could add even other papers if he wanted to."

"Nice. That would be really flexible. Tubby becomes a newspaper retail mogul and you become the head of a major software company."

Nathan grinned at that, then tilted his chair back and to looking at the ceiling. "I'll leave you to think about that," said Ellen. "I think I heard your Dad pull in and I need to go see if your mother needs any help in the kitchen."

The fellowship around the table was congenial and comfortable. The chicken cacciatore was a big hit with everyone, even Nathan. Ellen was glad to notice his comfort level with new dishes was increasing.

Ellen helped Trish tidy up the dishes afterwards, but then made her excuses. "I've got something I've got to do," she told Tommy. "The longer I put it off, the harder it will get. So, it's great to see you all, but I need to get going." She gave hugs and kisses all around and headed back to her apartment.

On the way the storm was clearly getting close. Lightning arced through the sky and the roar of thunder was uncomfortably close. Despite the weather, she wondered if she shouldn't stop by the Klamecks. It was Rika who said, after she'd overheard that conversation at Gabrielli's, that she should wait and see. She said, "if something else seems off, you'll know it." Well, today something really did seem off.

Maybe she would just pop in for a quick 'hi.' Then she'd go to her apartment and document the facts as she knew them.

Fat drops of rain were falling as she dashed up the driveway, holding her purse over her head. Lightning flashed so brightly she jumped, followed almost immediately by the sonic boom of the thunder. "That was close!" she said to herself. "Too close."

She banged on the Klamecks' back door.

"Ah, Ellen! Just the thing we need! Come in out of this weather! It looks like it is getting rather nasty out there." Rika seemed even more than usually glad to see her.

"I was hoping to catch you and see how you're doing. I had dinner with Trish and Tommy tonight, but I thought I'd say 'hello' before I headed upstairs."

"Your timing is perfect," said Rika. "We already have another visitor." Rob Powell came around the corner.

"Why, Rob! What are you doing here?" Suddenly she was conscious of her rather sodden appearance. Not that it should matter — he'd seen her in old overalls and a smelly old barn coat.

"I came to get some advice from the Sage of the Age. There's been a new development."

"Oh?" But Rika was already propelling her to the dining room table where the remains of some chocolate cake were in evidence. And Ellen couldn't help notice that there was a fourth cup already on the table into which Rika was now pouring wonderfully aromatic tea.

"You have an extra cup out. Who were you expecting?"

"You, of course," said Rika. "Who else? After hearing Robbie's story, it occurred to me that you might be coming by as well. Remember the Boy Scout motto: be prepared."

"Come in and sit down, Ellen," boomed Jonas. "Robbie has been giving us some fascinating insights into what happened today."

"Happened today?" she asked faintly.

"You knew my uncle, Bob Van Winkle, was in the plant today?" Ellen nodded. "At the risk of repeating what the Klamecks have already heard, Uncle Bob proceeded to chew me up and spit me out."

"That sounds ... unpleasant."

"He found out that we got three new orders from Wilco. Prime parts. Parts he would like to have for his own company, International Dynamics. Parts, by the way, that you played a major role in getting for Powell Manufacturing."

"But doesn't he understand how important those orders are to us? Doesn't us, not having those orders, mean that we're still on kind of ... shaky ground?"

"Mr. and Mrs. K know about the financial situation at Powell. I've told them everything; they know how important these orders are to us. And you're right: Uncle Bob does know how important those three orders from Wilco are to us. But that's not how he operates. He wants them for International Dynamics. Period."

"But doesn't he own a part of Powell Manufacturing? Surely it wouldn't be good for his investment if Powell went out of business."

"Right again, Ellen. It wouldn't seem like he would want to see us fail. But Mr. K may have some insight for us." He turned to Jonas who put down his tea cup.

"I did some consulting work with International Dynamics in the mid 70s. I understood that Powell manufacturing has several patents that International Dynamics would like to get its hands on. Not only that, but International Dynamics would like to have Powell's customers as well. So I do think there is some motivation, perhaps to force Powell out of business so that it can be acquired, patents and all, for pennies on the dollar. Bob Van Winkle's investment in Powell would suffer a loss, but what he would acquire would be far more valuable."

Ellen was quiet, processing what she just heard. Rob continued the conversation. "I came to see Mr. K to brainstorm ideas for blocking a takeover," he said. He continued, talking about poison pills and other strategies, things that Ellen didn't really understand. She interrupted him.

"How did Mr. Van Winkle find out about the Wilco order?"

"What?" Rob paused mid sentence.

"How did Mr. Van Winkle find out about the Wilco orders? You said he found out. How did he find out?"

"I ... I guess I don't know. Maybe Karl Smithson told him?" Rob was doing the talking, but Jonas was sitting very straight in his wheelchair.

"Why would Karl have told Mr. Van Winkle unless International Dynamics had also bid on those parts?" Jonas nodded at Ellen's question, but remained silent.

"I ..." Rob was having to think about this. He scratched his jaw line, then finally said, "Humph! I can't think of any other reason. What are you getting at, Ellen?"

"I think you know, Rob. I think International Dynamics was the company that underbid us by a few cents. I think Karl Smithson turned down the bids from International Dynamics, because, in his words, they weren't credible bids. They were our bids, just shaved by a few pennies. And I think Karl told your uncle that, and your uncle didn't like it."

"That would sure explain why he was so upset today. It was a very unpleasant day."

"I imagine it was. But, Rob, if this is all true — and I admit, it is conjecture, although rather plausible conjecture — then there is another thing to think about."

"What's that?"

Ellen glanced at Jonas. He was following the conversation with an intensity she had rarely seen in him. "Well, where did Mr. Van Winkle get the information about what Powell bid on the parts?"

"Where did he ... You mean, how did he ...?"

"Yes, that's exactly what I mean. Where did he get the prices we turned in so he could underbid them by pennies? I think the fact that all three parts were underbid by just a few cents implies rather strongly that he knew exactly what we had bid."

From his end of the table Ellen heard Jonas say quietly, "Well done!"

"I can't escape the logic of that," said Rob. "I guess Karl Smithson could have told him ..."

"That won't wash, will it?" Ellen pressed on. "Why would Karl tell Mr. Van Winkle what Powell bid on the parts, only to turn International Dynamics down? I can think of only one other plausible explanation." She waited for Rob to figure it out.

She could see the light go on in his eyes, followed closely by the terrible implication. "It means we still have a mole in the plant," he said. "And it isn't Kirby. So who is it?"

"I don't know, but I do have a tiny bit of information to add to this," said Ellen. "Remember me telling you about the conversation I overheard at Gabrielli's back in January?" Three heads nodded around the table. "Well, I heard one of those voices again today. At Powell Manufacturing. In your office, Rob."

"In my office? You mean that it was Uncle Bob — my Uncle Bob — you overheard talking at Gabrielli's?" His voice was tight, so tight it made him sound squeaky.

"Yes. I'm pretty sure." She paused. She might as well tell everything she knew. "And the person at Gabrielli's said he had a fly on the wall. Remember that?" Again three heads nodded. "A fly on the wall can mean several things, but to me it meant he had someone on the inside, someone who wouldn't be noticed, listening and watching."

Suddenly Rob slammed the flat of his hand on the table, making the teacups rattle. "And he said those very words to me today. He denied having a fly on the wall. Why, that dirty ..." His hands balled into fists on the table and the vein on his neck began to throb. "I accused him of having ears in the plant, and he said he didn't have a fly on the wall. Those were his exact words." He looked at Jonas, then at Rika and then finally landed on Ellen. In a voice that was pregnant with vulnerability, he said, "What am I going to do?"

Ellen reached across the table and covered his two balled fists with her smaller hands. "I don't know what we're going to do. But we'll face it together. You've got my support, Rob."

"My own uncle! I can't believe this!"

"Rob, let me ask you something. Where do you keep the information about the Wilco orders?"

"On my desk, in a folder ... Oh, no! You don't think ..."

"I'm afraid I do. Yesterday morning when I came to work I had the feeling things had been moved around on my desk. I didn't think much about it at the time, but is it possible that someone — Mr. Van Winkle's mole, whoever that may be — could have been into our offices looking for the pricing we submitted?"

"This just can't get any worse. I'm sure it's possible. The folder was lying on my desk and I didn't think a thing about that. I should have at least put it in my desk."

"I'm not sure that would have done any good. My information related to the Wilco order was in a file folder in my desk. But the desk isn't locked — anybody with access to the factory could have found it after I'd gone home."

"Who could be the fly on the wall?" asked Rob. He looked at the Klamecks, halfway expecting they would know the answer.

Just then there was another crash of thunder and the house was plunged into darkness except for the candles in the center of the table. "Oh, dear," said Rika. "An outage." She got up and lit several more candles in sconces on the wall and on the sideboard, giving the room a cozy ambience despite the ferocious storm outside.

"Mr. K, do you have any words of wisdom for me?" asked Rob.

"No, I can't say that I do. It seems to me that your internal consultant here has done a good job of asking questions, helping you reach your own conclusions." He nodded at Ellen. "What I have no clue about is who the internal spy, the mole, might be. But this is serious. It may be that you have to set a trap to flush him out."

"What do you mean, a trap?" asked Rob.

"Something like divulging some information, or leaving a document containing some false information lying around. Then you wait and see if anyone takes the bait. For example, you might bid on some other parts, and deliberately leave a fictitious price laying around. If the vendor gets a bid from another company that is based on that false price, it may help you narrow down your list of suspects. Right now I think we have to say that every employee in the factory could be a suspect, correct?"

"Yes, that's correct," said Rob. "And I see what you mean about setting a trap. I'll have to think about that."

"May I also suggest, Robbie, that you and Ellen have a secret word between the two of you? If you or Ellen suspect someone or something isn't quite on the up and up, you'll be able to drop this word into the conversation and alert the other. And you can do it without raising suspicions."

"I like that idea, Mr. K. Ellen, what word shall we use?"

"I have no idea. I'm not creative like that."

Rob snapped his fingers. "I've got it! We'll say opossum. That's easy to drop into a conversation since your nickname is Possum already. We'll add the 'o' in front of it to call attention to it."

"Wait a minute," said Rika. "I must interrupt. Ellen, you have a nickname?"

Ellen half laughed, and half wanted to hide her face in her hands. "They call me Possum."

"Why, for heaven's sake? An opossum is an interesting creature, no doubt, but why would they call you that?" Rika was amused.

"I'm glad you think it is funny, Rika. At first I really hated it. And the more I let on that I hated it, the more they called me Possum. I guess I've gotten to the point that I think it is kind of endearing in a strange way. Apparently the guys in the factory have a habit of pinning nick names on people they like. I guess it is a badge of honor."

Rika looked at Jonas as if to say, 'Who can figure these American's out?'

"You know about my nick name, right Rob?"

"Yes, but I don't know how you got it."

"Leonard shared his lunch with me one day because I forgot to make mine. We were just chatting and joking about things to eat and he talked about how his grandmother could make a possum pie. I think he was probably pulling my leg, but the next day I was Possum." She shrugged her shoulders. "I'm stuck with it, so I might as well enjoy it."

"I kind of like it," said Rob. "It's ... endearing." He poured himself a bit more tea from the pot. "Say, Mr. K, I've got an idea. You've sent Ellen on this quest to find the five principles of business information technology systems, right? Well, I propose that we call them the Possum Principles!" He saluted Ellen with his tea cup.

Jonas chuckled. "Possum Principles, indeed. Very droll, my boy." Then he became very serious. "Possums aside, you have a real problem at your factory. Having a mole in your midst is very bad. I encourage you to try to flush him out quickly. Your business will never be safe if you can't trust what might be being leaked to your competitors. And don't forget the code word, opossum. That is your signal to the other one that you're seeing something or interacting with someone who might be your spy, your mole. Is that clear?"

Both Rob and Ellen nodded. "Well then. That's settled," Jonas said. "I wonder how long this power will be off?" And, just as he said it, it came back on. "Oh that I only had such power!" he exclaimed.

Rika went into the living room and turned on the television. In a few minutes she came back. "Brad James on channel 27 says we are under a tornado watch, but that the bulk of the danger is past. The radar shows the stronger part of the storm is to our east now."

"Thanks, Mrs. K. Good to know. I really should be getting home to check on my mother and Mammaw."

Ellen got up to start clearing away the dishes. But Rika stopped her. "Ellen, why don't you see Robbie out. I'll take care of these."

Ellen got her coat and Rob retrieved his umbrella. They said good night to the Klamecks and stepped out into the blustery weather. "Ellen, I ... I thank you for what you helped me understand tonight. I don't like it. I don't like it one bit. But I'd rather know the truth than be blindsided later on." He turned to her in the faint light of the streetlamp out on Prospect street. Ellen could see his tortured face. Mist coalescing into drops on his cheeks that looked like tears.

"Rob ..." She didn't know what else to say.

Suddenly, awkwardly because of the umbrella, he drew her to him, held her, rested his face in her hair. Ellen's hands snuck around his waist, holding him, pressing her face into his chest, willing some of her strength into him to be able to face the days and weeks ahead. Neither of them spoke for a long minute. Finally, Rob said, "I guess I'd better get home." His voice was husky.

"Where are you parked?" Ellen said into his chest, not wanting to let go quite yet.

"Down the street. The usual place."

"I'll walk down with you."

"The storm. You shouldn't ..." But she cut him off.

"It's tradition. Besides, I'll be under this nice big umbrella with you."

Their mood brightened as they walked down Prospect Street, arm in arm. They arrived at the vacant lot and could see in the light of a street lamp that the storm had flattened many of the flowers. "But they'll bounce back," said Ellen to herself. "Just like we will."

As they arrived back at Ellen's driveway, Rob said, "We have some serious strategizing to do. But not tonight. It's late, I need to go home, and you need some sleep. We both need to think." He took her hand and squeezed it. "Thank you. You don't know what you mean to me."

Chapter 56
Rob and Ellen chat about Uncle Bob.

Ellen let herself sleep in the next morning. When she did wake, she was thinking about the problems at Powell, about the rat who was spying on them and who he could be, and about how Rob was doing.

She had just finished showering and dressing when she heard a tread on the stairs. She went to the door and found Rob with a box under his arm.

"Fancy a pastry?" he asked. "A man with facets might be persuaded to part with one, or even two, in exchange for an invitation to come in for a cup of coffee."

Ellen glanced down at the Klamecks' windows but there was no sign of a light in the kitchen. Oh, what the heck, she thought. Rob needs to talk. Was she lying to herself? Who cares! "For some crazy reason I made a whole pot of coffee this morning, even though I rarely drink more than two cups."

"Aw, I'm touched. You were expecting me." Maybe she was, maybe she wasn't. But he was here now. "Come in and sit down. I'll get some plates and another mug."

It was as natural as could be, Ellen realized later. Having Rob at her table, drinking coffee, chatting about little things, just felt comfortable, right. There was no pretense, no one-upmanship, no second guessing. They trusted each other and enjoyed each other, and the morning flew by.

They talked about music — Rob was a Led Zeppelin fan, but agreed with Ellen that Ravel's *Daphnis and Chloe* was a fine piece of music. They talked about places they'd visited, and places they would like to go. Ellen said she'd like to go to Sweden; becoming Rika's friend had made her want to see the country where she grew up. Rob said he had been to Sweden twice before, once to Stockholm and once to the western side. One trip was with his parents that had included Finland and Denmark as well. The other was a business trip to try to get some business for Powell Manufacturing that had been unsuccessful. He said he had enjoyed both visits, and hoped to go back himself someday.

Ellen asked how Shelby Lynn was handling the news of what they suspected her brother was doing.

"I haven't told her yet," said Rob. "I don't know how to tell her."

"Won't you have to tell her?"

"Yes, of course. It would be nice to have more proof. I'm convinced that we know what Uncle Bob is doing, but we don't exactly have a smoking gun."

"Didn't you tell me that your mother owns shares of Powell Manufacturing stock? This is none of my business, but does she depend ... I mean, is her livelihood ... Well, what I mean is, would she be hurt if Powell were to go under?"

"We never did finish that conversation we had back before Thanksgiving, did we? I was starting to tell you about the structure of Powell when ... Oh, when Kirby came in to take you on a date." Suddenly he was embarrassed.

"Yeah, I remember that day," she replied ruefully. "Would you like to know where he took me?"

"Uh, no. Not really. Yes."

"To a tractor pull."

"A tractor pull?" He almost choked, whether it was to keep from laughing or to hold his temper. "I don't know what to say about that."

"Wait, it gets better. Do you remember what I was wearing that day?"

"Well, I ... OK, I do remember. Because I thought how good you looked. You had on a nice blue blouse that looked really good with your eyes. Oh, and a rather short skirt, as I recall."

"You remember right. And would you like to guess what Kirby's mode of transportation was?"

"Oh, no. Seriously? Did he take you on his motorcycle?"

"He did. Can you imagine?"

"Well, now, I've never worn a short skirt, but I expect that was ... awkward."

"To say the least." Why am I telling him this, Ellen asked herself? Because, she answered, because he truly cares, and because he's laughing with me at the situation, not at me. "So tell me more about what you were going to tell me that day."

"Right. And, by the way, I remember saying that day that you had integrity, that I could trust you. If anything, I trust you even more now than I did back then." He gathered his thoughts. "I guess I'll start by saying that Uncle Bob is a man who wants to get his own way. He likes to take 'care' of people, but he wants to do it on his own terms." Rob motioned with his fingers to make air quotes. "So, yes, I think my mother would be hurt, but Uncle Bob would be there to rescue her, to take care of her. And that way he could do it on his own terms." He paused, thinking more. "I guess," he began again, tentatively, "That I don't like that, because then she'd be beholden to him. I'd rather that my Dad's legacy, the company he built, would be what sustains her financially, rather than Uncle Bob's largesse."

Ellen watched his eyes. They were half closed as he was thinking. But then they would open and look at her with an intensity that made it clear how very important this was to him. "My mother married my father, somewhat against her family's wishes. The Van Winkles are a well-to-do Lexington family. They run in just the right circles, hobnob with horse people, go to Keeneland for the spring and fall meets, belong to the right country club. That sort of thing."

"Your mother is an elegant woman," Ellen said.

"I'm glad you think so. I do, too. She comes by it honestly, going to finishing school and being brought up with southern hospitality in her veins."

"So how did she come to marry your father?"

"Growing up on the farm, he loved animals. He had already started his business — in the garage at Three Pines — but he went to a stock sale and saw Mother. She was with the ritzy folks in the stands and he was down with the horses, but he saw her and couldn't get her out of his mind. You'll have to get her to tell you about it some day. He pursued her until she finally agreed to go on a date with him."

"So they really did love each other, just like your mother said."

"Oh, very much! They came from different worlds, but once she decided my father was the one, she was ready to go anywhere to be with him, including move to Adams County and live in an old civil war relic of a house." He twisted his mouth in a comical way. "Her family wasn't so keen on the dirt farmer she married."

"So does that have anything to do with why your Uncle Bob would want to see Powell Manufacturing go under?"

"I would hope he wasn't that devious. But, in reality, yes, I think that plays a part in it. And, as Mr. K said, he wants to get his hands on Powell Manufacturing patents and Powell Manufacturing customers for himself." He looked at her again, making sure she was paying attention to him. "Ellen, he is a powerful man. When Mr. K says this is serious, he's right. We need to be careful. We may end up needing to set that trap he was talking about. And, no kidding, we need to remember the code word 'opossum' if either one of us suspects something is wrong. Deal?"

"Deal," she said, solemnly shaking the hand he offered her.

They speculated on who the spy could be. "Butch knows the most about the jobs we bid on because of his role," said Rob. "But I just can't see him doing something like that."

"Sandy, maybe?" asked Ellen. "Butch works for him. He might know quite a lot."

"Maybe ...," said Rob. "But he was at Powell before I even got there. I just can't see him being disloyal like that."

"One of the machine operators?"

"I just don't see how they would know enough. I guess one of them could have snuck into my office and looked at the papers on my desk, though." He paused. "I just hate this, Ellen. I hate suspecting people and looking over my shoulder. I just want a chance to do good work and bring in enough money to pay people a decent wage." He stared into his coffee cup for a long time.

"I want that, too," said Ellen. "For you. For all of us who work at Powell."

"Now," Rob said, draining the rest of his coffee and shaking himself out of his reverie. "How about a drive in the country? And then maybe some lunch at one of the wonderful little eateries we have in Kentucky? Do you have a scarf? You might want to bring one." Ellen looked at him. Why was he being so cryptic?

As usual, Rob had parked by the vacant lot. They walked arm-in-arm down the street. But instead of his usual Eagle, a bright red convertible with the top down was parked in the space. "What in the world is this?" asked Ellen.

"This, my friend, is a classic. It was my father's. A 1969 Ford Mustang. He had always wanted one and, after his business really took off, he bought one. He died just a couple of years later, so he didn't get to enjoy it much. We keep it in the garage and I'm allowed to drive it on special occasions. I thought you might enjoy the sunshine with the top down. Obviously the scarf is for your hair."

She smiled. Little things like that pleased her.

They ended up driving through horse country, which seemed fitting after the talk about Shelby Lynn's family. They admired the white fences and the elegantly appointed barns. "Nicer than most people's homes," Rob commented. They observed the stone walls in many locations. Ellen lay her head back, feeling the sun on her face, the wind through the strands of hair that had managed to escape the scarf, and feeling completely and totally at peace. Had she ever had this feeling since her parent's deaths? She didn't think so.

They did find a little country store at a crossroads and had a sandwich, piled high with shaved ham, lettuce, pickles and tomatoes. They sat on the swing on the front stoop of the store and ate their sandwiches while watching the cars go by. Rob kept one foot on the railing and gently rocked the porch swing as they ate. They discussed the relative merits of soft drinks. They both agreed that Ale-8-1 was a local favorite and justifiably so, but Rob also favored Cheerwine. "Cheerwine?" asked Ellen. "What's that?"

"A local drink from North Carolina," he replied. "Folks down there are crazy about it, sort of like we are about our Ale-8s."

"Well, that's something I'll have to try some day," said Ellen.

They ended up driving as far as Midway, taking back roads all the way and ending up at Weisenberger Mill on Elkhorn Creek. They lounged on the bridge, watching the water wheel and listening to its rhythmic splash-splash-splash.

As they were heading back to Laodicea, Rob looked over at Ellen and asked, "Hungry? Would you like to go to dinner together, or have you had enough of me?"

"Oh, no! I ..." She caught herself. It wouldn't do to be too forward. "I could eat."

"Where to, then? How about Gabrielli's?"

"Oh, that would be nice! I like Gabrielli's on a Saturday night. Everybody and his dog is there. It's a fun place to be."

"I agree. Gabrielli's it is, then." He managed to find a parking place right near the front, and, before Ellen could get her seat belt off, he was around on her side, opening the door. He held the door open to the restaurant and they stepped into the wonderful smells of yeast, garlic, and baking bread. The guys in the back were tossing pizza dough into the air in ways that always amazed Ellen.

She heard her name. She scanned the crowd and spotted Trish, Tommy, Nathan and Carrie sitting at a booth. "El!" called Trish. "Over here!"

"Oh, it's my sister and her family," Ellen told Rob. "Would you mind if we ..."

"I'd love to meet them," said Rob.

Trish was pleased to meet Rob and he and Tommy shook hands. Rob even shook Nathan's hand, saying, "I believe we've met before. At the factory?" Then he turned to the redhead and said "You must be Carrie."

"Yeth," she replied, not sure what to make of this stranger with her Aunt Ellen.

"Your Aunt Ellen thinks you're pretty special," said Rob. "So that must be true, right?"

"I gueth tho," the little girl replied, burying her head in her mother's side in a fit of shyness.

"Would you guys like to join us?" asked Trish. "Or is this like a date?" Her eyes twinkled wickedly and Ellen silently mouthed "watch it, Sis."

Rob looked at Ellen, half embarrassed and half amused. "Oh, I don't know. We just went for a drive and thought we'd get some pizza. What do you say Ellen? I'd love to spend some time with your family. Or do you want my many facets all to yourself?"

Trish looked puzzled so Ellen said, "Scoot over, Nathan." She grinned as Rob sat down beside her.

"Looks like you guys have ordered already," said Rob. "What would you like, Ellen? I'll go place our order." They ended up with a grizzly style pizza, hold the anchovies.

By the time both pizzas arrived, they were all chatting like old friends. Carrie lost her shyness when Rob showed her how he could fold a dollar bill into a talking fish. "That is really clever," remarked Trish.

"He has facets," said Ellen.

"Facets?"

"Yup. Rob Powell is a man of many talents. I did not know that paper money origami was one of them, but I am not surprised." She nudged Rob with her shoulder. "Tell 'em about your facets, Boss."

"Yup, it's true. According to Ellen, here, I have facets. Many facets. They lend to my natural charm and all-around perspicacity. I would say I'm one of the nicest people I know."

"Humble, too," said Tommy, and they all knew Rob was poking fun at himself.

Rob and Tommy got into a conversation about the ins and outs of Cincinnati Milacron injection molding equipment since the company where Tommy worked was installing a new one. That gave Trish the opportunity to quietly quiz Ellen about Rob. But Ellen just smiled.

At the end of the meal, Rob asked Trish and Tommy if they thought him buying everyone an i-c-e c-r-e-a-m would be out of line. "I know what that spells," said Nathan with some genuine enthusiasm in his voice.

"What doth it thpell?" asked Carrie.

"I think it would be fine," said Trish. "Carrie, Mr. Powell is asking if you'd like an ice cream cone. What do you say?"

"I thay yeth!" She looked at her dad, remembered his admonitions, and added, very seriously, "Thank you, Mr. Powell. Thank you vewy much."

So, before Rob drove Ellen back to her apartment, they all had an ice cream cone from Pemberly and walked around the town square licking their cones. Eight ancient catalpa trees, two on each side, anchored the square, giving rise to the local name, "Catalpa Square." Nate sagely explained to Carrie that the long cigar-looking things in the branches were actually the fruit of the tree. Tommy admired the Mustang and Rob obliged him by opening the hood. By the time Tommy was done looking it over, Rob said, "Man, you know way more about cars than I do. That's really impressive."

Trish squeezed Ellen's hand and whispered where Rob couldn't hear, "He's a keeper, El. He's a keeper for sure."

Chapter 57

Rob asks Ellen to get ready to go to Sweden.

Spring finally arrived in the Bluegrass with riots of flowers, trees displaying their first hints of green, and birds returning from their southern winter holiday. A pair of robins started building in the crook of the downspout outside of Ellen's dormer window where she could watch the daily progress. She was amazed at how well the two worked together, constructing the nest with unflagging zeal. Then, one day, a perfect light blue egg appeared in the nest. Each day a new one appeared until there were four. Then mother robin spent quite a bit of time keeping the eggs warm, even during the frequent storms that sweep through Kentucky in the Spring, sometimes sending everyone scurrying to their basements because of a tornado warning.

On those nights — and they often happened toward evening after the sun had warmed the atmosphere all day — Ellen would go over to the Klamecks. Sometimes Rika would call her. "They are saying there might be rough weather tonight, and I've baked cookies!" It was an excuse to get together. Even though there was a basement under the Klamecks' house, Jonas couldn't get down the stairs. So, instead, the three would hunker down in the requisite "interior room" playing Jotto or Hearts, keeping flashlights close at hand in case the power went out.

Ellen loved this time of year, when the days got longer and the world seemed to overflow with possibilities. It was light now well before she would have to be on her way to work, and she often took her coffee out onto the landing to listen to the birds and breathe the fresh air laden with the scent of rain and leaf mold, worms and early roses. A male mocking bird had decided the peak of the garage was the best vantage point from which to stake out his territory. "Mocking birds like to sing from something high," her father had told her. "And you can tell a mocking bird from a catbird because the catbird only repeats himself twice. A mocking bird sings the same borrowed tunes four or five times."

She had learned a lot about birds from her dad. Just leaning against the railing of the landing, sipping her coffee in the mornings, she could identify by sound, without ever seeing them, bluejays, pee-wees, chickadees, bluebirds, cardinals, nuthatches, flickers, and many more.

"Good morning, Gladys!" she sang as she came into work.

"Good morning, honey. How are you today?"

Ellen would replay some phrase like "Spring's in the air and all's right with the world" or "fit as a fiddle" or the new one she had learned from Annie, "finer than frog hair split four ways."

Work seemed to be settling into a pattern. Ellen was beginning to take the four Business Information Technology Systems principles she knew about and really put them to work. She worked with Whit Collette a lot to really understand how the SOLUTION/400 system worked. She followed processes through the plant. She even began to make suggestions for improvement. She tried, tentatively, to get Gladys to give up her Rolodex, but got such fierce pushback that she gave it up. At least for the time being. The entire factory was now fairly well covered with bar code readers, and she was beginning to think about putting a computer on a rolling cart in the receiving dock area so that the Receiving Department could log in parts right as they came off the transfer trucks.

She also did a lot of RPG programming, extracting data in various ways, looking for patterns and efficiencies. She continued to be a frequent and valued guest at the Rob's weekly staff meetings, presenting data about various topics as requested by one manager or another.

One day Rob brought Butch to her office and closed the door. "We've got an opportunity," he announced. "As before, this has to be kept very quiet. Only the three of us need to know about this, at least in these early stages."

"What's cookin', Boss?" asked Butch.

"We have been asked to make a bid. And this one is a big one, and a really good one." He looked from Ellen to Butch. "I won't say who the customer is, but I can tell you that it is overseas. The company is under some pressure from their US customers to add more American made components to their product, so they're interested in doing business with us. Wilco is a major supplier to this overseas company, and Karl Smithson recommended Powell Manufacturing to them."

"That's very nice of Karl," said Ellen.

"Yes, it is. We've impressed him with our ability to develop fair pricing for our products and our ability to deliver on time with excellent quality. You both have contributed significantly to that reputation. And, of course, Leonard is doing a great job over the Assembly line and Rachel is turning out to be a very good lead person."

"That's great, Boss. So when can we see the prints so we can start working up the pricing estimates?"

"I've got them in my office," said Rob. "Stop by in a few minutes and I'll give them to you. You guys know how to do this — you're experts at it. And I hope I don't have to remind you that we need the pricing soon and that this has to stay between the three of us. Understood?"

"Understood," said Ellen. "This is a great opportunity."

"Understood," said Butch.

"Butch, I've got something else to talk over with Ellen. How about I meet you in my office in five minutes, tops."

"Yessir, Boss!"

When he had gone and Rob had shut the door again, he asked, "Ellen, do you have a passport?"

"Uh, yes, I do, actually. My parents were going to take Trish and me to Mexico. But that was going to be between Christmas and New Years before … before they died. So I got a passport, but never used it. Why do you ask?"

"Because, if this goes down the way I think it will, you'll need to come with me so we can make a presentation to the customer, just like you did for Karl Smithson at Wilco in Dayton."

"Come with you, like, overseas?" Her butterflies were back. She'd not had the opportunity to travel much. She wasn't sure she was ready for this.

"Yes, overseas. I don't want to tell you where just yet because I want to limit the information that is out there. But I think you'll be pleased with the location. Besides, Powell Manufacturing needs you to do this. I need you to do this."

"I'll try, Rob. But, I'll be honest with you — I'm a little intimidated by going out of the country." But, if you were along, it wouldn't be quite so scary, she thought. It might even be very pleasant to explore a foreign country with this man. "I would like to do what I can, however."

"That's the spirit. When you go home tonight, can you check your passport to make sure it hasn't expired? If we need to get your passport renewed, we'll have to expedite it. I'm hoping that your passport is still current and there won't be any problems using it."

Later she called Butch. "Lunch? Do we have things to discuss yet?"

"I'm up for lunch," he replied. "Let me get some data together and I'll stop by to pick you up in about ten minutes."

They went to Fast Ernie's and got a table in the corner, away from prying eyes and ears.

"Rob thinks he's keeping it a secret where this customer is, but I think I know," said Butch.

"Really? Where?"

Butch unrolled one of the blueprints just enough to show a corner. "Recognize that logo?"

"Looks like a screaming hawk … Oh, wait! I do know that logo. It's on the car I drive!" Suddenly she was engulfed by the implications. If the customer was Saab, then … "Is it Sweden?" she whispered, and Butch nodded. "Let's do a really good job on this, Butch. I would be over the moon if we could get Saab as a customer."

They put their heads together and worked through lunch. When they were ready to head back to the plant they had a fairly firm idea about m-times and costs. "I want to check a few more details and then I'll write this up like I did before and give it to Rob, right?"

"Suits me," said Butch. "We're getting to be pretty good at this. But be sure and don't leave any papers lying around. Maybe even take them home with you so they don't fall into the wrong hands. I think I'll take the blueprints home, too."

"Good idea," said Ellen. "I feel like we've got to be really careful."

Later at home she found her passport in her envelope of important papers. The passport had a little under a year before it expired. Rob would be pleased. "Oh, why not?" she said to herself. "Why not tell him now?" She looked up the number in the phone book and found it under Harold Powell, Rob's late father.

"Hello? Is that Mrs. Powell? It's Ellen Murphy. ... I'm fine! How are you? ... I'd love to. You and the senior Mrs. Powell are wonderful. I really enjoyed the lunch ... Yes, let's do that. I'm calling to give Rob some information he asked me for at work today. Is he available? ... Yes, sure. I'll hold." She could hear Shelby Lynn calling for Rob.

"Hello?"

"Hi, Rob. It's Ellen."

"Mother said it was you. To what do I owe this pleasure?"

"It could have waited until tomorrow, but I thought I'd let you know that I did find my passport and that it doesn't expire for almost a year."

"Oh, that's great! That makes things a lot easier. Since we're talking where we can't be overheard, and I sure hope they haven't bugged my phone, let's do a little planning. I would like to go sooner rather than later. Strike while the iron is hot, if you know what I mean. Do you think we could get this pulled together in a couple of weeks?"

"Butch and I worked on it all day and I think we are very close to having it all nailed down. Certainly we'd have it by the end of the day tomorrow."

"That's terrific! Good work. So really the only holdups are to make sure our calendars are clear and to coordinate it with the customer. I don't know why I'm being so secretive about all this; I guess I'm just a little paranoid ..."

"With good reason."

"But I might as well tell you that we're going to ..."

"Sweden," Ellen squeeked. Don't appear over anxious, she chided herself. But she couldn't help it. The chance to go to Sweden with Rob, well, that was just a little more than a girl could keep bottled up inside.

"How did you know?" Rob was openly curious.

"Butch pointed out the logo on the blueprints to me. It matches the logo on my car. Therefore the customer must be Saab, which is located in Sweden."

"You really are quite the detective, aren't you? You're right, of course. Would you like to go to Sweden? With me? For business, of course."

"I would love to go to Sweden. I'd love to see the country Rika is from; I'm scared, but I'd love to travel; I'd love the challenge of winning this contract in another country."

"That's the spirit. I think it will be fun, as well as good business for Powell Manufacturing. If you can do the same kind of presentation to Saab that you did for Karl Smithson at Wilco, I have a very good feeling about this." They both were silent for a moment, enjoying the prospect before them. "OK, so tomorrow I'll get on the phone with Sweden and work out a time for us to come. They're six hours ahead of us, so I'll call early in the morning. Then, assuming we can figure out some days that will work, I'll have Gladys start arranging for the plane tickets with the travel agent. Is there any time over the next two or three weeks that won't work for you?"

Ellen pulled out her little pocket calendar and scanned the coming weeks. "No, nothing that I can see. You're probably the one with the tighter schedule. How long do you plan to be gone for? I don't even know how long it takes to get to Sweden."

"I think we ought to plan on two days in Sweden. I'd like to take more time than that, but I can't really justify it. We need to meet with the Saab purchasing folks and leave a second day for any questions we might need to have time to answer, but more than that isn't necessary. It would be nice to do some sightseeing, but this is a business trip."

"I'll just enjoy being in a new country."

"To go to Sweden you pretty much have to fly all night. We'd leave in the afternoon and arrive there the next day. We'll probably be pretty jet lagged, so I'd like to plan for one day to recover. But we'll see what they say. Coming home is an all-day affair. You leave Sweden very early, and get home late in the afternoon. And, of course, you've gained six hours flying west, so it makes for a very long day. All in all I'd say we'll be gone from Kentucky for five days."

"This is all so new to me."

"Are you worried?"

"No, not exactly worried. It helps to know you'll be along. You're a seasoned traveler. I wouldn't want to do it by myself."

"And I wouldn't want you to. We'll get the details ironed out tomorrow."

The conversation lingered. There wasn't really anything to say, and yet they both found plenty to talk about. Ellen realized she should be hanging up, but she didn't really want to. "Well, I'd better get to bed. Gotta go to work tomorrow, you know."

Rob laughed. "It's that slave driver of a boss you have. Sorry 'bout that. Good night, Ellen. Thanks for the phone call. Pleasant dreams."

"Good night," she whispered, and gently placed the receiver back in its cradle.

The next morning, Rob stopped in her office. "We're all set," he said. "The folks in you-know-where are very pleased that we're coming over. I think the fact that we're on this, and making the trip quickly, impressed them. Assuming Gladys can get the tickets, let's plan on leaving Monday, June 5." Ellen got out her calendar. "That will get us there on Tuesday as our day to get our sea legs under us. Then we'll meet the purchasing people on Wednesday morning. We'll have Thursday, just in case we need it, and fly home Friday the 9th. Does that work for you?"

Ellen consulted the mostly blank pages. "Works for me. I'm writing it down."

"Good deal." He winked at her. "This'll be good," he said.

Ellen and Annie had both brought their lunch so they headed to the cafeteria. They found Rachel already eating, so they joined her. "Girls," said Annie, "I want to ask you both a question." When she saw she had their attention, she asked, "Would you both be brides-maids at my wedding?"

Both Ellen and Rachel were delighted. "I would love to," said Rachel. "It would be an honor!"

Ellen was very excited, too, excited for Annie and her big day, excited that Annie thought enough of her to want her to be an atten-dant. Then she had a horrifying thought. "What day is the wedding?"

"June 10th, at my little church in Laurel Station."

"June 10th." Ellen pulled out her calendar again. That little booklet was getting a lot of use lately. "Oh, thank goodness," she breathed.

"What?" said Annie. "Is there a problem?"

"I was afraid there might be. I have to go on this business trip, and I was afraid I wouldn't be back in time. But I will be. I would love to be a bridesmaid, Annie."

"What kind of business trip?" asked Rachel.

"Well, I can't say much about it. I have to go with Rob — Mr. Powell — to visit a potential customer in Europe."

Annie and Rachel looked at each other. "Ooooooh," they mocked. "Going to Europe with Mr. Powell!"

"It's not like that at all, girls! You know me better than that, don't you? It's strictly business."

"Mmm hmmm," said Rachel, not buying it.

"No, I believe her," said Annie. "After all, look what she didn't do with Kirby when she had the chance."

"Yeah, I know," said Rachel. "Still, though. Going to Europe with Mr. Powell. Ooooooh," she mocked again.

Ellen smacked Rachel's hand. "Quit that, Rachel! You know there's nothing funny going on."

"I know," she admitted. "But a trip to Europe." She sighed. "Must be nice. Now, let's talk about bridesmaid dresses."

As Ellen was heading back to her office after lunch Gladys stopped her. "Ellen, honey, I got those tickets Rob wanted. The dates and flights he wanted were available. The travel agent will send them over tomorrow."

"Oh, thanks, Gladys."

"Now, honey, what's this all about? I'm not sure Kirby would like you traipsing off to Sweden with Rob."

"Uh ..." Ellen was speechless. How could she tell Gladys that she had no interest in ever seeing her nephew again? "It's just business, Gladys. That's all."

"Oh? What kind of business?"

"We're going to make a proposal to a possible new customer. If we get the bid, it will be very good for Powell Manufacturing."

"I'm sure it will be, honey. Good luck on that trip, and enjoy yourself a little, too, OK? Sometimes I think you work too much."

Ellen stopped by Rob's office. "I have a million questions," she said.

"Such as?"

"Well, what to wear, do I need to get shots, what do people eat, what kind of money do they use, won't I just be in the way. Stuff like that."

"First of all, you will never be in the way. I need you to do an explanation just like you did for Wilco. Create some charts that will make an impact. I'll sell the company, but you sell our capability, OK?"

Rob did his best to reassure her about travel to Sweden. No she didn't need shots. He'd help her with the Swedish krona. The food might be different but they'd find something they like and besides, hadn't Mrs. K cooked Swedish dishes for Ellen. "Oh, yeah. I forgot about that." And the clothes she wore to work would be fine. Swedish people have their own style, but they'll understand that Americans might dress a little differently. It would all be fine.

"I know we need to keep this quiet," said Ellen. "But can I tell my sister? Can I tell the Klamecks?"

"I suppose so. But, really, I am worried that someone — Uncle Bob and International Dynamics — will try something. Or whoever our mole is will pass along our pricing and they'll underbid us at Saab by a few krona."

"I won't tell many people. But Trish deserves to know I'll be out of the country, and I'd like to get some pointers from Rika."

"Agreed," said Rob. And they left it at that.

That evening Ellen had dinner with Trish and Tommy and the kids. After dinner, as Ellen and Trish were washing dishes, Ellen told her. Trish was surprisingly cautious.

"It sounds like a great opportunity and all, El, but ..."

"But what?"

"I mean I like Mr. Powell — Rob — but it worries me a bit the two of you traveling to Sweden alone together. You don't think he has something else in mind, do you?"

"He's going to an awful lot of trouble if those are his intentions. No, I don't think so. At all. Butch and I have been working very hard on the blueprints so that we can make a good presentation to the Saab purchasing people. It feels exactly like what it is: a business trip to try to get a big customer to buy from Powell Manufacturing."

"Do you want to go?"

"Oh, yes! Ever since Rika and I became friends, I've wondered what Sweden is like. So here's my chance, and the company is paying for it."

"Aren't you worried about flying that far? What if something happens?"

"I guess you and I are different about that. Ever since Mom and Dad flew us down to Orlando, I've been excited about flying. But you didn't much care for it. Neither of us have had much opportunity to fly, but I'm looking forward to it."

Trish hugged her. "I'm happy for you, then." She stepped back, still holding Ellen's shoulders. "My little sister is growing up, jet setting off to Europe with her handsome boss. You like him, don't you?"

"Yes, I do. But I would say it is more like we're just good friends. Nothing at all has happened."

"Maybe something will on this trip. It could bring you closer together. But it could … well, you know. Sometimes being too close, like being cooped up on an airplane for hours and hours, can drive two people apart."

"I guess we'll just have to see," said Ellen. "The main point is to get the business from Saab. Oh, and maybe see a little bit of Sweden along the way."

It was too late to visit the Klamecks by the time she got home from Trish and Tommy's house. So she had the fun of anticipating telling them the next day. Almost as if on cue, Rika came up the stairs just after Ellen had gotten home from work. "Would you come over and have dinner with us?" she asked.

"I would love to, because I have some news to share with you and Jonas." The sparkle in Rika's eyes mirrored her own.

"This sounds very exciting!" said Rika. "Can you be ready in half an hour?"

"Of course, but can't I come sooner and help out. I'd enjoy it …"

"By all means, dear Ellen. Come any time." So they ended up going across the breezeway together.

"Ellen has some news," Rika announced to Jonas as she entered through the back door.

"Oh? And what news is that?"

"I think I'll save it until after the meal," Ellen said imperiously. She almost stuck her tongue out at Jonas but thought that might be going a bit too far.

"Oh, ho! Playing a little game with us, are you, my dear? Well, we'll just have to see about that!" Jonas wheeled into the kitchen behind Rika and Ellen.

All through the final meal preparations and the meal itself, Jonas peppered Ellen with questions, each one more outlandish than the last. "You've learned to do a cartwheel. You're getting a kitten. You've memorized all of Shakespeare's sonnets. You've adopted a giraffe. You've joined the foreign legion. Hollywood wants you for a major motion picture." Ellen's giggles at each suggestion only encouraged him more. "You've converted to Hinduism. You're growing a third eye in the back of your head. There are little green men from Mars living in your bedroom closet." Finally, as Rika brought in dessert, Jonas said, "Well, I give up. I can't imagine what your news might be."

"I am going to Sweden on a business trip," she announced as she poured the tea while Rika served the cake.

Both Rika and Jonas couldn't have been more pleased. When she told them the purpose of the trip, Rika said, "That means you'll be going to Trolhättan. It is a lovely town. And will you be flying in to Göteborg?" She pronounced it almost like "YEW-teh-bory."

"I honestly don't know where that is," said Ellen. "I know we're not flying in to Stockholm, but to this other city."

"That will be Göteborg, the city where I am from," said Rika. "Oh how lovely! Jonas do you have one of your maps?"

Jonas excused himself and rolled into the living room. In a few minutes he was back with a folding travel map. They spread it out on the other end of the table; it was a map of the southern half of Sweden. Jonas pointed to the city. "But it says Gothenburg," objected Ellen. "Not that other city you were saying, Rika."

"That is because this is an English map. In Sweden we say Göteborg."

The Klamecks showed her the location of Trollhättan, the town that was the headquarters for Saab. They pointed out Lake Vänern, the large lake north of Trollhättan. "Since the 1800s there has been a series of locks just below Trollhättan," said Rika. "Now very large ships can sail from the Kattegat up the Göta älv — the Göta river — into Lake Vänern. And in July, they let the water spill over the old falls. I can tell you, that is an impressive sight to see."

The more they talked, the more excited Ellen became. While she was still apprehensive of the unknowns, she very much wanted to see the land of Rika's birth and bring home a nice big contract for Powell Manufacturing.

That night, as she was drifting off to sleep, she whispered to her mother and father. "Mom, Dad, I'm going to be doing some traveling. To Sweden, no less. What do you think of that?" And she knew they would have been pleased.

Chapter 58
The girls make bridesmaid dresses.

The news that Rob and Ellen were going to Sweden to try to win a contract with Saab didn't stay a secret for long. Very soon it felt to Ellen like everyone at Powell Manufacturing knew. There were those who were titillated by the fact that the head man was taking a pretty coworker to Sweden. There were those who were excited about the prospect of getting business with Saab. And there were the nay-sayers who thought it was an expensive trip with no hope for success.

Despite all the rumors flying around, Rob, Butch and Ellen had managed — or at least they hoped they had managed — to keep the actual pricing of the Saab parts a secret. When Butch told Rob that he and Ellen had taken their work home with them, far from prying eyes, Rob thought that was a good idea and started doing the same himself. Much of the final work of developing the cost estimates was conducted via phone between Rob, Butch and Ellen after regular work hours.

In the mean time, planning for Annie and Ronnie Dale's wedding was going into high gear. Annie, Rachel and Ellen often met for lunch in the cafeteria to go over details. Sometimes they would go out to lunch so Annie could check on some decorations or select the flowers she wanted to use.

The wedding was to be held in Annie's church, Laurel Station Baptist Church, a small country chapel in the southeastern end of the county. It turned out that David Palmer was the pastor who would conduct the service. "We don't want no fancy wedding," said Annie. "We just want to get hitched right and proper-like, 'in the sight of God and this company.' Brother David says it ain't about the wedding, it's about the marriage. Ronnie Dale and me, we want to make us a good marriage, one that'll last. The wedding and the reception will just last for an hour or two. The marriage'll last for a lifetime, Lord willin'."

"Amen," Ellen heard herself say. Rachel echoed her sentiment.

Rachel pressed Annie to say what kind of bridesmaid dresses she wanted her and Ellen to wear. Annie wasn't particular. "Whatever y'all will be comfortable with," she said.

"Well, what about your colors? A least tell us what colors to be looking at."

"Blue, I reckon," said Annie. "I'll be in white, of course." Rachel and Ellen had seen Annie's dress. It was simple and tasteful. Ellen thought it was just right for Annie.

One day when they were out for lunch Rachel had an idea. "Ellen, can you sew?"

"Not really … I mean I've tried to sew a few things, but …"

"Annie, what if me and Ellen sewed our dresses? We could buy the fabric at Wildmans and sew 'em up. That way they'd match and you could approve the color."

"Why, I think that's a fine idea," said Annie.

"Wait a minute!" said Ellen. "I can't sew."

"Course you can!" said Rachel. "You just don't know it yet. Have you got a sewing machine?"

"Well, actually, yes, I do. I have my mother's Singer. But really, girls, I'm all thumbs when it comes to sewing."

Despite Ellen's serious trepidation, they went looking for fabric and found a blue muslin that all three agreed was beautiful. Then they found a pattern that everyone liked. "Just enough cleavage to be interesting, not too much to be ugly," said Annie. The pattern had an empire waist and Ellen felt like she had seen that style before. Then it hit her: these dresses looked a lot like the costumes she had seen in the PBS dramatization of Pride and Prejudice. She found herself warming to the idea of sewing her own dress. And, before she knew it, they had decided to use her apartment as dressmaking central.

That Saturday the girls convened at Ellen's apartment. Both Annie and Rachel brought their sewing machines and soon every flat surface was covered with blue muslin, the thin translucent brown paper of the patterns, and assorted scissors, pins, needles, rolls of thread, and everything else related to sewing that one could imagine. They were giggling and enjoying themselves so much that they didn't hear the knock on the door.

Rika peeked in the door. "What have we here?" she asked.

Ellen looked up from her position on the floor on her hands and knees, cutting out the bodice under Rachel's watchful eye. "Oh, Rika. This is a nice surprise! Come see what we're doing. I want you to meet two of my very good friends, Rachel Hemingway and Annie Angel. Annie is getting married in a few weeks, and Rachel and I are to be bridesmaids. We're making our bridesmaid dresses."

"But this is too wonderful!" exclaimed Rika. "I'm delighted to meet you both, Rachel and Annie." She nodded at each woman, repeating their names so as not to forget them. "And congratulations to you, Annie. He is a fortunate young man. And you are a fortunate bride to have two such good friends."

"Don't I know it, ma'am," said Annie.

"Please call me Rika." She thought for a moment. "I wonder … it looks like you are a bit crowded. Would you like to bring your fabric and sewing machines over to my house where you can spread out a bit more?"

Annie looked at the other two. "What do you think, girls? We could do with a bit more room."

"Fine by me. And, if I know Rika, she knows a lot about sewing. Maybe she can make up for some of my inadequacies."

Rachel smacked Ellen's arm. "Listen here, you old heifer. You know more than you think you do. You're doing just fine cutting out that muslin. But, ma'am, if you've got a bigger table, it sure would be right handy in a few minutes."

"Well, that's settled then. I'll go put the coffee pot on and warn Jonas that he is about to be invaded by beautiful females."

They gathered up the fabric and notions and carried the sewing machines across the breezeway to Rika's home. Soon they were hard at it again, making sure the fabric grain was aligned and trying to figure out how to do the sleeves. Jonas was his charming self, welcoming the young ladies but then making himself scarce so that they could work.

The patterns were starting to come together enough so that
Rachel and Ellen were able to drape pieces over themselves to make
sure they were going to fit well. Rika was enjoying every minute of it
and turned out to be particularly adept at sewing in zippers.

Jonas wheeled into the dining room where the fabric was draped
and folded and where three different sewing machines were in various
states of use. "You ladies look like you're being very productive," he
said. "But I fear, my dear, that a man might starve down to nothing
and blow away."

Rika consulted her watch. "Dear me, it is almost one o'clock,"
she said. "I was having so much fun I completely forgot about
lunch."

"Oh, mercy!" Annie exclaimed. "Ellen, I brought over some
sorghum 'cause I was going to teach you how to make biscuits, too."

"Sorghum molasses?" asked Jonas. "Oh, what I wouldn't give
for some sorghum on biscuits made by a sweet young bride-to-be!"

"Hush, old man!" said Rika. "You watch your manners. How
about it, Annie? Would you and Ellen like to make some biscuits and
I'll throw together some lunch? Rachel, do you think we can afford to
take a break?"

"We're farther along than I thought we'd be by now," said
Rachel. "Let's do take a break so that poor Mr. Klameck here doesn't
perish from hunger."

"That's the spirit," said Jonas, winking at her. "Rachel, how
about you and I do some tidying while the other ladies go into the
kitchen?"

There was a knock on the door. "Will you go see who that is,
Ellen?" asked Rika.

Ellen opened the door and her heart skipped a beat. "Rob Powell! What are you doing here?" Ellen caught Rachel and Annie exchanging knowing glances.

"I was invited." He shrugged and grinned that lopsided boyish
grin that Ellen was beginning to appreciate on several different levels.
"Well, hello Rachel. Hi Annie. What's going on here?"

"Ah, Robbie. I'm glad you came," said Jonas. "The ladies are sewing bridesmaid's dresses and Rika is helping. We were just about to take a break for lunch."

"Your timing is perfect, Robbie," said Rika. "I invited him before I knew we were going to be sewing today," she admitted to the three girls.

"I was hoping to get Mrs. K. to tutor me in a bit of Swedish," explained Rob.

It ended up being one of those serendipitous times that are remembered fondly years later. Annie took Ellen into the kitchen and walked her through the process of making biscuits. Ellen knew where everything was, while Annie had the knowledge and experience. "Wait a minute! Wait a minute! Let me write that down!" said Ellen.

"Oh, girl, you can't make biscuits from a written-down recipe. You gotta do it by feel. Here, stick your hand in this and get the feel of it. That's about just right."

Rika kept a close eye on them and complimented Annie both on her skill as a cook and her ability to teach. She decided they should have a simple breakfast meal of scrambled eggs and bacon. By the time the bacon was ready to turn, the smell was driving everyone mad with anticipation. Jonas and Rachel straightened and folded the fabric pieces while Rob was pressed into service to "watch the bacon and make sure it doesn't burn."

Rika suggested they eat outdoors since it was such a fine day, so Ellen and Rachel set the table on the back deck as Rob finished the bacon, Annie pulled the biscuits out of the oven, and Rika scrambled the eggs.

Eating outdoors has a way of enhancing the flavor of just about any food, particularly when you're hungry. All six of them tucked in with a will and were soon complimenting Annie on her biscuits. Annie ran out to her car and brought in a quart of sorghum which Jonas eyed with gleeful anticipation. "The sorghum is for dessert," announced Rika. "Finish off the eggs, first," she told Jonas.

"Who made the sorghum, Annie?" asked Jonas. "I assume they're homemade."

"Oh, yes, sir, they are. My feller's daddy, Elmer Tease, stirs 'em off each fall. This is just about the end of last year's crop."

"Elmer Tease. Well, well. I've met him. How wonderful to be eating his sorghum molasses." Jonas lapsed into silence as he enjoyed their astringent sweetness.

During the afternoon, the dresses really started coming together. Rob was surprisingly interested in how sewing was done and even asked to try his hand on a scrap piece of cloth.

When enough of the pieces were in place, Ellen and Rachel were banished to the spare bedroom to put on the unfinished dresses for a final fitting. They came out like they were walking the runway to whistles from Rob and huzzahs from Jonas. Annie and Rika set to work, taking a little tuck with a safety pin here and marking places that needed to be let out a bit there. "Ow!" said Rachel when Annie pricked her with a pin.

They were then sent back to the bedroom to change back out of the dresses so that they could be completed. Annie and Rachel took care of the final stitching while Rika sat Rob and Ellen down and said, "Now, we will learn some important Swedish words and phrases."

Both were interested and apt pupils. Rika taught them to say *god morgon* (good morning) and *god dag* (good day). "And this one is very important," she said. "Swedes say it all the time. Say '*tack så mycket.*' It means thank you or, literally, thanks so much." She had Rob and Ellen repeat it until she was satisfied they had just the right lilt in their voices.

She taught them about the Swedish *krona* or crown. "That is the unit of money in Sweden," she said. She got out some coins and bills to show them what the money looked like. Ellen thought the paper money especially looked odd — various pastel colors on odd-sized paper. Rika explained that the letters "kr" would be used like we use a dollar sign, and that the three letter code for the Swedish krona was SEK. "Just like we use USD or U. S. Dollars here in the States," she said. She made them practice thinking about the exchange rate. "If something cost 70 *kronor*," she asked, "How much would that be in US dollars?"

Rob was quick and said, "A little over ten dollars."

When Rob told her they would be talking to the purchasing department at Saab, she taught them the word *köp*, which was pronounced more like 'scheop.' "You will think it should be pronounced 'cop' like a policeman, but there are many words that use the *köp* root, so watch for that."

By the time Rachel and Annie had completely finished the dresses, Ellen's head was swimming from all the new Swedish words. Her tongue felt like it was doing things it had never done before. She thought that Swedish was a beautiful language with its sing-song inflection but was ready to take a break when Annie asked if she would like to do a final fitting.

At first she demurred, but the others insisted so she trooped back to the bedroom to take off her comfortable clothes and slip the dress over her head. When she had zipped it up, she looked at herself in the dresser mirror. "It actually looks good," she thought to herself.

When she came out for the viewing everyone agreed. "It fits perfectly," said Rika, checking the fit of the sleeves, the position of the neckline and the length of the hem. "You girls did an outstanding job."

Annie hugged her. "Thanks for being my bridesmaid, Ellen. You look beautiful."

"I would venture to say that all three of you will look spectacular on the big day," added Rob. "Whenever that is."

"It will be the Saturday after we've just gotten back from Sweden," said Ellen.

"I see," said Rob.

"Mr. Powell — Rob — would you like to come to my wedding? You'd be more than welcome."

"Actually I'd like that very much, Annie. It would be an honor. Thank you."

Chapter 59
Ellen and Rob travel to Göteborg.

The big day had arrived.

Ellen brought her suitcase in to work with her and parked it in the corner of her office where it stared at her ominously as she tried to work. She found her pulse quickening. Nerves, she told herself. Travel nerves. But deep in her heart she knew this was a big deal. First time to a foreign country. First time across the Atlantic Ocean. First time in a really big airplane. First time traveling for hours and hours, and overnight to boot. First time traveling with her boss, if you didn't count that little trip to Dayton. And, to top it all off, there was a lot riding on this trip, a lot riding on her shoulders. Rob had shared with her how vital it was that they win this contract with Saab, and she was under no illusions that he was counting on her to present their data effectively and compellingly.

Nothing to be nervous about at all.

Whit Collette poked his head in her office and wished her a safe trip. Annie came by and hugged her and told her to travel safe. Even Leonard and Harvey made the trip up to the front office from back in the shop to wish her well. "You give 'em what for in Sweden, Possum, you hear?" said Leonard.

"I don't know if Swedes even know what a possum is," retorted Ellen. But she was very pleased with all the goodwill she was receiving from people who had become her friends.

She went out to tell Gladys she was going to pick up the job cards for the last time before she traveled, but Gladys wasn't at her desk, so she left her a note.

At noon, Rob came by carrying his suitcase. "Ready for the big adventure?"

"As ready as I'll ever be, I guess."

"Nervous?"

"A little bit," she admitted. She took a deep breath. "I'll be OK."

"I know you will. And I'll be with you to show you the ropes."

They headed out to Rob's car. He put their luggage in the trunk and then they headed out of the parking lot. "Quit being maudlin," Ellen chided herself as she gazed forlornly at the now-familiar factory that had become like a second home to her.

They checked in at the Delta counter at the Bluegrass airport in Lexington. The desk agent checked both of their passports. Not seeing any stamps in hers, the agent said to Ellen, "First time out of the country?"

"Yes," admitted Ellen.

"Oh, you'll love it!" The desk agent was enthusiastic. "Nothing like getting to experience new cultures, new food, new languages."

Their luggage was duly tagged and checked all the way to Göteborg. Ellen watched the green flowered pattern of her suitcase cruise down the conveyor belt behind the Delta desk and disappear into a hole. "I hope I see you again on the other end," she thought, shouldering her carryon bag.

"OK," said Rob. "Next is security."

Security was relatively easy. They had to show their boarding passes and their passports to the officer, and then again at the gate. And then they settled in to wait.

The first leg of their trip was very quick. A small ComAir propeller plane took them from Lexington to Cincinnati's airport. "It is actually in Kentucky," Rob said. "A lot of people don't know that the airport code CVG actually stands for Covington, Kentucky, not Cincinnati."

A Delta bus picked them up at Terminal C and took them to Terminal B for their international flight. The plane was actually labeled as Sabena Airlines, "Sabena and Delta have a codeshare arrangement," Rob explained.

They found their gate and Rob was telling Ellen about his strategy for traveling to Europe — eat a light meal on the plane, take a couple of aspirin, and try to sleep as much as possible during the night. "I brought an extra set of ear plugs and eyeshade, in case you'd like to try them," he offered. Ellen thought that was a good idea and Rob was in the process of pulling them out of his carryon bag when an announcement came over the intercom. "Will Robert Powell please come see me at the desk." It was the gate agent in a red Delta blazer.

Rob went to see what the problem was and came back with a sheepish look on his face.

"Is there a problem?" asked Ellen, almost sure that there was.

"Not really a problem … but kind of. They've upgraded me to first class. Apparently I've traveled enough that they bumped me. Which is fine except for one major problem."

"Which is?"

"That we can't sit together. I can tell them I decline."

"Of course you won't. You enjoy that. I'll be fine."

Despite her trepidations, it did turn out to be fine. Her new seat mate was a nice lady from Cincinnati who was going to visit her son who was in the Air Force stationed in Germany. She was kind and helpful and Ellen found herself relaxing a bit.

Supper was a rather non-specific bit of chicken and some uninspired carrots with a roll and tiny slice of chocolate cake. She wondered if Rob was eating the same thing in first class. Probably not. She was just finishing up, thinking about following Rob's advice to try to get some sleep, when he came strolling down the aisle, looking for her.

"How are you doing?" he asked.

"Fine. I've made a new friend. Rob, this is Mrs. Hisle. She's on her way to visit her son in Germany."

"He's in the Air Force," said Mrs. Hisle. "Pleased to meet you."

"I brought you something," Rob said. He laid three squares of expensive looking chocolate on her tray table. He touched her on the shoulder. "I hope you can get some sleep."

"Thanks," said Ellen. "You, too."

"Was that your boyfriend?" asked Mrs. Hisle after he had gone back to the front of the plane.

Ellen laughed. "No, no. Not my boyfriend. My boss."

"I wish I had a boss that would treat me like that. Take it from someone who's seen a thing or two: he likes you. Sure he's not your boyfriend?"

"Very sure. Pretty sure."

The flight attendant came and took away their trays and Ellen got out the earplugs and eyeshade that Rob had given her. She pulled her jacket over her arms and tried to sleep.

By the time the flight attendants were passing through the aisles offering glasses of orange juice and a bagel for breakfast, Ellen realized she had slept some. But not much. The seats were very uncomfortable and didn't lie flat. You had to sleep halfway sitting up and Ellen was quite restless. But she supposed she had gotten a couple hours of sleep. Now her eyes felt gritty and her mouth tasted like metal. She offered one of the two chocolates she had saved to Mrs. Hisle, but she declined. "Oh, no, honey. He meant those for you." The chocolate helped get the taste out of her mouth.

Rob came strolling back again. "Good morning, Ellen. How'd you sleep?" he asked.

"Not very well, I'm afraid."

"Me either. Good thing we gave ourselves the rest of the day before we have to be on top of our game tomorrow." Ellen looked at her watch. It was only 2:30 AM! What were all these people doing up? "Don't forget to set your watch ahead," Rob reminded her. "It is six hours later in Europe — 8:30 in the morning."

The plane landed at the Brussels airport and Ellen realized she was in another country. It was an odd feeling. Looking out past Mrs. Hisle to the buildings and vehicles of the airport, Ellen thought how different everything seemed. The signs were in French and the police cars were tiny and oddly marked. And the sun was shining even though her body told her it was still night.

They stood in line to go through passport control. The officer looked Ellen over, looked at her photo in her passport, then stamped it decisively and handed it back to her. He never said a word.

"OK," said Rob. "That's done. Would you like a decent breakfast now?"

"I'd rather not. I'm feeling a little queasy."

"I completely understand. We haven't adjusted yet. We still feel like it is the middle of the night. How about freshening up instead?"

"Now that sounds like a good idea."

They found a toilet and Ellen did her best to scrub her face and comb her hair. She had packed her toothbrush in her carryon bag, so she brushed her teeth as well. When she had finished, she felt a lot more human.

They located their next gate for the flight to Göteborg. Soon they were being called to board.

This time Rob didn't get upgraded. On the smaller plane from Brussels to Göteborg, there really wasn't a first class. The seats were the same, but the flight attendant pulled a curtain to separate the first class section from the rest of the seats. Ellen couldn't understand what all the fuss was about. "Free liquor," said Rob. "First class gets to drink, we have to pay for it." He looked at the serious expression on her face and laughed out loud. "Nope. We're not going to be boozing it up. Ok by you?"

Her relief was palatable. "Totally fine by me." She smiled.

This flight was definitely more foreign. It was an SAS flight. The announcements were made in Swedish, then French, and finally in English. Breakfast was unusual. It included some fish, some very dark bread, some sliced ham, and other things that Ellen couldn't definitively identify. She picked at the food, but did enjoy the strawberry jam on the tiny croissant.

They were sitting on the right side of the plane, and Rob began pointing out features on the ground below. "We're over Denmark now," he said. "See the sun in the east over the island where Copenhagen is located. And closer to us is the island of Fyn. I think I can make out Odense, the large city in the center of the island." There was water everywhere and Ellen could even see what looked like tiny toy boats out on the water. "They're actually huge container ships," Rob explained. "They look small from up here but they're massive up close and in person."

Ellen snuck a glance at Rob out of the corner of her eye. He was enjoying himself and, truth be told, she was enjoying herself, too. He was a good tour guide, keeping her interested and informed while letting her gaze out the window when she wanted to. He had suggested she take the window seat so that she could see more. That was turning out to be a lot of fun, looking down and the wispy clouds and the ships on the ocean, picking out the shoreline and the roads and towns.

Soon they were completely over water again. "That means we're getting close," said Rob. "We're over the Kattegatt, the big body of water that separates Denmark and Sweden." Ellen could feel the change in the attitude of the plane as the pilots eased the craft down toward Sweden and the Göteborg airport.

On the ground they waited patiently for their luggage to appear on the baggage carousel. Ellen began to fear that hers had gotten lost, but the green flower print finally appeared and Rob lugged it off of the belt for her.

They then had to go through passport control. The Swedish officer was more chatty than the one in Brussles. "First time in Sweden?" he asked in the same sing-song cadence that she had come to love about Rika's accent.

"Yes," she said. "I'm really looking forward to being here in your country."

"*Beundransvärd*," he replied. "Have a wonderful time." He stamped her passport soundly.

"*Tack så mycket*," she said, trying out the phrase Rika had made her practice over and over.

"Oh, ho!" he said. "You speak Swedish! *Varsågod*!" He smiled broadly and motioned for Rob to step forward.

They exited through the "nothing to declare" hallway. "That other hall is for people who are bringing in booze or cash," explained Rob. And then they were truly in Sweden, walking through the airport terminal, awash in strange accents, different kinds of clothes, and signs that were completely unintelligible to Ellen. But Rob seemed to know where he was going and he soon had the keys to a rental car. They stepped out of the airport into the fresh spring air that smelled very good after the stale atmosphere of the plane.

Rob found their car. "It's a Saab!" exclaimed Ellen.

"Of course!" said Rob. "It wouldn't do to go calling on the purchasing department at Saab driving anything else, would it?"

"Makes sense," said Ellen, admiring the lines of this trim new model. "Gunilla will be so jealous."

"Gunilla?" asked Rob, pulling on his seatbelt and adjusting the mirror.

Ellen laughed. "That's what I call my Saab back home. I don't know why." She shrugged her shoulders.

"That's a great name," he said, handing Ellen a map. "It fits. Now, Ellen, you're going to be the navigator, if you don't mind. You can read a map, can't you?"

"Of course," said Ellen. "My dad loved maps, and he passed that love on to me."

Rob pointed out the Landvetter Airport Hotel. "We'll come back here and spend the night our last night in Sweden," he said. "Our flight is so early on Friday morning, it makes more sense to be here, right next to the airport so we can fly home."

"That makes sense to me."

"Now, I believe I turn left out of the airport to take us toward Göteborg, yes?"

"Yes," Ellen confirmed.

"So be watching for the road in Göteborg that will take us north toward the town of Trollhättan."

"I see it," she replied. "It is route E45. But first we have to get through Göteborg."

Together they navigated the city and soon they were cruising along the banks of a large river. Ellen spotted a sign that said Göta älv. "Oh, that's the river Rika told us about," she exclaimed. "The one with the large ocean-going ships on it."

As if on cue, they rounded a bend and there was a very large ship, the size of a big building, working its way up the river. "Wow!" said Ellen.

"I agree," said Rob. "Wow!"

"Oh, double wow," said Ellen, pointing across the river to a castle perched on top of a hill. "You don't see those in Kentucky."

"You sure don't!" Rob smiled. "Enjoying yourself? Glad you came?"

"Oh yes, for sure. Yes!"

They passed a railroad yard with train cars that looked too short. They reminded Ellen of old movies she had seen that were set in Europe. Then she laughed out loud.

"What?" asked Rob.

"I was just thinking that those train cars made me think of movies set in Europe. And then I realized: we ARE in Europe." She laughed again and Rob chuckled along with her.

They passed a large building that was clearly a factory. The words 'Hygiene Paper' were painted on the side. "I wonder what that means," mused Ellen.

"Toilet paper," Rob replied and Ellen snorted.

"You're kidding, right?"

"Nope. Kinda makes sense once you think about it." Ellen got the giggles. Rob grinned at her and was soon laughing himself.

"How are you doing, Rob? Need to stop and stretch your legs?" Ellen asked after they'd been driving for a while.

"No, I'm fine," he replied. "Do you need a break? A pit stop?"

"No, I'm just worried about you. You're driving, and you didn't get much sleep last night."

Rob reached over and patted her hand resting in her lap. "You're really sweet. I'm fine, and thanks for caring."

Before they knew it they were pulling into the outskirts of Trollhättan. "It's like another movie!" exclaimed Ellen. "These little streets and the brick buildings. I can hardly take it all in!"

They found the Swania Hotel. A big swan on the sign for the hotel suddenly made Ellen realize what 'Swania' might mean in

Swedish. Rob pulled up to the curb in front and got the luggage out of the trunk. "How about you stay here with the luggage while I go park the car. Then we'll check in together."

Ellen stood on the curb fascinated to see the traffic comprised mostly of very tiny cars and the people walking on the street. They dressed differently. She could't quite put her finger on it. Perhaps it was the tendency toward narrow rimless glasses and shirts that were more tapered. Many of the women were wearing spandex leggings that Ellen thought left too little to the imagination. She hoped that Rob was right and that she'd brought the right kind of clothes.

Rob was back in no time and they stepped into the lobby of the hotel. The furniture and the decor were … different. "It looks European in style," she said to herself, then laughed again. "That's because we are in Europe, silly!"

The ladies behind the desk were very helpful and got them checked in without any problems. Their English was excellent, and Ellen tried her '*tack så mycket*' again and was met with approval by both desk clerks.

Then they headed for the elevators. They were both on the second floor, but, Rob explained, that was what we think of as the third floor. "Europeans count the first floor as the ground floor, then the floor above that is the first floor, and the one above that is the second floor. So, we're on the second floor, but it will seem like the third floor."

Ellen's room was one way and Rob's was the other. They made sure they knew each other's room number. "How about we give ourselves an hour to unpack and freshen up, then let's meet in the lobby and we'll go out for a stroll and a bite to eat."

"Sounds really, really good," said Ellen. "And Rob? Thanks for bringing me on this trip. I'm loving the experience and I would never have had this opportunity if it hadn't been for you."

"I'm very glad, Ellen."

Ellen's room was tiny — a single twin bed with a cunning little desk. "Like my apartment back home," she thought. The bathroom was tiny and the shower even tinier. There was an interesting hose attached to the shower head. Apparently you kind of hosed yourself off. The best thing about the room was that her window looked over the river and to the hills beyond. "Maybe I'll see another boat," she thought.

She had unpacked her suitcase and hung up her clothes to let the wrinkles start falling out of them. She took off her shoes and lay on the bed when the phone rang.

"Hello?" she said, trying to clear her throat.

"Ellen?" It was Rob.

"Oh, gosh! What time is it?" She looked at her watch and gasped. "Oh, I'm so sorry, Rob. I must have fallen asleep. I'll be down in a hurry."

"Take your time, Ellen. I rather thought that's what had happened. It is no problem at all."

Ellen scurried, got her shoes back on, brushed out her hair, and fairly flew to the elevator to meet Rob.

Chapter 60
On the streets of Trollhättan.

They stepped out into the streets of Trollhättan. As had become their habit, they walked arm in arm, observing the shops, the architecture, the people, the language. Everything fascinated Ellen. Everything entranced her. Hearing the people talking as they walked by, attempting to decipher the signs in the shop windows, observing how people interacted with each other, she savored it all.

They found a walking street where cars weren't allowed. A double row of trees graced the center of the street while pedestrians and bicyclists went to and fro in pursuit of whatever business brought them out on a Swedish spring day.

Rob allowed Ellen to try to take it all in, enjoying her naive delight in what she saw and heard. "You help me see things through new eyes," he told her. "You pay attention with all of your senses."

"Smell that?" said Ellen.

Rob sniffed the air. "A bakery?"

Ellen spotted a sign that said 'bageri.' "I bet that's it." She pointed.

"Let's check it out then."

They went into the yeasty atmosphere of a true bakery, where the breads and pastries were obviously baked freshly on the premises that day. They watched as women came in and purchased fresh baked goods for their families' suppers. Then it was their turn. The lady behind the counter said, "*Kan jag hjälpa dig?*"

"Uh ..." said Rob. "English?" It was tentative, almost apologetic.

"Of course." The lady's English was heavily accented, but they could understand her.

"We've just come from America," said Rob. "What should we try?"

The lady pointed out several pastries, but kept coming back to *pepparkaka*. Ellen tried not to get the giggles again. "Sounds kind of … unsavory," she snorted.

"You like. You try," said the lady firmly.

"We definitely have to have some pepper ca-ca!" said Rob, pulling out some Swedish kronor.

They made their purchase and Rob handed Ellen some money. "Here, take a little bit just in case you see something you want. Did you want to change more dollars into kronor?"

"I'll get my own Swedish money," said Ellen. "But where do I do that?"

"The hotel will change dollars for you, or we could stop in a bank. But, please, take this change. It isn't much, but a least you'll have a little spending money in your pocket." He insisted and Ellen reluctantly put the money in her purse.

They went out into the street again, munching on their *pepparkaka*. "Mmmph," said Ellen around a soft, fragrant mouthful. "It's really good! But what does it taste like? I know that flavor, but I just can't place it."

"Gingerbread," said Rob.

"Of course!" Ellen raised her hand to the sky and said to anyone who happened to be passing by, "How wonderful!"

They passed a toy store and Ellen told Rob she'd like to come back after she'd changed her money to pick out something for Carrie. "Sure, we'll do that," said Rob.

Suddenly Ellen grabbed him by the arm and pulled him into the alcove of a shop. "Opossum," she hissed.

"What?" gasped Rob, almost losing his footing, so abrupt was Ellen's movement.

"Opossum! The code word, remember?"

"Yeah, but what gives?"

"I just saw Gladys."

"Gladys? Gladys who?"

"Gladys Napier! From the factory!"

"What?! Gladys Napier? Here? In Sweden?"

"I just saw her across the street." She peeked around the edge of the shop alcove. "There. Looking in the window of that shop over there, that dress shop."

Rob peeked around the corner, too. "Oh, Ellen. Are you sure? I don't know …"

"I'm sure!" Ellen hissed. "But if you don't believe me, let's split up. We'll be less conspicuous that way. You check her out and we'll meet back at the hotel. But be careful! We don't want her to know we're on to her."

"What, like we're tailing her?"

"Yes, exactly! It makes sense, doesn't it? Why wasn't Gladys at work yesterday?" The set of her jaw challenged him for a better explanation.

"I … Well, I'm not really sure. She just said she needed some time off."

"Uh huh. Don't you see, Rob? She's the mole! It all makes sense. She's the spy! She knows a lot about Powell's business. Kirby is her nephew. She's been passing information on to some competitor!"

The woman they were observing turned around and they both ducked back into the alcove. The woman scanned the street, then entered the dress shop.

"Why don't you buy a newspaper or something and sit on one of those park benches over there where you can observe her when she comes out. When you're satisfied it is Gladys, come back to the hotel. I'll wait for you in the lobby. But don't let her see you!"

They split up, Ellen turning away from the direction of the dress shop so that she wouldn't be observed. She saw Rob head into a book shop to buy a paper, just as she had recommended.

Ellen had a few tense moments, realizing that she was both completely on her own and that she really didn't know which way was the way to the hotel. She wandered around a bit, and spotted the river between some of the buildings. "I know the Swania is on the river," she said. "That will help narrow it down." She made a few wrong turns, but then spotted the swan logo of the hotel and breathed a sigh of relief.

She found a quiet corner of the lobby and established herself there. She was fighting drowsiness again when she spotted Gladys through the glass doors of the hotel. She scooted lower in her chair and held her hand to her face. Perhaps Gladys wouldn't see her.

Gladys entered the lobby tentatively, scanning the room before she came all the way in. Ellen kept low in her chair and tried not to look at her. Looking directly at someone always seems to draw their eye, as if they can feel they're being watched. Ellen looked out of the corner of her eye, and then saw that Gladys was meeting someone who was just coming off the elevator. Ellen couldn't see his face, but she could see Gladys'. She was beaming, clearly glad to see the tall man she was meeting. They embraced and the man kissed Gladys full on the mouth. Gladys glanced furtively around the room. And then the man turned around.

It was Bob Van Winkle.

Ellen's heart sank, then did somersaults in her chest, then nearly gave out on her. Mr. Van Winkle and Gladys got onto the elevator, their arms around each other.

Ellen leapt to her feet and watched the elevator light. It stopped on the third floor.

She stepped to the front desk. "Excuse me," she said. "I think I just saw some friends of mine from America. Do you know any Americans on the third floor? What rooms are they staying in? I'd like to call them."

The young desk clerk was easily swayed by what Ellen hoped was a natural and authoritative tone. "Assume people will help you and they usually will," her father had once told her.

"*Åh ja.* Herr Van Winkle *och hans fru*, they are in room 317. That is one of our nicest rooms," she said proudly.

"Thank you. I'll just step over here and call them in their room." She sat in a chair in the lobby next to a house phone where she could keep an eye on the elevator and the front door. She raised the hand set to her ear and pretended to be talking on the phone.

Soon, as she expected, Rob came in. Ellen hung up the phone and quickly stepped over to him. "We've got an even bigger problem," she whispered.

"Yeah, you were right. It was Gladys for sure. I followed her and ..."

"Even bigger than that. Come on. We need to get out of the lobby where we might be seen. Can we go to a coffee shop or something?"

"Sure, but ..."

She was already dragging him by the hand back out of the hotel and onto the street.

"Wow, Ellen. I like a woman who knows her own mind, but this ..."

"Come ON!" Ellen said. "This is serious!"

When they finally got settled in the back of a coffee shop, Ellen told him what she had seen. At first Rob didn't believe it. But he came around as they talked, realizing that, despite the terrible implications, it made sense.

"Your uncle is married, isn't he?"

"Yes," said Rob. His face was so forlorn, so distraught, that Ellen took his hand. "To Aunt Alyson. But he's ... well, he's had several affairs."

"I know this is really bad, Rob. Really, really bad. But I think that's what has been going on. Your uncle has been using Gladys to spy on Powell Manufacturing. She's been the leak all along, and she's been passing the information to Mr. Van Winkle, who works for International Dynamics. We've suspected all along that International Dynamics is the competitor that has been underbidding us. And from what I saw in the lobby, Mr. Van Winkle and Gladys are close. Very close. They're probably ..." She paused, hardly able to form the word. "... lovers. The desk clerk only gave me one room number, not two."

Ellen watched, suddenly aware that Rob was about to lose his temper. She couldn't blame him. This was devious, underhanded, and just wrong on so many levels. But she needed to help him and she needed to do it now.

"Rob, tell me, right now, how are you feeling?"

"I'm mad. Really mad. So mad that, if he were here right now, I'd choke him." He crushed the paper coffee cup in his hand as if to demonstrate what Rob would do. And they both knew who he meant he would do it to.

"I'll bet you are mad. I'm mad, too. But we need to think now. It won't help if you lose your temper, right? I mean, let's work together to try to figure out our next move, OK?"

Ellen watched the emotions warring inside of the man sitting across the table from her. She saw the anger rise even higher as his face turned red. She watched the desire for revenge burn in him. And then she saw sadness creep in. She saw the hurt that could only be caused by a family member. Rob's face pinched in pain as he processed what had been done to him and to his mother and to his aunt and to everyone who worked at Powell. And then the pain gave way to resignation. Rob looked up at her. "What do we need to do?" he asked. He shrugged his shoulders and laid his hands on the table, palms up. "I'm lost, Ellen. I don't know where to turn."

Ellen placed her hands in his upturned palms and he immediately grasped on to her fingers. "I'm not sure what to do, either. But I think Jonas' advice might be helpful here. Is it time to set a trap?"

"Trap?" He was still recovering, still getting his temper under control.

"Yes. You remember. Like somehow we feed Gladys some false information. I'm not sure how we do that, but we'll think of something. And, maybe, we tell the people at Saab that we're trying to catch a mole. Do you think they would understand, or would that lose us the contract?"

Rob was still holding her hands across the table. As Ellen watched him, his eyes came back into focus. He looked directly at her and saw her, saw Ellen, instead of the pain and the hurt that was somewhere over her left shoulder that he had been looking at moments ago. He squeezed her hands lightly. "I see what you're trying to do here. You're trying to talk me down from losing my temper and get me to focus on finding a solution to our problem."

"Maybe I am, maybe I'm not. Is it working?"

"Maybe," he said dryly. "So run that by me again. The trap, I mean."

"I'm not sure how it is supposed to work exactly," she admitted. "But I think the idea is to feed some information to Gladys and then, if she uses it, it proves that she has been stealing information and leaking it to the competition."

"Like we would make up a false price list and somehow give it to Gladys, and … wait, how would we do that?"

"I don't know," said Ellen. "That's where I'm stuck. Back at the plant we could just leave a price list out on your desk or my desk. I think we know now that Gladys was the one who was going through our offices after hours — or even when we were just out on the factory floor. But we can't just leave it lying around here. So I'm stumped." She looked at him, hoping he would have a brilliant idea.

"Could we slip it under their hotel room door when no one was looking?"

"That's kind of obvious, isn't it? Wouldn't Gladys — or your Uncle Bob — not be suspicious?"

"I guess so," admitted Rob. "Could we enlist the help of the front desk ladies? They seem smart and eager to help. We could explain the situation to them, without revealing too much. I'll bet they could see to it that Gladys ends up with the fake price list."

"What would we say to them?"

"We could say we need to get some information to our friends, but that it is a secret and they mustn't know where it came from. We could ask the desk clerk to give an envelope to the lady in — what room did you say they were in? 317? — when the lady in room 317 comes to pick up her key. The desk clerk can say she saw the American gentleman drop it and ask her if she will mind taking it to him. It would be like Gladys accidentally received something that wasn't supposed to be meant for her. If Gladys takes it, we've already got the first bit of proof, since it will be marked with Powell Manufacturing. She'll know it didn't come from Bob Van Winkle. If she keeps it, that already tells us something. And then if she uses it ..."

"Yes, and how will we know she uses it? We assume she will give it to Mr. Van Winkle. What will he do with it?"

"Based on what has happened before, he will underbid our prices — our fake prices — by a few percentage points. For that Pentacore part, he underbid us by just half a percent. If he's true to form, he'll do it again."

"How will we know he's done that?"

"Yeah, I see what you mean." He stopped and thought for a minute. "I assume Uncle Bob is here to bid on the same parts we're bidding on."

"Yes, I was thinking that was probably the case. Otherwise why make the big trip over here? Just to steal pricing information which they could have gotten more easily back in Kentucky? Maybe to badmouth us to the Saab purchasing people? Maybe to have a fling with Gladys? And why, for pity's sake, are they at the same hotel we're at? Gladys knows which hotel the travel agent booked for us."

"I know the answer to that. The Swania is the only hotel in Trollhättan. They didn't have a choice. You'd think they would be more careful, though."

"Gladys was really scoping out the lobby before she came in. I really had to hunker down and hope that she didn't see me."

"Let's think now. I think we can assume Uncle Bob is here to make a bid on the same parts on behalf of International Dynamics. A minute ago, weren't you saying something about telling the people at Saab?"

"Yes, but I see a problem with that. Telling them we have a mole may make us look like we can't control our own factory."

"You're right. It wouldn't be good." He thought some more. "What if we give them a copy of our fake price list? We'll point out that the prices are quite different than our actual quotes. And then we'll tell them that, if they get a quote that is very close to the fake price list, it means that there is something bad going on, but we won't say what. We'll just say that the fake price list is a litmus test — we may have to explain what a litmus test is. If another company bids based on that fake price sheet, we'd very much like to have them tell us, and we'll explain more."

"Sounds a bit tricky. But I can't think of any better ideas."

"Maybe what we should do is play it by ear. We go prepared with the fake price list and, if it seems right, if we're able to establish a good relationship with the purchasing people at Saab, we'll put our plan into action. But we can always walk away if it doesn't seem like a good idea."

"You don't mean walk away from bidding on the work. That's what we came for!"

"Of course not. I mean we could walk away from setting the final piece of the trap."

"Oh. I'm with you, now." She realized they were still holding hands. She made no move to withdraw. "So how are we going to come up with the fake pricing?"

"Good question. We have your real pricing sheet, so I think we make a hand-written duplicate and adjust the pricing on that. A hand written sheet is likely to make it look like we've been doing some last-minute calculations. Maybe we even write 'updated pricing' on the envelope. It will make it seem that much more like an accidental opportunity for Gladys."

"I like that."

"And some of the pricing will be higher than our actual bids, and some will be lower. And some will be the same. That way we can tell Saab to watch for those particular parts and, if they follow the pattern we predict, we'll be able to prove that we have a spy in our midst."

"I think we're beginning to have a plan," Ellen said. "So, let's see ... I should probably hand-write the list as if I'm giving you some updated information."

"Yes! Good!"

"Perhaps you should be the one to talk to the desk clerk."

"I can do that."

"And maybe I can wait in a corner of the lobby and hopefully observe what Gladys does with the envelope."

"You'll have to be careful."

"I know. Maybe I could get a small mirror at one of the stores here and have my back to the desk while I watch for Gladys."

"Yes, OK."

"And then we've got to get ready for a totally great presentation tomorrow to Saab. Let's not lose sight of the main goal." She squeezed his hands.

He squeezed back and finally let go. "Right. Let's keep the most important thing the most important thing."

"Do you have a copy of the price list with you?"

"No, that's back in my room at the hotel."

"Maybe you had better work up what prices you want to use and then I'll copy the list in my handwriting."

"I tell you what. Let's go back to my room and create the fake price list. Then we'll put it in an envelope and I'll take it to the front desk while you get settled in to your watching post in the lobby. Then we wait. But what about supper? Are you hungry yet?"

"Not really," she admitted. "Let's get this done first, then get something to eat."

"Right on, Possum. Ready?"

It was a little awkward to Ellen, being in Rob's room, seeing his toothbrush and shaving kit on the shelf above the sink, seeing his shirts and pants hanging in the closet. But she tried to be professional. What would her mother or Rika say about this? She focused on the task at hand.

Rob made quick work of the pricing, leaving about half of the part numbers unchanged — "To keep it realistic," he said — and then changed a quarter of them up and a quarter of them down. Ellen copied his work onto a sheet of plain paper. Then she got an envelope out of the drawer of the desk with the Swania Hotel logo on it. She wrote 'Updated Pricing' on the front and solemnly handed it to Rob.

"Here is your bait, sir."

"I want to believe that Gladys and Uncle Bob won't take it. But I think I know better," he said. "OK, time for phase two in the lobby, right?"

"Yes. And I'm thinking I should go change into something a little more ... bland. Something where I'll fade into the background."

"Good idea. It's probably a good idea if the desk clerk doesn't connect the two of us anyway, so we'll arrive separately."

"Yes, and be careful. You don't want Gladys to see you. Well, actually, it doesn't matter if she sees you, but you don't want her to see that you've seen HER. You couldn't just pretend she isn't there. I mean, we're in Sweden for Pete's sake! What would you say? 'Oh, hi, Gladys. Lovely weather we're having over here in Sweden, isn't it?' And you couldn't just ignore her."

"You're right, of course. I'll be careful."

She went to her room and changed into a black skirt, dark hose, and a dark green blouse. She combed her hair in a different way, letting a lot hang in her face. She got out her sunglasses and, on a whim, she got out the Gideon Bible from her night stand for 'something to read.'

"Oh rats," she said to herself. "I forgot to buy a mirror. Oh well, it can't be helped."

Rob was just finishing at the front desk when Ellen stepped off the elevator. Neither Gladys nor Mr. Van Winkle were anywhere in sight. Rob didn't acknowledge Ellen, nor did she acknowledge him, but he did lay his finger beside his nose and nod ever so slightly as he passed her, heading to the elevators.

Ellen settled into position in a dark corner of the lobby and prepared to wait. She got out the Bible and pretended to be reading it as she scanned the room behind her dark glasses.

She began to wish they had eaten supper. The last meal she'd had was on the flight from Brussels. They'd had pepparkaka and some coffee, but that was about it for lunch. She looked at her watch. 5:15 PM. This could take a while. She sighed and told herself to be patient. This was a stakeout like on Columbo.

She began idly flipping through the Bible, which was fortunately in both Swedish and English, side by side. Something caught her eye: The Song of Solomon. Hadn't Annie told her she ought to read that?

Between glancing at the elevator every time it chimed and watching people come in from the street, she didn't get very far. She practiced keeping her face pointed toward the book while moving only her eyes which she hoped could not be seen through the sunglasses. Her intentions were to be as unobtrusive as possible while keeping a sharp lookout.

Around 5:45 the elevator bell dinged and Gladys got off. She scanned the lobby before heading to the front desk to leave her key. Ellen saw, without hearing what was said, the front desk clerk hand Gladys the envelope. Gladys was in the process of looking inside when the elevator chimed again and Mr. Van Winkle entered the lobby.

Ellen watched as Gladys motioned Mr. Van Winkle into a corner and showed him the envelope. He pulled out Ellen's hand-written notes. They both studied the paper for some time. Then Mr. Van Winkle folded the paper up, placed it back in the envelope, and put it in the inside pocket of his sport coat. He looked at Gladys and placed a finger to his lips.

Then they walked out the front door of the hotel and onto the street. As far as Ellen could tell, they had never even looked her way.

When she was sure they were well up the street, she took the elevator to the second floor and knocked on Rob's door. "Mission accomplished," she said. He motioned her to come into the room and closed the door.

"Tell me everything," he said.

So she repeated what she had observed. When she got to the part where Mr. Van Winkle had placed the envelope in his pocket, Rob sighed. "Well, that's that, then. We know for sure that Gladys is willing to pass on information she should not have to the officer of a competitor company. When we get back from dinner, I'll make a phone call back to Kentucky and instruct Rick Baker to terminate her. That alone is a firing offense. Are you hungry?"

"Starved."

"Me too. Where shall we go?"

"I have no idea. Just somewhere where Gladys isn't."

"Right you are, then."

They headed in the opposite direction from Gladys and Mr. Van Winkle and found a little restaurant that served what Ellen would have described as 'Swedish home cooking.' The potatoes were amazing — different, somehow lighter. They had a slightly nutty flavor and a texture that wasn't mushy. They made US potatoes seem like a poor second cousin.

For dessert Rob suggested *princess tårta*, a sponge cake with layers of whipped cream and a covering of green marzipan. Ellen could see where Rika got her inspiration for what seemed to be an infinite parade of fabulous desserts.

They were careful going back to the hotel, making sure they didn't accidentally run into Gladys or Uncle Bob. When they were safely on the second floor, Rob walked Ellen to her door. "Tired?" he asked.

"Exhausted. But before I turn in I want to go over my information for Saab tomorrow. I want to keep the most important thing …

"… the most important thing," he finished. "You did fantastic work today. I thank you. Can we meet for breakfast tomorrow at 7:00 AM? Our appointment at Saab is at 9:00, so that should give us time to eat and then get over to the Saab offices."

"Sure, that sounds good."

"All right. And now I'll say goodnight. Sleep well."

"Good night." She closed the door and forced herself to focus on tomorrow's presentation.

Chapter 61
The presentation to Saab.

Ellen thought she would have no trouble falling asleep. After all, she'd had very little sleep on the plane the night before and she was very tired. She'd scheduled a wake up call at 6:00 AM, but she had set her mother's travel alarm, too, just so there would be a backup. But when it came down to it, she just couldn't fall asleep.

She reviewed her presentation again. She tried reading. But she still tossed and turned. At 10:30 PM, she got up and looked out the window. It was still daylight. She remembered something from her physics class in high school that the days were very long in the summer the farther north you went.

She must have dozed because her wake up call from the front desk did wake her. She showered and dressed in the outfit she had selected for the big day. Then she headed downstairs. At first she was wary of bumping into Gladys, but then she realized that Gladys was probably being careful not to be seen. If she had no legitimate purpose for being in Trollhättan, then she would be the one wanting to keep out of sight.

She found the breakfast area for the hotel and was amazed at the variety of foods that were laid out. In the States it probably would have been cold cereal and, if one was lucky, some scrambled eggs made from powdered eggs, sausage, uninspired biscuits and pale gravy. The Swania had many types of cold cuts, a wide variety of fresh fruit, sliced vegetables, an incredible variety of cheeses, different kinds of breads and pastries, yoghurt, and plenty of things she couldn't even identify. People were helping themselves in a hushed, quiet morning sort of way. There was some light opera playing quietly over the loudspeakers.

She spotted Rob already sitting at a table.

"Good morning," he said, getting to hold the chair for her. "You look lovely. Did you sleep well?"

"Thank you, but I don't feel particularly lovely," she said. "It was hard to sleep with it being so light outside. I had the curtains closed, but it seemed like it was day all night long. Does it ever get dark here?"

"Yes, from about midnight to 3:00 AM — but even then it doesn't get very dark. We're up close to the arctic circle here. I'm sorry you didn't sleep well. Are you going to be OK for the presentation today?"

"Oh yes, I think so. I've shaken it off. I'm excited about what we might be able to accomplish today."

"I am too!" There was real enthusiasm in his voice. "How about some breakfast?"

"It looks very … interesting. And a little intimidating."

Rob laughed. "They put on a spread here, don't they? Let's go see what we can find."

As Ellen turned toward the buffet tables, she caught a glimpse of Gladys turning away from the door. Mr. Van Winkle was right behind her. She didn't think Gladys had seen Ellen spotting her, but she felt quite certain that Gladys had come to the door, seen Rob, and had quickly left. That made sense; it confirmed what she surmised Gladys would be thinking. She didn't tell Rob what she had seen until they were safely back at their table.

They both had coffee which was quite strong and rich. "Good Swedish coffee" as Rob described it. He showed Ellen how Scandinavians like to put slices of cheese, perhaps some cold ham or turkey, and perhaps some sliced peppers on a slab of dark bread. Ellen tried it and found it good. But she also got some strawberries and some cereal.

She told Rob about seeing Gladys. "I guess we would expect her — both of them — to avoid us," was all that he would say about it. He moved on to lighter, more positive topics.

She found herself enjoying breakfast, lingering over her coffee as Rob entertained her with stories about the baby goats and Henry and his grandmother. "I could get used to this," she sighed, and realized she'd said that out loud. She hadn't meant to.

"I could too." Rob smiled. "But I think it is time we go see if we can't win a contract."

They agreed to go up to their rooms for just five minutes to brush their teeth, and, whoever was ready first, was to come knock on the other's door.

In the car, Ellen was again the navigator while Rob negotiated bricked streets and roundabouts. Soon they were in a more industrial area and, even though the signs were in Swedish, it was easy to find the way to the Saab. Then Ellen spotted a sign that said inköpsavdelning. "It has that word Rika taught us, cop, in it. That's probably purchasing, don't you think?"

Rob pulled into a parking place and they got out of the car. Both of them took a deep breath, looked at each other and laughed. "Do I look as nervous as you do?" Rob asked.

"Even more so. You'll do great, Rob."

"And you'll do greater."

They entered the building and found a receptionist who was completely at ease with English speakers. "Yes, Herr Nilsson is expecting you. I will tell him you have arrived. Please have a seat."

They sat and Ellen watched the comings and going of people arriving at work, greeting each other in Swedish, going about their lives. It all looked so normal, yet so much was riding on this day, on what happened over the next hour. She couldn't help but be tense inside.

A man in a sport coat with tiny wire rimmed glasses approached them. "Are these the Americans from Powell Manufacturing?"

Rob jumped up. "Herr Nilsson, I'm Rob Powell. And this ..." Ellen held out her hand. "... this is Ellen Murphy, our Director of Information Technology."

"Please, call me Per," he said. "I am very glad to have met you. And thank you for making the long voyage here to Sweden."

"It is our pleasure," said Rob, shaking Per's hand.

"Please, come with me," said Per, punching in a code on the door lock to allow them into the inner office. They followed him down a corridor with offices on either side. It was clearly an office building, but it was not an American one. The furniture was more modern looking, the colors restful tones of blues and greens, the phones sleeker. The doors were a very light wood with different dimensions than an American door. The windows looked different. Even the paper on people's desks looked taller, narrower, and more streamlined.

Per waved them into chairs in his office around a round table. "I was just about to get a coffee," he said. "May I get you one as well?"

"That would be very kind," said Rob. Ellen didn't really want a coffee — she'd just had three cups over breakfast — but thought it might be polite to accept.

The little porcelain cups had the Saab logo on the side and each one came with a little saucer and a dainty stainless steel spoon. Everything, even the coffee cups, seemed just right, exactly designed for their specific purpose. Ellen realized she was sensing a culture of design that must infuse a company as well known for its innovative automobile engineering as Saab. *Tack så mycket,*" she said, which earned an appreciative smile from Per.

"Now," said Per, "Let me thank you again for coming all the way to Trollhättan. You have come about the parts we are putting out for bid, yes?"

"Yes," said Rob. "We understand that Saab is looking to source more parts in the United States to satisfy some of its dealerships and customers in America. We want you to know that, while Powell Manufacturing appreciates the opportunity, we intend to show you that Powell Manufacturing can produce these parts for you at a cost and with the quality you would expect from a Saab supplier, regardless of where it is located."

"That is all correct," said Per.

Rob launched into his story about Powell Manufacturing's history. Ellen watched as he wove a masterful story about his father starting the company, about the capabilities the company had, and about the sense of community among the workers. That last particularly seemed to resonate with Per. Then it was Ellen's turn.

She explained how the company had placed bar code readers virtually everywhere throughout the factory. Through those, she explained, she was able to monitor very closely the actual production times for every work center. "Our engineering department has reviewed the blueprints we have from Saab very carefully. We have analyzed each part for the machining, welding and assembly that would be needed for each one. And because we have very detailed information about the amount of time each operation will take, we can say with great assurance how long it will take to manufacture each of your parts. And so, when Mr. Powell shows you the cost for each part, you can be sure that those costs have been established based on real data, not on theoretical values."

"That's right, Ellen," Rob said, taking up the conversation. "Because we have so much real data about productivity and the manufacturing time for each work center, our confidence in these prices is very strong. Each one has a fair profit margin built into it, but there is no price gouging here. We believe that Saab deserves a fair price, and that Powell deserves to make a fair profit. Do you agree, Herr Nilsson?"

He smiled. "I'm Per. How do you Americans say it? Herr Nilsson was my father. And, yes, I agree, Rob. While I want the lowest price possible, I am also interested in quality and delivery to schedule. That means, as you say, a fair price, not necessarily the least expensive one."

"That's good. So let me show you the parts and the pricing." Rob retrieved a sheet of paper from his briefcase. "These are the prices in US Dollars for each part. Using yesterday's exchange rate, I've calculated the price in Swedish kronor."

It was Per's turn to pull out some sheets of paper. He was silent for several minutes while he compared the price on Rob's sheet with his own data. Occasionally he would say "mmm" or "ja." He made lots of marks on his sheet of paper.

He looked up. "These are good prices. Not so low that I do not believe them. And not too high. How is it your Goldilocks says? They are 'just right.' And I very much like your approach. What you are describing with the bar code is very interesting. We here at Saab are just beginning to explore adding bar code readers in our factories."

It seemed right for Ellen to add. "We are, perhaps, a bit like Pippi Longstocking. We don't live by anyone's rules but our own. We are perfectly fine being a little different."

Rob looked confused and Per burst out laughing. "I do not believe Herr Rob knows about our Pippi Långstrump, does he?"

"Perhaps not," said Ellen. "It is a children's book I read as a girl. Pippi Longstocking is a Swedish girl with red hair. She is very strong and — what would you say, Per? — a bit different. I'll lend you my copy sometime, Rob."

Per laughed again. "We like doing business with companies that are like Pippi Långstrump. Companies that keep their own rules. What are some of Powell Manufacturing's rules, Rob?"

Rob was quick on his feet. "One of our rules is that the customer is always right. Even if the customer is wrong, he is right." He smiled at Per and Per smiled back. "Another rule is that we don't take work we can't do well. Ellen can tell you of another customer we have who wanted us to take on some key parts for them. Before we said yes, we made sure we could manufacture the parts correctly and on time."

"That is very good," said Per. "Now, let us talk about quality. You'll notice that three of these parts ..." he checked them off with his mechanical pencil, " ... have very close tolerances. Tell me about your rules for quality."

"Every part that comes off of our Assembly line is checked by our quality assurance manager," said Rob. "We also check parts coming out of our welding department and especially out of our fabrication department." He turned to the pages for the three parts Per had indicated. "All three of these with the close machining tolerances would be checked in our fabrication department."

"I see," said Per. Immediately Ellen knew he was disappointed. It wasn't good enough. Rob must have seen it, too.

"These parts for Saab are very important to us, Per. We want to do the absolute best job we can for you. We've been studying statistical process control and getting ready to implement it. Would it help if the first parts we put under statistical process control were these parts for Saab?"

That's good, thought Ellen, but I don't know what statistical process control is. And I don't want Per to think we don't have our act together.

"By statistical process control, I mean that the machine operator himself would take these measurements for every part that was produced. We would create a chart showing the dimensions over time. Our understanding is that, statistically, we can predict if the tooling is going to produce a part that is out of tolerance in the future, even though it is still producing parts in tolerance today."

"That is much better," said Per. "We need some kinds of quality assurances like that. And you could send me those charts periodically, yes? Say, once each week?"

"Yes, absolutely," said Rob.

Suddenly Ellen had an idea. "Excuse me, Per, but may I ask Rob something?"

"Of course. Do you need me to leave the room?"

"No, no. Nothing like that. I've just had an idea and I want to see what Rob thinks of it."

"What is it, Ellen?" asked Rob.

"You know how the machine operators, Herb and Joe Bob and the rest, all use the bar code readers to record their production times. I think I have seen a machine gauge that works in a similar fashion. What I'm trying to say is that we could attach a gauge to each computer in the fabrication area and train the men to take measurements directly into the computer as they produce each part. The computer could create the charts off of real-time data that the men are collecting and even send those off to Per automatically."

"You could do that?" asked Rob.

"I think so. It hasn't been tried yet, but, yes, I think we would do it."

Rob looked at Per. "When she says she thinks she can do something, that means yes. She's just being cautious. I have yet to see anything Ellen couldn't do when she puts her mind to it."

"That would be very impressive," said Per.

"It just follows the third principle of Business Information Technology Systems." Per wanted to know more about that, so Ellen explained about her quest to find all five and that the third principle was that you should build data collection into processes that already exist. "Collecting quality dimension data as the parts are coming off of each work center would be a good example of the third principle in action."

"You will let me know when you find the fifth principle, yes?" said Per.

"I hope I'm letting you know sooner rather than later," said Ellen. "I too am eager to find that fifth and final principle."

"This is great, Per. It sounds like we are all on the same page," said Rob. "We'll start implementing the automated statistical process controls as soon as we get back to the States. Now before I ask you my big question, what other questions do you have for us?"

Per thought a moment. "I think you have answered everything I wished to know. So what is your big question?"

"What do we need to do to earn your business?"

Per smiled. "It is a fair question. You have done everything you need to do. I am very impressed with your approach and with your capabilities, especially as Ellen has described them. We at Saab must, however, talk to several other vendors and get their pricing before making a final decision. You understand. It is just business."

"Yes, I completely understand," said Rob. "May I then ask one other favor?"

"Of course."

"I am going to be very honest with you, Per. That is another one of our rules, by the way. No secrets. Everything should be done in the open. So I'm being open with you, Per." He stopped and Ellen felt herself projecting her strength to him again for what she knew was coming.

"We have recently discovered that we have a mole in our company. Do you know what I mean by a mole? A spy?"

"Yes, of course. Your President Reagan may be pursuing détente with Comrade Gorbechev, but we know about moles and the KGB."

"I'm glad you understand. This person has been giving information about Powell Manufacturing pricing to one of our competitors. In fact, we have lost business because our competitor simply underbids us without doing any of the careful analysis Ellen has shown you we do for each new part we take on. Most recently our competitor underbid us by one half of one percent. But that difference was enough for one of our customers to switch to a competitor."

"I do understand," said Per. "We had a case — I will not name any names — some years ago in which new Saab engineering designs were being leaked to our competitor, Volvo. It was a very bad situation."

"That is a very bad situation. Not unlike what we are dealing with, although on a smaller scale." He paused to make sure Per's body language supported his apparent understanding of Powell Manufacturing's situation. Per's face was engaged; his eyes were fully on Rob as he unfolded the situation. "I would like to ask you two things, Per," said Rob. "First, make sure that every supplier you talk to can demonstrate to you the kind of careful analysis we have shown you, an analysis that proves we have come by our pricing thoughtfully and with careful analysis. Second, I would like to give you a second price list." He pulled the fake price list out of his briefcase and wrote 'FALSE PRICING' across the top. "Per, this is not, and I emphasize not, our pricing. That information is on the sheet I have already given you. This false pricing is our attempt to catch our mole in action. You see, we have made sure that the person we suspect of being the spy has received a copy of this false pricing. I am asking you to consider letting me know if you receive a bid based on this false pricing schedule." Rob pointed out where the prices had been marked up and where they had been marked down. "If you get a bid that is just a small amount less than each of these false prices, you will know it came through a mole who has been sharing our trade secrets with our competitors." Per looked at him, anticipating the question. "Will you call me at the Swania Hotel here in Trollhättan if you receive a bid that appears to be based on our false pricing?"

Per looked at the fake price list for some time, tracing each price. He took so long that Ellen began to fear that he was either not understanding or that he was going to tell them to get out of his office. But when he looked up, he asked Rob, "You have artificially inflated this price, and this one, and these three here?"

"Yes."

"But that is not the actual bid."

"Correct," said Rob. "The bid we are presenting Saab with today is on this sheet." He pulled the actual pricing sheet from under the other papers.

"And these prices are artificially lowered?" He pointed to the others on the fake price list that had been decreased.

"Exactly. Again, those are not our prices. The real prices are on this sheet. These false prices are the bait in a trap we hope to use to catch our mole."

"Yes, I see." Per was silent again. Finally he said, "This is very serious, yes?"

"Very serious." Rob nodded.

Ellen could feel the tension in the room building. Would Per be willing to help them? Or had they gambled that he would, and lost? And, in doing so, had they lost the opportunity to win the bid for Powell Manufacturing?

"What is your room number at the Swania?" asked Per.

"Room 207. Ellen is in room 213. We will leave and go to Ladvetter on Thursday." Per wrote those numbers on the fake price list.

"To which of your competitors is the pricing being leaked?"

"I would rather not say," said Rob. "I am asking you to let me know if you receive a bid that seems to be based on these false prices I've given you. You don't need to tell me which competitor made the bid. But if I tell you which competitor we suspect, it may prejudice the results. I am not trying to prevent any of our competitors from making a bid to Saab or even winning the bid if their proposal is superior. I am only trying to prevent insider knowledge from unfairly changing the outcome."

Per looked from one to the other. Then he nodded. "Your integrity is admirable. I will do this." Per folded the fake price list and then folded it again. He tucked it in a drawer in his desk. "This is an unusual request," he said. "But I understand your concern. I am agreeing to the following: if I receive a bid that appears to closely resemble Powell Manufacturing's false bid, I will call your room at the Swania before Thursday. If the bid is received on Thursday or after, I will call you at your office in the US. I will simply tell you that Saab have received such a bid. I will not tell you from whom it has come. That small affirmation will allow you to know that the false pricing you gave to your suspected spy has been received by Saab through a competitor. What you do with that information is up to you. Is that acceptable?"

"Very acceptable." Rob stood up and Ellen followed suit. Rob stuck out his hand and shook Per's. "Thank you for understanding our situation. And thank you for being willing to help us out. I'm very grateful."

"I do not like rats, Herr Powell. If there is a rat, I hope that you will smoke him out."

"Thank you. And may I say that the main purpose of our visit is to earn your business. Ellen has explained to you in great detail why we are confident in our pricing. We would very much like to do business with Saab."

"Perhaps we can," said Per, ushering them out of his office. "*God dag*."

"*Tack så mycket*," said Ellen.

They drove back towards town in silence, each mulling over the meeting with Per in their own minds. Finally Rob said, "Well, Ellen. What do you think?"

"I think … well, I think that went quite well. We got our points across, I think he listened, and he was agreeable to help us smoke

Gladys out. It doesn't mean we'll get the business, but I think we did as well as we could have. What did you think?"

"I agree. I've been reviewing what we said, what we did. I don't know that I would have changed anything. I don't have an incredibly optimistic feeling about our chances of winning the bid. I'd give us a fifty-fifty chance right now. But at least, if we lose the business, it won't be because we didn't do the best we could." He reached across the gear shift and squeezed her hand. "You did really well, Ellen. Thank you. That reference to Pippi Whatshername was a good move."

"Longstocking. Pippi Longstocking. You're not so bad yourself. You answered him without hesitating when he asked you what the rules are at Powell Manufacturing."

"That was easy. I believe in those things. I guess I'd never had to say them out loud to a potential customer before, though." He laughed. "How about we go for a walk? All that being on our toes has made me feel like I need to blow off some steam. We could go for a nice walk, and then find a place for lunch. How does that sound?"

"Sounds good," said Ellen.

They parked the car in the garage and walked across the street toward the hotel. But Rob kept going down the sidewalk. "I talked to the concierge this morning," he said. "Apparently there are some nice walking trails along the canals. Would that be OK? Then we'll get a bite to eat."

"Would you mind if I changed shoes first?" asked Ellen.

"How thoughtless of me!" he replied, looking at her heels. "Let's both change into more casual clothes. That would be better, wouldn't it?"

Ellen just smiled. After she had changed into jeans and a simple sleeveless light blue blouse, she knocked on Rob's door. He had changed into jeans, too, with a crisp short sleeve button-up. "Much better," he said, and they headed out.

They rounded the corner of the hotel, heading towards the canal. A bell started ringing frantically and they watched as the drawbridge began to rise. "Oh, look!" exclaimed Ellen. What looked like a huge building was coming toward them. It was a ship so big that Ellen could scarce take in its size. It chugged through the drawbridge with barely enough room on either side to squeeze through. But somehow it did. Ellen looked up — it seemed to be many stories high, as high as the hotel or even higher. It took a surprisingly short time to pass through, and then the drawbridge began to lower again. When the traffic light turned green and the alarm bell had stopped ringing, traffic again began crossing the bridge, and Rob and Ellen crossed over on the pedestrian walkway. They stopped in the middle to watch the stern of the departing ship churning north toward Lake Vänern.

"That was something!" said Ellen. "I've never seen anything like that!" Rob took her hand and guided her toward the walking path that headed south along the canal bank.

It was a beautifully sunny day. The temperature wasn't overly warm nor was it particularly humid, quite a contrast to what weather in Kentucky could be like in the summer. They walked along, hand in hand over the graveled walk, simply enjoying the birch trees, the little yellow flowers, and the waterway to their left.

Another ship came by, smaller than the one they had seen.

The more wooded area gave way to commercial buildings. They were still on the banks of the canal when Rob exclaimed, "Look down there! I think that is a lock."

As they got closer, another ship began rising up before them, coming upstream through the lock. By the time they had gotten close enough, the upper gates of the lock were opening and another ship — this one looking more like a pleasure craft belonging to a rich tycoon — came sailing through. The gates closed and Rob said, "It looks like they're draining the water from the lock so they can bring in another ship from downstream."

That's exactly what was happening. In fact there were three ships waiting their turn to go through the lock. They leaned against the railing, watching the process. The water would lower in the lock, then the lower gates would open and the ship would enter. Then the water would rise until it was level with the upper side. Only then did the upper gates open and the ship move on upstream. And then the process would begin again.

When they'd seen two more ships go through, Rob asked, "Are you getting hungry?"

"Starved!" said Ellen. "All this fresh air is making me hungry."

"Great. I see a little restaurant over there."

They sat at a table in the open air, ordered sandwiches and orange Squash, and thoroughly enjoyed the boat traffic, the way the trees shivered in the breeze, and each other's company. Ellen sighed.

"What is it?" asked Rob.

"What is what?"

"You just sighed." He mimicked her, breathing out as she had done.

"Just that … well, just that could this day be any more perfect? I want to pinch myself. Here I am in the Swedish sunshine, watching boats go through locks in a canal, drinking orange Squash." She wanted to say 'with you.' But she didn't.

"Not worried about what Saab may say?"

A brief cloud flickered across her face, then vanished as if it had been hurried away by the Swedish breeze. "Not today. Not now, at least. Not here." Then she whispered, "Not with you," hoping he didn't hear.

He did, but he didn't immediately say anything. He just smiled his half smile, leaned back in his chair, and closed his eyes. "I agree," he said. He looked utterly relaxed.

Ellen was delighted by the simple way they could sit at a table in a little cafe without saying a word, and yet feel more connected than she had ever felt connected to anyone, with the exception of her parents.

"I don't want to, but I suppose we should be heading back," said Rob. "We need to see if Per has called." He stood up and offered Ellen his hand. She took it and he pulled her up. He didn't let go as they began walking back along the canal towards the hotel.

They took a different route back that ended up at a dam and what appeared to be a hydroelectric generating station. There was a rocky gorge with just a trickle of water running through it. They gazed at it from high above on the bridge over the chasm.

"I know what this is!" exclaimed Rob. "I saw a picture in one of the tourist brochures in my room. This is the original way that water flowed out of the lake. It must have been an impressive sight."

"Oh, yes. Rika told me that, in July, they have a big festival. They let water flow down through the gorge so people can get a sense of what is was like back in the old days."

It was late afternoon by the time they crossed back over the drawbridge and walked into the lobby of the Swania, tired and contented. "Any messages for Powell, room 207?" he asked.

"Yes, Herr Powell. There is a message." The clerk pulled a small envelope from the cubby hole above 207. Rob opened it. "It's from Per," he said. "He wants me to call him."

They went to Rob's room to make the call. "Too public in the lobby," he said.

Ellen sat on the edge of the bed while Rob sat in the chair by the desk and dialed.

"Hello, Per? Yes, this is Rob Powell of Powell Manufacturing. I had a message ... yes. Yes. Oh, I see. Thank you, Per. Not what I wanted to hear, but not surprising, either, I fear. ... Yes. ... OK. And what is that? ... Really? I am delighted. ... Yes, I will look forward to that. ... Yes, of course. Eleven o'clock? Yes, that would be fine. Thank you. Good bye."

He placed the receiver in the cradle and turned to Ellen. His eyes were bright. "Come here, Possum." He stood up. Ellen stood up and found herself in a bear hug. "We did it," Rob whispered. "We did it! We've got the bid. Per wants me to come by tomorrow and pick up the purchase order and sign the paperwork." He squeezed her. "We did it!"

The breath that Ellen thought she must have been holding for weeks, for months even, suddenly escaped from her lungs. The relief was physical, like the water pounding out of the locks as they lowered the water level. "Oh Rob. That's so, so good. Thank God."

"Yes, thank God," said Rob.

"And what about the bait?"

Suddenly Rob's elation was replaced by real pain. "Gladys took it, hook line and sinker. Per says a bid came in this afternoon that was almost exactly what we predicted it would be. It matched our false price list closely. He said it was blazingly obvious it had come through our mole."

"Oh dear." She laid her head on his chest. She knew what that meant. It meant he had to fire another long-time employee. It meant Rob's uncle was using devious tactics against his own nephew. It probably meant his mother's brother was cheating on his wife. It meant Rob had been betrayed. It meant all kinds of bad things. She wrapped her arms around him tighter, wishing she would take some of the pain away. "Oh dear," she said again.

They stood like that, breathing, regaining composure, gaining strength. Finally Rob said, "I need to make some phone calls." His voice was hoarse. "Would you mind?"

"Of course not. I'll go down to my room and put my feet up. We walked quite a bit today. When you're ready to talk some more, just knock on my door."

She let herself out quietly and tried to still her hammering heart by kicking off her shoes and lying on her bed with her eyes closed.

They ate dinner in the hotel's restaurant. The conversation was sparse, both keeping their own counsel and mulling things over in their minds. Occasionally one would say something and the other would respond. But there were long gaps where neither said anything. And Ellen was OK with that.

"We'll need to pack tomorrow morning," said Rob. "We'll relocate to Göteborg for the flight out Friday morning."

"Did you call back to Kentucky?" asked Ellen. "Am I right that you talked to Rick Baker?"

"Yes," replied Rob. "I talked to Rick. Gladys is no longer an employee of Powell Manufacturing. According to the schedule, she's supposed to be back at work on Friday. Rick will collect her keys and take care of the official termination when she shows up."

Later, Rob suggested, "Let's have a leisurely breakfast here at the hotel in the morning. Then we'll check out before we go to see Per."

The waiter encouraged them to have dessert, but they both declined.

"If Gladys is going to try to be back at work on Friday, she must be flying out tomorrow. Which may mean she's already left the hotel. I'm glad." She looked at him and the intensity of her gaze stopped him. "Do you know why?"

"Why?"

"Because I know you, and it would be easy for you to lose your temper right now. I can't say I'd blame you. But if you ran into Gladys or your Uncle Bob here in Sweden, well …" She let the thought hang there between them. They both knew what Rob was capable of.

Rob clenched his fist where it lay on the white tablecloth. And then Ellen watched as slowly, deliberately each finger relaxed until the fist was just Rob's hand, lying on the table.

"You're so good for me," he said. "I know I have a temper. But I'm learning to control it, thanks in no small measure to you. Yes, I might want to deck Uncle Bob. But I won't. It will be hard enough having that conversation with him back home. Let's just enjoy the time we have left in Sweden." He raised his drink glass. "To us. To a winning team. To getting the contract from Saab. To many more successful adventures." Ellen raised her glass and touched his gently. She wanted to echo 'to us' but she simply smiled.

As they were riding up the elevator, Rob said, "You asked if I had called back to Kentucky. I did. I made several phone calls — four to be exact. Everything is falling into place." He smiled enigmatically as he saw her to the door of her hotel room and said good night.

Chapter 62
Back to Göteborg.

Ellen slept well, waking up to the realization that her jet lag was over. "Just in time to repeat it going home," she said as she applied her makeup.

They enjoyed breakfast even more than they had the day before, now that they knew the ropes and weren't in a rush. By 9:00 AM they were heading back to their rooms to brush their teeth and finish the last of their packing. By 9:30 they had checked out of the Swania. "We hope you will return soon," said the front desk clerk, to which Rob replied, "We certainly hope to." They put their bags in the trunk of the car and Rob pointed out that they were very early for their meeting with Per at 11:00. He suggested Ellen might want to do her shopping.

She was delighted. Once again, they headed for the walking street, arm in arm, and found the toy store Ellen had spotted earlier. She ended up buying a doll in traditional Swedish clothes for Carrie and a board game called Bondespelet for Nathan. "It looks like it is some kind of farming game," said Ellen. "I'll let him stew a bit before he has to go to Rika for help with translating the rules." Rob thought that was just the thing. They moved on to a gift shop, where Ellen bought three tea cups and saucers. "One for Trish, and one for your mother and grandmother," she said. Rob suggested a traditional Dalarna red wooden horse for Tommy, and Ellen agreed. "He likes woodworking, and these little red horses are everywhere. I think he'd like that."

Their shopping done, they headed to the Saab plant and again, Per ushered them into his office and offered coffee.

Little was said about the spy other than for Rob to thank Per for his information and to note that "the matter has been dealt with back in the States."

They then moved on to more pleasant topics. Per gave Rob the purchase order which he signed in their presence, and he then reviewed Saab's standard Terms and Conditions with Rob.

"We had discussed statistical process control yesterday when you were here, yes?" said Per. "We are requiring that," he said, indicating the section in the Terms and Conditions.

"I understand," said Rob, looking at the wording on the page.

When he was done, they moved on to other topics. But Ellen said, "May I see that?"

Per handed her the document and Ellen read and re-read the paragraph. The wheels were beginning to turn in her head.

When they were finished, all three stood up and shook hands. "Per, it has been a real pleasure," said Rob. "I expect we will be talking frequently in the months and years ahead, and I look forward to it."

"As do I," said Per.

Now the mission was accomplished; they headed to the car and the road for Göteborg.

Ellen leaned against the glass as Rob drove, staring out the window. They had only been on the road once before, but it seemed familiar, friendly. Ellen found that a tear was threatening to spill out of her right eye. And then it did, coursing down her cheek and landing on the arm rest. "Is it possible to fall in love in three days?"

"What?" Rob wasn't sure he had heard her. And then he realized that he had heard her. "Yes," he said. "Yes, it is possible to fall in love in three days. Or even less."

"I love this country. I've only been here three days, and already I love it."

"Oh. Yes. It is a great place. Perhaps we can come back again. Would you like that?"

"Oh, yes. Oh, very much." They were down on the flat valley now, driving along the Göta älv. Ellen did a double take. Was that another ship? Yes! It looked like a building in the middle of the valley, but it was sailing up the river. "Oh look, Rob! Another ship!"

"I believe you've become quite taken with ships, haven't you?"

"I don't know a thing about them except that they are beautiful and majestic."

"You really are an amazing woman," said Rob. "Everything delights you. When I am with you, I see the world through fresh new eyes. You make it possible to bear all things, believe all things, hope all things, endure all things."

Ellen turned from where she had been gazing out the window, trying to commit every sight, every nuance to memory lest she should never get to come back again to this enchanted land. She looked at the man in the seat next to her. There was something about him, too. He may not have been enchanted, but then again, perhaps he was. She knew that he made her a better person. Made her try harder. Made her think deeper. Made her care more. "That's beautiful, Rob."

"Don't give me credit. It's in the Bible. But you do have that effect on me, Ellen."

Then, as if by mutual accord to deflect the direction the conversation may have gone, they began reviewing their meeting with Per.

"Are you satisfied with the order?" asked Ellen.

"More than satisfied. We got a really significant order. It all looks to be doable. And I don't mind telling you — this is the turning point for Powell."

"I'm very glad."

"I didn't see anything in the Terms and Conditions to be concerned about. It all looked quite reasonable and standard."

"About that," said Ellen, "I've been thinking."

"I always love it when you think."

"Hush, you!" She playfully swatted his arm. "I mean about those — what did you call them? — statistical charts."

"Statistical Process Control. It is a way of tracking the output of a process, usually a dimension, over time so that you can predict if a process is getting out of control and then won't deliver the quality and consistency you need."

"I kind of thought it was along those lines. I'll have to read up on that."

"I've got some books we can look at. Basically you make a chart with a high value, a mean, and a low value. The high and low limits are based on standard deviations around the mean." He looked at her.

"Yes, I know what a standard deviation is."

"So you make this chart. As long as the measurement is within the limits, the process is in control. But the minute it strays outside of the limits, you've got a control problem and a quality problem."

"I'd like to see some examples, but I think I understand. This idea of having a gauge to measure the dimensions, hooked to the computer much like the bar code readers — that could really help, couldn't it?"

"If I'm understanding you, it certainly could. What do you have in mind, Possum?"

"Well, I've been thinking about those gauges. What if we write a computer program to capture that data? Do you suppose people like Herb and David and Joe Bob would be able to take the measurements Per needs? If we did it right, the data would be captured right at the source, just like the Third Principle of BITS says it should be. And then, based on the fourth principle, we could extract that data and produce a chart like Per wants."

"Per would be ecstatic. Heck, I would be ecstatic. But do you think you could do it?"

"I'd need some help from Whit, but, yes, I think it is doable. We'll have to get to work on that right away when we get back."

"We'll have lots to do. But it will be good work, right? Solid work. Worthwhile work."

"That's important to you, isn't it? To have good work to do."

He looked at her again and held her gaze before he returned his eyes to the road ahead. "Very important. You really understand me."

They found a nice restaurant in Göteborg for dinner. Ellen suddenly realized it was Thursday and asked if *ärtsoppa* was available. "What's that?" asked Rob.

"Pea soup," said Ellen with a smirk.

Rob was dismayed. "Pea soup?" He was incredulous.

But the waiter said, "Naturligtvis, Fröken. Med senap och pannkakor."

Ellen grinned at Rob. "There may be a few things, Boss, that I know about Sweden that you don't know. It's Thursday," she said, as if that explained it all.

Then, of course, she had to explain what Rika said Swedes eat on Thursdays. And, of course, Rob had to change his order, too. So they had pea soup together as their last dinner together in Sweden, followed by Swedish pancakes and lingonberry jam.

Finally, they drove out to the airport. Rob returned the rental car and they wheeled their luggage across the street to the Landvetter Airport Hotel. "I'll have to get my gifts incorporated into my luggage," said Ellen.

"Will you have enough room?" asked Rob. "If you don't, I would be able to take something in my suitcase."

They checked in and headed to their rooms. "How about a coffee before we turn in?" asked Rob.

"That would be nice."

The hotel coffee shop had lots of candles and good Swedish coffee. They delayed and procrastinated. Ellen didn't want the evening to end and it seemed that Rob felt the same way.

Finally he said, "I suppose we had best get to bed. We have to be up very early in the morning. We just have to go across the street, but it will take a while to get through the line."

Ellen stifled a yawn. "I suppose you're right. But I'm having such a nice time, I hate for it to end."

Rob walked her to the door of her hotel room. Ellen put her key in the lock and opened the door, then turned. Rob stood there, awkwardly, like he wanted to say something. They were standing very close together and Ellen suddenly realized that she could invite him in to her room. No one need ever know and she could experience things that she now knew she very much wanted to experience. And experience with Rob. There was heat in the moment. It may have lasted only a few seconds, but Ellen felt something new, something strange, something frightening, something exciting, that she had never felt before. She almost held out her arms. She almost held the door open wider. Her instincts told her that Rob was thinking the same thing. It was a moment where the whole world hung in the balance, where there was a fork in the road, where anything was possible, but only one choice could be made.

And then she remembered her decision. Trish had said, "Right place, right time, right person." She knew that Rob was the right person for her. But this was not the right time nor the right place.

Rob's voice was low and throaty. "Good night, Ellen. Pleasant dreams." And then he did take her in his arms and held her for moment, pressing his cheek against her head. And then he turned away toward his own room, leaving Ellen breathless and floating.

Ellen didn't sleep well. Possibly it was nerves about traveling. More likely it was the potential for what might have happened last night but didn't. She was glad it hadn't, or was she? She thought of Rika. How far are you willing to let him go? She had realized last night that, were it not for the decision she had made months ago, she would probably have gone much further than she intended.

She got up long before her wake up call, showered, and examined herself critically in the mirror. Could a man like Rob Powell desire her? It certainly seemed like he had last night.

Rob was in the lobby already when she came down with her luggage. "How'd you sleep?" he asked.

"Not great. And you?"

He shrugged his shoulders. "Not particularly well. Travel nerves, I guess. Or something else. I don't know. Did you get everything in your suitcase?"

"Yes, it all fit. I had to be careful with the teacups. I wrapped each one in a ... well, let's just say they are well padded."

Rob grinned. "They may not need as much padding as you think."

They checked out and walked across the parking lot. It was already daylight even though it was hardly yet 5:00 AM.

The departure hall was a busy place with lots of people and their luggage waiting in line, even at this early hour. Ellen was fascinated by the departure boards. It looked like they were made of little decks of cards with each of the letters of the alphabet — including those odd Swedish vowels å, ä, and ö — and numbers on them. Whenever there was an update on the board, the little decks would begin rhythmically clicking as the cards were being turned, one by one, to reach the right one for each character.

When it was finally their turn at the desk, the clerk checked their passports and printed tags to go on their luggage. "Going home?" she asked.

"Yes," said Rob. "But sorry to leave Sweden."

"I hope you will come back soon," she said.

"We intend to. Thank you. Did you get the seating change I requested?"

"Yes, Herr Powell. And here are your new boarding cards."

They then headed up the escalator to the lounge to wait for their flight to be called.

The lounge was nice. Rob settled Ellen at a little table and brought her some coffee and a little Swedish pastry. "I want to remember everything," said Ellen, sipping her coffee. "Absolutely everything. The taste of the coffee. The sounds of Swedish being spoken everywhere. The signs, the design of the furniture, the way the light looks different here. Just everything." She gestured widely as if to encompass the entire country of Sweden in one full sweep.

Rob caught a hand and held it. "I'm so glad you were willing to come on this trip. Not only for what we've accomplished together — which is significant — but because we got to do it together. I was able to see Sweden through your eyes, and I've loved it."

The boarding announcement for first class came over the loudspeaker. "Come on, Possum. That's us."

"No it's not. We're in coach. Unless they upgraded you again."

Rob showed her the boarding passes in his hand. "See?" he said. "First Class. For both of us."

"But how ..."

"I called last night and made the change. A girl like you deserves to fly home in first class."

"But didn't that cost …"

He waved the question away. "After the business we landed? It was an easy decision. You're going to sit in first class next to me and you're going to enjoy every minute of it." He tried to hold a serious expression. "Is that clear?" He couldn't hold it and the seriousness gave way to joy as they stood and he held out his arm. She took it.

She leaned her head against his shoulder. "You're a nice guy."

"And I've got facets. Don't forget the facets."

"Oh, you definitely have those. You could really spoil a girl."

"I intend to," he said, as he handed the boarding cards to the flight attendant at the door.

First class exceeded Ellen's expectations. She declined the champagne that was offered, but was impressed with the fresh orange juice that arrived in a beautifully designed rounded glass. The seat was wide and comfortable. "Just like a lounge chair!" she exclaimed. And best of all, Rob was sitting next to her.

Rob again suggested she take the window seat, so she got the joy of seeing the rising sun to the East as they began their climb out of Göteborg. The sun shown on the Kattegat like a diamond necklace draped between Sweden and Denmark.

Preparations for breakfast began, first with a steaming hot hand towel that they used to wipe the sleep out of their eyes and clean their hands. This was followed by actual tablecloths, draped right over their tray tables, and real silverware neatly arranged on the mini table. The food was served on china plates, not a little aluminum pan like in coach, and the flight attendant kept bringing hot coffee and offering fresh baked rolls out of a basket. Ellen was like a child in a toy store and Rob enjoyed every minute, observing, commenting where appropriate, and smiling a lot.

It seemed they had only finished up breakfast when the captain announced preparations for landing in Brussels. As they walked

through the Brussels international concourse arm in arm, Ellen noticed several people that looked at them and smiled. She smiled back.

They were in first class on the big plane from Brussels to
Cincinnati, too. "How did you manage all this?" asked Ellen.
"I made some more phone calls last night," said Rob. "One call
was one I hadn't been able to complete the afternoon before, but I got
through this time. And I was able to arrange for first class on the first
two legs. Unfortunately the ComAir plane from Cincinnati to Lexington doesn't have a first class, so I hope you can allow yourself to fly
coach on that last hop."
"I will attempt to maintain my dignity while lowering my newly
established standards," she replied.

After the plane achieved cruising altitude, the passengers and
crew all seemed to settle in for what they knew would be a long trip.
"At least the seats are very comfortable," thought Ellen. "Maybe I
can make up some of that sleep I missed last night." That made her
think of the tiny but significant vignette in the hotel hallway last
night.
She flipped idly through the magazine in the seat pocket in front
of her. But soon the magazine fell idle as her thoughts drifted away to
yesterday. To the things that had happened on this trip to Sweden. To
the things that had happened since she had taken the job at Powell.
To the person she had become. Was becoming. She thought about the
future. For the first time in many years — perhaps since her parents
had died — she wanted to plan for the future, not just manage to get
through. But she didn't know how.
Her life was like the jet airliner she was on, hurtling through
time, but not knowing exactly where she was or where she was going.
"Ellen," said Rob. With an effort she brought herself back to the
present reality, the pattern of the fabric on the seat back in front of
her, the arrangement of the glasses on the console between them, to
Rob's hand resting idly near her. "Ellen, I need to ask you an important question."

Jonas had said to her many times that she had good instincts. Her instincts were telling her now that this was important. She turned to him in the dim light of the first class cabin. The window shades were lowered and people were dozing or watching the movie. She admired the line of his jaw, the whiskers that betrayed an early morning with no time to shave, the laugh lines and wrinkles around his eyes, the firm set of his lips.

"I'm listening Rob."

Chapter 63
The Fifth Principle.

Rob took Ellen's hand. "This is neither the time nor the place," he said. "But I can not wait any longer. I have to know the answer to a question."

"What question is that? I'll help if I can."

"I certainly hope so. You remember I said I had made some phone calls day before yesterday."

"Yes. To take care of terminating Gladys."

"That was one of the phone calls. But I made three more. One was to my mother."

"Of course. You wanted her to know things had gone well with Saab."

"That was part of it, but not the most important part. I also called Mr. and Mrs. K."

"Oh, that's nice. Are they doing OK?"

"Yes, they're fine. But I wasn't able to reach the person for the most important phone call."

"And who was that?"

"Your sister."

"My sister? Trish? But why …"

Rob didn't answer her question but kept on talking. "I didn't reach her yesterday, but I did reach her last night after we headed for our rooms. Ellen, I hope you know how much you have come to mean to me. When I am with you, I feel like I can accomplish anything. With you I no longer have that gnawing loneliness that has been a part of my life for years. With you I can laugh. With you I can be myself. You're smart, you care about people, you see things through eyes that I can only imagine. You make me a better person. A better man."

"Are you saying I, too, have facets?"

"Facets! My darling, you have so many facets that you are a shimmering, glittering diamond. There is no jewel that compares to you. You are the finest gem that a man could hope to possess. And that's what I'm trying to say to you." He reached for her other hand, holding them both and looking intently into her eyes. "Ellen, I have fallen in love with you. I love you more than life itself, and I can wait no longer. Would you consent to marry me? Would you allow me the great privilege of being your husband? Would you let me care for you, be your best friend, be your lover, keep you, honor you, nurture you?"

Rob held her gaze. The cabin, the other passengers, the background roar of the air molecules streaming past the fuselage, the flight attendants passing quietly through the cabin, the Vacant light on the lavatory door, all of it faded into insignificance as she looked at the man she had been afraid to admit she loved. He was too far above her. He was from a family that owned a company. He was a well-traveled man, a sophisticated man. Rob Powell was a man she could only dream about, but never, ever hope to actually be with. And yet here he was, in seat 4B, asking her to marry him.

His gaze never wavered. He was waiting for an answer.

"You really want to marry ... me?" The last word was a tiny whisper. The insignificance with which she viewed herself would not allow her to speak about herself in any other way.

"More than anything. I think I have loved you from that first day at the factory when you fixed my keyboard. Can you possibly learn to love me, too?"

"I think I already do. I just can't admit it to myself. You really want to spend the rest of your life together with me." It wasn't a question so much as a statement to herself, as if she was testing it in her mouth to see if it rang true.

"I want to spend the rest of my life with you. I want to set up housekeeping with you. I want to have children with you. I want to grow old with you. Ellen, you are the one, the only one, and if you say no I will be consigned to being a very lonely man. But I know this is sudden. I hope you'll forgive me for springing this on you at 39,000 feet, but I'm about to burst with the love I have for you."

"What will Trish say …"

"I talked to her last night. Your parents are deceased, but I wanted to ask someone for permission to ask for your hand. Trish and I had a long conversation last night. She sends her love and says to tell you she's very happy. I hope you're happy, too."

"I am happy, Rob. Very happy. Just pinching myself to get used to the idea."

"I also spoke with my mother and grandmother. Of course I wanted their blessing. They're thrilled. Over the moon. I don't think they believed I would ever get married, and then when they found out it was you I'd fallen in love with, they were ecstatic. They really like you. Love you, even."

"And I love them. They're both so kind to me. And you talked to the Klamecks? About me?"

"Yes. It wasn't so much that I wanted their permission, or even their opinion. But I thought they would want to know that I'm going to do my darnedest to take away the best renter they ever had. You should have heard Rika shout! She was overjoyed."

It was very awkward with the console between them, but Ellen managed to put her arms around him and Rob held her. Then, without thinking, she realized he was kissing her and she was kissing him back. "Our first kiss," she whispered.

"Right here in first class on a Sabena flight at 39,000 feet," he replied. "So can I take that as a yes?"

"Oh, yes," she said. "A thousand times yes."

"Then I have something for you," he said, rifling through his carryon bag under the seat in front of him. He pulled out a little box and opened it. Inside was the daintiest band of gold with a small blue stone. "Will you allow me?" he asked. He slipped the ring on her finger. It fit perfectly. "It isn't what you deserve. You deserve the biggest diamond money can buy. And when we get home I will go down on one knee and ask you properly, but I … well, I just had to know. You've made me very happy. So happy!"

"I'm even happier than you are," she whispered looking at the stone. "You don't need to go down on one knee. And I don't want another ring. This one is perfect. Where did you get it?"

"After we went walking down by the locks, I knew I couldn't wait any longer. I made the phone calls and then I went shopping. I found this little ring in a jewelry store on the walking street. The blue stone with the yellow gold reminded me of the colors of the Swedish flag. I think Sweden will always be special to us. Would you like to come back here on our honeymoon?"

Suddenly Ellen's butterflies were back. A honeymoon. And all that implied. "Rob," she said quietly, staring at the ring on her hand. "There's something you need to know about me." He was quiet. She didn't look at him so that she could find the courage to continue. "I've ... I've never been with a man. I don't know anything about ... about, you know."

He gently lifted her chin so that she was looking at him. His eyes were twinkling even though his tone was serious. "About sex?" He smiled. "I confess, I don't know much about it either. I hear it is wonderful when two people are married and in love. But since I've never been married, and never been in love before now, I'm as new to all of this as you are. I figure we'll have all of our lives to figure it out. And I only want to do that with you."

"But I don't want you to think I'm one of those women who ... well, there were some rumors flying around about me and Kirby. I don't suppose you knew about that, but I wish you could believe me that nothing happened."

"Of course I believe you. I heard the rumors, but I knew they couldn't be true. Even while you were seeing Kirby I loved you and I knew you weren't that kind of girl. I only hoped you wouldn't get hurt."

"But he took me to the Campbell House. He had ... expectations. He already had a hotel room."

"I know."

"But how do you know? It was awful and then Kirby started spreading rumors that we had slept together and I was so afraid of what you would think and I didn't want ..."

Rob touched her lips with his finger. "I know, Ellen. I know the rumors weren't true. Remember? I was the one who drove you home from the hospital that night after your date with Kirby. It was obvious to me that something had happened but that you didn't want to talk about it. Then, when the rumors started flying around at the plant, I knew. I knew what Kirby had planned and what he was trying to convince people had happened. And I knew that it was completely false, because you were with the Klamecks at the hospital and I took you home to your own apartment."

What felt like a physical spring wound up inside her suddenly released. So often — too often — it seemed she had been holding on to something that was worrying her, eating away at her and she didn't even know it. What Rob thought of her meant a great deal to her. And now that she was going to be his wife, it meant even more. To realize that Rob really did know, because he drove her home that night, not because he was just saying it, was like releasing something very tight inside her.

She smiled and sighed. Then she snuggled up to the side of the man she had come to respect and admire — at least as much as the console between them would allow. For just a moment she wished they were back in coach where there the only barrier between two seats was a movable armrest.

"There is a lot to think about," she said.

"You mean a wedding to plan?"

"Yes, that. But where are we going to live? Are we going to live in your bedroom at Three Pines?"

"I hardly think so. I want to have a little more privacy than that with my gorgeous new wife."

"And is it OK if I continue working at Powell Manufacturing? Won't that be awkward?"

"We'll figure it out. We have all kinds of changes coming, what with the new Saab parts and ..."

"That's it!" Ellen snapped her fingers and it was her turn to sort through her carryon bag.

"What's it?"

Ellen pulled out the notebook Jonas had given her so many months ago. She turned to a fresh page and wrote:

Principle Five: The business information technology system must be designed in such a way so as to allow it to grow and change easily, adapting to changing business conditions.

Rob was looking over her shoulder. "That's it. Of course. Well done, Possum. You've found all five. This quest is complete, just in time for another quest."

"And what quest it that, oh man-of-facets?"

"Actually there are several. The quest to turn Powell around and place it on firm financial ground. The quest to add new capabilities to the computer system. And the most important quest of all: the quest to learn how to be the absolute best married couple we can be. I'll look forward to being on that quest with you. For life."

Ellen snuggled in to Rob's shoulder and found herself simply overrun with pure joy. Tomorrow would be Annie's wedding to Ronnie Dale.

And after that, there would be another wedding to plan.

Epilogue
1997 — Eight Years Later

Ellen found a parking place right in front of Pemberly. "How about some ice cream, Doralynn?"

"I like ice cream, Mommy."

"I know you do, sweetheart. Just a little treat before we go home to fix Daddy's dinner. Maybe we'll catch Mr. Klameck inside." She looked in the rear view mirror. "Is Soc still asleep?"

"Hey little baby, is you asleep?" The way Doralynn said it made Ellen smile; she was mimicking the way the child had heard grownups talk to babies. "Him's waking up, Mommy," she said.

"OK, then. Here we go to get some ice cream." Ellen opened the rear door to get Soc out of his car seat and unbuckled her daughter from her harness. She hoisted the baby onto her hip and took Doralynn's hand.

At the counter in Permberly she ordered the smallest dish of ice cream with sprinkles for Doralynn and the same but with hot fudge for herself. She looked around for Jonas, but he wasn't there. But she did spot another familiar face. "Whit Collette, what are you doing here?" He had his chin in his hand, idly stirring his half-empty cup of coffee. "You OK? Want some company?"

Whit looked up. "Oh, hi Ellen. Long time no see." His enunciation was flat. It wasn't the Whit that Ellen knew from their time together at Powell Manufacturing. "Sure, sit down." He vaguely waved his hand at the empty chairs. "Hi there. You're Doalynn, aren't you?"

"Yes I is," she said, climbing up onto a chair.

"Thanks, Jimmy," Ellen said to the young man who set the ice cream in front of them. Then she turned her attention back to Whit. "How are things going at Lark Logistics?"

"Not so good," Whit signed. He looked up at her. They had been good friends during their mutual time at Powell. They still were.

Whit had been offered a great job at Lark Logistics about a year after Ellen and Rob had gotten married. He had taken it, with Rob's blessing. Whit still remembered Rob's words as if they had been spoken yesterday: *I'll never stand in the way of an employee trying to better themselves. We've been lucky to have you for all these years, Whit. I wish you the very best of success.* Whit briefly toyed with the idea that, with Ellen staying home now to raise her children, he might be able to get his old job back.

Ellen was waiting. She knew he would tell her, and he might as well get it over with. "I lost my job today," he said. "Laid off. No severance pay. Nothing. I haven't even told Peggy."

"Oh, no!" The genuine gravity of the situation was not lost on Ellen. Now, as a stay-at-home mom herself, she understood what it meant to be a single income family. Whit's wife Peggy had left the workplace when their first daughter arrived. Now, five daughters later, the loss of Whit's income could be serious indeed. "And your oldest is in college, and the next one is just about to start, isn't she?"

Whit nodded. He had been sitting at a table in Permberly, thinking of all the ways they would have to cut back and sacrifice until he could find other work. "I just don't know what to do." He said it to his coffee cup, imagining himself drowning in there with no one to throw him a life preserver.

Ellen touched his hand. "I can't presume to know what you're going through," she said. "Although I do know what it is like to try to make ends meet when there isn't enough rope to hold on to. But you're a smart guy, Whit. I have confidence in you."

Whit sighed. "Thanks, Ellen. I think I'll be OK. It has just hit me hard, and I'm still digesting it." He looked out through the front windows of Pemberly to the catalpa trees on the square, stark and bare with their pods rattling and twisting in the keen February wind. "I'd better get home and break the bad news to Peggy. Great to see you, Ellen. Maybe next time I'll be a bit better company."

Ellen watched him go without the usual spring in his step. "But," she thought to herself. "I know Whit Collette. If anyone can make a silk purse out of this sow's ear, it's him."

Watch for

The Catalpa Club

by Martin Ramsay

coming soon from Narrow Gate House Publishers
narrowgatehouse.com

www.ingramcontent.com/pod-product-compliance
Lightning Source LLC
Chambersburg PA
CBHW031957060726
47497CB00015B/93